PRAISE FOR
PRAISE

Winner, *The Australian*/Vogel's Literary Award, 1991

Winner, Commonwealth Writers' Prize for Best First Book (Pacific Region), 1992

Shortlisted, Victorian Premier's Literary Award, 1992

Shortlisted, Adelaide Festival Award for Literature, 1992

Shortlisted, Canada–Australia Literary Award, 1992

'McGahan's book is a bracing slap in the face to conventional platitudes and hypocrises.' *Weekend Australian*

'Candid and unembarrassed, McGahan's work throbs with an intensity.' *New Zealand Herald*

'*Praise* is one of those books that takes a hefty bite out of a piece of subject matter, chews it to a pulp and then spits it out.' Peter Craven

'McGahan's gritty, unflinching *Praise* is one of few Australian novels of the 90s that really matter.' David Marr

'A tour-de-force revelation of life in the slow lane of drugs and sex and alcohol.' *Weekend Australian*

PRAISE FOR
1988

'A fiendish and eventful psychological novel . . . hugely satisfying.' *New York Times Book Review*

'The pre-eminent Australian road novel.' *The Australian*

'Untamed and frankly shocking. When *1988* is dismissed as "another" young man's angsting book by reviewers deaf to the stylistic magic of this book, it makes the joke even funnier.' *The Age*

'The glue that holds it all together is McGahan's tremendous narrative skill. *The White Earth* is a long book, but there is nothing sprawling about it. A lean, intelligent and incisive novel.' James Ley, *Sydney Morning Herald*

'The novel is beautifully structured, filled with parallels and reverberations which come back to haunt and illuminate the reader as the story unfolds.' Katharine England, *Adelaide Advertiser*

'A great Australian story embracing national themes that should engage us all.' Lucy Clark, *Sunday Telegraph*

'Impressive . . . A well-wrought, meditative reflection on Australia's colonialist demons.' *Publishers Weekly*

'The contemporary setting notwithstanding, these characters have a timeless quality and could have stepped from the pages of a Dickens novel.' *The Age*

PRAISE FOR
UNDERGROUND

Shortlisted, Queensland Premier's Literary Award, 2007
Shortlisted, Best Science Fiction Novel, Aurealis Awards, 2006

'A corker of a book. On the surface it's a tense, engaging political thriller, but there is no hiding from its articulate critique of Australian society.' *Herald Sun*

'A delicious romp through an Australia both familiar and deeply disturbing.' *Courier Mail*

'A fast-moving and sometimes outrageous action-adventure novel . . . It is, without doubt, McGahan's most nakedly political work so far.' *Sydney Morning Herald*

ANDREW MCGAHAN was born in Dalby, Queensland, and died in Victoria in 2019 at age fifty-two. His first novel *Praise* (1992) won the 1991 *The Australian*/Vogel's Literary Award and the regional prize for best first book in the Commonwealth Writers' Prize. His second novel was the prequel *1988* (1995), and his third novel *Last Drinks* (2000) was shortlisted for multiple awards, including *The Age* Book of the Year and *The Courier Mail* Book of the Year Award, and won a Ned Kelly Award for Crime Writing. In 2004, *The White Earth* was published and won the 2005 Miles Franklin Literary Award, the Commonwealth Writers' Prize for the South East Asia and South Pacific Region, *The Age* Book of the Year (Fiction) and *The Courier Mail* Book of the Year Award. It was also shortlisted for the Queensland Premier's Literary Award for fiction. McGahan's fifth novel, *Underground*, was published in 2006 and was shortlisted in the Queensland Premier's Literary Award for fiction and for the Aurealis Award. In 2009, *Wonders of a Godless World* was published to acclaim and won the Aurealis Award. McGahan's award-winning writing also includes stage plays and the screenplay for the movie version of *Praise*.

THE
RICH
MAN'S
HOUSE
ANDREW
McGAHAN

ALLEN&UNWIN
SYDNEY • MELBOURNE • AUCKLAND • LONDON

First published in 2019

Allen & Unwin
83 Alexander Street
Crows Nest NSW 2065
Australia
Phone: (61 2) 8425 0100
Email: info@allenandunwin.com
Web: www.allenandunwin.com

 A catalogue record for this book is available from the NATIONAL LIBRARY OF AUSTRALIA National Library of Australia

ISBN 978 1 76052 982 6

Internal design by Sandy Cull, gogoGingko
Set in 11.7/17 pt Berkeley Oldstyle by Bookhouse, Sydney
Printed and bound in Australia by Griffin Press, part of Ovato

10 9 8 7 6 5 4 3 2 1

FOR LIESJE

▲

AUTHOR'S NOTE

THIS IS MY LAST BOOK.

An author can't always say that with certainty, but as I'm in the final stages of dying as I type this, it seems a safe bet. It's a finished novel—I wouldn't be letting it out into the world if it wasn't—but I can't deny that my abrupt decline in health has forced the publishers and I to hurry the rewriting and editing process extremely, and that this is not quite the book it would have been had cancer not intervened. That doesn't help with any flaws you might find in the story, but it might explain them, and for once I can fairly plead—I was really going to fix that!

PROLOGUE 1

Introduction from *The Cloven Sky—A History*,
Roger Fitzgerald, 1991

Dutch master-seaman and ocean-going explorer Gerrit Jansz, born 1605, was very nearly one of those unfortunates whom history overlooks.

For centuries, indeed, it did overlook him, robbing him of the honours usually granted to mariners who make great discoveries: first, the fame of the discovery itself, and second, the right to name the new landmark, be it a river, or a strait—or, in this case, an island.

Or more to the point, a *mountain*.

Instead, for many years, the fame of discovering the Wheel went to French sea-captain Marion du Fresne, who, in 1772, driven by bad weather to the south of the then barely known isle of Tasmania, happened upon the great massif rearing in all its solitude.

Then again, du Fresne himself can also be considered cheated by history, for although he named the mountain, the name he chose never stuck. The actual name can be traced instead to the English navigator and explorer, James Cook, who visited the massif five years after the Frenchman. Cook did not rename the mountain, respecting du Fresne's claim, but all the same it was Cook's journals, published after his death, and containing a crucial printer's error, which gave the mountain the peculiar title by which it has been known ever since.

English and French historians debate whom is really owed the credit, Cook or du Fresne, but the truth is that Gerrit Jansz beheld the Wheel long before either of them, well over a century earlier in fact—in 1642. And yet a combination of self-doubt, politics and bad luck conspired to keep his discovery a secret for another three hundred years.

▲

So, who was Gerrit Jansz?

Very little is known about the man; his place of birth, his earlier life, are all a mystery. He was a seafarer in an age of seafaring, and until 1974, if he was remembered at all it was not for any deed of his own, but merely for being a senior member of an expedition led by the far more famous mariner and explorer, Abel Tasman.

The expedition in question was a voyage to explore and map the coastline of Australia. Not that such a country then existed, the landmass was instead known variably as Terra Australis, or the Great Southern Land, or later New Holland. In 1642, its shores were mainly a matter of guesswork on world charts, so the Dutch Council of the Indies dispatched Tasman to correct this failing.

His fleet consisted of two vessels. One was the flagship *Heemskerck*, a war-yacht of one hundred and twenty tons, upon which Tasman himself and navigator Frans Visscher resided. The other was the *Zeehaen*, a fluyt (or transport ship) of two hundred tons, upon which the most important figure was the influential merchant and draughtsman Isaac Gilsemans. All three of these men would emerge with renown from the voyage. Remembered more rarely was the fact that the *Zeehaen* was captained not by Gilsemans, but by a master named Gerrit Jansz.

Jansz is listed on the expedition's roster as being thirty-seven years old, and 'of Batavia', which is now Jakarta. There is nothing else. His captain's log of the voyage with Tasman survives, but it is a technical document and mentions little of his private life. It can be inferred, however, that he had worked largely in the Dutch East Indies (present day Indonesia) before being selected to captain the *Zeehaen*, and that he was a keen amateur geologist and mathematician.

But it is with the log of the *Zeehaen* that the quirks of history began to conspire against Jansz. Had that log been published and widely read as soon as the fleet returned home, the full import of certain passages within might have become apparent. However, the log was not Jansz's property—as neither were those of Tasman, Visscher and Gilsemans. All such records belonged to the Council of the Indies, who had commissioned the voyage, and *their* prime interest was not to publicise the expedition's findings. Rather, the findings were confidential information to be used by the Council to advance Dutch trade and influence.

Official secrets, in other words.

Hence, reports were slow to be released. In time, however, Tasman, Visscher and Gilsemans all published accounts of the voyage that earned each of them varying degrees of fame. Jansz published nothing, and his log faded quickly into obscurity, as did the man himself.

Yet oddly enough, it would turn out that Jansz's log was the only original document of the voyage that would survive to the modern day. The other logs have all been lost, but Jansz's was rediscovered by Dutch historians in 1973, filed inexplicably amid a collection of ancient shipyard schematics, but in good condition. Finally, scholars could read the document in full, and what they found there astonished them.

Even then, history was reluctant to embrace Jansz, for when the news was released to the world in early 1974, it was immediately declared that the log must be a fraud, a hoax. It was just too timely, too convenient, given what was taking place on the Wheel at that moment.

The log was quite real, however.

And it changed everything.

▲

The accepted history was this.

Abel Tasman's expedition set out from Batavia on August 14, 1642, and first sailed west to Mauritius and thence south to catch the roaring forties, which then bore them east again, in search of land. Mistakenly assuming that the bulk of Terra Australis lay further south than it actually does, Tasman aimed to sail along a latitude line of more than fifty degrees. Striking poor weather, however, he turned further north: luckily, or he would have missed even Australia's southernmost point, the great island that would later bear his name, Tasmania.

But that was yet to come. For now, a string of storms struck the fleet—it was late spring in the southern hemisphere, but the weather in the Southern Ocean can turn foul at any time of the year—and on a dark night the two ships became separated. The *Heemskerck* under Tasman managed to hold its course to the east, but the *Zeehaen*, under Jansz, was forced further south once more. It was a full six days before the gales cleared, and Jansz could turn his ship safely north again.

Tasman, in the meantime, had made his great discovery by sighting a wild and rugged land: the west coast of Tasmania. He was worried about the disappearance of the *Zeehaen*, but trusted that Jansz would make his way east eventually, and so got on with exploring the new shore. And indeed, ten days after it had vanished, the *Zeehaen* at last reappeared, riding up unharmed from the south-west.

After much celebration (and the naming of a nearby inlet as Reunion Bay) the fleet spent a further four days in Tasmanian waters, mapping the island's western and southern shores. They then launched off eastwards into the Pacific to make further discoveries, New Zealand among them. In time, Tasman would return by a northern route to his beginning point in Batavia, having sailed fully around the Australian mainland without actually ever sighting it. But he had at least thereby proved that the Great Southern Land was a freestanding continent.

Such was the accepted history—until Jansz's log was discovered. Before then, no account had ever been given of the *Zeehaen*'s ten days alone upon

the southern sea. It was assumed by historians that nothing of importance had occurred in that time. But something had, even if no one at the
time, not even Jansz himself, realised it.

For their first six days alone, the log reports (laconically, in Jansz's
native seventeenth-century Dutch, only the gist of which will be given
here) that the *Zeehaen* battled wind and wave, driven always either to the
south or the south-east. In all that time, scarcely a scrap of blue sky was
seen. But on the sixth night the gales calmed and the clouds blew away,
and on the seventh morning there came a clear sunrise.

Jansz was awake and on deck in the pre-dawn light. (The draughtsman
Gilsemans rose late that day—a pity, considering what was about to tran-
spire: a sketch of the scene might have proved invaluable.) A swell was
running still, but lessening, and the breeze, though light and shifting,
seemed to be setting to the south-west, which would help the *Zeehaen* on
its return to the north. For the moment, however, the ship and its crew
were merely enjoying the respite from the storm.

Jansz had just checked the ship's chronometer to note the time, then,
as his gaze roamed the grey horizon, something due south of the ship
caught his eye: a sudden glow that was brightening, a sliver of dusky red
on the edge of the world, vivid, but far, far away.

'I bethought it the top of a cloud,' writes Jansz, 'which, ascending to a
great height, was catching the unrisen sun.'

But the more he looked, the less Jansz thought the glowing red sliver
to be a cloud. For one, there were no other clouds at all in the south.
Nor was it the shape of cloud form: neither the cauliflower cumulus of a
storm, nor the diaphanous sheet of high-level cirrus. Instead, it looked
for all the world like a crest of rocky land, the uppermost line of a great
ridge flushing with the first light, except so far away that its edges were
softened by distance almost to mist.

Unearthly. In all his time at sea, Jansz had never seen anything quite
like it. For many minutes he studied the distant sliver wonderingly as its
colour changed from red to purple, and then near to blue, fading all the

while as the light grew in the sky, till it was only the faintest of blurs. Was it land or not? Should he investigate? It lay in the wrong direction— south, not north—and he was already off course as it was. But if it was land, then surely it should be investigated? Jansz could not decide.

But then a warm light broke across his face and he turned to see the sun lifting above the eastern horizon, the sails of his ship flushing orange. A thought struck him. He consulted the chronometer and saw that since he had first sighted the glowing sliver in the south, over twenty minutes had passed. That settled it then. The shape in the south—and it was all but invisible now in the haze of daylight—could only be a cloud.

Jansz reasoned it out in his log. The object lay due south of the ship, on the same longitude, so it should have experienced sunrise at roughly the same time as the ship. And yet that pale sliver to the south had been sunlit a full *twenty minutes* earlier than had the *Zeehaen*.

There was only one way to explain that: altitude. An object—a cloud, say, or a mountain—that reared to great heights above an observer would always see sunrise before that same observer. And as it happened, Jansz had made something of a study of this effect.

His subject had been a particular mountain in Java, a mountain with white rock at its peak that glowed particularly brightly every sunrise. Local Dutch geographers had assured Jansz that the mountain was (translated into modern terms of measurement) some twelve hundred metres in height, and observing the mountain over several dawns, Jansz had noted that the sunlight reached its peak almost exactly one minute before it shone upon the world at sea level.

So he had a figure of ready reckoning. For every thousand metres in height, the sun rose about fifty seconds earlier than at sea level. (There are adjustments needed, as Jansz knew, to compensate for the different rate of spin of the Earth's surface between, say, a position on the equator and one nearer the poles, but that need not be explored here.) Jansz had used this reckoning while observing storms at dawn, and so had measured thunderheads that rose to a fantastic thirteen thousand metres, greeting the sun near to twelve minutes before the lower lands.

Thirteen thousand metres was already far higher than any earthly mountain rose. But the red sliver that Jansz beheld that morning, for all that it looked like the top of a mountain, had been sunlit for close to *twenty-one minutes* before dawn reached the ship.

That suggested a height of twenty-five thousand metres! Stupendous, even for a cloud, well beyond any precedent in Jansz's experience. And for a mountain—well, it was impossible.

The thing was a cloud, and only a cloud. To think—as Jansz wrote in his log—he'd almost dashed off to the south, chasing a useless mirage. Congratulating himself, Jansz turned his ship to the north, to make his rendezvous with Tasman four days later.

So it was that the greatest discovery of the Southern Ocean would not be made for another century, and by another captain.

Still, given the data in Jansz's log, there can be no doubt about the truth. His own estimated position at the time translates to a spot three hundred kilometres to the south-southwest of Tasmania's south-western-most point. Looking directly south from that position, he can have beheld only one thing, not a cloud, but the summit ridge of the Wheel, meeting the dawn. The first human ever to do so.

And strangely enough, his rough estimate of twenty-five thousand metres, as little as he could credit such a figure himself, was accurate to within less than a tenth of a per cent, out by a mere seventeen metres. It would not be bettered in precision until the modern day of global positioning satellites.

Not bad for a man history almost forgot.

PROLOGUE 2

Introduction from *Reaching for the Hand of God*,
by John Soliola, 2007

NOVEMBER 14, 1974. The four men slept through their last night before the summit attempt—or pretended to sleep, for with the goal this close, it was a steady soul indeed who could manage to drift off. But in any case all four were at rest, unspeaking. Other than their breathing and the rustle of sleeping bags, the only sounds in the hut were the humming of the compressors and heaters, and the occasional venting of exhaust.

From outside, nothing. No gales battered the aluminium alloy walls; no snow or hail pattered upon the aluminium alloy roof. Not this high up. Up here, the great silence held forever over all.

By the inner airlock door, beneath a stencilled monogram that read *H-122*, there glowed a chunky digital readout. Embossed labels were glued alongside lines of orange electric numbers that occasionally flickered and changed.

```
Time, AEST . . . . . . . 2.40
Alt, M . . . . . . . . . 24,590
Int Temp, C  . . . . . . +15
Ext Temp, C  . . . . . . -63
W Av Vel, km/h . . . . . 4.6
W Max Gu, km/h . . . . . 7.9
```

```
Int AP, ATM  . . . . . . 0.75
Ext AP, ATM  . . . . . . 0.04
Int Ox, %  . . . . . . . 25.8
Int CO2, % . . . . . . . 0.06
Ma Integ, %  . . . . . . 100
AL Integ, %  . . . . . . 100
```

In other words, all was well. The hut—a stout, pressurised, prefabricated structure roughly the size and shape of a small caravan, and known formally as a HAEV, a High Altitude Environment—was doing its job, protecting the men from the stratospheric night. Outside was lethal, airless cold and a barrenness harsher than any desert, but within, the men slept, or did not sleep, upon a padded, electrically heated floor, breathing at ease in the oxygen-enriched air, surrounded by ample supplies of food and water.

At three a.m., an alarm sounded. If any of the men had genuinely been asleep, they all stirred now. Two hours of preparations began. First, breakfast and ablutions. Then, the painstaking checking of equipment—inspecting first the hut itself, then each of the four men's pressure suits, including all the associated tanks and batteries and seals, and back-ups for each, searching for even the smallest flaw or malfunction. Finally, and only when everything had been declared Condition Green, came the donning of the suits, each man taking at least fifteen minutes, even when assisted by the others.

At five a.m. the four were ready to go outside. They looked, at a glance, like four astronauts about to step into space—which, after all, was not so far from the truth. But these men weren't astronauts, they were mountain climbers, and they were still on Earth, if only just. Not that it made their task any easier. Indeed, getting to the Moon had been simpler in many ways than getting this close to the summit of the Wheel. Five years had passed since Armstrong had taken his great step for mankind, with Mars presumably to follow one day soon, yet *still* there remained this one point on the home planet upon which no man had ever set foot.

9

In any case, on closer study, the men's pressure suits were rather different to those the Apollo astronauts had worn, although they had in fact been made by the same firm, the David Clark Company, which had been in the business ever since the US military began sending planes into the high atmosphere. Indeed, the climbers' suits—HTF11 (High Terrain Function) suits—were the more advanced models.

The Apollo pressure suits, for instance, the A7L series, were notoriously inflexible, barely adequate for the simple movements of walking on the Moon. True, all pressure suits face such limitations; stiffness is the trade-off for supplying full air pressure within a self-contained suit. But mountain climbing demands flexibility. So David Clark had gone back to their drawing boards and—after intensive experimentation—had come up with a range of original artificial fabrics for the HTF series, giving the climbers more freedom.

There were other important differences besides, especially as regards the life-enabling equipment in the backpack sections, for survival in *near* space is a less complicated affair than in actual space. Thin air, for instance, even at only five per cent of the atmosphere at sea level, is better than no air at all. Thin air can be pumped by a battery-powered compressor into a small, pressurised tank to provide constant breathing air to the suit, whereas an Apollo suit, surrounded by vacuum, had to carry its entire air supply in a larger, heavier tank.

But this is no place to go into all the technicalities. Suffice to say that in being more flexible and more lightweight and more easily powered than any pressure suit that had gone before, it was the HTF suits above any other advance that had enabled this expedition, and these four climbers, to approach victory where all else had failed.

Final checks complete, the men turned to the door. One of them thumbed the airlock controls to release the catches, then opened the door, allowing the men to step into the airlock, an anteroom chamber that was nearly as large as the main room. Stacked here were all kinds of supplies in boxes, cans and flasks, wrapped tight against the room's periodic depressurisations, while various tubes and cables ran through the walls to feed the compressors and heaters within both chambers.

The men closed the inner door, and turned to the outer. It boasted a small, thick window. Through the glass a turquoise darkness sparkled, freezing even to the eye. One by one, the men lowered and latched their visors and switched on the environmental functions of their suits; air pockets inflated and pressed against skin in imitation of air pressure, other fabrics contracted to the same effect; heating and cooling systems kicked in, and breathing systems too. They were ready for the outside.

The four checked all systems one last time, as per the drill. Finally one of them worked the controls by the outer door, and with a thumping sound, air began to drain from the chamber. It took only a few moments. Then the light by the outer door was blinking green. External and internal pressures were equalised.

The men opened the outer door and stepped through into the near-space of altitude twenty-four-and-a-half thousand metres.

At lower levels on the mountain, such an exit might entail beating one's way against jet stream winds of incredible force, or digging one's way up through an overnight ten-foot dump of snow, or feeling cautiously through fog so thick as to be night-dark.

But here, there was none of that. Hut 122 was above all such weather of the world. Nothing more than a mild breeze ever blew here, or could blow, and the air was so thin that that breeze was undetectable anyway, especially through the suits. Nor did snow or rain ever fall here, or cloud ever gather. None of these things *could* happen. At nearly twenty-five kilometres altitude, the atmosphere was dead to weather. It was dry of all moisture, permanently frozen at temperatures far below zero, and utterly sterile.

As was the landscape.

Naked rock was all that greeted the four men, the stony surfaces without lustre or sheen. Nor was there any glint of ice, for even the trace moisture that had been contained in the rocks themselves, millennia ago, as they lifted inch by inch into the sky, had long since been sublimated away into the parched air. Far below—fifteen kilometres down the mountain—there was snow and ice aplenty, entire glaciers, but up here near the Wheel's peak there was only desolation.

It was a landscape closer to the surface of Mars than to Earth. Hence NASA's eagerness to be involved in the expedition: climbing the Wheel was a perfect rehearsal for a future Mars landing.

And yet the Wheel was no wide dusty Martian plain. The four mountain climbers were perched on a knife-edge of stone that climbed precariously into the pre-dawn sky, gulfs of infinity dropping away on either hand, only a misstep away.

Such was the summit ridge of the Wheel, a hellish flesh-less backbone, narrow and rugged and cleft with many chasms. To the south, beyond the hut, it dropped away in jagged rises and falls, towards the far-below ocean, invisible for now in the darkness. To the west lay an abyss of empty air and a night untouched yet by any predawn light, but to the east the approaching sun outlined the very curve of the planet, the atmosphere, seen from almost beyond it, glowing as a golden mist.

But the men ignored the approaching sunrise. Their gazes were raised northwards, to the brightly coloured stars above, and the shadow that loomed stark against them. Here the ridge leapt up in a series of cliffs and precipices, until far above, still some four hundred vertical metres higher than their campsite, a twisted fist of blackness marked the crest of the ridge: the pinnacle of the mountain.

There it was. The summit of the Wheel, the famed Hand of God, the focal point of immeasurable tonnes of stone, reared so painfully from the earth to pierce the stratosphere and to rear exactly—as far as anyone had so far measured—twenty-five thousand and seventeen metres. Far away in the Himalayas, the world's second highest mountain, Everest, long ago defeated, was less than half that height.

The four men stared for a time. Carbon monoxide–rich exhaust puffed periodically from their breathing units, crackling as the moisture within it froze instantly in tiny clouds of man-made snow before just as quickly sublimating. But otherwise the air was etched with a razor clarity, the peak above just beginning to glow in anticipation of dawn—not the pearly pink-white of a snow-capped peak, but rather a deep red upon black, as if veins of blood flowed through the rocky faces above.

Three hundred and thirty-two years had passed since Gerrit Jansz had spied the growing fire on the horizon, and not realised what it was that he saw. Now the four men beheld the same sight, but from so close that as the light strengthened they could discern individual seams and clefts in the summit above, as if in arm's reach. Before this day was out, if all went well, they would stand upon that strangely shaped pinnacle, so like a human hand, where no man had stood before.

No man, nor any other creature neither. No bird had ever soared so high, no animal or insect had ever scaled the twenty-five kilometres from below. Only humanity had ventured even this close—and that at a terrible price. The slopes of the Wheel, far below, were littered with dozens, hundreds, of unrecovered corpses, the remains of climbers who had died in their assaults upon the mountain. The history of disasters and failed attempts stretched back over a hundred years and more.

Non-climbers had also made attempts. Twice in the 1950s, high altitude balloonists had tried to soar to the summit, each time to meet with horror and death. And in the 1960s, both the USA and the USSR sent their highest-flying aircraft—spy planes—to pass over the summit at hypersonic speeds, the motors of their cameras whirring, to see what they might of the mysterious Hand of God up close.

And yet despite all such efforts, the only knowledge that had been gained of the summit were a few dissatisfying photos, more enigmatic than revealing. The Wheel's uttermost tip twisted upon itself in a way that hid and shadowed its own form: the Hand of God was not open to the world, but enclosed, keeping its secret. The spy jets could not pause in midair to get better shots, and no helicopter could fly even half as high as needed. A rocket, perhaps, at vast expense, might have risen aloft and detached a landing module to approach the Hand—but no module known could then thread the space between the fingers.

The frustrating truth was this: the Wheel was too high for any aircraft to reach, and yet too low, too awkward, for a rocket to make a practical landing. If the great peak was to be defeated, it must be done the old-fashioned way, by human sweat and strain, labouring slowly up through the stone and ice and thinning air, camp by camp.

As these four men indeed had done. These four—and many others. Some six hundred climbers had taken part in the two-year campaign, ferrying the many tonnes of supplies and equipment ever higher up the Wheel's flanks. They had ascended by two separate paths, each redundant for the other to safeguard against destruction by landslide or avalanche, and each strung with pressurised huts every few hundred vertical metres. The huts were linked by power cables and heat-jacketed water lines that ran all the way back down to the mountain's foot, to ships docked at the harbour, housing great generators and water pumps.

As well as the six hundred climbers, the expedition employed at least as many support staff stationed at Base Camp or upon the ships that stood permanently offshore. And hundreds more had contributed to the assault from afar: the engineers who crafted the HTF suits and the HAEV huts, the staff in the supply depot in Hobart, the administration and publicity staff, a documentary film crew—the list went on, thousands of people in all, adding up to the greatest campaign ever mounted against the Wheel. All of it, so many man-hours and so much expense, just to place these chosen four at the foot of the summit.

The daylight grew, dawn hurrying forwards, hard and bright. Far below, deep in the swamp of gas that was the atmosphere, sunrise was a murkier affair. Likewise, from sea level, the stars at night were blurred and muddied. But up here, over ninety-five per cent of the atmosphere was beneath the climbers' feet. There was no pollution, no vapour, no clouds, so the stars shone more fiercely and with deeper colours than could be dreamed of below; and when the sun cleared the horizon it leapt up white and blinding in what seemed an instant.

As it did now. Light as harsh as a camera flash washed the peak above, turning it from red to white-gold, and then swept down the summit ridge like a silent avalanche. As it neared, the men lowered the alloy-tinted shades of their helmets. The world turned all to glare for a moment—and yet still freezing, for no warmth came with the sun—then their eyes adjusted, and the summit stood exposed in the morning, the rock a dull carmine now against a blue-black sky blasted clear of stars.

Unspeaking, the men moved forwards and came quickly to the foot of the first sheer rise. A steel-rope ladder waited there, leading upwards, for in fact the lower two hundred metres of the final ascent had already been climbed. In the week preceding this day, three preparatory teams had already set out from Hut 122 to ready the way. First had gone a climbing team, breaking a new route up the ridge, and leaving lines and ladders behind them. Two supply teams had then followed, carrying and depositing, two hundred metres up, a stash of batteries and other supplies, ready for the summit team to employ.

The four men, one by one, set their feet and hands to the ladder and began to climb. Nevertheless, even so assisted, they progressed only slowly, with the exaggerated care that had become the norm for climbers in bulky suits that could easily overbalance, and wearing helmets of glass that, for all that they had been specially toughened, would still break if smashed hard enough against stone.

There were other reasons for caution as well. To those who have not been there, the higher altitudes of the stratosphere, free of winds and weather and ice, may sound like an *easier* place to climb, compared to the lower, windier, snow-bound regions of normal mountains, especially with a HTF suit to keep one warm, and to provide air.

But those who have done it know differently. The lack of wind, for instance, is more disconcerting than comforting, for it reinforces the sense of *thinness* to the air, the sense of emptiness yawning all around, the sense that there is nothing to support you. The atmosphere, at sea level, is in fact a cushion, even if most people never notice it. The thick air supports, cradles, protects. If you fall from a cliff, it is dense enough to slow your plummet to a terminal velocity of only a few hundred kilometres per hour. Fast, yes, but sometimes, just sometimes, survivable.

But at twenty-five kilometres up, all that protection and cushioning is gone. A climber is naked in the near vacuum. It feels somehow all the easier to trip and topple. And should one actually tumble over the edge of the mountain into the abyss, then for the first few thousand metres of your descent there will be virtually no air resistance to slow you down. Lacking any hindrance, a human body can—merely by falling unassisted— approach the speed of sound. And should frail flesh and blood, at that speed, graze against the sharp stone of a cliff, well . . .

The silence, too, of high altitude is disturbing. The air is so thin in the stratosphere that it can barely transmit sound, so even a rock struck upon a rock is no more than a distant tapping. Oh, the shriek of a gale and the thunder of avalanches have their own terrors, but silence works blackly on the mind, reinforces the vast emptiness of the heights, waiting to ensnare the climber. It's made worse by the suits, for *they* are noisy; they gurgle, hum and blare with static from the communications system. But that's all interior sound. Nothing comes from *outside*.

That, and the flat, stark light, can make the whole high-altitude world seem distant and faraway. Unreal. For a climber this is a perilous sensation: mountaineers need above all to be in contact with the mountain they are ascending. Not only physically, but emotionally. To feel detached from it, to *be* detached from it, only increases the likelihood of a mistake. Many have been the climbers on the Wheel who, even while walking along a level ridge in calm stillness, find themselves sweating terror in their suits, all but paralysed, so tenuous does their grip feel on the mountain and on the thin air surrounding them.

But for all that, the four men ascended now without incident for two hours, slow and cautious but untroubled on the ladders, and so reached the storage cache two hundred metres up.

They were now at twenty-four thousand seven hundred and ninety-five metres—leaving two hundred and thirty metres to the summit. Two hundred and thirty metres of virgin, unclimbed territory, most of it sheer and difficult. It would be slower going from here.

The men took a last assessment. All their suits were functioning nominally, and amid the cache of supplies all the batteries were fully charged. Effectively, keeping safety margins intact, they had twelve hours to reach the summit, with as much time again to descend. Hopefully it would take less time than that, but even if they must climb or descend in darkness, they had flashlights enough to do so.

All was as ready as could be. The four men were hand-picked, the best climbers from among the six-hundred-strong assault team. They would take turns breaking a new route up the final pitches, leaving behind lines and ladders as they went. Barring unforeseen problems, the entire four-man team should stand upon the Hand of God before sunset. And in the days to come others would follow, team after team ascending to the summit, in reward for the years of labour they had put in.

The four set off again, hopes high.

But as it would prove, only one man alone would gain the summit that day. And he would be the last to set foot there to this day.

BOOK
ONE

1

A FUNERAL

DEATH IS THE GREAT INVIGORATOR. It awakens and stirs those left behind—the deceased's family, their colleagues, their dependants, whomever is bound to them in any way—like a slap across the face of a sleeper. Everything that has seemed fixed up to that point, loves, grievances, financial affairs, breaks loose the instant that the individual in question dies, and a thousand eventualities that were impossible before—whether to be dreaded, or desired—suddenly come into play.

So it was for Rita Gausse upon the death of her father, even though they had barely spoken in years. Aged forty-five, she had, in the previous decade, fought the storm of her life to the point where she had wrested out a small haven of calm for herself, a port amid the whirl, and was finally catching her breath a little. But the news of her father's passing, little though it meant to her at first, would break her lashings and hurl her bodily out to sea again—literally.

She learned of that death only a few hours before it appeared in headlines around the world, the dateline April 17, 2016. Not front-page headlines, but headlines all the same.

Acclaimed architect dies in home of Walter Richman—or words to that effect, always mentioning the name of the famous client, of course, followed by the minimal details. *Influential architect Richard Gausse has been found dead at age 78 in the newly completed home of billionaire*

Walter Richman. Gausse designed the controversial, multi-hundred-million dollar residence on Theodolite Isle in the Southern Ocean, and had been overseeing the final stages of construction. He was known to be suffering ill health and Tasmanian police who attended the scene report no suspicious circumstances. Gausse leaves behind his second wife Amanda and their three adult children, George, Jerome and Erica, and Rita, daughter from his first marriage to Candice, predeceased. Richard Jerome Gausse was born in 1938 in Rose Hill, Sydney, to Belgian migrant parents and studied architecture at the University of Melbourne. Most famous for his 'buried' style of design, he first rose to fame in the 1960s with . . .

And so on.

It was Amanda, second wife, estranged but not divorced, who had called Rita with the news.

'The old bastard has croaked it, luv,' were her first words over the phone, pronounced in what sounded like an exhalation of nicotine. Amanda was Sydney high society, but her speech patterns were pure fish-and-chips. 'His heart again, they're telling me. As if he had one, right, luv? You and me know, god help us.' She was crying through the cigarette drags, and laughing too, in a fond, bewildered way.

'Amanda, are you okay?' Rita asked. 'Have you got someone there?'

They had always got along, stepdaughter and stepmother. Better in most ways than either of them got on with father and husband.

'Oh, I'm fine. Erica's here, and the boys are coming over. It's you I'm worried about. All alone down there. What are you going to do?'

The two women were a thousand kilometres apart. Amanda, propped up no doubt on her overstuffed couch in her Elizabeth Bay apartment with its harbour views, and Rita standing in her pyjamas staring out over her living room balcony to the dim valley of the Maribyrnong and the orange night-glow of the Melbourne skyline beyond. It was three in the morning, but Rita had not been asleep. Even in this second and far more respectable career—a veterinarian now five years graduated and specialising in emergency care—she was as nocturnal as she had ever been, working night shifts at an animal hospital across the river in Kensington. 'What *is* there to do, really?' she replied. 'I mean, for now. I know there'll be the funeral, later, I suppose. Are you going to . . . ?'

'Oh, yes, I'll see him buried nice and proper, course I will. At least, when we get him back from that god-awful rock. Did you know about that job, luv? When did you talk to him last?'

'Not since before he started there, I think. I'd heard about it though, it was always in the news.' And how the old Rita would have railed against him for being involved in such a project: by all the gods, he couldn't have picked anything worse. But the new Rita, thankfully, had remained indifferent.

They talked details for a few minutes, then, after further protestations of concern, and offers of accommodation in Sydney from Amanda, the two women hung up on each other.

Leaving Rita to gaze out at the night. And to think—*So, he's dead. Dad is dead. I have no father.*

How did that make her feel?

In truth, other than a mild sense of surprise, the news had so far roused little emotion in her at all. Unless, of course, she was in denial, and masking a deeper grief or rage within.

But she didn't think so. There was no call for any consuming grief or shock: his death hardly came out of nowhere. He had never been in good health since his first heart attack in his late sixties, and then the cancer scare at seventy-two. He ate all wrong, drank too much . . .

As for rage, well, there wasn't much anger left. She no longer blamed him for the way things had gone. Not since her own . . . well, fall from grace. They had made up in their fashion, after not speaking all the way from Rita's twenty-first birthday to her fortieth. And during the lunches and dinners of their rapprochement they had got along amiably enough. If they hadn't kept in close contact since, well, it didn't signify any great hatred, or any great issue unresolved. It just was.

She searched herself again. No, there was no repressed wail of emotion hiding inside her. Her father was dead now. Her mother, long before. There was nothing else to be said. Certainly, she could see no reason why it should change anything in her life.

She poured herself a glass of white wine and drank it in his honour while sitting on the balcony, watching the river; the cat, Simon—a rescue from the clinic—on her lap. Then she went to bed.

▲

The funeral, a fortnight later, was an event, as of course it would be, given Richard Gausse's fame within the architectural world and the long list of his rich clients, and given Amanda's love of a party.

The grand Centennial Hall at the Sydney Town Hall was host to the formal ceremony and eulogies. A confirmed atheist (one trait Rita had always shared with him), there would be no farewelling of Richard Gausse in a church. The following wake was a gorgeously catered affair for three hundred of his closest friends and clients, hosted in a huge marquee in the grounds of Richard's own cavernous mansion in Rose Bay. The place had sat empty of late, but proved useful now.

Rita attended both. She did not speak at the funeral, only watched all the eulogists up on the stage, and at the wake she felt slightly apart from it all, the one orphan of the family now, compared to her stepsiblings, an out-of-towner, lost among the glamour of the Sydney elite. True, she had been born and partly raised in Sydney, and she knew many of the faces, and some even remembered her. But she had never truly thought of Sydney as home: the family had been away so much when she was a child, travelling about the world for Richard's work, and at eighteen Rita had officially fled the city in the process of fleeing her father.

Meanwhile, she got thoroughly, if genteelly, drunk at the wake. Yes, her drug-taking days were behind her now, but alcohol remained a lifeline, as necessary as it had ever been. So her recollections the next morning were hazy, no more really than a disjointed assortment of moments from the whole day.

One instant was an encounter in the Town Hall just after the ceremony, memorable purely for its awkwardness. Rita had been momentarily stranded with a duchess-like acquaintance of Amanda's, who, in a stab at conversation, made three faux pas in a row. The first, mistaking Rita for one of Amanda's own children, was the urgent inquiry, *I'm told his first family was rather unstable; wife and daughter both. Is the daughter here, do you know?* The second, forging on bravely in the face of Rita's admission that she in fact was the daughter, was the breezy observation, *Oh, well, I so wanted to meet you. You're the one who wrote that strange book, the one that had you prancing around naked in the hills, or something similar, aren't you? Can we expect another one soon?* And the third, flailing after Rita's frosty reply in the negative, was the tentative, *And you're married, you have children of your own now . . . ? Oh, no wait, that's right . . .* At which point Amanda had returned to drag the fool woman away.

Another image—from much later in the night, as the party was winding up, with Rita well in the pleasant grip of red wine—was of a very svelte couple, younger than her, in their thirties maybe, whom she had found herself talking with, discreetly but unmistakably inviting her back to their place for a threesome, an offer she had pretended not to understand. At her father's wake, for heaven's sake!

But two other memories loomed larger, and both of them, strangely, involved her father's client—his last—Walter Richman.

The billionaire himself had not attended the funeral—considerately, in Amanda's view, as she told Rita, for if he *had* shown up, then the ceremony would have gone from an A-list-but-tastefully-restrained party to a full-blown media circus. Instead he had sent a video message to be played in the hall during the orations.

It was the last of several such recorded testimonials from famous clients based overseas. Rita had ignored the others, for from her seat in the front row alongside Amanda and her stepsiblings, the big screen, hanging almost directly above, was hard to see. In her abstraction, she hadn't cared anyway about what strangers had to say regarding the no-doubt hideously beautiful mansions and office blocks her father had designed for them. But when Richman came on, something about his voice, booming through the hall, made her crane her neck and actually look at him, looming giant overhead, and listen.

She knew his face, of course, lean and wry and somehow battered, hair cut long and still lusciously black, even though he must be in his seventies by now. Who in the world didn't know that face? Still, it was different to see it like this, not in a news broadcast or on a front page, but in a privately filmed clip, shot—where? In the house her father had built for him? It was impossible to say. Richman was sitting forward on a couch in a dimly lit room, the background in soft focus, anonymous.

'Richard Gausse was my friend,' rolled the voice, rich and low, with its effortlessly confident American accent, New York–genteel. 'And I say that at a time in life when men don't easily make friends. But in the short while that we worked together, on one of the most difficult projects imaginable, we truly formed a bond. Indeed, in the last years of his life, I was perhaps his only intimate companion, and learned much of his heart. And so to Amanda and to all of his children, George and Jerome and Erica, and Rita, I say this: though he was separate from you physically, you were all very much in his thoughts—increasingly so, as his health failed. And he was haunted by sadness and regrets of which he can never now speak to you. But I hope that you can remember him well, as I do.'

For a moment more Walter Richman stared earnestly, compellingly, at the camera. Then the image faded, and he was gone.

What a strange thing to say, Rita thought, as the ceremony moved on. To claim, in such a public forum, to be in possession of the final intimacies of a dead man, in front of his own family. *Weird*. But no one else remarked on it throughout the day.

And the last, and strangest memory of all, also involved the billionaire. Very late in the night, not long after Rita had escaped the lure of the threesome couple and was gathering her things before calling a taxi to take her to the hotel, a woman approached.

'Ms Gausse?'

Caught unawares, Rita threw back her head somewhat dizzily to get a look at the woman. She was no one Rita recognised, no one she had noticed throughout the day, even though she was quite striking; of middle age, perhaps, but trim and fit, her poise graceful in some indefinable way, her dress impeccably black, her legs clad in supple knee-length leather boots, her hair a bright dyed-blonde cropped very short.

'Yes?' said Rita.

'If I might introduce myself, my name is Clara Lang, and I work for Walter Richman.'

Rita stared in surprise. The woman's accent was international, mostly US but mixed with a trace of European, German maybe, or Dutch. And on closer inspection there was something strange about her face: her nose was shaped as if it should be one of Nordic fineness, but there was a sudden bluntness to its tip, a marring of some kind.

'Oh, yes,' Rita said, after a gap. 'What do you do for him?'

The woman gave a quirked smile, and Rita knew, the way the drunken do, that *she* was sober, had not taken a drink all day. 'I'm the chief of his private staff, although the title he prefers is major-domo. I manage his day-to-day affairs. He sent me to be his representative here today. I've passed on Mr Richman's condolences to your stepmother and stepsiblings already—but I did not want to miss *you*. You especially.'

Rita swayed a little, flushed and self-conscious now. 'Well, that's very kind of you.' But couldn't this have been done earlier, instead of now, when she was leaving, and so damn woozy?

The woman nodded as if understanding. 'In truth, I wanted a moment alone with you, away from attentive eyes and ears. I have a private message for you from my employer.'

'From Walter Richman?'

'Yes. He has a request to make of you.'

Another sway. 'What?'

The woman's calm gaze seemed to note the sway, and her lopsided smile came again. 'Well, this isn't the best time to discuss it. Not at your father's funeral service. And you're about to leave anyway, I see.' Her hand slipped deftly into a small handbag and produced a card, held it forwards. 'In two weeks from now, I'll be in Melbourne on business. Perhaps I could meet with you then in more relaxed circumstances?'

Rita took the card, noting that the woman's right hand was missing its little finger, a slim white scar the only remainder. Half of the fourth finger was missing as well. 'If you like, yes.'

'Good. I'll call you. I have your number, if you can excuse the liberty. Your stepmother's legal people gave it to me.'

And with a nod, the woman withdrew, slipping off towards the exit without giving anyone else in the milling crowd a glance.

Which sent Rita baffled to her taxi.

When she woke the next morning, hungover and wrung out, with those calm eyes, blonde hair and a maimed hand hovering in her mind, she might have thought the encounter was only a dream, tacked onto her memories of the actual party. Except that when she went through her bag, the card was there, plain but elegant.

Clara Lang, it said.

And nothing else but a mobile phone number. There was no email address, no job description, no title, no company or function. But it proved at least that she was real. Her, and Walter Richman.

But what could it all be about?

Rita gave a mental shrug. Time would tell, and she needed to get going. She was due back in Melbourne for work and had a tedious twelve-hour drive down the Hume Highway ahead of her. The trip would have been just an hour by air, of course, but there was no point reminding herself of that. Even now, after everything else she had repudiated and dismissed from the old days, she could still not go near a plane.

She made for the shower.

2

DEPORTED

Section of article,
Sydney Morning Herald, 2004

Daughter of Architect Detained at LA International Airport

Rita Gausse, daughter of renowned architect Richard Gausse, has been detained by authorities in Los Angeles after disruptive behaviour on her United Airlines flight from Melbourne. Reportedly under the effects of alcohol and other unnamed substances, Ms Gausse was restrained during the flight by staff and passengers. She has been denied entry to the United States and will be returned to Australia. It is understood that Ms Gausse, who was travelling with a female companion, was intending to visit the USA as part of a promotional tour for her recently published book, the . . .

3

AN INVITATION

TRUE TO HER WORD, WALTER Richman's major-domo phoned a week later to set up an appointment.

Where, Clara Lang wanted to know, would Rita like to meet? They could make use of a conference room at the major-domo's hotel—the Park Hyatt, by the cathedral—or meet in a restaurant or café. Or would Rita prefer to play host in her own home?

Rita was ready for this. She had by then researched the name Clara Lang and confirmed that the woman was indeed who she claimed. While not exactly famous, she was, as the right hand to Walter Richman, certainly a known figure in the corporate and society world. There was even a Wikipedia entry about her.

It was brief, but enlightening. Born in Germany in 1963, she had lived in the USA since age eleven, which explained the accent. In her younger adulthood she had been a professional mountain climber, which added up too, seeing she now worked for the most famous climber of all time. However, a serious injury (unspecified) had led her to cease mountaineering in 1990, after which she had studied economics and business, developing a role as a corporate consultant, training young executives in teamwork efficiency and problem solving. It was via this avenue that she had come to meet Walter Richman in 1996, who took a liking to her—one climber to another, presumably—and offered her a job on his personal staff; a staff which, twenty years later, she had now headed for a decade.

All legitimate, but the question remained for Rita: where to meet? The thought of this forbidding woman—former mountain climber (a very good one, according to the article, a pioneer in a time when female climbers were a rarity) and now steward to one of the richest and most powerful men in the world—sitting down for coffee and biscuits in Rita's modest Ikea-furnished apartment, with Simon, the regulation woman-living-alone cat, rubbing and purring around her ankles . . . well, no, it wouldn't do at all. And yet the notion of encountering the major-domo in some sterile hotel conference room, or over a white tablecloth in a stiffly formal five-star restaurant, was even worse.

So Rita settled on a café near her flat, down on the river—home ground, but to some degree neutral. Clara Lang agreed readily, although admitting that she was unfamiliar with exactly where the Edgewater Estate development might be found. 'It's not far,' Rita assured her, 'only seven or eight kilometres west of the city. Fifteen minutes in a taxi.' Or, she supposed, in a corporate limousine.

On the appointed day and hour she left her flat and made the short walk to the rendezvous, descending the steep street that led from her apartment block on the lip of the Maribyrnong valley down to the riverbank. It was a beautiful sunny autumn morning, and the river itself was glinting coolly blue as it curved through parklands towards Footscray and its junction with the Yarra beyond.

At the base of the slope was Edgewater Square and a small area of cafés and restaurants, including Rita's regular haunt. She arrived five minutes early to find Clara Lang already seated at a table on the deck in the sunshine. Her clothes matched the setting. Rita had half expected business attire, but instead Walter Richman's emissary was wearing jeans, heavy hiking boots and a T-shirt, an unneeded jumper slung over the back of her chair. She was staring out over the water, but turned as

Rita approached, and rose quickly, an economy of movement apparent in her, a mountain climber's litheness perhaps.

'Rita,' she said, hand extended. 'So good to see you again, on such a nice day.'

They shook hands lightly, Rita fleetingly aware of the absence of the major-domo's little finger. Casually dressed or not, Clara Lang looked every inch assured and capable. The set of her narrow face was cool, Germanic in its self-possession, and it was only the odd blunting of her nose that gave any hint of fallibility.

With the greetings exchanged, and Rita settled, and their coffee orders taken, the major-domo nodded towards the view, walkers and cyclists moving on the riverside paths. 'I have visited Melbourne many times, especially in the last few years, and yet I never knew it had a second river. I thought there was just the Yarra.'

'You're not alone in that,' Rita replied, noting that the major-domo had pronounced *Melbourne* correctly, without the mis-emphasised first syllable and the elongated second syllable common to Americans. 'The Maribyrnong often gets forgotten. It was an open sewer for most of Melbourne's history, although it's been cleaned up a lot lately as the western suburbs have gentrified.'

Clara nodded, shifting in her chair to consider the café complex around them, the Edgewater square beyond, and behind that the glass-and-steel townhouses and apartment blocks of the estate, crowding up the slope. 'Yes, this certainly all looks new. What was here before?'

'Right here? This area was a munitions factory and storage depot. There's still an old magazine intact behind those buildings over there. But further along the river there were abattoirs and tanneries and chemical plants, all types of heavy industry.'

'You would not guess it now,' Clara observed. 'Which really is a deceit, to my mind,' she added, with a bluntness that made her seem quite German indeed for a moment. 'Generic redevelopments like this, they give no sense of place or time or history.' But her smile was good-humoured as she eyed Rita. 'I only say that because it's not the sort of place I would have thought the daughter of so daring an architect as your father would choose to call home.'

Rita suppressed a sour smile. Well, no . . . there was a time when she would not have expected it either, a time when she would have scorned an estate like this, a stock-standard middle-class ghetto without a trace of architectural substance, or even of basic homeliness.

'It's a matter of budget more than choice,' she lied primly. 'Early on in their careers, vets don't earn a fortune. They don't in their later careers either, most of them, come to think of it.'

'Early in your career?' Clara considered. 'Yes, of course, it's easy to forget, but you have started late as a vet, haven't you. After your . . . former profession came to an end.'

So she knew about that. Lord. Now the major-domo would ask why Rita—after such a 'shall we say alternative' past—had chosen to become something as practical and mundane as a vet.

But in fact Clara didn't seem interested in earlier lives. 'Where do you work now?'

Rita pointed to the far bank of the river and the inner suburbs beyond, and explained about the hospital and the night shifts.

'You enjoy night shifts?'

'I do, yes. Plus it's only me these days, so it doesn't matter if my hours are unsocial.'

Again, the major-domo showed no inclination to pry, leaving *only me* and *these days* unquestioned, or perhaps she already knew about all that too. She was looking at the water again. 'These walking trails along the river. Do you use them?'

'I do. Further upstream there are some nice parks. You can go for miles.'

'You're a keen walker?' Clara enquired, with a look that was sizing up Rita's physique.

'I suppose so.' There was no supposing, Rita walked a lot. It was one of the few habits she had kept from the old days, although now she restricted herself to urban routes. But although she was fit enough, there was no denying that she was somewhat more full-fleshed than the trim major-domo. 'What about you? You used to be a serious mountain climber, I saw online. Do you still climb at all?'

The ironic smile came again. 'No, I don't do much climbing anymore, or even much serious walking. I'm forced to rely on the gym.'

'No spare time?'

'That too,' agreed the major-domo, and folded her maimed right hand over her left.

And suddenly Rita had it. The undisclosed injury mentioned in the Wikipedia article—it had to be frostbite. Rita knew next to nothing about mountaineering, but she knew about that at least, how climbers often ended up with extremities frozen solid, later to turn black and rotten and require amputation. And, yes, facial features too, like the tip of a nose. Not that two lost fingers and a blunted nose would ruin a climbing career—but Clara had mentioned walking. Her toes.

Rita glanced at the major-domo's shoes. The heavy hiking boots gave nothing away. But Rita remembered now that the major-domo had also worn long boots at the funeral, and that there had been an upright formality in the way Clara had walked away that night. She had thought it was a natural stiffness, but what if it was rather something careful, something artificial, learned in a rehab ward?

Rita's gaze lifted, found the other woman watching her steadily. At which point the coffees arrived to break the moment. After their first sips, the major-domo straightened and took on a brisker tone.

'Before we come to the business at hand, I should say first that I knew your father quite well. We worked together often in the last few years at the Observatory. I liked him very much.'

'I'm glad,' Rita replied. 'But then you must know he and I weren't very close.'

'He mentioned that, yes, though of course it's none of my business. But if I might enquire, what has happened to his ashes? I forgot to ask Amanda what she intended to do with them.'

'He requested in his will that his ashes be released into the surf at Clovelly beach in Sydney. It was his favourite place to swim. I don't know if Amanda has done that yet, though.'

'Ah. His will. Did you know that I was a signatory to it? He made some alterations to it a couple of years ago, and I happened to be at hand. I remember that he said he was making changes to his bequests regarding you. And of course he died a very wealthy man.'

Rita blinked. It was shock, yet again, like watching Walter Richman on the big screen at the funeral, to find that a stranger was so intimately involved with her own family affairs.

'Yes,' she said, 'he told me he was going to do that. I wasn't in his old will, from the days when we didn't speak at all, but after we made up he wanted me back in. I told him his money should really go to Amanda and her kids, they were far more central to his life than I was. So he promised he would keep my bequest small. Which he has.'

Out of all Richard Gausse's fortune, garnered over a lifetime of designing for the rich—the commission on Richman's house alone had been close to twenty million—Rita had been left just five hundred thousand dollars, along with some art works that had belonged to her mother. Rita was grateful for this frugality. The money would pay off the mortgage on her flat and leave her a nice amount of cash in reserve, but it was not so much that it would distort the newly won balance of her life, not so much that it could tempt her towards . . . old ways.

'I'm glad he respected your wishes,' said Clara. Then the bluntness again. 'Is it because you did not approve of his style of design—an offence against nature, I remember one critic called it—that you did not want to share in the money he made from it?'

'It was one of the reasons we fell out,' Rita answered carefully. 'I had stronger opinions about things then.'

36

'Still, at the same time you must have been aware of his genius, even if you didn't approve of it.'

'I don't know that I was, or that I am even now. Genius doesn't equal being right. And like you said, I wasn't the only one who thought his projects were abominations.'

The smile. 'Well, in greatness there is always controversy. Which brings me to the house your father designed for my employer.'

Rita had to nod. 'It's been controversial all right. Not many houses have caused a whole government to fall.'

The major-domo's shrug was cursory, an unspoken, *Well, yes, if you consider a Tasmanian government to be of any consequence.* 'All that fuss will soon be forgotten. Greatness is what endures. And trust me, the Observatory is your father's greatest work. His masterpiece.'

'Well, I wouldn't know, would I? Your boss has kept it all so secret. No photos in the papers, no articles in the magazines. I haven't seen a single shot of the interior anywhere, only a few exterior snaps of the mountain, and only from a distance, which tell you nothing.'

'Ah, but that's exactly the point,' said the major-domo, 'that's exactly why Mr Richman has sent me. I'm here to extend an invitation to you to come and stay in the Observatory, to come and see your father's work firsthand, as Mr Richman's personal guest.'

Rita sat back, genuinely surprised. She had not known what to expect from this meeting, but she had never suspected this. 'Me? Walter Richman wants *me* to come and stay with him?'

Clara nodded. 'It's in memory of your father, really. A few months from now Mr Richman will be hosting a huge party at the Observatory, a house-warming if you will, with hundreds of guests flown in, but before then he'll be holding a smaller private celebration for those who helped make it all possible. The chief builder, the interior designer, people like that. Obviously, as the architect, your father would have been the guest of honour. But now that Richard is gone, Mr Richman is hoping you will attend in his place.'

'But why on earth me?' Rita protested. 'Why not Amanda? She's the one you should be talking to. Or one of Amanda's children, for that matter. They were all of them closer to Dad than I was.'

'Perhaps. But Mr Richman's conversations with your father have convinced him that you would be the most appropriate.'

'What conversations?'

'To that I am not privy. I only know that it's you Mr Richman wants.'

Rita was shaking her head. She was not going to go, of course. It was impossible, for one inarguable reason of which the major-domo would not be aware. But even without that, she didn't *want* to go, not to spend an evening, or a whole weekend perhaps, standing in her father's place, among those who had worked with and admired him.

'No,' she said. 'Ask Amanda, she's the right person for this.'

'I understand that Mr Richman intends to invite only you, or no one from your family at all.'

Rita bridled. 'He can't force me.'

'Of course not! It isn't meant that way at all. Mr Richman merely believes that you are the only one your father would want in attendance, if he were alive still to give an opinion. The invitation is testimony to your father's esteem for you, no more.'

And what was she to say to that? What esteem? What could her father have said of her that impressed Richman so? Rita would have thought that someone like herself—her old self, that was, for she assumed it was mainly her former life, with all its extravagances and dramatics, that her father had discussed with Richman—would be held in disdain by a hard-headed multi-industrial billionaire. True, her father would have told Richman that she had since disowned her old beliefs, that she had straightened out, that she was okay now . . .

Okay now? Rita turned her head a moment, to take in the view along the river. It was an unremarkable scene, a tamed waterway in a tamed valley, people strolling along its bank in the sunshine. Ah, but to her old self . . . to her old self it would have looked very different. Her old self would have seen through the surface to the secret beneath.

This landscape, the whole western half of Melbourne, seemed to a casual observer to stretch out flat and bare and dusty: dull when compared to the eastern side of town, which rose, hilly and green, to meet the Dandenong ranges. But the flatness was a lie. In truth, the Maribyrnong River and its tributaries cut the plain into a maze of valleys and gorges. Freeways bridged those gorges heedlessly, but to a walker like Rita, following the minor roads and the bike tracks and the green belts, the western suburbs were a constant series of surprisingly steep descents and climbs, always down to and then up away from water.

But that wasn't the great secret. The secret was the plain itself, for the western half of the city sat upon the edge of a vast and rare geological oddity: the remains of a giant volcanic flood. From six million years in the past up until only a few thousand years BC—well into the era of living human memory—a multitude of gentle volcanos had pulsed out billions of tonnes of lava across the landscape, drowning a huge expanse under a layer of rock sixty metres deep. This basalt inundation, hundreds of kilometres across in all, was the third largest of its kind in the world, with only examples in India and the United States, the Deccan Plateau and the Snake River Plain, occupying a greater territory.

And right here, sitting in this little café, that flood was visible in cross-section. Here the humble Maribyrnong had carved a gorge through the basalt, a trench that reached all the way down to the ancient bedrock. Oh, the gorge had been worn since by wind and rain, and then quarried by man, smoothing its sheerer sides down to gentle slopes, but even now as Rita gazed at the settled valley and its green parks, she could still picture the ancient floods of lava, piling one upon the other.

And if the *younger* her had wandered up this same gorge, say three hundred years ago, when only the Aboriginal population had weighed lightly upon the country, before the thousands of other humans swarmed in: well, the presences here, forged in their unique fires and then unearthed by the river, would have been *potent*.

She blinked, came back to herself.

Jesus. Presences?

She returned her gaze to the table, and to Clara Lang, waiting for a reply. And Christ, she was over-thinking things. Richman's invitation was surely nothing more than it seemed, an act of politeness for the sake of her father's memory. Not that it mattered either way.

She shook her head at the major-domo. 'I'm sorry, but whatever Dad told Mr Richman, I still won't be going. It's impossible.'

'But why?'

'There's no way to get there but by air or by sea.'

'That's right. But we'd take care of all that. We could either fly you first class to Hobart and from there by Mr Richman's own helicopter, or—'

Rita swallowed. 'I don't fly. Not even in first class, and certainly not in a helicopter.'

'You don't fly at all?'

'Not ever.' Not in twelve years, at least. And she set her jaw to show that, no, she did not want to talk about why.

But Clara only shrugged. 'Then by sea. Mr Richman has a fine ocean-going yacht. We could arrange for it to pick you up right here in Melbourne. It'd only be a three-day voyage . . .'

Rita was shaking her head again. 'Unless his yacht is the size of a cruise liner, no way. I don't go to sea either. Not in anything small, at least.' Not, she added silently, with fewer than a thousand people around her for company . . . okay, for safety, for *protection*. Not that she believed that nonsense anymore, but some things were visceral beyond reason.

The major-domo's expression was now one of intrigued curiosity. 'That is indeed a pickle. Mr Richman's yacht is very large, but there's no denying it's not quite an ocean liner.'

'There you go then. I'm sorry, you'll have to pass on my thanks for the invitation, but—'

Clara lifted a hand. 'However, Mr Richman *is* a majority shareholder in several cruise lines, and hence part owner of some of the biggest ships in the world, several of them operating right here on scenic routes to the Wheel. So I wonder . . .'

The biggest ships in the world? With a sinking heart Rita saw her mistake. She could argue all she liked, but it would be futile now. By refusing the invitation on the grounds of the impossibility of transport, she had—in the world of the super rich, where no practicality could not be solved with money—already agreed to go.

And for a moment, as the major-domo murmured on about state-rooms that could be made available and ships that could be diverted, a part of Rita stood back in awed consideration.

The awe was not for the fact that she would be going to meet one of the most famous and wealthy men in the world. She had encountered, during her childhood and adolescence, more than enough celebrity clients of her father's to know that there was usually nothing inspiring in person about the wealthy and famous. Often, quite the opposite. So, no, Walter Richman himself did not overly daunt her.

But his home did.

Or rather its location. For a visit to Walter Richman's house on its remote isle also meant a visit to the nearby wonder of the world, the Wheel. And something in her quailed at *that* thought.

In fact, something in her had always quailed at the thought, for through all the wanderings of her earlier life, roaming across Australia and exploring its wilder areas, she had never visited the wildest part of all: she had never taken a trip to see the Wheel. She could have done so easily at any time: every summer, thousands of tourists took cruises from Melbourne or Sydney, or joy flights from Hobart, for that very purpose. And in those days she *did* still sail and fly.

So why hadn't she ever gone? What doubt or fear or warning had sounded in her back then?

Perhaps it was just that she had always been wary of mountains, wary of the grander scales of geography. Her art, back when she had believed in it, had been about more intimate landscapes, the human-sized contours of hills and gullies and creeks and caves, not the over-towering scenes of the great mountain ranges of the world. As for the Wheel, which dwarfed even other mountains, let alone humans, well . . . the old her had instinctively known that it was no place for her, that she would not be able to look upon it without succumbing in ways she could not control.

It was, simply, *too much*.

But now? Could the new her look upon the mountain of all mountains with safety?

And then—rather shockingly, for how could she have forgotten it?—Rita remembered that the man she would be going to meet, Walter Richman, had *climbed* the Wheel, the only man ever to do so. She had been just three years old that historic day in 1974, but she remembered gathering with her parents around the TV to watch the grainy footage of the final dramatic ascent, the four climbers in their space suits setting out for the summit, but in the end only the one man making it there, the lone figure, standing, arm raised within the very Hand of God.

And abruptly she found the thought of meeting that same figure, even forty-two years later, even as an old man now, very daunting indeed.

4

HOW THE WHEEL GOT ITS NAME

Excerpt from *Reaching for the Hand of God*,
by John Soliola, 2007

The first human acknowledged by history to have set foot upon the Wheel was a British naval officer by the name of William Bligh.

Yes, *that* William Bligh.

The *Bounty*, however, and its mutiny, were still far in his future. Bligh was only twenty-three when he landed on the Wheel, and not yet a captain, or even a lieutenant, but only a promising young sailing master serving on the sloop HMS *Resolution*, under a far more renowned sailor than Bligh himself would ever become, one Captain James Cook.

The year was 1777. Cook was on his third voyage of exploration in the southern Pacific, and had two ships, the *Resolution* and the *Discovery*, under his command. He was determined during this trip to make a landing on the mountain isle, which had been discovered five years earlier by the French explorer Marion du Fresne.

Du Fresne had been unlucky. Forced south of Tasmania by bad weather, he had sighted the Wheel and sailed to its foot, making the official discovery long after Jansz's enigmatic glimpse. But with bad weather continuing, the French captain had been unable to make a landing there to claim the mountain for France. All he could do was roughly map the island's shoreline, and name the mountain on his chart: *La Grande Crete*

Rouge. Then, with a Gallic shrug perhaps, he sailed on for his intended destination, New Zealand.

Strangely enough, Cook himself passed to the south of Tasmania just a year after du Fresne, in 1773, on the second of his great voyages to the Pacific. However, he did not happen to sail sufficiently south to sight the Wheel, nor did he go looking deliberately for the mountain, for he had not heard anything at that stage of du Fresne's discovery.

This was because du Fresne himself had met with a violent death in New Zealand, along with many of his crew. The survivors of the disaster did not reach France, or make their findings public, until after Cook had already departed on that second voyage. So it wasn't until Cook returned to Tasmanian waters in 1777, aware by then of du Fresne's discovery, that the English captain could make his own visit to the great mountain, determined to be the first to set foot there.

Initially, the weather was kinder to the British than to the French. Cook sailed his two ships up to the Wheel under a bright summer sky and upon calm summer seas. The mountain was, in Cook's own words, 'the most stupendous vision of all my years at sea.' But he was puzzled. Du Fresne had named the mountain *La Grande Crete Rouge*, which Cook translated loosely as the Great Red Wall.

But why *rouge*? The lower half of the mountain was draped in a white and blue mantle of ice and snow and glacier, while the appalling upper heights, rocky and forever bare, seemed to be coloured mostly a basalt grey. There was a tint of ochre to the stone, yes, but still, there was little actual *red* to be seen anywhere on the massif.

Perhaps, Cook mused, things had been different at the time of du Fresne's visit. The snow cover might have been lesser then, revealing more of the native stone of the lower slopes, which might well be reddish. But in any case, Cook let the name stand in du Fresne's honour, though he dropped the *Grande*, as the mountain's greatness, he thought, was self-evident. The Red Wall, he inscribed on his charts.

For the next two days, in perfect weather, Cook sailed all about the Wheel, carefully mapping its shoreline but finding nowhere suitable to land. Instead, he alighted finally upon the single other landmass that keeps the great mountain company there upon the southern sea, a smaller island that rises ten kilometres to the west of the Wheel, and which possessed, even then, a rough natural harbour.

Cook named this island Theodolite Isle, for here he and his surveyors could take accurate bearings to measure the height of the Wheel across the water. The Wheel's summit was not visible from Theodolite Isle's shore, so to better site his instruments, Cook had his men climb part of the way up the island's own mountain, a great spire of rock that lofts nearly three thousand metres high. This pillar is itself an impressive feature, but of course is dwarfed by the Wheel nearby. Cook, in honour of its usefulness to him, named it Observatory Mount.

The result of all these measurements? Du Fresne, without the luxury of solid land beneath him, had estimated a height for the Wheel of (in today's measurements) twenty-four thousand six hundred metres. Cook's calculation was twenty-four thousand nine hundred and fifty. Both were short of the actual summit, and, interestingly, neither were better than Jansz's incidental guess some centuries earlier.

On Cook's fourth morning in the vicinity, the weather holding fair, though a high overcast was moving in from the west, he decided it was time to set a man upon the Wheel itself.

It was no easy task. The shoreline of the mountain—on Cook's new map, the massif formed a great crescent arc, forty-five kilometres end to end, its tips pointed to the west—was virtually harbourless along both its east and west faces. Everywhere, steep slopes plunged directly into deep water. The west shore was at least somewhat less sheer than the eastern, but in turn was pummelled ceaselessly by the prevailing swells of the Southern Ocean.

Cook could find only one place to put men ashore. It was a spot on the western face, near enough to the centre of the arc, where a chunk of mountainside had in some past age slid into the sea, leaving a scooped hollow at the waterline, fringed by a low reef of rubble that rose just enough to take the brunt of the waves. In its natural state this haven was unfit to host Cook's large ships, though there was the promise that it might, after large-scale sea works, one day do so. In the meantime, it did at least offer shelter for smaller craft to put in and run aground.

Cook launched two boats, placing them under command of his fourth-ranked officer, the *Resolution's* young sailing master, William Bligh, who had declared himself eager for the adventure.

A skilled seaman, whatever his future flaws, Bligh made short work of the landing, timing his run between swells to thread his two craft through a gap in the outer reef to gain the inner anchorage. The water there was awash with foam and prone to surges, but on the far side of this uneasy harbour, a huge slab of rock tilted gently down from the mountainside, where the boats could be run up and dragged clear of the water.

Sixteen men stepped ashore, Bligh the foremost, as he noted proudly in his diary. Then, with a ceremonial firing of a pistol, and a fluttering of a flag, the mountain, and the island it formed, was claimed for Great Britain in the name his highness, King George III.

It was a far-from-welcoming locale, however. The men were perched on a naked slope with no way to move to the left or right, where cliffs reared forbiddingly. They could only go upwards. Bligh led the way, taking his party to the top of the slab, and then up an exposed ridge so steep that the men were bent double, as if climbing a ladder. In this fashion they reached a narrow shelf that looked out over the sea and the ships below from a height of about one hundred and fifty metres.

Here they paused while the *Resolution's* naturalist, George Forster, made study of the plant life. There was surprisingly little. Moss and lichen grew on the rocks, a few grasses and stunted trees grew in stony cracks, and birds could be seen wheeling about the cliffs, but that was all. Other isolated sea mounts Forster had studied were either thick with plant life, or were crowded rookeries for seabirds, or were the breeding grounds for sea-going creatures such as seals or penguins. In comparison, the lower slopes of the Wheel were strangely barren.

Forster made note of all this, but could offer no immediate theory as to why the area appeared so shunned by life.

Bligh, meanwhile, had spied an out-thrust of rock shaped like the buttress of a gothic cathedral rising some fifty metres above the shelf; a natural platform at its end promised a fine view. The party had no real mountaineering equipment, but determined to be the first to reach this landmark (later to be known as Bligh Rock or Pulpit Rock or Rock of Martyrs) Bligh set off accompanied by two game seamen.

Climbing hand over hand, they eventually reached the aerie at over two hundred metres above the sea. This would prove to be the highest point gained by the first assault upon the Wheel, and it ended as many future assaults would end—in disaster.

They had by then been two hours on land, and even as Bligh reached the platform he realised that the calm weather of the last several days was beginning to break. A grey pallor had come over the sea, and a chill was robbing away the warmth of the air. In the sky, the high sheet of overcast had ridden swiftly up from the west, and directly overhead its forward edge was now encountering the immovable barrier of the Wheel. High above, cloud broke and swirled slowly against stone and ice.

But that slowness was an illusion of distance. What Bligh did not know—could not know, for it would not be fully understood by meteorologists until two centuries later—was that when certain high level jet-stream winds collided at just the right angle with the vast western face of the Wheel, those winds were deflected, focussed and accelerated fantastically down the mountainside. All Bligh knew was that whereas there had been only a warm breeze blowing all morning, suddenly, out of nowhere, a cold gale began to bluster down from above.

It was time to get back to the boats.

Leading his two companions, Bligh descended as fast as he dared to the shelf. The other thirteen men were already climbing down ahead of him, making for the waterline. By then the wind was howling, and chips of ice and stone were pelting alarmingly from above. The leading group made it to the boats and one craft set off in waters suddenly perilously choppy, while the other waited for Bligh and his companions.

They could not wait long. The wind was hitting the ocean like a great hammer now, driving the water first away from the shore, then back again in ever-greater swells. These waves had begun to crest and crash as Bligh reached the boat. The young officer made it aboard with a leap, but the two men behind were not so lucky; the craft was swept away before they could follow. Bligh made several attempts to return for them, but the wind and the waves were too wild. He was forced to retreat, shouting orders to the two left behind that they were to withdraw to somewhere higher and safer up the mountain, and await rescue.

With that, Bligh departed. It was only under the greatest duress that his boats made it back out to sea and to the waiting ships—and then the ships themselves were hard put to ride out the growing storm, which developed in violence beyond all experience. Icy gales howled down from the upper reaches of the Wheel, and the *Resolution* and the *Discovery* were forced to flee westwards, heeled hard over with only storm sails raised. It was only when they were well past Theodolite Isle that they moved beyond the worst of the buffeting, and could heave to.

There they held throughout the afternoon until darkness fell. All night the gales raged in their fury. Also, a deep moaning could be heard coming from the direction of the Wheel, rising now and then to an enormous piping and whistling: the voice of a far-off hurricane. And strange flashes could be seen high in the night, great sheets of blue, as if of lightning, illuminating the remote upper flanks of the mountain, though there were no storm clouds present. Cook postulated in his journal that it was perhaps some strange and monstrous cousin to St Elmo's fire—though this explanation did little, he admitted, to dispel the unearthly menace of the sight, or to make any less terrible the howling of the wind.

But towards dawn the storm finally eased, and by sunrise the wind had dropped and the sky was clear. Cautiously, Cook took his ships back east, and finding no adverse conditions, returned to the landing point of the day before, where the two sailors—their names were Barnabas Clover and Orald Makepeace—had been marooned.

There was no sign of them.

Bligh was sent ashore again, with a search party. The tilted slab was bare of any trace of the men, as was the shelf above, the most obvious place for them to shelter. But one of the searchers spied a shred of colour high upon the buttress of rock that Bligh and the two men had climbed the day before. Up went Bligh once more, but what he discovered was confounding. The men were not there, but they *had* been, for jammed hard into a crevice were two sets of clothing: pants, shirts, jackets, shoes, everything. Clothes, but of the men themselves, nothing.

What had happened? Why had the men ascended to the exposed buttress? Even in calm weather the climb was a precarious one; in the storm of yesterday it would have been horrifying.

Had they been *forced* to do so? Had the waves, driven beyond all comprehension, threatened the shelf, itself a hundred and fifty metres high, and compelled the men on to the buttress? And even if that was so, why had they removed their clothes? Why had they rendered themselves so defenceless in such bitter wind and cold? And where were they now? Had the gale finally plucked them from the height? Or had the sea risen *two hundred metres*, and swept them away?

The questions were never to be answered, for despite a full day's search, no further signs of Barnabas Clover or Orald Makepeace, not even a smear of blood or a tuft of hair, were to be found.

Sorrowful, Cook sailed off eastwards the next morning, leaving the Wheel and the mystery behind. He had only ever intended this visit to the mountain to be a detour. Despite all its wonders of size and terror, the Wheel offered no prospects for settlement or exploration. Cook and his ships had more important business waiting in the Pacific.

It is worthy to note that Cook, and later explorers, found no suggestion that the Wheel had ever been previously visited or inhabited by humans. Nor has any modern investigation. The indigenous nations of present-day Australia and New Zealand make no claim over it. Separated from the nearest land by over two thousand kilometres of deep ocean, the Wheel, it seems, has stood eternally apart from humanity.

▲

It was some years before the *Resolution* and the *Discovery* returned to England (leaving Cook himself dead in Hawaii) and it was then that the misunderstanding about the mountain's name arose.

The source of the problem was Cook's account of the voyage, published posthumously. Not that it was his fault. Cook's writings on the matter were perfectly clear, calling the mountain The Red Wall. And so it is inscribed on his original charts. However, thanks to a careless typesetter during the printing of the first edition of Cook's journal, the Red Wall became, on the new map, The Red *Wheel*.

It was an obvious error, one that was corrected in later editions. But in one of those quirks of history it was the erroneous name that prevailed, first purely as slang, later as the mountain's title de rigueur.

Why was this so? Perhaps the mistaken name endured merely out of a sense of black humour, for which mariners and mountain climbers alike are known. And after all, when viewed on a map, the great crescent described by the mountain does indeed look like one half of the rim of a giant wheel, with little Theodolite Isle forming the hub.

But perhaps there was an even deeper recognition in play. For as the years would show, the mountain would treat those who challenged it, seafarers and climbers alike, much as it had the luckless Clover and Makepeace—that is, with a mysterious and unremitting cruelty. And in this regard, could it not be said that the mountain was akin to the infamous instrument of medieval torture, the *breaking wheel*?

Either way, the name stuck.

▲

But forget Clover and Makepeace for a moment: the Wheel proved no friend to *any* of its discoverers. Consider the fate of Gerrit Jansz, the first to glimpse the mountain, but doomed to centuries of obscurity rather than being given the fame he deserved. Or consider du Fresne, credited with the find, yes, but dead only a few months afterwards, killed by Maori warriors before he could stake his claim to history.

Or consider James Cook, most famous mariner of his age, likewise cut down in Hawaii, only months after *his* visit to the Wheel.

And as for Bligh in his later years, well . . .

Need we go on?

5

ARRIVAL

THE MOOD ON THE SHIP was an unhappy one. Even secluded in her executive suite, Rita could sense it. One glance at the sky from her private balcony—tastefully fitted out with a bar, fire-pit and six-person spa—was enough to tell her why. Low cloud spread from horizon to horizon, and according to the weather forecast it wasn't going anywhere soon.

For her three thousand fellow guests on board the *Southern Wanderer* the clouds represented a disaster. This was the very last cruise of the autumn season. In only two days the waters about the Wheel would close to recreational traffic for the winter, and the *Wanderer* must return to Melbourne. But if the skies did not clear before then, then the Wheel itself—which had hidden stubbornly behind the clouds for a day already—might not be sighted at all. And there were no refunds. The weather was in the lap of the gods, not the cruise directors.

The Wheel *was* visible, of course—at least, its lower slopes were. The *Wanderer* had been roaming back and forth along the mountain's eastern shore all day, close in to cliffs that tilted back sheer from the sea. But with the cloud base at only fifteen hundred metres, the upper ninety-five per cent of the Wheel remained obscured, the world's greatest mountain reduced to no more than a dark wall, receding away for dozens of miles to either hand. Vast, yes, but what an anti-climax.

The ship had left Melbourne five days previously, with Rita as its most reluctant and nervous passenger. In the six weeks since her meeting with Clara Lang, her misgivings and fears about this entire enterprise had only grown. But she had been unable somehow to change her mind and refuse, so she had arrived at Station Pier as promised to board the ship.

In fact, she arrived by limousine, another example of Walter Richman's generosity regarding her travel arrangements, or perhaps his way of ensuring that she did not chicken out at the last moment.

At the check-in desk, nothing was too much trouble for Mr Richman's special guest. The first officer himself escorted Rita up to her suite, a five-room apartment on the uppermost accommodation deck. It was usually either reserved for use by the cruise line's own directors or was rented for fifteen thousand dollars a night. And it came—Rita was embarrassed to learn—with its own butler and housemaid.

She pleaded to be assigned to a plainer room, but her escort only laughed. The ship was otherwise fully booked, he explained, but, in any case, these were Walter Richman's direct instructions, and not for a first officer, or even the captain, to dispute.

So Rita resigned herself. As for the domestic help, the butler assured her—after directing her unpacking—that she need not concern herself with gratuities for himself or the housemaid. Mr Richman had already taken care of that item, and very generously at that.

The *Wanderer* sailed just on sunset, slipping across Port Phillip Bay in the twilight and passing through the heads into Bass Strait just as night deepened. Rita watched the land pass from her balcony. The evening was calm, and during its crossing of the bay the great ship had glided along as smoothly as a ball on glass—but once through the heads, the vessel began to rock gently on the ocean swells.

A light sweat broke on Rita's forehead, and an uneasiness woke in her stomach, like seasickness—but it wasn't seasickness, it was dread, a fear that the old madness would reach out of the past and assail her. Her eyes searched, ready for unusual waves to rise from the sea, their secret natures revealed to her alone; or for a storm, newborn and aware, to swell and come ravening forwards, battering uniquely at *her*.

That's how it had been her last time at sea, twelve years ago now, when she had booked passage for herself and Anne back to Australia, after their disastrous flight into LA. The US customs authorities had intended to simply throw them on the next flight home, but Rita had begged and wheedled until they allowed her time to organise a sea passage instead. There was no way she could have boarded another plane, she would have collapsed in screaming fits. A ship was the only way she could imagine making the return trip. A big, sturdy ship. A *safe* ship.

But there were no cruise liners that sailed from Los Angeles to Australia direct, so Rita's only option was to book their passage on a commercial vessel, taking one of the few spare cabins that such craft sometimes sold to wayfarers. And while the ship was certainly big and sturdy—in fact it was huge, a seventy-thousand-tonne container vessel— it did not turn out to be safe. Not for Rita at least.

She should have known. She should have realised that there would be problems. There were not enough people on board. Rita and Anne were the only passengers, and otherwise there was just the thirty crew. The vessel was an empty tub, deserted of human life, and it was human life that Rita needed around her, if she was to be protected from the sea. Seventy thousand tonnes of cold, dead steel was useless.

Oh, the voyage wasn't as bad as the flight had been. The presences of the ocean were as immense and untameable as those of the air, yes, but they were deeper and slower in mood than the monster that had buffeted the LA flight. Still, the voyage was bad enough, and it lasted three weeks. Rita was rigid and sleepless throughout, under assault from what seemed to be an endless parade of gales and squalls and swells, their consciousnesses hammering angrily against her own.

She was suffering through detox, too. They had no cocaine, leaving alcohol as her only defence, meaning that she spent the days either drunk, or hungover, or crazed with stress. And no doubt it was those three weeks locked in a cabin with an alternatively ranting or whimpering partner that finally convinced Anne—if the LA flight hadn't already done so—that things were over, really over, between them. She said her goodbyes to Rita the instant the ship docked in Sydney.

Rita had learned one thing, however. Two days short of Sydney, their ship crossed paths with a cruise liner outbound for the South Pacific, a big vessel with several thousand passengers. The two craft passed within half a mile of each other. The day was rough and squally, and Rita's demons had been torturing her as presence after presence fleeted by— but she noted that those same squalls were mysteriously calmed as they passed over the liner. Not calmed *physically*, of course, the wind and waves slapped just as hard against the liner as against Rita's ship. But the *presences* of the squalls, in the face of several thousand human souls, withdrew sullenly into themselves, and were silent.

Rita swore to herself then that if—*if*—she was ever forced to sea again, she would do so only amid a similar crowd. Not that she intended to go to sea again, or for that matter to ever again leave the Australian mainland, by *any* means of travel. She swore that, too. And for twelve years she had held to her vow. But now here she was, on a ship venturing by night into the wilds of Bass Strait, one of the most storm-strewn stretches of ocean in the world. No wonder she was nervous. What if she was wrong? What if, after all these years, she found that the protection of the crowd was not enough, and that she had put her head into the lion's jaw?

But in fact that first night passed without event. The weather stayed fair and Bass Strait remained benign, and by the next dawn the *Wanderer* had rounded the north-east corner of Tasmania. From there they spent a leisurely day tracking down the east coast, lingering by the cliffs and spires of first the Freycinet and then the Tasman peninsulas, before crossing Storm Bay to Bruny Island. By evening light they passed down Bruny's sheer coast to its many-pillared tip, and then on to the Friars, a tiny collection of seal-crowded isles that were the last southern outliers of Tasmania. Then, leaving all shores behind to the north, the *Wanderer* steamed on directly into the wilderness of the Southern Ocean.

Now the weather kicked up a little. After all, autumn was almost gone and winter was nigh. Waves reared, the wind blustered cold, and clouds scudded overhead. But the *Wanderer,* a mammoth craft fitted with the latest in stabilisation gear, was equal to the challenge, forging on smoothly into the swell. Not only did Rita remain free from seasickness, but her older malady held off as well. She could not say whether this was because she was truly rid of it after so long, or because the thousands of people around her were crowd enough to drown out any other influence, or because, to be honest, she was half-drunk much of the time. But either way she sensed no awareness in any of the passing storms, and perceived no consciousness in the rolling waves.

She spent the days in her suite, reading novels or staring at movies on any of the four giant screens, sipping wine all the while. The ship offered other diversions—rock climbing, wave surfing, ice skating, live shows, a casino—but none appealed, even less so did the idea of company. She stayed in for every meal, delivered by her faithful butler, and refused even the standing offer of a seat at the captain's table.

Otherwise, she waited—along with everyone else—for the Wheel to appear.

According to the ship's enthusiastic guidebook, the mountain should have made its entrance on the morning of their second day at sea. Keen-eyed passengers, said the book, could hope at dawn to spy, peeping over the southern horizon, the summit of the Wheel, 'ethereal, glowing red in the light of the unrisen sun', even though the mountain would still be several hundred kilometres away at the time. (In perfect conditions, informed the book, the peak of the Wheel could sometimes be visible from close to an astounding five hundred kilometres distance.)

But though Rita was up and watching from her balcony, the southern horizon that morning was a haze of broken cloud and sea spray, and nothing of the great peak was visible. No matter, assured her butler, no doubt at some point during the day the sky would clear and the Wheel would reveal itself, marching slowly up to its impossible heights.

Only it never did. The clouds remained all day, only to blow away frustratingly at nightfall, and then by the next dawn, infuriatingly, fog had come instead, followed by rain. By then the chance to view the great wonder from afar was gone anyway. Late that afternoon, in a steady, depressing downpour, the ship came within the lee of the Wheel's eastern shore, and the first part of the voyage was over.

The mountain loomed immediately above them now, and should have been a spectacular sight, climbing away to the stratosphere—but, other than its dreary lower ramparts, the Wheel remained as invisible as ever in the clouds. And so it stayed for the next day as well, the rain and the fog and the cold equally miserable and unending, which left the ship and its passengers only one more day before they must depart.

Rita's butler brought her a report from the main dining rooms of the passengers' mutterings. Why did the *Wanderer* have to hasten away, why couldn't they stay until the cloud finally cleared? Why was the deadline for departure so strict? Why were these waters closed to cruise ships for three months a year? By whose authority?

Well, answered the staff patiently, it was done by authority of the Australian government, to whom these waters belonged. As for the exact reason why, sadly the staff did not have that information at hand—but every passenger had a theory of their own. Some said it was for security purposes: there was a secret military base on Theodolite Isle, *everyone* knew that. Others said it was environmental: certain schools of fish bred in these waters in the winter and must not be disturbed. Or maybe it was whales, not fish. And, anyway, said still others, there was no point hanging around in winter, the weather was always like this, raining nine days out of ten. In fact, it was crazy to have come this late in autumn in the first place, the cruise line should never have allowed it.

But Rita's butler, after he had recounted all such theories, gave an austere wink. 'Pure bunkum, of course. *You'd* know the truth of it, ma'am, I'm sure, being a friend of Mr Richman's and all.'

Rita didn't know anything, but hardly felt she could admit to it, and so remained, like the other passengers, in ignorance.

However, there was at least one special treat in store for everyone. The captain announced it on the eve of their final day: the ship would be making a detour to the waters on the *western* side of the mountain— normally restricted territory. What was more, they would be visiting, and actually landing at, the mysterious Theodolite Isle, home not only to various secretive installations (the nature of which the captain was not at liberty to divulge) but also to the newly completed residence of the famous Walter Richman. Such a docking, in fact, was a privilege that had never been granted to any cruise ship before now. And it was all for the sake of a particular passenger now on board.

Rita, hearing this announcement over the intercom in her suite, could only wince. Lord. After a build-up like that, the whole ship would be watching in fascination when she disembarked. Maybe she should have taken the damned helicopter after all.

The following day produced the same clouds and rain as the two previous, but in the early afternoon the *Wanderer* steered south to the endmost cape of the island, and circling around it, entered the Wheel's western waters. This, as everyone knew, was the famous side of the mountain, the side where all the history had been made, where Cook had landed, and where the great climbing expeditions of the thirties and the fifties and the sixties had tried and failed to scale the peak, before the final epic victory, Walter Richman's victory, in 1974.

It was also, the guidebook said, the more physically dramatic side of the island. Oh, yes, the eastern face was spectacular in its own right (at least when it was not hidden by cloud). But because of the curve of the Wheel's great crescent, bent back like a giant bow, the flanks of the

East Face receded from the viewer, making this aspect of the mountain seem austere and remote and chilling.

The West Face, however, was another matter. The guidebook, with a reverent tone, promised passengers 'a grand stadium of nature' and 'a titanic stage set for the drama of history'. And for all the hyperbole, the book for once was right.

Now, as the *Wanderer* forged forwards, the great arc of the Wheel seemed to enclose the ship rather than recede from it. The mountain's upper heights remained hidden, but even so, the great wall rising to the base of the clouds and curving in a half-circle forty-five kilometres across was a profound sight. The crescent enfolded an immense space of ocean, dark and wild, and yet the water might have been the sands of an enormous arena, roofed overhead by the vast canopy of the clouds.

In the centre of this gargantuan amphitheatre, just visible through the sea mist, rose a lonely hump of land, from which a single mount rose like a pillar to meet the clouds. This was Theodolite Isle, the Wheel's sole companion in all the wilds of the southern sea, and the only habitable land for a thousand miles in any direction.

It was also home to Walter Richman, and Rita's destination.

She studied the isle from her balcony as the ship made its way across the inner sea of the great arc. Rain started to fall again, and it was near freezing out in the open, but she was too intrigued to retreat indoors. The great pillar of stone, she knew, was Observatory Mount. It lofted some two thousand eight hundred metres above the sea, sheer sided and narrow as a finger, and in any other part of the world would have been a wonder in its own right. But here, only a tenth the size of its awesome neighbour, it was reduced almost to insignificance. But only almost.

And to think, someone had conceived to build their house atop its peak, to claim that lonely grim spire as their *home* . . .

But of Walter Richman's house as yet nothing could be seen—the cloud cut off the top of the finger as neatly as a scissor stroke. And Rita could almost feel the frustration of the other passengers on the *Wanderer*, foiled yet again by the overcast skies as they lined the decks and balconies below her, their necks craned upwards in vain.

The island drew closer. Its eastern shoreline formed a natural harbour, and the waterline within was crowded with port facilities and sheds and one tall crane rising. Behind the harbour the land rose gently, a road winding up the slope, lined with various buildings, some small and anonymous, some larger and industrial looking, and one that appeared for all the world to be a large resort-style hotel. Beyond all this lay the Mount, stabbing upwards abruptly. Not so much like a finger, Rita decided; rather, it was an immense incisor tooth belonging to some great titan long dead and now decaying in the sea, the island formed by the monster's huge jawbone, and the Mount a last surviving fang.

The ship was slowing now, swinging its bow towards the mouth of the harbour. The haven—its name was Port Fresne—was not entirely natural, Rita could see now. The enfolding wings of the shorelines had been reinforced and lengthened by walls of concrete and piled stone. Much of the work, to Rita's untrained eye, seemed only newly finished. Even so, and despite the port and all the buildings, the whole island, with its great prominence of rock towering up, and with the grey sea all about, looked a wild, forsaken place, barely touched by man.

The *Wanderer* was at a crawl now as it entered the harbour, the ship far too large seemingly for what was only a small body of water. But doubtless the captain was sure of his room to navigate. Indeed, its bow and aft thrusters churning up froth, the *Wanderer* now performed a stately pirouette of some ten minutes' duration to turn about on its axis, and then slip slowly sideways to come up flush against the one dock in the port that was long enough, just barely, to host it.

Back when all this was being organised, Rita had at first assumed that the *Wanderer* would merely stand off from the isle while a launch took her ashore. But it had been explained to her that the seas were usually too rough outside the harbour to safely bring a launch alongside, meaning that the ship must enter the port and dock. But she wasn't to worry, the docking would be purely a routine procedure.

Now, however, having watched it all, and sensing the tension about the ship, Rita could tell that this was not routine at all. It had been a challenge of navigation. And the mortification grew in her at the enormity of so much bother for her sake—not just this docking, but the whole trip, the tens of thousands of dollars wasted to free up her cabin, the diversion of the ship from its usual route, the interference in the lives of its thousands of passengers, all of it just to deliver *her*.

What did that say about her host? What kind of person arranged all this just to ensure the arrival of a single guest? Even for a billionaire, it seemed outrageously extravagant. So why was Walter Richman so determined, so eager, for her to be here?

Well, she would find out soon enough. He might even be waiting for her right now down on the dock. Uneasiness swept through Rita. She did not feel ready. She looked down over the rail, but from her vantage could not see the gangway immediately below, only the dock workers to the fore and aft, securing the *Wanderer*'s lines.

She sighed, and turned back to the suite, just as the knock came on the door: the first officer once more, arrived to escort her down.

6

RICHMAN UNAUTHORISED

Excerpt from feature article by
Alannis Harris, *New York Times*, 1989

. . . which leads to the question that is often asked: how did Richman become, befitting his name, so damn rich?

The answer is that he inherited his wealth.

Yes, he has multiplied that inheritance several times over since, but much of Walter Richman's money was really earned two generations back, not by his father, multi-millionaire industrialist Berthold Richman, but by his grandfather, Horace Richman, who first lofted the Richman name to prominence.

Horace himself grew up comfortably middle class in the late nineteenth century, a third-generation American of English heritage, son of a prosperous Pennsylvanian farmer and landholder. Horace, however, had no interest in farming: his tastes were academic. Scholarships to first Andover and then Harvard saw him graduate in law. He never practised, however, moving instead immediately to join the federal civil service. His forty-five-year-long career peaked with the Washington-based posting of Deputy Secretary for Economic Affairs, making him second in rank in the entire Commerce Department, and frequent advisor to several presidents.

Horace's son Berthold (always known as Bert) was thus raised in a heady atmosphere of power and influence. He attended the same fine schools and colleges as his father, but was no academic, and had no interest in civil service. Having witnessed many a meeting between his reserved and proper father, acting for the bureaucracy, and a collection of charismatic entrepreneurs, ranging from cashed-up industrialists to flat-broke confidence men, Bert knew which side of the street he wanted to work. He was going to do business, not merely administrate it.

Of course, it still helped to have a rich dad. In 1935, at age thirty-one, Bert secured a 'loan' from his father (the debt was never called in) of thirty thousand dollars, a fortune at the time. He used the money to invest in steel and armaments, with perfect timing, given the looming troubles in Europe. By the end of World War II, having secured several key contracts for the construction of tanks and military transports, Bert had increased his holdings fifty times over. By then he was diversifying into mining, manufacturing, trucking and shipping. And he never slowed down. In 1950, he was one of the richest men in the United States.

Meanwhile, in 1945, Bert had married wealthy New York socialite Rebecca Wells, daughter of US senator Douglas Wells. Thirty years old, known for her hot temper and heavy drinking, Rebecca had struck up a tempestuous affair with Bert—no angel himself—and when she fell pregnant, the two decided to marry. The child was born five months later, in December 1945, New York City.

A boy, christened Walter Flagstaff Richman.

His parents' marriage was not a success. Their relationship remained permanently stormy, riven by arguments and alcohol and vastly differing ideas about life. By 1950, Bert and Rebecca were living apart, although they never divorced.

Walter would be their only progeny.

He resided mostly with his mother throughout his childhood, but seldom in one place, for Rebecca was a devoted worldwide traveller. She was also a keen skier, visiting resorts throughout the USA and Europe, which was how Walter received his introduction to alpine landscapes. He was a talented skier, but as he matured he showed more interest in going up mountains than skiing down them. In the French Alps, at the age of twelve, he began training under some of the great Chamonix climbing guides of the era. When he was fourteen, Walter and his mother flew to Australia to take a scenic cruise to the Wheel. The boy came away awestruck by what he saw, and more enamoured with the idea of climbing than ever.

Then, in 1960, Rebecca was killed in a skiing accident in Switzerland, and Walter, fifteen years old, was forced to return to New York to live with his father. The two were almost strangers to each other, and the next few years were troubled, for Bert thought it was time his son put aside the jet-set lifestyle and buckled down to economic studies and to learning the family business.

It soon became plain that Walter indeed had a ready head for finance, but to his father's disappointment, the youth couldn't seem to shake the climbing bug. He was forever sneaking away from school or from his father's office to go rock hopping with other disreputable types who shared the hobby. And on holidays he always managed to arrange, without his father's knowledge or financial aid, to get himself included on climbing expeditions to more serious mountains in the Rockies or in Alaska.

His father did all he could to hinder this, but at age eighteen Walter came into his mother's inheritance—she had left her own considerable fortune solely to him—and now that the youth was privately financed, there was nothing the senior Richman could do to stop his son going climbing full time.

In the seven years that followed, from 1963 to 1970, Walter relentlessly roamed the world's high places, bagging peak after peak, sometimes as a solo climber, but more often as part, or occasionally leader, of a team. By the age of twenty-five, from Everest on down, he had knocked off six of the ten highest mountains in the world (the Wheel aside) and his reputation as a climber was spreading white-hot through mountaineering circles.

But so was another reputation.

He was not a man liked by his fellow climbers. Indeed, those who climbed closely with him on an expedition seldom did so a second time. That he was arrogant and selfish and ambitious to the point of recklessness was not so much the problem—name a successful climber who wasn't some, or all, of those things. Nor was it that he was unpleasant company: he could, most claimed, be quite engaging, at least on a short or casual acquaintance.

The problem was his dishonesty. He was rich, yes, and funded many of the expeditions in which he was involved, but he was also cheap. For instance, he skimped far beyond sensible economy on vital supplies and equipment for the rest of the team, although his own gear was always first rate. He was notoriously slow in paying the wages of camp staff, even the wages of the all-important Sherpas, if in the Himalayas. Verbal agreements were often dishonoured, and even signed contracts were barely respected. And when challenged, he was quick to resort to lawyers and counter-suits.

More annoying still was his grandstanding. Talented a climber as he undoubtedly was, he seemed compelled to ram that talent down everyone's throat. He was notoriously greedy in claiming credit on team climbs, forever eager to be seen as the key player in any ascent, even if it had patently been a group effort. Worse, his self-aggrandising extended even to that gravest sin of all in the climbing world: claiming or implying that he had bagged certain peaks or difficult routes which in fact he had not.

This last habit was particularly baffling, seeing that his real achievements were so impressive anyway. As one climbing companion wrote, having spent a week with him once, blizzard-marooned in a two-man tent in a high camp,

> *He was the damndest person to understand. He was always going on about money and about getting ripped off by everyone around him. I suppose it's because he knows that everyone else knows how rich he is, therefore he thinks people are always trying to take him for a ride. And he wouldn't shut up about how good a climber he was, how he was better than everyone else. Christ, I knew that he really was a good climber, as good as anyone I ever saw, but it was like he was terrified that, again, because he came from money, no one would take him seriously no matter what he did.*

But worst of all—and you only realised this after spending a lot of time with him—he was boring. Fucking deathly boring. You couldn't have a conversation with him, you could only sit there and listen. He never listened back. His eyes turned into blank walls if you tried to talk about yourself. A few days locked in with someone like that, you start going mad.

But for all his flaws, Richman's money, in the cash-starved world of mountaineering, meant he never lacked for new climbing partners, even when the old ones stormed off in disgust.

As for romantic partners, he had no lack there either. He was young, wealthy, undeniably handsome, with all the dash and glamour of a daredevil mountaineer, and charming when he wanted to be. But in all those years no long-term relationship developed, and in truth there was hardly the time, so rarely was he away from climbing for any protracted period. His first love remained the mountains.

Then, in December 1970, Bert Richman, only sixty-six years old, died suddenly of a stroke. The bulk of his estate—controlling interest in a vast collection of industries, plus investment and real-estate portfolios—passed directly to his son.

Walter, who had been about to start an expedition in the Andes, abandoned his plans and flew to his father's home in New York. For fully four months he holed up there, consulting with his father's financial associates and company directors, and also with a legion of more mysterious experts. The business world held its breath: what would the twenty-five year old do with such an immense burden thrust upon him? Could he cope? Or was his father's empire doomed?

Walter's answer, when it came, would horrify the stock market to such a degree that it caused the largest crash of 1971.

But it would make climbing history.

7

ALIGHTING

IT WAS NOT WALTER RICHMAN who greeted Rita when she stepped off the gangway into steady rain. It was Clara Lang, sheltering under a large umbrella and offering a second to Rita.

'Welcome to Theodolite Isle,' the major-domo said, her smile lop-sided as she raised an eye to the huge ship looming over the dock. 'I'm glad that you made it without any trouble.'

'I feel ridiculous,' Rita replied, but glad at least to see a minimally familiar face.

Clara Lang laughed. She was dressed in a dark grey suit under a black raincoat, with a scarf thrown around her neck against the cold. 'Why? All those people, they're dying of envy, and of curiosity too.'

Rita spared the ship an upward glance and saw a thousand faces staring straight down at her, every rail and balcony packed with people, the expression on every face almost identical. *Who is this woman? Why is she so important that we had to stop here for her?*

She ducked her head. She had been assured by her butler and by the first officer that the staff were under order not to reveal her identity to anyone—and she believed the assurance.

Still, what if one of those people up there simply recognised her? Oh, it was unlikely, she knew. Even in the days of her minor fame, she had been careful with her public persona, wary of the unstable types she might attract. She had not put her picture on the back of her book, and her online presence had always been minimal. True, there were newspaper photos from the LA incident. But it was all more than a decade past; her clothes, her hair, they were completely different now.

Still, someone might know her. And she did not want to be known, not in attachment to the Richman name and all its false glamour. She had earned her anonymity, and wanted to keep it.

'Shall we get going?' asked Clara, with a nod towards a car that was waiting at the rear of the dock. A steward from the ship was already placing Rita's bags into its boot.

Rita nodded and they set off under the umbrellas, the rain battering furiously for a moment. There was no one else visible on the dock or among the sheds, other than the workers attending to the *Wanderer*'s ropes. But away beyond the bulk of the ship, in a sheltered corner of the harbour, two other craft were moored mid-water. One was a squat and functional-looking ocean-going barge. The other was a huge, sleek, luxury yacht, gleaming a splendid gold in the grey light.

'Was that my alternative ride?' Rita asked as they went, indicating the yacht.

'Obscene looking thing, isn't it?' nodded the major-domo. 'The *William Bligh*. Mr Richman gave it the name. A joke, I assume. It's quite new.' They came to the car, a black luxury sedan, and she pulled open the front passenger door. 'Believe it or not, that's the first yacht he's ever owned. He always thought the idea was ridiculous—whenever he wanted a boat, he just leased one. But now that he lives on an island, it does come in handy to ferry guests to and fro. Along with the helicopter. There's a pad down here, of course, but the more exciting one is up top.'

Rita looked up towards the hidden peak of the Mount, the sheer cliffs thrusting brutally into the clouds, and felt her stomach roll. It was unthinkably bad to be in a helicopter at any time, so naked to the forces of the air, but to be stuck in one while the pilot was trying to land upon some tiny platform high on a windblown peak: utterly awful.

A deep horn-blast rent the air, making her start, followed by two blasts more. Back across the dock the gangway had been hauled in, and the sound of frothing water was scaling up as the *Wanderer* prepared to pull away. Rita slipped into the passenger seat, watching the ship, while the major-domo crossed around to the driver's side and got in.

'I hope you don't mind that I'm the only one who came down,' Clara said. 'I could have brought some of the others along to say hello, but I didn't think you'd want a big fuss made.'

Rita shrugged. 'To be honest, I was worried it would be Richman himself.'

'Oh, he's not actually here yet. He'll be flying in tonight from Hobart.' The smile again. 'But there's no need to be nervous. He's quite a normal person when you meet him. No ogre, certainly.'

'I'm glad to hear it,' said Rita. She waited as the major-domo started the car and swung it around to head towards the Mount. Then added, 'So the others are all here already?' Rita had been told in advance of the guest list for Richman's small gathering, but the names had meant little to her.

'Oh yes, Kushal and Madelaine got in last night. And Eugene has been here all along, fine-tuning the last of the smart systems.'

They drove in silence a short time. The road—tarmac, freshly laid—curved around the arm of the harbour, climbing as it did so. Sheds and huts slid by, some with aerials sticking up, some surrounded by high fences with locked gates. Though the arrangement had appeared ramshackle from a distance, up close Rita could see that everything was neat and well maintained.

'So all this down here,' she said with a gesture to a building they were passing, a Quonset-hut type structure, 'still belongs to the military? What do they do here exactly? Or is it all secret?'

Clara shook her head. 'There's no military here, that's just one of the rumours we don't deny. It helps to keep the tourists away.'

'None at all?'

'Oh, there was once. Back before the days of satellites there was a US tracking station here, quite an important one. It caused all sorts of trouble in the nineteen fifties, because the mountain climbers attempting the Wheel in those days needed to use the port here as their base, and the military didn't like sharing the island one bit. But the Americans are long gone. The Australian weather service took over the island in the seventies, in cooperation with the Lighthouse Commission. But they're gone too; the weather equipment and the lights are automatic these days. Otherwise, well, there have been people living here one way or another since the early eighteen hundreds. There is history everywhere. The very first settlement was a whaling station, and you can still find a few rusty old iron rendering vats lying around, even from those days.'

'But if there's no military, why the regulations that close the waters here over winter?'

'That goes back to the fifties again. When the US set up their tracking base here they wanted privacy while they did their calibration tests and so on, so they got the Australian government to close the waters around the Wheel for one full winter—and from there it just stuck, year after year. The military were happy, it gave them three months of privacy out of every twelve, and afterwards the weather people felt the same. It was just so much easier for everyone, not having to worry about climbers or cruise ships getting into trouble here in winter conditions.'

'And now?'

'Well, when Mr Richman acquired the lease to the island and agreed to shoulder the expense of maintaining the weather and navigational equipment, as well as improving the port facilities, one of his conditions was that the winter ban remain in force. It was part of the great attraction for him of building his home here, the fact that for at least three months a year he has the Wheel to himself.'

Rita felt dimly appalled. It was one thing that the military and government departments could lock a wonder like the Wheel away for a quarter of every year, but for *one man* to do it?

70

Clara might have been thinking something similar. 'The conditions of the lease are confidential, I should add. As you can imagine, it would have made all the protests even worse, if people had known. As it was, the trouble only really began when Mr Richman announced his plans for the Observatory. But in fact he'd already been in possession of the island for ten years by then, with no one the wiser.'

Rita had to nod. She remembered the protests all too well, because of the involvement of her father's name. Environmental groups, nationalist groups, climbing groups, and others beside had all reacted with fury when construction of the Observatory was announced. Hue and cry was raised. Sovereignty of an Australian landmark was being handed over to an American! Observatory Mount, historic since the days of Captain Cook, was going to be torn apart and desecrated! Why, it was as outrageous as if Walter Richman had been granted the right to move, lock and stock, into the Sydney Opera House! It must be stopped!

Alas—said both governments involved, the federal and the Tasmanian—everyone's hands were tied. The lease had been arranged under earlier administrations, the terms were watertight, nothing could be done. And after all, while yes, the Wheel was a National Park and protected, Theodolite Isle had never been anything of the sort. It had already been used for all manner of purposes, from carving up whales to serving as a junkyard for mountaineering expeditions. Far from desecrating the place, Richman would actually tidy up two centuries of accumulated mess, and also improve the port. In truth, it was a great deal for the nation.

Of course, everyone understood what was really going on. Richman was pumping money into the coffers of the relevant political parties, lots of it. Legal challenges were mounted, fleets of protest boats blockaded the harbour at Theodolite Isle, unions placed work bans on construction, the High Court made rulings, and the kerfuffle drove the sitting Tasmanian government from power at the subsequent election. None of it made any difference. Richman's house was delayed by a year maybe, but it was built all the same, and Australian voters got the message, if their history hadn't made it clear already: billionaires make their own rules.

In the rain, the car was approaching the top of the rise now. Clara Lang pointed out the last two buildings that lay before them.

'On the right,' she said, indicating a large concrete structure, screened by young pine trees, 'is the power station. It is diesel-fuelled and big enough to power a small town, which this place effectively is. And on the right'—she nodded towards the multi-storey hotel-like building—'is the accommodation and recreation block. It has been home to the construction crew these last five years or so, and will be home from now on to the household staff and general island workers.'

Rita asked, 'How many staff are there? How many people live on the island?'

Clara considered. 'The household staff consists of about sixty people: cooks, cleaners, maintenance workers, various technological special- ists. Some of them have their families here during their rotations. Then there are the power station staff, the port facilities staff, the security staff, the island groundskeepers—in all, that comes to about another seventy people, some with families also. All together, there can be over two hundred people living here, depending on the season.'

'You weren't kidding about it being a town,' Rita said.

The major-domo was nodding. 'It's a lot of people, I know. But when you're up in the Observatory there's no sense of a crowd. Up there, you wouldn't know that Base even exists.'

'Base?'

'That's what everyone calls the town down here. Officially it's Port Fresne, but everyone just says Base. Observatory up top, Base down below. And up top, you feel like you're alone in the world—you can't see anything of Base, or hear it. There's only the sky and the wind and the view. All credit to your father's amazing design.'

Rita leaned forwards a moment to stare up through the windscreen in hope of catching a sight of the Mount's peak far above. The rain had eased a little, but the cloud still defied her, chopping off the upper Mount clean. But presumably the Observatory was not visible from this angle in any case, if Base was invisible from the residence above.

They drove on. The road led them by the accommodation block, then passed through a gate in a high fence. They entered now into a formal landscape of heaths and grasses and small pines, and of sculptured rock terraces, dripping with water. 'Do you like it?' Clara enquired, driving slowly now to give Rita a chance to see. 'I do. It is what is known as a sub-Arctic style of garden. Which is apt, for here on Theodolite we're as far south in latitude as the tip of South America. The Antarctic Circle itself is only a thousand kilometres further south.'

'It's lovely,' said Rita, feeling cold.

Finally, the foot of Observatory Mount loomed up through the rain, a wall of wet stone leaping massively. The drive became a circle, passing beneath a large awning that extended out from the Mount's foot, roofed in slate and supported by a heavy timber frame.

'This is the front door,' said Clara, pulling up beneath the awning. Warm golden light bathed the vehicle from overhead. 'So to speak, anyway. The journey up starts from here.'

Under the shelter of the awning, a path of flagstones led to a portico set into the Mount. The doorway was a great carven arch, almost like the entrance to an ancient cathedral, its two huge wooden doors folded back. From within, more golden light streamed out into the grey day.

A young man emerged as they climbed out of the car, with the air of having been waiting for them. Clara made the introductions. 'Rita, this is Eugene Morris. He's Mr Richman's private technical consultant, and there's one or two small items he'll need to attend to before we go on.'

'I'm the IT nerd, is what she means,' the man said, offering his hand. 'Pleased to meet you, Ms Gausse, and welcome to the Observatory.'

Rita shook the hand, noting that he looked very much the part. He was maybe thirty, had boyishly long blond hair, a pale clean-shaven face, thick glasses, and his dress was casual, a rawhide leather jacket over a T-shirt, jeans and sneakers. Rita was not normally one for IT types—they could be so superior—but for once she felt an immediate liking, if only perhaps because of his broad accent, which marked him as Australian.

'Let me get your bags,' he insisted.

The bags retrieved, the three of them passed beneath the archway and entered what Rita could now see was a foyer, not unlike that of a grand hotel. To the left was a discrete counter, upon which a computer terminal glowed, while to the right, leather armchairs and sofas were arranged before a baronial fireplace in which a great fire blazed. Dead ahead, where in a real hotel a bank of elevators might have waited, another great arch opened, and through it a wide hallway receded away to what seemed to be infinity. Except it wasn't a hallway, it was a tunnel—its walls panelled, its floor laid in stone tile, its ceiling hung with tasteful chandeliers, but a tunnel all the same, piercing deep into the mountain.

Eugene ushered Rita to the counter, his air apologetic. 'Now, Ms Gausse, I do have one request on behalf of Mr Richman before you go on up. I'm assuming you have a mobile phone?'

'Yes.'

'May I have it for a moment, please?'

Rita retrieved her device—an iPhone, two years old and somewhat battered—from her coat pocket and handed it over. 'Why?' she asked, not with any hostility, merely curious.

The IT expert was plugging the phone into the computer. 'Well, as you'd understand, Mr Richman is an immensely public figure, and so has to be cautious about his personal safety. He would be one of the most tempting targets in the world for a kidnapping, especially in a remote location such as this. Under the advice of his security team, therefore, he has been careful to keep the interior layout of the Observatory secret. There is no greater tool for a prospective kidnapper, I'm reliably informed, than to know the interior of a target's house.'

He was fiddling with Rita's phone now, tapping something on the screen.

'To that end,' he continued, 'it's forbidden to take photos within the residence upstairs. Now, it's easy enough to ban cameras, but these days, cameras aren't the main worry: it's phones. And we can hardly demand that all visitors give up their phones. After all, we have excellent cellular access here, if I say so myself. So the least invasive way, we've discovered, is to install a simple app on everyone's devices.'

'An app? For what?'

He smiled. 'All it does—while your phone is in range of the wifi or cellular network here in the residence—is disable your phone's camera. Everything else works exactly as normal—texts, email, browsing, whatever. But you can't take videos or photos.'

He was handing the phone back. Rita, in her surprise, could not even tell if she was annoyed. 'There's an app that does that?'

'Well, *we* have one, but it's not in public release. It was a special favour from the folks at Apple to Mr Richman, who is an old friend and investor. Don't worry, I'll wipe it from your phone when you leave.'

She had recovered a little now. 'And will you be scanning my luggage too?'

The smile crinkled. 'We could, of course. We have the equipment right here. But there's no need. Your luggage was thoroughly x-rayed on the ship when you boarded, and just now when you disembarked. That's how I already knew that you don't have a camera.'

Rita gave up and turned to the major-domo enquiringly: what was next?

Clara was reassuring. 'That's it for the security checks. But it's some way yet to the Observatory itself, so just so you know, there are bathrooms here, if you wish to freshen up before going on.'

'I'm fine.'

'Then this way, please.'

Clara now ushered Rita through the inner arch. Parked in a discrete alcove just within were three golf carts, upholstered in burgundy leather.

'We could walk if you liked,' she said, 'the tunnel is only three hundred yards long. But with the luggage we may as well ride.'

Eugene had trailed along with Rita's bags. He loaded them onto one of the carts, then gave a small wave. 'I'll be up later,' he said to the major-domo. And to Rita, 'I'll be seeing you again at dinner tonight, but if you have any trouble in the meantime with the facilities in your suite, let me know.' Then he disappeared back into the foyer.

'Where are we going?' Rita asked, staring into the vanishing perspective of the tunnel. 'I thought we'd be heading *up*, in a lift.'

'We will be,' answered Clara. 'But not yet. It makes sense when you think about it. The lift shaft goes all the way to the top of the Mount, so that means it has to begin directly *beneath* the Mount's peak, not here on the outer edge of the mountain. So, to go up, first we have to go in.'

Rita hadn't thought of that. But of course it was logical. She slipped into the cart. 'It must be a hell of a shaft, if it goes all the way to the top.'

The major-domo nodded, taking the driver's seat. 'Two thousand five hundred metres, straight up. The Mount is two thousand eight hundred metres high, but we're already at three hundred metres here.' She put the cart in gear, and turned smoothly into the tunnel, the electric motor all but silent. 'However, you must not think of it as a normal lift, the same as you would find in any high-rise building. This is something quite different. The design is borrowed from diamond mining, where shafts can go down for many thousands of metres. Mr Richman owns one or two such mines, so he had the expertise to do something similar here.'

'I see,' Rita commented faintly. 'Well, I suppose it's better than having to take the stairs.'

'Actually, there *are* stairs. There's a second shaft aside from the main one, and apart from housing the service elevator, it is also home to an emergency staircase. Like a fire escape. Best hope you never have to use it though; the flights are steep, and there are thousands upon thousands of steps. I'm told it's the longest internal staircase in the world.'

The cart rolled smoothly down the tunnel. The road was of flagstones, but to one side a railing fenced off a carpeted walkway, lit by sconces set into the panelled walls. The air was warm, artificially heated presumably, scented with tones of wood and stone. And once again a sense of unreality washed over Rita. The *cost* of all this. An entrance hall so big you had to drive down it. A staircase—not even meant for regular use, a mere back-up safety feature—that was the longest in the world. An elevator borrowed from diamond mines. Just so that one man could build a house atop a mountain. It was staggering in its extravagance.

Which was strange, because in all that she had read about Walter Richman since receiving his invitation, he was *not* a man known for extravagance, not of the vulgar, gold-plated cars and diamond watches and vast mansion kind. And yet now in his old age he had embarked upon building the most expensive private residence in recent world history. Maybe Roman emperors had conceived of more indulgent projects, or Louis XIV perhaps with Versailles. But otherwise . . .

Clara seemed to be aware of her train of thought. 'Trust me, you haven't seen anything yet.'

Ahead, the end of the tunnel was in sight, widening out into an area of brighter illumination. As they drew closer, Rita could make out another parking bay, and another archway. Beyond was a spacious salon furnished with armchairs and couches, and a wood-panelled bar. There was no sign of the lift. Then, as the major-domo drew the cart up to the parking bay, Rita realised with a shock that the salon *was* the lift.

Clara was amused as she turned off the cart, following Rita's gaze. 'I told you not to think of an average elevator. Go on through.'

They climbed out. Rita collected her bags and ventured through the arch. At the point where it opened into the wider room there was a line visible across the floor, a fine gap of darkness. Beyond, the couches waited, wide and deep, arranged around a large oriental rug, and at the bar decanters and bottles glistened on the shelves.

'Take a seat and we'll be underway,' said Clara. She attended to two large doors that slid smoothly from either side of the arch, closing off the room. That done, she pressed a button set in a panel on the wall—there was only the one—and after a pause of some seconds, with barely the slightest jolt or sound, Rita realised they were moving.

Clara lifted a hand to the bar. 'A drink of any kind?' she enquired. 'The ascent takes about seven minutes. It can go faster in an emergency, but then not quite as smoothly.'

Rita found that her mouth was dry. They were really going to climb fully two and a half kilometres up a single shaft, dangling on no more than a steel cable, while an abyss grew beneath them all the while. No amount of sumptuous furniture and fine oriental rugs could change that. She longed, suddenly, for a long swig of wine.

'Just a water,' she breathed.

'It's perfectly safe, of course,' the major-domo reassured her as she opened a concealed refrigerator within a cabinet. 'It's already been running for three years and more, you know, without a flaw.'

'How did they do it?' Rita asked, casting around for any distraction from her nervousness, scarcely feeling their motion upwards but also terribly aware of it, of the gulf opening. 'I mean, how do you actually dig a giant shaft from the bottom of a mountain to the top?'

Clara handed her the water. 'It's really rather ingenious, if you're interested. The method is called raise-boring. At the bottom, you dig a tunnel to the centre of the mountain—the tunnel we just came through. Then by helicopter, piece by piece, you lift a drilling rig to the top of the Mount. Then you drill a *small* shaft, say half a metre wide, down to meet with your tunnel. And now comes the clever part. You attach a big reaming disk, eight metres across, to the bottom of your drill shaft, and slowly haul that disk back *up*. It spins as it goes, carving out a much bigger shaft, and meanwhile all the refuse falls back to the bottom to be hauled out through the tunnel. Very elegant and cost effective. Though I won't lie, at two and a half thousand metres, the two shafts we dug here were pushing the technology to its limits.'

It was more information than Rita needed, but she clung to it anyway. 'Why isn't this car round then,' she asked, 'if the shaft is round?'

'Practical reasons,' the major-domo replied. 'You still have to build a gantry inside the shaft, within which the elevator runs, and a square gantry is easiest. Plus, a square gantry leaves space around the edges of the shaft which can be used to run cables and conduits for power and water and waste disposal and the like.'

Which all made sense, but the ascent was all Rita could think about. How high were they already? And yet the strange thing was, there was nothing for her to be afraid of here, not even the old her: no matter how deep the shaft, it was not open air, it was not a natural void where deadly presences might dwell. But her nerves were singing. And why did her head feel so thick and slow?

Then her ears popped, and she thought *of course*, it was only the change in altitude. She sipped on her water, and as she swallowed, her ears cleared further still. *Snap out of*, she told herself.

'You might notice a few effects as we go,' Clara was continuing. 'Two thousand eight hundred metres is not a height that normally poses any great risk of altitude sickness—you generally have to go well over three thousand before that becomes an issue—but travelling from sea level up to twenty-eight hundred all but instantaneously like this can make people a little light-headed and dizzy sometimes.'

Yes, that was all it was, just the speed of the ascent affecting her. The other thing, the sense of vertigo and dread, that was just vapours, just her inner ear and her lungs adjusting to the thinner air . . .

'Almost there,' said Clara after a time.

Rita had closed her eyes. She opened them, saw the major-domo staring expectantly at the panel on the wall. A barely perceptible slowing made itself felt in her stomach. There was no elevator 'ding' of arrival, but a green light blinked on the panel.

'And we're here,' said Clara.

Another set of sliding doors stood on the opposite side of the room from the first set. Clara opened these second doors, then moved to one side. 'You're okay? Are you ready?'

Rita rose cautiously, but the dizziness had departed now that the motion had ceased. Beyond the doorway was a rectangular foyer, windowless and austere, carved out of the native stone. An archway opened from it to the left. The only furniture was a high stone bench, or perhaps it was a low table, cut, like the room itself, from the bedrock. And the only decoration was a painting on the right-hand wall—a large dark canvas, very old-looking, and crowded with figures and faces.

For the moment, however, Rita was interested only in what lay beyond the foyer, for through the archway a golden light was streaming, not artificial, but natural. Sunlight. She moved from the elevator into the foyer and then to the archway. She stared at what waited beyond, took a further few steps forwards, and then stopped.

'My god,' she said.

Clara had followed to stand at her side, her smile serene. 'Didn't I tell you?'

8

THEORIES OF DESIGN

PORTION OF THE TRANSCRIPT OF a lecture delivered by Richard Gausse to the North American Institute of Architectural Historians, Boston, 2010.

And so, we come at last to the subject for which most of you have no doubt been waiting—the house that I am currently designing for Walter Richman.

First, some caveats. For one, construction is only just now beginning on the site, and as any architect will tell you, the design as it currently stands will certainly undergo some alterations in the building process.

Second, I am bound by certain limits of confidentiality. For reasons of both security and privacy, Mr Richman has only given me permission to discuss his residence with you on the understanding that I will not divulge any precise details of the house's layout. Nor am I to show you any accurate schematics of the design. But never fear. A general description will be enough, given the extraordinary nature of the structure.

You will all, of course, be familiar with Observatory Mount, standing near to three thousand metres high upon the historic Theodolite Isle, at the foot of the world's highest mountain, in the remote Southern Ocean. A more beautiful, rugged and wild prospect is hard to imagine.

It is not by any means a virgin site, however. For the last two centuries Theodolite Isle has been continually inhabited and put to a wide variety of uses, commercial, military and civil. In the process, even the summit of the Mount, though much less trampled than the rest of the island, has witnessed its fair share of construction and alteration. By the time our surveyors arrived, the summit was already littered with a motley collection of old weather huts and empty generator bunkers and defunct satellite dishes, the detritus of years past. But that said, no one until now has tried to erect a permanent habitation upon the peak. A house. A home.

A house, I call it. But the word is perhaps misleading, for when I say 'house', many here will no doubt picture a structure that rises above the ground, a building that sits on top of Observatory Mount, as out of place as an unfortunate pimple. But in my design, nothing will extend above the level of the summit. Indeed, in silhouette, the Mount will appear exactly as it has always appeared. It could not be otherwise. I have no wish, despite what my critics say, to change the mountain in its essence. My design has its roots in the desire to respect the mountain, not to injure it.

Those of you familiar with my life's work will not be surprised by this. I am famous, if I may use that word, for what has become known as an 'enfolded' or 'buried' style of architecture. Put simply, I prefer, wherever possible, to build into the earth, to delve within it, rather than to construct on top of it. I have designed houses that extend into sheer cliffs, or into gentle hillsides, or into flat desert ground. I have delved into the slopes of a great sand dune, and beneath the roots of an immense redwood tree, and once even dug into the ice of the Antarctic cap. The variations are endless. But the crucial thing about all my design is, first, that it seeks to respect and preserve the environment in which it is built, and, second, is that it makes a fundamental break with the standard concept of what a building, a residence for humans, a house, actually is.

Consider this in terms of the matrix—the space in which a structure exists. A standard house creates its own matrix as it is built. Foundations are laid, a floor is put down, the walls rise, and a roof goes on. There is no matrix except the house itself. Hence everything must be connected, every surface perform a double duty. The ceiling of a lower level is also the floor of an upper level. Interior walls are shared between rooms, and every corner and angle must match up within one set of external walls.

An enfolded house, however, is built within an already existing matrix—in this case, the solid rock of Observatory Mount. There is no need now for surfaces or walls to be shared. A floor need only be a floor, a ceiling need only be a ceiling. Rooms can be dug wherever we like, as large as we like, and need no relation or connection to other rooms beyond a communicating passage. Angles can take any form we please, and levels need not be stacked upon one another in storeys. In short, there is, for the architect, an utter freedom to create within three dimensions.

In some ways, it's easier to think of this sort of home as a burrow, rather than a building: a free-floating collection of chambers set within a matrix and connected by tunnels. Of course, the places I design are nothing like burrows—they are not dark, or cold, or maze-like. And that's where the skill of this form of architecture lies, to make these homes feel light and open and completely natural in their form and function.

Such a house I have designed for Walter Richman—and I say with confidence that it will be the greatest work of my career.

But down to the details.

Let us examine the house in the manner of a visitor arriving there for the very first time. How, for instance, will such a visitor even reach the top of Observatory Mount? Until now, it has only been possible by climbing. True, the Mount is not in fact a difficult mountain to climb by professional standards, and a regular route has been carved out over the years, involving ladders and stairways cut into the stone, so that even non-climbers can make the ascent with relative ease. Still, this is hardly adequate, hence we have installed elevators, of a scale and magnificence unlike any other, running up shafts some two and a half kilometres high.

All very well. But this affects the design of the residence immediately, for while our visitor can enjoy their ride to the top in heedless comfort, the architect must find space at the top of the mountain for the great winches that draw the elevator cars up and down, and space for the motors that drive the winches. And likewise, although electrical power for the house will be provided from a station at the foot of the mountain, several independent back-up generators, each one as big as a truck, must also be installed somewhere at the top of the Mount. Then there are things like water tanks and pumping plants and air-conditioning stacks—all of which will be of industrial scale, given the size of the residence.

On any normal build, all these utilities would require ugly protrusions or extensions from the house itself—but here we have no such problem. Winches, generators, tanks, no matter how vast, can be secreted within the central mass of the peak, completely out of sight from the main body of the house. And out of earshot too, with as much as ten or twenty metres of solid rock to act as dampener between utility spaces and the nearest living quarters. On a day-to-day basis, our visitor, and the residence's occupants, will not even know that such equipment exists.

Hidden away also will be an entire complex of domestic storage facilities. Wine cellars, larders, cold rooms, linen closets, laundries—all the necessary impedimenta of a stately house can be tucked away inside the rock of the Mount. The same goes for the service tunnels by which the staff will access such facilities. Oh, and another 'by the way'—as you can by now begin to guess, a lot of excavation will be involved in this build. Where will all the discarded stone go? The answer is down the shafts and out into the harbour, where the fill will be used to reinforce the dock facilities—which have been, up until now, somewhat deficient.

Anyway, back to our visitor. When their luxurious elevator ride is over, what will greet them? At first it will be a plain foyer, quite modest in size. It is only when they exit that foyer that they will get their first glimpse of the residence's true scale—the Entrance Hall.

And trust me, it will be a shock.

For Observatory Mount, as it approaches its summit, narrows into a wedge-like ridge that will incorporate the Entrance Hall—a single great chamber lined either side with giant windows, allowing light to flood in.

Anyway, this is what our visitor will see—

Note—Mr Gausse's address is here interrupted by shouts and commotion from the rear of the hall, a party of protestors having made a clandestine entrance. The group, representing various environmental bodies opposed to construction taking place on Observatory Mount, was armed with water balloons and paint bombs and proceeded to attack the crowd. Security was soon on the scene, but it was some time before order could be restored, and Mr Gausse declined to resume his address, other than to respond to the protestors before departing the podium.

Desecrating the Mount? What are you talking about, you fools? Nothing I could do could pay the Mount more homage.

9

THE TOUR

RITA STOOD IN A GOLDEN glow, the rays of the westering sun cast in vast slants through tall windows. She had forgotten, after the time spent in the dim lighting of the foyer and the tunnel below, and then during the long elevator ride, that it was still day outside. Nor had she considered that in their two-and-a-half-thousand-metre ascent they would have risen above the rain and cloud. But here she stood, aloft in the open sky.

And also, within a cathedral.

That was her first impression—that she stood at one end of a soaring gothic church. Of course, it wasn't that, there were no pews, no altars, no icons of saints; it was a place of purely secular worship. Yet in the leaping arches, and in the tall pillars, and in the towering windows ranged down the sides, each ten times her own height at least, she might well have strayed into some great cathedral of old.

The size of it! The space had to be near to a hundred metres long, carved out of the ridge that formed the Mount's crest. The ceiling followed that ridgeline in all its jagged leaps and thrusts, an organic steeple no man-made church could ever rival. The great pillars, single spans of stone left by the excavation of the interior, marched in two lines down the centre and met overhead in arched ribs, between which, fifty metres overhead, glass panes opened directly to the sky.

Clara Lang had waited politely for some moments as Rita absorbed the sight. Now the major-domo said, 'This is the Entrance Hall. You're catching it at a good time of day. The afternoon sun really sets the interior alight. And, of course, the view outside is something extraordinary.'

'Yes,' breathed Rita.

To the left, displayed in sections through the row of tall windows, was a deck of low cloud, the roof of the rainy day below, extended westward to the horizon, bathed orange in the afternoon light. Here and there rose towers of cumulonimbus, palaces lofting above misted lowlands, each casting long shadows eastward. And high above, a sheet of icy cirrus shimmered with rainbow colours, through which a marbled network of fractures showed blue-black glimpses of the winter sky. It was a cathedral of cloud dwarfing even the cathedral of stone.

And yet it was as nothing compared to the view to the east. There, revealed to Rita at last, and defying comprehension, rose the Wheel.

The mountain filled every window on the right side of the Hall, seemingly within hand's reach, even though it was kilometres away, so crystal was the air. Its immense West Face was a multitude of landscapes and colours all in one: sheer cliffs frowned a reddish grey from far above; vast slopes of snow reared dazzlingly white; shadowed couloirs waited dark and ever frozen; and great glaciers perched blue above silver falls of tumbled ice. It was overwhelming, as if an entire continent had been upended to ninety degrees and was hanging there by magic.

And yet this was only *part* of the mountain, for even now the Wheel's ultimate height remained unfathomable. The veil of high cirrus, which the peak pierced as sharply as a titanic blade, hid the uppermost reaches. Rita remembered reading somewhere that even the highest of clouds could only reach about halfway up the Wheel, which meant, incredibly, that the hidden summit might lie twelve or thirteen kilometres higher still. So much stone, lifted so remote into the air.

It was too much, she had to look away, back to the safer majesty of the Entrance Hall, to stop herself from becoming dizzy.

And indeed, two people were now approaching across the Hall, striding down the central aisle between the pillars: a middle-aged man in a grey suit, and a young woman dressed in black and white. The two paused before the steps leading up to where Rita and Clara stood, and the man gave a brief bow.

'Ms Gausse, welcome to the Observatory. My name is Bradley, and I'm the house manager here. If there's anything you need during your stay, you have only to let me know. Giselle is the maid on duty in your wing of the residence, and she will take your bags to your apartment now, as I understand that Ms Lang is eager to take you on a tour of the house before you are shown to your quarters.'

'If that's okay with you,' the major-domo added. 'Just so that you can orientate yourself.'

Rita nodded, awkward in the presence of domestic staff. 'Yes, of course.'

Bradley gestured—in another time and place, Rita supposed, he might have been called a butler—and the maid took up the bags.

'If there's nothing else for the present, Ms Lang?' the house manager enquired.

'Thank you, no.'

'Then we'll be out of your way.'

And the two domestics marched away again down the long hall.

Watching them go, Rita noticed now that the floor, which she had thought was inlaid with coloured patterns, was in fact bare stone, polished to display the natural swirls and lines within the rock of the mountain. To either side of the central aisle, great rugs were spread, hosting suites of couches and low tables. But the main ornamentation of the Hall was art. Paintings hung everywhere, from the pillars, and upon the walls between the great windows. And sculptures of all sorts stood on podiums, some works in groups, some standing alone.

'Shall we start the tour?' Clara asked.

Rita nodded, and followed the major-domo down the stairs.

Clara waved a hand to the exhibits. 'As you'll have noticed, Mr Richman is a keen appreciator of art. What you see here is by no means his entire collection, of course—he has a gallery in New York, open to the public—these are just a few of his favourites. We won't stop now, there'll be plenty of time for you to look at them later, but you probably already recognise some of the more famous works.'

They were walking down the aisle towards the far end of the Hall, where another great arch opened to some further vast space. Rita glanced about at the art. *Did* she recognise anything? She was no expert. But certainly, the works appeared to be the kind normally found in great museums, the styles classical, medieval, Renaissance. But she wasn't really looking, her attention was drawn ever and again to the eastern windows, and to the vertical wonder that was the Wheel.

The major-domo, following Rita's gaze, gave a nod. 'It's not the clearest of days, sadly, so you can't see the summit. But never fear, you're bound to get a good look at it sometime during your stay. The forecast is for finer weather in the next day or so.'

Two-thirds of the way down the Hall the aisle split to pass around a large oval opening in the floor, into which a curved staircase descended. Lights illuminated the stairs, but the chamber below, whatever it might be, was in darkness. Moreover, a chain was stretched across the upper landing—no real barrier, but the meaning of it plain.

'Down there is the Museum,' Clara explained as they passed by. 'It's not quite ready for guests yet; we're waiting on a last important exhibit to be installed. But it'll be open before you leave.'

They moved on to the southern arch. Before passing through, Rita paused and looked back to see the Hall from the opposite perspective. It amazed her anew, so soaring, so light-filled and yet so naturally embedded within the mountain. But what she noticed most now was the humble foyer at the far end. From this angle it seemed less a mere antechamber and more a kind of sanctum, a focal point for the Hall— like a cathedral's chancel or apse. The little chamber shone gold in the sunlight from the windows, as if the beams had been directed there on purpose. And taking on the air of a sacred altar was the enigmatic stone platform that she had first noticed—too high to be a bench, too low to be a table. And the thought struck her: why had her father put that there?

The thought was chased by a realisation: her father had designed this entire Hall. This beautiful, wondrous space. He had conceived it, dreamed it up from nothing, created it from blank stone. Her father, whom she had dismissed for so long, along with all of his works.

Rita lowered her head. Then, aware that the major-domo was waiting, she turned and followed her through the arch.

'The Atrium,' Clara announced.

The space they had entered was almost too vast, and too complicated, to take in at once. From the archway, the great room spread beneath an enormous dome of carved rock and glass. On the far side of the space other grand rooms opened and expanded away—Rita had a fleeting impression of a library and a dining hall. But what captured her gaze most was an immense well that opened at the centre of the room, right beneath the crest of the dome, its rim lined by a stone balustrade. Dropping into the well was the most fantastic staircase she had even seen.

It appeared at first—as Rita moved to the balustrade to see better—as if the structure was some mad kind of M.C. Escher illustration brought to life. Circular flights of stairs curled impossibly around other circles of stairs in a puzzle without end, the twined serpents forming a great column of stone that plummeted away into dimness.

Clara came to the rescue. 'Unnerving, isn't it? This is the Double Helix Staircase. It's two spiral staircases entwined in each other: whichever flight you take, it never meets the other one, though they both get you to the same place. A brilliant design, but in truth your father can't take all the credit. This one is inspired by a similar, if much smaller, example in France, in the Château de Chambord. And that one was designed by an architect even greater than your father. Leonardo da Vinci.'

Fighting vertigo, Rita followed the spirals with her eye, down and down. It took a notable mental effort to sort the pattern out, but yes, she could see it now, that way each helix curved in opposition to its twin. As the two stairways descended, the great tower they formed was joined by bridges that leapt out from landings positioned deeper within the well. Rita counted four such landings, widely spaced out, before a bottom could be glimpsed, maybe a hundred metres below, making the Double Helix Staircase as tall as a skyscraper. Christ, would she have to walk up and down the monstrous thing just to get around the place?

The major-domo was ahead of her once more. 'Don't worry, there are also elevators—everyday, normal elevators—between all the levels. The stairs are great fun, however. And gorgeous to look at.'

Rita suppressed a sigh of relief.

The major-domo gestured to the rest of the Atrium. 'Where we're standing now is the Great Landing. Three of the grand public rooms open from this level. Behind us, of course, is the Entrance Hall, while over there is the Saloon, which extends on into the Library. Over there is the Dining Hall. And in the middle . . . Well, can you guess?'

The Saloon and the Dining Hall were subsidiary caverns opening from the Atrium. Between them, where there should have been a dividing mass of solid stone, instead gleamed walls of glass, blue and shimmering: daylight filtering down through a great depth of water.

'Is it a giant aquarium?' Rita hazarded.

Clara shook her head. 'It's the bottom of the Terrace Pool—the Terrace is directly above us. There's a bigger pool, an indoor one, down on the recreational levels, but this one here is open to the sky. Shall we go up and see? We reach the Terrace this way.'

The major-domo led Rita to a cast-iron spiral staircase that rose from a corner of the Great Landing to a balcony that ran around the base of Atrium dome. Rita ignored the vertiginous view down into the well, and instead studied the dome immediately overhead. It must be flat from above, for the windows that pierced it were shafts cut into the stone, deeper about the outer edge of the dome than the inner.

A doorway opened from the north of the balcony. The two women passed through it, climbed another short flight of wide stairs, and emerged into what Rita at first thought must be the open air, so bright was the light. In truth, it was another enclosed space, carved from the Mount's summit. But here almost no native stone was left, only a lattice-work that formed the frame for walls and roofs made entirely of glass. The effect was of a giant greenhouse—and indeed, many leafy plants and ferns grew here in raised beds, bathing in the sunshine.

'This is the Conservatory,' explained Clara. 'The Terrace is lovely, of course, but given our altitude and the local climate, it's usually too cold or too windy to go outside, so this serves as a sunroom.'

Wicker furniture was scattered about, and a bar waited at the rear, set into a cave-like recess. But Rita's gaze went to the sky, revealed more fully than even in the Entrance Hall. The clouds and the sinking sun and the staggering rampart of the Wheel were all still performing their ballet of magnificence, but there was a new element added to the dance now, a sense of air and movement. A wind was blowing beyond the glass, its presence betrayed by streamers of cloud, wisps of mists no more, that were sailing sedately just above the Conservatory roof.

'This way,' Clara beckoned.

Outside spread the Terrace. To reach it, however, Rita saw that a strange portal must be negotiated. It consisted of a short passageway of thick glass, at either end of which was a solid-looking door, one opening to the inside, the other opening out.

'It's an airlock,' Clara explained. 'Just one of the things you have to get used to up here. Every exit that opens to the outside is the same, and it's a necessary precaution, trust me. The winds up here can get truly violent. If we had only normal doors, we'd have gales running wild through the house. But don't worry, it's all quite simple. The first thing to do, before going out, is to check on the weather. Here.'

She was indicating a small display set beside the inner door. It was glowing green, and bore a list of figures, the top three of which were, *Temp, –3 C. Wind Av, 11 kph. Wind Max, 24 kph.*

'Nice and mild, for now,' the major-domo observed. 'But you don't have to worry about the exact numbers, all that really matters is the screen colour. If it's green, then it's safe to go outside. The screen will flash orange if conditions get more serious, say, if the temperature drops below minus twenty, or if the wind starts to gust over forty. Orange is a sign to think twice, and to rug up good and proper. And if conditions get worse than that, say minus forty, or a wind over seventy, the screen goes red. Don't go outside then. The doors automatically lock at that point anyway and will only open with a manual override. So never fear, if things are really bad, you can't accidentally blunder out into it.'

Rita was staring out to the Terrace, which even in the glowing afternoon sun looked cold and terribly exposed. 'What if the wind suddenly rises when you're already out there?'

Clara smiled, reassuring. 'The override will always let you in, but there's little chance you'd ever get caught by surprise out there anyway. The most sophisticated Doppler radar available is monitoring the Wheel at every moment, and warnings will sound on the Terrace and all balconies if any dangerous winds are on the way down.'

Rita didn't understand. 'On the way down?'

'On the way down from the mountain. That's where our weather comes from, around here. It's complicated to explain in detail, but the gist of it is that the Wheel, being so high, sticking right up into the stratosphere, can create some unusual and dramatic effects. One of them is that it can drag very powerful winds down from the upper atmosphere, and direct them towards us here on the Mount. I'm talking about jet-stream winds. Do you know what a jet stream is?'

Rita nodded, hoping her expression gave nothing away. Did she know of the jet stream?! Christ, did she!

'Well, you'll understand then,' said Clara. 'You wouldn't want to be out there when one hit. But you can't miss the alarm. It sounds whenever the radar detects any mass of air descending the Wheel's western face. I'll show you.' She pressed the screen of the weather display and a keyboard flashed up, upon which she typed in a code.

Immediately, a voice awoke within the Conservatory, resonating from unseen loudspeakers; a woman's voice, calm, but serious in tone. 'The following alarm is a drill. Repeat, the following alarm is a drill.' And after a pause of some seconds a shrill tone blared out, not overloud, but un-ignorable, and the recorded voice returned to declare, *Emergency. Strong winds approaching. Seek shelter. Emergency.* After which the alarm trilled once more, then fell silent.

'You hear that, you get inside,' said the major-domo. 'There's no need to panic, you'll have several minutes at least. Just move calmly and get in here undercover. Then you'll be fine, whatever comes.' She glanced up at the ceiling. 'Don't be fooled by how delicate this all looks; that glass is heavily reinforced.' Another smile. 'Shall we go outside?'

Rita swallowed her dread. She had to do it at least once, she supposed. 'Lead the way.'

Clara nodded to an alcove near the airlock in which maybe half-a-dozen long heavy coats, fur-trimmed, hung on hooks. 'There're always overcoats here, if you don't have one with you. But I don't think we'll need them for just a quick jaunt.'

She lifted the latch. It was a sliding door, and pushing it aside, she ushered Rita through, then closed it carefully behind. 'It's a failsafe system,' the major-domo commented. 'The outer door can't open unless the inner door is shut, and vice versa.'

She opened the outer door and the two women stepped through into the clear air of the mountaintop. Cold sang against Rita's face, but not bitter in that first instant; rather it was refreshing after the warm stillness of inside, the breeze tasting faintly of salt, even two thousand eight hundred metres above the frigid Southern Ocean.

The Terrace spread before them, laid in flagstones. 'This was originally a natural hollow in the peak, even before it was levelled out during construction,' said Clara. 'Which is why this spot has been used so often over the years. It was a good place to set up weather shacks and satellite dishes and the like. All gone now, of course.'

What remained was a wide court utterly open to the sky, without roof or awning of any kind. Nor was there any furniture, other than benches cut here and there into convenient protrusions of rock. Only one feature broke this puritan simplicity; a large circle of wind-ruffled water: the Terrace Pool. It was shaped to look like a naturally formed pond in the stone, and the surface steamed slightly.

'It's heated, of course,' said the major-domo, as they approached the water, 'otherwise it would freeze. And there's an even warmer spa there in the corner, beautiful on a cold night. But be warned, if you're not a good swimmer, the pool is very deep at this northern end, close to ten metres, reaching all the way down to the Atrium below, as you saw.'

They paused a moment to peer into the depths, but of the chambers below, nothing could be guessed.

Clara led them on, towards the eastern side of the Terrace. Here, a chest-high parapet of stone formed a protective railing. Beyond it was an open gap of air, and then the Wheel.

They drew near to the edge, and Rita had to take a slow breath to still her terror. She tried to keep her eyes on the icy heights of the Wheel, not the fall that was opening below her. But vertigo was inescapable, even looking upwards, so appallingly did the mountain rise and rise. To let her gaze lift too high was to feel herself tugged towards the heavens, as if gravity was reversed and she would fall into the sky.

But when she gave in and lowered her gaze—they stood against the parapet now—it only fell through the middle airs without finding any purchase at all, an eagle plummeting, until, perhaps a thousand metres below her, the eternal rain clouds blanketed the ocean beneath. And even worse: as she stared down, a mocking wind oozed up the side of the mount and curled around her throat, cruel and cold.

It was impossible to believe, in awful moments like this, that there had ever been a time when she had not suffered with heights. But there had been, there had. For her first three decades, Rita had been free of all vertigo, unafraid to stand at a cliff edge, unafraid of flying. But then had come the hideous trip to LA, during which, amid her breakdown, she had learned—staring wide-eyed, clear through the fuselage of the plane—just what kinds of presences could stalk the wild upper airs.

Nothing had been the same since. Even now, over twelve years later and an atheist to the very religion that she had founded, even now, it was so easy to feel, in the wind as it crept up the mountainside, those same presences, so malign, so untamed, so hateful of all intruders into their realm, prowling in the great abyss of air at her feet.

'You okay?' asked Clara.

Rita had stepped back, hands to her eyes to block the terrible sight. 'I'm fine,' she said, fighting the nausea. 'Just bad with heights.'

'Ah. Is that why you don't fly? But you really don't have to worry, you're perfectly safe here—you'd have to voluntarily climb up and over the wall to be in any danger whatsoever.'

But that was the thing, of course, with vertigo. The conviction that you might do exactly that, voluntarily jump, lost in the spell.

Rita calmed herself, however, with another deep breath, and a further step back from the parapet. She turned towards the end of the Terrace. 'And what's up there?' she asked.

The great wedge of the Mount's summit ridge, which had widened around the Terrace, narrowed again to the south. At the same time it leapt up in a great mass of stone, a giant tooth that towered maybe forty metres over the Terrace. This tooth was, in fact, the true and final summit of the Mount. At its base, stairs ran up to a porch and a doorway set into the stone; and above the doorway the rock was punctuated with windows and recessed balconies, rising even to the very tip.

'That's Mr Richman's private residence,' said Clara. 'The Cottage. It's his retreat away from the rest of the Observatory, a more intimate space for him and his family, much cosier than the grand rooms below, though just as well appointed, and with the finest views of all.'

Views? Rita could imagine. From within that upraised tooth the open air would call horrifically on every side. Her gaze went to the blunt peak, and she realised that it had been cut away, replaced by a domed roof or room that seemed to be made entirely of glass.

The major-domo too was staring up. 'I'm afraid our little tour can't take in the Cottage. Entry there is only at Mr Richman's invitation. But it is extraordinary in places, that topmost chamber in particular. I won't try to describe it—hopefully you will see it yourself one day. But I'll say this much, its nickname is the Lightning Room.'

▲

The rest of the tour, inevitably, was anticlimactic.

Oh, there were further wonders, back inside. The Saloon and the Library and the Dining Hall. The Double Helix Staircase, descending which was like being swallowed by a vertical maze. The Cavern Pool, for indoor bathing, which was an immense cavity hollowed from the mountain, hosting not only a full-size Olympic pool but also a wonderland of artificial waterfalls and dark whimsical grottos. But everything paled compared to the cold wildness of the view from the Terrace.

Last on the list was the Games Arena. It opened off the lowest landing at the bottom of the Helix Staircase, and was, Clara promised Rita as they came to its entranceway, perhaps the most remarkable feature of the entire Observatory, little though its title suggested it.

But upon hearing the name, a memory stirred in Rita, and she paused, making the major-domo stop too. 'Isn't that where my father died? I was told it was in some kind of sports hall or gym.'

Clara's expression turned mortified. 'You're right, it was in the Arena. I'm so sorry, I didn't think.'

'What was he doing there, do you know? I mean, with his heart, he wasn't playing sport, or on an exercise machine, was he?'

'No, it was nothing like that. The Arena wasn't even fully finished at the time. He was just there inspecting construction, as far as I know— and that's when he had the heart attack. It was Mr Richman who found him, when he came down for his morning run. He called for help immediately. There are always medical staff down at Base, and they got to your father as quick as could be, but there was nothing they could do.'

Rita nodded. It was all as she had been told. A heart attack. And there was certainly no reason to avoid the place where it happened. She wasn't superstitious about things like that.

And yet . . .

Clara added, 'But in any case, of course, we can skip the Arena if you'd rather. You can come here any other time.'

'I would rather leave it for now,' Rita admitted, 'if it's all the same to you.' And quite apart from anything else, the truth was she was weary of staring in awe at the spectacle of the Observatory. There was only so much grandeur you could take in, sometimes.

Clara pressed no further. 'In that case, we're done. Oh, there's plenty more I can show you later if you're interested, some of the hidden areas that keep this place running, like the winch room, which is impressive. Or I could give you a tasting tour of the wine cellar, or the cheese room. But enough for now. I'll show you to your apartment. And there's no need for a long climb up the stairs again, we'll take the elevator.'

They were standing at the foot of the great well in which the Double Helix Staircase rose, towering intricately above them. Ignoring the stairs, Clara led Rita to a door in the outer wall of the well. It opened to a small lift, as conventional as any hotel elevator, and in it they rode up to the first landing below the level of the Atrium. There, two guest wings ran off in opposite directions, one north, one south. Taking the southern way, they passed down a corridor of lush carpet, the walls decorated with paintings. The corridor curved slightly, its further end hidden, and sets of double doors opened along the left wall. At the third such doorway the major-domo paused and put a hand to the latch.

'I hope this will suit you,' she said. 'Kushal and Madelaine also have apartments in this wing. I only tell you so you don't think you're alone down here. I know how easy it can be to feel isolated in this place, as if no one else is here. But rest assured, other people are around.'

Rita nodded, realising that indeed a vague unease had been rising in her. Apart from the house manager and the maid whom they had met at the beginning of the tour, they had not, in all the grand rooms and hallways, encountered another soul.

The major-domo pushed open the door, ushered Rita through. 'Well, here we are.'

The apartment was huge, at least four times the size of Rita's own back in Melbourne. A brief exploration led by Clara showed that it possessed two stately bedrooms (Rita's bags were waiting in the largest), two opulent bathrooms, a fully fitted-out kitchen, a dining room, and a sprawling living space filled with couches and armchairs, all of it fronted by a glass wall, twenty feet high, facing east to the Wheel.

The two women end up in the kitchen. 'There are basic supplies in the fridge and the pantry,' concluded Clara. 'Coffee and tea and so on, and breakfast stuff like milk and cereal. For most other meals during your stay Mr Richman hopes you'll be joining him and the other guests. But if there's anything else you want stocked here, you only have to ask. Just dial housekeeping—it's nine on the phone there. And if you're hungry at any time dial the kitchen, that's number eight. There's always a chef on standby when guests are in residence.'

Rita could only nod, almost faint with luxury by now.

'As for dinner tonight, it will be at eight in the Dining Hall—but pre-dinner drinks will commence around seven in the Saloon. Will you be able to find your way there, or would you prefer I come and collect you?'

'Oh, I can find the way, I think.'

'Then I'll leave you to settle in. Unless there's anything else?'

'No, thank you. And thank you for showing me all around. It's . . . well, it's all amazing.'

'Thanks to your father, yes.'

Rita saw the major-domo to the door, closed it behind her, and with a relieved sigh turned to face the apartment once more.

So—she was here.

Already the real world felt a million miles away and a thousand years ago—and she had five days yet to get through. Rita had not wanted to stay so long when all this was being arranged, but somehow, resist though she might, it had gone from being a weekend visit to a few days and finally to five.

The real world . . . Yes, this house was surely *not* the real world. The Observatory might be made of solid stone, but it was a piece of fantasy, a billionaire's indulgence. And yet, it was also what her father had spent the last years of his life designing. His masterpiece.

So, what did she think of it?

She wandered slowly through the living area, noting the solidity of the floor beneath the carpet, the quality of the furniture and of the appliances, the precise lines of every edge and corner. This apartment alone was perfect in its beauty and proportions.

But as for the rest of the Observatory . . . that she couldn't decide upon. She could not even settle on what to call the style in which it had been fashioned. Time and again during the tour she had been reminded of Gothic cathedrals, with all the soaring arches and pillars of stone, and all the ornate follies carved from the rock . . .

And yet the style was not really Gothic. After all, the purpose of those old cathedrals was to inspire, in man-made walls and roofs, the same kind of awe that a natural wonder would. The great cathedrals were *artificial* wonders, built to bring the faithful, via awe, into the presence of their god. But here, the Mount already *was* a wonder. Her father had not raised walls to create awe, instead he had tunnelled cunningly to dazzle the mind with the hidden innards of the earth. His purpose had not been to create an artificial mountain, it had been to reduce a real mountain to human scale.

So, no, not Gothic. But what, then? In truth, she could see hints of so many styles here: contemporary American hunting lodge, mixed with Swiss chalet, mixed with French Chateau, mixed with German baronial schloss. Yet it was none of these things. Not as oppressively male as a lodge, not as clinical and sparse as a chalet, not as fanciful as a chateau, not as darkly louring as a schloss . . . It was its own style, unrivalled anywhere else in the world, and how could it be rivalled, for there was only one Mount, and only one Wheel, towering above.

Rita sighed. What did style matter, and what did it matter if it was to her taste or not? The question was this—and she could not help but ask herself in the old way, in the way she had sworn that she had given up—was she *okay* here? Did she *feel* anything here?

Anything *wrong*?

Oh, she knew well enough what the old her would have thought of the Observatory. She would have called it an obscenity, and felt only pain here, her own, and the pain from the stone all around. Now she searched within herself for that same pain . . . but there was nothing. Despite the moment earlier on the Terrace, none of her old senses were active—the stone around her felt as dead as stone surely always was.

Wasn't it?

Rita stared at the glass wall. Beyond it was a narrow balcony, running the full width of the apartment. It was recessed snugly into the Mount, sheltered by an overhang of rock, and had a high parapet of stone, but even so it looked, to Rita's gaze, a terribly exposed position, naked to the wind and to the long plunge to the sea below.

Dare she go out there? It could be accessed by another of the airlock doorways. Beside the inner door, the little display was glowing green for safety, as had the display upstairs.

She moved close to read the figures. *Temp, –5 C. Wind Av, 18 kph. Wind Max, 37 kph.* A little colder, then, and a little windier than it had been on the Terrace some half an hour ago.

She glanced at her watch. It was just past five o'clock, and the winter sun, hidden behind her to the west, would be setting. She could not see the sky from this angle, however. The entire glass wall showed only the immensity of the Wheel's western face, ten kilometres away across the air. If she wanted to see the sky, she must go out.

Steeling herself, she slid open the inner door, passed through, closed it, proceeded to the outer door and slid it open too. Then, her gaze lowered warily, she stepped out onto the balcony.

The cold slapped at her again, but within the hollow of the balcony there was little direct wind. She took a step to stand as close as she dared to the balustrade, then looked out.

The Wheel rushed at her all over again, its ramparts of ice and snow and stone seeming to be toppling forward. Then the vertigo eased, and she could study the face in all its multi-coloured vastness. Directly opposite her the cliffs and snowfields were now a deep blue, shadowed as the sun sank below the horizon. Higher up, the shadow paled, and the snow and ice turned from deep azure to pale cerulean, and then finally to a dim white, before flushing red perhaps eight or nine kilometres above her, where the dying sun still shone.

Higher still the cirrus clouds remained, bathed pink from beneath. But now, here and there, the bank was breaking up, and through the gaps she could glimpse sections of the upper half of the mountain. Ten, fifteen, twenty kilometres above her, inconceivably distant, bare faces of grey stone shone softly on the edge of space.

And higher yet, bright in the sunlight, another bank of cloud hid the ultimate summit. Except, how could any cloud be so high?

Or in fact—?

Rita's breath caught.

She was not looking at cloud. She was looking at something solid, a faraway ridgeline glimpsed through a shifting rent in the cirrus, two lines that steepled to a point, a blunt, misshapen apex infinitely remote, etched against the blue-black, as far away as the Moon. She could scarcely believe it, but it had to be—it was the summit, the very Hand of God, thrust high in the middle stratosphere . . .

Then the gap in the cloud shifted and closed, and the vision was gone. Rita shuddered. What a hideous, lifeless place that final ridge looked from where she stood. Impossible to imagine that it was of this world at all, or that men had ever stood there.

No, she reminded himself. Not *men*. Only one *man* had ever stood there. One man alone, out of all the thousands who had tried.

And she was about to have dinner with him.

10

ABOUT THE HAND OF GOD

Excerpt from *The Cloven Sky—A History,*
Roger Fitzgerald, 1991

The name by which the summit of the Wheel is known, the Hand of God, (or, less commonly, the Palm of God) did not come into vogue until the 1930s and owes its origins to the development of telephoto lenses.

Of course, long before the 1930s photographers were capturing images of the Wheel. But though early photographs could show the lower slopes of the mountain in detail, the uppermost ridge and the oddly shaped knob of the summit remained indistinct. People were also studying the mountain through telescopes in the early years, but these too failed to give a definitive view. This was partly due to the limitations of early spyglasses, and partly to the fact that the viewers were usually standing on the decks of rolling ships. There is only one stable platform in the vicinity from which to view the Wheel, the peak of Observatory Mount (the Wheel's summit is not visible from the lower parts of Theodolite Isle) and for most people that was out of reach.

But in 1931, new distortion-corrected telephoto lenses came on the market, and in 1932 an expedition armed with such lenses set up camp atop the Mount, and so made the first comprehensive photographic studies of the peak. Almost as soon as the first shots of the summit were published, the phrase 'Hand of God' entered the mountaineering lexicon.

For what the photos seemed to show—though in truth, the imagery was still infuriatingly imprecise, more suggestive than definitive—was that what had appeared from afar to be a blunt knob was in fact a knurled upthrust crag. And that crag looked (from the angle of Observatory Mount, at least) for all the world like a half-clenched fist. The thumb was especially prominent, its scale hard to fathom, but most likely about three times human-height, the fingers more generalised, but seemingly curled in a shadowed overhang, perhaps even a cave. And between thumb and fingers was an open flat space—a palm.

So: a giant fist of stone, so large that a man might stand within it, thrust like an offering upwards to heaven from the top of the tallest mountain on the planet—what else was it ever going to be named but the Hand of God? It's not known who exactly coined the phrase, but the credit hardly matters, the illusion (if that's what it was) was so potent that everyone who beheld those first photos came to the same conclusion.

Almost as quickly came the legends.

If those curled fingers really did form not merely an overhang but an actual cave, there at the apex of the world, then what was *in* the cave? What secret, what mystery, did it conceal? Climbers in that era were only scrabbling about the Wheel's lower flanks, not even daring to fantasise yet about reaching the summit, but everyone else—fiction writers, fabulists, religious fanatics—could leap to the Hand of God in their minds and populate the cave with all manner of creatures and artefacts.

Jesus lived there, having ascended to the cave after his crucifixion, to await his second coming. Likewise, it was the abode of King Arthur, waiting to be the Future King. Buddha meditated there on the edge of space. Mohammed had been transported there briefly during his revelations. A whole host of Hindu deities call the cave home. Any number of human shamans and charlatans claimed to have travelled there in astral fashion. And when the flying saucer craze of the nineteen fifties kicked off, the Hand of God became the landing site for aliens of all types, or the laboratory to which they carried their abductees.

In other tales, the cave was the final resting place of the Ark of the Covenant, carried there by the cherubim to place the relic safely beyond nefarious human hands once and for all. The Holy Grail, of course, was hidden within the Hand, as were the prototypes of Mesoamerica's crystal skulls, and the complete annals of Atlantis.

The maddening thing was, short of going to the summit in person, or overflying it by aircraft, there was no way to dismiss all this nonsense and confirm what the Hand truly looked like. Even up until the 1960s no aircraft could safely fly so high, and the best mountain climbers were still well short of the top. So idle myth-making could proliferate.

The most famous of all the tales, of course, was the 1959 science fiction novel by Arthur C. Clarke, entitled *2001: An Odyssey of the Wheel*, which was even more famously made into the classic 1967 Oscar-winning film of the same name, directed by Stanley Kubrick.

The novel postulates that the Hand of God is not in fact a natural formation, but was carved hundreds of thousands of years ago by a visiting alien species. These aliens, travelling the galaxy in search of intelligent life, had found Earth lacking any such as yet, but noted that one of the many ape-type species showed promise of developing intelligence one day. The aliens also took note of this particular ape's prehensile thumbs and dexterous fingers, knowing how critical a 'hand' or similar utile organ was to the development of technology in all the other intelligent worlds they had visited.

So, says the tale, the aliens fashioned a message for us, the beginnings of a trail that we could follow to find them, when we were ready for such an encounter. They carved the likeness of a hand into the highest mountain on the planet, knowing that we would be drawn there by the likeness, and that we would need advanced technology to reach it. (They could have chosen no better place. On any other mountain, their sculpture would have been quickly hidden by snow, or eroded away by wind and rain and the cracking of ice. But at a height that places it far above the weather of the world, the summit of the Wheel is inviolate.)

Within the hand itself, so the story goes, inscribed in stone beneath the curled fingers, the aliens left key mathematical symbols that would direct humanity to the next waypoint along the trail. This next waypoint was another hand, carved in a crater hidden from human eyes on the far side of the Moon, the 'dark' side of the Moon, reachable only when humans were capable of leaving Earth's orbit. This, in turn, would reveal further signs that would take us to the depths of the galaxy.

Both the novel and the film were huge successes, and that success fuelled much interest in the Hand of God. But even by 1970 no climbing expedition had yet reached higher than twelve thousand metres on the Wheel, not even halfway to the summit.

But then the United States military took a hand. In December 1967, six months after *2001: An Odyssey of the Wheel* hit cinemas, and after securing permission from the Australian government, on a fine summer's day (it wouldn't have mattered if it wasn't fine, as the weather ceased above ten miles anyway) an SR-71 Blackbird spyplane, crewed by pilot Major William Lawson and RSO Major Gilbert Martinez, flew two passes over the Wheel at just under Mach 3 and an altitude of eighty-five thousand feet, less than a kilometre above the Hand of God.

Cameras whirred at each pass, and the world waited in fascination. The photos that resulted were as clear and sharp as anyone could wish, showing the Hand in monochrome precision.

And yet . . .

Nothing was really answered. The summit, even from this new over-head angle, still looked uncannily like a giant human hand, and the curl of the fingers completely hid the hollow that lay beneath them. And even though the second of the Blackbird's passes was to the west of the summit, so as to look sidelong into this apparent cave, still there was only dark-ness at the mouth of the cavity, a shadow cast by the hand's thumb, and its inner recesses remained beyond view.

The Hand of God, said the conspiracy nuts and the true believers, was giving the US military the finger.

There was great demand for another over-flight, and for a photo to be taken at the right time of day for the sun to be shining into the recess, but the US authorities somewhat huffily refused. They had wasted enough hours on a militarily insignificant mountaintop; it was time they got back to the serious business of Cold War spying. Not to be outdone, the Russians carried out their own over-flight six months later (unauthorised but monitored by US radar) with a MiG-25, but few properly developed versions of their photos ever made it to the West, and those that did were no more definitive than the American shots.

And so, the myth-making could continue, for seven more years at least, until Walter Richman stood upon the Palm of God in person.

How he came to be there alone is itself an extraordinary story, covered elsewhere. All that matters for now is that he was seen, by those watching from below, to leave the Palm and to disappear briefly into the cavity beneath the fingers, before emerging again. Which should have settled the matter. But when Richman came down from the peak, to everyone's amazement he refused to reveal what he had seen there. And though he had taken plenty of photos of the view looking *out* from the Palm, he took no images at all of the Hand itself, or of the cave.

Why not? Why his enduring secrecy, when so many are so eager to know the truth? Through his many interviews in the years since, and in his own published writings, Richman has given the same answer. He maintains he keeps silent out of respect for the mountain. He says that whatever he saw within the cave—and he confirms it really is a cave—will forever remain between himself and the Wheel. 'The mountain has been defeated,' is his typical summation on the matter, 'but I think we owe it the honour of keeping its last secret.'

Thus, the mystery remains, and to this day fantasy has been left free to populate the Hand of God as it sees fit.

The truth, of course, is no doubt perfectly mundane. Any serious thinker knows there is no Hand on the Moon, and no alien message waiting on the Wheel. There are no gods or goddesses or hidden treasures there either. Almost certainly, there is nothing in the cave within the Hand of God other than frozen, sterile rock.

But the other truth, infuriating as it may be, is that only one man in all the world can say so with total certainty.

And he won't.

11

INTRODUCTIONS

RITA LEFT HER ROOM AT five minutes past seven. She had showered and changed and then waited an uneasy hour, flicking unseeing through cable channels on the living room TV as night fell outside, and mercifully (but why did she think of it as merciful?) the Wheel faded from orange to grey and then to no more than a shadow, a wall beyond the wall of glass.

Now, in the deserted corridor outside her apartment, she was struck once more by the quiet of the Observatory. She deliberately paused a moment to listen. It was not in fact a total silence: a barely perceptible hum hovered at just the audible threshold, the murmur, no doubt, of air conditioning and heating, the vibration of distant equipment in kitchens and lift shafts and generator rooms, no matter how well insulated and dampened. No active building could be *noiseless*.

And yet, the quiet, it seemed to her, was surely the best that money could buy. She had visited many great houses in her youth, in company with her father attending to his wealthy clients, and most of those buildings had possessed, when they were not hosting parties or large gatherings, the same awful quality: *emptiness*. A hollowness rang in the ear, footsteps echoed on wooden floors, voices floated ghostlike from distant rooms. There was a sense of unused and unwanted space all about, and an inhibition about making any noise oneself.

But here . . . here the quiet was a more assured one, a more carefully designed one. There was no hollow ringing in the air, no distracting echoes of voices or footsteps or clatter from some other place, no sense indeed that there *were* other places, or that there was anyone at all beyond this single corridor to disturb, even if she yelled out.

Rita was enough of an architect's daughter to note the subtle baffles built as decoration into the ceiling and walls to break up reflective surfaces and deaden echoes, and the use of carpeting and wall hangings to dampen noise. But no doubt this rich silence (yes, that was the word, *rich*) was due mostly to the buried nature of the structure, to the mountain itself that enfolded the building, that had swallowed it . . .

She shook her head at herself, set off down the hall. Not swallowed. The mountain had done nothing of the kind. It was men who had burrowed into it, not the other way around.

And that was another question: in all this excavated vastness, did she feel lost at all, did she feel small? Did she feel intimidated, wandering about on her own within the belly of such a beast? It would signal a failure in the design if she did. But no, the hallway, as she walked down it, was sized just right, not so narrow as to feel tube-like or claustrophobic, not so large as to feel impersonal and cold. The colours of the carpet and the wall hangings were warm, the lighting was intimate. Her clever father had made this tunnel in the rock feel human-sized and safe.

But then she came to the hallway's end, and the well of the Double Helix Staircase. She had known it was coming, of course, but even so the vertigo beat dizzyingly in her chest as she stepped out onto the landing and the walls swept suddenly away from her, both up and down, rising from and falling into the awesome central bore.

Here was no comfort or intimacy; here was awe and inspiration, the staircase seeming to twist itself up from the depths, supported only by the sheer dynamism of its shape. Far below was a pool of darkness; high above, the windows of the Atrium dome were black with night.

But up and down the walls of the well a thousand points of light burned, tiny stars that formed serene galaxies floating around the stairs. It was, Rita could not help but think, *beautiful*. Whatever it was her father had wrought within the mountain—even be it monstrous, indulgent, a crime against nature—there was beauty here, first and foremost.

Eschewing the lift, she crossed the bridge to reach the closest arm of the Helix Staircase. Below, the spirals descended into the glowing darkness, but she turned her eyes to the night sky above, and climbed.

Beautiful, yes . . . but beauty that was to be seen by so few people. After all, this was not a public monument, nor a church, nor even the foyer of some corporate headquarters monolith that the public could at least peer into through the glass. This was a private home.

Why did they *do* it, she wondered, climbing slowly up the winding way. Why did the rich build things like this staircase, live in places like the Observatory? No lifestyle, no matter how exalted, truly called for a private home bigger than say four or five times the size of an average family house. So why did the super wealthy construct these vast palaces with their entry halls and ballrooms and guest wings, most of which would sit idle for ninety-nine per cent of the building's life?

Were they that insecure? That desperate to display their money and their power? And that tasteless to think that a big building was the best way to do it? Surely a *secure* billionaire would never bother. Why, even Richman himself, for most of his life, had derided the very concept of a grand home, refusing to build himself a single mansion despite the fact that he could have afforded dozens. Surely that was the wiser path. And yet, here in his senior years, even he had succumbed . . .

No. As she had before, Rita thought it again: she did not understand the rich. And as she would never *be* rich, not billionaire rich, she never would understand them. Maybe the very condition that enabled a person to make billions also made it irresistible to them, or necessary, to build grandly. Maybe the fact that she couldn't understand mansion-building was the very flaw in her that prevented her from becoming rich. Maybe one could never exist without the other.

And maybe that was nonsense. Twenty metres up, and slightly out of breath, Rita emerged into the Atrium.

Music had come floating down the stairs to her—jazz, mellow—and she had half expected to be greeted by the sight of a live quartet. She had even been disappointed that Richman would opt for such a vulgarity at what was meant to be a casual dinner. But no, there were no musicians in sight, the music was merely playing from unseen speakers.

She turned to the Saloon. Behind the gleaming wooden bar, a white-shirted barman was assiduously engaged in the perfect cliché of polishing glasses. In a huge hearth a fire was blazing warmly. And there, arranged upon a cluster of couches set before the fire, were three people, two of whom Rita knew: Clara, and the IT expert Eugene, who had tampered with her phone. The third was a woman of middle age.

'Rita,' called the major-domo, seeing her and rising from the couch. 'Come and join us. Eugene you've already met, but let me introduce Madelaine Reynard, our chief interior designer.'

Rita took the woman's extended hand. Though stylishly attired in a black dress and shawl, she was not quite what Rita would have imagined as an interior designer, for her frame was squat and solid, and her large face was dourly frowning.

'Pleased to meet you,' Rita said.

'Oh no,' the designer returned, with a frank stare, 'it's my pleasure to meet *you*, Ms Gausse.' Her sombre gaze flicked briefly to the major-domo, as if to share some ironic point, then returned to Rita. 'My sympathies upon your father's passing. We worked closely together in the last few years, as designer and architect always must.' She had a notable accent: French, beneath an American-style English. 'He was a great man.'

Rita bowed her head politely.

'A drink?' asked Clara.

A fresh round was ordered for everyone from the bar; Eugene drinking beer, the three women selecting various white wines.

'Your work here is beautiful,' Rita ventured to Madelaine, for the designer kept staring at her.

'Thank you,' was the unsmiling reply. 'I am very happy with the result. Indeed, as far as I was concerned, my work here was finished. Done. Yet here I am again, at Mr Richman's request.'

Clara hastened to explain to Rita. 'Well, yes, of course, the work *is* finished. And this weekend is mostly just a celebration of that. Still, Madelaine and Kushal—Kushal, as chief builder on the project—have also been invited in somewhat of a professional capacity. You might say this gathering is the final handing over of the house, an inspection tour to sort out any last niggles, before the grand opening a month from now. There might be a couple of things yet that need some reworking. Your father, too, of course would have been here, if he'd been able.'

'But instead of your father,' commented the designer, addressing Rita, 'we have you.' The tone of the observation was too formal to tell if disapproval lay beneath it, or something else. 'The daughter, who has a certain fame of her own, though not for architecture. I have read your book, Ms Gausse.'

Rita flushed in surprise. It was the last thing she had expected. 'That was all long ago.'

'Now, now, Maddie,' Clara was smiling. 'We promised we wouldn't bring up Rita's book if it's not something she wants to talk about.'

'Of course,' nodded the designer. 'We have only just met,' she added, with the directness of a second language, 'and I am being rude.'

There had been discussions about her book? How strange. And yet, after all, these people had been friends of her father's, it wasn't so fantastic that they would look up a book written by his daughter.

Still, it was embarrassing.

To cover her unease, Rita asked of Madelaine, 'Do you work full time for Richman, or was this just one contract?'

The designer's expression did not change. 'I have maintained my own company for many years now, but in truth I no longer have any clients other than Mr Richman. There is no time, I am too busy. As you may understand, Mr Richman owns many buildings, private and corporate, all around the world, and is always constructing more.' She glanced up and about at the great space around them. 'But this Observatory, of course, was of a different scale.'

'Yes, I can see that,' Rita said. 'Yet you've managed to make it feel very welcoming and comfortable on the inside.'

The designer looked surprised. 'But why not? Comfort is everything!' And finally some warmth touched her lips. 'As long as comfort is not mistaken for clutter. That I will not stand.'

'Did you also do the interior decoration then, as well as the interior design?' Rita enquired.

'Oh yes, down to the last detail of furnishing, be it a footstool or the cutlery or the soap holders in the showers. Some architects consider even such minor trivialities as their province, but thankfully your father was not such a one, and was happy to leave the interiors entirely to me. And thankfully too, Mr Richman is not one for ostentation. He may have chosen the most extravagant location in the world—a mountaintop, for the good lord's sake, in this terrible wilderness—but he is a sensible man when it comes to his bathroom fittings.'

Rita nodded, glanced up to the high dome. 'All this blank stone. It must have presented some unique challenges.'

Madelaine's gaze was more approving now. 'The worst part was the outdoor areas. How do you humanise a space so cold, and so windy? The gales up here, Ms Gausse, you would not believe! The balconies, the upper deck, they were fiendish to design in any usable fashion— and then to have to put up with those hideously ugly airlock doors!'

Her indignation was so forlorn, and her pout so childlike on such a stern face, that everyone had to laugh.

'And here's Kushal at last,' noted Clara, her eyes going to the stairs.

Rita turned to see a large middle-aged man of sub-continental appearance striding towards them, dressed in a casual suit and a red shirt. He had a full head of swept grey hair, and a toothy smile.

'My friends,' he declared, arms outspread. 'How good to see you all again.' And coming up, he lowered his arms to extend a hand to Rita. 'And this must be the esteemed Ms Rita Gausse.'

Rita accepted the handshake as Clara made the formal introduction. 'Rita, this is Kushal Mangalam Ambini, chief of construction for this and many other of Mr Richman's building projects.'

'Just Kushal,' the man reassured Rita. 'And may I say it is an honour to meet the daughter of the father. Richard was a wonderful fellow, and of course brilliant, we had many fine days working together. And creativity runs in the family. I have read your book, Rita—if I may call you Rita—and I was most fascinated by it. Most intrigued.'

'Thank you,' she replied, taken aback again. Had *everyone* read her book?

'Kushal,' warned Clara, 'I've already reminded Maddie that Rita is not to be pestered about ancient history. This is a social gathering.'

'Of course! I only say it to let her know that we are not *all*'—and here he tipped a wink to the designer sitting stoically by—'sceptics on such matters. But in any case, a whisky or I shall die!'

He whirled away to the bar, leaving Rita to take her seat again, disconcerted. What possible interest could her book—her delusional manifesto upon the otherworldly, written eighteen years ago—have to people like these, to hard-headed construction professionals?

But when the builder returned, all smiles and with a large whisky in hand, he made no further mention of Rita's past beliefs. 'Tell me,' he said, collapsing on the couch beside her, his eyes, slightly reddened, twinkling mischief, 'what do you think of your father's work here, if you can forgive its shoddy construction for my part, and also Maddie's awful paint scheme and terrible carpets?' His English was typically

Indian in its properness. 'The Observatory itself, I mean in its raw form before we all ruined it, as your father first conceived it, do you like it?'

'It's . . . it's a little beyond an off-hand opinion, to be honest.'

He seemed to understand. 'Exactly! A building like this—how do you judge? Oh, I know there were millions of fools out there doing exactly that. The protests! The abuse I suffered during construction! "Leave that precious mountain alone!" A pile of rock! I ask you? But of course, once anyone is *here*, once they *see* it, well, their tongues are stilled.'

Rita could only nod.

Kushal pointed towards the great wedge of glass that divided the Saloon from the Dining Hall: the lower depths of the Terrace pool. The water within was illuminated by recessed lights of many colours, and streams of bubbles were rising from the bottom: as they rose they glimmered red and green, before disappearing into a darkness over-head, as if they were sinking into an abyss rather than rising towards the open air.

'You see that? That pool? That's what I mean about my terrible van-dalism of your father's design. I did that, not him.'

'It wasn't in the original design?' Rita asked, relieved in a way, because it was a touch that hardly seemed like her father.

'Not like this! Not as deep. It was shallow at first, and there was only solid rock down here. But I said, Richard, please, allow this. I'm no swimmer, I just float, you know, I don't go underwater, so I need a way to watch beautiful women when they go bathing.'

'And my father agreed?'

'Oh no! He was horrified. But Mr Richman saw the joke, and I got my way. But oh, the trouble we had over that damned pool and the ice up there—I tell you, a bad dream. Even heating the water isn't enough, it kept freezing over. We had to put in those bubble streams to keep the surface agitated at night—though at least they look nice in the lights.'

Even as they gazed, the darkness at the top of the pool suddenly flared into brightness. A glare awoke too through the windows of the Atrium dome. Light was flooding the Terrace above.

'Ah,' said the builder. 'The helipad lights. Our host approaches.'

Rita stared up. In the glow of the spotlights, she could now see wisps of cloud racing across the top of the dome, across the Terrace. It must be getting quite windy outside; she'd had no idea, there was no sound or vibration within. But lord, a helicopter was really going to be landing out there in the wind and fog, all the way up *here*?

A noise intruded now from outside, kept low by the Observatory's sound insulation, barely enough to compete with the background jazz, but unmistakable: the thrum of a helicopter. Reflections of light flashed red and blue through the high windows, then came a glimpse of a white body and blurred rotors passing over the dome. The thrum of rotors continued for a few moments more, then died away.

'Right on schedule,' said Clara, with a glance at her watch. 'I'm sure he'll go to the Cottage first to clean up, but he shouldn't be too—ah, there we go!' The major-domo's phone had just chimed in her pocket. She took it out and inspected a text message. 'Ten minutes, he says.'

Rita looked at Eugene, who had been sitting silently through the last few minutes, perusing data of some sort on his own phone. 'How does this all work, by the way?' she asked, curious. 'How do we get such good phone reception and internet way the hell out here?' Only an hour ago Rita had received a phone call from her house- and cat-sitter back in Melbourne, one of the young nurses from the vet hospital, with a question about Simon's food regime, and the reception had been perfect.

The IT expert slipped his phone away, shrugged companionably. 'Well, it's possible for anyone in theory. Satellites cover even remote parts of the ocean these days, and offer a full range of internet access for ships at sea. But the bandwidth is limited, so it's not cheap, and it's usually not very fast, especially when demand is high. Of course, money isn't an issue for Mr Richman, but more to the point, he's a major stockholder in the company that owns the satellites in question, so we have as much bandwidth as we want, and as fast as can be.'

Rita nodded, noting yet again that when you had enough money, so many of the everyday inadequacies simply faded away.

'The whole place is a technical marvel, truth be told,' Kushal enthused. 'Communications, security, environmental controls, there are all sorts of wonders buried away in the tunnels and back rooms. And yet sitting here there is no hint of any of it, so you'd never guess.'

The conversation ran on about the Observatory and its marvels: about the nearly seven kilometres of passageways and service tunnels that riddled the upper Mount, only a third of which were ever meant to be seen by guests; about the internal artificially lit hydroponic garden growing fresh salad vegetables right here in the residence; about the natural springs that had been found during construction, which now provided all the mega-litres of water needed for the pools.

The discussion was only interrupted at last by a new arrival; a man emerged purposefully from the Dining Hall, and, with a shake of his head to the barman, came over to the group.

'Kennedy,' greeted Clara.

'How goes it all here?' the newcomer enquired, not sitting down. He was middle aged but muscular, with cropped grey hair and a reddish face. His eyes flicked over the five of them, lingering last on Rita.

'No problems,' the major-domo said. 'How was the flight in?'

'Getting iffy, if you ask me. But the boss was keen to land up here.' The man hitched at his belt. For all his brawn his belly was notable, and something about his suit was ill-fitting across the shoulders. His eyes were still on Rita. 'This is our special guest, I assume?'

Clara nodded. 'Rita, this is Kennedy Boland, chief of Mr Richman's security team.'

The man shrugged a greeting. 'Don't be intimidated by the presence of armed guards around Mr Richman, Ms Gausse.' His accent was middle American, deep-voiced, with a twang that slurred the *Ms* to the point almost of insult. 'As I hope you understand, a man of his position would be a tempting target for kidnappers or terrorists.'

A gun, Rita thought. Of course. His coat was ill-fitting because of some kind of shoulder holster beneath it. But that was odd, for surely a professional security aide would have his clothes tailored to hide those kinds of protrusions? And yet this man, who presumably was one of the best in his field, if he was security chief to Walter Richman, was wearing a suit that looked too tight, and cheaply made.

'Of course, I understand,' Rita answered coolly. Then she added, 'But is there really much risk, here in such a remote location?'

He considered her starkly. 'Here more than anywhere. A helicopter could land suddenly, full of kidnappers. A boat might come out of the night full of terrorists. The remoteness is a weakness as much as a strength. There're no police out here. No help. It's just us.'

Eugene smiled with what might have been a deliberate flick of his long hair. 'Never fear,' he said to Rita, 'we're not *totally* blind here. All flights within five hundred clicks are tracked by radar down at Base, so no landing can be a total surprise. And even if a chopper full of gunmen did touch down out on the Terrace, all the exterior doors are emergency lockable, bulletproof and blastproof. All nearby shipping is tracked too, down to small yachts, and the harbour can be closed with five minutes' warning by raising chains across the mouth.'

Kennedy's nod was distant. 'All decent measures—if they work as they're meant to. But no system is foolproof.'

Clara spoke to Rita. 'Kennedy is ex-military intelligence. It's his job to know everything that goes on around Mr Richman.'

Eugene cocked an eyebrow to the security chief, almost mocking. 'So how many people are in the building right this second?'

Kennedy didn't blink. 'Twenty-two.'

Rita could not suppress a surprised glance, and the security chief's pale eyes latched on to her instantly. 'The five of you sitting here,' he said, 'me, Mr Richman in the cottage, the barman there, a waitress standing by for you all in the Dining Hall, a chef and an assistant chef in the kitchen, two systems managers in the control room, five cleaners on duty in the lower levels, and four of my own men patrolling the exit points and the upper deck. Twenty-two in all. First thing I did when I got off the bird was to consult the duty roster, and then check that it was right.'

It wasn't even a boast, simply a description of a fact.

'Twenty-two is a skeleton crew, really,' Kushal observed. 'There'd be more here by day. Cleaning staff, cooking staff, maintenance staff for the air-conditioning plant, the heating system, the electrical systems, the winches, the pools and spas and filtration systems. And that's not to mention the staff down at Base. The power plant, the radar shack, the docks, the warehouses, gardens, port security. It's endless.'

Rita had to say it. 'And all of it, all these people working and living here, all the security, all the money it takes, just because one man wants to make his home on a rock in the middle of nowhere?'

'Well,' said a voice coming up behind her, 'what's so wrong with that?'

She spun. Her back had been to the Library, and approaching from that direction was a figure familiar from a thousand newspaper photographs and video clips: Walter Richman, billionaire, conqueror of the Wheel, man of history, but *real* now, in the flesh, and that changed everything.

'Hi,' he said to her, 'I'm Walt.'

12

HOLY BRIBES

Extract from feature article 'One Man's Mountain'
by Antony Narev, *Sydney Morning Herald*, 2014

So how did Walter Richman do it? How did he become the only man to ever stand atop the Wheel? I don't mean, how did he climb the mountain itself—as interesting a story as that is—I mean, how in the hell did he convince the three other climbers with him on that last fateful day to hang back just below the peak, and to let him summit alone?

Mountain climbers are hardly retiring types, and with a peak in plain sight are not known for a willingness to let anything get in their way. Summit madness, it's called, and it has lured more than one climber to an untimely death, pushing on to some taunting crest even as night is falling and the weather is closing in and the oxygen is gone . . .

But somehow, Richman convinced three of the best climbers in the world to stop short of the most prized summit in all history. He had no excuse involving safety or survival. They had reached the final approach well within their schedule, and with plenty of daylight and oxygen to spare. He did it simply for the sake of gratifying his ego, for no better reason than to let him later claim, 'I was the only one!'

Even more remarkably, in the years following, he seemed to convince the world that he was right to do so, that he wasn't acting out of pure narcissism, that it wasn't one of the greatest acts of bastardry and betrayal ever committed in the climbing world—that he wasn't, in short, as one anonymous climber further down the mountain called him 'a deranged, selfish fucking cunt'—but rather, somehow, that he had done the right thing, even the noble thing.

Gobsmacking, really. Except, this is how con men always work. They not only rip you off, they make you thank them for ripping you off; they make you *love* them for it. And whatever else he may be, Walter Richman is most certainly a con man.

But to fully grasp the enormity of what happened that day on the summit, we have to go back a little, to April 1971 in fact, some four months after the twenty-five-year-old Walter Richman had unexpectedly inherited his father's staggering fortune, and to the day that he announced, at a specially convened press conference, exactly what he planned to do with all that power and money.

He was going to climb the Wheel.

That's right, he repeated to the crowd of disbelieving journalists, most from financial newspapers, he was going to lead an expedition to defeat the greatest mountain the world. It would be an effort that would involve hundreds of people, demand a host of technical innovations in several fields, and would take three years at the least—an undertaking as big, in its way, as NASA's landing on the Moon.

The first journalist to splutter out a question in response to this ignored the whole preposterous idea completely, and demanded instead to know what Walter planned to do about his father's empire? Who was going to run it, while he was off tilting at windmills?

'Oh, I will,' Richman responded casually, as if managing one of the largest multi-national multi-industrial concerns in the world would be no trouble at all. 'In my spare time, that is.'

Stocks immediately plunged on markets right around the globe. It was awful, said the wise heads of the business world, it was everyone's worst fears realised. The young fool was going to squander his father's fortune, a vast economic enterprise would be left rudderless, its capital frittered away with no hope of return, and all to do what? Climb a tower of rock and ice in the middle of nowhere? Madness.

But in fact, the wise heads had it wrong. Richman set about organising his mammoth expedition with extraordinary energy and flair—and with a canny knack for sharing the financial burden around among a long list of corporate sponsors and technical partners (who, incidentally, would spend years chasing down money owed to them by the expedition, long after the mountain had been climbed).

It soon became apparent that rather than embarking on a folly, Richman was instead engaged in what was becoming the great project of the age. After all, space had been broached and the Moon reached, the deepest trenches in the ocean had been visited, the wilds of every continent explored. What was left for man now to achieve but to set foot upon that last untrodden spot of his own planet?

Strangely enough, Richman himself, in all his mountaineering career up to that point, had never climbed an inch on the Wheel, even though his contemporaries had made ascents there as high as twelve thousand metres. Indeed, Richman had only even *seen* the mountain once, during a cruise in his youth. He now claimed that this omission was deliberate. 'I've been saving that mountain until I was ready to go all the way to the top. Why climb half a peak? I want it all.'

He put the call out, meanwhile, for other climbers to join his team—and they answered, signing on in their hundreds. Richman's reputation was not good among his fellow climbers, but this expedition was simply too big to ignore. What was more, as news leaked out about the technical advances he was making with his new high-altitude climbing suits, it seemed more and more likely that he really might succeed. There had been other great attempts on the Wheel, but none like this, none with NASA as a partner, and none with limitless wealth to back it up.

Work began at the Wheel itself in early 1972. There was little climbing initially; the first months were spent in stockpiling supplies on Theodolite Isle and on improving facilities at the notoriously fickle Bligh Cove upon the shores of the Wheel itself. The latter involved excavation of the sea floor, and the building of concrete walls to create a proper deep-water port, for Richman's plans called for the berthing of two large ships in the cove for months at a time, in all weather.

With money no object, it was all done by June 1971, and the two ships took up station. One was a twenty thousand tonne former cruise liner, renamed the *Artemis*, after the Greek goddess of mountains. Its purpose was to serve as accommodation for the support staff and for the climbers when they were off duty. The other ship was a converted oil freighter, renamed *Vulcan* after the Roman god of fire, and it would be a floating power station and pump house, feeding electricity up the mountain, and fresh water too, through heat-jacketed pipes.

Why were electricity and water considered so vital, even at the huge expense of laying cables and pipes all the way up the Wheel? The answer is simple: one of the heaviest burdens that normal climbers must haul up a mountain is fuel, either in the form of oil and gas for cooking and heating, or—for pressure-suited climbers—in the form of batteries to keep the suits running. To have electricity on hand, for cooking, heating and recharging, would simplify things vastly. Another great burden is drinking water. True, on most mountains snow can be melted as needed, but on the Wheel, above the fifteen thousand metre mark, there *was* no snow, it was drier there than any desert. So piped water too was a necessity.

In July 1971, climbing began. Not serious climbing, however. On the lower slopes a path was already well laid out. Most earlier expeditions had also started at Bligh Cove, and taken this same route up the West Face. In truth, the expedition did not even consider this early stage to be part of the climb, but merely the 'walk in', to use a Himalayan phrase, leading to the establishment of a Base Camp. In this case, Base Camp was founded at five thousand one hundred metres, on the great ledge that runs for miles across the West Face at that altitude, smooth and level and thirty metres wide, known in the climbing world as the Plateau. Many earlier expeditions had used the Plateau likewise—it was littered with the remains of old camps—but the Richman effort would in time see a thriving small town develop there, narrow, but with all mod cons, and with a population close to a thousand.

The real climbing began in November. In rotation, teams of four climbers at a time set out from the Plateau to carve new routes up the slopes of the West Face, laying fixed lines behind them as they went. This would be a 'siege' campaign, with teams repeatedly ascending and descending the mountain, building camps higher and higher until at last the summit was within easy reach of the final camp.

It was now also that climbers began to don their suits, Richman's game-changing High Terrain Function suits. Of course, they had not needed these in the thicker airs below Base Camp. And even above the Plateau, from five thousand to eight thousand metres, they wore only lightweight versions of the suits, not yet fully pressurised. Many climbers in fact could have survived without even those as far as nine thousand metres; it had been done before. But climbing to nine thousand metres unaided is an exhausting, body-wasting, often lethal process. Richman wanted his climbers fit and healthy at all times, not hollowed-out wrecks, so from five kilometres on it was suits only.

Trailing the climbers, two lines of HAEV huts also crept up the West Face from Base Camp. The duplication was a precaution, in case avalanche should wipe out one line or the other. On each line, the huts were an average of about three hundred vertical metres apart, though there was much localised variation dictated by the terrain. Likewise, the two lines of huts were usually held about a kilometre apart horizontally, although as the lines ascended beyond the precipitation limit at fifteen thousand metres, this distance was reduced as the risk of avalanche was gone and even the threat of rock fall lessened.

In all, one hundred and twenty-two huts would be painstakingly installed. This involved, for each hut, hauling its ninety-four individual components—frames, panels, seals, internal fittings, pumps and other machinery—as far up the mountain as necessary, then locating or clearing (sometimes by explosive) a large enough piece of level ground to host it, followed by construction and connection to the water and power network, and finally stocking with supplies, to leave it ready for habitation. It was tedious work, and, as with all things on the Wheel, dangerous. It took five months for the climbing teams to gain the previous high mark of any other expedition, twelve thousand metres—and cost the lives of four climbers, caught in two different avalanches. But as the experience of the teams grew, and as they began to reach heights above the worst of the weather, the ascent accelerated, pushing into completely virgin territory, twelve, thirteen and fourteen kilometres up.

Walter Richman himself was also by then active on the climb. He had overseen the early stages of the campaign from his headquarters in New York, visiting the Wheel only intermittently. But after the completion of Base Camp he transferred his office to an executive suite on the *Artemis*, and placed his name on the climbing roster.

From then on, his routine was much the same as any of the five hundred other climbers on the list. First, from the *Artemis* it was a three-day hike up to Base Camp. (Helicopters could land on the Plateau, but it was a risky procedure and reserved for emergencies.) After a day's recovery, climbers would then don their lightweight suits and begin the ascent proper, laden with whatever their assigned burden happened to be: supplies or a pack of panels for a hut or perhaps a chemical toilet. Climbers were expected to ascend between five hundred and a thousand metres in a day, before resting overnight in the established huts. Ascending and descending teams slept in alternating huts along each line. In a pinch, a single hut could sleep eight climbers, and in a full emergency, could squeeze in sixteen, briefly.

At eight thousand metres, a High Base Camp had been established, where a small population of technicians lived and worked in a collection of large HAEV workshops. Here, climbers were issued with the full HTF suits that they would wear for the rest of their ascent. From High Base

Camp they then pushed on, day by day, hut to hut, until finally they reached the last hut in the line. At this point they might merely deliver their load and immediately descend, or, if they were lucky, they might be assigned to route-breaking above the hut.

The latter was the prize assignment, as it meant real climbing, breaking new ground on virgin faces, with no fixed lines laid ahead. Otherwise, the climber, load delivered, merely faced the long descent back to Base Camp and then to the *Artemis* for a few days R and R, before starting all over again. By the later stages of the expedition, with the leading huts placed high on the Wheel at twenty kilometres and above, a full ascent and descent could take five or six weeks. So, any chance to do real climbing at the top, amid so much tedious up and down work, was precious.

Many climbers, indeed, could not bear all the laboured waiting for such a brief chance, and so quit. Others, whose individualistic mountaineering ethics were offended by such a massed and coordinated assault, by its bureaucracy, and by its building of so much infrastructure on the mountain—vandalism, one disgruntled critic called it—also resigned in disgust after a few times up and down.

But most remained, and climbed with a will. For the reward was worth any price—a chance to stand at last upon the very Hand of God. This was key. Richman, at the campaign's beginning, had promised that every climber involved would be allowed their own moment of victory on the Wheel's peak. In other mountain campaigns, the summit was usually attained only by a single assault team, gaining all the glory, while the support teams missed out. But on the Richman expedition, *every* climber who had contributed would get their chance at the top. After all, once the network of huts was complete, and once the initial assault team had gained the summit, it would be no great matter to keep the whole system in operation for a few months longer, the time it would take for the rest of the climbers to rotate up and have their own turn.

You couldn't say fairer than that.

Even so, many wondered who exactly would be in that initial assault team, for even if everyone else got to reach the top eventually, the *first* to do it would be the ones the world remembered.

That Richman himself would be in the team was a given; after all, he was paying for everything. (So at least it was thought.) But who would be the other lucky three? Expedition management's only comment was that everyone's climbing hours were being logged and assessed, and when the time came, the best climbers would be chosen.

Of the expedition's slow, perilous ascent up the last ten thousand metres of the Wheel's western face, passing from the familiar air and weather of the troposphere into the alien world of the stratosphere, this brief account will not try to tell. The successes, the disasters, the deaths, are all well attested. Suffice to say that in November 1974, two years after the establishment of Base Camp, Hut 122 was completed and stocked at an altitude of twenty-four thousand six hundred metres, just a touch under five hundred vertical metres from the summit.

All now lay ready for the initial assault team's final ascent to the Hand of God. That team, of course, had been chosen some weeks before the hut's completion, to ensure that they would be only a few camps below on the day that 122 became operational. As expected, leading the team was Richman—and in truth, as he had by then put in as many climbing hours as anyone, there was no reason he should not be there.

But the other three members were interesting choices. For a start, though all three were excellent climbers, none were *elite* climbers. There were dozens of far more renowned and more expert mountaineers on the roster, all of whom had put in their fair share of the work. But instead Richman selected three climbers less experienced than himself—and for that matter, younger. Richman was twenty-eight, none of the other three was older than twenty-four. And last, though this was not known at the time, the finances of each of the chosen three was parlous. One was newly-wed and newly a father to twins, heavily over-mortgaged on his house in Australia. Another was trying to prop up a failing hiking business in the USA. The third had a chronic gambling problem.

The question has to be asked thus: were these circumstances known to *Richman* when he made his selection, and did they influence his choice? The answer, given the events, seems plain.

Richman's summit team left Hut 122 on the appointed morning, and climbed without issue to the supply dump earlier established two hundred metres higher up the ridge. From there, taking it in turns to go lead, they climbed laboriously, over six hours, up a last sheer face to reach the final approach. There now remained only a walk of some ninety metres along a knife-edge spine angled at about thirty degrees. With Richman in the lead, the team set out. But halfway along the spine, with the Hand of God in full view, Richman paused and turned, seemingly to address his three companions following behind.

At the same moment, radio connection with the team was temporarily lost. Only the TV telecast, shot from the top of Observatory Mount via telephoto lens, remained continuous, showing the four huddled in apparent discussion. The consultation lasted ten minutes, after which Richman turned and pressed on alone up the spine. At the same time, the radio link with the team was re-established.

The three left behind climbed no closer, though they recorded events with their cameras. And so Richman covered the last fifty yards by himself, and at 3.15 p.m. on 14 November 1974, he stepped all alone onto the palm-of-a-hand-like platform that sits between a thumblike protrusion to one side, and a curled-fingers overhang on the other: the first man to stand within the famous Hand of God.

He remained there for half an hour, making speeches over the radio for posterity and posing for photographs taken by the three men lower down. He ignored all questions from expedition headquarters, descended finally to join the other three men, then continued on down to Hut 122. Whereupon he soon declared, via an announcement from expedition management, that all teams on the mountain, even those ascending, must immediately begin to descend to Base Camp, and that no support would be given to anyone who tried to press on for the top. The summit of the Wheel was now officially *closed*.

As can be imagined, the climbers further down the mountain were disbelieving and outraged. They had been promised their moment on the summit, how dare Richman take that away! Several teams rebelled, and set off upwards from higher camps in defiance.

But Richman and his team disabled Hut 122's power and water linkages as they left, rendering it useless. They then did the same to the next hut down. This put the summit beyond any last-gasp sprint attempt, even for the most foolhardy, and with no fresh supplies being sent up, by order of Richman himself, there was nothing to be done. Complain all they might, the rebel climbers could only withdraw.

They went bitterly. So great was the hatred for Richman that when the summit team was only three kilometres down the mountain, an armed security team was sent up to escort them the rest of the way. By the time they reached High Base Camp they had retreated behind an impenetrable wall of bodyguards, and Richman was speaking to no one apart from his own media connections. Upon reaching Base Camp, the four were whisked away by helicopter, and that was that. Walter Richman had stolen the Wheel for himself, and gotten away clean.

To this day, Richman's three companions have never spoken a word in public of their part in the adventure. So—what *did* the billionaire say to them, that afternoon upon the summit ridge?

Richman's own version—issued in a press release from the *Artemis*—went like this: while climbing the final ridge a realisation had come to him. He saw suddenly that it would be wrong for more than one climber to stand in the Hand of God, let alone for hundreds of climbers to do so. It would, he realised, reduce something sacred and otherworldly to little more than a trampled tourist spot. So he had decided, even as the summit came in view, that only one man—to represent all the hundreds in the expedition—would go to the peak, and that it was fitting that this one man, as leader of entire enterprise, be himself. Oh, he knew it would be unpopular with his fellow climbers, but that was a burden he was prepared to accept for the sake of the mountain.

The other three climbers were, supposedly, so moved by Richman's revelation that they agreed to stand back and let him go on alone, even though the summit lay plain in their sight. For which nobility, said Richman, they should be forever applauded.

Which is all very well. But even though none of the three have ever made any definitive statements to deny Richman's version, it became evident in the months following the expedition, through a series of investigative reports in major climbing magazines, that each of the three had come into a considerable amount of money.

Ten of millions of dollars, in fact.

Which can lead to only one conclusion. Richman had bribed them that day on the ridge. He had offered them *so* much money, that even with the summit and eternal fame a mere fifty yards away, they had succumbed. He may even, perhaps, have threatened them with worse alternatives if they refused his offer, knowing their financial straits.

Either way, they accepted. Older climbers, no doubt, might have resisted; more famous and financially secure mountaineers might have shouldered Richman aside and charged for the summit regardless. But the three younger, inexperienced and economically struggling men that Richman had chosen to be present that day looked at the immense riches on offer—and bowed their heads. And so Walter Richman got his wish, to be the only man in history to defeat the Wheel.

And no one was *ever* going to follow him. With amazing speed, in the wake of the great ascent, the twin lines of HAEV huts, and the electrical cables and water pipes that fed them, were dismantled and carried down the mountain. High Base Camp and then Base Camp came down too, and last of all, the two support ships that had spent nearly four years in Bligh Cove hauled anchor and sailed away.

This was—according to Richman—an act of environmental guardian-ship, done to ensure that the Wheel was returned to its natural state. But common opinion in climbing circles was that Richman was merely ensuring that no one else could use the huts and the camps and the other gear to one day repeat his achievement.

For all these crimes, Richman has remained a loathed figure ever since among the mountaineering community. He has never climbed seriously again—no expedition or team would have him. And yet, in the wider world, he has not only escaped opprobrium for his actions on the Wheel, he has become—by some at least—admired. He is seen as a figure of restraint and wisdom. A conservationist, even.

It helped that his was the sole voice of the expedition. The contracts of everyone else who signed up for the campaign expressly forbade them from talking to the press or publishing their own accounts, either during the climb, or afterwards. And though of course plenty *did* talk about it publicly later on, those who were too outspoken and too critical of Richman were aggressively pursued by his lawyers.

So the official version of the expedition was Richman's to control. He wrote two books, one a general history of the campaign, the other a more personal retelling, both of which cast him as the undoubted hero, the man who had saved the great mountain from an undignified ravaging. There was also a documentary series and a feature movie, both funded and approved by Richman, and both exalting him.

In short, in the battle for public opinion, Richman easily outgunned his critics. Oh, the world knew well enough what he had done, the promises he had made and broken, the bribes and the lies, and all for no better reason, despite his fine talk, than to gratify his own ego.

The world *knew* all that.

And didn't care. They loved him anyway. They loved his charm. They loved his sheer villainous chutzpah and his refusal to be apologetic, and they loved the impotent fury of those who spoke out against him. They loved him as only other super-celebrities are loved, and gave him the same grace: the right to be above moral judgements.

In the forty years since, he has flourished in the radiance of that adoration. He has grown ever richer, ever more famous, ever more beyond reproach, no matter how questionable the nature of his business dealings. Until, at last, with no other worlds left to conquer, he has returned to the Wheel, the site of his ascension long ago, both literally and figuratively, and with his billions he has purchased it.

Or as good as. He has purchased Theodolite Isle, the only access to the Wheel, and will build his monstrous house there upon its height. And in doing so he will claim the Wheel, a wonder that should belong to all the world, to all of *us*, as his private property.

13

OVER CIGARS

THE WORLD'S RICHEST MAN—well, *one* of the world's richest men—smelled of leather and wood, and, ever so faintly, of something evocatively chemical that Rita finally decided was jet fuel.

Such at least was the conclusion she came to after three hours in Walter Richman's presence. She had been trying to place the third scent ever since the moment of their introduction in the Saloon, when she had risen, disconcerted, to shake his hand.

He had drawn her in close, the way some men do, his free hand touching lightly on her shoulder, and she had received her first physical sense of him: his surprising tallness; the strength of his long, weathered face; and finally, the composite masculine smell about him that somehow was the essence of wealth and power. All of it came in an instant, along with a single flash of naked scrutiny from his grey-blue eyes.

Then he had released her and declared to the room, 'Shall we get straight to the food? I'm starved!'

They had eaten in the grand Dining Hall; four courses, predictably superb but thankfully not overly avant-garde; the setting candlelit and intimate, despite the room's huge size. Richman was seated at the head of the table and Rita was placed at his right hand, so that occasionally, as he leaned towards her to emphasise some point or other, the mysterious chemical tang, sharp but pleasant, had wafted over her again.

Now, with the meal completed, and the group having returned to the Saloon for post-dinner drinks, she had pinned down the answer.

It was whisky that did it. Richman had opened a bottle of a certain fabulously rare single malt from the Scottish Highlands to offer around, and the aroma of whisky had always reminded Rita of petrol. She declined the whisky, but it was then that she realised: *fuel* was the third scent that accompanied Richman. The other two, leather and freshly sanded wood, came no doubt from some expensive brand of cologne he had splashed on before coming down to dinner. But the third was accidental: jet fuel, clinging to his clothes after his trip in his helicopter. So yes, she had been right about that much, it was a moneyed smell.

But the scent was lost now in any case, giving way to clouds of smoke, for Richman, Kushal and Madelaine were indulging in cigars along with their drinks. Eugene, though not smoking, was on whisky as well. Only Clara and Rita had stuck with wine at this late stage, Rita opting for a chardonnay—Russian River *not* Napa Valley, according to the barman, whatever that meant—and Clara choosing a red.

It was a restful moment. The six of them (Kennedy had not been present at dinner, busy presumably with security matters) were reclining in chairs and couches set at a safe distance from the Saloon's giant hearth. A bright blaze was burning there, great logs of some aromatic wood crackling—Theodolite Isle was treeless, so the wood must have been shipped in for this single purpose, at who only knew what expense—and around it the rest of the Saloon was lost in dimness.

The snugness of the setting—the soft couches, the whisky, the fire—was heightened by the fact that *outside* the wind had been rising all evening and was now moaning audibly about the Observatory. Whenever Rita looked up to the windows of the Atrium dome, she could see wraiths of icy fog racing across the Terrace above. Occasionally a deeper thrum would signify an even stronger gust, and the very stone foundations of the Mount seemed almost to tremble underfoot.

'It's nothing out of the ordinary,' Richman assured Rita, catching her glance up to the high windows as for a moment the moan of the wind became a thin shriek. 'In fact, for this time of year, it's an average night. You ought to hear it when a gale *really* kicks up. Even through the triple-glazing. But it's a wonderful sound, don't you think?'

He was reclining on the same couch as Rita, having invited her to join him when they all settled. He was dressed casually in a white shirt and green corduroy pants, and she was struck again by how vigorous he appeared, his pose lithe and relaxed, his hands large and well muscled, his hair grey but shoulder length and lustrous. She would have guessed him to be a hale sixty years old at most, if she hadn't known he was seventy-one, and she supposed that—were she a person of a different persuasion—she might well have found him attractive.

'Yes,' she said, 'you must like the wind, if you plan to always spend winters here. At least, I read somewhere that you plan to.'

He laughed. 'It's true. My wife and kids think I'm mad. Why don't I come in summer? What do I possibly see in it at *this* time of year? But they have never been climbers, any of them; they don't get how good it is to be in some *weather* once in a while.'

He had already apologised to Rita for the absence of his wife, even though Rita knew—as Richman must have known she knew, it was quite public—that although he was not actually divorced from his second wife, they lived separate lives. As for his children, the second marriage had produced two sons and a daughter, all adults now, but none of them had accompanied their father either. Nor had any mistress, though Rita had no doubt there must be one tucked away somewhere in his life, if not several: Richman struck her as a man who made conquests easily and frequently. But at least she felt sure that he had no designs on *her*, even if he was unaware of her sexuality. She had detected not a hint of flirtation in his manner towards her all evening.

But otherwise he had been a charming and attentive host, full of solicitation about her father's passing, expressing gratitude that she had been able to come all this way, and enquiring in detail about her voyage on the *Wanderer,* the latter followed up by an amusing story about how he came to invest in the cruise line. He had also revealed a little of his plans for the following few days—in particular that there was to be a rehearsal for a big laser-light and fireworks show that would feature at the formal opening of the Observatory in a month's time.

'Trust me,' he promised, 'it'll be something you've never seen before. I've got a team of twenty pyrotechnic people on the island at the moment, working up and down the Mount, and a dozen lighting specialists too.' And then, after a pause to glance at the others. 'There's a little business to attend to as well, while we're all here. But that can wait. Tonight is strictly for everyone to get to know each other.'

Except, of course, everyone else already knew each other, didn't they? Rita was the only stranger here. It would have made her self-conscious, but the other guests, like Richman, had all seemed to be at pains to make her feel welcome. Kushal and Eugene in particular had been cheerful and friendly and inquisitive, and even Madelaine had maintained a cool politeness. Most relieving of all was that no one had made any further demands to know her opinion of the Observatory, this vast thing that these people had together created. Richman forbade it.

'No one pester Rita about the house,' he had ordered during dinner. 'We'll give her a day or two at least to get used to the place. Then we'll see what she thinks. Until then, leave her be.'

For Rita's own part, five glasses of wine had also helped settle any tension she had been feeling at the evening's start; it had almost even dispelled her awe of Richman himself.

Still, she was not completely won over by him. He was very much the amiable host at the moment, but there had been hints of the Walter Richman she had learned about from reading the business section of the newspapers, where his reputation was a decidedly mixed one of ruthlessness combined with a hot-tempered narcissism.

It was in the little things. At one point their waitress had brought out the wrong bottle of wine, and Richman had broken off from his conversation to correct her, his voice suddenly cold and curt; not rude exactly, but indicating by tone alone the relationship of master to servant. And towards Rita herself, for all that he seemed attentive, she was aware always of a distraction in him, a sense that when she replied to his questions he was not fully listening, that his hearing was directed elsewhere, his eyes always on the verge of darting away.

She suspected he was monitoring the conversation among his other guests. And after all, they were not really *guests*, were they. They were staff, they were his hired hands. And though his interaction with them seemed perfectly relaxed and jovial on the surface, there was something else just beneath: a supervisory watchfulness on Richman's part, and a wariness on the part of the others, their gazes always returning to their benefactor, as if reading his mood.

Or perhaps Rita was just imagining it. But she had to admit, there was an existential intimidation in the mere presence of a man like Richman, for all that he was being friendly. How often were you in the company of someone so powerful they could, at a whim, either grant your every wish, or destroy your life completely? How could you *not* watch your tongue in such a situation? And she noted too that while she had accepted every offer of wine made by the staff, the others had been more circumspect, taking only one or two glasses at dinner. And Richman himself, before his whisky, had only downed a single glass.

But fuck it, why should she worry? Billionaire or not, she didn't want anything from him—it was he who wanted *her* here, not the other way around. And it was not as if she easily intimidated anyway. Only a few weeks back, at work in emergency, an over-muscled over-tattooed six-foot-six Hell's Angel had brought in his hideously injured Rottweiler at three in the morning—the dog run over and at death's door, the owner in an alcohol-fuelled rage, yelling threats at the nurses that if the dog died then everyone in the clinic died. Rita, a foot and a half shorter than him, had stared the great fool down and told him to shut up and grow up and get the hell out and let her do her job. He had blinked at her in shock a moment, then obeyed as meekly as a lamb, shuffling off to the waiting room, blowing his nose on tissues the nurses gave him, while Rita got on with the business of saving the dog's life. You saw it all in emergency. So why should Richman's wealth bother her?

As if on cue, the billionaire, his cigar smouldering in an ashtray as he swirled his drink in its deep glass, alarmed her by asking, apropos of nothing, 'Anyway, tell me, what made you choose to become a vet? It's a far cry from what you used to do.'

So, had Richman had read her damn book too? 'Maybe because it *is* a far cry,' she answered.

'I've never been one for pets,' he mused, eyes on the fire, 'never in one place long enough.' He glanced at her again. 'So, you *disowned* all that stuff from long ago? Your father said something along those lines.'

She took a steadying sip from her glass. 'I outgrew it, that's all. I was running off the rails.' And she had an entirely unwelcome flash of memory, of the pale faces of the other passengers on the LA flight, staring at her as she raved, all bloody and stark naked.

'But that was just you personally?' he pressed. 'You and the drugs and things? It wasn't your *beliefs* that were the problem?'

She considered. 'Well, not exactly, I suppose, no. Not in themselves. It was where I took those beliefs that was the problem. But once I got my head clear, I dropped all that stuff too.'

'Fair enough, fair enough,' he nodded, but again, with that distracted air, as if he was part of some other discussion. 'Well, I'm not trying to pry. I just wondered. Your father talked about it all. I think he regretted being so harsh about it, back in those days when you fell out. He thought he could have been more understanding, given how it started.'

But Rita did not want to talk about that, not how it all started, oh no. She changed the topic. 'I didn't mean to be rude before, you know, when I was saying how crazy it was for you to build a house up here.

I was curious, that's all, as to why you went to so much bother and expense. Why it was so important for you to live here.'

That got his full attention. 'Expense and bother? You're not kidding.' He took up his whisky and drank, as if reflecting on the costs. Rita had read that he was worth in the vicinity of seventy or eighty billion US dollars, but still, the Observatory had to represent an extraordinary drain on his resources, a blind investment on a project that could never return a cent to him. All for a house that he planned to live in for only a few months every year. 'But as to the why . . . is it just because of my history with the Wheel, you're asking? Am I here out of nostalgia? Am I just another old man returning to the scene of the triumphs of his youth?'

'So it isn't that?'

He smiled. 'Maybe it is. Why pretend that those days *weren't* the most exciting of my life? Do you think if Neil Armstrong or Buzz Aldrin got the chance now to build a house on the Moon—or somewhere right next door to the Moon—they wouldn't go for it?'

Rita blinked. It was an interesting proposition, not only in itself, but because it revealed that Richman thought of himself in equal terms to the men who had walked on the Moon. And yet, why should he not? He was as famous as them, and in his way even rarer than them. Twelve men had walked on the Moon, but only one had stood atop the Wheel.

'That is,' the billionaire considered further, 'Aldrin would go for it, at least. I always get the feeling he could keep going back into space forever. I'm not so sure about Armstrong. He seemed to put the Moon behind him, once it was done. The same way I gave up climbing mountains. Once you've done the ultimate, why repeat it?' His eyes met hers briefly. 'I know them both, you know, Buzz and Neil.'

Rita sipped more wine. Jesus, of *course* he knew them. There were all those photos of the three of them together, taken in the months after the Wheel expedition. Richman had been feted all over the world; he'd met presidents and royalty and movie stars, and yes, astronauts . . .

'But if it was really just nostalgia,' he went on, 'if it was just to see the Wheel again, then I could just have moored my yacht here for a few months. That would have satisfied any pangs for the old times, and would have saved me a fortune as well, not to mention several years of my life, which at my age is a consideration not to be sneered at.'

She said, 'Why then?' And was aware, suddenly, that the others around the fire, who had been chatting among themselves, had fallen silent now, and were watching their employer with attention.

Richman frowned. 'Well, in one way it's the same reason that I climbed the mountain in the first place—because the notion came me and wouldn't go away. The human will defines itself, you know, and needs no other reference. But in addition to that, to me it doesn't feel that I've come *back* to the Wheel at all. It's more that I've never left it. There's a link between me and that old monster out there, formed on the day I reached the summit. I don't talk about it much'—this, with a glance to his other listeners—'but it's true. I'm the only one who has ever stood there in the Hand of God, the only one who has seen the mountain's final secret. That's a privilege and a responsibility, and the Wheel, I think, respects the fact that I've kept its secrets ever since. I feel—there's no other way to say this—I feel that it wants me here. That this is the place where I should see out the last years of my life—last decades, hopefully—and where, when the time comes, I should lay that life down.'

His tone was levelly sincere, as if his motivations were nothing but deeply held. Spiritual, even. But again, the caution nagged in Rita. When he talked of standing alone on the Wheel's summit he made it sound as if his being alone there was by fate's decree, as if circumstance had forced that burden upon him, rather than it being something that he himself had insisted on, to the outrage of all those other climbers.

'And, of course,' Richman added, 'when it came to an architect to fulfil my dreams here, your father was the only choice.'

And it was decent of him to keep praising her father, except—the doubt again—who was he really praising? Richard Gausse? Or himself, for being clever enough to *hire* Richard Gausse?

She asked, 'How did you know of his work?'

'Oh, I visited the house he built for Maurice Berthier in the Pyrenees, and saw the potential his ideas might have, if given raw material as grand as the Mount here. And also the funds to make it possible.'

'Maurice Berthier?'

'You haven't heard of him? He's one of the Rothschilds, a lesser one, true, but still, very rich. And a keen amateur climber.'

Kushal addressed Rita from the couch opposite. 'And you don't know the house your father built for him? But it's famous! *La Maison de la Colline*, it's called. It's cut into a crag that juts up out of the Pyrenean foothills—a less dramatic version of the Observatory, you could say, though with its own charms, and in beautiful surrounds.'

Rita kept her voice neutral. 'No, I've never heard of it. I can only guess my father designed it during the time we didn't speak—which was quite long. I made no effort to keep track of him then.'

Richman bent his head towards Rita. 'He was so happy that the estrangement ended, you know. He talked about you a lot, especially in this last year or so. He was very reflective about things. Maybe he felt his time coming, I can't say. But that's one of the reasons I wanted you here this weekend. I'm sure it would have made him happy.'

Rita felt a fleeting puzzlement. *One* of the reasons? Wasn't it the *only* reason she was here? In honour of her father's memory?

'I still wish I'd got there earlier on the morning of his attack,' the billionaire was musing sadly. 'The doctors assure me there was nothing anyone could have done, that it would have been too late, but even so. He should have been here this weekend, sharing in this triumph. It was always my intention to have this small gathering at the completion of the build, before the big party, just to especially thank those most responsible for what we've created here. Indeed, I'll say it now—my

143

thanks and congratulations to all of you.' And he raised his glass to the others. Kushal, Madelaine, Eugene and Clara all dutifully raised their glasses in return.

'As to the next few days,' Richman continued, 'I want you all to simply relax. Eat, drink, swim, admire the finest view on the planet. Indulge yourselves. For the time being, we're on holiday!'

Smiles and nods came from his audience, and above, on the Terrace, the wind rose once more to a sob, before falling away.

But Rita was struck again by a sense of incongruity. These people patently were not on holiday. They were professionals, and this all had the air very much of a work meeting. Indeed, she was aware of a sense of impatience around the group, a falseness in the way they were all draped on the couches about the fire, the way that feet tapped restlessly, the way glasses were swirled but seldom raised to lips.

The mood was directed mostly at Richman, as if his four employees secretly resented him for wasting their time. But some of it, Rita had the disconcerting feeling, was also directed at her, as if there was something they were waiting for *her* to do or say.

But what, and why? How could anything that she did or said really matter to any of these people?

She finished her glass, caught the ever-watchful eye of the barman, and nodded for another. It would be her last, most likely (in company at least, she may well have a nightcap back in her apartment); the evening was surely drawing towards its close.

But she was wrong about that, for barely had her glass been refilled when Richman sat up abruptly. 'But I'm forgetting, you haven't had a full tour yet, have you, Rita?'

She hesitated. 'Well, Clara showed me . . .'

'Yes, yes, the rest of the house—but not *my* part of it. You haven't seen the Cottage yet.' He glanced up to the Atrium dome. 'Yes, it's a clear night out there for all that it's windy. So why not now then? Shall we take a visit to the Lightning Room?' He leapt up from the couch, addressed the group. 'C'mon, we'll all go! Bring your drinks.'

Rita was flustered, sensing more strongly than ever the impatience in the others. 'No, really, it doesn't have to be now. Everyone else here has surely already seen it anyway . . .'

The billionaire was having none of it. 'Are you kidding? They *love* showing this place off to new people for the first time. And the Lightning Room, well, it's something special. You'll see.'

And dutifully, Richman's staff all laughed and nodded, and climbed to their feet.

14

NOT A MOUNTAIN

**Article by Abe Jenkins, from *Climbing* magazine,
November 1976**

There is an oddity about the much-celebrated Richman expedition that many have noted: of the six hundred and more climbers who took part in the epic assault upon the Wheel, hailing from all corners of the globe, not one of them was a Sherpa. The ethnic group widely held to produce the best climbers in the world, men who grow up with the Himalayan giants as their playground, had no representation whatsoever in the greatest climbing challenge that history has yet seen.

Why was this?

In fact, the Sherpa weren't the only group missing from Richman's roster. There were also no Spanish climbers. The Spanish, however, were excluded at Richman's own instigation. (It was the billionaire's rather petty revenge for certain stories that were circulated about him in the Spanish climbing community some years earlier.) The Sherpa, meanwhile, were most certainly invited to be part of Richman's great enterprise. And the wages would have equated—in the poverty-stricken part of the world from which the Sherpa hail—to a respectable fortune. And yet, to a man, the Sherpa refused.

Why?

Well, first, a little history. The Sherpa people, a minority of Tibetan heritage, are mostly inhabitants of Nepal, through which the central

Himalayan ranges run, though Sherpa are also to be found in the neighbouring states of Tibet, Bhutan and India. Ever since international climbers have been visiting the region, they have sought the help of Sherpa locals to get to the tops of the high peaks.

At first, that help was mostly in the form of guiding and load carrying. But gradually it emerged that the Sherpa's high-mountain abilities marked them down for more serious duties. Born and raised at altitude, they were physiologically attuned to the thin air, and were also tireless and loyal climbing companions. By the early 1950s, they were being enlisted as full climbing members by expeditions in the Himalayas, and with success. When the greatest mountain in the region, and the second highest in the world, Mount Everest, was finally conquered, one of the first two men to stand upon its summit was a Sherpa, Tenzing Norgay.

The year was 1953, and Norgay's companion on Everest's peak was English climber Thomas Bourdillon. Both men were part of a team entitled the British Everest Expedition. This was a large campaign consisting of a dozen climbers and dozens more support staff but, as with all Himalayan expeditions, it was scarcely heard of outside climbing circles. World attention, when it turns to mountaineering, is only really ever interested in the Wheel, and in the latest news, often disastrous, of the expeditions assaulting its defiant ramparts.

So neither Bourdillon nor Norgay earned much fame from their achievement. However, the skills of Sherpa climbers had forever been proven, and when Bourdillon and his British compatriots turned their attention to an attempt upon the Wheel, it seemed only obvious that they should enlist the aid of the Sherpas once again. In 1956, thus, the British Wheel Expedition was formed, and when, late in that year, over a hundred climbers and support staff were landed on Theodolite Isle, thirty of them were Sherpa climbers, led by Tenzing Norgay.

The expedition, the largest that had made an assault upon the Wheel up until that point, was not, of course, aiming for the mountain's summit, which was far out of reach for the technology of the day. Their aim was instead the famous Black Band, a landmark on the West Face which stands at just over ten thousand metres. This was more than a kilometre higher than the summit of Everest, higher than anyone else had ever climbed, and would push the limits of the basic oxygen equipment available to the climbers to the utmost limit.

In the event, the expedition would meet with mixed success. One of its climbers, New Zealander Edmund Hillary, indeed reached the top of the Band to set a new record for altitude. (True, there is some debate as to that, but let's let it stand for now.) Alas, he then died on the descent, his body never to be recovered. But whatever the expedition's achievements, they were attained without the help of any of the Sherpa, for by that stage all thirty of them had gone home to Nepal.

What happened?

The Sherpa *began* the climb, sure enough. In the preparatory stages of landing at Bligh Cove and getting the expedition gear up to Base Camp on the Plateau at five thousand metres, the Sherpa climbers were as active as any other. However, once Base Camp was established and the expedition readied for the harder ascent towards the Black Band, the Sherpa, through their spokesman Tenzing Norgay, requested to be excused.

Expedition management was astounded. The Sherpa wanted to go *home*, just when the exciting climbing was about to start? What on earth was wrong? Was there a problem with their wages, their food, their camp accommodation?

None of that, answered Norgay, *we just don't want to climb here, thank you.*

Pleaded management: But why *not*?

We don't like this mountain, said Norgay. *It is not a mountain as we know other mountains. It is something else.*

Which only flabbergasted management all the more. What did he mean, not a mountain? Of course the Wheel was a mountain. Look at the damn thing, it was biggest bloody mountain in the world.

No, answered Norgay calmly. *Chomolungma is the biggest mountain in the world.* (Chomolungma is the Tibetan name for Mount Everest, translated as Mother of the World.) *The biggest true mountain. It can be a cruel mother, as we know, who have suffered upon its slopes. But it is a mountain as other mountains are mountains. The Wheel is not.*

Management: All right, what is it then, if not a mountain, for heaven's sake?

Norgay: *That I do not know. But I have climbed upon it enough now to know that I recognise nothing here, I do not feel at home here, I sense no kinship from the stone and snow and ice here, as I do at home in the Himalayas. The Wheel is alien to me, to all of us, and we do not wish to remain here.*

Management: Is it that you've lost your nerve, is the Wheel just too big for you?

Norgay: *To not fear a mountain is to be a fool. But it is not fear driving us now. The rest of you may succeed here or you may not, I don't know. But I will not stay here. None of us will.*

And from that position Norgay and the rest of the Sherpa would not be budged. After some weeks of argument and stalemate they were duly shipped home, and the expedition continued without them.

So, what did Norgay mean?

How can the Wheel *not* be a mountain, as other mountains are?

Was it a philosophical or religious position? The Sherpa are Buddhists, but that doesn't necessarily explain it. Buddhism's relationship with the natural landscape is a complex one, sometimes with moral overtones, but there's little in Buddhism that would suggest that parts of the natural world can be declared *not* of the natural world.

So it seems that Norgay and the other Sherpa were talking only as climbers, as roamers in the high places of the world, as lovers of the thin air and the freezing cold. They rejected the Wheel as *mountaineers*, refusing it categorisation. Which brings us back to the same question. How is the highest mountain in the world not a mountain at all?

It's a riddle that remains unanswered, even twenty years later. Norgay and his compatriots have seldom spoken of it since, and all younger Sherpa, when they are offered, as Richman offered, the chance to go climbing on the Wheel, only shrug and answer much as did Norgay. *We have no interest in that place.*

But whatever the solution, it is most certainly not that the Sherpa were or are *afraid* of the Wheel. Fear does not rule the Sherpa climbers. To this day in their homeland they prove that by continuing to climb and die on the pitiless slopes of their Mother Everest.

Indeed, consider this. The Sherpa climbers risk all for a summit which to the rest of mankind is the lesser challenge, a second-prize peak. While climbers on the Wheel ascend to fame and fortune, the Sherpa labour in thankless obscurity. So who, really, is the braver?

15

THE LIGHTNING ROOM

RICHMAN'S PRIVATE QUARTERS LAY BEHIND a secret door.

The door was accessed from the Library, which Rita had already explored with Clara. It was a welcoming, windowless cavern to the rear of the Saloon. Walls of tall bookshelves rose on every hand, laden with leather-bound volumes—antiques, Clara had explained to Rita, collected by Richman for their age and rarity. Moveable ladders set on rails gave access to the upper shelves, and here and there arched alcoves formed inviting reading rooms lit by dim lamps.

But Richman led Rita and the others through all this without a glance, and so came to a final alcove that was backed by a bookcase filled with especially fine-looking red-leather-bound tomes. The arched entry to the alcove was flanked by two life-size marble busts that were positioned atop solid wooden pedestals.

'Do you recognise them?' Richman asked Rita.

Rita looked for a moment at one bust and then the other, but aside from noting that both of the faces were male, she was at a loss. They might have been any historic figures from the ages.

Richman nodded. 'They're mountain climbers. This one is George Mallory, and this one Edmund Hillary. They were two of the great pioneers in the early days of climbing on the Wheel. Each climbed the highest that anyone had ever climbed in their own eras. Mallory made it to almost nine thousand metres in the nineteen thirties, and Hillary made it over ten thousand metres in the nineteen fifties. Both of them died on the mountain, sadly, but what they achieved was still incredible, given the primitive equipment available at the time.'

The names meant nothing to Rita. But then, she was no climber.

Richman grinned suddenly. 'Now watch this. I got the idea from the old TV version of Batman. Couldn't resist.'

He pushed on the forehead of the right-hand bust—Edmund Hillary. The entire likeness tilted back on a hinge to reveal a glass panel set flat atop the pedestal. Richman pressed his thumb to the glass, and in response, the rear bookshelf of the alcove slid smoothly and silently aside. Beyond waited what was evidently an elevator car.

'Just a little joke,' Richman said, as the others murmured laughter. 'Still, it's not bad as security either, having a secret door. Of course, even if someone knows the secret, they'd still need their prints on file to get in. Apart from this elevator, the only other way up to the Cottage is via the Terrace, and that door is print-activated too.'

They were all filing into the car, spacious even with the six of them. On the panelled wall, a brass plaque bore three buttons only. The bottom one was marked *Staff* and presumably descended to some lower domestic level. The middle said *Library* and the top, *Cottage*. Richman pressed the top button, and the door slid shut.

They rose in silence, the lift mechanism barely a hum in the background. A sense of unreality possessed Rita. This quiet elevator car, the people she was with, the whole last three hours she had spent— it was impossible to believe that it was happening not in some luxury city hotel, but rather in a fantasy palace carved from a mountaintop far away in the wilds of the Southern Ocean. It was just too strange.

But when the car slowed and stopped, and the door opened, the mountain wilderness was all too apparent once more.

To one side a threshold led into the Cottage proper, but Rita's gaze went to the opposite wall. This was made of glass and overlooked the

Terrace, which was lit now only by a glow coming through the windows of the Atrium dome underneath. Beyond, windblown and unearthly, the night waited, a gulf of nothing around the mountaintop.

'Christ,' Rita had to say, going to the glass and staring down. Beside her, an airlock door opened to the top of the stairway that ran down to the Terrace. The weather display, she noted, was glowing orange for caution, no doubt because of the gale blowing, though out across the bare court below the only evidence of the wind was the swift ripples that were sheeting across the darkened surface of the pool.

'It's something, isn't it,' said Richman at her side. 'It's one of my favourite views, even though you can't see the Wheel from here. Makes you feel you're flying above the Mount.'

It did, and for an instant Rita's gaze lifted from the Terrace to the night all around, and like a flash she was staring through the transparent walls of the plane on the LA flight, and seeing all over again the monstrous presences that called the middle skies their home.

'Anyway, come on through,' her host was saying. Suppressing a shiver and a passing weakness in her knees, Rita turned away and followed the others through the inner threshold.

What lay beyond was . . . well, if not exactly the open plan living area of a typical family house, done in a kind of neo-American Ranch style, then it was something not wildly distant from that.

The space was unevenly ovoid, mirroring the shape of the tooth of stone from which the Cottage had been dug. There was a sunken lounge area with couches set before a brightly burning fire; a dining area, railed off, containing a table and a timber bar; and backing it all was a spacious and gorgeously appointed kitchen.

'My home,' the billionaire said simply to Rita.

It did indeed look homely, certainly as compared to the vast splendour of the great halls below; a retreat that spoke of privacy and casual ease. Not an *average* home, sure enough, not with its unique shape and the raw stone of the walls; not with furniture that was of the very finest leather; not with a kitchen that glowed with state-of-the-art appliances; and not with the tall windows that opened all around, dark now, but which would no doubt offer staggering views by day—but even so.

Richman didn't linger. 'This way,' he said, leading Rita and the others across the living area. 'Still three floors to go yet.'

In the centre of the room rose an ornate ironwork scaffold with a narrow elevator car held within. It was in the style of the old-fashioned elevators found in Victorian-era hotels or apartment blocks, perhaps a genuine antique rescued from some grand building of the past. Around the elevator ran a staircase of matching wrought-iron, likewise ascending.

They took the stairs. One level up they came to a landing from which two hallways extended. 'This is the family floor,' Richman expounded to Rita. 'It has three bedroom suites, one each for the kids.' They kept climbing. 'And this floor,' he added as they reached the next level, 'houses my own suite and my private office.'

The stairs and elevator both terminated here. Doors opened from either side of a broad landing, but both were shut. At one end of the landing a picture window occupied the entire wall, the glass dark now, but if Rita had her reckoning right it faced to the Wheel and by day it would offer yet another amazing vista. And at the landing's other end a final narrow set of stairs spiralled up to—

To what?

'This way,' said Richman, going to the stairs. He wore an anticipatory smile, matched, Rita noticed, by some of the others.

'The Lightning Room?' she asked.

The billionaire only beckoned her upwards. The stairs curved into the solid rock of the ceiling, and then into blackness. It was like climbing the turret of a medieval castle. Dim lights in the walls grew dimmer as they rose, and after several turns they came to a heavy curtain hanging across the way. Beyond was near darkness, aside from a barely discernible fluorescence that outlined the steps to prevent tripping. 'Just a little further now,' came the voice of Richman, sepulchral.

They circled one more time about the shaft, and then—

Then they stepped into the open night, into midair, into a sky flung with stars, onto a platform that had no roof and no walls or rails on any side, only the gulf and the fall to ruin. Rita's legs almost buckled as the realisation and terror reared in her. There'd been no warning! No one had told her that they were venturing out onto such an exposed aerie, naked to the night and the wind and the freezing air—

Except, it was still warm. There was no wind—that is, she could hear it moaning and thrumming close by, but she could not feel it on her face—and around her the others were chuckling.

Glass, she realised, it was all glass. Now that she looked for it, outlined against the stars was a gossamer framework in which the panes must reside, reaching up and overheard in a vault.

The terror slipped away, replaced by wonderment. She was standing on the pinnacle of the Mount, like a climber who had just achieved the summit, two thousand eight hundred metres above the sea, and there was nothing, north, south, east or west, to hold back the sky.

And what a sky! She turned in place, staring up. The wind still roared and sang, but there were no clouds anymore, no shred of fog to obscure the heavens, and stars were everywhere, undimmed by any rival light, for there was no moon, and a shoulder of the Mount's peak blocked any light from the Observatory below. Such was the clarity in the heavens that it seemed to Rita that even faint nebulas were visible, cobwebs against the bright scatter. But most spectacular, nearing the zenith, was the sash of the Milky Way, somehow three-dimensional in its proximity and shot through with pinpoints of red and green and blue.

And matching the Milky Way for vastness and glory, rising from the east to meet it almost overhead, was the Wheel. The great mountain was illuminated only by the starlight, but even so an ethereal green glow seemed to infuse its appalling faces of stone and ice. Perhaps it was an actual glow, some pale but gargantuan version of St Elmo's fire, or perhaps it was some type of aurora effect, here so near to the Antarctic.

But either way, there the Wheel stood, a titan with its snout tilted to the sky, the shrouds of earlier all blown away.

Gazing up, still not sure if she felt only wonder or maybe also dread, Rita became aware of the others moving around in the darkness. Some were even sinking down; why, they were sitting. Yes, with her eyes slowly adjusting to the night, she could see now, there were armchairs scattered about the glassed-in chamber. There was even a large low shadow that must be a bed. Richman could sleep up here if he chose, with the infinite stars for a roof, like camping in a tent of glass.

'Well,' Richman asked, a tall shape at her shoulder. 'What do you think?'

'It's incredible,' she answered, quite honestly. 'But . . . why the *Lightning Room*?'

A dark arm rose, pointed. 'You see that?' He was indicating the peak of the spider's web of framework that supported the glass. The structure, and indeed the room beneath it, must have been near to ten metres across, rising to a point high above them. There the lines converged, and a solid spike arrowed up stiffly.

'That's a lightning rod,' Richman said.

'You mean, lightning hits right *there*?'

The shadow at her side was nodding. 'This whole room is a Faraday cage—and believe me, it's necessary. Storms hit the Mount all the time, the Wheel seems to breed them, and the Mount is a lightning magnet. You realise that you are *on* the peak. Apart from the tunnel to give access, and the erection of the glasshouse, very little was done up here, aside from smoothing a few lumps out to level the floor.'

The sense of nakedness assailed Rita again. To be exposed on such a high loft, with no more protection than glass . . .

Richman laughed quietly. 'But don't worry, that's not just any old glass. It's quadruple-glazed to keep out the cold, and proof against wind and rain and even hail. And that frame might look like it's made of nothing, but in fact it's constructed from a special metal superalloy, one of the toughest substances in the world, which is why it can be so thin.'

She swallowed. 'And you've really seen lightning hit?'

It was another shadow, from one of the chairs, who answered: Eugene. 'Hell, yes. I set up a surge detector to monitor how often exactly. In the four months I've had it running, we've had two hundred direct strikes up here. For any given storm, it averages five or six hits.'

'I've been up here at the time,' Richman confirmed. 'It's something you've got to see, to hear, to feel, if you hope to believe it. The clouds, the updrafts, the electrical imbalances building, you're right *in* it, and then, boom, the world ignites . . . but you're completely safe every second. The rod links to a metal cable which grounds directly to rock.'

A queasy sensation flipped Rita's stomach. Completely safe? With storm clouds forming *around* you? With lighting striking a few feet above your head? Oh, she remembered enough of science lessons to know that it was true, that the strike would be safely grounded by the rod into the bedrock of the mountain, harmless to anyone inside.

But her old self . . . her old self had once believed things that went quite beyond science. And that old self was horrified. To taunt the power of a storm that way, to mock the presences born within all that violence, to recline under glass in a comfortable chair, and to employ all that force and fury for no more than your own entertainment . . .

For the old Rita, that would have been foolhardiness beyond belief.

'But, of course, it's not for storm watching that I use the room mostly,' the billionaire said, his head in silhouette, tilted to the stars. 'It's for nights like this. I sleep here as often as not in clear weather, and there's no better sight to wake to in the night than this.'

'And in the morning?' Rita enquired, glancing about, for there was no sign of any curtains or blinds fitted to the walls and ceiling.

A shrug. 'The glass is electro-chromatic, and can be set to dim as daylight approaches. Pretty old hat, these days.'

The voice, accented faintly French, of the designer came from where she lounged. 'We have used various forms of switch glass all through the Observatory, especially in the grander spaces where there are big walls of glass or skylights that would be difficult to cover otherwise, when the sun is too bright. It's a useful technology, to be sure, but a rather sterile one. That's why, for the private quarters and other intimate spaces, we have generally used more traditional blinds and curtains.'

Kushal interjected. 'Is it just me, or are there clouds forming way up there?'

He was staring up at the Wheel, and everyone now followed his gaze.

High, high above them, the great curved rampart that was the Wheel terminated in a crest against the stars. But whereas only five minutes earlier that crest had been a remote shadow, now a caul of pale white was coalescing there, a faint sheet of cloud, hanging just above the summit. Even as they all gazed up, it seemed to shimmer more brightly, wave-shapes glowing as if lit from within.

'What *is* that?' Rita could not help but ask, amazed at the delicate beauty of the sight. She could swear that there was even a hint of colour, iridescent, in the different bands of the sheet.

Richman let out a whistle. 'You don't see *that* every day. It's a nacreous cloud.'

Eugene said, 'But I thought there couldn't be any clouds that high, not at the level of the summit anyway. That's right in the stratosphere, there's no moisture for clouds to form.'

'Normal clouds, no,' said the billionaire. 'But nacreous clouds—they're sometimes called a polar stratospheric cloud—are different. Very high, and very rare. They're made up of chemicals from the ozone layer. No one is really sure how they form, but the Wheel sees them more commonly than most parts of the world. We had atmospheric scientists along with us, during the expedition, trying to study them.'

'But what makes it glow that way?' asked Madelaine.

'I'm guessing the Moon,' Richman answered. 'It must be rising. We can't see it; it's on the other side of the Wheel. But the time is about right. We're just short of the third quarter, so it'd be pretty bright as it comes up.'

They all watched in silence for a time, sheer beauty holding them spellbound. Richman must have been right about the rising Moon, for slowly, minute by minute, the silhouette of the whole upper Wheel was becoming more defined, the outline glowing dimmest red, a penumbra cast from the invisible eastern horizon. And about the summit, the pearl cloud glimmered ever brighter in ripples.

The billionaire broke the silence. 'I've been *in* one of those, believe it or not.'

Kushal was disbelieving. 'Inside a cloud like that?'

'Just the once. We were at about twenty-four thousand metres, from memory. It was very weird. You get used to having no weather up there. Then one morning there was this wind blowing, and a bizarre fog all around us. The air was so thin you couldn't *feel* the wind, mind you, but you could see it—the mist was streaming by in all sorts of colours. There was some worry about our pressure suits, actually, as those clouds can be quite acidic. But we got through okay in the end.'

Rita felt a shudder of insignificance as she stared up, the realisation hitting her as if for the first time. The man beside her had *been* up there, up on that impossibly remote summit. It was as if she was standing with Neil Armstrong and both of them were staring at the Moon.

Where he had *walked*.

It was hard to accept, and even harder to broach. She would have liked to ask Richman, as any curious child might, what it was *like* up there. But she couldn't, it was a question both too immense and too small. He must have been asked it ten thousand times since he climbed the Wheel, and he must have a dozen automatic responses at his call. And how could it really be answered anyway, other than by clichés? Amazing, wondrous, inspiring—all equally meaningless.

He said, 'We didn't learn that much about nacreous clouds even then. It's still largely a mystery as to how and why they form, though we do know that they represent severe disturbances in the middle stratosphere. Which can, as it happens, be a precursor to severe weather down here in the troposphere, a day or two later.'

'You think we're in for a storm?' Eugene asked. 'I was checking the forecast for the Southern Ocean just this afternoon, and there was no mention of anything all that severe on the way.'

The billionaire shrugged. 'Maybe. The link isn't direct. We saw a couple of these types of formations during the expedition. Once, the worst storm of the whole climb hit the lower mountain a day later. The other time nothing happened at all. So who knows? But you've been here long enough to know the forecast doesn't count for a lot when it comes to the Wheel. The mountain makes its own weather.'

Silence followed for a while. Eventually the pearl cloud about the peak began to lose its iridescence, fading to a monochrome grey, as if the angle of the rising Moon on the far side of the Wheel could no longer summon the colours of earlier. Then it was gone.

'A final nightcap in the Saloon, I think,' said Richman.

They descended the way they had come, back down through the stone tunnel, down the cast-iron steps to the lower level of the Cottage, and from there by elevator to the Library and the Saloon.

Where they found the security chief Kennedy waiting for them at the bar. He was sipping a soda water and talking with the barman.

'You've been up to your idiot glasshouse, I take it?' he asked, addressing Richman.

The billionaire smiled to Rita. 'Kennedy hates that room. He's the toughest man I know, afraid of nothing. Except thunderstorms.'

The blunt face of the security chief showed no amusement. 'I'm not afraid of thunderstorms, I respect them is all.' And to Rita he added, 'I saw a man get hit by lightning once. Wasn't pretty. The odds might be low, but storms are nothing to play around with—and there's certainly no need to court trouble deliberately, lighting rod or no lightning rod.'

'I quite agree,' Rita said, meaning it.

Kennedy seemed slightly surprised. He gave her another look. 'So, you're saying you didn't like that room?'

Something in his tone brought Rita alert. She said, 'It's impressive. But I'm like you, I wouldn't go up there in a storm.'

His eyes held hers. 'And on a night like tonight? Not a storm to be seen. Did you pick up any vibrations, say?'

'Vibrations?'

Richman cut them off. 'Leave her alone, Kennedy. I promised we wouldn't harass her for opinions about the place yet.' His tone was entirely genial, but Rita didn't miss the flash of resistance in the security chief's face before Kennedy relented.

The barman now took their various orders for coffees or digestifs. And to drink them they settled once more in the couches by the fire, for though the Saloon was not by any means cold, for those who had been up to the Lightning Room the memory still lingered of the freezing night and the wind beyond the glass, and of the great icy rampart of the Wheel rising—so the flames beckoned warmly.

But the conversation was desultory, the climax of the evening having come and gone. Rita soon found herself suppressing yawns. She had begun this day, she recalled, in her cabin on the *Wanderer*.

Richman too seemed to have lost his enthusiasm; his manner was restless and detached. When Rita finally spoke up to say that she was tired, he nodded as if he had been waiting for the announcement.

'Right, right,' he said. 'It's been a long day for all of us.' He rose, leaving his glass of port barely touched. 'Now, I may not see much of you tomorrow, Rita, my schedule is pretty full—but never mind, you've got the whole Observatory to enjoy, and the others for company. But tomorrow night the party starts for real. Clara, if I might grab you for a few minutes upstairs? There are some details we need to discuss.'

A general movement began. Kennedy departed for another security sweep. Madelaine declared she would accompany Rita down to the guest wing and likewise retire. Kushal said he would have a last cigar, and Eugene volunteered to keep him company with a final whisky. Richman made his goodnights and swept off to the Library, accompanied by Clara. The barman was packing up behind the counter.

Goodnights complete, Rita and Madelaine made their way to the Helix Staircase and began the descent. They did so in stiff silence at first; of all the people Rita had met so far here in the Observatory, the designer was the one with whom she had the least rapport.

But to break the silence she said, 'So Richman will be working while he's here? He mentioned his full schedule tomorrow.'

The stout Frenchwoman nodded. 'He'll be on the phone or in video conference all day, most like. Usually his schedule is broken into fifteen-minute intervals, and each slot will be always be full.' She raised an eyebrow to Rita coolly. 'I hope you realise how unusual tonight was. I've never seen him take an entire evening off before, not just to sit around and chat to no purpose. He did it just for you, you know. He is determined to be welcoming and to put you at ease.'

Rita was somewhat staggered, first by the thought of a day plotted out down to every quarter hour, and second that someone like Walter Richman had broken his own regime just for her. She said, 'But of course it's all really for my father's sake, isn't it? I'm just his stand-in here.'

Madelaine gave a snort. 'You must not think that your father and Richman were friends. Walter Richman does not have friends, only employees who are of service to him, and your father's service was complete, even before he died. It's *you* he's interested in now.'

'But *why*?' The question came out more entreatingly than Rita had intended, but the puzzlement had been mounting in her all evening. Why had these six strangers been at pains to be so nice to her? Why did she matter to these people—to Richman most of all?

Madelaine considered a moment. Then she asked a strange thing. 'The matter that Kennedy raised, about the Lightning Room. You did not feel anything . . . unpleasant . . . about that place?'

'Should I have?'

'Not to my thinking, no. But . . . well, some people are bothered by such things, if they know about them. A man died in that room, during the construction. Died in a very unusual fashion. Do you know of it? It was in the news, though not all the details.'

Rita shook her head. This was the first she had heard about it. She had made no effort, after all, to keep up with the news about her father's work. 'What do you mean, in an unusual fashion?'

'Well, I did not see this myself, and it was rather hushed up, but I gather that the man was a security guard, and he was alone on the site. All the other workers had been sent down from the top levels because of severe weather. They always kept a security guard up here during the build, because there was trouble early on with protestors.

'Anyway, for some reason the man went up to the Lightning Room. It wasn't glassed in then; it was open to the sky. And he got trapped. There was a manhole hatch covering the access tunnel in those days, and somehow it shut behind him and he couldn't get it open, though he was found with his hands on the latch. But meanwhile, the storm was at its worst and there was hail, incredibly large hail, and he had nowhere to hide from it. It seems he got his skull bashed in.'

Rita blinked. 'Awful,' she said.

The designer nodded. 'The stranger thing, though, was that he was found naked. His clothes were all neatly folded at the bottom of the tunnel. That's what had everyone so mystified. In a terrible storm, at temperatures well below zero, he went up to an exposed height, totally nude. Why on earth would he do that? People have been mistrustful of the room ever since. Some say they get bad feelings there. That's what Kennedy was asking you about. He was being wilful. He knows why Richman asked you here, and he does not approve.'

163

Rita shook her head. 'So why *have* I been asked here?' she demanded, but it was dawning on her now. All that talk about her book really should have warned her. Her damn fool of a book.

They had reached the level of the guest wings. 'It's not my place to say,' demurred the designer, 'it's up to Richman. But I will tell you this. I must be honest: when I read your book, I thought it was nonsense.'

'I think it's nonsense too,' Rita replied levelly. 'Obviously I didn't think so when I wrote it, but I was only twenty-four then, and in a very different state of mind. Now I'd rather that it didn't exist. I'm hideously embarrassed whenever it's brought up.'

Madelaine appeared surprised. They had arrived at Rita's door, and the Frenchwoman paused there, rounding about to study Rita more closely, looking up from her six inches less in height. 'Seriously? You don't believe those things you wrote anymore?'

'No.'

Madelaine's expression turned perplexed. 'Then I really don't know what use you'll be to Richman, whatever he is hoping.'

With a ghost of a smile in apology, she raised a hand in farewell, then strode off down the passageway towards her own suite.

BOOK
TWO

1

THE PROMISE

Introduction to *The Spawn of Disparity*
by Rita Gausse, 1995

Everyone has felt it at some point in their lives: an indefinable sense of awe at the scenery of the natural world. A tall mountain rising to catch a sunrise while all around you is dark; a canyon opening before your feet, plunging away precipitously; a waterhole nestled in some secret forest glen, the only sound a hypnotic drip of water.

In such situations something in the human spirit becomes aware of an *otherness* in the scene it is beholding, aware of a singularity and preciousness that it cannot quite identify or grasp, but which stirs up wonder and reverence, sometimes even unease or fear.

Why is this?

Why, for instance, should the sight of a mountain evoke any emotion in us at all? A mountain is only a prominent pile of stone. Why should the view over a great canyon, which is only an elongated depression in the ground, stimulate us so? Is it because such things are beautiful? Perhaps, but that only raises the next question: why do we think mountains or canyons or waterholes are beautiful?

Is it because they are wild and untamed? But there is nothing inherently wild about a canyon; it is only erosion at work. The same could be said of any waterhole, no matter how captivating. And there is nothing untamed about a mountain, it is merely a wrinkle in the landscape cast up by either plate tectonics or volcanic processes. Besides, we can look at a piece of scrubland or a jungle gully in which no man has ever lived, and which indeed *is* wild and untamed, and feel no awe at all.

And yet consider this. Take a mountain around which a city has been built—Table Mountain at Cape Town in South Africa, for instance, or the soaring stone spires of Rio de Janeiro. People still consider these features impressive, yes, but do they look at these mountains and spires with the same wonderment that they would if the peaks reared alone in the wilderness? No. Something about such mountains and spires, with houses on their flanks, and roads and streetlights all about, does indeed feel *tamed* and *non*-wild. They are, in a word, diminished.

So what's going on? What is it that we are perceiving when we feel that something is awe-inspiring? Is it a question of wilderness, of the lack of human presence? Is it a recognition of something bigger than us, or older than us, or apart from us in some other way? Is it an appreciation of danger and physical threat? Is it some primal memory in us, longing for a freer past that we have long since lost as we civilised ourselves? Is it all these things together, or something else entirely?

Well, I have the answer. It's not one that most people expect, or will find easy to believe, but I can't help that—a closed mind is a closed mind. But there are already many who know I speak the truth, many who have sought me out to employ the special talents I possess, talents that were vouchsafed to me, terrifyingly, when I was sixteen.

Those people were in trouble, and this book is for those who are likewise in trouble, those who are in discomfort and fear, experiencing the deeper and darker side of what lies behind our awe of certain natural landscapes, and who need guidance on how to respond.

I promise, I can help you.

2

LUXURIATING

RITA AWOKE TO SNOW.

She had left the great glass wall of her bedroom uncurtained the night before; with the Wheel filling the entire view eastward, there would be no sun peeking in to wake her at dawn. As it turned out there would have been no sun anyway, for when she opened her eyes she saw only a field of grey through which snow descended in silent flurries towards the unseen ocean over two-and-a-half kilometres below.

She stretched in her bed; it was king size and superbly comfortable, the sheets a deliciously soft linen. The entire bedroom was as snug as a cave, its dark walls and lush carpet shutting out the freezing morning beyond the glass. Lingering indulgently, she stared at the falling white flakes and listened to the distant mutter of wind from the balcony. Then, on the bedside table, her phone dinged with a text message.

It was from Clara Lang. *Good morning. Just reminding you that lunch is in the Conservatory at 1 pm. Otherwise the morning is all yours. Remember, the kitchen staff are at your disposal for breakfast!*

Hmm. A room-service breakfast, and a morning with nothing in particular to do. So, this was the life of the idle rich . . .

Smiling, Rita rose and went to the shower, where she enveloped herself in steamy water that jetted from four different directions, ignoring for now the bathtub, which was the size of a small pool.

169

Refreshed and wrapped in a fluffy bathrobe, she wandered into the living room, and stared out at the snow. It was no great blizzard, the flurries came and went in veils, and in the clearer moments the lower slopes of the Wheel could be seen off to the east, wet and glistening. If anything, the weather seemed to be clearing.

Even so, she would not be venturing out onto the balcony any time soon. The weather panel by the airlock doors showed green, but it was still windy out there, and the temperature was minus twelve degrees Celsius. Who needed that after a warm shower?

She turned to the kitchen. It had everything necessary to fix a basic breakfast of her own—but what the hell, she was a billionaire for a day. She dialled room service, and ordered poached eggs with toast, spinach and hash browns on the side.

'Yes, ma'am,' was the answer. 'We'll have that up to you in about fifteen minutes.'

In the kitchen a gleaming coffee machine waited, its instruction manual sitting politely alongside, but she dug beneath the counter and found drip-filter equipment, then proceeded to grind the beans and make herself a coffee, straight and black.

Sipping it, she took another lap around the apartment, noting the perfect proportions of the rooms and the perfect placement of the furniture, and the warm, steady silence.

She was, she realised, at a loss as to what to do with the morning—or with the following four days ahead of her.

She was not used to idleness anymore, that was part of the problem. Since the great change in her life of twelve years ago, she had worked, worked and worked. First for a year to complete her secondary education as a mature-aged student, after ignoring it so appallingly in her late teens. Then through the five years of her vet degree, all the while holding down a variety of part-time jobs, as she had come away from the collapse of her old life and the split with Anne with only slender financial resources. (She had, of course, refused to ask her father for money.)

Then the *real* work had started. Her first internship at a veterinary hospital had made university look like a breeze, with fourteen-hour shift stacked upon fourteen-hour shift, rotating from day to night with scarcely a day off in between, let alone a holiday. Indeed, in the five years since graduating, she had taken barely six weeks leave out of the twenty she was due, and even then, only in dribs of three or four days at a time. It was only of late, really—now that she finally had a measure of confidence in her own abilities in the emergency ward—that she had been able to imagine stepping away from the job for a proper break.

So she had taken two weeks off for this trip, even though she would be only five days at the Observatory. And that made this, it seemed to her now, something of a significant juncture, a still point of reflection after the long mad dash of rebuilding herself from the ground up.

She was at the window again, gazing out to the snow. It had thickened momentarily, an opaque wall of dancing particles, some falling, some rising as the wind eddied about her balcony.

Another reason, of course, that she had not taken any extended holidays in the past ten years was the problem of what do with such a break when it was just *her*, alone. Her last real trip, all her real trips, had been with Anne. She had dated no one since, not seriously. Oh, there had been sex, yes, she wasn't a fucking nun, and even some longer-term flings; there were the clubs she frequented with the circle of friends she had made at university, or hook-ups arranged via apps on her phone. But no one had claimed her heart the way Anne had, and Rita was not sure she had even wanted anyone to—she'd had other priorities.

But now, well, the rebuilding phase was over, that was a fact . . . and she wasn't getting any younger.

It was strange to think about really. What did she want? *This* Rita Gausse, this sensible, independent professional woman, living her ordered, quiet life in her ordered, quiet, river-view flat. What sort of partner would *this* Rita choose, if she could?

Not someone like Anne, that was for sure. In a way, Rita herself had *become* Anne. That was not to say that Anne had been staid or quiet or dull. She had been anything but! Yet she had always been the more grounded of the two of them, the saner. The old Rita, spinning wildly further and further away from her own centre, had needed that. But the new Rita didn't need grounding. Didn't need Anne.

Even so, she still missed her sometimes, god only knew. And right now, on this dim grey morning, in this warm luxurious hideaway, with the snow falling outside and the wind murmuring deliciously cold through the glass, and the great soft bed waiting . . . well, lord.

The doorbell chimed, and Rita forgot about past loves and future holidays.

Breakfast was here!

▲

Afterwards, she decided she would go for a swim. Not in the pool up on the Terrace obviously. It was hardly outdoor weather, though by the time she finished breakfast the snow had stopped. She would visit the Observatory's indoor pool, the Cavern Pool as it was called. Her glimpse of it during yesterday's tour had been intriguing.

So she dressed, then packed her bathing suit into a light bag she found in the wardrobe, and made for the door. In anyone else's private home, or even in a hotel, she would have walked to the pool with her suit already on under a bathrobe, or hell, with just a towel thrown over her shoulder. But somehow that didn't feel right here. It would show a gauche lack of . . . well, not breeding maybe, but of familiarity with wealth.

Amused at herself, she went out into the passage. The usual quietness greeted her, the hallway deserted, not even the impression of a footprint visible on the thick carpet, as if there was no one else in the whole building. And when she came to the Helix Staircase and looked up and down the great twisting monolith to the levels far below and the great dome of the Atrium above, there was still not a soul in sight.

She descended one of the barrels of the staircase, trying not to feel self-conscious in her solitude. The silence didn't help. It was not oppressive. Not exactly. Indeed the space was calm and spacious and well-designed. But it was there, and it was bigger than her.

The Helix Staircase itself was also disconcerting. There was a parallel flight of stairs entwined with your own that you could never see or meet, and it was all too easy to imagine that someone was secretly ascending or descending those stairs, invisible to you. A trick of the mind only, maybe, but nagging and persistent. When Rita came at last to the bottom, the recreation level, she could not help but dart a quick glance back up at the great tower, as if to catch a face staring down at her from some high railing. But again, there was no one.

'Why, hello there.'

She spun. From this lowest landing there opened only two passages. One led, as Rita remembered, to the Cavern Pool. The other she had not been down yet, for it led to the Games Arena, which she had yesterday declined to visit. Emerging now from this latter hallway, dressed in shorts and T-shirt and running shoes, mopping a sweaty head with a hand towel, was the youthful IT expert, Eugene.

'Oh,' Rita said, 'good morning.'

'Swimming or running?' he asked, with a nod to the bag she carried.

'Swimming. You've been running?'

'Oh yes. I do ten kays every morning. Usually earlier than this, but I slept in after last night. Richman is down here most mornings too.'

'Ten kilometres? Around and around on an indoor running track? That must get a bit tedious.'

Eugene paused in mopping his head. 'You haven't seen the Games Arena, I take it. There's nothing tedious about running in there. You really should go and have a look.'

She glanced down the passageway. But no, she still did not feel ready to view the place of her father's death.

'Maybe some other time,' she said.

He hesitated, perhaps remembering belatedly. 'Oh. Well, have a nice swim. I'm for the shower. See you at lunch.' And with a spring he started up one spiral of the Helix Staircase.

Rita watched until he vanished from sight, then she was alone again, the silence all the more intense for having been broken. Finally, she turned and followed the hallway to the Cavern Pool. The lighting grew dimmer as she rounded a single bend and came to a set of wooden swinging doors, almost like lights going down before a curtain opening on a show. Then, pushing through the doors, she was borne into an underworld of stone and water as fantastical as any theatre.

Before her spread a paved terrace, beyond which a vast body of water opened, blue-green under a ceiling of native hewn rock. First there was an Olympic-sized rectangle, marked into lanes for those who wanted to swim mundane laps. But on the far side of this functional space the pool widened out into a lake of sheer whimsy. Around its shore rose a tiered complex of ponds, water splashing from the higher to the lower—no silence here, the air was alive with the laughter of cascades. Elsewhere flooded tunnels, shimmering with light, wound away into the rock to ends beyond view; and in other places again grottoes beckoned enticingly, some of them intimate little caves with hot spas bubbling within, others misted and secret behind waterfall entrances.

Lovely.

But also deserted. Rita could see no one in the water, nor any clothes or towels draped on any of the cane chairs that were arranged poolside. She explored a little. At the rear of the terrace a fire burned in a hearth. To one side a doorway led off to a line of private dressing rooms and toilets. On the other side of the terrace another doorway led to both a sauna and a steam room, as well as a chill-looking plunge pool. But she found nobody using any of these facilities. She was alone.

And the more she looked, the more extravagant the emptiness felt. There was no sign that anyone had visited the pool before Rita today, and maybe no one would have come at all, if not her, but still, everything was in readiness. The fire was burning—the flame was gas—just so that if someone should drop in, it would be there to welcome them. Lights were on everywhere, even in the steam room and sauna. And she could only begin to imagine the size of the filtration and pumping systems that lay behind the pool and the waterfalls; all of it kept running merely on the off-chance that someone might show up for a swim.

The wastefulness of it seemed extraordinary. But then what did wastefulness matter, she supposed, when there were billions of dollars at hand? There were no childproof fences here either. It seemed money could bypass every concern, even the strictest of zoning laws.

Time to get in. Rita slipped into a dressing room, changed, and re-emerged. Dropping her things on a chair, she moved towards the steps that led into the water. And who cared whether the pool was an obscene indulgence or not, it wasn't her money that had been spent on it, so why judge? The truth was she found it all marvellous, a fairyland lake hidden within the mountain. It had been dug out by machine, yes, but the cavern felt uncannily natural. And unlike any other indoor pool she had ever visited, there was no smell of chlorine, no waft of warm humidity—the air held only a cool, flinty scent.

But the water, as she set foot on the first descending step, was pleasantly warm, and utterly clear against a greenish floor. Subtle lighting, below and above the waterline, made the whole pool glow gently. She took a few more steps, up to her thighs, then sank deliberately and pushed off from the stairs, surfacing a few yards out.

It was delightful, just warm enough without being cloying. She put her head down and swam a few strokes, staring down at the lines, her eyes not stinging at all. But it wasn't lane swimming she wanted. She lifted her head, studied the vault of the stone roof overhead, then considered the grottoes, and finally the tunnels that wound off into gloom like newly discovered underground rivers. How far might they run?

With a gentle breaststroke, she chose the nearest opening and glided inwards. The rock ceiling arched low over her. She almost had to laugh. To think, she was swimming along a watery tunnel that was set two and a half kilometres up in a spire of stone!

Ridiculous. Who would even think of such a thing? Except, well, her father *had* thought of it; or perhaps Richman had, and it had been made *real*. And here she was, the only person using it.

The thought gave her pause. She put her feet down and found the water to be only chest deep, which was reassuring, even though she was a confident enough swimmer, for the main pool was already out of sight behind her, lost around the curve of the tunnel.

But good lord, she wasn't an explorer venturing down some uncharted subterranean waterway—this was all man-made. She was perfectly safe. She forced herself onwards, taking long languid steps now rather than swimming. So gloomy had it become that overhead, on the rock ceiling, pinpricks of luminosity stood out like glow worms. But surely they weren't *real* glow worms. Were they?

She drifted on. Around another turn the light ahead grew stronger, and there came the sound once more of falling water. Increasing her pace, she turned a final bend and was shocked to see daylight before her. Real daylight, sky and clouds, bright. Her stomach flipped, for it seemed that the tunnel simply debouched into open air, that the river in which she swam must simply flow clear out onto the face of the Mount, there to fall, in a dreadful cascade, to the sea far below . . .

She drew in a breath, calmed herself. Of course it wasn't open air. She was looking at a wall of glass set flush into the side of the Mount. And though the water seemed to flow over a lip into nothingness, and though she could hear the sound of it falling, in reality it must be a trick, an infinity edge set just short of the glass wall.

But it was an uncanny illusion. She drifted closer. The view was to the west, an immensity of ocean and sky. On the other side of the glass, only feet away, a last flurry of snow was scurrying along the cliff face, a bizarre counterpoint to the warm water in which she floated, but beyond, the western sky was pale blue, clearing to sunlight.

Rita waded as close to the window as she dared, and found that in fact it leaned out somewhat, so that the nearer she came to the infinity edge, the more she could see down and down and down to the ocean. Her senses were all in a tangle, her wet skin telling her she floated in a pool that was held secure within solid stone, her eyes and gut exposing the truth of the precipice below. God, for all its wonders and beauty, this house was a terrible place for those afraid of heights!

But she lingered all the same, studying the ocean far below, slate grey and veined with white. Nowhere in that vast, bleak field of grey could she spy a ship or any other sign of mankind. Indeed, it was probably one of the least-travelled expanses of water in the world, for no trade routes ran this far down into the Southern Ocean, and when the tourist cruises came to see the Wheel, they did not venture west of it.

The only ships that might appear out there would be fishing trawlers, or research vessels on their way to bases in Antarctica. It was one of the latter, the Australian Antarctic vessel *Aurora Australis*, that would be picking Rita up four days from now, on its way home to Hobart after its latest sojourn to the ice. Richman had called in certain favours—Rita didn't know of what sort—to get the ship detoured. It did not normally carry non-research passengers, and its crew would no doubt resent the imposition, but all Rita cared about was that the ship was big, and that it would have plenty of people on board.

But that was four days away yet, and after a while of staring out at the last few flakes of snow, and at the empty ocean rolling away, Rita began to feel cold despite the warmth of the water.

She turned and waded back through the tunnel to the main cavern. To banish the last of the chill, she put her head down and swam four stiff laps of freestyle, up and down one of the lanes. Then, breathing hard, she made her way to the stairs. Once on dry land, she took up a towel from a waiting pile and stood in front of the fire to dry. And while rubbing at her head with the towel, she heard it. Or thought she did.

She stopped, listening. The cavern was both echoey and yet sound-absorbing, the patter of the waterfalls camouflaging the greater hollowness. And now, beneath the splash of water, she heard it again. A woman's voice, muffled and distant, but crying out.

Rita strained to listen. What were the words? Was it *Hello?* Or was it *Help?* She couldn't be sure. And where was it coming from?

She stared about. Not from the dressing rooms, nor from the sauna, nor from beyond the main doors, nor from the grottoes or tunnels. If anything, it seemed to be coming from the fire—that is, from some-where behind the fluttering gas flames.

She examined the hearth, frowning. To the left of it was an alcove lined with shelves holding more towels. Stepping into that alcove now, Rita discovered that one side of it was a false wall, hiding the entry to a short passageway that ran off further to the left.

It ended in a closed door.

Hello? she heard more clearly now, though still muffled. *Hello, can anyone help me?* The tone was not, as she had at first thought, one of fear, but rather of impatience and frustration.

Hesitantly, Rita moved down the passage, and tapped on the door. It bore no sign or marking, but she guessed that it must be a staff entry. 'Hello? Are you okay in there?'

Silence.

Rita paused a moment longer, then tried the door. It had no lock and swung open at her push. Immediately, a hum was in the air. She was looking down a plain corridor, the walls lined with unpolished concrete. Along one side ran bare metal pipes and plastic electrical conduits, and a short distance ahead the passage opened into a large machine room of some kind. Rita propped the door open—there was a latch for the purpose—and, feeling like she was trespassing, crept forwards.

'Hello?' she called. 'Hello?'

The hum grew louder. She came to the machine room. It was crowded with what she assumed must be plant equipment for the pool. Large steel pipes emerged from the wall and joined with other pipes attached to esoteric metal boxes and tanks that might have been filters or pumps, or even boilers for the steam room.

There was no one there. But to the right another passage opened off the room, and even as Rita stepped towards it, a woman poked her head around the corner, and blinked at Rita in surprise.

'Where the hell did *you* come from?' the woman demanded. Then, glancing past Rita to the corridor Rita had just come down, she added, 'Wait, where does *that* go? I didn't see that before.'

Rita was not quite sure what to make of this. 'Um—I came from the pool.'

'The pool?' The woman shook her head disgustedly. She was plump and fiftyish, and dressed in a grey smock, a cleaner's uniform by the look, her accent Australian. 'Christ, I'm miles out of my way. But bloody hell, I *looked* in here and I swear I didn't see that door.'

'Are you lost?'

'Lost? I've been wandering around in here for a bloody hour! When I got to this place it was the last straw, which is why I started bawling out for someone to come and get me. I couldn't even find a damn intercom to call for help.' She beckoned to Rita and pointed down the passage from which she had emerged. 'Look at it. How would you like to have to negotiate these damn tunnels day in and day out?'

Rita looked. The passage extended for maybe thirty metres, lit only by sparse bulbs overhead, the walls lined with more pipes and conduits. Other passages opened from it to the left and right, and at its furthest end was a landing for a stairwell that went both up and down.

'Looks awful,' Rita agreed.

The woman shuddered. 'I hate it. I shouldn't be anywhere near here, I was in the B Guest Wing, vacuuming, and I was just trying to get to the break room for a coffee! I must have taken a wrong turn somewhere, then I couldn't find my way back.' She looked at her watch as if to confirm the worst. 'Jesus, it really has been an hour!'

'Aren't there signs to show the way?'

The cleaner rolled her eyes. 'There are, but they never make sense to me. I swear I follow them properly, but I get lost anyway. Everything looks the same and it's always so damn dark in there, and hot too, with all the vents and pipes. You wouldn't believe how much water and heat has to be pumped around this place just to keep a few people warm . . .' She pulled herself up, gave Rita a sudden look. 'You're a guest, aren't you.'

'Yes, I am.'

'Oh lord, sorry to have bothered you then. It's the first rule, never bother the guests; don't even talk to them unless they talk to you first. I'll get out of your hair. The pool is down this way, you said?'

'Just through the door.'

'Good. We're not supposed to use the public areas to get around, but I'm not going back that other way again!'

They retreated the way Rita had come, emerging through the alcove to reach the poolside, where everything was as Rita had left it.

The cleaner shook her head as she stared about. 'I still can't believe I'm so far off! Did I interrupt your swim?'

'I'd just got out.'

'Oh. Good. Well, I'm sorry again—and thank you for coming for me, it must seem very stupid to you, getting lost where I *work*.'

'Not at all. I didn't like the look of those tunnels either.'

'Stupid damn maze. Who on earth would design a house this way, I ask you?' The woman turned towards the main exit, then hesitated, turned back. 'You're all alone down here?'

Rita nodded.

The cleaned glanced to the door of the spa section. 'You're not . . . um . . . you aren't thinking of using the steam room, are you?'

'I don't know. Why?'

The woman looked reluctant. 'I wouldn't, that's all. Not after what happened. They say it's perfectly safe, and always was. I know even Mr Richman uses it, so it must be. But still.'

'Why? What happened?'

'You don't know? Well . . . I shouldn't be telling you, I guess . . . but someone died in there. He was on his own too. So I just thought . . .'

'Died? How?'

The woman shook her head. 'He was a staff member, but I'd be lying if I said I knew all the details, there're all sorts of rumours about it. An accident, we were told. Anyway, if you're a guest, then you're a friend of Mr Richman's. You could ask him. Cheerio.'

She turned, marched to the swinging doors and banged through them, leaving Rita nonplussed. And alone once more.

She stared about the Cavern, hearing once more the gentle splash and mutter of falling water from the cascades. But the effect did not quite ring true anymore, now that she knew about the tunnels that lay behind the cavern walls, with their great steel pipes humming, and the heat and the darkness, miles and miles of it apparently. What a place to get lost. No wonder the poor woman had been so upset.

But as for her talk of a death in the steam room, well, it sounded like a tragic event, yes, but deaths were hardly unheard-of in saunas and spas. Maybe the person had been old, or overweight. All that steam, it was a strain on the body, and some people just couldn't cope.

It was certainly nothing to get spooked about.

Yes . . . but then this was the second death in the Observatory that Rita had been told of. The man in the Lightning Room that Madelaine had mentioned, and now another in the sauna.

But no, wait, it was three deaths in fact, because of course she was forgetting her own father.

Three people dead in the one house. That was different.

Wasn't it?

She glanced at the sauna doorway again. Richman himself still used the steam room, the cleaning woman had stated. So it must be safe. And Rita was no believer in *ghosts*, never had been, even back when she had believed in all the other mad things.

But no, she didn't want a spa. Never had wanted one. With a shrug, she headed for the change rooms to get out of her suit.

3

FALLING MAN

Excerpt from *Reaching for the Hand of God,*
by John Soliola, 2007

In all, twenty-two climbers died during the Richman expedition upon the Wheel. Of those, seven were killed in avalanches, three in rockslides, three in pressure-suit failures, four in a single horrific HAEV hut blow-out, and five by falling. Each of these fatalities was, of course, its own tragic tale of ill fortune or misjudgement. But it was one of the five deaths by falling that was perhaps the most cruel and haunting of all.

The incident took place just three weeks before Walter Richman stood on the summit. The victim was an Australian climber by the name of Matt Yale, commonly known as Red. Cheerful and popular, thirty-one years old, married with two school-age children, he was an experienced mountaineer, having climbed extensively in New Zealand and the Himalayas and upon the Wheel itself before signing up with the Richman campaign. At the time of the accident he had logged seventeen ascents and descents on the mountain, all of them without trouble.

On 21 October 1974, however, at an altitude of twenty-three thousand nine hundred and fifty metres, all that changed.

The location was Hut 119, set high on the mountain, at the base of the final summit ridge. The hut itself was only newly installed: indeed, Red's team was carrying the last load of supplies that would make the hut officially operational. It was an exciting, expectant time for, as everyone knew, the expedition would only need to construct two or three more huts now before the final assault on the summit could begin.

(Note: the system of having two lines of huts, one as a backup for the other, had been abandoned for the narrow last two kilometres of the ascent, the two lines meeting and climbing on as one.)

The day before the accident had been unremarkable—as unremarkable as any day can be high in the stratosphere. Red's team had overnighted at Hut 118 before donning their HTF suits for the three-hundred-metre climb to Hut 119. The route was well marked and laid with guide ropes, and each man was carrying some twenty kilos of rations that would complete the stocking of the higher camp. They arrived mid-afternoon, unpacked and stored their loads, then spent the night in the hut, with the intention of descending at dawn to make way for the next team, an assault crew, who would begin the harder work of pioneering a new route up to a prospective Hut 120.

The night passed smoothly, as did the morning ritual of checking and donning their suits. They emerged a half-hour after sunrise. However, during the final external inspection of the hut before departure they discovered that overnight a malfunction had occurred with the water line. The coupling that attached the heavily jacketed and heat-traced piping to the valve in the hut wall had not sealed fully—or had come loose under pressure—and a leak had occurred. Not a major leak—cut-off valves would have activated with any large surge of flow—and most of the water that had escaped had evaporated away in the thin atmosphere, but a crust of ice was still visible around the partially detached coupling. A new coupling would have to be installed.

This was an inconvenience at most. The problem had occurred before at other camps, and there was a spare coupling ready and waiting in the hut. It was a matter of half an hour's work to attach the spare to the water line, and reconnect it. Two of the men re-entered the hut, leaving Red and one other climber outside. Red was walking along the water line, inspecting it for any further sign of damage, while the other climber took advantage of the break to admire the view.

For good reason. Hut 119 boasted the most spectacular outlook of any of the camps on the mountain. For a start, it was only the second hut to be sited on the summit ridge, after the long zigzag route up the West Face, giving it open views to both east and west. But more than that, Hut 119 was sited at the very top of the awesome Grand Couloir.

For those not familiar with mountaineering terminology, a couloir is a vertical gully or chute in a mountainside. If narrow and sheltered enough, they can sometimes offer a safer and simple route up a steep face. But at other times they can be even sheerer and more deadly than the face into which they are cut. The Grand Couloir is of the latter sort.

There are in fact *three* large couloirs on the West Face of the Wheel. Two slightly smaller but still immense couloirs can be found to the north and south of the centreline of the face, and are called, predictably, the North Couloir and the South Couloir. But the Grand Couloir, positioned close to the centreline, just south of the summit, is the undisputed king.

The West Face is, of course, itself steep and sheer, but it is not utterly vertical. However, from a beginning point just below the summit ridge, a channel has been cut—as if by some godlike hand wielding a mighty chisel—which drops straight down, bare and terrible, for fully eight thousand metres. And at its base, heaped in what is by then a dark, uptilted canyon, there awaits a deadly fan of razor-sharp scree.

What formed this great scar on the mountain is not known. Some theorise it was created by an ancient landslide, others that it was a trench in the ocean floor, millennia ago, before the Wheel was lifted above the water. Whatever its origins, the Grand Couloir's vertical walls present a dire obstacle. No one has ever tried such sheer and technical climbing at such an extreme altitude, and it's doubtful anyone ever will.

The Richman expedition had certainly made no attempt to do so. For the last seven kilometres of the ascent, their route had passed safely to south of the Grand Couloir. Only now, as they traversed back northwards along the summit ridge, were they coming close. In fact, Hut 119 sat directly above the Couloir, the ridgeline at that point forming a giant overhang, a roof over the terrible chute below.

Little wonder then, on that fateful morning, that Red's companion took a moment to stare about at the incredible prospect on offer. But it meant that he did not see exactly what happened next.

What he *heard*, over the radio in the helmet of his suit, which linked all four climbers of the team, and the team to Base Camp, was Red give a muffled exclamation, followed by a strange scrabbling sound, and then an alarmed cry for help. The climber turned to look, but found, astoundingly, that his companion had vanished.

Then, over the com, the screaming began.

▲

What had happened, it emerged during the later inquiry, was this. A greater amount of water had leaked from the defective coupling than the team had realised, and not all of it had evaporated. A steady trickle had dribbled from the hut down the westward side of the ridge—i.e., towards the top of the overhang above the Grand Couloir—mostly evaporating as it went, but leaving behind a very thin sheen of ice, bonded fast enough to the rock to resist immediate sublimation into the frigid air.

This sheen of ice would have been difficult to see at the best of times, but on a west-facing slope, shortly after sunrise, cast into shadow, it was all but invisible. At such a high altitude, with so little air to diffract or diffuse light, shadows are deeper and darker than those at sea level. So, all unknowing, Red, in his inspection of the water leak, must have taken one step too far into this shadow, and suddenly found that the footing was ice slick beneath him.

He fell—but not only fell, he then *slid*. For the slick of ice actually ran a full ten metres, all the way from the hut down a steady forty-degree slope to the edge of the overhang, which, even worse, had a slight uptilt at its lip. Without hope of purchase, Red accelerated swiftly down this slide, flew up over the lip, and sailed helplessly into space.

(Had the day progressed normally, once underway the four climbers would have been either roped to each other or clipped to fixed lines to prevent such falls. Freshly out of the hut, and on 'safe' ground, however, no one had clipped on yet.)

But even *this* wasn't the worst of it.

Usually, in a fall from a high face, a climber is dead long before they reach the bottom. Few cliffs are completely sheer, and so the falling body will slam and bounce against the slope as it descends, hitting with such speed and violence that not only is the person soon rendered insensible, their bodies are completely torn apart.

Red was not to be so lucky. The walls of the Grand Couloir *are* almost completely sheer, and he had fallen from an overhang, some distance out from the face. Even worse, he had been thrust still further out by the speed of his slide. So he hit nothing. Red simply fell, a stone dropping straight down into a hole eight kilometres deep.

And he fell *fast*. In the thin atmosphere above twenty kilometres high, there is virtually no air resistance to slow down a falling object. Experimental jumps from high-altitude balloons have seen skydivers fall, for brief periods, in excess of the speed of sound. Red would have reached similar velocities, the sides of the couloir flashing by in a terrifying rush. And even that wasn't the worst, for if he had merely fallen to the bottom of the couloir and smashed into the scree there, at least his ordeal would have been over in little more than a minute.

But he didn't hit the bottom of the couloir. Instead, as he reached about the eighteen-thousand-metre mark, Red at last began to meet some air resistance. Indeed, *wind* resistance. For on that day a strong jet stream happened to be blowing, striking the West Face dead on. Part of the jet stream was being diverted down the mountain, but most of it was being diverted *up* and *out* from the face, and it was this torrent of up-rushing air that Red encountered. It slowed him down, yes, but it also thrust him further out and away from the mountain. So much so that even as he reached the level of the base of the couloir, he was already by then clear of the entire West Face and moving further out all the time.

And so he kept falling.

In the end, he would miss the mountain completely. In an epic five-minute descent, dropping twenty-four thousand metres, Red would travel *horizontally* some fourteen kilometres to the west—slamming down finally in the ocean a mile and more from the shoreline. By then, in the denser air, he had slowed to a terminal velocity of around only two-hundred kilometres per hour. But this lesser speed was, of course, more than enough to kill him when he hit.

But even *that* isn't the worst of it.

The worst of it was that Red was fully conscious all the way down. For every second of those five minutes.

The microphone of his com system remained open for the whole descent. The range of the HTF suit radios was only a few kilometres, so he soon passed out of the hearing of his shocked companions at Hut 119. But as Red fell, he was picked up successively by receivers at lower huts, each of which sent a signal by hardwire down to Base Camp, where everything from every channel was recorded. So there is a playback available of Red's every utterance on the way down.

It makes for harrowing listening.

At first, as his teammates at Hut 119 heard, there is his exclamation as he slips, and then a cry for help as he is sliding down the ramp, followed—as he sails off the lip—by incoherent screaming.

This resolves after about fifteen seconds into a series of gasps and expletives, the tone of which is sheer disbelief. By then Red had already fallen over a kilometre and was still accelerating, his body whirling in a flat spin which would have left him completely disorientated.

At about forty seconds, however, as he began to encounter the up-flowing jet stream, Red's spin, either by accident or design, slowed and stabilised. He ended up in a spreadeagled position, head slightly down and forward, and in this pose continued for almost the rest of the descent, with a clear view of the land rushing by beneath, and of the ocean rising, inevitably and inexorably, to claim him.

On the recording, after the confused swearing and panting, there comes, at about the time that his spin ended, a silence. Then, at the one-minute mark, comes actual speech.

Red: *Fuck. Oh Jesus. Fuck. No. No.*

In the background is a thin whistling, the air rushing around his helmet, only a distant whine at first in the higher altitudes, but becoming a dull roar as he descends into thicker air.

Red: *Oh fuck no. I'm fucked. I'm fucked.*

And still he is falling past the mountain.

At the one-minute-fifty mark another voice intrudes, an emergency hail broadcast across all channels. By this time, expedition management had been alerted, and now Geoff Lodge, who was the chief of operations on duty at Base Camp that morning, gets on the line. Lodge himself was indoors and could not see Red, but he was receiving constant updates via radio from other observers sited either on the Wheel, or on the main observation post on Observatory Mount. The babble of these watchers can at times be heard in the background.

Lodge: *Man falling, man falling. Can you hear me? Can you hear me? This is Geoff Lodge at Ops. Respond with your name if you can.*

Red does not seem to have been aware until this moment that his com was still on and his mike open, but now he responds wildly.

Red: *It's me, it's Red! It's Red. Help, I fucking fell. I fucking fell!*

A brief silence follows. In interviews since, Lodge has made the admission that he had not expected the falling man to actually answer, and having made contact against all likelihood, he now had little idea of what to say or do.

Finally—

Lodge: *Red, I hear you. I hear you. Are you hurt?*

Red: *No! But I'm fucking dead, man, I'm fucking dead!*

Lodge: *I . . . Jesus. (Garbled interruption in background.) Okay, okay. Red, listen, can you clear the shoreline? Can you make it to the water? If you can, we can get a boat out to you.*

Red: *I don't know! Maybe. What fucking difference does it make? I'm gonna hit too hard. Water won't save me!*

Lodge: *Spreadeagle yourself. Get a glide going. If you can make it to the water there's a chance, if you hit right, if there's some chop to break the surface tension. It's windy out there, it might work.*

Red: *Fuck. Fuck. Okay, okay. I can try. Maybe. I think I've got a glide going already. I can hold this. I don't think I'll hit the mountain.*

At this point, now two minutes thirty into the fall, and at about eleven thousand metres, Red was fully in the grip of the updraft from the jet stream. Perhaps he could feel himself being pushed out and away from the mountainside, hence his optimism.

In fact, Red's glide average ratio, from his fall to the place of impact, would end up at roughly point seven to one—that is, for every seven metres that he travelled horizontally, he fell ten metres vertically. In years since, with wing suit flying having become a popular pastime for thrill seekers, jumpers have been able to achieve much greater glide average ratios, easily two to one or even three to one and more. But for an unintended fall, and in a non-aerodynamic suit, Red's ratio was impressive.

There follows garbled and crossed lines on the com for the next minute, as Lodge engages in hurried conversations with watchers on Observatory Mount and with safety crews on the ships in Bligh Cove, in regard to a rescue boat. Red interjects with further expletives and terrified denials as the ground and the ocean loom closer.

Then, at three and a half minutes, the *Artemis*, the expedition accommodation vessel, cuts in.

Artemis: *Artemis here. Geoff, we've got Frieda coming in, we got the news to her and she's on her way. Can I put her on?*

Lodge: *Red, do you hear that?*

Red: *Frieda? Oh fuck, oh fuck.*

The Frieda in question was Red's wife, who also worked for the Richman expedition as accommodation coordinator on the *Artemis*. She lived permanently on the ship, though the couple's two children only visited the Wheel during school holidays, and hence were spared the ordeal of witnessing their father's death.

When the crisis began, a messenger had been sent to find Frieda and bring her back to the *Artemis* radio room. She comes online at three minutes and fifty-five seconds into the fall. Red was then at five thousand metres and had just over a minute to impact. On the tape there is a muddle of voices, then a woman's voice cuts through.

Frieda: *Honey? Matt?*

Red: *Frieda? Oh Christ honey, I'm so sorry, I fell, I didn't mean to, I—*

Frieda: *It's all right, it's all right, you're gonna survive this.*

Red: *Oh god, I dunno, I'm gonna hit so hard. Frieda, you and the kids, I'm so sorry, I don't wanna leave you—*

Frieda: *Then don't. Do what they say. Glide as much as you can, and when you hit the water—*

(Garbled interruption.)

Lodge: *That's right, Red, when you hit the water, try to go feet first. You'll break your legs but that'll absorb some of the shock.*

(Garbled interruption)

Observation Post: *I can see him now, naked eye. Christ, he's gonna hit way off shore, a mile at least. Get that boat out there.*

Frieda: (crying) *Oh god. Matt, hang on. Don't leave me, don't—*

Red: *It's coming, it's coming, oh Jesus. Frieda goodbye I'm sorry I love you I love you oh shit oh—*

Red's com cuts off at this point, though he is still some ten seconds short of impact. Observers later reported that he seemed to shift in his falling stance, presumably to orientate himself feet first to the water. He lost control of the manoeuvre however, and instead slipped into a rapid head-over-heels spin. The G-forces of such a tumble would have been horrendous, and may have damaged his com relay.

191

The last portion of the tape continues.

Frieda: *Matt? (A scream.) Matt? Matt?*

Silence.

Observation Post: *He's hit.*

Lodge: *Confirm?*

Observation Post: *He's down. I've got the spot marked and the boat is on the way.*

Unidentified male voice, off mike: *Christ, you see how hard he hit? Spinning like that, no fucking way he survives, no—*

The feed cuts off abruptly.

But those final words were all too prophetic. Cartwheeling at over two hundred kilometres an hour, Red hit the water head first and vanished in a soul-crunching splash. The watchers on the Mount did not see him resurface. The rescue boat reached the spot within two more minutes, and divers were in the water within a minute more, but to no avail. Red was gone, and his body would never be recovered.

It was assumed, at the following inquest, that his HTF suit had most likely fractured upon impact, then filled with water. Even if Red had not been killed instantly, he would have been helpless against so much dead weight dragging him down. The ocean in that area is two thousand metres deep, and the seabed is riven with narrow canyons and swept by strong currents, so a full recovery effort was never launched.

Three weeks later, Walter Richman stood within the Hand of God on the summit, and the Wheel was finally conquered.

4

DEATH AND ART

AT ONE P.M. RITA LEFT her apartment to attend her lunch appointment in the Conservatory.

Other than the brief exchange with Eugene, and then the encounter with the woman in the Cavern Pool, she had spoken to no one all morning. And once again, as she came to the well and began to climb the Helix Staircase—the lift was available, but the great staircase was still too fascinating to ignore—Rita encountered not a soul, her only companion the confident silence of her father's design.

But hiding behind that silence, she knew now, lay the Observatory's tunnels, thrumming with machine noise. And those tunnels were everywhere. On her way back from the pool she had searched for other entry points that might betray them, and behold, they were legion. Some were discreet and camouflaged: doors set flush into wood-panelled walls, or masquerading as full-length mirrors. Others were concealed behind false angles in decorative alcoves. But now that Rita knew what to look for, they all were visible to her discerning eye.

She tried a few of the doors and found none were locked. Invariably they opened to plain concrete corridors that ran off into gloom, but the only indication as to where those corridors led were cryptic markings on the backs of the doors. The tunnel nearest her own apartment, for instance, opening from a small nook in the main hallway, was marked UH-GWA. The best she could guess from this was that the GWA might refer to Guest Wing A. But otherwise, who knew?

In any case—she thought, as she circled about on the stairs—there was something about all these tunnels that set her teeth on edge. It was not that she was blind to the need for service passageways in a house so large. But the intent here seemed so naked: that the grand spaces should not be ruined by the appearance of anything so mundane as *staff*, that the peace and quiet of the guests must not be offended or disturbed, that the employees, as reminders of menial things, should be banished from sight to scurry in a dark underworld of noise and steam. Something in Rita—perhaps it was only a relic of the long-dying Australian sense of egalitarianism—revolted a little at the notion.

Which was ironic, for when she finally reached the Atrium, the first people that she encountered in fact *were* staff.

Of a kind, anyway. The house manager, Bradley, was leading a group of four men across the landing towards the Dining Hall. The four were all dressed alike in work gear of overalls, boots and safety helmets, and toting plastic crates stuffed with wires and cables.

'Good afternoon, Ms Gausse,' declared the house manager, apology in his tone. 'Don't mind us, please, these men have an urgent task on an eastern balcony, and this was the quickest way.'

'Something wrong?' she enquired, as the men trooped past, barely sparing her a glance.

'Oh no,' the manager reassured. 'These are just fireworks specialists for tonight's show. A few last-minute details to be attended to.'

'Ah. Any hints about tonight then?'

Bradley smiled. Rita still did not know if it was his first name or last. 'I'm afraid not, ma'am. Other than to say that the weather is looking like it will be clear this evening, which is a relief.'

'Oh. Well, I have a lunch . . .'

'So I understand. In the Conservatory. The others are already there, I think. But excuse me, I must escort these men to where they need to be.' And with a nod he moved after the other four.

▲

Lunch was an á la carte affair, the five of them—Rita, Clara, Kushal, Madelaine and Eugene—lounging on cane chairs set around a circular table laid in white. Chat was polite as drink and food orders were taken, the topics consisting of the weather—clearing now—and the magnificence of the views which beckoned on every hand through the Observatory's glass walls: the sky and the sea and, of course, the Wheel.

But as they settled in, the major-domo enquired as to how Rita had spent her morning, and that led to Rita reporting on her visit to the Cavern Pool and her rescue of the cleaning woman.

Kushal responded with indignation. 'I cannot believe that she could be lost in the way you say. The service passages are complex, yes, but they are no maze. They are marked with perfectly clear directions.'

'Then why do the staff keep going missing in them?' Eugene enquired with amusement. 'Happens all the time.'

'Because they are inattentive. They cannot read a simple sign. They must be walking in their sleep to go so astray.'

Rita then moved on to the tale the cleaning woman had told her, of the dead man in the steam room. It was a topic she might have avoided had Richman been present, out of fear of embarrassing her host, and also she did not want to get the cleaning woman into any trouble, but surely it was okay to discuss with these others. It wasn't *their* house.

Even so, she could see the uncomfortable glances being shared about the table as she spoke. 'So is it true?' she concluded, asking the question of all of them. 'Did a man really die in the steam room?'

Clara sighed reluctantly. 'Well, yes, there was an unfortunate event down there several weeks ago. One of the pool maintenance workers was found dead in the steam room. It was very sad.'

'How did he die? Was it an accident?'

The major-domo shook her head. 'There was no malfunction of the steam room, if that's what you mean. When the body was found, everything was functioning exactly as it should, temperatures within normal ranges. Nor was he trapped in any way. The door is not even capable of being locked. But for some reason he stayed in there for a considerable length of time, and well, that's obviously dangerous. It was very upsetting. And though, as I say, there was no malfunction, Mr Richman had the room completely stripped back and refurbished in any case, so you mustn't think there's any risk now.'

Kushal was shaking his head again, annoyed. 'There was no need to replace anything. The steam room was fine. The man was obviously suicidal. He sat in there deliberately until it killed him!'

'How long are we talking about?' Rita asked.

Kushal shrugged. 'He was missing for over a day before someone noticed his clothes piled outside the door.'

'Twenty-four hours in a steam room,' mused Eugene.

Madelaine sipped a soda water, expressionless. 'He was a horrible sight when they found him, I'm told. They say his skin had cooked through and was peeling off in large pieces. And the smell!'

'I heard he wasn't quite dead even then,' added Eugene. 'He only *died* when they lifted him, and he fell apart.'

'For pity's sake,' reproved Kushal. 'That's nonsense and you know it is. He was dead of heat stroke, that's all. And that's bad enough.'

Rita said, 'His clothes were outside? He was naked in there?'

Clara gave her a curious stare. 'Is that so strange? It's a steam room, after all.'

'I was just wondering,' Rita replied. 'Wasn't the man they found dead in the Lightning Room naked too?'

This drew another round of stiff glances about the table. 'You know about the Lightning Room?' Clara enquired.

Rita was careful to not even glance at Madelaine, her informant. 'I remember it being in the news a while ago.'

'Ah. But you didn't mention it last night, when we were up there.'

'It hardly seemed the right time. I didn't want to be rude.'

'No,' Clara conceded.

'So, with my father that makes it three people that have died up here in the Observatory. Is that weird?'

'Well, you must remember,' said Kushal, 'this whole island has been one massive construction zone for the last four years, an engineering project as big as any in the world. With so many people around, deaths—either accidental or natural—are inevitable.'

A sudden flash of intuition came to Rita. 'Have there been *more* than three deaths? Since construction began?'

The builder's eyes met hers briefly before skewing away. 'Yes, more than three. But I'd rather not discuss the actual number. It would be misleading to a layperson. Let's just say it was within the expected norms for a project of this size. Construction is a dangerous business. Though be assured, all safety codes were followed.'

Madelaine sipped again from her glass. 'Maybe sometimes a site is just unlucky.'

'Unlucky?' Rita echoed.

Kushal said, 'There's no such thing as bad luck in construction, just bad planning. But sometimes the workers get a silly notion in their heads about this site or that being jinxed. It doesn't even have anything to do with the accident rate. I've worked on projects where we had injuries every other day, and no one was bothered by it, but then I've worked on projects where there's hardly been a finger scratched, and yet everyone was certain that the site was bad luck, cursed by some local god or other. I'm talking about India here, mostly, but I've seen the same thing all over the world in different forms, East and West.'

'Local gods,' noted Madelaine, with a cool glance to Rita. 'Our guest would know all about those, wouldn't you, Ms Gausse?'

Rita said, 'It's not a phrase I ever used, even back in the old days.'

The designer nodded a concession. But Rita could not help being aware of the unease that remained around the table.

She said to them all, 'I'm not bothered that people have died here, if that's what you're worried about. I don't believe in ghosts or curses any more than I believe in local gods.'

Clara said, 'It's not that we think you're bothered. It's just that Mr Richman specifically asked us to not discuss this matter with you— or to talk about your book—until later.'

'Why later?'

'He intends, I think, to bring the matter up himself when he decides the time is right. For now, he does not want your exploration of the Observatory to be distracted by irrelevancies, no matter how tragic. So, would you mind if we let the subject be, for now?'

Rita thought a moment. 'One last question. When my father was found, *he* was fully dressed, wasn't he?'

The major-domo's expression remained deadpan. 'Of course.'

▲

Lunch was done by three p.m. They would not be required for anything further, the major-domo informed them, until seven p.m., when Richman expected to see them all on the Terrace.

The others dispersed. Eugene had IT problems to fix. Kushal was off to make a call home to India. Madelaine planned, she said, to meditate. Clara had been summoned to attend her master. Rita, at a loose end and sleepy after the meal, which had included several glasses of wine on her part, decided that a return to her apartment and a nap were in order.

But after descending to the Atrium, she turned aside on impulse and passed through the arch into the Entrance Hall. She had not revisited the great chamber and all its artworks since her arrival. She would spend a moment now taking a better look.

Once more she experienced the sensation of stepping into a secular cathedral. But she noted another aspect now: a curious quality to the light. There was a lambent, almost underwater feel to the Hall. Outside, the weather was clear now, the winter sun bright, so the Hall should have been filled with harsh sunbeams and hard shadows. But instead everything was softened, the shadows stripped of any real contrast.

It was the windows, she realised, and the transparent panels in the ceiling. They looked like common glass at a glance, but they couldn't be, for all of them showed the sky differently. Through the windows facing east, the daylight was a pale green; overhead it was deepening aqua; and through the western windows the sky was an indigo field on which the sun shone a vermillion disk.

Of course. This must be Madelaine's photoelectric 'smart' glass in action, muting, filtering and diffusing the hard daylight into something softer. Well, it was certainly effective. When combined with the colour of the walls and pillars, carved of the Mount's blue-red basalt, the glass transformed what might have been a hall filled with dreary afternoon glare into a magical underwater world that was both enticingly dim and yet aching with clarity.

No doubt the filtering served to protect the valuable artworks in the Hall, too.

Rita commenced the long stroll down the aisle, gazing left and right at the paintings and sculptures. The stairwell that led downwards into what Clara had called the Museum was still closed by a chain, so presumably the last-minute installation the major-domo had mentioned was still ongoing.

Some of the works were obviously modern, and many others looked classically Greek or Roman, but the bulk of the collection, especially the paintings, appeared to Rita's untrained eye to be from the medieval and Renaissance periods. And for all her lack of specialist knowledge, she grew increasingly awed by what she was seeing. There were no helpful labels to assist her here, as in a public gallery, only the scrawl of the artists' signatures on the paintings themselves, and not always even that. But surely *that* painting was a Raphael, and surely *that* one was a Rembrandt, and surely *that* one was a Picasso?

Then there were the sculptures and other works. The slender marble youth with the David-like eyes—that couldn't be by Michelangelo, could it? And was that tortured-looking figure in bronze a Rodin? And displayed in a glass cabinet, could those yellowed pages, densely hand-written and interspersed with illustrations of medical dissections, have been penned by anyone other than Da Vinci?

Rita did notice a theme emerging. Mortality. The more she looked, the more it seemed that death, either as a literal figure, or as an abstract concept, dominated most of the images about the Hall. And not only death, but death's companion woes. Suffering. Illness. Even torture.

Perhaps this was just the preoccupation of the relevant art periods, especially the medieval, when death and torment were more daily real-ities. Still, it was strange, in this contemporary setting, to be walking past illumination after illumination of ancient figures being disembowelled, or crucified, or hung, or scalded with hot irons, no matter how artist-ically, or indeed religiously, the image was expressed.

And then there was the centrepiece of the collection. Rita had noted it on the day of her arrival—the great dark painting hanging in the other-wise unadorned nave-like lobby at the end of the Hall, drawing the eye from every vantage point. She was pulled towards it now, inevitably.

A flight of three broad steps led her up into the lobby. To her right, the doors of the main elevator were shut, hiding the two-and-a-half-kilo-metre plummet of the lift shaft. In the centre of the room the altar-like block of stone rose from the floor, blank and enigmatic, too high to be a seat, as she had noted in puzzlement last time, too low for a table.

But she recognised what it really was now. It was her father's sig-nature on the building. She had almost forgotten, so long had it been since she had toured his buildings with him, but he had always liked, in his designs, to place somewhere in the building a non-functional extrusion, be it a rough hemisphere emerging from a wall, or a blunt pyramid extending down from a ceiling. It was his way of referring to the earth and rock from which his designs were dug, the unfinished and non-practical nature of the shapes demanding attention and acknowledgement. Often his signatures were hidden away in corners, secrets to be discovered, but here in Richman's Observatory, his greatest work, he had placed his signature in the very foyer with this solid unmissable oblong.

Smiling to herself at sudden old memories, good memories, Rita circled around the block, her hand lightly caressing the stone. Then she turned and, resting her thighs against the artefact, leaned back and considered the great painting that hung above it.

It was big, maybe ten feet by six, painted on wooden panels, medieval in style and darkened with age. And its subject, unequivocally, was death. In scenes that sprawled across a brown, blasted landscape of ruined fortresses and dead trees, a horde of skeletal figures, some with scythes, some with swords, some with nets or spears, were rounding up and slaughtering dozens upon dozens of fleeing, wailing, screaming men and women.

It was an *orgy* of death, inflicted in a multitude of ways and to all manner of folk. In one corner, an armoured king pleaded in vain as Death held an hourglass above him, sand run out. In another corner, richly clad dinner guests were ravaged and hauled up from their table by the relentless skeletons. In a third corner, a lone figure knelt to be beheaded. In the fourth, two Death-figures rang a funeral bell. In the background, battles raged and ships sank at sea. And in the centre, a rampant image of Death mounted upon a pale and bony horse rode swinging a scythe gleefully as a crowd tried hopelessly to flee from it, herded into a giant, open-mouthed coffin . . .

Surreal, Rita thought. Mad and surreal. What on earth could Richman want with this Dark Age piece of morbid fancy, hanging in pride of place?

'Do you know the artist, and the painting?' came a voice behind her, startling.

She turned, and found the security chief Kennedy standing on the other side of the stone altar, gazing at the painting with a tight smile.

'No,' she replied, trying to appear unruffled. He had come up without a sound, so must have trod softly down the Hall, and yet a latent energy in him seemed close to the surface, as if he had just dashed here at speed, or come from a fist fight. It was something about the brightness of his eyes, and the tension in the way he stood.

But his voice was perfectly calm, placid even, in its controlled American drawl. 'It's called, you won't be surprised to hear, *The Triumph of Death*. And it's by a sixteenth-century Dutch artist named Pieter Bruegel the Elder. I don't know who the fuck the younger Bruegel was. But this is the elder.'

Rita turned back to the painting once more, nonplussed as much by the security chief's manner as by his information. A figure was plunging into a lake, a millstone tied around its neck. Wild dogs pursued a naked man. A gallows lurked in the distance, a victim dangling from its crossbeam.

Kennedy spoke again. 'Can you tell what it is that Richman likes about it so much?'

She shook her head. It was a vast and striking work, even a master-piece for all she knew, but what in the world was there to *like* about it?

'I'll give you a hint,' said Kennedy serenely. 'It's a particular object in the painting. You can find the same object in a dozen or so other works here in the collection, some by Bruegel himself, who had a par-ticular fondness for drawing it.'

Rita glanced back into the main Hall and all its portrayals of suf-fering. 'The only common theme I can see in here is different ways to die.'

'You're close,' the security chief nodded, his eyes too bright. 'I'm talking about a *particular* way to die. A specific device of torture.'

Rita stared again at *The Triumph of Death*, could only shake her head hopelessly.

'There,' said Kennedy, pointing to the upper right corner of the painting. 'See? Those things that look like cart wheels, stuck up on poles.'

Rita stared more closely. There were indeed several of the strange objects depicted in the middle distance, like wagon wheels, as Kennedy had said, stuck atop tall poles. And now she could see that human figures were bound to the wheels, spreadeagled and wretched, exposed naked to the sky.

'They're *breaking wheels*,' said Kennedy. 'Of all the medieval punishments, they must have been the worst. First your limbs were deliberately fractured; then your stomach was slashed open and your entrails laid bare; then you were hoisted, tied and helpless, into the sky for the birds to get you. First, they'd peck out your eyes, then they'd eat your guts alive.'

Rita stared in horror. 'It was a real thing? They actually did that to people?'

'What do you mean, real?'

'I mean, it's not just an imaginary torture that was made up later, something fake to use in waxwork dungeons, like the iron maiden?'

The security chief shook his head. 'Do you see an iron maiden anywhere in that painting? No, Bruegel was depicting only the real deaths of his time: hanging, war, starvation, all perfectly factual.'

Rita had to agree. The wheels looked utterly matter-of-fact in their depiction, drawn from life, for all their ghoulishness.

And then she saw it at last, the answer to Kennedy's original question, obvious really. 'That's why Richman has this hanging here,' she said. 'It's all about the mountain, that's what you mean. The breaking wheel is meant to be some kind of metaphor for the Wheel the mountain?'

The security chief nodded with a sudden sourness. 'A metaphor. Sure, that's what it is. A motherfucking metaphor.'

Rita looked away uneasily. Was something wrong? Was he angry about something? It was impossible to tell. She said, 'So Richman thinks the mountain is like a torture device?'

'I think,' said Kennedy with an air of precision, 'it's more a question of ordeals. Ordeals that must be endured and overcome.' He took a slow glance back into the Hall. 'Most of the art in here is about that. But *The Triumph of Death* is the key. Richman went to extraordinary lengths to get it. It's a famous picture, you know. It was in a state museum in Madrid, and they were *very* reluctant to part with it. But money, and I mean hundreds of millions, talks.'

Rita still could not pick what it was that was different about the security chief today. She said, 'I'm surprised he sees the Wheel, the mountain, in such morbid terms. I would've thought he would think about it in more positive ways.'

Kennedy snapped a short laugh. 'You don't understand. The breaking wheel means pain and defeat for its victims, just as the Wheel the mountain has meant pain and defeat for all those who've attempted to climb it. Except for one man, that is. Except for Richman. He's the only one who has ever stood atop the Wheel, the only one who has beaten the world's greatest mountain. And to beat the Wheel is to beat the breaking wheel. You follow?'

'To beat death, you mean?'

'I suppose I do.' Kennedy had moved closer to the painting, studying the skeletal figures striding amid the dying masses. 'I've watched the way he looks at this. It's called *The Triumph of Death*, yeah, but when Richman hung it here, it was his own triumphs he had in mind.'

'You're saying he thinks he's immortal?'

The security chief shrugged. 'Isn't he? You think his name will ever be forgotten? You think Neil Armstrong's name will ever be forgotten? But it's more than that.' His over-bright eyes roamed the corpse-strewn landscape. 'Anyone else, like you or me, when we look at all the different deaths happening in this thing, somewhere in there we see ourselves.

We *know* we won't be allowed to escape it; we *know* we're gonna die. But not *him*. I've watched him stare and stare at this picture a dozen times, looking from death to death to death, and he always smiles, because you know what—I'm sure he has *never* seen himself in it. Everyone's death is represented there, except his own.'

Rita studied Kennedy a long moment. His hands were on his hips as he searched the painting (and what death did he see for himself depicted there?) the pose drawing back the coat of his ill-fitting suit. She could catch a glimpse of a shoulder-holstered gun, and also, strapped to his belt and held in a clipped pouch, a pair of stainless-steel handcuffs.

She said, 'You seem to have inferred a lot about Richman from his artwork.'

His eyes never left the painting, and his Midwestern drawl seemed to slow down even further. 'Oh, never mind me. I'm only talking this way because I just snorted a huge fucking line.'

She stared at him.

He gave her a glance, bright and contemptuous. 'Why should I care if you know? Who are you going to tell? Anyway, I seem to recall you had a thing yourself for the nose candy once—at least, if my old friends in US Customs are to be believed.'

Rita suppressed a shudder. Well, yes, of course he would know about that, it was on the public record. But it was still crass of him to throw it in her face. She said, 'I don't care what you do. But I'm surprised Richman hasn't noticed.'

His gaze was on the painting again. 'I normally wouldn't touch it on duty. But in this fucking mausoleum, what else is there to do? There's no threat on the horizon of any kind. Richman is holed up in his Cottage, and my only job is to keep track of the staff. Oh, and one guest. Did you enjoy your swim this morning?'

Rita started. He'd been watching her?

His expression remained deadpan, despite the fever in his eyes. 'There are cameras everywhere, at least in the public zones. You can't be surprised by that? There're cameras in the staff tunnels too—though somehow we missed that little cleaning lady when she got lost. She's been fired, you know.'

'*Fired*? Why?'

'For talking to you. Christ, cleaners are the last people who should be seen or heard. It's actually a problem we've had with a lot of the Australian staff here; they don't do subservience well, think they can talk to goddamn anyone.' He shrugged. 'Or maybe it's because she told you about the corpse in the steam room.'

'*Richman* ordered her fired for that?' Rita pressed, appalled at the idea.

The security chief barked another laugh. 'Of course not. He doesn't bother with the firing of fucking *cleaners*. I fired her. Or at least, I instructed the House Manager to do it. No, as of this moment, Richman knows nothing about the whole encounter. Nor do I plan to tell him. I'd advise you not to do so either. He would not be pleased to hear it.'

'I wasn't supposed to know about the steam room?' Rita asked, still outraged. 'Or about the man in the Lightning Room either?'

Kennedy nodded. 'Not yet you weren't, at least. But oh well, spilt milk . . .'

'Why? What does it matter?'

'You'll see. When Richman decides it's time for you to see.' He straightened, gave *The Triumph of Death* a final glance. 'You know something? I've only just noticed this—every single death in this painting is the result of an act of violence.'

Rita was distracted. 'What?'

'I mean, there's nothing *natural*,' he explained patiently, eyes still cocaine bright. 'No act of god, like. I don't see anyone here dying because of a flood, for instance, or because of a forest fire, or a tornado. There're no deaths here by any force of nature at all. It's all deliberate murder and killing.'

'So?' asked Rita, bewildered.

'So, do you think Richman has noticed? If not, it's a bit of an over-sight, wouldn't you say?'

'I don't—'

'I *mean,* this painting is really only about the triumph of one sort of death. And that means Richman might have missed the point completely.'

And before Rita could demand anything further of him, Kennedy had turned away and gone striding away down the Hall.

THE QUESTION OF PRESSURE

Article, *National Geographic*,
July 1972, by Robyn Fay

In the far wilds of the Southern Ocean, two days by ship south of Tasmania, an extraordinary collection of men and materials is being gathered to attempt what has hitherto proved impossible: to defeat the highest mountain on Earth, the infamous Wheel.

Of course, Walter Richman and his quest scarcely need introduction here. The expedition has already been covered extensively in this publication, and its progress, once climbing begins, will be tracked closely. The purpose of this article is to discuss the particular challenges that the Wheel poses for Richman and his team.

That the Wheel is a perilous place is no news either. In the last two centuries, nearly two hundred climbers have died upon the mountain's slopes, and it is doubtful that even Richman's lavishly supplied and technologically advanced attempt will be fatality free. Even to set foot upon the Wheel's lowest shore can be deadly, as the first men to do so, the hapless companions of the young William Bligh, Barnabas Clover and Orald Makepeace, could attest if they were able to speak from beyond the grave. They were the first of the Wheel's casualties, killed by one of the mountain's notorious storms only a few hundred metres above sea level.

Indeed, in many ways the foot of the Wheel is as dangerous as the summit. It is a dreadfully exposed position, lying beneath twenty-five kilometres of slope that is overladen with ice and rock and snow, all of it liable to avalanche or landslide at any time. Ancient debris paths on the Wheel's lower flanks, some miles wide, are grim indicators of the devastation that has been wrought there in ages past.

But only in ages past, luckily. To our great fortune, the current era finds the Wheel and its geological region in a period of prolonged stability. While minor falls do regularly pepper the lower slopes, there has been no major collapse in recorded history. But ten thousand years ago, or twenty, a Richman-type expedition would have been dodging huge avalanches from day one—yes, and the tsunamis those avalanches throw up.

But up to ten thousand metres, the Wheel, steep and cruel though it may be, is a mountain like any other mountain. But *above* ten thousand metres (and recall, the second highest mountain in the world, Mount Everest in the Himalayas, tops out at just under nine thousand metres) the Wheel transforms into a territory that for humans is far more deadly and alien.

Why is this?

The most important consideration is *air*. Or, more to the point, the lack of it.

Now, as everyone knows, air gets thinner the higher up you go, which is why it gets harder to breathe. That difficulty in breathing can cause headaches, nausea and fatigue, as well as slowing down digestion and degrading sleep. At high altitude, above six thousand metres or so, an unprepared human will lapse into unconsciousness, and even acclimatised individuals can suffer life-threatening complications, such as pulmonary oedema (fluid on the lungs) which can cause death by suffocation, or cerebral oedema (fluid on the brain) which causes migraines, hallucinations and blindness.

Ancient peoples attributed the unpleasant symptoms to the actions of displeased mountain gods, or to curses for transgressing on sacred ground.

Modern science has a different explanation, and it's not just that there is less air to breathe. Breathing consists of two processes. One is *expiration*, the expansion and deflation of the lungs that draws in and expels air. The other is *gas exchange*, where elements from the inhaled air pass through the delicate membranes of the inner lung and move into the blood that is being pumped through the lungs by our hearts.

Oxygen forms twenty per cent of Earth's atmosphere, and powers most of our bodily functions. Gas exchange ensures an ample supply of oxygen into the blood, and expels our body's waste product, carbon dioxide. And this is the key: the gas exchange is driven by differences in *pressure*.

Put very simply, there is less oxygen in the blood flowing through our lungs than exists in the inhaled air, and the difference in pressure forces the oxygen from the air into the blood, which is where we need it to be. (Likewise, the difference in pressure forces the carbon dioxide *out* of the blood and into the air in the lungs, which we then exhale.)

But as a climber ascends a mountain, even though the percentage of oxygen remains the same in the air, the overall air pressure coming into the lungs grows less; the *pressure* of the oxygen is less, and so the exchange of oxygen through the lung membranes slows, and less of it gets into the blood. And when that happens, bodily functions suffer.

The body has ways of coping with this. It can produce more red blood cells, which are particularly good at absorbing oxygen, to make up the difference. This is what happens during the 'acclimatisation' phase of climbing a mountain. If a climber goes slowly, and spends several days or a week or two at middle altitudes before going very high, their body has time to produce the extra red blood cells, and so is better prepared for thin air.

But there are limits. Regardless of acclimatisation, most climbers will begin to suffer severely above about seven thousand metres, where the air pressure, and hence the oxygen pressure, is less than half that of sea level. At this height, the body gets so little oxygen that it begins to waste away, effectively slowly dying, hence the name 'the death zone'. And so most climbers at this point will use what is known as supplementary oxygen.

The climber wears a mask attached to a pressurised gas cylinder, inhaling an extra two or three litres of pure oxygen per minute. The mask is not sealed against the outer air, so the general pressure within the lungs remains the same, but nevertheless the oxygen flow increases the *percentage* of oxygen in the air reaching the lungs, which boosts the oxygen transfer process.

But individuals do vary. While most ascents of Everest, at eight thousand eight hundred and forty-eight metres, have been achieved using oxygen, several daring climbers in recent years have made the summit entirely under their own steam, using no supplementary oxygen at all. On the Wheel, climbers have reached as high as nine thousand five hundred metres unaided, but only in the greatest distress and at peril to their lives. It would be fair to say that the absolute limit for an unaided climber, no matter how fit or acclimatised, would be ten thousand metres, no more.

But interestingly, even with supplementary oxygen, the limit is not much higher, lying somewhere towards about thirteen thousand metres. At this height, air pressure drops to under ten per cent of sea level. Even with an oxygen mask, the pressure of gasses entering the lungs is now so low that no matter how high the oxygen *percentage* is, the *pressure* of it is less than the pressure of the oxygen already in the blood, and so the gas transfer process fails.

Indeed, it begins to reverse. Rather than oxygen flowing from the lungs to the blood, it begins to leak from the blood into the lungs, the prolonged effects of which would clearly be fatal. Of course, long before that point, a climber would have collapsed. Thirteen thousand metres is really only a theoretical upper limit. In practise, no one has climbed higher, using supplementary oxygen alone, than just over ten and half thousand metres, only a kilometre higher than the record of climbers going unaided.

How then does the Richman expedition seek to climb to *twenty-five thousand* metres? At the summit of the Wheel the air pressure is effectively zero, and an unprotected human, far from being able to breathe (and quite apart from the deadly cold) would find not only his blood evaporating through his lungs due to lack of pressure, but every fluid in his body likewise boiling and seeking to escape his very skin.

An awful fate. How to avoid it? Wear space suits, of course. But the real solution to the problem lies with that key word *pressure* once more.

Like astronauts in space, the climbers in Richman's team, when they venture high on the mountain, will be wearing special pressurised suits. The exact pressure and ratio of oxygen inside these suits is yet to be determined (space-walking astronauts, for instance, breathe pure oxygen at one third atmospheric pressure) but the effect will be the same. By enclosing their bodies in airtight suits, they can maintain the air around them and hence in their lungs at a high enough pressure to ensure that oxygen can be easily absorbed into their blood. The fact that their suits will also protect them from the extreme cold of high altitude, and from the extreme solar radiation, is more a bonus than anything else. Pressure is the crucial function.

Now, the Richman expedition is not the first try this. Several expeditions in the late 1960s made similar attempts on the Wheel using full pressure suits. However, as the suits in question were rather primitive, the best height achieved was just over twelve thousand five hundred metres. This is impressive enough, being halfway up the mountain, and a record that stands to this day: and yet nevertheless a disappointment. It remains to be seen how high the Richman expedition will get, but it's beyond doubt that *their* pressure suits represent a leap forwards in high-climbing technology.

To examine this, we must now pass to the laboratories of NASA and of their affiliate designers, the famous David Clark company . . .

6

ENTERTAINMENTS

WAITING FOR RITA WHEN SHE returned to her apartment, propped up on a side table in the entry hall, was a gold-printed invitation. It read: *Your presence is requested upon the Terrace this evening for a Carnival of Flame and Fireworks, and an Ascent of the Wheel. 7 pm. Dress warmly!* And, hanging from a hook on the wall beside the table, a fashionable coat had magically appeared, full-length and fur-trimmed, accompanied by a matching pair of calf-high boots, and a fur-lined hat.

All of which, it turned out, when Rita tried them on, fitted her perfectly. And attired thusly (though only carrying the coat and hat) she duly set out at seven that night and climbed to the Atrium and then on upwards still to the Conservatory.

Her first glance through the glass walls out to the Terrace gave an impression of flames flickering and people moving about, but before going out she paused at the airlock doors to read the weather screen. The colour was green, the temperature minus eleven degrees Celsius, the wind no more than a breath. In other words, she thought, shrugging on the coat, it was as balmy a night as could be hoped for there on the Mount.

Donning the fur hat last of all, she passed through the doors and emerged onto the Terrace. The chill air nipped immediately at the bare skin of her face, but the sensation was delicious when the rest of her was so enfolded. And before her lay . . . why, it was like some lavish scene from Hollywood.

Fires burned everywhere, flaming bright in the freezing darkness. Some were great bonfire flares rearing from the tops of stone pillars, others were more comfortably sized blazes set in stone bowls around which couches were gathered, others again were tiny jets of coloured flame burning within lanterns or at the tips of candelabras set in alcoves. No corner of the Terrace was left unilluminated—not even the pool. Flames burned there too around the water's edge, and in the middle, by some trick, fire even seemed to spring from the water itself.

All the fires were smokeless—presumably they were gas-fed—but there was just enough movement in the icy air to everywhere set the flames dancing and flaring, making the golden light across the Terrace undulate and shift hypnotically. And through this glow ran traces of steam that rose from the heated waters of the pool, a gorgeous mist that shimmered and hid and revealed.

Through this wonderland strode Walter Richman, hands out to greet Rita. 'How do you like it?' he said, genuinely excited, it seemed, with a sweep of his arms to encompass the fires all about.

'It's beautiful,' she replied quite honestly. 'But I'd hate to see your gas bill.'

'You'd be horrified, sure enough,' he laughed. 'But we have plenty in reserve in the tanks down at Base. The whole island gets its power from natural gas, as a matter of fact—an LNG carrier stops here every month or so to fill us up. Of course, we don't light all these fires every night, and some of them are only temporary anyway—but this is how it will look for the big opening party, more or less.'

'So, is this the 'carnival of flame' that was mentioned on the invitation?'

'It's the beginning of it, yes. The fireworks part is still to come.'

'And an 'ascent of the Wheel'? What on earth is that going to be?'

He shook his head. 'All in good time. After dinner. Then you'll see.'

He led her over to the others, who were grouped around a bar that stood near the eastern edge of the Terrace. A laid dinner table flanked by tall flaming pillars waited beyond. The position would by daylight have offered a stunning view of the Wheel, and for Rita an appalling one, for beyond the low parapet there was only the great plummet away to the sea, but for now, dimmed by the bright flames, both the fall and the mountain could only be guessed at in the shadows. Likewise, though the sky was clear, the stars were for the moment reduced to only pale echoes of the brilliant constellations that they had all witnessed last night in the Lightning Room.

Rita exchanged greetings with the others: Kushal, Madelaine, Clara and Eugene. The mood among them was much brighter than it had been at the terse lunch. No doubt the fantasy setting, and the expectation of the show to come, had something to do with that. And also, maybe, it was the addition of Richman to the group. Without him—there was no denying it—Rita and the others were a cast without the leading actor—there was an irritating irrelevance to everything they did and said. But with Richman present—and a cheerful, voluble Richman at that—there was a focus to it all.

Eventually they sat down to dinner. Rita was once again placed at her host's right hand, and the billionaire was once again particularly solicitous towards her, asking all about her day and her exploration of the Observatory. In reply, she made no mention of her encounter with the cleaner, nor, when she spoke of the Cavern Pool, did she detect any change in Richman's manner that might indicate he was aware of the incident, or of the woman's firing.

'I love that pool,' he enthused. 'I do twenty laps there most mornings, and then I warm-down with a few rounds of slow breaststroke through the tunnels. It's wonderfully meditative.'

'Was that the idea behind the design?' Rita asked.

'Oh yes. There's nothing more calming then swimming inside a cave—I found that out years ago on some of my expeditions. The pool up here is fine and spectacular, but floating under an open sky is not the same as within a rock-bound space.'

'You might be right.'

'Of course, I do a hard run, five miles, in the Games Arena before the swim,' Richman continued. 'Have you visited there yet?'

Rita shook her head. 'Not yet.'

He was briefly serious. 'Your father. I understand. But I hope you can overcome your aversion—the Arena is truly a marvel, a tour de force in its own right. You mustn't miss it.'

'I'll get there,' she promised.

Even Kennedy, when the security chief appeared, seemed almost cheerful in the flame light. He arrived as the dinner plates were being cleared away by the waitress and bent to Richman's ear to murmur a few quiet words, to which the billionaire nodded in satisfaction.

'So how many people in the building right now, Kennedy?' enquired Eugene from the end of the table, playing what appeared to be a familiar game with the security chief. 'Must be a lot.'

Kennedy straightened. 'Fifty-five. Get off your ass and go check it if you like.'

The IT expert laughed.

'Why so many?' Rita asked.

Kennedy gave her a glance. 'Tonight's show, of course. We've got the fireworks teams here, and, well, other specialists too. You'll see.'

It was interesting. Watching him, it seemed to Rita that the intensity had gone from Kennedy's eyes, but they remained sharp nonetheless, with no sense of coming down. Perhaps the security chief had other drugs to help cope with the after-effects.

'Meanwhile, have you given Mr Richman your opinion of his art collection, yet?' Kennedy asked her, a twitch of mockery on his lips. And in an aside to his employer he added, 'I happened upon Ms Gausse in the Entrance Hall earlier today. She was especially interested in *The Triumph of Death*.'

'Ah,' said the billionaire.

'An intriguing work,' commented Kushal from across the table. 'Though very grim. But no doubt the artist's intent was to warn of the inevitability of death, and hence to say, enjoy life while you may, which is not so grim a message after all.'

'That's one way of looking at it,' Richman agreed with a smile. 'But it's not quite what appeals to me. What I admire about the work—about most medieval art—is an understanding that I think modern society has largely lost. Namely, that pain and mortality are not meant to be strangers to us, but are in fact our most constant companions through life. Confronting them both, accepting them, striving in defiance of them, cheerfully, and in full knowledge of inevitable defeat, is the whole *point* of life. Otherwise, we really are just livestock, dumb and terrified, being herded by death towards the abattoir.'

'Or victims upon a breaking wheel?' Rita asked, for the billionaire was still watching her.

'Or that,' he nodded.

A recklessness took hold of Rita. 'Of course, it must be easier to not fear death when you're already so famous that no one will forget your name for generations, and when you leave behind a building like this one as a permanent legacy.'

He laughed. 'Nothing is permanent, sure as hell not fame. As for this place, I don't kid myself. As soon as I'm dead, my beloved children will flog it off as quick as they can to the highest bidder, if one can be found. Likely as not it'll end up as a hotel for honeymooners, or a backpacker lodge for mountain climbers. But the running costs will ruin anyone who tries to maintain it, and so inevitably it'll become neglected and run down, and eventually it'll be abandoned. A hundred years from now, as regards this place at least, I'll only be remembered as the fool who sank a fortune into a folly.' His smile was winning. 'The point, again, lies in not giving a shit about any of that. In *my* lifetime, whatever it takes, this place will shine, because I say that it will.'

There was more laughter around the table, but Rita had a sudden uneasy image of exactly what he was describing, of this same luxurious Terrace upon which they sat, but now all desolate and broken and covered in ice as the wind whistled over it. But the desolation wasn't a century in the future, or fifty years, or even ten. It was sooner than that. Much sooner. Tempting fate, she thought. Richman, in his confidence, was tempting the fates.

'But speaking of maintenance,' the billionaire said abruptly, with an elaborate glance around, 'what's happened to the damn lighting up here?'

Taken aback, everyone looked. It seemed that, unobserved, the fires about the Terrace had been dying away. It must have been gradual, or surely someone at the table would have noticed, but now even the largest of the blazes dwindled to flickers, and night came to the Terrace. Overhead, the stars, barely visible earlier in the evening, were bright.

'Is there a problem with the gas, I wonder?' Kushal ventured.

But before anyone else could speak, a low thump detonated from somewhere below them; then, with a whistled shriek, something shot up from below the western rim of the Terrace and climbed into the night, trailing sparks. High, high it rose against the pale backdrop of the Milky Way. Then—

BOOM. A golden flower exploded, flaring silver as it spread against the darkness, then frittered away in embers falling towards the distant sea.

'Ah,' said everyone around the table, and rose to their feet as one.

A fusillade of detonations followed, the fireworks launched apparently from lower balconies of the Observatory, so that the rockets leapt into view without warning from beneath the Terrace. First they filled only the western sky, but then the north and south, and finally to the east, so that the summit of the Mount soon seemed to be surrounded by a thunderstorm, the clouds formed of boiling smoke, the lightning flashing multi-coloured.

Richman was laughing. 'This is only the beginning!' he cried to them all. 'Watch the rockets; follow the path they make!'

The starbursts were now confined to the eastern side of the Terrace. One by one, the rockets were arcing further and further away from the Observatory before they detonated, soaring ever deeper into the gulf of darkness that lay between the Mount and the Wheel.

Away, away went the starbursts, the gazes of everyone on the Terrace following, until there was an appreciable lag of a second or two between the blossom of the flower and the BOOM of its ignition. And then three seconds, then four. And now the starbursts were lonely showers of light out in the void, getting further away still. And also lower, descending gradually in the dark, explosion by explosion, until each starburst came below eye level.

Rita grasped it at last. The detonations were moving towards the Wheel, tracing a path, burst by burst, across ten kilometres of night.

Now indeed the rockets were no longer even being launched from the Mount. Dim flares of red on the surface of the ocean far below told of launches from what must be barges or boats moored there for the purpose. Fiery stalks marked each rocket's ascent, reaching up to the middle airs between the Mount and the Wheel before the flowers bloomed.

'They're not just any old fireworks, either,' Richman continued, as the crack of the explosions faded with distance, even though the fusillade was unceasing out there in the void. 'They're twice as big as the shells used at public events, and shooting three times as high, up to over a kilometre.'

Yet for all their size and explosive power, the starbursts were shrinking away inexorably as the kilometres grew between them and the watchers—already they must have crossed halfway to the Wheel. Indeed, now the bulk of the mountain itself, lost before in the glare of the fireworks, was becoming a presence once more, a deeper shadow than the night, and vast beyond all reckoning compared to the shrinking starbursts that crept towards it.

Rita was aware of a strange, muffled, doubling of sound now, as if more fireworks were exploding than could be seen. She realised that it must be echoes, each explosion reaching her once directly, and then many seconds later reaching her again, reflected off the great wall that was the Wheel.

She shivered. The breeze was blowing more chill across the Terrace, the last of the smoke had cleared and the smell of powder departed. The faraway starbursts continued, almost at the foot the Wheel, and how small the silvery flowers had become, tiny spring blossoms against a louring monolith. The thump and mutter of explosions was still audible, but the effect had become ghostly and sad, lost in so much immensity, and Rita shivered again.

'Keep watching,' Richman warned. 'We're getting to the good part now.'

The rockets were no longer being fired from barges, it appeared, but rather were lofting up from the foot of the Wheel itself. It must be from Bligh Cove, there was nowhere else along that inhospitable shore where the pyrotechnicians would be able to set up their equipment.

The light from the explosions was now revealing, in flashes of lurid red and green, the landscape of the Wheel itself, giving glimpses of faraway stony cliffs and icy crags. But it was only a tiny portion of the great mountain. To the left and right of the fireworks, and far above them, the bulk of the Wheel remained in darkness.

There came at last a final flurry of starbursts, which must have been dazzling and deafening up close, but which from this distance was only a dispassionate glitter, fading to nothing, followed by a muffled crescendo of faraway thunder, echoing on itself. Then it too died, and the night and the darkness and the quiet leaned in, victorious.

Except, no.

For at the point where the last fires had faded, far across at Bligh Cove, a new and improbable light was rising, not an explosion, but a steadier, more piercing glow, tinted green. And simultaneously, on the

Terrace, a deep peal of sound suddenly woke—a swell of music played on hidden speakers.

'Ha!' laughed Richman.

The glow at Bligh Cove was now a dazzling pinpoint, like a giant magnesium flare seen from afar. And belatedly Rita saw, stabbing out from some hidden position below her on the Observatory balconies, a pale rod of light glittered in the darkness, catching on the smoke from the fireworks. It extended in a straight line all the way across the ten-kilometre gulf to the bright point at the foot of the Wheel.

A laser, of course; she was seeing the beam of a laser. She could now detect additional beams lancing out from the Observatory, another four or five ghostly lines, all of them focussed on Bligh Cove, which was glowing ever brighter. The music—a soundtrack of strings and key-boards—trembled as if in anticipation of some momentous beginning.

And suddenly, in the flickering manner of laser writing, the words *Bligh Cove* appeared at the focus of the beams, inscribed in glowing green upon the mountainside. Rita drew a breath of amazement. Why, to be read at this distance, the letters must be enormous, dozens of metres tall.

But now the focus of light was distorting, elongating itself—a glowing line was striking out from Bligh Cove, climbing the Wheel's lower slopes. It jagged this way and that, but crept ever upwards, leaving behind an unbroken green trail. Once it paused and widened into a dot, like a mark on a map, before moving on. Higher up, it did so again. And all the while the music on the Terrace swelled in accordance.

'What is—?' Rita began, but caught herself, for even as she spoke, a third dot was forming on the laser-lit line, and beside it more words appeared written in light. *Base Camp.*

And suddenly she understood. The laser show was marking the route by which Walter Richman and his expedition had climbed the Wheel!

It was obvious now, the way the glowing green line cut back and forth in switchbacks in some places, or in others plunged straight up. Rita dimly remembered her history lessons. There had been a supply camp at Bligh Cove, but Base Camp had been on the great ledge called the Plateau, five thousand metres up. And between there had been subsidiary camps. That's what the unmarked dots must represent.

The green line was now climbing above Base Camp. In fact, it had split into two lines which took separate though roughly parallel paths upwards, strung with dots along the way, sparse beads on a necklace. Rita remembered the two lines of camps that had been run up the mountain, with dozens of huts set along either path, refuges where the climbers could rest in pressurised air, with running water on tap and electricity to recharge the batteries of their suits.

She stared, utterly fascinated as the laser-illustrated route ascended ever higher. In those long-ago lessons, Rita had been shown photographs of the mountain with the route the climbers took clearly marked, and she had been quite uninterested. But this was entirely different. This was three-dimensional; this was alive, with the Wheel right there before her, and the scale of it all, the truth of what Richman and his team had done, was staggering.

Up, up climbed the twin lines, bright against the bulk of the mountain. The night remained too dark for any detail of the West Face to be seen, and the laser lines illuminated nothing but themselves, but even so, ridges and cliffs and couloirs could be guessed by the way the lines either crabbed sideways or leapt upwards. And they were climbing so *high*, it was impossible to believe the Wheel could really be that tall. Yes, its shadow was ever present in all its grandeur, but the bright line of ascent defined the terror of its heights all anew.

The strings of the soundtrack swelled across the Terrace as the lines rose. Rita did not recognise the piece, and wondered, with a kind of horror, if it was original, if Richman had ordered it composed just for this memorial to his great achievement.

And still the lines, dotted with camps, continued to etch their paths upwards. She could hardly imagine how the effect was achieved. How many lasers were involved? How powerful were they? How was it that the twin lines, even as they now approached the summit, twenty kilo-metres and more above her, still seemed as crisp and bright as the lines on the lower slopes, which were so much closer?

Far above in the night, just below where the two great shoulders of the Wheel met against the stars, likewise the two green lines had now drawn together. This single line progressed swiftly to the summit ridge, where it jagged leftwards and climbed on. Until, just below the hump of the Wheel's pinnacle, a last dot appeared, and a third piece of writing was cut in light, fine and far away, but just distinct enough to read. *Hut 122.*

The last camp, Rita knew. The hut from which the man standing beside her here and now on the Terrace had, all those years ago, set out with three companions to reach the peak.

There the line went now, a bright scratch somehow drawn from twenty-five thousand metres distance, creeping along the crest of the ridge towards the summit. And as the line at last reached the very Hand of God (though of course it was much too far away to see any details of the palm and the fingers) and as the music swelled to ecstasy, the entire diagram of lines and camps drawn across the Wheel flared bright and golden in triumph, a pathway to heaven, and the summit blazed like a new star.

For a long moment it held like that, then in a blink it vanished, a switch thrown to off.

But the show was not over. Colours danced all over the Wheel for a confusing instant, the beams of the lasers swinging wildly through the smoky airs about the Observatory. Then a new pattern of lines coalesced on the mountain, forming not a route this time, but arms, legs, shoulders, a head . . . it was a man, a figure in outline, drawn across the entire West Face, a giant standing twenty kilometres tall.

It was Walter Richman.

The figure possessed no recognisable facial features, for all Rita knew such detail was beyond the capacity of the laser projectors, and in any case, the figure wore a helmet. But she knew it was Richman anyway, for the image was a copy of one of the most famous photos ever taken, a shot of Richman standing upon the pinnacle of the Wheel, snapped by one of his companions waiting on the ridge below. The photo showed him turned half away from the camera, a bulky form in a pressure suit, his head tilted to the sky, a climbing axe draped over his shoulder. It was an image that had always projected victory, humility and exhaustion all at once. And now that same image flickered in glowing green outline across the vast screen of the mountain he had conquered.

On the Terrace, Richman was applauding. 'Yes, goddamn it. Yes!'

Slowly, the titanic figure turned, its shape flickering as the lasers redrew, and faced the Observatory. A hand the size of ten football fields raised, and waved to the watchers.

Around Rita, the others laughed and applauded, and Richman whooped his joy, but Rita, staring at this monstrous apparition, felt something chill and dreadful awake in her gut.

This . . . this was awful.

The giant now bowed to the watchers, a god acknowledging its worshippers, and then, with a final flourish from the music, it straightened and faded away. The multiple beams of the lasers disappeared, leaving the air around the Observatory empty, and across the ocean the great wall of the Wheel was dark once more. The show was over. But it gave Rita no recourse from the sick feeling.

It was more than awful . . .

She gulped at the cold air, feeling flushed and nauseous and dizzy. What was wrong with her? Was she falling ill? Had she drunk too much? But no, it wasn't a physical discomfort exactly, it was more as if . . . as if some moral sense within her was in revolt, as if she had witnessed something indecent, and was sickened now with the shame of not having stopped it.

She shook her head. What did she mean by that? It had been entertainment, that was all. A party trick, vast and complicated and technically a marvel, but just a trick and no more.

The lights were coming up on the Terrace now, and Richman was receiving congratulations from his guests. 'Thank you, thank you,' he was saying. 'Of course, there'll be somewhat more fireworks on the actual night. And the laser show will have some commentary to explain about the route up the mountain. But you get the gist of it.'

The vertigo was withdrawing from Rita a little, thank the lord. But even so she felt hollowed out and cold, and soiled somehow.

The billionaire turned to her at last. 'Rita? It's a wild extravagance, I know. But after all, if you're going to throw a party then—' He paused, looked at her more closely. 'Are you okay?'

Disgust had overcome her again. An extravagance? To spend what must have been hundreds of thousands of dollars, no, more likely millions of dollars, for the amusement of just six people? You could not call that merely extravagant; it was *degenerate*. But that wasn't what really bothered her. It was Richman's money, after all. He could waste it how he liked.

'I'm fine,' she said, wiping cold sweat from her forehead. 'I think it was just watching all those lights in the dark. Made me a bit dizzy.'

'Would you like a glass of water?'

'No, thank you.'

What she wanted was to be away from him. Loathing filled her, not for his wealth, but for his ego, for the sheer vastness of his conceit.

That was what repulsed her so much about the show she had just witnessed. The staggering vanity of it. Richman had projected his own image, twenty kilometres tall, upon the mountain. He had turned the mighty Wheel, and all its towering grandeur of snow and ice, into a screen on which to glorify himself. And he expected *congratulations* for it.

Faintly she said, 'It was a wonderful show, though. Amazing.' Because how else could she rid herself of such narcissism? Praise was the only way to make him leave her alone.

He was nodding. 'Everyone told me it couldn't be done. It was beyond laser technology, they said, at that distance and scale. But it's like anything else, you don't take no for an answer.'

No. And wasn't that the irony of invincible egotism—how often it *did* get the apparently impossible done, by sheer force.

'Anyway,' the billionaire said brightly, turning to the others. 'Now that we're done with the festivities, we can get out of the cold. Dessert is being served in the Conservatory—shall we go in?'

So ushered, the others made off towards the airlock doors. Rita, however, hung back. Clara, passing by, gave her a questioning look.

'I'll be along in a minute,' Rita said. 'I just need a breath of clear air after all that smoke.'

The major-domo nodded politely and moved on, leaving Rita alone, aside from the bar attendant and the waitress, who were now cleaning up.

Wrapping her coat tight, Rita wandered away along the eastern edge of the Terrace. It felt very cold now, the breeze beginning to stiffen into a wind. Back by the bar there was still light—but elsewhere none of the fires that had been ablaze before Richman's show had been reignited, leaving the Terrace abandoned to the wind and the night.

Chilled to the bone, Rita came to a small protruding balcony that jutted out over the eastern drop. In her distraction she dared even to lean against the rail at the outmost point, the wind curling up at her from the two and half thousand metres of darkness directly beneath. Ignoring it all, she stared across the gulf to the shadow that was the Wheel.

And she felt it then, emanating from the mountain, the way she could feel sunlight even when her eyes were closed. Only now it was as if she had turned her face towards a cold lightless sun, one that radiated only a single baleful emotion.

She drew a breath, unnerved. An image came to her, as clear as if she had just lived it. She was standing—impossibly—on the bitter summit of the Wheel, high above the Earth. And from that vantage she beheld the green flicker of laser lights searching up from far below, coming closer, closer, until suddenly the Hand of God was bathed in an icy green glow.

It was hateful, that light, in her vision. It was alien, a light where no such light, hard and artificial, had ever shone before. It was the intrusion of something man-made where mankind did not belong.

No, the intrusion of a single *man*. A man who long ago had defeated the mountain. A man who had returned now to tunnel into the native stone and to build his home mockingly at the mountain's foot. A man who, in ultimate insult, had carved his own image in light upon the Wheel's hide.

Rage at that enormity flowed in storm waves from the mountain. Rage, and yet it seemed to Rita that there was satisfaction too, an eager certainty that retribution was coming. Not yet, not now, not when the man was as protected as he was, but soon, when he was alone, or nearly alone, then—

Rita blinked, staggered back as if she had been hit, so appalling was the image that flooded her mind. But then it was gone, gone without a trace, as was all sense of otherness or enmity.

Blinking still, she strove to remember what the last shock had been, but there was nothing; it was a dream forgotten instantly on waking. All she knew was that the whole thing, the vision of the mountaintop, the sensing of emotion, had been like . . .

Oh no.

Like the old days, that's what it had been like. When she had believed that she could . . . commune . . . with the bedrock of the hills.

But oh Christ, that was done with. She didn't believe that anymore. There was nothing to commune *with;* she knew that perfectly well now. And anyway, even at her most delusional, she had never communed with an entire *mountain*, let alone a monster like the Wheel, and never, ever, from ten kilometres distance. Even by the logic of her old madness, that was impossible on every level.

And yet . . .

'Ma'am?'

Rita started. It was the young barman, braving the chill away from the heaters, his upper half clad only in a thin white coat and shirt and bow tie.

'Ma'am, would you like a last drink of anything, before I close down the bar?'

She shook her head. 'I'll be going in now. Thank you. I'm fine.'

He nodded and withdrew.

Rita took a shuddering lungful of the cold air, felt her head steadying once more. She glanced back up at the Wheel, and felt—nothing. Only the cold and the wind. The mountain itself was an inscrutable shape of blackness against the stars, and in no way could she imagine what it would be like to stand upon the peak, or to resent the intrusion of mankind.

Of one man.

She puffed the air out.

No way at all.

And thus reassured, if only shakily, she turned from the Wheel and sought the safety of the doors, and the warmth and light within.

7

THE THEORY OF PRESENCES

Extract from *The Spawn of Disparity*
by Rita Gausse, 1995

Let's get this out of the way then, straight up.

I think it's important to state exactly what I believe from the outset.

I am not fearful about this.

I do not need to dance about the truth, or prepare the way for delicate souls who will have trouble accepting what I have to tell them. Fuck the delicate souls—these things are facts; they don't need to be sugar-coated, nor should they be wrapped in cheap mysticism.

So here it is. In short, there are invisible non-human presences, non-human forms of consciousness, all around us in the landscape.

Let me stress the term *non-human*. They are not ghosts of humans departed; they not human-related spirits of any kind. Indeed, let me say further, they are not even of organic origin. They are not in any way related to animals or plants. They are *inorganic*. They are born only of stone, or of the atmosphere, or of water. They do not breathe, or need food. They will exist, I am certain, as readily on lifeless Mars as they do here on Earth. Perhaps more readily, in fact, for reasons that will become clear.

But here is the next important point: these forms of awareness do not exist in just *any* piece of stone, or in any patch of sky, or in any reach of ocean. They are born only when something *unusual* happens within a landscape or environment. They are a consciousness that comes into existence when change occurs; they are defined by it; their first thought, so to speak, is not *I think therefore I am* but rather *I am because I am not as everything else is.*

Some examples will help explain. You are wandering through a forest. The ground gently rises and falls, there are trees and creepers everywhere, birds sing; it's all very nice, but you feel no sense of anything special. Then you come upon a deep fold in the land, and descend into a gully of overhanging cliffs. It comes to a dead end, where a deep rock pool waits, water dripping into it from the stone walls above. You are alone there, cut off from the rest of the forest, and all is hushed and still and cold.

Now you sense something, an otherness to the landscape, a hush, an awe.

Or you are hiking across a desert plain. It is stark and bare and striking in its own way, but it leaves you untouched. Then you come to a lone pinnacle of stone, raised long ago by some volcanic or geological upheaval. It is not dauntingly tall, maybe only forty or fifty metres high, but as you walk around it, noting how strange and isolated it is there amid the flatness of the desert, you once again begin to sense something *else*, something that dwells there, not human, not animal, not plant, that you cannot name.

Or take one of the most common experiences of all. You are in your backyard, gazing up at the sky and the clouds, and all is as normal. Then a storm approaches, the great thunderheads advancing from the horizon to loom over you, the air stirring, lightning flickering, thunder rumbling— and something in you awakens at the sight, something in you quickens, you feel dwarfed by a manifestation that is alien to you, bigger than you, indifferent to you.

In all these moments, what you are sensing is the *presence* that inhabits these landscapes or phenomena. Your own awareness is interacting— imperfectly, blindly—with the alien awareness that was created by the formation of the forest gully, or by the raising of the stone pinnacle, or by the brewing of the storm. Your human consciousness is detecting— confusedly—inhuman consciousnesses that are born of violence and change and difference. You are sensing, as this book is titled, the spawn of disparity.

Thus, they are not *everywhere*. In a landscape with a thousand mountains, for example, only a mountain that stands out from the others will have a presence within it. This is easily tested. Travel through some mountainous region where, as you go, snowy peak appears after snowy peak. You will find that amid so many mountains, summit after summit will excite no special awe in you. But eventually there will be one—not necessarily the highest—that is different, either standing alone and apart, or rising more sheerly, or at stranger angles, and *that* mountain will stir a response in your heart. *That* mountain, forged differently from its fellows, will hold a presence within.

I should say here that the presences that inhabit mountains, or storms, are about the largest that the human soul can detect. I suspect that there are larger presences in larger formations—continents for instance, and whole oceans, maybe entire planets. But if so, those presences are simply too huge, too diffuse, for any human mind to comprehend. We have not the perspective—though perhaps astronauts, who have looked back upon Earth from a distance, would beg to differ. On that I cannot comment.

Now, what are these *presences* exactly, you ask? Well, it may be easier to begin the answer by explaining what they are not. They are *not* merely a human type of consciousness trapped in a rock. Banish all notion that they think or feel or experience the world as we do. They are alien to us in every way, non-living, non-corporeal, non-pretty-much-every-concept-we-have of awareness. Yet they *are* aware, of themselves, and of their surroundings.

And though they are not living as we understand it—they do not eat or drink or reproduce—they *are* mortal; they do die. They exist only as long as the formation that gave birth to them itself exists. When the gully is weathered away, so is the presence within it. When the pinnacle is worn down, its awareness is worn down too. When the storm blows itself out, nothing *other* is left behind.

Presences exist, and they die. Their life expectancy, however, is nothing like ours. The time between their birth and death can be a million years, or a few hours, or—say, in the case of the giant rogue waves that form upon the ocean, rearing vastly up before collapsing into foam—even a few fleeting moments. Time has no meaning to presences. A millennium or a microsecond, all is the same. And they do not fear their end, or resist it—except in one unique manner, which we will come to.

But why do I call them *presences*? Why that name, over the alternatives? After all, there are many names that could be used instead.

Humans have called these awarenesses *gods* or *demons*, *spirits* or *elementals*. I could do the same, borrowing any number of such divine titles from a hundred different mythologies.

But I don't think it would be wise. To call them divinities would be misleading. Quite apart from religious dogma, we humans tend to envision our gods and demons as essentially just pumped-up versions of ourselves. Supernatural beings, yes, powerful and frightening and mysterious, and endowed with all sorts of hidden knowledge and motivations, but still beings that think and reason much as we do.

But as I've said, the presences of which I speak are in no way human: they don't lust or fall in love or crave power; they don't feel hot or cold; they have no gender. They are not alive in any way that we are. To repeat, they are inorganic.

Should we therefore simply *call* them inorganics, as does the famous shaman (or fraud, take your pick) Carlos Castaneda? Certainly there are echoes of presences in his writings. But alas, his other-dimensional beings, for all their inhumanness, are still imbued with human-like motivations of greed and control. Indeed, Castaneda's inorganics are closely tied to humans (they farm us, basically) whereas the presences of which I speak, if left to themselves, have no interest at all in humanity.

What then of the old term *numens*, which dates back to classical times, and was the name given to bodiless, sexless, inhuman consciousnesses that were believed to inhabit the landscape, and which it was wise for humans to honour and placate? That sounds very close, surely, to the meaning I'm after. And likewise, what of animism, and of other eastern religions and philosophies which see gods within hills and mountains, such as the sacred peaks of the Himalayas. Indeed, such mythical concepts can only have grown from a keen appreciation of the concept of presences as I now seek to explain it.

Still, 'numens' is a term I have elected not to use. For one thing, numens and other animistic gods inhabit not only hills and rocks and rivers, they also abide in living objects like trees and forests, or sometimes even in man-made objects, like statues or crossroads. Also, while they live within a landscape, they are viewed as separate *from* that landscape, able to move, for instance, to other mountains or trees, if encouraged, rather than being entities that are *of* the landscape, with no discrete existence beyond it. It is a subtle but crucial difference, as I will show in later chapters.

In short, therefore, having examined and discarded every known term that refers to inhuman presences in the landscape surrounding us, I have settled, if reluctantly, upon the word with which I began. In fact, it came to me in childhood, in those first terrifying moments that I was enlightened, against my will, to the true nature of the world.

Yes, *presences* may be an unsatisfying word, too general in its meaning, but by that generality is at least neutral and free of so many of the misleading implications that other terms carry.

Oh, and there is one last avenue of terminology that it is important to reject immediately and completely. Presences have nothing—*nothing*—to do with the notion of Gaia, or with any sense of Life Force or Mother Nature, or with environmentalism. Remember, they are non-organic. They do not rely on the system of photosynthesis; they do not care about global warming, or about preserving forests, or about saving the whales. The scurrying life of plants and animals is of no consequence to a consciousness that is born of motionless stone, or of shifting air masses, or of the upthrust of an ocean wave.

233

That said, however, there is one crucial aspect of life that does matter to them, and that is *conscious* life, human life, in other words, for only humans are truly conscious. Why does the human mind matter? For a simple and brutal reason: it can kill a presence before that presence's due time.

To an inorganic awareness, the proximity of an organic awareness is toxic. And the proximity of massed organic awareness—i.e., a crowd of humans coming into close contact with a presence—is toxic *fatally*.

In short, we humans, us, our very thoughts, are poison to the presences we encounter.

And that's where all the trouble starts.

8

PREMONITIONS

RITA WOKE TREMBLING AND FLUSHED to her third day as Walter Richman's guest.

It was a hangover. She had drunk far too much the night before. On top of what she had imbibed during dinner, she had gulped down several wines with dessert, and then indulged in whisky and port with Kushal and Eugene. And, ah yes, she remembered now, once back in her apartment, she had drunk another wine on her own. No, two wines, actually. Or had it been three . . .

It was almost, she noted ruefully, as if she had been drinking in self-defence.

In the old days, alcohol had been her first resort when she had wanted to escape the presences around her. Other drugs—pot, cocaine, LSD and the like—only heightened her awareness of them (that was one way of putting it, another might have been that those other drugs *created* her awareness of them) but alcohol, mercifully, had always been deadening, shutting her special senses down. So, in drinking so much, had she been making a pre-emptive strike last night? Washing away the memory of her episode on the Terrace, and ensuring that it was not repeated?

Maybe. Maybe not.

Either way, she was paying for it now. She swung gingerly out of bed, swayed her way to the shower, and under the hot blast of the four

235

nozzles began to feel a little better. Afterwards, she ordered bacon and eggs and coffee. She really could get used to daily room service, she noted bleakly, taking the first hot sip of the long black.

And then there it was: the rest of the day to be filled. Her only engagement was for dinner—another formal affair in the Dining Hall, she had been told—otherwise she was free.

What to do?

A swim?

Or a sauna perhaps?

In the steam room where the man had died, cooked through in his own skin?

But she did not think she could face the Cavern Pool. There were few better hangover cures than a swim or a sauna, and it wasn't as if she was seriously put off by the story of the dead man. But the thought of venturing down there all alone again, through the empty halls to the great dark cavity dug from the heart of the Mount, silent except for the splash of water, and beneath that, the hum from the hidden machinery in the tunnels . . . no, not today.

The upper pool then? It was heated, after all, and refreshingly open to the sky. But when Rita gazed out through the glass walls of her apartment, the sky itself was a washed-out grey, drear and uninviting, and the weather panel by the balcony door warned of strong winds and bitter temperatures.

Again, no . . .

The plush couch in the living room beckoned, and the huge TV screen with its full suite of cable and streaming channels. Later, she promised herself, going to the couch and sinking into it and reaching for the remote, later she must get out and do something, or meet someone, but for now, for the rest of the morning at least, she could curl up and indulge.

But she did exactly that—turning the fire on, fetching a soft blanket to snuggle under, nibbling on some high-quality chocolate she found in the larder, locating a few favourite old shows to watch—the hoped-for sense of comfort and cosiness refused to eventuate.

The hangover was partly to blame. It lingered stubbornly. But it seemed to be more than just that. Something else nagged at her, a nameless tension, as if somewhere, just beyond her hearing, a drill whined, or an alarm wailed, or a dog barked, or a baby cried, making it impossible to relax.

Occasionally, she found herself all of a sudden sitting up and turning to the windows to stare out at the Wheel, as if some half-heard report had come from that direction. But there was never any actual sound, and the Wheel was always as it ever was, an immutable wall of grey and ochre and white. Oh, doubtless the West Face, overburdened with so much stone, must crack and groan constantly, and the many glaciers, grinding slowly in their beds, must at times split and shatter and shed ice in great crashes, but from this distance there was nothing to see, and nothing to hear. The Wheel was silent.

And yet, *something* emanated from it, Rita's ragged senses told her. There was an echo of what she had felt last night (though in truth she couldn't remember exactly what she had felt last night, the alcohol she had consumed since had dulled the memory), something increasingly strained and drawn out and expectant. Something—

Goddamnit, no.

Stop it.

What she was thinking was impossible, even her old self would have said so. No presence could be so strong, no presence could make itself felt across such a distance . . . And there were no such things as presences anyway. She had made it all up, when she was young and hurt and furious.

The ring of the house-phone was a welcome distraction. Rita muted the TV and answered. It was Clara. 'If you're not busy this afternoon,' said the major-domo, 'we can fill in a gap in your tour.'

'Tour?' Rita echoed, not understanding.

'The Museum—it'll be ready for viewing in a few hours. The last piece we were waiting for arrived yesterday; they're installing it now.'

'Oh . . . well . . .'

'Are you fixed for lunch? We could meet in the Conservatory for a bite, if you like, before visiting the Museum. Or I could simply meet you there, say at three, if you'd rather eat on your own.'

'Yes, I think I'd prefer that, I'm actually a bit tired after last night,' Rita said with inward relief. A simple sandwich in the apartment would be much easier in her current mood than lunch with company. 'I'll see you at three then.'

'Very well. I'll be waiting.'

▲

Both of them were prompt, meeting within the arched doorway to the Entrance Hall.

'I didn't even think to ask before,' Rita said straight up. 'But when you say museum, what sort do you mean? A museum to what?'

The major-domo blinked. 'You're right, I never said. Well, you won't be surprised. It's a museum to mountain climbing. More specifically, a museum to the Richman expedition and the Wheel.'

'Ah.' And that certainly made sense, although Rita greeted the news with a sinking heart. She did not think she would be all that interested in a museum stuffed with climbing memorabilia at the best of times, even less so now. Lunch had not helped much. She still felt hungover and nervously irritable, on edge for no cause she could pin down.

Yet Clara was smiling as she ushered Rita through the archway. 'I can guess what you're thinking, but it's worth your while, really.'

They passed down the Hall, ignoring the artworks, and came to the stairs that led below. The chain that had previously blocked entry was now gone.

'Down we go,' said Clara.

They descended. It did indeed feel as if they were passing from the main body of the great cathedral to its secret subterranean catacombs. The stairs described three turns through the solid rock, leaving all light of the upper world behind, before reaching the bottom.

A low, wide chamber awaited them.

It was quite windowless, lit only with an orange light from braziers set on the walls. Squat pillars ran off in rows, supporting a flat ceiling; it was at least fifteen feet high, but felt low after the soaring space of the Hall above.

It was a showroom, Rita realised, designed to display not itself, but the exhibits within. A museum to mountaineering, to the expedition that had conquered the Wheel, so the major-domo had called it. But Rita could see that it was really a museum to one man, Walter Richman.

He waited at the foot of the stairs, across an expanse of red carpet. There, upon a podium, stood an upright slab of stone carved into human shape and imprinted with a life size photographic image—the same image indeed that Rita had seen inscribed upon the Wheel in the darkness last night, twenty kilometres high: the famous photo of the triumphant mountaineer standing upon the summit of the world.

And next to Richman's likeness, on a matching podium, was a high-altitude climbing suit, standing freely as if a man was inside it even now. And Rita knew, even before asking, what it must be. 'Is that the one?' she said as they approached the display. 'The one he was wearing, on the summit?'

The major-domo nodded. 'It is.'

'And is this what you were waiting for?' Rita guessed. 'The final installation?'

Another nod. 'Mr Richman didn't consider the Museum complete without it. He loaned it to the Smithsonian Air and Space museum in Washington, back in the eighties, which is where it's been ever since, in pride of place, I'm told. But of course he always reserved the right to take it back, and they have other suits they can use, if not quite as special as this one. It was a complicated procedure, however, getting it here, and there were delays, hence the curators only finished their work on it this morning.'

Rita was circling the suit slowly now. She could not deny her fascination, having only ever seen photos or film of the strange attire, never the actual thing up close, let alone the only suit to have made it to the summit. (And where, she wondered, did they keep the pressure suit that Neil Armstrong had worn while he walked on the Moon? Was it also at the Smithsonian Air and Space museum? Wherever it was, at least it couldn't be taken away at whim—it had always been government property, not private.)

The suit was certainly big, looming over her with arms akimbo like an outsized wrestler, made even more ominous by the gold mesh screen of the helmet hiding the emptiness within. Richman himself was tall, at least six-foot-two, and between the helmet and the thick-soled boots, the suit must add three or four inches to that. And it was bulkier than even the famous photos made it look, especially with the great rectangle of the combined battery pack, air compressor and tank on the back.

Amazing to think that climbers had scaled all manner of cliffs and sheer slopes in such a get-up. It looked as if it would be difficult even to walk in, let alone to clamber up rock faces.

'I've worn one of them myself, you know,' the major-domo commented, as Rita completed her first lap. 'Only a modern replica, of course. I was much too young to be any part of the original expedition. But it was a working copy.'

Surprised—for she had all but forgotten that Clara had herself once been a professional mountain climber—Rita stared at the other woman in frank assessment a moment. The major-domo, though comparatively tall and fit, still appeared diminutive compared to the hulking HTF suit.

'It was a smaller model than this one, of course,' Clara added, aware of the meaning of Rita's stare. 'They do come in different sizes. And it was only to walk around in, I didn't climb in one.'

'What was it like?' Rita asked.

'Well, they're more flexible than they look. Certainly an improvement on the NASA suits of only a few years earlier. But I won't kid you, I wouldn't much like to try a difficult ascent in one. Your centre of gravity is all off; your peripheral vision is poor; you get very little tactile feedback from your hands and feet, which can be vital in climbing. In fact, you feel cut off from the whole world, almost like you're trapped in there. It's hard to get into, and harder to get out of, especially with any speed. I'll confess, I got a little claustrophobic. And occasionally they do fail, depressurising catastrophically. They were very brave people, those expedition climbers, to tackle a mountain like the Wheel in these things.'

Yes, Rita mused. Whatever else she might think about Richman and his wealth, it could not be denied that there was courage and daring in him. Self-interest, certainly, but bravery too.

She was still studying the suit. It had obviously been cleaned and polished since its days of use, but even so, signs of wear were visible: subtle dents in the backpack, scratches upon the glass of the helmet, faded stains and marks on the fabric of the torso, and notches worn in the heels of the boots—boots, she reminded herself, which had stood upon the Hand of God, on the black airless edge of space.

Was this what Clara thought so important for her to see? Was the point of this visit to impress upon Rita the courage and character of the major-domo's employer? Had Clara sensed Rita's . . . well, disgust, with the billionaire last night? And set herself the task of proving to Rita that Richman had other and better qualities?

She glanced at Clara, but in fact the major-domo had already turned away from the suit and was staring off towards the rest of the exhibits, a guide waiting politely but eager to move on.

'What next?' Rita asked.

All manner of cabinets and displays waited in the dim reaches of the room, but Clara nodded to an object placed in the centre of the chamber, the largest installation of all. In another setting, Rita might have thought it was an old-fashioned caravan, one of the curved silver types, with its wheels and axel stripped off so that it sat flat on the ground.

But she knew it was no caravan. 'Is that a real hut? One used on the mountain?'

'It's *the* hut,' the major-domo replied. 'Hut Number One Twenty-Two. The one Richman and the rest of his team set out from to reach the summit, and the one they came back to when it was done. It was on loan too, not to the Smithsonian, but to the Australian National Museum in Canberra. They were sad to give it up, because they couldn't find a replacement. The huts are rarer than the suits. They were dismantled as the expedition withdrew from the mountain, and the parts and panels were thrown away or recycled—that skin is a titanium alloy and worth quite a bit of money. As far as I know, only six fully complete huts still survive in museums around the world.'

Rita had moved to the hut. The hatch-like door bore the number 122 in faded paint. Through a small thick window, little was visible.

'It's open,' added her guide. 'You can go in. It's allowed. Just pull the latch.'

Rita did so; the door was surprisingly light. Stepping in over the sill, she found herself in a narrow chamber that took up about a third of the structure, a second hatch leading to an inner room. The room was filled with paraphernalia: pumps and filters of various sorts; a collection of crates and bagged supplies; a chemical toilet and washbasin, and finally, two high-altitude suits, the same as the one outside, but hanging limp, like human carcasses, from cradles on the wall, charging cables attached to their battery backs. Two further cradles, empty, suggested that the room was in fact intended to host four such suits. This antechamber was, in short, a multifunction porch—part disrobing room, part utility room, part storeroom and part toilet.

Carefully, Rita took a few steps inwards and peered through the inner hatch. Here, obviously, were the living quarters of the hut. One wall bore a rudimentary kitchen, with an oven and sink, another wall bore communications devices and weather-observation readouts. There were fold-out tables and shelves, and everywhere cabinets of all shapes in sizes were jammed in corners and across the low ceiling. On the floor, there was plentiful room for the four thin, narrow mattresses that had been spread out there.

Fascinating. Everything was cramped, yes, but in other ways it seemed absurdly large and luxurious for a structure that had perched on a cliff twenty thousand metres high.

She retreated through the doors. 'How did they ever get this up the mountain?'

'Piece by piece,' said the major-domo. 'It demounts. If you look at the skin, you can see it's made of panels bolted together. Each hut breaks down into roughly one hundred loads, with even the biggest—the main air compressor—still small enough to be carried by one climber. It took a lot of trips, but when it was all done and assembled you had a pressurised environment with heating, electricity and water, where four climbers could rest and relax overnight while their HTF suits recharged in the docks.'

Rita was circling the hut now. On the side and at the rear there were valves and couplings protruding through the walls, to which were attached lengths of thick insulated hoses or cables.

'Those are the power lines,' Clara went on, 'and the water lines, the latter jacketed and heated to prevent freezing. Both lines ran all the way back down to Bligh Cove where the support ships generated the power and pumped the water. In effect, the expedition built a town on the mountain—but instead of the buildings being collected together in a square or a circle, they were strung out in two parallels streets, each twenty-five kilometres long. Well, only twenty kays actually. The hut system only began properly from the Plateau onwards. But you get the idea.'

'Amazing,' Rita observed faintly.

Clara shrugged. 'It was brute force. Against that kind of logistics, no mountain stands much of a chance. Not even a mountain like the Wheel.'

Rita looked at her. 'You don't approve?'

The major-domo repeated the shrug. 'It's not my kind of climbing, that's all.' She inclined her head towards the next exhibit along the aisle. '*This* is more in my line, if you want to know.'

Rita turned to the display in question. It consisted of two glass cabinets. In one, set on a metal frame, there was an old-fashioned looking climbing axe. The other cabinet contained only a tattered black leather-bound notebook.

'Do you know what these are?' Clara enquired, and her tone caught Rita's attention, for it was tinged now with a certain Germanic awe.

'No,' she answered.

'The axe belonged to George Mallory. You can see his name scratched on the shaft. And the notebook belonged to Edmund Hillary.'

The names echoed in Rita's memory. The same two men were memorialised in the marble busts in the Library, at the entrance to Richman's private domain. She said, 'They're climbers who died on the Wheel, right?'

A solemn nod. 'They were pioneers, both of them. Mallory wanted to be the first man to climb above thirty thousand feet. Everyone talked in feet then. Thirty thousand feet is about nine thousand two hundred metres. Higher than any other mountain on Earth, even though it's not even halfway up the Wheel. Hillary came later, in the fifties, and his aim was to go beyond ten thousand metres. By then, people were starting to use metres more.

'Of course, either figure is just a number. But as it happens, there is a band of black rock that runs right across the Wheel, starting at just above nine thousand two hundred metres, and reaching up to just over ten thousand metres. It's not really *black*, but it's distinctive—I can show you later, back outside—and it gave them a target. Mallory knew that if he could reach the bottom of the Black Band, he would have achieved his goal. And twenty years later, Hillary knew that if he could reach the top of the Band, then he would have achieved his.'

'And did they?' Rita asked. Her knowledge of the history of the Wheel did not extend beyond Richman's expedition, apart from knowing that there had been a litany of failed attempts previously.

The major-domo shook her head. 'That's just it. No one is sure. Both men were lost in storms on the final days of their attempts, along with their climbing companions, and none of the bodies were ever found. All that ever turned up of Mallory was his axe, found just short of the Band, just *short*. But was he heading up when he lost it, or heading down? No one can say. As for Hillary, some years after he was lost a notebook was found fixed in the ice high up on the Band, wrapped tightly in oilskin. It turned out to be his climbing journal, the book in which he jotted down his notes every day, and the final entry says—well, look, you can read it for yourself.'

The book was open, and across the two visible pages was scrawled a single word in pencil, the letters large and jagged, as might be formed clumsily by a heavily gloved hand.

Success???

'Those question marks are the problem,' said Clara. 'What do they mean? Did Hillary reach his goal, before the storm took him? Or not? Was he confused about where he was? Or do they mean something else entirely? We'll never know, and in a way it doesn't matter. Whether or not Hillary or Mallory reached their targets, the truth is they failed, both of them. A climb is only successful if you make it back down alive.'

Rita stared at the scrawled word, trying to imagine the conditions in which it had been written, in what kind of howling winds or blizzard, and in what state of mind by the writer, with death threatening all the while. But it was impossible to grasp, there in the safety and warmth of the Museum.

She glanced at the major-domo, caught her eyes intent upon the relics of the lost climbers. 'You admire these two men particularly?'

Clara's nod was unembarrassed. 'They were pure climbers. They had few of the advantages and comforts that later climbers used, though Hillary did employ oxygen. They climbed only in small parties, not in teams of hundreds, and they climbed against a mountain they knew they could never beat. Its summit was forever beyond their skills, yet they climbed all the same. They set themselves targets that were essentially meaningless, just lines on the mountain, but they were prepared to die in the attempt to reach them. Yes, I admire them. Oh, I acknowledge what the Richman expedition did, but that wasn't climbing, that was an industrial process against which even the Wheel was helpless. But men like these two—they fought bare-handed against giants.'

Rita blinked. 'Did you ever attempt the Wheel, when you used to climb?' And how was it that she had never thought to ask this before?

'Oh yes,' Clara answered.

'How high did you go?'

'To the top of the Black Band. With just one other climber, alpine style, which means no pressure suits, and with oxygen assistance only for the last thousand metres or so. It's where I got all this.' She lifted her hand briefly to display the lost finger, then touched the frostbitten blur of her nose, and finally gave a glance down to her feet, enclosed as ever in calf-high sturdy boots. 'A storm caught us. Truth be told, we nearly died for our troubles. But they were the most magnificent days of my life.'

Rita stared in fascination. 'Has anyone climbed higher than that without a suit?'

'Not much higher. Beyond ten thousand metres, it's simply not practical, above thirteen thousand it's a scientific impossibility. To go further would need another huge Richman-style effort with suits and huts, and all the money and manpower that includes. So these days, the top of the Black Band is about as far as any climbers go, if they even make it that far. Indeed, since the Richman expedition, only seventy people have beaten the Band, and made it back alive. Another fifty and more have died trying.'

Rita shook her head in wonder. 'No wonder you came to Richman's attention.'

Clara nodded, and yet frowned minimally, as if the accolade was not entirely a happy one.

They had moved on again, to the last of the exhibits in the main aisle.

Richman was the subject once more. It was a piece of relief artwork, cut from wood, a series of peaks shown in silhouette—seven of them, the greatest obviously the Wheel in the centre, with three lesser mountains represented on either side.

At the tip of each mountain was an inset photo, each an image of Walter Richman standing upon that mountain's summit. The photo for the Wheel was the same iconic image as usual, the others however showed different versions of Richman, mostly a younger man, wrapped only in climbing gear, not in a pressure suit, much more human, his face bare, other than snow goggles perhaps, and his smile white and triumphant, his hands in several shots bare to the cold, giving a thumbs up.

'It's the Seven Summits,' Clara explained. 'Richman is the only one to complete the set.'

'The Seven Summits?'

'It's not the seven highest mountains in the world, if that's what you're thinking. It's the highest mountain on each of the seven continents.' The major-domo touched each mountain in turn with a single finger. 'The Wheel, obviously, is in Australian territory. Then there's Mount Everest for Asia, Kilimanjaro for Africa, Mount Vinson for Antarctica, Denali for North America, Aconcagua for South America and finally Mount Elbrus for Europe—though he did Mount Blanc as well, as there's argument over whether Elbrus is really Europe, seeing as it's in Russia.'

'Richman climbed them all?'

'He'd climbed most of them by the time he was twenty-three and began the Wheel expedition. He only had Kilimanjaro and Vinson left to do. They were his last two climbs.'

'Is it such a big deal? You can just walk up Kilimanjaro, can't you?'

'True, although it's no stroll. But most of the seven are much tougher climbs. It's not as hard as climbing the seven actual highest mountains in the world, which are all in the Himalayas, apart from the Wheel, but the Seven Summits is still considered quite an achievement. Indeed, Richman was already famous before the Wheel for having done the likes of Everest and Denali and Aconcagua at such a young age. Only people like Messner and few other stars of that era were more highly regarded.'

And yet, there was not the tone of admiration in Clara's voice as had been there when she'd spoken of Mallory and Hillary.

'How do you rate him, honestly?' Rita asked. 'Purely as a climber, I mean. On his own. Not as leader of a huge expedition team.'

The major-domo gave another shrug. 'I've never climbed with him, so I can't say with any fairness. Self-evidently, he was very good.'

'But?'

A sigh. 'But from what I've heard and read, he was never . . . popular . . . with other climbers. I don't mean during the Wheel expedition, when he was the boss. No one is ever all that happy with the boss of such climbs. No, I mean earlier, when he was climbing with small teams in the Himalayas.'

'People didn't like him? Why?'

Clara had become reluctant but answered all the same. 'When selfishness puts lives at risks, or costs lives, then the mountaineering community is not very forgiving.'

'Lives?'

Another reluctant pause. 'There was a story told about his Everest climb. I don't suppose you'll have heard of it, Everest accounts never seem to get beyond the climbing world, as compared to stories about the Wheel. Anyway, this was in 1971. Richman was the only climber to summit Everest that year, and only the twenty-first person to do it ever, which for so young a man, just a youth really, was an astonishing achievement.

'It should have made him a hero. But within a few months rumours began to circulate, stories about a tragedy that accompanied his climb. The expedition was a small one, four Western climbers and eight Sherpas, very lightweight compared to most parties that had tackled Everest at that stage. They took the southern route. On summit day the first assault team, Richman and the Sherpa Nawang Tsering, set out from their high camp on the South Col, with the second assault team in waiting to try the next day, if Richman and Tsering failed.

'Well, Richman stumbled back into the South Col camp thirty-six hours later only half alive. When his companions finally got some sense out of him, it emerged that Richman had indeed summitted, but alone, and that Tsering was dead.

'As you approach the summit of Everest along the south ridge, the last barrier for a climber is a low cliff called the Bourdillon Step, named after the first climber to scale it, and indeed the first climber to summit Everest, back in the fifties. According to Richman, he and Tsering reached the Step in good time, and managed to ascend it, and from there it's usually only a half-hour slog uphill to the summit. But apparently Tsering was exhausted by this point, and couldn't go any further. Sitting down, he told Richman to press on, saying he would wait for Richman's return, so that they could descend together.

'Now all of this is happening at about eight thousand eight hundred metres, which is well into the death zone of air too thin for the human body to survive on. Both men were on supplementary oxygen, but don't think that's anything like using a pressure suit. Oxygen will give you a boost, yes, but you're still at very low atmospheric pressure: just breathing, let alone climbing, is hard work. The cold too is appalling, and worse if you aren't keeping warm with exercise. So it was a dangerous thing for Tsering to do, to just sit and wait like that. There's every chance indeed that his oxygen mask was malfunctioning, which would explain his exhaustion, and make his sitting there all the more deadly. But it was the choice he made.

'Richman pressed on alone and reached the summit in the early afternoon. He took over a dozen photos of himself there—by his own account he was on the summit for almost an hour—and no one has ever disputed that he actually made it. On the descent, he found Tsering exactly where he had left him—about two hours had passed by then—and together the two of them now set about descending the Step. It should have been easy enough, as they had fixed ropes on the way up.

'But something went wrong, and Tsering fell, and fell badly. The Step is only about ten metres high, but that's enough. Maybe he had stiffened up while sitting there in the ice for so long, maybe he was just too oxygen-deprived. Anyway, by the time Richman got down to him, it was obvious that Tsering's injuries were fatal in the circumstances, for one of his legs was badly broken, and he was coughing up blood, unable even to sit up, let alone get to his feet.

'Understand, there was nothing Richman could do to help him, no way to get him down the mountain to medical aid. At that altitude, there is no possibility of a climber having the strength, when so oxygen-deprived himself, to carry another human being. Tsering died within the hour. Even so, Richman remained with him, despite night coming on and a freezing gale arising, until around midnight, when he finally continued his descent.

'He was out of oxygen himself by then, and in the darkness and the storm he barely made it down to the South Col and to his team-mates, who had been waiting anxiously. It was immediately obvious to them that he was in no fit state to descend the rest of the mountain alone—it would take both of them to help him to Base Camp, still three thousand metres further below. And so, giving up their own summit attempt, they struck camp and began to lead Richman down, finally reaching Base

Camp successfully some twenty-six hours later. As for Tsering, they had no choice but to leave him where he fell.

'Richman recovered eventually with no permanent ill-effects, and at first no one blamed him for Tsering's death. Yes, maybe they should have turned back when the Sherpa first collapsed, but after all, he insisted that Richman go on, and accidents can happen at any time, especially so high up. More to the point, climbers are often loath to judge another climber's action when they weren't there themselves to judge the conditions and situation.

'But in fact there was another party on the mountain that day, a Spanish team, who were also taking the southern route, and who, in a team of four climbers, arrived at the South Col at the same moment that Richman and his two companions were departing, and who spoke with them briefly.

'Communication was limited between the two groups, due to language differences, but the Spanish at least understood that Richman had successfully summitted, and also that a dead body awaited them further up. The next morning the Spanish climbers set out for their own attempt, and got as far as the Step before deteriorating weather forced them back—for good, as it turned out. But they spent an hour at the Step, and two of the party climbed to the top of the cliff and inspected the ridge beyond, and what they found, and later reported, was perturbing.

'Tsering's body was there all right, at the bottom of the Step, just as Richman had said. But it did not seem to the Spanish that he had died quickly. His only obvious injury was the broken leg, and that had been splinted roughly—apparently by Tsering himself, to judge by the knots. He was found sitting up, and around him, neatly arranged, were his spent oxygen bottles and even some food wrappings, stuffed into a crevice. And at the top of the Step, meanwhile, the Spanish climbers found only one dimly visible set of tracks leading away to the summit, and then back again, with no sign that Tsering had ever stood there, let alone sat down and waited.

'None of this came out immediately, and when it did, it was only in a Spanish climbing magazine of limited circulation. It was a few months more before it was noticed in the wider climbing world. But there was no doubting its significance, for the implication of the Spanish account was pretty bad, in respect to Richman's own version.

'Yes, Richman had certainly summitted. But had Tsering really climbed the Step safely and only fallen on the return? Or had the Sherpa fallen on the way *up* the Step, and then had Richman, instead of returning immediately to the South Col to fetch the other two climbers— the three of them together might have got Tsering down—stubbornly pressed on to the summit, and only returned to the injured man some hours later, to find that by then Tsering was too insensible to move? If so, then the question of blame was a much acuter one; to abandon an injured man who might well be saved, purely for your own glory? That is *not* good mountaineering.

'There were mutterings about it all in the climbing community, and even a few hints dropped in the press—but the problem was that by then Richman had inherited his father's fortune, and was now fabulously rich and putting together the expedition against the Wheel, hiring climbers and specialists by the dozen. No one in the mountaineering world could dare offend him, not if they wanted to be part of it. Not a single Spanish climber, for instance, was ever hired on the project. No one else wanted to be blacklisted, or sued for that matter. And so the affair got slipped under the rug.

'And after all, who knows? It all may have happened much as Richman claimed. The observations the Spanish made were hardly proof. The tracks above the Step could have been altered by wind and weather, making it look like only one set, rather than two; the rest of it, the splints on Tsering's leg, the eaten food, might have been Richman's doing.

'No one could ever be certain. But it was never forgotten. And it didn't pass unnoticed, when the Wheel was beaten, that again only Richman actually made it to the top.'

Rita was staring. Clara had given this whole long account without pause or change in emotion, without even looking away from the depiction of Richman and his Seven Summits. But there was no doubting her attitude to the tale.

Rita said, 'You think it's true, don't you, the Spanish version.'

The major-domo glanced up at last. 'I didn't when I first came into Richman's employ. Why would I? The man was a hero of mine, and the job offer came at a very low time for me, after my surgery. I was grateful, and excited too. Oh, he had a tough reputation. I'd talked with plenty of older climbers who had worked with him. His temper was famous, and he was obsessed with his public image. But as I said, ego is hardly rare in that world. What I couldn't believe was that a man like Richman would ever directly lie about the death of a climbing partner—a partner whose life he might have been able to save.'

'And now?'

'Now I'm not so sure. I've seen enough, working for him . . . well, to make me wonder.'

'Like?'

Clara's gaze was almost sad. 'Don't mistake me. I don't intend to suggest that he is in some way monstrous. Yes, as do all businessmen of his level, he sometimes acts with great ruthlessness, even brutality in a commercial sense, and he can be very selective with the truth when it suits his purpose. I accept that. I expected it when I started this job. I am not so naïve. That the powerful and the rich lie and cheat to stay rich and powerful is hardly a surprise.

'What I did not expect was that beyond the lies and the cheating can sometimes be not mere rationalisation or expedience, but . . . well, call it delusional belief. A place where the lies and the cheating in fact

253

become, to the beholder, the truth. Where manipulation of others, contempt for others, becomes in itself a virtue.'

'It sounds like you mean he's clinically sociopathic or something.'

'Do I? Perhaps. I'm no psychologist. I only say all this as . . . well, an apology of sorts. I convinced you to come here, on Richman's insistence, as his loyal employee. But in fact, at the time I met you, I had already decided to leave his service. I'll be going very soon, within a month or two, after his big party. I have not told him yet, but I am decided nonetheless. And as one whose loyalty is no longer absolute, I say to you: be cautious of him. He has not been at all honest in his reasons for bringing you here.'

Rita had come to this conclusion herself, but it was still a shock to hear it stated so baldly. 'What does he really want then, for heaven's sake?'

'He has concerns about this Observatory, about its construction, and about many incidents that have occurred here, and he thinks that you can advise him and Kushal and Madelaine how to fix it.'

Rita was gazing in disbelief. 'You mean, he thinks there are'—*oh, just say the word, damn it, say it aloud for the first time in years*—'presences here? But he can't believe that. *I* don't even believe it anymore.' But ah, even as she said it, she felt again the throb against her forehead, the nagging toothache on the edge of her senses of something that was building—something malign, and it came, even here in his crypt, surrounded by rock, she could not be mistaken, it came from the great face of the Wheel.

The major-domo looked away. 'He does not confide in me totally, so what he believes in his heart I cannot say. But I thought in fairness you should be warned. Sometime, quite soon I would imagine, now that you've had a few days to get to know the Observatory, he will broach the subject. At least now you can prepare for that moment.'

A sudden realisation came to Rita: she did not know where in the Observatory the major-domo lived. Clara had never mentioned it. Certainly she had no apartment in Rita's guest wing. So, where? Was she housed in the other guest wing, perhaps? Or—as personal aide to Richman—did she have a room up in the Cottage? She would need to be near him, true. But was it only as his personal aide? *He does not confide in me totally. What he believes in his heart I cannot say.* There was something deeper about the way those words had been spoken.

Rita found herself blurting out the question before thinking. 'Are you sleeping with him?'

Clara's glance was sidelong and somehow amused. 'Sleeping with him? Are we so clichéd, you mean, the boss and his secretary? Well, it's none of your business, of course, but no, I'm not. Our relationship is close, yes, but it has always been a professional one. It's really not sex that a man like Mr Richman is looking for in his employees. Other things are much more important. Like loyalty, as I just mentioned.'

'Sorry,' Rita stumbled. 'I don't know why I asked that.'

'Oh, you're not so far off. Staff such as myself and Kennedy are, in some ways, more intimate with Mr Richman than even any of his wives or mistresses. We certainly spend more time with him. Most days I'm the first face he sees of a morning, and the last face of a night.'

A powerful image struck Rita, of evening time in Richman's bed-chamber, after Kennedy had made his final security sweep; of the billionaire in his walk-in-wardrobe, undressing for the day and changing into his silk pyjamas, calling out his last orders and dictations to Clara, waiting modestly out of view in the suite's doorway. And then of Richman falling heedlessly into his vast king-sized bed, while Clara slipped away to her own more simple, monastic quarters.

'But it's of no matter,' said the major-domo brightly, shrugging the topic aside. 'I truly didn't mean to alarm you with all this talk—I just did not think you deserved to be taken off guard.' She glanced around the underground chamber. 'In the meantime, I'm happy to show you around the rest of the exhibits, if you're interested—it's a fine collection of memorabilia, and not just of Richman's own achievements.'

Rita gazed around at the cabinets and displays, noting all manner of paraphernalia displayed there, coils of rope and battered backpacks and heavy jackets and down suits, and axes and pegs and boots with spiked attachments, and camp stoves and ration tins and snow goggles … and no doubt each piece had some significance and importance. But no, somehow, she was no longer interested.

In truth, her hangover was back in full force; no, not the hangover, the other thing, the uneasy gnawing in her stomach, the building tension that had no release. 'Actually,' she said, apologetically, 'what I could really use is a cup of tea.'

Clara was immediately attentive. 'Aren't you well? We'll go up to the Conservatory, and I'll order up a pot. We can come back here any time.'

What Rita wanted was to go back to bed. But then she thought maybe the major-domo was right, maybe the open vistas of the Conservatory, the view out over the sea, would help clear her mind. Maybe she would even venture out onto the Terrace for a breath of fresh freezing air. The Wheel would be there too, of course, but perhaps it was better even to face that head-on than to hide away within the rock.

As for the question of presences and of what Richman really wanted with her, well, she wouldn't be seeing the billionaire until tonight at the earliest, so that matter could be put aside too.

'The Conservatory would be nice,' she said, and together they made for the stairs.

THE STORMS OF THE WHEEL

Excerpt from *Reaching for the Hand of God*,
by John Soliola, 2007

Nowhere on Earth has more deadly weather than the Wheel. Temperatures on the mountain can go as low as minus seventy degrees Celsius, and the gale winds that on occasion descend from the high slopes are the strongest that have ever been measured. Worse, the volatility of conditions—the swiftness and unpredictability with which calm blue skies can transform to a raging tempest—is unparalleled anywhere else on the globe, so much so that weather forecasts are all but useless.

Disaster can strike at any time.

The reasons for this are manifold. For a start, the Wheel sits alone, thousands of kilometres from any other landmass, halfway between Tasmania and Antarctica, in the midst of the Southern Ocean, which is itself the most cold and exposed and windblown stretch of sea anywhere in the world. Gales and swells circle the globe there without interruption, and winters are long and dark and brutal. Even a normal-sized mountain located where the Wheel is would be wild, bleak and frigid place.

But of course the Wheel dwarfs all normal mountains. At twenty-five thousand metres, it rears clean through the troposphere and penetrates fully thirteen kilometres into the stratosphere, a part of the atmosphere that is entirely alien to the realm in which humanity exists. But just as important as the Wheel's height is its orientation. The great wall formed by the mountain stretches roughly north to south, which means that it forms a barrier lying athwart the prevailing east-west winds that blow in that part of the world. And this is where the trouble, as far as the weather is concerned, really starts.

Usually, when a mass of moving air encounters a mountain or a mountain range, it can simply rise over the obstruction and carry on with its journey. However, there is a limit to how high any air mass can rise, and that limit is called the tropopause, which is both the border and the barrier between the troposphere and the stratosphere.

We won't delve too deep into the complicated field of atmospheric mechanics here, but put simply, the tropopause is a permanent temperature inversion that places a lid on all the air below it. The height of this inversion varies as you move from the equator to the poles—it can be as high as fifteen kilometres, or as low as eight. But at the latitude of the Wheel it sits at about twelve thousand metres.

This means that when eastward-flowing winds strike the Wheel, they *cannot* simply rise and flow over the mountain as they would elsewhere in the world, for when they attempt to do so, they are blocked by the tropopause. Instead, the winds must wrench themselves to the north or to the south to go *around* the mountain, or they must flow down the mountain and reverse themselves to blow *westwards*, causing all manner of turbulence and tumult.

This situation becomes critical when it involves jet streams. Jet streams are bands of high-level, eternally blowing winds that together form a great system that redistributes heat and moisture throughout Earth's atmosphere. They are extremely powerful, raging at speeds of up to three hundred kilometres per hour. There are many known and named streams, and at the latitude of the Wheel, the stream in question is called the Polar Jet.

The Polar Jet blows endlessly west to east around the Antarctic Circle at an altitude varying between nine and eleven kilometres. For much of the time this stream flows safely to the south of the Wheel, but all jet streams meander in their course through the seasons, and it happens that every now and then the Polar Jet bends to the north and so encounters the obstacle of the great mountain.

Now, in most parts of the world, with the exception of the highest peaks of the Himalayas, jet streams sail above all land features and are at most slightly diverted by even the biggest mountain ranges over which they cross. But at the Wheel, the jet stream slams head-on into a solid wall.

Hence, the stream must divert in some direction. Sometimes the stream will bend upwards, and indeed, though it can cannot climb *over* the Wheel, it will rise with such force that it briefly breaches even the tropopause and ascends several thousand metres beyond the barrier, reaching as high as eighteen kilometres before dying out. These rising winds can also carry moisture into the otherwise barren stratosphere, where it precipitates, which explains how the Wheel boasts a permanent snow cover at otherwise improbable altitudes, all the way up to seventeen thousand metres.

More commonly, however, the Polar Jet does not go upwards, it veers either left or right to howl across the West Face and then spills over the lower shoulders of the Wheel to the north or south. There, it rips across the ridgeline as a shrieking gale that makes such exposed positions too deadly to stand or even crouch upon, let alone climb.

In all these cases, the lower slopes of the mountain are left almost unscathed. But sometimes, when the winds strike the Wheel at just the right angle, the Polar Jet is diverted not upwards or left or right, but straight *downwards*, pouring down the West Face like an invisible avalanche.

To climbers caught on the Face in such a situation, a comfortable ascent in calm air can turn, in the space of minutes, to a nightmare fight for life in a hurricane gale that is trying to blow them off the mountain. Indeed, until the installation, during the Richman expedition, of Doppler wind-detecting radar upon the nearby Observatory Mount, which can give climbers at least a few minutes' warning of descending gales, these surprise downdrafts were the leading cause of disaster upon the Wheel.

But the deadliest zone created by diverted jet-stream winds does not, in fact, lie on the slopes of the Wheel at all, but instead westward and out to sea. This unfortunate position happens to be the peak of the afore-mentioned Observatory Mount.

The explanation is this. If the Wheel was an actual wall, perfectly flat both vertically and horizontally, then the diverted winds would simply stream down to the base to batter against the sea. But of course the Wheel is actually a slope, which means that the winds flow down at an angle and are thrust westwards across the sea once they reach the bottom. Towards Observatory Mount.

More importantly, on its north–south axis the Wheel forms a vast curving arc, the mouth of which faces to the west. So, as the winds push out from along its forty-five-kilometre shore, they are also directed, because of the curve of that shore, to converge towards a central point. This conver-gence and crowding together of winds results in a huge acceleration and amplification of wind speeds within an increasingly narrow lane of air. And that lane aligns perfectly with the peak of Observatory Mount.

Indeed, if certain weather conditions are prevailing in the lower atmo-sphere around the Wheel, then, on rare occasions, the falling downdrafts can be accelerated far beyond their original velocities. Remember, jet-stream winds can easily reach two or three hundred kilometres per hour, which is bad enough, but at the focal point of Observatory Mount hyper-magnified winds have been measured at sustained speeds of nearly five hundred kilometres per hour, with gusts reaching even higher.

The single strongest gust of wind ever recorded anywhere on Earth, by direct measurement of a properly calibrated and properly functioning anemometer, was caught in August 1984 at the weather station then emplaced atop Observatory Mount. It clocked in at an astonishing five hundred and twenty-eight kilometres per hour.

This is terrifying stuff. It is likely that winds within severe tornados do reach similar speeds, though such measurements have been made only indirectly. But in any case, a tornado is soon come and gone. Atop

Observatory Mount, steady gales in excess of four hundred kilometres per hour have been known to blow without let for hours. In the wind stakes, thus, the Wheel rules horrifyingly supreme.

But perhaps it is best to let some examples from the history of the mountain speak as evidence.

In 1965, fewer than ten years before Walter Richman's expedition finally made it to the summit, its climbers protected by their high-altitude suits and huts, an expedition was mounted by a French team under the auspices of the legendary Maurice Herzog, who in the 1950s had led the first team to summit a peak above eight thousand metres in the Himalayas. Having lost most of his toes and fingers to frostbite on that occasion, Herzog was not one of the climbers in the 1965 attempt upon the Wheel. But it was his name, and his then position of French Minister for Sport, that helped raise the funds and equipment necessary for a serious attempt upon the mountain.

Although the equipment was as advanced as the times allowed, it was considerably inferior to that available to the later Richman expedition. Nor were the logistics of the Herzog attempt anywhere near as vast as those of Richman's. The French, for instance, did not have the capacity to run electricity and water to their higher camps. For this and other reasons the attempt was most likely destined to fail, even if conditions on the mountain had been friendly.

Conditions were not friendly. In fact, the weather was uniformly bad. Meanwhile, neither the pressure suits nor the habitats functioned as well as hoped, and supply lines up the mountain proved all but impossible to maintain. In the end, the expedition topped out at only twelve thousand two hundred metres. This was the highest that anyone had climbed to that point in history, and indeed it was the first time that climbers had penetrated, if only just, into the stratosphere. Still, it was a disappointing thirteen kilometres short of the summit.

However, just before the expedition was abandoned an occurrence truly cruel and bizarre took place.

ANDREW McGAHAN

At the time, a team of two climbers was pushing up from what was then the highest camp, at twelve thousand metres, in order to establish a new camp above. Roped together, they had been labouring up an eighty-degree pitch for some two hours in fine and sunny conditions. They had just crossed over the twelve-thousand-one-hundred-metre mark, when the leading climber, Henri Paillon, paused to wait as the lower climber, Pierre du Gast, came up on the line Henri had just fixed to the face. As he waited, Henri looked out westward to admire the view.

What he saw made his heart—until that moment safely warmed against the subzero temperature by his suit—freeze.

It was, in Henri's own words, a *'riviere noire du vent'* ('river of black wind'), curling towards the Wheel out of the south-west. It was not actually black, he would later explain, nor even tacitly visible. He sensed it as much through some unknown faculty as through his eyes. Or perhaps, as others have suggested, there was a natural form of the Schlieren optical effect in operation that day in the upper atmosphere, by which the normally invisible fluidic motions of the air became visible. Either way, Henri somehow *knew* that a thousand metres below himself and his fellow climber, a vast swathe of furiously disturbed air was bending out of the south to blast upon the mountain.

He was seeing the jet stream.

Henri stared for maybe a minute in silence, morbidly fascinated. But when the northern edge of the river began to impact the southern flank of the Wheel, kicking up a storm of racing snowdrift, there was no room left for doubt, and his paralysis broke.

The wind was real, and it was going to hit them, there on the exposed face.

He shouted a warning to Pierre, still some ten metres lower down the pitch. They must both retreat at all speed to their camp below. There, a firmly anchored pressurised fibreglass 'tent' was waiting, designed to withstand hurricane force gales. They could hope to ride out the storm inside. But if the jet stream caught them in the open . . .

So they began as rapid a descent as possible. But in their bulky altitude suits progress was torturous, and they had moved no more than twenty metres before the Polar Jet, slipping swiftly northwards across the West Face, began to blast the mountain a kilometre below them. And most of the blast was deflected *upwards*, straight at the hapless climbers.

Along ridges and upon sheer faces, updrafts are common enough, and at times can be fierce, even on lower mountains. But this was a jet stream, of a force beyond anything other climbers had ever experienced. Paillon and du Gast were in a predicament unequalled in history.

They weren't alone on the mountain, of course. The expedition had camps strung all the way down the West Face, three of which were also caught up in the jet stream blast. But the climbers in those camps were safe in their reinforced habitats, the tents themselves further secured in the lee of rock crannies or ledges. Henri and Pierre were trapped on an open face, with no means to secure themselves other than an ice axe each, and the fixed line they had just laid. Against winds that were estimated later at over four hundred kilometres per hour, and perhaps even greater, these frail defences were useless.

Paillon, the higher of the two men, and the only survivor, soon lost sight of his companion in the blinding snowdrift. In any case, he had no time to consider du Gast's fate, he was too busy battling for his own life. The wind became so strong that he was forced to turn and face head *down* the slope, merely to hold his position, his axe embedded as deep as it could go and his body stretched out upwards beyond it, flailing about in the gale like a rag.

How long he held on like this he did not know. But abruptly there came a violent tug on the rope that connected him to du Gast. Du Gast had begun the storm *below* Paillon, but now the line spun Paillon about and dragged him *up* the cliff. For a bewildered moment he scraped upwards across the stony face, the rope dragging him, until by merciful luck he slammed rearwards into the underside of a rocky outcrop and jammed there, immoveable.

It was an agonising position. He was bent backwards, pinned by both the force of the wind and the pull from the rope, his spine so contorted that his face was to the sky. Later it would prove that three of his vertebrae were crushed, and two ribs broken. But it was the sight above him, vanishing and reappearing through the storm of raging spindrift, that struck Paillon with true horror.

Twenty metres overhead, attached to the other end of the rope, suspended in midair by the force of the gale, was the shape of a man.

It was Pierre. Clipped firmly to the line by his harness, the climber soared birdlike in the gale, tugging *upwards* still against the rope, for all that he and his suit together weighed over one hundred and twenty kilograms.

A human kite.

From below Paillon could not see his companion's face through the glass of du Gast's helmet, but from the movements of the man's limbs Paillon was sure that his friend was still alive. Time and again, du Gast's hands seemed to reach determinedly down along the rope to grip it, as if the airborne climber hoped to drag himself hand over hand back down to Earth. But ever and again a ferocious gust would blast his hands up and away, his ice axe, still tethered to his wrist, flailing about uselessly.

The grotesque spectacle went on, Paillon later estimated, for fully a minute at least, with Paillon himself helpless to intervene. Then du Gast's flailing ice axe cut square across the line, severing it clean. His last link to Earth cut, du Gast lofted skywards, borne by the hurricane. He was still alive, Paillon was sure, and still trying desperately to claw his way down the rope, even as it billowed up all around him.

He vanished into the whiteout, and was never seen again.

A week later, the expedition was abandoned. Although Paillon survived the gale, which blew for some hours before subsiding, and although other climbers did establish several higher camps above twelve thousand metres, the heart was gone from the team. Already short of funds, and having already suffered too many casualties from equipment failure, avalanches and storms, du Gast's awful fate was the last straw. The French went home.

That wasn't the end of his story, however. In the years following there was much typically morbid speculation within the climbing community about du Gast's fate. Where had his body ended up? To what place had the jet stream carried him?

Had he, for instance, been hoisted clear away from the slopes of the Wheel to fall to his death out to sea? Or had the wind deposited him somewhere higher up on the mountain? And if so, how high? Fourteen thousand metres, sixteen thousand metres, eighteen thousand metres? Even higher?

More intriguingly, could it be that he *survived* his ride upon the hurricane? Could it be that he found himself, wherever he landed, still fit and able to climb? What if—to let imagination run—he touched down somewhere within range of the Wheel's summit? He was wearing an altitude suit, after all, and though it was an inferior model to those that followed, it would have been capable of life support, for a few hours at least, even at twenty-five thousand metres.

So could it be, could it possibly be, that in fact Pierre du Gast, and not Walter Richman, was the first man to stand atop the Wheel, even if he did not then live to make it back down again?

Does his body—so certain wistful climbers like to speculate—even now lie within the cave upon the Hand of God? After all, Walter Richman alone of mankind has looked into that cave, and to this day has not revealed what he saw there. Indeed, does this explain *why* Richman won't reveal what he saw, because what he saw was proof that he was not after all the first person to stand there?

It's a nice fantasy. But alas, it is, of course, impossible. For one, not even the strongest updrafts caused by a jet stream striking the Wheel have ever been recorded to rise above the eighteen-thousand-metre mark. And even if du Gast was deposited somehow unharmed at that extreme upper limit, he could never have climbed the seven kilometres to the summit in the last few hours left to him.

In any case, he most likely landed somewhat lower down. For although du Gast's body was never discovered, climbers from the Richman expedition did indeed find a tattered fragment of old rope at an altitude of sixteen kilometres, where no rope should be, as no one, before the Richman climbers, had ever been that high before. It was not proof of anything, as it was an ordinary piece of climbing rope that could have been used by a dozen expeditions aside from the French one, and it could have been blown there by some other gale. Still, very probably it was a piece of the fateful line that had tethered du Gast kite-like in the last minutes of his life.

Which would mean that he rose, after the line broke, fully four kilometres in that awful gale. The terror he must have felt during that journey defies description. And most likely he died then upon final impact with the mountain, or from suffocation, if, as seems likely, his suit failed amid the trauma.

Still, he might *not* have died immediately. And while it seems certain he did not gain the summit, if he did survive the deadly ride on the wind, and landed upon the mountain at sixteen kilometres high or thereabouts, then he deserves his place in history. Because, for the few hours remaining to him, he was the highest and loneliest man of his age.

▲

The second account of the storms of the Wheel concerns an expedition that took place thirty years earlier than Herzog's, and which was attempting to climb a different part of the mountain. In fact, it was attempting the other *side* of the mountain: the little known and rarely essayed East Face.

Now, the Wheel's East Face is akin, in mountaineering circles, to the far side of the Moon in the field of astronomy. Oh, everyone has seen photos of the Moon's far side, but only a handful of astronauts have beheld it with their own eyes, and none at all have ever walked there. Likewise, though dozens of cruise ships pass beneath the East Face every year, and in film and photography it is as familiar as the West Face, very few climbers have ever made any serious attempt to scale it.

The reasons are simple enough. The East Face is sheerer than the West, and the outward tilt of its slab formation makes it even more inhospitable to the climber; the eastern shoreline of the Wheel is utterly without harbour to land or house supplies; and higher up there is no convenient large ledge, such as the Plateau on the West Face, where an advanced base camp can be built.

All indisputable facts. But there is also a final, less tangible reason that so few climbers are attracted to the East Face. It feels—there's no other word for—*lonelier* than the West Face. Yes, the West Face is hardly welcoming, but because of the arc shape of the Wheel, with its north and south extremities bending to the west, a climber on the West Face feels somewhat enfolded by the mountain, even if that enfolding can at times feel downright oppressive.

On the East Face, however, a climber feels much more naked and exposed, for on this side the arc of the Wheel curves *away*. Whatever section of the face you happen to be climbing feels like an out-thrust spine upon which you dangle vulnerably. Also, the East Face only gets direct sunlight in the morning, cold and weak, and is in shadow by noon, followed by a long, gloomy descent into evening, a situation loathed by most climbers. The West Face, by comparison, though dark in the morning, basks in glorious sunshine throughout the afternoon and well beyond sea-level sunset.

No wonder then that the East Face is so friendless. Even so, there are always a few daring or foolhardy souls who relish the chance to defy the unpleasant and the difficult, and over the years there have been at least a dozen serious attempts made upon the grim eastern slopes. Most such expeditions failed without achieving much of note, and no one has ever climbed beyond ten thousand metres on the East Face, but one attempt has indeed gained immortality. It did so not for the altitude gained, however, but rather for the fiendish disaster that ended it.

The year was 1934, and a particularly masochistic Italian team was trying to be the first to ascend to serious heights on the East Face. At that time, no one had climbed beyond four thousand metres on the Wheel's eastern side, and the Italians' ambitious target was a prominent spike that protrudes from the centre of the Face at just over seven thousand metres, called ever since, even though the Italians did not reach it, the Roman Pillar.

It was hard going from the beginning. Merely getting the expedition's supplies ashore on that long harbourless coast was an ordeal, and then, even with a base camp established, it was a torturous crawl upwards for the eight-man team on the hostile outward-tilting slabs. Nevertheless, after six weeks, they were nearing five thousand metres. It was then, however, that the weather intervened.

Unlike the West, the East Face is not exposed to the prevailing winds, either at high or low altitudes. Rather, it is a lee face, and so could reasonably be expected to be sheltered from the storms that batter against the west flank of the Wheel.

Things aren't so simple in reality. It's true that the East Face never endures winds like those that howl across the West, but that is not to say that the weather is always calm there. As the prevailing winds (and the jet stream) are compressed and diverted around the north and south shoulders of the Wheel, they find themselves in a 'vacuum' on the east side. And so, as water flowing around a boulder in a river will form whirl-pools on the far side, the great air streams likewise create gigantic eddies across the Wheel's East Face.

Most of the time, these eddies are relatively mild affairs compared to the tempests of the West Face, but they still make for peculiar effects, as the Italians in 1934 witnessed and recorded. Most notable were the cloud formations: long barrels of white cumulus that revolved slowly like enormous breakers at a beach; or strange cap-like clouds that stacked upon themselves like the roofs of Chinese temples, first one stack, then another, diminishing as they extended to the horizon; or clouds that curled in intricate filigree and spirals, like some infinitely expanding Mandelbrot set in the sky.

Meteorologists have names for these various formations: wave clouds, lenticular clouds, rotors, cirrus Kelvin-Helmhotz clouds are just a few. They take shape in the air currents swirling downwind from mountains, but—as ever—in the lee of the Wheel these effects are far greater than anywhere else in the world.

Adding to the weirdness of it, for the Italians, was the fact that from noon onwards, the vast pyramid shadow of the Wheel itself would begin to creep across the ocean, casting the middle airs into shade even though all above was sunlight and blueness. The clouds in those middle airs were thus forever dancing between light and dark, blazing bright and then fading again as they rose or fell or moved east, until late afternoon, when the Wheel's shadow seemed to engulf the whole world, and the eastward view became a netherworld place of grey mists, while far overhead the sky burned red with sunset.

But on the day of the final disaster the Italians were to witness something quite beyond all these ordinary wonders. The cause of it cannot be known for certain, but from the description it would seem that the jet stream was again in play. Most likely the Polar Jet was hitting the West Face, and at such an angle as to ensure that the gale was diverted upwards over the left and right shoulders of the Wheel. This would create roaring, rising torrents of air at either shoulder, which in turn would create a vast zone of turbulence *between* the shoulders, i.e. all across the East Face. And as it was summer, this turbulence would have drawn warm moist air from sea level high into the cold altitudes, creating clouds and precipitation.

But ignorant of such upper atmospheric mechanics (a field still in its infancy in 1934) what the Italians saw was this: on what had otherwise been a calm and warm day, abruptly, early in the afternoon, titanic thunderheads began to form to their left and right. Accompanying this was a far-off high-pitched noise, as of some vast machine whirring at incredible speed. Had it been twenty years later, they may well have compared the sound to a mighty jet engine roaring high on the mountain.

Impressed by the spectacle, but not particularly alarmed, the Italians continued with the day's work. Two of the climbers were near five thousand metres, pushing upwards, with two more in support a thousand metres below. The other four members of the team were resting at Base Camp, two thousand metres lower still.

But as evening approached the storms on either side grew unabated, until they were super-cell size, black burgeoning monsters, each swollen so hugely that between them now a gap of only a few kilometres remained, through which the climbers could still look east to a darkening horizon. Thunder rumbled continually as lightning brooded and flickered within the depths of the great thunderheads.

Then lightning started sizzling *between* the thunderheads, running horizontally from one cloud to the other, cutting directly in front of the astonished Italians. Indeed, because the centre of the East Face was outthrust between the two storms, the great dazzling bolts were passing only dozens of metres away from the cliffs to which the climbers clung. By rights the lightning should surely have been grounding in the mountain itself, but it went only from storm to storm, as if each thundercloud was the electrical opposite to the other, and irresistible.

Thunder battered the face with deafening cracks, shaking rocks loose in perilous falls. The four high climbers had by this point retreated to their tents, one camp at four thousand eight hundred metres, the other at four thousand. But these offered dubious shelter. As the gap between the storms narrowed further, gusts of winds began to buffet them. At first it was only random blasts of air that blew this way or that, savagely plucking at the tents. But then a more sustained gale settled. For the two climbers in the higher camp, the wind was blowing down the face. But for the two climbers in the lower camp, it was blowing upwards.

And finally, the crowning strangeness. From the edge of each thunderhead a sinister protrusion began to extend towards the storm opposite:

a twisting, seething tube of rapidly spinning cloud, fringed with white spray. As the climbers above and below watched in amazement, these two extrusions joined into one, and so formed, writhing between the thunderheads, an impossible thing: a horizontal tornado.

For what followed, we have only the testimony of the climbers at the higher camp. From their point of view, the tornado was below them. It now drew closer to the face, twisting sinuously and whistling demonically all the while, and began to slowly descend, its outer edge rubbing directly against the mountainside as it went, kicking up snow and stones in a fury. Said one of the two climbers later, it was like watching an enormous rotating scrubbing brush running down the face and sweeping it clean.

An apt description, for as it went, the tornado swept the two climbers in the lower camp clear off the mountain. The next day the shredded ruins of their tent, still holding their mangled remains within, would be located floating sadly in the sea.

For the moment, however, all the climbers above knew was that the tornado raged unfettered until at last the two storms, swollen into the stratosphere by now and sending enormous shrouds east across the heavens, grew fat enough to swallow the vortex and join together as one. The East Face was then engulfed in darkness, rain and hail.

The two surviving climbers clung on through a miserable night. And even when the storm faded and dawn at last came, they still faced a perilous descent, for the storm had blown away all intermediate camps and fixed lines. Indeed, if not for the other four climbers at Base Camp, who ascended quickly to help, the two might indeed have perished.

But in any case, once everyone was safely down, and the two dead bodies recovered, there was no question of beginning the campaign all over again. The six survivors packed up their gear, radioed for their ship and retreated in mourning.

And to this day, the two dead climbers remain the only fatalities ever recorded of a tornado that came at its victims sideways.

▲

The final of these three tales of wind and weirdness upon the Wheel does not in fact take place upon the mountain itself, but rather upon its accompanying lesser peak, Observatory Mount—the Child of the Wheel, as it is sometimes called. But if Observatory Mount is indeed the Wheel's offspring, then, as the following account will demonstrate, the larger mountain is a punishing parent.

Observatory Mount was first climbed in 1895. Although sheer sided and impressive to behold, it has never been considered worse than a moderate ascent for experienced mountaineers. By 1950, the year in which this event took place, it had been climbed dozens of times. Indeed, the island from which the Mount rises had been permanently inhabited since the early 1900s, when a lighthouse and keepers' huts were constructed at what is now the port and township of Base. And even before then, whaling stations had provided a seasonal population.

Still, in 1950, there were as yet no permanent structures on the Mount's summit. This was about to change, however, and the driving force was the Australian Bureau of Meteorology. Planners at the Bureau had decided that it was time to install a manned weather station atop the Mount, for they had begun to appreciate just how unique the Wheel and its environs were in meteorological terms, but were limited in their understanding by the poor data currently being collected there.

A construction team was assigned and arrived on Theodolite Isle in December. It consisted of thirty men. Half of them were climbers, to get the team to the top of the Mount, the rest were carpenters and weather specialists, to build the actual station.

A month was spent in fixing a route up the Mount, complete with steel guide lines and ladders and stairways, so that even a novice climber could ascend without difficulty. A further two month's work saw a large accommodation hut and a smaller weather hut nearing completion on the summit. (For historians, the larger hut was placed roughly where the

Terrace Pool of Walter Richman's residence would later be sited, while the weather hut, and the recording instruments, were positioned higher up on the knob that Richman's Cottage would subsequently occupy.)

Both structures were built only of timber, but as stoutly as possible, and with hipped roofs to withstand gales, for extreme winds across the summit had already been reported by earlier climbers. Similarly designed huts had been used in Australia's Antarctic territory, at Mawson's camp at Cape Denison, for instance, the buildings of which by then had lasted several decades against temperatures of minus forty degrees Celsius and gales up to three hundred kilometres per hour.

But, with the project all but complete, several days of squally weather, atypical for late summer, descended, during which strong winds battered the Mount, rendering the ascent dangerous. Work was postponed, and everyone except for three men retreated from the summit. The remaining three bunkered down in the accommodation hut to see out the storm and keep any damage in check. They had supplies enough and plenty of oil for heating, so did not feel themselves in any great danger.

On the fourth night of the unsettled weather, however, the Polar Jet swung out of the south, hit the higher ramparts of the Wheel, and came ravaging down upon the Mount in full force.

Not that the men on the summit knew that this was what was happening. In 1950, jet streams were not yet fully understood, and the interaction between them and the Wheel even less so. All they knew for certain was that the blustery conditions worsened abruptly in the darkness from an inconvenience to something more terrifying than any of them had ever known.

Senior carpenter Raymond Jones, of Launceston, Tasmania, was one of the three, and later recorded an oral account of the event.

It'd been windy up until then, sure enough, but that shack had kept us snug and warm all through, no worries. We were all asleep when things turned bad, about two a.m. The first I knew of it I thought it must be an earthquake, the hut was slamming back and forth like the ground under it was shaking. But then I got my head around the incredible noise from outside—not an earthquake, it was the wind, roaring away like a tidal wave collapsing or something.

We all piled out of bed, amazed at how much the shack was groaning and shuddering with every gust. Up until then, even the strongest blow hadn't bothered it—we built that thing solid—but now it was flexing like those oak posts were just pine sticks. God knows what the wind strength was. Charlie wanted to go up to the weather shack and look at the anemometer—we'd installed it only a week before—but I put paid to that. No one was going outside, no one was even going to try to open the door, even though it was on the lee side. It sounded goddamn terrible out there.

We waited and it got worse and worse. I've never heard anything like that awful wind. It scaled up from a roar to a banshee scream to a . . . well, I know people always use freight trains when they talk about winds in hurricanes and the like, and they're right, but it's not just any freight train. Imagine the biggest, nastiest diesel engine you ever thought of, out of control and running wild down a hill at a hundred miles an hour, screaming straight at you, and the driver has got the air horn blasting as loud as it can go, and you're just standing on the rails only an instant from getting hit—that's what the sound is like, not just loud, but evil and metallic somehow, like iron screaming, and it's terrifying because you could swear you're going be killed right now, and then right now, and then right now . . .

Anyway, after maybe an hour we knew the shack wasn't going to last, the roof was jittering all around and the joists were cracking. We would've been goners if we'd been in there when it went. But of course we had a last resort we could use. It was a natural feature in the summit, a cavity in the rock that was just nicely shaped to form a kind of basement. We'd built the shack right over it, even snugged the shack down into the hole a little for security, and then built a trapdoor into the floor. So we dropped down there now. It was a pretty rough and ready space down there, just naked stone, it was only ever meant for storage, but it would give us shelter if the shack above went.

And went it did! We'd only been down there ten minutes when the freight train up above turned into ten freight trains, all with demon opera singers on board, shrieking at the top of their lungs—and with a crash the whole hut ripped away above us, roof, walls, even half the floor. Some of the stuff in the cellar went flying up too, and we might have gone with it, if we hadn't been under the part of the floor that held. Also, we had jammed ourselves into the narrowest part of the cavity, a crevice really, at that end of the basement.

So now there it was, the night and the wind right above us, all open. If you can imagine what it would be like looking into the mouth of some black howling hell just a foot or two over your head, then you might get an idea of it. Charlie and Mike, they were deeper into the crevice than me, under an overhang—we were all squeezed in as tight as we could go—so it was really only me who could see up into the throat of it.

Christ I was scared. I could feel myself being sucked upwards all the time, not by the wind exactly, but by some kind of weird vacuum effect—my ears were popping like crazy from the low pressure.

I would've gone too, if it hadn't been for Charlie and Mike hanging on to my belt for dear life. I had bruises around my gut for weeks afterwards, and back in the crevice the other two got so battered about against the rock walls that they ended up all bloody. And though we were all shouting and screaming at each other the whole time, I don't remember hearing a single world. In amongst all that insane din, it was as if we'd all gone deaf and dumb at the same time.

It felt like we held on for years like that, but when the blackness above began to turn grey we knew that dawn was coming and that it'd actually only been about three hours. And thank god the wind began to ease off about then too. It was like . . . it was like a wind that bad needed darkness to blow, and that it was being driven away by day. I dunno, but either way, by full light it was over. Things were still windy, but the great bloody freight train was gone.

We climbed up, all of us in shock and still not hearing quite right, to see what we might see. There wasn't a trace left of the two huts, other than the holes we'd drilled as foundations—no other sign that anything had ever been there. The whole summit was swept clean, even the rock looked like it had been sandblasted to bleeding. But maybe not. I was a bit shook up, and nothing looked right to me really.

Anyway, there we sat, all trembling and dazed and terrified that any minute the wind might come back, and there we were still when the other blokes climbed up from below to rescue us. The wind hadn't hit down there, but they'd heard the dreadful din coming from the summit all night, so they came up first thing.

Never been so glad to see other faces.

Other than the superficial injuries mentioned, the three men survived without any lasting harm, but as noted in the account the weather station had been obliterated. It was another two years before a second station was built, and this time the huts were bunkers, fashioned of reinforced concrete and excavated into the solid rock for further protection. This second station stood for the next fifty years, withstanding several similar windstorms in that time, and recording the world record wind gust along the way.

It was only when Walter Richman began the construction of his residence atop the peak that the old bunkers were finally demolished—the steel guide lines and ladders and stairways removed to prevent anyone climbing the mount ever again, and the crevice in which Ray Jones and his two companions had sheltered from the demon gale enlarged fifty times over to form a swimming pool.

10

ON THE BRINK

IN SEARCH OF THEIR CUP of tea, Rita and Clara climbed without talking from the Museum up to the Entrance Hall. When they reached the top of the stairs, however, they found they were not alone—voices were echoing and a mass of feet tramping. The two women had to stand back a moment as a group of about a dozen men clad in overalls and black T-shirts trooped by towards the foyer at the Hall's furthest end. The men were all heavily loaded with bags and boxes, or pushing large silver crates along on trolleys, the crates bearing the logo 'Skyfire Pyrotechnics.'

At their rear came the house manager, Bradley, as well as Eugene and Kennedy, the latter with one ear to a walkie-talkie as he strode along.

'Everything all right?' Clara enquired.

The security chief rolled an eye minimally. 'Log jam getting everyone down to Base. This is the second load of the fireworks boys—the first lot went down in the service lift no trouble, and the lift came back up fine, but now there's a glitch, something or other is out of alignment, so the engineers down at Base are holding the elevator up here while they check the telemetry. It's taking forever, so meanwhile I'm sending this lot down in the main lift.'

Clara glanced ironically at Bradley. 'Don't the house protocols insist that the main elevator is only for Mr Richman and his guests, and that all staff or visiting workers are to use only the service lift?'

'They so insist indeed,' replied the house manager, with an austere look to Kennedy.

'He already told me,' growled the security chief. 'But these guys have a ship waiting in the harbour that's already overdue; it was supposed to be gone by noon. So fuck the protocols. Bradley can ride down with them if he's so worried the marble floor might get scuffed, heaven fucking forfend.'

'I'm riding down too,' grinned Eugene. 'I've been waiting an hour up here; I was supposed to be down at the mainframe straight after lunch.'

Kennedy shook his head ill-temperedly. 'He's not the only one. We should've had the whole change of shift done an hour back, but everyone is stuck because of the service elevator. If it's not fixed soon I'll be sending the bloody cleaners and dishwashers down on the main lift too, and to hell with the silk carpets and the velvet on the couches.' And with that, he and Eugene and the house manager moved off, Kennedy's walkie-talkie crackling all the while.

Rita and Clara watched them go a moment, then continued in the opposite direction. 'Is that common?' Rita asked. 'The lift breaking down, I mean?'

'It's happened once or twice. But thankfully never both lifts at once.'

Rita rubbed a hand against her brow, the hangover headache, or whatever it was, getting worse by the minute. 'If they did both go, there'd be no way down but those stairs you talked about, right?'

'Well, it wouldn't come to that even then. If both lifts failed the next option would be a helicopter ride down, from the helipad. There's always a chopper on standby down at Base. It's all fail-safe. So the stairs would be very much a last resort, I'd say.'

Jesus. A helicopter ride or a climb down two kilometres of stairs. Rita didn't fancy the thought of either. But she said no more.

They came to the Atrium and climbed the small spiral staircase to reach the Conservatory. Through the glass walls and ceiling, the wide world swung into view.

Rita squinted painfully at the brightness. The dull covering of cloud from the morning had now largely broken up. Westward, a mid-level bank still lingered, riven by great shafts of sunlight that cast shining patterns on the sea, but overhead the sky was clear apart from a few fleeting cumulus, and to the east the Wheel reared in all its immensity, naked of any cloudy ornament, brutal in the sunlight.

'I'll order the tea,' said Clara, making for the bar. It was unstaffed at this mid-afternoon hour, but a house phone sat on the counter.

Rita, left to herself, turned fully to the Wheel, determined to face the worst, opening herself to it—could she truly feel an emanation there, radiating from the stone and the ice? Or was she being foolish? But what she sensed was only confusing. There was nothing coherent, no *presence,* if that's truly what she was looking for. But the tension was still there, unfocussed, below any threshold of sight or hearing or sixth sense, but still grating, still nagging at her like fingernails dragging on a blackboard.

She suddenly remembered the Black Band the major-domo had mentioned, the landmark that climbers had set as their target. It was curious, Rita thought, that she hadn't noticed it herself already. She searched for it now, figuring that at about ten thousand metres high it should lie roughly between a third and half of the way up the mountain. Though in truth from this perspective, with the face of Wheel tilting away from her, it was hard to judge exactly.

She let her gaze rise slowly, starting from the lower slopes of the great mountain, as a climber would, below the snowline even, where the smattering of vegetation, stunted trees and grasses, gave the face a bluish hue. This gave way to the vast snowfields of the lower heights; unimaginable tonnes of snow packed thickly all across the forty-five-kilometre arc of the Wheel, dazzling white in the clear air. Above that came the broad horizontal fracture across the face that formed the great ledge known as the Plateau, at five thousand metres. And above that more snowfields, then finally the rockier, even sheerer cliffs of the middle face, where ice clung instead of snow, and where, in couloirs and plunging valleys, huge glaciers hung precipitously.

But upwards still travelled her gaze, leaping in instants vertical miles that it would take a climber days to master. At last, where the snow and ice began to thin towards the barer upper half of the mountain, there it was. Not a *black* band, but a greyish strip that ran level across the face, the stone notably duller than the ochre and red to be found elsewhere. By Clara's description the band was nearly a kilometre thick, but from so far below it looked narrow, a line drawn by some gigantic pen, like a border. And so it was, for in truth it marked the divide between the habitable lower part of the mountain, and the airless, inhuman part that reared above, clear into the stratosphere.

And god, even this lesser landmark, not even halfway up the Wheel, seemed to Rita impossibly high and remote, now that she knew that men had indeed climbed so high up with scarcely any aid at all, no pressure suits, but only flimsy oxygen masks. She felt dizzy just contemplating it, and to steady the sudden nausea took a seat at a table.

At the bar, the major-domo (who had climbed to that distant Black Band, Rita reminded herself in wonder, at the price of a finger and the tip of a nose, and the loss of some unknown part of her feet) put down the phone, frowning.

'That's odd,' Clara said, 'no one in the kitchen is answering.' She peered over the counter. 'But actually, all the fixings to make tea are back here anyway. Shall I go ahead and boil the kettle?'

'If you want,' Rita answered faintly. 'But really, just a glass of water would be fine.'

But the major-domo was now among the cupboards. 'Here we go. Hmm.' She held up a small black glass jar. 'Yellow Gold Buds tea. Not too extravagant for your tastes, I hope?'

Rita didn't know what this meant—was Yellow Gold Buds an expensive brand? She only shook her head, the ache behind her eyes lancing more sharply than ever. What was wrong with her? She had never had an attack like this before, not even in the old days. In the old days she had always known where the sensations, the bad vibes if you will, were coming from, and also what they meant. But now she was only bewildered, distracted unbearably.

As Clara attended without fuss to the tea, Rita rubbed her temples hopelessly, staring at the floor like a victim of seasickness. When she dared a glance up at the Wheel again, vertigo leapt at her, so that it felt the entire mass of the mountain was toppling forwards, and she had to look away again quickly.

'Here we go,' said the major-domo at last, placing a steaming pot and cups upon the table, accompanied by milk and sugar.

At the same moment, Kennedy appeared at the top of the stairs, his walkie-talkie still in hand. 'Tea? Haven't you got any damn coffee?'

Clara ignored this, filling cups. 'Got everyone down?' she asked the security chief.

'The fireworks crew, yes, but there's still the change of shift staff—they're all milling around at the service lift like a herd of cattle.'

'Ah. Is that why I couldn't get an answer from the kitchen? I did wonder.'

'It's not just the kitchen staff, it's cleaning and maintenance too, and my own boys—'

He broke off as his walkie-talkie squawked, and for the next minute engaged in an esoteric conversation with the distorted voice on the other end. A conclusion was reached, after which he put the device in his pocket with a sigh.

'That's it, then. They just got the service lift working at last, and of course now everyone wants down at once. Problem is protocol says you don't go down until your replacement has come up, just to be sure every station is always tended. But it's a fifteen-minute wait for the lift to go down and come up again, and it turns out some of the staff are starting annual leave today and are supposed to go out on the same ship with the fireworks crew, and it absolutely has to get going or else

. . . so what the hell, I've sent them *all* down. I think we can survive a quarter hour up here without cleaners and kitchen hands.'

Clara nodded smoothly. 'Well, do you want some of this tea or not?'

The security chief sank into a seat. 'It's not that gold-plated shit again, is it?'

'Yes, I'm afraid that's all I can find.'

'Jesus. Fine then.'

A third cup was produced. For a few moments the three of them sipped on the tea, the two staff members chatting about in-house topics. Rita paid little attention. The hot liquid in her cup had no taste (was it really gold-plated?) and her eyes were drawn repeatedly to the sky and the Wheel, searching. It felt to her as if thunder was rumbling constantly just beneath her hearing—or was it just the throbbing in her head? The ache was a migraine now, all-encompassing, body and mind.

Finally, Kennedy's walkie-talkie rasped a few words, and he rose. 'That's everyone down. I'd best go and meet the crew coming up. Thanks for the tea.' He was at the top of the stairs when he paused again. 'You know, if that fool Eugene was here, he'd love this, because right this second, with the firework teams gone, and with both staff shifts down at Base, there're only six people in the entire Observatory right now. Us three here, Kushal and Madelaine, and of course Richman himself. I don't think there've ever been so few as that at any moment since I started here.'

And he was gone.

'The place does feel empty,' Clara remarked, sipping the last of her tea.

Empty. *Empty.* The word rolled about Rita's scattered mind, but it wasn't the right term; there was a better one; not empty; not empty . . . but *vulnerable.*

She blinked. Now why did she think that? Vulnerable to what? The headache was making her paranoid. But the feeling wouldn't go away.

Clara was gathering up the cups. 'What did you think of the tea? Supposedly this stuff was once served only to Chinese emperors.

Apparently it's harvested by hand with golden scissors on a single day on a single mountaintop, and then the leaves are genuinely dipped in gold. It's meant to be for flavour and good health, they claim, not just to be outrageously pretentious. But I don't know. All I do know is that this single pot would cost you a hundred dollars in a restaurant. And yet it's the only tea Mr Richman drinks . . .'

It was all so much prattle to Rita, with her aching nausea. She couldn't care less about the tea. Kennedy's statement was still resonating, like a hateful song replaying in her head. *Only six people . . . I don't think there've ever been so few . . .*

And suddenly Rita had it; suddenly she made the connection between the words and her unease. Of course, how could she have been so dense? She had written an entire book about this; she had believed it once, implicitly. It was all about the numbers. Presences were affected by the proximity of human minds, especially by *many* human minds. A crowd made them weak, debilitated, helpless. But when there were *fewer* minds about, then presences could . . .

Oh no.

She started from her seat, but it was already too late. With an almost audible twang, the pressure behind her eyes snapped, and she was free of pain, free of the sense of foreboding and suspense. Because the waiting was over, the *preparation* was over.

'We have to get out,' she gasped aloud.

Clara stared at her in amazement.

Then the long disaster began.

11

THE SMALLEST OF THE BIG

**Extract from *The Cloven Sky—A History*,
Roger Fitzgerald, 1991**

The Wheel is the most unusual mountain in the world. The highest, yes, being well over twice the height of Mount Everest, the next in line. But it is also singular in other properties. It is, for instance, far steeper, far sheerer, than any other comparable mountain.

Improbably sheer, in fact.

Now, measuring the steepness of any mountain is a complicated business, as generally mountains do not rise from base to peak with a regular slope, the way a pyramid does. Nor is it always possible to define exactly where the base of a mountain is, if for instance it exists as part of a complicated range or massif, or if it sits atop a much vaster plateau.

But by any measure, the Wheel is extraordinary. Mountains like Everest and K2, say, while possessing sheer and awesome faces on some approaches, can, on other routes, be virtually walked up, following inclines that average as little as thirty degrees. (This is steeper than it might sound, by the way. Thirty degrees—zero degrees being flat, and ninety degrees being vertical—is a severe slope. It's walkable, but not easily. And by the time you reach forty-five degrees, you'll be scrambling on hands and knees.)

Of course, no one just walks up Everest or K2, because whatever the slope, there's the cold and the thin air of high altitude to contend with, not to mention ice falls and avalanches, all of which make the upper

284

reaches of such mountains difficult and deadly. Still, the *average* slope of most of the great mountains in the world, combining their sheerer cliffs with their gentler inclines, comes in at around fifty or sixty per cent. Yes, there are vertical faces to be found on these mountains, defying even the best climbers, but such faces seldom rise more than a few hundred metres, and the biggest in the world (away from the Wheel) are no more than a thousand metres or so high.

Now consider the Wheel. It has just two faces, the East and the West, divided by a single central ridge that rises in a roughly north–south line. We'll discuss the central ridge later, as climbers rarely venture there. It is the two faces that matter.

They are *astoundingly* steep.

The sheerest is the East Face. From the waterline to the summit, it climbs twenty-five kilometres vertically in only six kilometres of horizontal distance, an average slope of seventy-seven degrees. The West Face (which is the most commonly climbed) is only slightly gentler, rising to the same height over seven kilometres, and so checking in at about seventy-five degrees.

Remember, these are *averages*. There are, of course, steeper and gentler sections as a climber progresses. But as an average, a slope of seventy-five degrees and over signifies, in practical terms, a single cliff twenty-five kilometres high.

Such a thing is barely comprehensible, given our knowledge of rock and its weight-bearing capacity. In theory, no known rock is really strong enough to maintain integrity in such a face. Put simply, the stone at the bottom of a cliff so high and steep should be crushed by the appalling weight of the rock above, and bit by bit the whole face should have collapsed an age ago. The fact the Wheel has not collapsed (at least not entirely and not yet) is self-evident, but we'll get to the theories as to why that is in a moment.

Meanwhile, what of the Wheel's central ridge? Why *don't* climbers venture there, when it is patently less steep than either of the faces?

Indeed, following from the northern tip of the mountain to the summit (the North Ridge, as it is known) the horizontal distance is some twenty-one kilometres, a mere fifty-one-degree average slope. From the southern end (the South Ridge) it is twenty-four kilometres horizontally, which gives an average slope of forty-seven degrees, even more eminently climbable.

The answer lies in that term *average* again. For the North and South ridges do not ascend in a smooth diagonal. They are, in fact, fantastically jagged, with pillars and peaks leaping up continually, riven by great rifts in between. To ascend one of these ridgelines therefore is to be forever climbing and descending a progression of smaller faces, each of which is sheer. Indeed, it has been calculated that to reach the summit via either ridge would involve twice as much hard climbing as going by either of the faces.

Of course, in practice, almost all expeditions have attempted just one route, and that is a direct line up the West Face. Why the West? Well, there are several reasons, but the one of interest to us here has to do with the unlikely matter of *slabs*.

What on earth—asks the non-climber—are slabs? And how do they affect a mountain?

Well, begin by imagining a pyramid again, a stepped pyramid, four-sided. Now, to walk to the top of the pyramid up any of its sides would take exactly the same amount of effort and skill, yes?

But now imagine that the pyramid has been tilted twenty degrees to one side—say, to the east side. This time, when you try to walk up the pyramid, each face will be different to ascend. The north and south faces will still be okay to climb, although it will feel a little strange, as each step will be tilted twenty degrees to the left or right. Even the west face will still be climbable, as each step will tilt twenty degrees *inwards*, towards the face, so that even if you stumble, you'll only fall forwards against the next step.

But the east face will have become very uncomfortable to walk up, for now each step tilts twenty degrees *away* from the face, so that any slip or misstep will tip you outwards and backwards, perhaps even toppling you clean off the pyramid.

So it is with mountains sometimes, if not quite as obvious as the example just given. As a face ascends in great pitches and slabs of stone, the ledges that are formed may have a predominate slope one way or the other. Sometimes they lean *into* the face, sometimes they lean *away* from the face. Inward-tilting slabs, and the V-shaped ledges they form, are friendly to climbers, as they provide secure resting places. Outward-tilting slabs, with their upside-down V overhangs, are more exposed and more dangerous.

So it is with the Wheel. The West Face is an inward-tilting face, while the East Face tilts out. But how did this come about? How can a mountain as immense as the Wheel *tilt* at all? And to return to the earlier question, how does this great pile of rock even hold together, when the laws of geology suggest it should long ago have fallen apart?

The answers to both questions are linked to the past. And to begin the explanation, a crucial distinction must first be made: in geological terms, the Wheel, the biggest and tallest mountain the planet has ever known, is not, in fact, really very big at all.

What was that?

Not very big?

It's true. Indeed, the Wheel, far from being big, is the very *smallest* of its geological brethren.

Okay, what's that supposed to mean? Who or what are these brethren I'm talking about?

Well, it's *not* other mountains.

Indeed, the Wheel is not a mountain at all in the sense that other mountains are. All other mountains in the world owe their existence either to volcanic activity, or to the action of tectonic plates. Tectonic plates are the vast, continent-sized slabs of the Earth's crust that, in their slow creep and thrust, constantly reshape the surface of our planet. As these monsters shove against each other, their edges rear up in wrinkles that we call *mountain ranges*.

But the Wheel is not merely the upraised edge of one tectonic plate or another. It is not a wrinkle. It is itself an *entire* plate, upended.

A tiny plate, albeit. Most tectonic plates are much, much bigger. There are seven so-called major plates—the Pacific Plate, the Indo–Australia Plate, the Antarctic Plate, and so on—and each of them is thousands of kilometres wide or long. Then there are about ten minor plates scattered between the larger ones, and finally a dozen or so micro plates squeezed between yet again. But even those plates labelled as micro are usually still pretty big, at least several hundred kilometres from side to side.

But the Wheel plate—in its original horizontal form—is thought to have been only about sixty kilometres across. Just *sixty*. It was the merest flake of a thing, floating light as a leaf upon the hot magma underbelly that is the world's innards.

This was about two hundred million years ago. At the time, the Wheel plate formed part of the ocean floor somewhere to the south of modern-day Australia. And, of course, it was anything but a leaf. Sixty kilometres wide and roughly circular in shape, it was also about sixteen kilometres thick (average for tectonic plates) and, made of the most common stone in the world, a tough, dense basalt, it would have weighed billions of tonnes.

But the Wheel was also positioned between two much vaster plates, the mighty Indo-Australian Plate, and the equally mighty Antarctic Plate, each of them about sixty million square kilometres in size, dwarfing the Wheel by a factor of tens of thousands. Nor were these two great plates standing still; both were in motion, which made for a complicated life for the Wheel, caught in the middle.

At least the two bigger plates were not butting heads directly, which would have simply crushed the Wheel to nothing in between. Instead, the Antarctic Plate was marching eastwards across the bottom of the Indo-Australian Plate, while the Indo-Australian was in fact pulling away from the Antarctic to head north. This made for relative calm along most of the boundary, but the Wheel was trapped in an odd north–south kink between the plates, and *there* the forces involved were much more abrasive, as unimaginable weights of rock jammed and contorted awkwardly against other unimaginable weights of rock.

For many millions of years, the Wheel was simply bruised and spun about by all this shifting and straining. But about seventy million years ago (in fact, at the same time that the Himalayas were starting to rise, caused by the Indo-Australian Plate, far away at its northern rim, beginning to crash violently into the Eurasian Plate), by outlandish chance something different happened, something that has never happened anywhere else on Earth.

The Wheel *caught* on underlying and overlaying corners of the Indo-Australian and Antarctic plates, and, as the bigger formations kept pushing by one another, the tiny flake began to rotate on its vertical, rather than horizontal, axis. Its western edge dipped down, its eastern edge reared up.

It was not an instantaneous process, of course. It took millions of years, but gradually the entire Wheel plate was tipped onto its side, to become in essence an upright disk, a giant coin standing on its rim, sixty kilometres in diameter and sixteen kilometres thick.

Or, as it could be called, a *wheel*. (Though of course the mountain was given its strange name for entirely different historical reasons.)

But sixty kilometres? Was the newly raised Wheel really ever that high?

No. Nowhere near that. For a start, the lower edge of the plate had sunk into the underlying mantle even as the upper edge rose, so that only one side of the disk was reared upwards—reaching at best thirty kilometres high. But that was thirty kilometres above the *ocean floor*, not above sea level. As the Southern Ocean was then and still is now about four thousand metres deep, that leaves an ancient height for the Wheel of twenty-six kilometres at the utmost, before time and erosion began their work.

Nor did the great disc rise cleanly and in one piece; the stresses involved were literally Earth-shattering, and great fragments of the Wheel broke away, or sheared off in cataclysmic avalanches, as the inexorable rotation continued. This fact would be more obvious if the ocean around the

Wheel did not hide the vast litter of rock debris that lies about the great mountain's feet, as well as drowning the great chasms that the rotation tore open here and there.

(The only such piece of debris visible above sea level today is, of course, Theodolite Isle. It is thought to be a particularly large fragment of the plate that broke off quite early in the rotation process, then itself bizarrely upthrust.)

In the end, of the ancient plate that began its life sixty kilometres across and sixteen thick, all that remains today is an upraised rim that lofts twenty-five kilometres above sea level, and which extends forty-five kilometres north to south, and twelve kilometres east to west. And the plate is not 'flat' anymore. The torsion acted upon it by the Indo-Australian and Antarctic giants *bent* the north and south ends of the Wheel in a westward direction, resulting in the familiar arc the mountain describes today.

Nor did the plate ever become entirely upright. It was left with a lean to the east at an angle of about seven degrees. Hence the inward- and outward-tilting slabs of the West and East faces.

So that's one puzzle solved.

This entire process is thought to have taken about twenty million years, after which . . . well, nothing much. After so much upheaval, the Wheel was finally released by the grip that had upended it, and in the fifty million years since has been left in relative peace. The two bigger plates continue their movements, but the Wheel, now lubricated by the ring of its own debris, has slid smoothly between them. Which is not to say that the region is utterly stable. There is evidence of periodic earthquake activity through the millennia. But in the modern era there have been amazingly few tremors detected, and those only minor.

But still, how do those towering cliffs of basalt endure? Even without earthquakes, they should, as mentioned, be crumbling under their own weight. While basalt is indeed considered a hard, enduring rock, other rocks like granite are stronger, and yet no granite monolith has ever risen beyond a few thousand metres in height without eventually collapsing. How does the Wheel manage it?

Well, it's all about the *type* of basalt. Basalt, an igneous rock, is typically made up largely of minerals like quartz and feldspar, combined with a smaller mix of other minerals such as iron and titanium. Its actual hardness will rely much on the precise ratios of these various minerals within the rock.

Geologists have thus studied the basalt of the Wheel with interest. Intriguingly, they have discovered unusually high ratios of titanium there, but more importantly they have detected the trace presence of a very rare mineral that is normally only found deep within the Earth, called eclogite.

Eclogite, a supremely dense and tough mineral, not unlike diamond, is a metamorphic variant of basalt that forms under the immense pressures of the inner mantle, say fifty kilometres deep and more. It is rarely brought to the surface, and when it is, freed of the underworld pressures, it usually reverts to other basaltic forms. Yet minute flecks of the mineral pervade the basalt of the Wheel.

How this can be is not quite known, but somehow, in the torturous process by which the Wheel was created, a profuse and stable form of eclogite managed to suffuse the plate. It's thought that this is part of the explanation as to how the Wheel remains so sheer. In short, the very immensity of the mountain's own weight has helped to create a high-pressure mineral within the stone that in return is tough enough to bear the weight that created it.

A bizarrely circular process.

Or, a wheel within the Wheel.

And a final note. Eclogite in its pure form is crimson or pink in colour. While its presence in the Wheel basalt is minimal, for those seeking the secret behind the unusual red hue of the mountain's stone, here too perhaps—in the unprecedented fury of the Wheel's formation—lies the answer.

12

THE RED WHEEL

THE VIBRATION CAME WITH A rush of rumbling and buzzing and shaking underfoot all at once. Rita's first thought was that some vast piece of machinery—maybe one of the lift winch mechanisms—was running amok somewhere within the Mount.

But then Clara was up out of her chair and shouting, 'Earthquake!'

She dragged Rita away, both of them reeling across a solid floor that, impossibly, was leaping and shuddering and making their knees buckle. Their destination turned out to be the airlock doors leading out to the Terrace—the major-domo threw the inner door open, and then crouched under the metal lintel, pulling Rita down beside her as the quake clattered on, a steam engine tearing itself apart.

Then it was done. The mad concussions ceased abruptly and the floor became fixed stone once more. Silence fell, aside from a few final tinkles and clangs from the bar. The teapot and the cups had all fallen off and smashed on the floor.

Rita and Clara huddled a moment longer, then straightened slowly, staring around.

'Just a tremor, I think,' said Clara, a little shakily. They were cautiously venturing out from the doorway. 'I don't see any major damage.'

Nor could Rita. In the bar, several glasses and bottles of wine had fallen from the shelves and smashed, but throughout the rest of the

Conservatory all the tables and chairs remained upright, and none of the hundreds of glass panels that made up the walls and the ceiling had fallen or shattered, or even cracked. Also, the lights were still on.

'Even so,' said the major-domo, 'I think we should get out from under this roof for the next few minutes, in case there are bigger aftershocks.'

Rita nodded. They passed back through the airlock, along the way seizing two of the coats that hung on the adjacent rack.

Outside the cold was like a tonic, the slap of it on Rita's face settling her jangled nerves. But she already felt better than she had all day—exhilarated, relieved, the hangover banished at a stroke, and with it the nagging toothache of foreboding that had bothered her since waking. Was that what it had been all along? Had she merely been sensing, subconsciously, the build-up of the stresses within the earth?

'Do you get quakes often here?' she asked. They had walked out to the centre of the Terrace, staring about in search of any damage, but other than some strange ripples still washing back and forth on the surface of the swimming pool, there was no visible evidence of the tremor at all.

'No,' said the major-domo. 'In fact, there's a seismic monitoring station down at Base—there has been since the military days—and its records show that this whole zone is actually remarkably stable, given that it's a plate boundary. I know because Mr Richman had structural engineers look into it before construction began. Of course, the Observatory was still built to the highest quake-proof standards. You'd be safe here even against a big tremor.'

Rita supposed it was true. Certainly, the stone beneath her feet felt secure once more, although the memory of the floor leaping under her like a skittish living thing was difficult to shake.

Clara had pulled her phone from her pocket. 'It really all looks fine up here. But it might have been worse down at Base. I'll check with Eugene, seeing as he just went down there.'

Rita gazed away to the Wheel while Clara dialled. The mountain loomed amazingly vivid and close out here in the cold air, gigantic beyond conception as it rose away to the edge of space. But for once she found nothing oppressive in its size, nothing ominous. Her mood was too buoyant. Yes, she had been full of dread before the quake struck, convinced of all sorts of perils. But now she felt only light and ener- gised, as if she had just escaped an unpleasant duty, or avoided some deeper danger, with no more than a minor shake and scare.

Or had she? A faint voice of warning sounded somewhere inside her. Was her sense of relief a little madcap, foolhardy even, the oblivious joy of some small creature that eludes the swooping hawk, and yet does not see the plunging eagle?

There was a mist on the Wheel.

She blinked, stared again. No, she wasn't imagining it. All across the snowy regions of the great mountain a diaphanous veil sparkled, blurring the icy cliffs and the hanging glaciers. Rita understood sud- denly. It must be a great flurry of snow and ice shaken loose from the mountainside by the earthquake, like glittering dust.

It was beautiful.

'And no one is hurt or anything?' the major-domo was saying into the phone, presumably to Eugene down at the bottom of the Mount. 'Good, good. Well, I'd say we dodged a—'

A great rippling, crackling sound suddenly washed across the Terrace. It was like a rapid series of detonations, loud, but coming from faraway and softened by the distance. For a moment Rita could only think that there must have been fireworks left unexploded from last night, and in some weird delayed effect, they had been set off by the quake.

But there were no fireworks. The sounds—the crackling was going on and on—was coming across ten kilometres of air, from the Wheel.

'Jesus,' exclaimed the major-domo, both into the phone and to Rita. 'What *is* that?'

Rita was staring. Something was happening on the mountain, high up on the centre of the face, near the top of the snowpack. The mist there appeared to be in motion, a more coherent mass now, more solid, creeping slowly down the sheer slope. And the faraway crackling had merged into a dull roar.

Except—

It wasn't mist that was falling.

'Shit,' breathed the major-domo, her right hand, holding the phone, dropping to her side.

It wasn't mist, it was the mountainside itself. All across a huge section of the central face—Rita couldn't begin to guess how big a section, but it must be kilometres wide—the very bedrock of the Wheel seemed to be slumping, sliding and falling, churning up great dirty-white clouds of debris. From this distance the immense mass seemed to inch its way downwards, but the roaring that filled the air ever more loudly gave lie to that apparent slowness.

'Avalanche,' said Clara softly.

Rita understood at last. It was not the mountain itself that was falling, it was ice and snow. An avalanche. A big one. And of course, part of her reasoned, it should be no surprise. The earthquake had struck the Wheel as well as the Mount, and on any steep, snow-covered mountain the result of such a shaking would be all but inevitable.

And yet the scale of it!

Rita had never seen an avalanche before, but she suspected that in most mountain ranges even the largest avalanche would scarcely be visible from a vantage point ten kilometres distant.

But this . . . this was like watching the sky itself fall. It wasn't just a single slab of snow that was moving, or a single chute that was unloading, or a single overhanging ice ridge that was tumbling; it was everything on the central face. On the open slopes entire snowfields were in motion; in the ravines where glaciers lurked, snouts of ice were toppling forwards, shattering as they went, the broken chunks slamming into the frozen cliffs below and setting them loose as well. It was *everything*, slumping, plunging downwards, leaping and jagging from slope to slope, jostling in a mad rush to reach the distant sea.

The roar was all pervading now, like a gale blowing in Rita's face, and yet still the titanic collapse was growing. On both the left and right its edges were racing outwards, great slabs of white breaking away and dragging their neighbours with them. Nothing could stop it; nothing could block its dreadful spread; no crevice or couloir was wide enough. Even the Plateau, the long, wide ledge that ran across most of the West Face at five thousand metres, was no hindrance. As Rita stared, the leading edge of the avalanche reached the great shelf and overflowed it, not even slowing.

And still it grew. The avalanche now stretched across the entire central face, from far out on the southern shoulder to the middle of the north ridge, an expanse that must be thirty kilometres wide.

She spared a glance to Clara. The major-domo, wide-eyed, was mouthing something. Rita couldn't hear the words but she thought it might be *Oh shit, oh shit, oh shit,* over and over like a mantra. Clara was afraid? But why? As a mountain climber, she must have seen avalanches before, and though the collapse was a cataclysm, yes, it was also safely ten kilometres away across the ocean.

Rita swung her gaze back to the grand spectacle, and forgot about everything else. Lord, how many millions upon millions of tonnes of ice and snow were falling now? How many *billions* of tonnes? Avalanche? No, she decided, it wasn't just an *avalanche*; *avalanche* was far too small a word. Yet she had no word for what it truly was.

But now—had it been sixty seconds since the vast movement began?— there was a new and stupendous aspect to behold. At the centreline of the Wheel, the leading edge of the collapsing mass was ravaging down the last thousand or so metres of the face—burying the scant trees there in an instant—to slam into the ocean. In immediate response, great towers of water began rising up, the creep of their ascent and then fall betraying the tremendous size and weight and violence of the process.

The thunder grew even louder as the impact upon the sea spread left and right, falling ice piling upon falling ice, until a vast arc of the

Wheel's shoreline was lost behind fountain walls of spray. And this was from only the leading edge of the collapse—above it a whole mountainside of ice was still in mid cascade, runaway and unstoppable.

Rita became aware that Clara was poking feverishly at her phone.

She stared, amazed that the major-domo could think of texting—yes, she was texting—at a moment like this. Clara caught her eye and explained at a shout over the thunder. 'All that ice—all that volume—hitting the sea; it'll send a wave this way! A tsunami! It could hit down at Base! I tried to ring Eugene, warn him, but he doesn't answer! So I'm trying this instead!'

Rita was taken aback. A tsunami? A *tsunami*. But they were things that happened in other places—in Asia, in Japan, she had seen videos. It couldn't be happening here, right now, right in front of her.

She returned her disbelieving gaze to the Wheel. The thunder was eternal, but in fact the collapsing face was mostly hidden now behind a cloud of ice and snow that had been thrown up by the tumult, climbing like a cumulonimbus. The impact upon the ocean was all too visible. All along a thirty-kilometre curve of shoreline the sea was swelling and withdrawing, as if in horror, from the land, shoved aside by the countless tonnes of ice crashing from above. The fact that the displacement of water was visible at all from this distance only proved how vast it was—and already a white line could be seen forming at the forefront of the bulge, forging outwards from the Wheel.

A wavefront.

'Fuck, fuck, *fuck*,' yelled Clara in fury at her phone. 'No answer! Nothing!'

Rita had no memory of moving, but somehow both of them had crossed to the eastern edge of the Terrace and were now at the parapet. The drop away to the ocean was as appalling as ever, but Rita's fear of heights was lost in the face of the disaster across the water. The wave was thrusting slowly out from the Wheel's shoreline now, a sinister up-swelling that had formed into a bowed line dozens of kilometres long. And it was not *slow*. It must be racing across the sea.

Towards Theodolite Isle.

How long would it take to cross the ten kilometres? She had no way to calculate. But already, even as the wavefront moved out from the Wheel, Rita could note a terrible thing. Because of the way the mountain curved in a gigantic amphitheatre shape that focussed upon Theodolite Isle, the wave too would focus upon the island. So the surge would amplify as it came, building and crowding upon itself as it narrowed upon the one central point . . .

And behind it, still the avalanche roared on, still the ice piled and piled into the sea. The lower half of the Wheel was lost now behind the thunderhead of snow blown up and out by the collapse. The underside of that cloud was shadowed blue-black, but its upper reaches dazzled white as it soared towards the stratosphere, ten or fifteen kilometres high, matching the mountain itself for grandeur.

It was a scene fit for the world's end, but the cloud was harmless in essence. Rita's gaze was drawn back to the ocean below, to where the true danger lay. The forefront of the tsunami swell was sweeping towards her, flattening out as it reached the deeper waters, but all the more threatening for that. Rita knew enough of such things to understand that when it reached the shallows again, as it neared the shore of the island, the wave would rear with renewed fury.

Clara was punching other numbers into her phone now. 'Why the fuck doesn't anyone answer down there? They've got to get people into the lifts and get them to safety up here with us!'

Did they even know they were in danger down there? Could they see what was coming towards them? Up here, far beyond the reach of even the most fantastical wave, she and the major-domo could see it all. But down at sea level the wave might not even be visible yet.

She watched it coming. It was halfway across the gap now, a swollen arc converging relentlessly upon the hub of the island.

'Get out of there!' Clara was yelling. She was leaning over the parapet, staring down wildly, as if her warning shout might reach the town below. But Base was not visible from anywhere up here; it was hidden by the shoulder of the Mount, and it was certainly beyond the hearing of any human voice, all as Rita's father had designed. 'Get out!'

The wave was three-quarters of the way across now. It was not really a single crest, it was a great swollen bruise freshly inflicted upon the sea, the water latent with a hideous, compressed power. There was nothing to be done from up here, no life-saving action to take. But surely those below must see it now, only a few miles offshore, looming from the sea? Surely by now people were running, climbing, dashing madly for any high ground they could find?

But there was so little time, the surge was racing so fast, and already its forefront was beginning to rear and froth terribly as it neared the shore. How high was the wall of water rising? Rita could not tell, but a new note had come to the thunder, an underpinning boom and thud, like surf on a beach, but amplified ten-thousandfold.

Rita too was leaning over the parapet now, but even so the forefront of the wave was passing from her view beneath the Mount's shoulder. Her final glimpse of it was of an improbable cliff building from the sea, water cascading down its face even as it rose higher, surely dozens of metres tall, no, scores of metres, and more . . .

Then it was out of sight, and to Rita there was only the bloated surge of its wake to stare at for five seconds, ten, twenty—then she felt it. The very stone beneath her trembled like an earthquake anew, not so much the effect of single concussion, but of a vast violent *push* against the Mount's foot.

Long moments later, an enormous rush of sound swept up over the Mount and engulfed her, a crash of booming and rending and smashing, and even, Rita was sure, of human wails.

Nor did it die away. The terrible din went on and on, for this was a flood, not a mere wave—a great swathe of the ocean displaced and shoved massively forwards by the titanic volume of the avalanche. And the flood would not end until the avalanche that drove it, ten kilometres away, ended too.

Rita raised her horrified stare. How long had it been since the collapse began? Five minutes? Ten? It felt like an hour, though it could not possibly have been as long as that. But ah—thank god—it did now seem that perhaps the tumult over on the Wheel was finally exhausting itself. Through the storm cloud of swirling debris it was hard to see what was happening on the lower face, but a bass note to the thunder was dying away. And yes, all along the Wheel's shore, the great fountains of water were falling back. Surely that meant that the last of the descending ice and snow had finally finished its long plunge to the sea.

Even so, the shockwave of water that had been sent out still had to run its course. For perhaps five minutes more Rita and the major-domo could only watch and listen as the ocean surged and roared about the island, drew back, then surged again. Only gradually did the surges lessen and the coherence of the flood break apart into cross-currents that roiled and conflicted with each other, and slowly, slowly, faded.

The thunder of earlier also dwindled at last, leaving an aftermath echo, the lesser cascade of the floodwaters sulkily retreating into the sea. The ocean all about was now a muddy wash of foam and of flotsam swept from the island. Rita did not want to study the wreckage too closely.

She looked up at the Wheel once more. Smaller, subsidiary slides of ice and snow were still moving here and there on the face, but the great snowstorm cloud was drifting southwards now on the winds of the world, thinning as it went.

So—was it over?

Clara was staring dully at her phone. 'I've got no reception anymore. Nothing. The whole system must have been knocked out. Christ, people must be dead down there. Lots of them.'

Yes, people would be dead. But Rita couldn't process the thought properly. Shock was sinking too deeply into her; she felt only a cold hollowness, a complete exhaustion of her emotions.

'Clara? Rita?'

It was Kushal, emerging through the airlock doors. Behind him came Madelaine. Each of their faces was pale and drained, staring.

'Did you see?' Kushal asked, and Madelaine's wide eyes echoed the tone of the plea. *Did you see what we saw? Was it real? Did it really happen?*

The major-domo nodded. 'We saw.'

'And down at Base?' the builder pressed. 'Do you know? Are you in contact?'

To which Clara only shook her head.

On the other side of the Terrace a door was flung open at the top of the stairs that led up to Walter Richman's private Cottage, and the billionaire himself emerged. For once, in contrast to his usual air of assured calm and command, he looked as stunned and bewildered as everyone else.

'Are you all okay?' he enquired, descending the stairs. 'No one is hurt?'

'We four here are fine,' Clara replied. 'But I haven't seen Kennedy. As for everyone else down at Base, we don't know yet . . .'

'When the quake began Kennedy came up to the cottage,' said Richman. 'He's okay, I sent him to the Control Room to see if he can contact anyone. But it must be bad down at Base, real bad. The lights went out at the same time that the wave hit, so the power station must have been taken out, and you know what that means—the station is higher above sea level than almost all the other buildings down there. So if *it's* gone . . .'

'So is everything else,' finished Clara, the understanding dark in her eyes.

Richman was gazing at the Wheel, shaking his head. 'It shouldn't be possible. An avalanche of that scale, it's . . . it's unprecedented. But god, look at that mountain, will you! Look at the colour! It's like it's stripped itself for battle or something.'

Rita followed his gaze. The last of the avalanche thunderhead was shredding away now, a mushroom cloud long after the atom bomb has exploded, revealing more and more of the Wheel. There was still snow and ice upon the West Face, by no means had *all* of it fallen. But the mountain was changed nonetheless, denuded of much of its protective coat of white. Great reaches of native rock now stood bare.

And Richman was right: the colour! For now that the cloud was gone the afternoon sun was striking the face full on, lighting the newly bared rock with a glow that seemed almost preternatural. And for the first time Rita understood—really understood—why the mountain was named what it was.

She had always known the Wheel's full title, of course. But even after seeing the mountain firsthand, she had thought it was a name given more in romance than in accuracy, for before now there had really been only the faintest of a rose blush to behold here and there where the rock was exposed.

But now—now she saw the truth! Indeed, the French explorer, sea captain Marion du Fresne, who had discovered and named the Wheel, must have seen this same truth too. He must have happened upon the mountain after some earlier avalanche had scraped the West Face as bare as it was now.

La Grande Crete Rouge.

The Great Red Ridge.

Red. That was key.

Red. The colour blazed from the stone, as deep and fierce in the sunlight as patches of fresh blood splashed amid the remaining stretches of white. It was as if the hide had been flayed from some titanic beast to reveal the livid muscle beneath. But—so it seemed to Rita's eyes—far from being hurt, the beast itself was glorying in its nakedness, rearing with renewed dominion over an ocean that was still all in tumult.

Richman was right again; it *did* look stripped for battle. Worse than that, it looked . . .

Rita felt it then, in a sickening rush, and knew that the whole question of whether she believed in her special senses of old, of whether she had rejected them or not, was irrelevant. For it was as undeniable to her as the sun. Palpable, a single emotion was radiating from the naked face of the mountain.

Satisfaction.

The Wheel was pleased with itself, pleased with what it had just done. But not only that. Rita also detected a sense of anticipation in the titan as it gazed down at the tiny human figures standing atop the little Mount, a dark, gleeful expectancy for something even more terrible that was yet to come.

The earthquake and the avalanche and the giant wave that had swept over Base below, killing who knew how many people, these were not the culmination of the great mountain's malice—they were merely the opening flourishes.

For the six of them who remained, the Wheel had only *begun* with its breaking.

BOOK
THREE

1

THE LA FLIGHT

IT HAD BEEN A BAD day even before they got to the airport and found the flight delayed. Truth was, it had been a bad week. It shouldn't have been, it should have been an exciting, happy period, because everything was coming together, everything they had wanted: the book tour, the whole US market, the big-time at last, the fame, the money that would follow . . .

Instead it had all been a pain. The packing and repacking; the last-minute hunt for a house-sitter to look after the garden and pets after the friend they had organised had to pull out suddenly; the even more last-minute dash to attend to Rita's lapsed passport. And Anne was in a foul mood throughout. The two-month trip couldn't have come at a worse time for her; she was at a crucial stage of editing a manuscript by one of her favourite writers, and now was being forced to hand it off to a colleague. Then there was the muddled disaster of the going-away party that neither of them wanted to host anymore, but at which they drank too much anyway, and snorted too much, meaning only more time lost to hangovers and fights . . .

A shitty week, in all, and in a way—even though she hated air travel—by the time they were in the cab to Melbourne airport, Rita was actually looking forward to the flight. Because at least everything was done now, and for the next sixteen hours they would be able to relax.

More to the point, so keen had her new US publishers been to get her to the States they had chimed in with Business Class tickets, so those sixteen hours would pass in pampered comfort.

But barely had they settled into the Qantas Club Lounge at Tullamarine when the announcement came that their flight would be delayed by some hours due to a maintenance issue with the aircraft.

Her nerves immediately back on edge, jammed into an uncomfortable corner of a couch (as even the Qantas Club was crowded that day) Rita's first reaction was to flag a passing waiter and order a glass of champagne. To which Anne sighed, 'Oh for Christ's sake, you're not going to get drunk already, are you?' And it went downhill from there.

The delay ran fully six hours (a part needed to be flown in from elsewhere) and Rita did indeed get drunk in the meantime. And why not? It was not as if she needed to be sober for anything; there was only the flight ahead, and after that, a hotel room waiting in LA. She wasn't due to meet with her publicity team for a full two days after touching down.

And anyway, Rita *always* had a few drinks before flying. Anne knew that, and knew why, too. The alcohol was necessary to dull Rita's special senses before take-off, to blot out her ability to detect presences. She had learned that lesson in her youth, in the months after her great revelation. Flying sober, encountering the presences of the air with her mind wide open and aware, was *awful*.

She well remembered her first flight in the wake of her mother's death. The plane had passed around the edge of a thunderstorm, and encountered severe turbulence. Locked in the flexing, leaping metal tube that was the aircraft, the younger Rita had been overcome by waves of hostility that originated from *outside* the plane, from a presence in the thunderstorm, malign and wild, that wanted to hurl the intruder from the sky. It was only the force of the jet engines, and the cunning give and flex of the fuselage, that was preventing the plane from being torn apart.

Rita had wanted to scream, or vomit, or go dashing madly along the aisle, anything but sit there strapped into her seat as the plane shuddered and the attendants staggered by, their smiles brittle. If it had gone on for more than a few minutes she would have. But that was the saving grace of air travel. In an airliner moving at nine hundred kilometres an hour, contact with any presence was at worst a fleeting one. And so the plane had moved beyond the turbulence before it—or Rita's control—broke.

But it was enough to make her dread flying. And so when she was a little older, and understood presences and her reaction to them better, Rita had begun to self-medicate with several strong drinks before and during a flight. Alcoholically dulled, she could fly untroubled by any malevolence through which the plane might pass. And she had come to trust that the plane always *would* pass through. That for all their loathing of humans trespassing in the upper airs, the presences there were not strong enough to do any serious damage to a modern jet.

The LA flight was about to prove that belief wrong, alas, but she didn't know that yet. All she knew, there in the Qantas lounge, was that of course she must have a drink or two before take-off, and that Anne also knew that perfectly well, so why the hell was she being so snooty and disapproving about it?

Ah, but then Anne was disapproving about almost *everything* these days . . .

Okay, yes, so the timing of this trip was inconvenient for her, but that wasn't Rita's fault. It was the US publishers who had changed the dates, moving the tour six weeks forward. But Christ, Anne worked in publishing herself, she knew how these things went.

It was typical, really, of how their whole relationship had been lately. (So ran Rita's thoughts as she moved from her fourth glass of champagne to her first of chardonnay. Anne was drinking too by then, but much slower, and without looking at Rita.) Typical of how Anne had started to resent Rita's work, and the way it dominated their lives.

It hadn't been like that at the beginning. Anything but. When her book was first accepted for Australian publication, and the publishers had assigned her an editor, Rita had been nervous about her initial meeting with the woman. She had pictured a hardened chain-smoking professional aged fifty or more, a sergeant-major type used to whipping young first-time authors into shape, and also completely cynical about Rita's claims and theories.

But instead it had been Anne, only a year older than Rita herself and surprisingly shy, not hardened or cynical at all. Far from dismissive about the book, Anne was oddly reverent. She *believed* it, accepted that it was real, that Rita's abilities were real. She was fascinated by Rita. Which certainly made the editing process easier than Rita had expected.

In return, Rita found Anne insanely sexy, in a tight, repressed, bookish sort of way. There was a settled submissiveness to her that contrarily promised—and indeed delivered, when it came down to it, one night after they'd known each other a few weeks—a wickedly dirty nature underneath.

In short, they fell in lust and love, though they managed to keep the affair secret until after the book was published. It would have been unprofessional otherwise, Anne had insisted primly.

Through the years that followed, in addition to being Rita's partner, Anne had assumed the role almost of acolyte, of dutiful disciple to Rita's prophet. She had put her own career on hold, leaving her secure in-house post and going freelance, just so that she could follow Rita around to the distant corners of the country and assist in the ritual lustrations.

The book had tripled Rita's business. It had not sold all that many copies, perhaps, hidden away in the Alternative Philosophies section of Australian bookshops. But it made an impact where it needed to, with free-thinking and spiritual types who were *troubled* by ghostly things they could not explain. Through Rita's website and blog the requests had begun to pour in. Help us, please.

Indeed, Rita began to find herself something of a cult figure. In time, she was receiving requests even from overseas, in particular from the USA. She made two trips there, her flights paid by desperate clients, and on the second trip she also appeared at a string of small alternative festivals. Finally, a large American publishing house became aware of her, saw the possibilities, and signed her up.

Now they were predicting big things. Huge things. In the post 9/11 world of 2004, they said, New Age thinking had never been more popular, and *Spawn of Disparity* was something truly original, something that would stand out from the crowd and sell by the bucketload. By the truckload.

So they promised, anyway, and Rita was eager to believe them, even though she was quite sure that her American editors (unlike Anne) privately considered her ideas to be pure bunkum.

That was fine. But Rita had become aware throughout the US negotiations that Anne wasn't quite the believer she had once been either. The drugs had something to do with that. Oh, Anne was no teetotaller, and she knew that cocaine and LSD could help Rita, that they heightened her special senses for the lustrations. (Not that Rita had mentioned that in her book!) But even so, Anne was plainly beginning to wonder if it was *just* about the work.

And okay, truth be told, there had been a lot of coke lately, and not just at the lustrations, but at parties too, with friends. Or, more truthfully, even when it was just the two of them at home alone.

But what the fuck. It wasn't causing any problems. They had the money; they could afford the drugs, and Rita's constitution was famously tough; it could handle anything she threw at it. So Anne's fears were groundless in that respect.

But her disapproval had other facets. The most disturbing was that she seemed to suspect lately that Rita wasn't always being entirely honest with her clients, that Rita's descriptions of the presences she encountered, and of how she placated them, was a little . . . well, made up.

A suggestion Rita angrily refuted, of course. Because it wasn't true. Or it was hardly true. But okay, yes, maybe once or twice, even with the help of the drugs, she hadn't been able to interact with the presences the way she normally could. But dammit, she was only human, wasn't she allowed to have a bad day at work like anyone else? So if she covered for herself by telling a few fibs, so what?

And okay, at other times, she could tell straightaway that there was no presence in a place to which she had been called, no matter what the clients insisted. In the old days she would simply have said so and gone home. But now that she was famous, now that her clients paid a fortune just to get her to visit their properties, what was she supposed to tell them as they waited eagerly, watching the ritual of their hired priestess? Should she announce they had wasted their money? Should she give it *back*?

No, surely it was better to declare that it had all worked as promised, that the presence had been addressed and assuaged. After all, as there had been no presence in the first place, it was all benign enough, just an elaborate kind of Feng Shui . . .

Ah, but although the clients might fall for these white lies, Anne did not. She knew Rita much too well. She said nothing aloud, but it was in her eyes, a growing disappointment and doubt. The faithful acolyte was starting to question if her prophet and priestess might in fact be an outright fraud.

Then there was all the sex.

Not *their* sex. *Their* sex was an increasingly rare event these days. No, the sex at the lustrations, with the clients, was the problem.

It didn't happen every time, of course, and god knew, it had never been about sex in the old days. But there had always been nudity, from those very first few times when Rita had experimented with what would become her lustration ritual. The nakedness undoubtedly helped, undoubtedly put in her closer contact with the surrounding landscape and the presences in it. But, well, why deny it? It had felt good too, in a sensual way. And later, with the drugs, it started to feel fucking great.

Anne had been turned on by it too, Rita was sure. Originally. In those days it had been a private thing, just the two of them alone, the clients having been sent safely away. They would both end up naked, and in their shared elation after the communion with the presence, as often as not the ritual ended with some outright fucking.

Which was fine enough. But then the clients started joining in. At first, they were merely present as observers. Then certain clients wanted to take a more active part, joining in the nudity as well—and at the prices they were paying, how could Rita refuse? And that was fine too, but in this last year, especially since cocaine had taken over from LSD as Rita's stimulant of choice . . . well, it didn't bear thinking about too closely.

It had happened only three times in all, each time with a different couple, but some of the memories were a little sordid, in all honesty. Again, Anne had seemed a willing enough participant on the first occasion. She was not naturally into group, let alone bi, sexual encounters, but the coke had helped, god knew, and she had always been willing to please Rita, so she'd gone along. But the second time it happened, in Rita's hazy replayed memories, Anne had been less an active participant . . . and on the third, she was entirely uninvolved.

The upshot of all this was that six months ago Anne had declared that she was taking back her old in-house editing job, which meant she would be less free to travel with Rita. There was a row about that, but it ended with renewed declarations of love, and a night of just the two of them in bed, like the old days, and the promise that they would make the upcoming US book tour into a fun, shared holiday.

At the time it had felt like a good solution, a break that would get them entirely back on track. Later, as Rita—without Anne now to hold her back on her working trips away—spiralled deeper into the alcohol–coke rotation (and okay, it really had been out of control a little, even Rita herself could tell that), and as Anne withdrew into her editing, the book tour had come to feel like it would be a last-ditch attempt to save the whole relationship. And now, drinking fast in the Qantas Lounge with take-off delayed another two hours, according to the last announcement, it felt like a disaster only waiting to unfold.

Even so, Rita could never have imagined that it would unfold with such speed, and such spectacular awfulness, as it did on the plane.

▲

By the time boarding was finally called, there was a decided sway to Rita's step as they made their way down the tunnel, but if the flight attendants noticed anything they made no comment—they even served her a pre-flight glass of wine.

The plane was a 747, with the business class section in the hump— the layout old-fashioned by 2004 standards, three aisles of two recliners apiece. Rita and Anne were seated in the right-hand aisle, but they could have sat anywhere really. After all the delays, which had seen several groups of passengers assigned to other flights, the section (indeed the whole plane) was more than half empty.

They taxied to the runway. This was usually a stressful moment for Rita, a time to steel herself against what might be to come in the upper airs. Knowing this, Anne would normally nestle an arm under Rita's for reassurance, just before the plane began its acceleration down the tarmac. She did not do so today, however; even that simple gesture was beyond them. But in any case, Rita was drunk enough not to care. Airborne, she ordered another drink as soon as the seatbelt light went off.

And then kept them coming. As Anne had the window seat— Rita avoided windows, she had no desire to look out from on high—Rita could order without having to reach over her to do it. Indeed, Rita might have been flying alone, with a stranger sitting beside her, for all that they interacted. Anne had her headphones on and spent most of the time buried in the pages of a book. Rita drank and flicked through the channels on her entertainment screen.

And so several hours passed. Eventually, Rita found herself becoming drowsy. In another reality she might have gone to sleep, and still been asleep when the incident later occurred, in which case everything might have turned out differently—the flight, the US book tour, her career, her relationship with Anne, everything. But she didn't fall asleep. Instead, she got up and swayed her way to the toilet. And it was while she was in the bathroom, seated on the bowl, that she discovered the cocaine.

Her hands had been moving about distractedly and encountered a small bulge in the top pocket of the suede waistcoat she was wearing. Nonplussed, she dug it out and was appalled to behold a small plastic bag of white powder. Then—holy mother of god—she remembered why it was there.

It was from the going-away party. She had worn this same waistcoat. Late in the night, the supply of coke that she had laid on for the guests had run low, so she had sent out for more. When it arrived, the delivery boy had given her a little bag gratis, a gift from the dealer, he said, for a loyal customer. Something with an extra kick.

Rita had promptly stashed it away in her pocket, saving it for herself and Anne to try later, when everyone else had left. But she and Anne had argued after the party and gone to separate beds, and Rita had forgotten all about the little bag.

Now she gazed at it in awe and gave a shaky laugh. Christ, she had been about to land in LA with coke in her pocket! What a nightmare that could have been! Detention, arrest, deportation, who knew? Thank heavens for this bit of luck then, thank god she had found it. All she had to do was flush it down the toilet and the bullet was dodged.

Except, well, why flush it?

There was still eleven or twelve hours left to the flight, and she was already bored to death, especially with Anne not talking to her. It would do no harm if she held on to it for the next few hours, as long as it was all gone—all used—before they landed.

Once considered, the notion was irresistible. Much later, looking back, Rita would realise just how drunk she must have been to think it was a good idea, given what cocaine would do to her special senses. But at the time all she had felt was a sense of righteousness, an almost angry defiance, as she studied the little bag, as if this was the perfect way to show Anne that she could and would do whatever she liked to enjoy herself. She wouldn't even *tell* Anne, she would just ride out the rest of this dreary flight in the bright hazy mist of a coke high.

So without further hesitation, she finished her ablutions, drew out three lines on the counter of the bathroom, and had her first snort.

Walking back to her seat she felt fantastic, the lethargy of five minutes earlier burned away, the sway gone from her step. Anne didn't even look up as she resumed her seat, and Rita didn't give a fuck. She ordered up another drink, chatted brightly with the attendant a moment, then got back to cruising the TV and movie channels, the coke buzzing in her head all the while like some secret sex toy.

So passed another several hours, the time now sweeping by at a grand pace. Rita didn't even feel mad at Anne anymore; she had benevolently risen above it. Once, when Anne herself rose and went to the toilet, then returned, still frostily refusing to meet Rita's eye, Rita even smiled at her as she edged by to her seat. This bought a surprised glance, but also, Rita was sure, a softening of the tight hunch of Anne's shoulders, the beginning of rapprochement.

Oh yes, everything would be fine once they were in LA and the flight and all the bother was finished with, once it was just the two of them and a big hotel bed. And with that pleasant thought, Rita rose for a trip to the bathroom and another three lines of the coke.

Back in her seat again, it finally occurred to her, through the euphoria, that her special senses should be more alert now. So, was there anything to be detected out there in the high atmosphere, mid-flight? With a devil-may-care inner shrug she cast her awareness outwards deliberately, searching for any hint of a presence anywhere near the plane.

And found . . . nothing at all.

Well, she had been drinking, still was drinking indeed, so maybe even the coke wasn't enough to rouse her sixth sense today. And yet her awareness didn't feel dulled, it felt as sharp and lively as the rest of her: there was just nothing out there.

She searched for the next half hour or so, intrigued. The plane flew on as smoothly as if it was on rails; she didn't think she'd ever been on a flight so smooth. Which made her wonder—had she been wrong, all these years, to be so afraid of flying? Had she needed to dose herself with alcohol all these times? Had those few early bad experiences given her the wrong idea, were the upper airs in fact mostly deserted of presences, deserted of danger?

An hour later—Anne was asleep by then, but her head had briefly rested on Rita's shoulder, and yes, surely everything was going to be just fine between them—Rita rose and visited the bathroom for the last of the coke. Afterwards she stuffed the little bag, now empty, in the disposal.

Then, as she was walking, no, *gliding* really, down the aisle back to her seat, the cabin dim and silent, nearly everyone else asleep, her head trilling with pleasure, the demon struck.

Suddenly she wasn't gliding, suddenly she was *flying*; she was airborne, her legs flailing for purchase. At the same time came a deafening, wrenching metallic thud, the whole aircraft seeming to contort and slam, though she was weirdly unaffected by it, suspended in midair. Then with another wrench the floor leapt up and rammed into her unready legs, and she was spreadeagled painfully on the carpet. Her head hammered into the armrest of an adjacent seat, hard enough to set her ears ringing.

She rolled away, dazed, but understanding at last what was happening. Turbulence!

All about her people were starting awake. Some, thrown from their seats, looked bewildered and pained, others were still strapped safely in their chairs but were nevertheless digging themselves out from beneath displaced blankets and pillows.

Rita staggered upright, and made two steps towards her own row where Anne's head was craning up in puzzlement, searching for her presumably. Then, again, with another wrench, she found herself aloft. This time her head whacked agonisingly against the ceiling. She caught a glimpse of other bodies in midair, and of luggage lockers springing open and bags floating out weightlessly. Then she and everything else was hurled to the floor once more with a crash.

In the shocked silence that followed, the seatbelt chime sounded with a faint ding, and the cabin lights flicked back on, bright.

'Rita! Come on!'

It was Anne, just two rows away now, leaning out and extending a hand. Rita floundered forwards in a half crawl and allowed herself to be dragged into her seat. She strapped herself in just as the plane leapt violently again, luggage flying and glass smashing in the galley. Held fast by the belt, Rita felt her stomach lift and fall in a rollercoaster motion, then she was staring at the blood on her hands and clothes, wondering where it had come from.

'Ladies and gentlemen,' announced the calm voice of the captain over the PA, 'our apologies about those bumps, we've obviously hit a bit of rough air. But there's no need to—*Damn!*'

The plane was heaving wildly again, this time not only shifting up and down, but also rolling sharply to the left, so that Rita felt for a moment she was dangling sideways from her seat, with the left side of the cabin a pit below her. Finally things righted themselves, and the jet flew on.

Rita put a hand to her head, found a huge lump there, wet. When she lowered her hand there was fresh blood bright on her fingers. Jesus, she'd split her fucking scalp open. This was ridiculous; it wasn't a bit of rough air; this was dangerous.

The plane bucked savagely again, not once, but repeatedly, slam, slam, slam, as if deliberate blows were raining upon it. And it came to her then, finally, overwhelming her shock: there was something *outside* the plane, something that was attacking it.

Of course! How had she not recognised it sooner, how had she been so blind? She had been through this before, after all. There was a presence out there, huge and strong and violent. It must be bad weather. Their flight path must have brought them within the clutches of a thunderstorm.

Anne was pulling Rita's head towards her, inspecting the wound. 'Christ, you're gonna need stitches there, I think.'

'The window,' Rita demanded. She could feel the hostility from the thing outside like sunburn on her skin. 'I wanna see what's out there!'

Anne's window shade had been shut, all the cabin's window shades had been shut, to help people sleep. She pulled it up now. Rita stared across her to the glass, frowning in disbelief. She had been expecting to see the boiling folds of a thunderhead out there, for what else could have given birth to a presence so powerful?

But there was no storm. There was only the horizon, dull orange with an approaching dawn, and a clear sky. How could that be? Or was the upheaval on the other side of the plane? But when Rita stared across to the left side of the cabin, she saw that passengers there had likewise thrown their shades up, and the sky was clear that side too.

'But that's crazy,' Rita breathed to herself. The presence was so palpable; its enmity towards the plane so ferocious; it was *there* somewhere.

'What's wrong?' Anne was asking.

The plane shook again, sinking then leaping up, and rolling right then back to the left, the two women thrown ragdoll about their seats as frightened cries rose and more glasses crashed.

'There's one of them here,' Rita hissed when she could speak, not needing to say the word *presence*, not to Anne. 'I don't understand how, though. There's no weather out there. But I can *feel* it.'

Anne was staring at her in confusion. 'How can you feel it? You've been drinking for hours. That's the whole point of drinking, isn't it?'

At which point Rita had to explain about the cocaine, at the same time wondering how she could have been so stupid. To snort coke on a *plane*? To expose herself to exactly the presences that were the most upsetting to her? Madness!

But Anne was appalled for a different reason. 'You brought coke with you? Are you fucking insane? Are you that fucking addicted?'

'No, no . . . It was by acci—'

Slam. A massive blow from beneath sent the 747 surging upwards, pressing Rita down so hard the wind went from her lungs. Then *slam* again, and the plane was corkscrewing downwards—Rita could see the ceiling contorting with the strain—and the last luggage lockers were spewing out their contents, and something heavy—food trolleys maybe—were smashing back and forth in the galley.

Worse, this time the aircraft didn't right itself. The plunge continued, and the four engines could be heard roaring now, though whether they were trying to raise the 747 back up again, or drive it down even more quickly, an emergency dive, Rita couldn't tell. She couldn't think, the hammer blows came too fast, throwing her head back and forth.

And then *slam*, something seemed to snap behind her eyes, and she discovered that she could see right through the tube of the fuselage to the open air beyond. Fuck, had the plane split open, was it tearing apart, were they all about to die?

But no, in a moment more she realised the truth. It was not actual sight she was experiencing; it was a *virtual* sight; it was her special senses reacting to the overwhelming presence that surrounded the aircraft. The entity out there was so potent that even through the solid walls of the 747's body, it was imprinting itself on her retinas.

She gazed in a transport of horror. There was no thundercloud, no storm, the upper airs were clear—and yet she could *see* it, a great river of force that was wrapped about the plane. It was vast, extending ahead of them endlessly, and for thousands of metres above and below, a monster of wind, an invisible hurricane, roaring in great bands both vertical and horizontal, with brutal updrafts matched side by side with downdrafts, and it held the 747 within its grasp like a toy.

Later, back in Australia, Rita would learn about jet-stream winds, and about a phenomenon called Clear Air Turbulence, or CAT for short. In rare instances it could be extremely dangerous to aircraft, and once, over Japan in the 1960s, it had torn an airliner completely apart, killing all on board. Rita's own flight, while not as bad as that, would be one of the worst recorded, with several serious injuries to passengers. An investigation into the incident would report that the cause was a freakishly strong offshoot of the Northwest Pacific Jet Stream that had pushed unusually far south, catching the Qantas flight unawares.

But Rita knew none of that now. She saw only a titanic, howling monster in the sky, and knew that it was intent on destroying the plane. That it *would* destroy the plane, unless—

'I have to stop this!' she gasped.

Anne was a rigid shape at her side, hands clutched to the armrests. 'What?'

'You know what I mean.'

Anne's eyes, already wide with shock, blazed with disbelief. 'Are you kidding?'

'No.' Then Rita was fumbling at the release catch of her seat belt as the engines screamed in futility against the ceaseless buffeting.

Anne's fingers clutched at Rita's, her shout over the noise both terrified and furious. 'Are you crazy? It's just turbulence, Rita! It's bad, but it's just fucking turbulence! It's nothing to do with you! There's nothing out there! You're just drunk and off your head on the fucking coke!'

Rita slapped her hands away. Anne was a fool. Anne couldn't see through the solid walls of the plane like Rita could. Anne couldn't see the invisible talons that were wrapped gleefully about the jet and which were slamming and slamming it, each time the wings flexing almost to the snapping point.

She was free of the belt and up at last. Anne screamed, 'For Christ's sake, sit *down!*' But Rita ignored her, went reeling down the aisle as the floor lurched and rolled underfoot. At any moment she might be thrown against the ceiling, she knew, but she felt better now that she was taking action. All she needed first was to find something sharp.

She came to the galley. Two trolleys had broken free and many of the shelves had popped open, strewing all manner of food and cutlery across the floor, the mess shifting with every thud and heave of the plane. Two flight attendants, strapped into their jump seats, goggled at her.

'Ma'am,' cried one, 'you have to return to your seat; you can't be in here!'

She ignored them too, searching through the chaos for what she needed. But none of the knives looked sharp enough. She needed . . . oh good lord, what a fool she was; she didn't need a knife. And she bent to pluck up the broken stem of a wine glass.

The attendant who had warned her had unbuckled and risen, approaching Rita sternly. 'Ma'am,' she said, 'I really have to insist—'

Rita sliced at her casually with the glass stem, cutting a line through the woman's blouse and across the top of her shoulder. 'I'm trying to help, you stupid cunt,' she said. 'Get away from me.'

The woman went flailing back, just as the plane corkscrewed again, and Rita momentarily danced midair before landing amazingly upright. The second attendant, horror stricken, was rising now too, but Rita turned away. She needed a moment alone, and there was only the one place—she ducked into the bathroom once more, and locked the door.

A lustration, that was their only hope, the only way to save the plane. The pilots would not be able to do it; that was evident. She could still see through the walls; she could still see the monster that gripped them, spanning the entire sky. The jet was diving again, engines shrieking over the human screams from the passengers, the pilots trying to get below the turbulence, but the monster was holding them aloft almost effortlessly, the winds howling upwards as the plane strove to go down.

Rita tore off her waistcoat and top and hauled down her skirt, baring herself to the titan in the sky as she had bared herself to a hundred different presences at a hundred different lustrations. Wedging her legs between the toilet and the wall for stability, she thrust her awareness out, offering her mind, open and defenceless, to the thing out in the air.

Hatred poured into her, unreasoning, boundless hatred, unlike any she had experienced before. This was nothing like communing with an ancient presence from the land. This beast would live and die within hours; its every passion was fierce and new, and though it knew nothing of humanity, still it hated this artificial thing that had trespassed in the sky, and hated too the pinprick annoyance of the human minds that rode within the device. It wanted only to crush the aircraft and extinguish the life within it.

But there was something else it might accept. Something else presences always accepted.

With practised ease, even despite the bucking of the bathroom about her, Rita slashed a cut across her left breast, parallel to a mass of other hairline scars drawn there. (They were hardly noticeable at a glance, she had always been careful to not cut too deep. And anyway, Anne had once found them erotic, had loved the feel of them under her tongue.)

Then, knowing that one cut would not be enough (not this time) Rita shifted the glass to her left hand and sliced her right breast the same way, offering up twice the blood to the monster.

The hatred faltered, roared back, faltered again, unsure—she had the thing's attention now. Its inhuman thought had recognised that this human was different, that this human *mind* was different, that she understood the crime of their trespass here in the high air, and was ready to atone for it, to beg forgiveness, to pay a price in her own flesh . . .

Slam. The plane wrenched savagely sideways, tipped, and seemed to Rita to roll completely over, for she felt she was bouncing across the bathroom ceiling. But that was surely impossible, a 747 couldn't perform barrel rolls like a stunt plane. Then she was in a dishevelled heap on the floor, and the monster was roaring its malice outside, unsated.

Not enough, she realised, she had not offered enough. Without further thought, she slashed two cuts at her bare thighs, and let more blood flow. *There,* she flung skywards, though not with actual words, *there, I offer more than I've offered any presence ever before. I pay the price for this plane and all these people!*

Rita did not know, even now, after so many lustrations (and this in fact would be her last) why it was that presences so respected the shedding of blood. They were not organic themselves, did not bleed or suffer physical pain, and yet when her special mind made contact with them, and when she offered her own pain in exchange for their anger at humanity's trespassing, they accepted the coin.

Would this monster do the same? Rita waited, not daring to breathe. The 747 continued to lurch and heave, and there was a labouring, off-tune tone to the engines now, as if they had been damaged. But the massive hammer blows had ceased.

Yes. The monster remained in the sky, but it was relenting, relenting, allowing the 747 to skim lower and lower, the vibrations smoothing out until . . . Until, thank god, it was dropping clear into the empty air beneath the great twisting stream of wind.

They were free.

Rita at last became aware of another hammering, so much softer than the din of the monster that it had been inaudible until now: the pounding of fists on the bathroom door.

'Ma'am, ma'am!'

Then came a scrabbling sound around the hinges. Wasn't there some way that attendants could remove bathroom doors in emergencies? Laughing, Rita rose and threw the latch back, shoved the door open. The two attendants gave way. Why, they were scared of her! Rita waved the glass stem lightly. 'It's okay. It's okay now. I stopped it.' They backed away further still, aghast. Rita had no idea why. She walked out, turned to face the rest of the cabin. 'It's all right,' she told everyone. 'We'll be just fine now.'

Pale faces stared at her in horror, not least of all Anne's, who had risen and was in the aisle, her hand to her mouth.

Puzzled, Rita glanced down at herself. Oh, of course, she was naked, and there was blood everywhere. But silly people, that was the point;

that was how she had done it. Anne knew. Rita lifted the bloody glass stem once more and pointed. 'You don't have to worry. She can expl—'

Which was when a large athletic-looking man—Rita seemed to recognise him and thought he might be a famous sports star of some sort—rose from his seat and, with apparent satisfaction, drove his elbow into Rita's temple, knocking her out cold.

▲

She would wonder, ever after, if the little bag of coke had been spiked with something. After all, the delivery boy on the night of the party had mentioned something about it having an extra kick.

Well, it had been a kick all right.

By the time Rita woke, mildly concussed from the blow to her head, she was trussed up in her seat, with her ankles and wrists bound with plastic ties, and the 747, its engines still sounding wrong, the aisles still a mess, was descending for an emergency landing in LA. At the first stirring of consciousness she had actually felt a wave of relief, for my, what an awful dream she'd had. But of course, on waking properly, she found herself bound and bloody, and Anne silent at her side, face tear-stained, and oh god, it was real . . .

Upon landing, everyone else—even the injured—was held in place until transit authorities could board the plane and escort Rita off under armed guard, Anne trailing behind. Then followed forty-eight hours of misery. She was questioned by various uniformed men, then sent to doctors who took samples of her blood and discovered high levels of alcohol and cocaine, then sent back to the uniforms who informed her of the denial of her visa, and who finally stashed her in a holding cell to await the first flight that could be found to take her back to Australia.

It could have been worse, Rita knew. The attendant she had slashed with the wine glass could have pressed assault charges. Her acts of mayhem in the air could have been construed as terrorism. She could have been held indefinitely in LA to face the nightmare of the US justice system. Being sent home was the very best she could hope for, and she owed that to the turbulence. It had been pretty frightening, everyone agreed, and so her actions were mostly put down to a hysterical panic attack.

In the end, the authorities even accepted that she could not possibly get on a plane again after what had happened, and so allowed her to book passage home on a ship instead. Not that the voyage home was any picnic, either. It was its own slow-moving nightmare. And not that anything was going to fix things now between Rita and Anne.

'It's over,' Anne told her when they docked in Australia. 'Unless you check into rehab. I think it's over anyway, but I won't even speak to you again until you're off all this shit. Goodbye.'

Rita checked herself into rehab, but Anne was quite right, it was over anyway.

Everything was over.

For one, after just a week of total sobriety in the facility, Rita realised that her special senses had vanished. She thought at first that maybe, after the horror flight and the terrible voyage, they were just burned out, that they would return in time. But nothing came. Of course, there were no presences to be found around a suburban rehab clinic anyway, but still, she had always been able to pick up at least an echo from the landscape, no matter where she was.

Now, there was only dead air.

That was frightening. What was more frightening was the realisation—as she went through her drug history with her counsellor—that of all her lustrations of the last three or four years, of all her communions with presences in the wild, not one of them, not one, had been performed without the influence of either LSD or coke.

In truth, she could not even remember the last time she had sensed a presence at all without the aid of a hallucinogen or a stimulant. God, even back in her late teens she had been on pot most of the time.

It wouldn't be since she was sixteen maybe, since the very beginning, that she had sensed a presence while utterly sober and straight.

But in that case . . .

Was it possible? Had it *all* been because of the drugs? Had it all been just one long mind-fucked delusion? Those early experiences, no, she hadn't taken any substances then—but Christ, she had been *naturally* screwed up in those days, a teenager in the midst of god knows what hormonal chaos, her mother dead in horrible circumstances, her emotions a train wreck. So had even her *first* experience been a delusion as well, a way of coping with the trauma?

Was it *all* bullshit?

Two months later, when she checked out of the clinic on a bright sunlit morning, clean and sane and subdued, she went to find out.

She drove up to the Dandenong Ranges and to the town of Olinda. From there she walked a mile or so into the Ranges national park. At a certain place, unmarked by any sign, she left the graded track and its steady stream of hikers and struck up into a rainforest gully, daring the snakes and leeches.

And there, where it had always been, she found the little rocky glen that she had discovered years ago, led there by her newly awakened senses. It was a secret corner of the hills, rarely troubled by humans, where a small stream trickled over a sheer ledge. Behind the trickle was a neatly shaped cave, moss-lined and as cosy as a small room. There was even a platform within that was perfect as a bench.

Rita sat there now, listening as hard as she might with her mind. The presence that she had discovered here had never been a strong one. The glen was too modest a place, too minor its uniqueness, to be host to a greater awareness. But the little entity had always acknowledged her, every time she visited, and there was no reason it should have died away, so rarely did other minds ever intrude here.

But she could not feel it now. The glen was lovely, the trickle of water calming, the solitude an aching pleasure after the clinic. But there was nothing more. No awareness, no presence. At which Rita could only conclude, there never had been.

She let out a sigh.

Time to start life over, then. Time to move on from this nonsense, this arrogance and self-righteousness, this self-absorption. Time to move on from what tore her apart. Time to grow up.

She walked back to her car.

▲

It wasn't that simple, of course. It was two very bumpy, lonely and difficult years before she sorted herself out enough even to enrol in her vet course.

But that was the moment it started. And for the next decade, she was untroubled—at least, overtly—by any hint of the presences of her old life.

Until, that was, Walter Richman summoned her to his awful house, and the Wheel fell.

2

TAKING STOCK

THE LAST OF THE AVALANCHE cloud had dissipated and the setting sun had slipped behind a bank of cloud, dulling the great red face of the Wheel and dropping the temperature even further below freezing, by the time Rita and the other four, Richman, Kushal, Madelaine and Clara, finally left the Terrace and retreated to the warmth of the Conservatory.

Inside, the silence rang hollow in Rita's ears, her memory still overwhelmed by the thunder of the collapse and of the tsunami—and by the cries, real or imagined, of the dying down below.

Richman stared appraisingly at the ceiling and walls. 'The lights are on again, so I'm assuming Kennedy has got the generators running.' In explanation to Rita, he added, 'There's an emergency back-up system here in the Observatory, enough to run the lights and the heating for weeks. So we don't have to worry about freezing just yet.'

Rita wasn't worried about freezing, her only thought was to get down off this exposed mountaintop as soon as possible. 'What about the lift?'

The billionaire shook his head. 'To run the main lift, or even the service elevator, you need the Power Station online. But anyway, until we know how things stand down at Base, we couldn't use the lifts even if they were working. The shafts might be damaged by the quake, or even

329

flooded down at the bottom. But I'm going to the Control Room right now to look into all that.' He glanced to the others. 'You can all come along, if you like. We're in this together.'

Everyone nodded. The billionaire in the lead, they descended to the Atrium and then moved into the Dining Hall. At its end they passed around a corner into a concealed servery area, and then on through a set of swinging doors into a large commercial kitchen. To one side of this, a concrete-lined service hallway ran off into gloom. Following it, they passed around two bends and reached a landing from which stairs climbed both up and down. They went down one flight and came to another landing, from which more service passages ran off on all four sides.

But these were really service *tunnels* now, Rita noted, for no daylight would ever reach down here. Even the fluorescent lights were dim, the conduits for the wiring visible along the bare walls. From somewhere below—the stairway continued down—she could hear a steady roar that she assumed was the generators. But Richman led them along one of the tunnels and the sound faded.

They came at last to a closed door. It bore no sign to identify what might lie behind it, but there was a panel and keyboard beside the door handle. After entering a security code and then having his thumbprint read by the scanner, Richman pushed the door open, and ushered them to follow.

Beyond was a large chamber that was lit mainly by the many computer screens that glowed upon three ranks of desks and by server banks that blinked in red and green along the walls. Other walls bore lockers and whiteboards and all manner of charts and schematics. The burr of cooling fans, and the faint smell of warm electronics, filled the air. *The Control Room, just like NASA,* thought Rita.

At one of the desks, bent over a keyboard in front of a terminal and flanked by a rack of video screens that displayed the footage from seemingly dozens of security cameras, was Kennedy.

'Everyone good?' the security chief enquired without turning his head.

'Good,' Richman replied. 'You got the generators going, I see. How else do we stand?'

Kennedy gave a grunt. 'Generators are fine, sure, but there must have been a nasty electrical surge up here when the Power Station went, because all the fuses were tripped when I came in. I've flipped them all back, but I dunno, half the systems seem to be permanently fried or otherwise screwed up. I'm still trying to work it all out.'

'Any news on the lifts?'

'Wrecked, for all I know. They were both down at Base when the wave hit, and I get no response from either one. If the water was high enough to kill the Power Station, then it probably flooded the bottom of the shafts too.' He glanced up, his stern face set in wonder. 'You know the Power Station is about four hundred metres above sea level, right?'

'I know,' nodded Richman. 'What about the emergency stairs? They in one piece?'

'Doesn't matter if they are. We can't get to them. According to the data here, the security doors for both of the elevator shafts activated when the power went, and now I can't open them.'

'Shit,' said the billionaire, crestfallen.

'Shit,' concurred Kennedy.

There was a pause, with Kushal and Clara likewise suddenly stony-faced at this particular piece of news, leaving Rita puzzled.

She asked, 'Security doors?'

It was Clara who explained. 'There are only two access points to the Observatory, the two lift shafts, the main and the service. Even all the old climbing paths up the outside of the Mount were dismantled when construction began. So, as a precaution, in case kidnappers or terrorists ever get control of Base and try to come up here, the upper exit of each shaft can be sealed off with blastproof doors. It makes the whole Observatory impregnable. But now it seems they've activated when they shouldn't have.'

331

Kennedy shook his head. 'No, they were doing what they're supposed to do. They're designed to shut if the power fails. The thinking is that in a kidnapping or terrorist attack, the Power Station might get sabotaged. So at the first hint of a power failure, the doors slam shut automatically. Of course, we're supposed to be able to open them again from this room, but that's one of the systems I was talking about. It's fried. Those doors aren't moving.'

'So we're stuck up here?' Rita demanded, the dread in her urgent once more.

'Not *forever*. Just until we sort it out. Which we will. I wouldn't let anyone go down the stairs yet anyway, not until we know more about conditions at the bottom. There could be flooding, or the stairs might have been damaged by the quake. So just relax, we'll all be sitting tight for the time being.'

Kushal enquired, 'Can you tell anything at all about what's happening down there?'

Kennedy waved a hand to the wall of video screens. Many of them displayed shots from around the Observatory, but the lower eight screens were either black, or displayed only static. 'Not a single feed active down there,' he said. 'Short of hanging over a balcony to see for myself, I can't tell a thing.'

'Well, then, shouldn't we do that?'

Walter Richman smiled humourlessly. 'You wouldn't be able to see anything. To get a view down to Base or even catch a glimpse of the harbour, you'd need to do some mountaineering. You'd have to climb over the parapet up on the Terrace and then traverse all the way around the shoulder of the summit to the south face—that's the only place you could see Base from. True enough, it could be done, there's some climbing gear down in the Museum. But I wouldn't be rushing to that option just yet.' He glanced to his security chief. 'What we need is Eugene up here; this stuff is his specialty. He definitely went down with all the others before the quake?'

Kennedy nodded bitterly. 'He did. And so did the other two maintenance guys who could have helped. By protocol, this room is supposed to be manned every second. But fool that I am, I let everyone go down; I thought it would only be for ten minutes. So the six of us here is all we've got.'

Richman let out a puff of air. 'That's a fuck-up, Kennedy. No mistake.'

'No one knows it better than me, sir,' said the security chief, head bowed.

But the billionaire did not seem terribly interested in blame. 'All right. Nothing to be done about it now. The generators are going, that's the main thing. How much fuel have they got?'

Kennedy raised his head, pointed to some readings on one of the computer screens. 'The tanks are full, so that gives us at least a fortnight of emergency power. Heating, lighting, refrigeration and so forth are all secure. Of course, we lose some less critical systems. The lifts are gone, as we know, and the heating of the pools, for instance, is out.'

'Food and drinking water?'

'Fully stocked, more or less. Again, that means enough for a fortnight at the very least, by the protocol, probably far more in reality, given that there are only six of us. The rule book assumes three times as many people here, as a minimum. We won't have to worry about starving for a month and more. Not that it'll come to anything like that, of course.'

'Communications?'

'None with below, and the internet and the phones are out, so there's no communications with the outside world just yet either. The whole hub at Base must be shut down or lost. I've still got my radio here, but none of my men are responding on it. If they're not dead down there, then I'm assuming they lost their radios in the flood. But we're not without options. Once we dig out the satellite phones, we'll be able to get in touch with Hobart and call up some support. Even if the harbour is wrecked, they can still land a rescue chopper up here.'

'There *are* satellite phones here then?' queried Richman. 'There was supposed to be at least one in the emergency kit in the Cottage, but it wasn't there when I looked. Where are the rest of them kept?'

Another frown from the security chief. 'I don't know. I haven't looked yet. But they sure as hell have to be here somewhere.'

'Well, let's make that priority one. And priority two, we need to get those security doors open, so we can go down and see what the damage is at Base. You work on the doors, Kennedy.' He turned to the others. 'The rest of us, time to start opening some of these lockers. Let's find those phones.'

They set to. Rita, for one, was glad to have a task that could distract from her shock and sense of foreboding—and glad too that Richman, surely no stranger to extreme challenges, had recovered and seemed to be in calm command once more.

But the following hour brought only frustration. The searchers tore open every locker and cabinet in the Control Room, and then hunted through two adjacent storerooms that were filled with first-aid gear and other emergency supplies—but nowhere did the promised satellite phones appear.

Richman was furious. 'I saw the damn things not two months ago down at Base during the final fit out, eight of them, charge packs and all. They were supposed to be installed up here six weeks ago at the latest. If the fool responsible has left them down below, if they're still sitting there now, or washed away, I'll sack him if he's not already dead.'

No one laughed.

The only remotely useful devices the search turned up was four pairs of walkie-talkies, of the kind that Kennedy and his team used.

'Better than nothing, I suppose,' was the security chief's assessment of the radios. 'They have a range of maybe twenty miles from up here across the open ocean, but that's only useful if a ship is passing by and listening on the right frequency. Likewise, we could talk to Base, but only if someone down there is alive and in a state to hear us.'

Clara took up one of the handsets. 'Well, I can check for a passing ship anyway. I'll be up on the Terrace if anyone needs me.'

She went. The others remained behind, watching impatiently as Kennedy strove to open the security doors. But he was no expert, and no matter how he fiddled with fuses or rebooted various computer systems, nothing he tried could bring the unlocking mechanism back online.

'The doors really *are* shut?' Richman checked finally. 'It's not a mistake; we're not just getting false readings from the blown equipment?'

Kennedy shrugged. 'It's no mistake. But go down and see for yourself, if you like.'

At length, they did just that. Leaving Kennedy in the Control Room, the other four set off to inspect the service elevator shaft in person.

It lay several levels below, down through the tunnels, and even amid all the other confusions and horrors of the day, Rita found the descent an unnerving experience. The passages and stairways seemed endless, burrowing ever deeper into the Mount, marked at various junctions only with the arcane codes of letters and numbers that she had noted on her previous investigation. No wonder the poor cleaning woman had ended up lost at the pool!

But Richman appeared to know his way unerringly. They passed the generator room as they went, a clamour coming from within, along with a heavy smell of diesel, and through an ajar door Rita glimpsed a line of great behemoth engines, twice her height, labouring in the gloom as exhaust fans hummed nearly as loudly as the generators themselves.

Then it was on, down away from the noise into a colder, quieter section of the tunnels. At last they arrived at a final wide landing beyond which no stairs descended. Along three of the walls metal roller doors were marked *Storage One* through to *Storage Three*, and on the ceiling ran rails for a crane. The fourth wall formed a large threshold, identified by a sign overhead which read *Service Elevator and Emergency Stairs. Caution, Long Steep Descent.*

But that threshold was barred now by a grey metal slab that had slid down from a housing above—a slab that was proof, so Rita had by now learned, against bullets, grenades and even rocket launchers. It was held in place by great electromagnetic locks set within the bedrock of the Mount, out of reach and quite immune to any interference other than a coded electronic order from the Control Room.

'Well,' observed Richman, 'it's shut all right. And there's no manual override.'

Kushal was nodding unhappily. 'I told you that was asking for trouble.'

Richman shrugged. 'Kennedy advised that a manual override would be too dangerous. It could by worked by any staff member, say a traitor in league with attackers from the outside.'

'A traitor could just as easily open the doors from the Control Room,' Kushal argued.

'The Control Room is a secure area, open only to half a dozen people at most, much more closely vetted than the general staff. If one of *them* is a traitor, then the whole place is compromised regardless. No . . . from a security standpoint, this was the smart move. We just didn't take into account an earthquake, followed by avalanche, followed by a goddamn tsunami big enough to take out the Power Station and burn out the electronics that control these things.'

Rita paid all of this little heed. She was staring uneasily at the security door, thinking not so much of the wisdom or folly of its installation, but rather of what lay hidden behind it.

There would be no elevator carriage waiting, she knew that. It had been caught down at the bottom during the quake. There would be just the empty shaft, a two-and-a-half-thousand-metre-deep hole plunging down through the mountain, a cable dangling into the blackness, falling, falling . . .

That, and the stairway.

But no ordinary stairway, she knew. It would not be walled-in all around, impossible to fall from, as would be found in any normal high-rise. No. How had Clara described it earlier? *More a series of ladders than a staircase.* A series of ladders, two and a half thousand metres high. The shudder such an image sent through Rita was terrifying both in the dread and fear of the expanse and yet also in its simultaneous vertiginous allure, reaching out, trying to draw her in and down . . .

No. She would rather wait even for the terror of an evacuation by helicopter from the Terrace, than venture down such a stairway. Or perhaps, even better than either, simply linger up here for as long as it took for the elevators to be restored to operation. There was a month's worth of food, after all.

Except, the idea of lingering in the Observatory was no relief either. Indeed, now that she was trapped here, however temporarily it might be, she wanted nothing more than to be gone. All her resurgent senses groaned with certainty that something awful was going to happen here. But even so, to take the stairs as escape . . . no. Not them. Not yet.

Anyway, the door was shut.

They spent another hour down in the bowels of the service area, searching each of the three storerooms for the elusive satellite phones. The rooms were filled mainly with furniture or with pallets of bulk items like toilet paper. There were six enormous TV screens still in their boxes, presumably awaiting installation somewhere, a huddle of gleaming new refrigerators, even a spare grand piano hulking under a blanket. But there were no smaller appliances or technological items, and no phones.

Finally they retreated, weary and claustrophobic after so long in these dim, bare-walled caves. It was by now nearly seven p.m., only three hours since the earthquake, but already that seemed an age ago and a different world. They returned first to the Control Room, where Kennedy reported that there was no change—they remained incommunicado—then they climbed back up and out to the main levels, through the Dining Hall to the Atrium.

'We could all use a drink, I bet,' Richman declared, heading for the Saloon.

Up here, it was almost possible to believe that nothing had happened. The air of luxury still prevailed, most of the lights were on, a fire was laid ready to ignite in the great fireplace, the mellow recesses of the Library still beckoned enticingly.

But not everything was as usual. The great transparent wedge that divided the Saloon from the Dining Room, the base of the Terrace Pool, would normally have been floodlit from within and glittering like an undersea fantasy as the bubble streams rose to the surface. Now, under emergency power, it was unilluminated. In daytime light would still have filtered down from the surface, but with night above the pool was black, an ebony monolith, making all the spaces around it, the Dining Hall, the Saloon, the whole Atrium, feel smaller somehow.

But no matter. Kushal set to getting the fire going, and Rita, along with Richman and Madelaine, circled around behind the bar to inspect the state of things. As it happened, the wine fridge was still powered, and so even amid disaster the chardonnay was being kept at the perfect temperature.

They had all just settled into couches with their drinks, the fire flaming up nicely, when Clara appeared, descending the stairs from the Conservatory. She was dressed in one of the long outdoor coats, her face pinched with cold and anxiety.

'Any luck?' Richman asked, though the major-domo's expression was answer enough.

Clara shook her head, going straight to the fire, hands outstretched. 'I've been transmitting maydays over a dozen channels and more, but so far no one has responded. Not a squeak.'

'Well, it was always a long shot.'

The major-domo nodded. 'I waited till full dark to be sure, but there are no lights out at sea, not in any direction. Other than that, all I can say is that it's getting colder and colder out there. I think there might be some weather coming.'

Rita turned her gaze to the great glass panels overhead and the view of the sky. All was night out there, except for on the eastward edge of vision: there, faint and high above, in the upper reaches of the atmosphere, a wisp of gossamer pink glowed. It was the peak of the Wheel, catching a last vestige of the long-past sunset, and around it once more a nacreous cloud was shimmering pale.

So high, so cold, so strange. A primal part of Rita reacted with a shiver, as if she had spied the approach of some black and deadly storm of ice.

'So what now?' Kushal asked.

Richman sipped a whisky. 'We wait.'

Kushal gave a sigh, considered the glass in his own hand. 'It hardly seems right though. Many must be dead or injured down below—and yet here we sit, unharmed, drinking whisky. It feels . . .'

'Obscene,' Madelaine filled in for him. She lifted her glass in turn. 'Nevertheless, short of jumping over the edge, there's nothing we can do to get down there or to help anyone. We can't even help ourselves. We're trapped, who knows for how long.'

'Oh, four days at the most,' declared Richman casually. 'Don't worry about that.'

'Four days at the most? How can you be so specific?' asked the designer.

'Well, it could be sooner,' the billionaire replied. 'If we find the satellite phones, or if we can get the security door open, then we could be out of here by tomorrow. But even failing all that, there's no need to fear a prolonged imprisonment.

'Consider the situation. I, for one, have already missed half a dozen business calls that I was due to make to people around the world, people who were waiting for me to do so—and I'm not a man to miss calls that I've set up. They'll already be wondering what's wrong, and trying to find out.

'And that's just me. The rest of you no doubt had similar arrangements, and people who will be wondering by now why you've gone silent. And that's not even considering the hundreds of folk down below, and all their worldly affairs.

'And even that's not all. The earthquake will have been measured in Tasmania, and seismologists there will be trying to contact the seismic station here and wondering why they can't. Plus we have a weather station down at the port and other maritime facilities that are meant to report in regularly, and won't have, if it's as bad down there as we think.

'So trust me, for a whole host of reasons, a lot of people will be turning their attention to this island even as we speak, and putting two and two together. By late tomorrow morning I'm quite sure that a plane or a chopper or a fast ship will be dispatched to investigate. We could easily see a helicopter landing up here by lunch time.'

Madelaine was frowning. 'Then why did you say four days at the most?'

'Well, even in the absolute worst case, in which for some inexplicable reason no one notices that we've been cut off and no one is sent to look for us, we'll still be fine, because a ship is due to dock here then.' The billionaire gave a nod to Rita. 'It was all arranged a month ago. It's Rita's lift home, the *Aurora Australis* on its return trip from Antarctica to Hobart.

'It's due three days from now. True, the *Australis* doesn't keep as tight a timetable as some vessels, given the ice sheets and other arctic hazards, but it was on schedule last I heard from it earlier this week, so if it's not here exactly on time, I'd expect it to be no more than a day late. So let's say four days at the utmost, before the outside world discovers our predicament here, and the rescue starts. So you see, there's little to worry about.'

So relaxed was his assurance, and so reasonable his argument, that Rita felt her own fears recede a little. Truly, what harm *could* they come to in a mere few days, here in such a stronghold, provided with stores and supplies enough for far longer than they would need them?

'In the meantime though,' Walter Richman concluded with a winning smile, 'we do have to fend for ourselves. The first concern is dinner. There's a fully stocked larder back in that kitchen, but I don't claim to be much of a cook, other than the basics. In my mountain-climbing days that meant not much more than beans or stew or instant noodles. Anyone interested in volunteering?'

Kushal gave a laugh. 'Why not? If everyone is agreeable, I still remember a recipe or two from my mother—as long as your cooks have the right spices, mind, and some golden basmati!'

And so the bizarre evening progressed, somehow cosy and pleasurable for all that everyone knew a mile or so below them there must be ongoing chaos and suffering. The camaraderie was fed by a make-believe air of roughing of it, of living by candlelight during a storm, and by glass after glass (in Rita's case at least) of superb wine.

They ate casually, the meal spread out on the low tables of the Saloon, with music playing on the bar sound system. Kushal turned out to be an excellent cook, serving up a feast of two curries, lamb and chickpea, along with coconut dal, all accompanied by fragrant rice and pappadums.

Not that all practicalities were forgotten. Periodically, Richman went off to visit Kennedy in the Control Room, to see if there was any progress with the security door (once also to take him some food). And several times Clara departed to try her walkie-talkie again on the Terrace, or to continue the search for the satellite phones as she remembered possible hiding places in which no one had yet looked.

By eleven p.m., however, it was clear that the emergency stairs were beyond reach for now, and that the quest for the phones was hopeless. It was decided that nothing further could be done that evening. Kennedy would remain on duty in the Control Room, in case someone below somehow re-established contact, but otherwise the rest of them should go to bed, and wait to see what the morning heralded.

Even then, everyone poured a final nightcap, lingering by the fire for a last half hour to marvel at the day they had just lived through.

'Tell me, Walter,' Kushal enquired of Richman, the builder sipping on cognac by then, 'would you have even attempted to climb the Wheel, if you had known avalanches on such a scale were possible?'

The billionaire was staring sombrely into the flames. 'I don't think I could have justified the risk, no. Oh, we accepted there was an avalanche danger, of course we did. And sure enough we had some big falls, some that took out multiple huts at a time, and claimed several lives too. But that display this afternoon? Something like that would have killed *all* of us, even sunk our ships. Little though we knew it, obviously we were lucky that whole time.'

Clara was musing over a sauterne. 'I do remember reading a theory about mega-avalanches on the Wheel. It was in an article somewhere. But they were talking about the past, millions of years ago, when the Wheel was still being shaped by great quakes and landslides. There was no suggestion that anything like what we saw today has happened in historical times, certainly nothing has been recorded in the last few hundred years. So I wouldn't say that you were lucky back during your expedition, Walter, instead I'd say that *we* have been incredibly *un*lucky today. It's got to be a one-in-a-thousand-year event—no, a one-in-a-hundred-thousand-year event.'

'That certainly would make it bad luck,' Richman agreed thoughtfully. He gave a sudden glance to Rita before returning his gaze to the fireplace. 'Even worse luck that the quake hit at exactly the moment it did, exactly in the ten-minute window in which there were unusually few people up here.'

'What on earth does it matter how many of us were here exactly?' asked Madelaine in some annoyance. 'What are you talking about?'

Richman looked mildly at the designer. 'You read Rita's book, didn't you?'

Rita flushed silently. Not the damn book *again*. But she did not interrupt.

'I read it, yes,' said Madelaine, 'though only quickly, I admit. I might not have absorbed every last detail. But what of that? What does her book have to do with how many of us are here?'

'Well, the phenomena Rita discusses in that book, her *presences*, are supposedly more likely to manifest and act when people are alone, or in small groups. Presences are much weaker, by her theory, if there's a big crowd around. And think about it: there has *always* been a crowd up here, twenty or thirty people, until just one brief instant this afternoon, when it dropped to six. Going by Rita's logic, you could argue that it's a suspicious coincidence that the quake happened to strike just at that moment.'

'You could argue it if you believed any of that nonsense,' Madelaine replied. Then added, with a look to Rita, 'But even she no longer believes the things she wrote. She told me so herself.'

Rita shifted reluctantly. She had indeed said that to Madelaine. And up until today she would have repeated it. But now, after what she had witnessed from the Terrace, after the hateful, gleeful expectation she had sensed in the Wheel . . .

She said, 'I'd rather not talk about any of this. I'm sure it's no help to anyone.'

Richman smiled. 'Oh, Rita still believes it all, Madelaine, and always has, whatever she tells you, whatever she tells herself. Otherwise she wouldn't have refused to fly here in a helicopter like a normal person, she wouldn't have demanded a ride on a cruise ship instead. Deny it or not, she's still too scared of her invisible beings to fly, or even to go to sea without the security of having hundreds of people, hundreds of minds, around her for protection.'

Rita met this with a stare. 'It isn't that simple,' she said. But went no further. For how could she explain without delving into her whole sorry life story, and they did not need to hear *that*.

'Well, never mind.' Richman drained his glass. 'Maybe this is all by chance and maybe it isn't, but it hardly matters, we'll be out of here by tomorrow night, whatever the mysterious forces might intend.

The Wheel has done its worst, after all, and we're still fine. So I'm off to get some sleep.'

And with a wink to Rita, and a nod to the others, he rose and strolled off to the Library.

After a moment's hesitation, Clara drained her glass and followed after him.

3

THE THIRD MAN FACTOR

Extract from 'Strange Tales of the Wheel',
George Wilkins, 2005

Third Man factor stories.

Every mountain in the world has them. At some point or other, some hapless individual or small group of two or three climbers, will become lost on the high slopes, stranded there by storm or mishap. Isolated from all other human help, close to death in the cold and the dark, they will despair. But then—behold! They encounter a mysterious only-half-seen figure that leads them somehow to safety before vanishing, leaving them shaken but alive to tell of the event to other awed, fascinated climbers.

They have met the legendary *Third Man*.

The phenomenon is quite well known in other situations too—anytime, indeed, that humans find themselves on the brink of death. It could be someone lost and dying of thirst in a desert. It could be a sailor forsaken and drowning at sea. It could be a victim trapped and fighting for breath in a burning building. The Third Man can appear anywhere, and to anyone in mortal peril. But something about mountains and icy landscapes in particular seems to summon the vision.

The incident which led to the name is as good an example as any. In 1916, the famed polar explorer Ernest Shackleton, his ship trapped and crushed in the Antarctic ice, his crew stranded on a desolate shore far from rescue or resupply, set out in a small boat with a few companions to reach the nearest hope of help, a whaling station seven hundred miles away on South Georgia Island. After a horrific storm-filled voyage, they finally reached the southern shore of the island—a frozen, mountainous place—but salvation was not yet at hand. The whaling station lay on the *northern* side of the isle.

Now, South Georgia is a long, thin landmass; narrow north to south, but much more extended east to west, with a jagged shoreline. To sail all the way around to the whaling station would thus have meant yet another torturous voyage for the weary mariners. So Shackleton decided to take the shorter route and go directly overland, on foot. This would mean a twenty-mile trek across the island's pathless interior, climbing, along the way, a range of high, icy mountains. A desperate venture. Even for men well fed and equipped such a route would have presented a stern challenge. For men hungry, exhausted, wet and cold, it might well prove to be fatal.

Even so, Shackleton set out with two others. And after thirty-six hours of tribulation the three of them, with almost no mountaineering equipment to speak of, did indeed manage to conquer the inner range and reach the whaling station to summon help. In time, all of Shackleton's crew would be rescued, a miraculous achievement, celebrated ever since. But later the explorer would report an interesting thing about the crossing of South Georgia.

In their extremity, as he and the other two men struggled amid the ice and rock, Shackleton had become convinced that there were *four* of them on the long march, not three. The other two men revealed that they also had felt this. All of them had known they were only three, but they all *felt* a fourth, a companion comforting and supportive, though silent and never directly seen, who stayed with them as far as the whaling station, then disappeared.

The tale became well known, and was referred to by the poet T.S. Eliot in his landmark work, *The Waste Land*, with the following haunting passage.

Who is the third who walks always beside you?
When I count, there are only you and I together
But when I look ahead up the white road
There is always another one walking beside you
Gliding wrapt in a brown mantle, hooded
I do not know whether a man or a woman
—But who is that on the other side of you?

Eliot had changed the numbers involved, and so, in time, the phenomenon, which many later explorers and adventurers would report, and which by rights should have been the Fourth Man, came to be known instead as the Third Man factor.

The history of mountaineering has since abounded with examples of the phenomenon. Almost always in such tales, the Third Man is a helpful influence. Usually this is only in the sense of the companionship it offers, silent and unseen at one's side, or waiting somewhere up ahead perhaps in the snow, promising companionship; the conviction that one is not alone, despite the fact that you are very much alone, and in deep peril.

But sometimes the Third Man is of more overt assistance. A voice may speak to the stranded climber, encouraging them to continue up or down the mountain, or warning them that they must not rest any longer, but move on, before they lose the ability to move at all. Sometimes the voice will point out a new route that must be taken, or warn of one that must be avoided, sometimes it will even seem to physically push a climber along. Mostly, the Third Man is anonymous and faceless, but there are tales in which the visitor, though unseen, is held to be a dead relative or some other absent loved one.

Unsurprisingly, many of the individuals who experience the phenomenon find it to be a deeply spiritual encounter. There is talk of guardian angels and spirit guides. Others are content to attribute it to the hallucinations of an oxygen-starved brain, or point to theories about consciousness and bicameral minds. But however you explain it, the Third Man, wherever and whenever it appears, is almost always a benign, indeed a life-saving, visitation.

But not on the Wheel.

On the slopes of the world's highest mountain, something else seems to be afoot.

Something malign.

There is no shortage of examples—Third Man tales from the Wheel are legion. This in itself is hardly surprising, the Wheel being the most dangerous mountain on the planet, a place more than any other where climbers are likely to find themselves lost and hallucinatory and close to death. But what is less expected is that the reports brought back of the Third Man—at least, from those who survived the encounter—are universally negative ones.

Some of the tales speak of an acute sense of hostility that comes from close at hand, a resentment that seems uniquely personal, almost as if a figure was beside the climber, glaring in anger. Others speak of an actual figure, elusive but glimpsed on the edge of vision, that seems to be hunched as if ready to spring and attack, a deranged demonic presence, causing climbers who behold it to flee in haste, whatever the risks to their safety. There are no friendly companions in these tales, no silent but supportive figures, only creatures that promise hatred, and, if given the chance, violence.

Other tales report more overt incidents. Ropes that were securely tied somehow become untied. Necessary items left in tents in high camps—oxygen or cooking fuel or food—will inexplicably go missing, even though there is no one else high on the mountain at the time, nor any scavenging animal or bird that lives so far up. Few of these incidents cause fatalities, maybe—but then, such reports only come from those who made it off the mountain alive. Who knows how many of the unexplained deaths on the Wheel, or the disappearances of climbers, may have been because of a rope that somehow became loosened, or from lack of an oxygen bottle where one should have been waiting?

The dead tell no stories.

But in any case, it is widely agreed that the most disturbing of all the many Third Man stories from the Wheel is that of the tragic demise of the Japanese mountaineer Keizo Yuko.

Born in 1960, Yuko was too young to take part in Walter Richman's massive assault on the Wheel in 1974. Indeed, although Japan boasts a strong climbing culture, relatively few Japanese climbers took part in Richman's venture, owing to the rule that all climbers must be fluent in English, the notion being that the expedition could not afford to have any language confusion in emergency situations. But already a keen climber at fourteen, Yuko followed the assault breathlessly, and swore that one day he too would climb upon the world's highest mountain.

As soon as he was old enough, he cut his teeth first on the Japanese and European Alps, then progressed to the Himalayas in the early 1980s, bagging three eight-thousand-metre peaks in quick succession. Then, considering himself ready at last, he turned to the Wheel. The great mountain was by then no longer undefeated, of course, but there were still challenges aplenty upon its lower slopes.

Yuko arrived there in the summer of 1984, a junior member of an eight-man Japanese team. They were one of only three teams on the mountain that year, historically a low number. In truth though, in the decade since Richman's triumph, the count of serious expeditions had been even lower most years. It was understandable. Now that the mountain was beaten, some of its allure was gone. Also, most of the climbers of the 1970s generation had worked for Richman and so had more than satisfied their own curiosity about the Wheel. It wasn't until the next generation matured— those who like Yuko had missed the Richman affair—that teams began to visit the mountain once more in greater numbers, eager to carve out their own achievements there.

The goal of Yuko's team was to be the first ever to ascend to Black Summit Three. This is one of the many subsidiary peaks set along the Wheel's North and South ridges. Black Summit Three is on the South

Ridge, a lumpish pillar that rises about eighty metres above the general ridgeline to nine thousand two hundred and twelve metres, set some eleven kilometres to the south of the Wheel's actual summit. Its name refers to the fact that it is the lowest of the three notable sub-peaks that exist within the range of the famous Black Band.

The other two Black Summits, being higher and more prominent, had by 1984 already attracted climbers and been defeated. Black Summit Three was the last that was virgin. So it was that Yuko's team, looking for an untrodden feature on the Wheel that was within their range (given that their expedition was small in scale and lacking any kind of high-altitude suits—although they did plan to use oxygen above eight thousand metres) set their sights on the otherwise unremarkable spire.

Their route was a traditional one in its early stages, tracking up the fixed lines and ladders of the West Face to the Plateau at five thousand metres, where they established a base camp. From there they angled south, following Richman's route for a time, but then cutting away much further southwards across rarely climbed territory. They founded Camp One at six thousand metres, and then Camp Two at seven thousand metres, by then directly beneath their target, though still more than two kilometres short of it in altitude.

Now the most difficult climbing began for Yuko and his seven companions, in high, thin air. They did not ascend directly upwards, however, where the face was particularly sheer. Rather, they traversed still further south across a series of cracks and ledges, aiming for the lower end of a chimney (a groove a few metres wide and deep, cut into the face) that runs back northwards at a steep angle for many hundreds of metres, all the way to the ridge-top, not far from the base of Black Summit Three.

It was a long way around, to be sure, but the chimney offered by far the safest final approach to the ridge, so much more sheltered and secure compared to the open face. The chimney's lower end, however, was to be strictly avoided, for it debouched into the terrifying abyss of the South Couloir.

This feature, the third of the Wheel's three great couloirs, is a huge vertical gash cut into the West Face about twelve kilometres south of the central line. It is three hundred metres across, delves the same distance back into the face, and it drops, sheer-sided and dreadful, from the top of the ridge to halfway down to sea level, four thousand metres in all.

Like the other great couloirs, it has never been climbed or even attempted. Indeed, Yuko's party would be treading closer to it than anyone had before at that point in time. Wisely, however, they did not intend to actually stray onto its deadly precipices.

Fate planned differently, alas.

Six weeks into the expedition, Yuko and his climbing companion Kasuya Noguchi, ten years Yuko's senior, reached the base of the chimney at just over eight thousand metres, some one hundred metres to the north of where it opened into the couloir. Here, they intended to drop supplies to establish Camp Three before descending. In days following, other pairs would finish establishing the camp, then the team could turn north and begin to climb up the fifty-degree sloped groove towards Black Summit Three.

But even as Yuko and his partner began to unload their packs, one of the Wheel's notorious clear-air storms struck the West Face.

Now, during the Richman expedition, Doppler wind radar had been installed on Observatory Mount to monitor the Wheel and warn of any descending jet-stream gales. But that facility had been unmanned since Richman's departure (it would not be permanently operated until 1990) and so there was no warning for the Japanese climbers.

In mere minutes, conditions at eight thousand metres went from calm and clear to a hurricane gale shrieking down the face, kicking up a blizzard of spindrift snow and reducing visibility to zero.

The pitch the two climbers had just ascended was sheer and difficult, and even though they had left fixed lines as they came, they knew it would be impossible to descend so exposed a route in such conditions, so they decided to bivouac and ride the storm out. They had a small tent and supplies for several days, carried for just such a situation, and the overhang of the chimney offered shelter from the gale and from any associated avalanche.

Thus they bedded down with some confidence, despite the fury of the wind screaming just beyond their little eyrie. They were also in contact, via radio, with their fellows further down the mountain, the closest of whom were two climbers at Camp Two, a thousand metres below, while the other four were spread between Camp One and Base Camp. While concerned, no one in the team saw any reason to panic. The Wheel's clear-air storms were terrible, but they seldom lasted more than a day or so.

Unfortunately, this time the wind did not let up for five days straight. Worse, it combined with a front of moist air that came sweeping in from the west on the third day, resulting in heavy snow and hail. Avalanches soon forced the climbers at the lower camps to withdraw to the safety of Base Camp, but retreat remained impossible for Yuko and Noguchi, trapped by the exposed face below them.

They had no oxygen with them, as it had not been planned to begin using the gas until the next pitch further up the chimney. At eight thousand metres, the human body, lacking any breathing assistance, cannot sleep or digest food. It is, in effect, slowly dying. Such conditions can be endured for short periods, which is what enables climbers without gas to make brief forays up as high as nine thousand metres and beyond. But after five days in their tent, sleepless, oxygen-deprived and malnourished, the two climbers were now entering desperate straits.

At last, on the sixth day, the wind relented, though the region of the chimney remained lost in snow and cloud. Yuko and Noguchi emerged from their cocoon to find that the fixed line by which they had intended to descend had vanished completely, stripped away by either wind or avalanche. They had no other ropes left. So it was that, severely weakened, and already suffering from early stages of frostbite on their hands and feet, the two climbers were now faced with an unsecured descent on a sheer face.

It was a deadly danger, but they had little choice. They doubted they could survive another night at eight thousand metres, nor could they hope for anyone to come up and rescue them. With the snow falling unabated, the lower approaches were still being swept with avalanches, and none of the climbers at Base Camp could yet risk ascending.

They began the descent, but only a hundred metres down the face they reached an impasse, a bulge that they had barely managed to pass on the way up, and which, in their degraded state, they could not now cross. In a last attempt to swing himself around the obstruction, the older climber, Noguchi, fell—and by outrageous fortune, saved his life. For despite a plummet of some fifty metres, he landed in soft fresh snow on a ledge at the foot of the pitch. Though knocked insensible for several hours, when he came to he found he had suffered no worse than severe bruising, and could continue his descent.

Higher up, Yuko, after calling down to his friend for some time and hearing no response, feared the worst: Noguchi must be dead. Yuko decided, in his grief, that the face was un-descendible. He spent the last of his strength returning to the chimney, and to the tent he and Noguchi had left behind.

There he spent a sixth night alone, increasingly ill and delirious, and quite unaware that below, Noguchi had regained consciousness and was staggering his way down through snow and constant avalanches to Camp Two. As Yuko had the pair's only walkie-talkie, there was no way for Noguchi to let anyone know he was alive.

The seventh day dawned windless and snowless and bitterly freezing, decreasing the risk of avalanche at last. The other four climbers of the team finally set out from Base Camp, and by midday had reached Noguchi at Camp Two. He was all but comatose, but they were able to give him oxygen and hot soup, reviving him enough that two of the climbers could begin to escort him further down. The other two then began the ascent towards the chimney, a kilometre above still, in search of Yuko.

They did not yet know if he was still alive. He had made no radio contact since the night before, and though the two rescuers were in clear air as they passed seven thousand five hundred metres, just above them a dense layer of cloud hung motionless right across the West Face, hiding anything that might be happening at eight thousand metres and within the chimney. Still, it was imperative that they at least try to reach him.

Finally, however, their radio crackled into life with a faint voice. It was Yuko. His diction was slurred, like a man heavily drunk, but he could be understood. 'Base Camp, Base Camp,' he said. 'Yuko here. We will try again to descend. Noguchi says he has found a new way, if we go down the chimney.'

The two rescuers stared at each other. *Noguchi*? How bizarre! It seemed that the climber above was hallucinating that his partner was still with him. 'No,' replied one of them urgently. 'Noguchi is already down. He is safe. Stay where you are, Yuko. We are coming for you, with oxygen.'

There was silence for a time, then Yuko came back, his voice stronger now and more certain. 'What are you talking about? Noguchi is right here with me. He has reconnoitred a path down the chimney, to the south, and says it is quite easy. I only have to follow him, and we can get down.'

Now the two rescuers were alarmed. A route southward down the chimney would only lead to the open mouth of the South Couloir, and a sheer drop of nearly four thousand metres.

'No, no!' they responded even more urgently. 'Do *not* go down the chimney. Noguchi is *not* with you. You are imagining it. Stay where you are; we will be with you with oxygen by nightfall.'

Now the climber above grew angry. Of course Noguchi was with him, he insisted, why were they trying to trick him into believing otherwise?

'Put him on the radio then!' one of the rescuers demanded, hoping to demonstrate to Yuko that he was alone. 'Let us talk to him.'

But Yuko only said, 'I can't. He has gone ahead down the chimney. He is calling to me now. I must hurry up and follow him.'

Silence followed. The rescuers peered up in frustration, but the cloud above remained impenetrable. What was happening up there? Was Yuko actually following his illusory comrade down the chimney? Was he even now drawing near to the place where the groove debouched without warning into the gulf of the couloir? Would the confused climber see the danger in the fog before it was too late?

Time and again as they scrambled upwards, the rescuers shouted warnings into the radio, but it was another hour, just as they were nearing the cloud level themselves, before they received a reply.

'It's all right now.' Yuko's voice, though only a whisper, came through clearly, for after all, the range was now only a few hundred metres. 'We're nearly down. Just a few more yards, and I'll be clear of the chimney.'

The two rescuers looked at each other aghast. Clear of the chimney? That meant he would be stepping blindly into the plunging emptiness of the couloir, and to his certain death.

'No!' they screamed, into the open air now, hoping that their shouts would reach Yuko more emphatically than over the radio.

And then the walkie-talkie crackled again, but this time the voice that came on was Kasuya Noguchi himself. He had by now, with his two helpers, descended to Camp One. He and the others had been listening to the radio conversations of the higher climbers, and Noguchi had recovered enough to try to help his former partner. 'Keizo! Listen, it's me, Kasuya! You're alone up there. I am not with you. You must stop and wait for the others!'

A wrenching silence.

Then, from the lone climber, 'Kasuya? No. That can't be you.' The voice was awful to hear—exhausted, haunted, but still doggedly sure of itself. 'I can *see* you. You're just there, ten yards beyond the end of the chimney. You're *beckoning* to me.'

The words chilled the listeners with horror. There was nothing for anyone to stand on ten yards beyond the end of the chimney. There was only the open air, and the long, long fall.

'I'm coming to you now,' said Yuko.

There followed a clunk as the walkie-talkie was dropped to the ground. Somehow, the channel remained open and sending. The listeners heard the sound of shuffling steps growing distant. Then, barely audible, came Yuko's voice.

'Kasuya? Why won't you look at me?' Another scrabbling step, and the sound of small stones bouncing off into infinity. 'Why won't you—'

There was a frozen pause. Then came three short, ragged cries. Cries filled with—what? Terror? The sudden return to sanity, there on the brink of the precipice, and already overbalanced? Did the ghost figure finally turn and show its face?

No one will ever know.

The two rescuers nearest the couloir glimpsed a blur of a figure dropping away within its appalling depths, spinning madly, arms and legs flailing. But even so, they continued their ascent to the chimney, to be sure that it was empty.

As it was.

The malefic Third Man of the Wheel had come, done his work, and vanished once more.

4

WAITING

RITA WOKE SLOWLY TO THE growl of something like thunder, a subterranean throatish sound, as if some vast beast was shifting its bulk and breathing low as it hunted in the mist and darkness.

Mist and darkness. She opened her eyes to a dim featureless space, bewildered a moment as to where and when she was. Then she remembered: she had drawn the curtains the night before as she went to bed, wanting to shut out the night and the great shadow of the Wheel against the stars.

The rumble came again, an afterthought trembling, and the notion rose in her, listening as she lay, that it was the Wheel that was the hunting beast, the mountain that was growling in its throat, a menace even from ten kilometres away.

She blinked, the dream state fading to rationality. Aftershock. It must be an aftershock, a settling after yesterday's earthquake. And that was bad enough, without thinking of beasts . . .

She rose and pulled back the curtains—and saw that one part of her dream at least had been prophetic. Overnight, fog had come.

And it was a heavy one. The wall of mist through the glass was not the bright grey of a light morning fog that would burn off with the sun, but rather the brooding jet slate of the underside of thunderstorms. She could barely see the furthest side of her balcony, and beyond that, nothing. Nor was this pre-dawn gloom. A glance to her watch on the bedside table confirmed that it was almost nine a.m. The sun was long up, but the Observatory was shadowed in deep, deep cloud.

And wrapped also in cold. The weather panel reported that the temperature outside was a brutal minus nineteen degrees Celsius. Thank the lord the heating in the Observatory was still working. They were quite safe and secure. And yet . . . as Rita stared again into the gloom, still the dream sense of foreboding pervaded her senses. It was the Wheel, she knew. For all that it was invisible in the cloud, it loomed in her mind as a threat—indeed, even a greater danger now that it was unseen.

She shuddered and turned away, feeling weary and raw and unready for any of this, for the day that lay ahead. The hangover didn't help. She had gone to bed at three, having yet again drunk far more than was good for her, an entire bottle here alone in the apartment, on top of all she had imbibed up in the Saloon with the others. It seemed indecent to think of it now, all of them downing Richman's fine wines when people down at Base were injured or dead. But then, what else had there been to do? And anyway how else was she to shut down any possibility of . . . *sensing* . . . things she did not want to sense?

But what now? Staying drunk all day, or until rescue came, was hardly the answer . . .

She jumped suddenly as an electronic squawk blared from somewhere in the flat, followed by a cough and then a hollow amplified voice.

'Rita? Rita, are you up? It's Clara here. I'm on the intercom. Can you hear this? If you can, go into the living room, you'll see the panel there.'

Wondering, Rita moved into the living room. There, unnoticed until now, set into the pillar dividing the space from the kitchen, was a black panel that held a speaker and numeric keypad.

'To answer,' boomed Clara's disembodied voice from the speaker, 'just press the button marked *Talk* and speak into the panel.'

Rita found the button, pressed it. 'Hello?'

'Oh, good. I hope I didn't wake you, but you said last night you'd be up by now.'

Rita had said that? She could not recall. She pressed the button again. 'It's fine, I was awake. You gave me a bit of a shock though. I didn't know there was an intercom system here.'

There was a pause that seemed somehow embarrassed, and Rita had the sudden feeling that they had also discussed this last night. 'Well, there was never any reason to use the intercoms before; it was easier to text or phone. But now that our mobiles are useless, and with the internal phone system down, the intercom system is all we have left. But anyway, we're calling a meeting in the dining room to discuss our options for the day. There'll be breakfast too. In half an hour?'

'I'll be there,' Rita said.

Twenty-five minutes later, showered, and with a hurried coffee sitting uneasily in her stomach, she was ascending the Helix Staircase.

And there was no escaping it, she mused as she climbed, staring up at the vast cavity of the Well, the windows in the dome far above shrouded in grey: the Observatory felt different now.

Oh, it had always felt huge and imposing, but it was only now that it felt *empty*. Somehow, the knowledge that dozens of staff moved and worked within the place, even if they were unseen, had given the great residence a sense of occupancy. Now that Rita knew there was no one in the service tunnels or the kitchens or the offices, now that she knew there were only six of them in all those acres of rooms and hallways, *now* she felt a cold vacancy to the house, an outsized, inhuman sense of scale that no cosy heating or clever interior design could dispel.

She came to the Atrium and heard voices. The others, with the exception of Kennedy, who presumably remained in the Control Room, were all awaiting her at the dining table, Richman and Clara each looking bright and fit, Kushal and Madelaine with a rather more dishevelled air that perhaps matched Rita's own state. Pots of fresh coffee and tea, and several trays of toast and a selection of cold meats and preserves were spread out for breakfast.

'Any news?' Rita asked as she came to the table, returning various nods of greeting.

Richman, at the table's head, was as suave and assured as if yesterday's disaster had never happened. 'We still have no outside communication, and no way to get down, if that's what you mean.'

Rita took her seat. 'But you still think rescue will be coming for us today?'

'I expect so. Of course,' he added, with a nod to the greyed-out windows, 'if this murk doesn't lift, then even when a helicopter arrives it won't be able to land up here. It'll have to land at the pad down at Base. But at least that will be a beginning.'

'That's if the helipad down at Base is even still functional,' Kushal put in, in the tone of resuming an earlier argument. He gave Rita a sombre look. 'We still have no idea how bad things are below. It's worrying enough that we can't go down—but what I find more ominous is that no one has come *up*.'

Richman was sceptical. 'It's a two and a half thousand metre climb. Would you labour up a flight of more than ten thousand stairs—ladders, really—if you didn't have to? They may well be fine down there, apart from a little water damage, and be rightly assuming that we're fine up here too.'

Kushal shook his head in turn. 'You saw that wave, things will be far worse down there than just a *bit wet*. Someone should have come up here by now seeking medical help. The fact that no one has suggests that there is no one left who can.'

'But they couldn't get in anyway, could they?' asked Rita. She was gingerly buttering a slice of toast, though she had little appetite. 'Wouldn't they be blocked by the security doors?'

'Yes,' answered the builder, 'but we'd still see them. There's a security camera at the top landing of the stairs; they'd show up on that, even if we couldn't let them in. Also, there are intercom panels at the top and the bottom of the stairs, plus more spaced out in between, and no one has used them.'

Richman shrugged. 'We can play guessing games all day. Until we can get down those stairs and see for ourselves, it's all irrelevant. Hell, I was thinking I really would climb over to the south face and at least have a look down—but as long as this fog hangs around, there's no point even in that.'

'How long will the fog last?' Madelaine asked. 'Do we have a weather report?'

Clara said, 'We lost weather reports when we lost the internet and the satellite TV.'

'What about a radio?'

The major-domo shook her head. 'We don't have any radio receivers. That is, obviously, we have the two-way radios, the walkie-talkies. But nothing you could pick up an FM or AM station on. It's a weird situation, I know, but in this digital age, there was just no call for something so old-fashioned up here.'

'Wonderful,' said Madelaine with a grunt. 'So here we sit in digital ignorance.'

Richman sat up more sternly. 'We haven't been totally idle. Kennedy has been working away in the Control Room, and thinks that he'll be able to trace the burned-out relays that control the security door and replace them. It's taking a lot of trial and error; he's no more an electrician than I am—but we can hope that he'll succeed eventually. Kushal, after breakfast, you could go and help him. You must know something of electronics, you're a builder after all.'

Kushal laughed uneasily. 'A little, a very little. Plugs and wires were always my weak point. I had experts to look after that for me. But of course I'm willing to do what I can.'

'And the rest of us?' asked Madelaine. 'Surely there is something we should be doing?'

Richman shrugged. 'The best advice I can give for now is to keep your ears open. Without any radar or other communication, the first any of us will know of a rescue team is when we hear either a helicopter circling about, or, if a ship arrives, a horn blast from down in the harbour. Otherwise, well, it was Clara who provided breakfast, but there's still lunch and dinner to be prepared. Volunteers?'

So they settled in for the day. The breakfast finished, Richman departed for the Cottage, to do what there Rita did not know, but he went alone, unaccompanied by Clara. Meanwhile, Kushal went off somewhat sheepishly to assist Kennedy, so it was left to the women, Rita, Madelaine and the major-domo, to clear the table and do the dishes.

Even after that was done, by unspoken agreement the three of them did not disperse: the notion of returning each to their own far-flung quarters was too lonely. Instead they held together against the uncertainty of the day, wandering into the Saloon and stoking the fire once more to a comforting blaze. There they remained until noon, either talking or drinking coffee or gazing out at the grey.

All the while they followed Richman's instructions and listened. But although occasionally one or another of them would lift her head attentively as if in response to some sound from outside, nothing definite ever emerged from the silence, no reassuring throb of helicopter rotors, no warning blast of a ship's siren. From time to time, Clara took a walkie-talkie out onto the Terrace and ran through the radio channels, but she received only static in reply.

Then it was time for another foray into the kitchen to prepare lunch. Madelaine ferried the sandwiches down to Kushal and Kennedy, and returned with the report of only slow progress on the door. Clara attended to Richman in the Cottage, and brought back no report at all.

Once the lunch tidy-up was complete, the chardonnay came out again, and the three women sat about the fire contemplatively. 'So tell us, Clara,' Madelaine enquired after a time, filling everyone's second glass, 'are you as confident as Richman that rescue will really come today?'

The major-domo, reclining in her chair, had her booted feet resting on the edge of the hearth. Her gaze seemed faraway. 'Walter likes to imagine the world as it should be, organised and swift. I'm not the same. I know the world is often confused and slow. So no, I don't expect a quick rescue. I think it will take all of today at least before any serious alarm is sounded. By tonight, maybe someone will demand action, but even then, they won't send a helicopter straightaway, they'll wait until daylight and morning.'

Rita spoke up, having noted the major-domo's use of the more intimate *Walter*. 'How is he holding up? Richman? I know he seems confident. But this whole project, the Observatory, the town at Base, everything he's spent the last few years on, lies in ruins now, doesn't it? I know nothing up here has been damaged, but if Base has been wiped out, then surely the Observatory isn't viable anymore.'

'Oh, he'll rebuild,' said Clara simply. 'He's already told me that. Money is no object when it comes to this place. He refuses to be beaten by anything that concerns the Wheel. Ever.' Her voice caught. 'But lord, people are *dead* down there. Hundreds of them maybe. Just for the sake of his stupid *house*.'

Attuned to the conflicting emotions in the statement, Rita gave a glance to Madelaine. Did the designer know that the major-domo planned to soon leave Richman's service? Could it be spoken of openly?

Madelaine, however, was only gazing at the windows and the fog. 'But tomorrow?' the designer pressed of Clara, as if she hadn't even heard the last exchange. 'You're sure by tomorrow someone will come?'

'Perhaps,' the major-domo sighed, sitting up, the moment gone. 'If this cloud lifts.'

But the fog didn't lift. All afternoon it remained, unmoving, as deep and still as if all the windows had been painted over. At about three thirty, stifled and bored, the three women at last went up to the Conservatory, donned jackets from by the doors, and ventured out onto the Terrace.

It had warmed only slightly through the day, and the temperature stood at minus twelve degrees Celsius, but as it was windless, this was not unbearable. Still, the Terrace was a gloomy sight. There were no lights on, no fires blazing in the pits or the hearths, and up here the embedded underfloor heating was not powered during emergencies, so ice had formed over every surface, congealed out of the freezing mist.

The mist itself was even more oppressive now that they were out in it: visibility was no more than ten yards, making even the open Terrace feel claustrophobic. And yet conversely it also felt terribly exposed, at least to Rita. She was all too aware of how slick the icy floor had become under her feet, and she could not help but imagine some awful, slipping, sliding accident that would send her careering into one of the parapets and then straight over the edge, to plummet endlessly, wailing, into the silent greyness.

Except it wasn't silent. There were *sounds* out there. Some were local to the Terrace, ice cracking underfoot, or sometimes, more mysteriously, from where no one was standing. And sometimes a soft, insidious clatter came from beyond the parapets, like pebbles or flakes of rock pattering down sheer cliffs. And that was probably only ice too, sheering away from the flanks of the Mount.

But from further afield in the gloom came a low sound that had nothing to do with ice, it was altogether vaster, a low-toned howl, like wind piping in some huge hollow tube. What it might be none of them could at first guess, but turning from point to point to locate the source, they decided it came from the east. In other words, from the direction of the Wheel.

Finally, Clara gave a slow nod. 'It comes from very high up, I think. I've heard something like that before, in my climbing days.'

Rita was staring into the fog. Though the darkness was no deeper eastward than westward, she could sense or imagine a more profound shadow rearing there, giant.

'I was in the Himalayas,' Clara went on, 'part of a team trying to climb Kangchenjunga—that's the third highest of the Himalayan peaks, just a few hundred metres lower than Everest. One night as we were at Base Camp, at near to five thousand metres, there was a sound like this sound now, coming out of the darkness. It was dead calm where we were, but in the moonlight we could see up to the summit ridge, and up there a great plume of snow was being torn off the mountain. That's what we were hearing, the wind over the peak. We were four thousand metres below, but even so, the howling was terrible. Suddenly, I did not want to climb the mountain at all.'

'And did you?' Rita asked.

'No. The weather turned bad the next day, and stayed bad for weeks. We never got above six thousand metres. But I remember that sound.'

Madelaine had her head cocked in fascination. 'You think there's a gale blowing higher up on the Wheel? Even though it's calm here?'

'If there is, and if we're hearing it from *ten* thousand metres away and more, then I don't like to imagine what kind of wind it is.'

But then the sound faded again, and silence reigned once more.

They came to the pool. Normally it would be floodlit in such a gloom, as well as illuminated internally, sparkling blue-green and steaming invitingly, no matter the chill of the air. But now it was unlit, the water frigid and black, a rime of ice creeping inwards from the edges.

'Will it freeze over?' Rita wondered.

'Probably,' said Clara. 'With the heating off, there's nothing to stop it.'

'Will it freeze *solid*?'

'I'd think not. Even under emergency power I gather that there's still a certain amount of heating applied at the base, to keep the internal plumbing from freezing, which would damage the pipes. The top will freeze, I'm sure, but not the whole pool.'

There seemed no point staying any longer, so they retreated carefully across the icy ground and went back inside.

▲

At four thirty p.m., with the greyness outside beginning to deepen to black as true evening drew near, there was finally a development.

The Saloon intercom crackled into life. 'Heads up, girls.' It was Richman's voice. 'Kennedy has got the door open. Come down and see.'

They exchanged glances. The billionaire's tone did not sound celebratory.

They rose and trooped off through the Dining Hall to the service tunnels, then down through the maze—Clara confidently leading the way—past the Control Room, empty now, and on to the uttermost depths and the service landing.

There they found that the heavy steel slab that had blocked the service elevator shaft had now withdrawn upwards into its slot. Revealed was a large rectangular threshold, opening onto a narrow landing, beyond which a dark vacancy yawned, cold and echoing. Richman, Kennedy and Kushal were on the landing, standing at a rail and peering down, into the shaft. 'Come on,' beckoned the billionaire. 'You won't believe this.'

The women filed in, Rita the hindmost. She had tried, coming down, to prepare herself for this, knowing that she was likely to find the shaft and stairway unsettling. But even so . . .

She found herself on a concrete platform that jutted out into a vast vertical tube hewn from the inner heart of the Mount. The far edge of the platform matched up with a square tower of scaffolding that rose within the greater circle, fixed by multiple anchor points to the curved walls. This square tower was divided into two rectangular shafts. The left shaft was for the service elevator. Guide rails ran down it, and a thick cable dangled from a chute in the roof overhead, above which, presumably, lay the winching room with its great engines and fly-wheels. At the platform's edge, sliding doors of wire mesh, closed now, prevented the careless from stepping over the lip when the carriage was not there to receive them.

Down the other shaft within the great scaffold ran the emergency stairs, accessed by a simple gap in the railing, open to the void.

'Mother*fuck*,' said Clara, who had reached the railing first. Reluctantly, but drawn inexorably, Rita inched to the rail, gripped her hands on the banister, and forced herself to look.

And oh god . . . it was *awful*.

She had been warned, sure enough. The stairs were not really stairs, she had been told. And it was true. What she beheld was a series of ladders, narrow, bare and steeply angled, that switched back and forth as they descended within the scaffold tower, joined each to each by only the tiniest of landings made of naked squares of metal grating.

There was nothing *solid* to any of it, no proper railings, no floors that weren't merely screens. And around this matchstick structure opened the immense emptiness of the shaft, falling and falling in vanishing perspective to its invisible base, two and half thousand metres below in the darkness. Oh, there were lights in the shaft, pinpricks mounted on the scaffolding, but they did nothing to illuminate—all they did was give dimension to the terrible abyss as it sank.

But all of that Rita might have borne, whatever her private terrors. None of that was the worst. The worst was that the stairs were—

'You see that, Clara?' commented Walter Richman. 'Can you explain that? I've been asking Kushal, and *he* sure can't.'

Kushal shook his head, defensive. 'It should not be possible. The specifications took into account the threat of earthquake. All the anchor points are rated for much higher torsion than yesterday's little tremor could have produced. It makes no sense.'

'And yet,' said Richman, 'there you are.'

Rita was battling with nausea, so revolting was the sight. About fifty metres below, just where the gloom of the shaft began to dim details into a blur, one entire flight of stairs had come loose from its lower landing, and was now hanging about forty degrees askew, its last step dangling over the gulf. And even further down, at the limit of visibility, a second flight of stairs had come similarly free.

'There must have been some particularly bad flexing within the shaft,' Kushal was musing. And Rita understood his defensiveness now—this was his job; he had *built* these stairs. 'It's a little understood field, in fact, the effects of torsion upon structures attached within a confined shaft. In any case, the specs we were given were clearly insufficient.'

'We're not interested in blame just now, Kushal,' Kennedy said testily. 'All we want to know is, can we still risk climbing down there?'

Madelaine expressed at least a little of the horror that Rita was feeling but couldn't voice. 'Go down that? Are you crazy?'

'Oh, I think it could be done,' pondered Clara, her gaze moving carefully over the stairs, a mountain climber assessing an untested face. 'If only an occasional flight is loose, then it'd be no great feat to climb down to the next one, using the scaffolding. But if multiple flights in a row have come away further down, it might get tricky. Even so . . .'

'You'd actually try it?' asked Madelaine, her expression awe stricken.

The major-domo tilted her head. 'I'm just saying it would be possible.'

'We're not all mad fools like you bloody climbers,' commented Kushal. 'I'm not going down there no matter what.'

Richman spoke again. 'For the moment no one is going down. If it turned out that there was no other choice, then maybe I'd let Clara try, if she really wanted, and if we rigged her up with safety gear. Certainly she would be the best choice among the six of us. If I was ten years younger, sure, I'd be willing to give it a go myself, but there's no arguing with old age, and you others have no climbing experience at all. That only leaves Clara. But there's no need for any heroics yet. We'll at least wait to see what tomorrow brings. Come the morning, we'll probably have a helicopter landing on the Terrace, in which case the state of these stairs will be irrelevant.'

Rita remembered to breathe. It had been out of the question, of course, that she would ever go down those terrible stairs herself—but even the thought of Clara going down, expert climber though she once was, had been making her head throb with anxiety. Thank god it had been ruled out. The only dim surprise was that Richman, no matter his age, hadn't volunteered himself first, at least if only to then be talked out of it by the rest of them.

Clara, meanwhile, had been staring intently into the depths of the shaft. Now, to Rita's renewed alarm, she leaned far out over the rail and cupped her hands around her mouth. 'Hello!' she called. 'Hello below! Is there anyone down there?'

The others all froze. Echoes of the call sounded ghostly from the depths, then silence settled, chill, and watchful somehow.

Everyone listened again, straining to hear some far-off shout from below. But the only sound was a kind of seashell whisper, immense and hollow, that rose up the shaft on a creeping breeze. The more Rita listened, the more it sounded, disturbingly, like the faintest of breathing—the mountain itself inhaling and exhaling through this artificial throat.

Kushal shuddered. 'This place gives me the creeps. I'm going back up. If we're stuck here another night, then it's time for a drink.'

And so they abandoned the stairs.

▲

Madelaine cooked dinner that night, her version of beef bourguignon, along with the last of the fresh bread that the house chefs had baked yesterday morning. Once more, they ate casually in the Saloon, and afterwards lounged about sipping on drinks.

The mood was grimmer, however, than the previous night. There was no air of making-do this time, of impromptu camping out, no post-disaster sense of euphoria. For all the comforts of the food and the drinks and the fire and the soft leather couches, there was a palpable undercurrent of impatience.

The change was most notable in Kushal. The builder was normally indefatigably cheerful and talkative, but tonight he was all but silent, slumped in an armchair, with one hand wrapped broodingly around his whisky glass. From time to time he would rise and stride impatiently to the windows to stare out, as if hoping to find that the fog had cleared. At other moments Rita would catch him sitting rigidly, his head tilted as if listening, perhaps for the unlikely sound of a helicopter arriving by night.

If so, no sound ever came, nor did the fog against the windows shift or lift.

Finally it appeared Kushal had had enough. In a lull in the conversation between the others, he sat up abruptly and said, 'Are we going to talk about it? Are we going to address what's happening here?'

Richman considered him a moment, then said mildly, 'What do you mean?'

The builder waved a hand to the surroundings. 'I mean, how it is that we've been stranded here—and what we should do about it. Or,' he added, giving Rita a stare, 'what *she* should do about it.'

'Me?' said Rita.

The billionaire looked at them both, said only, 'I still don't see what you're getting at.'

'You don't?' Kushal challenged. He was, Rita noted, somewhat drunk. 'Here we are in this impregnable palace of yours, and it's supposed to be foolproof; there are backups for the backups. No matter what, we're supposed to be able to leave whenever we want. There are three ways at least: by the lifts, by the stairs, or by helicopter.

'But look, one by one we've lost each of those three. A tsunami floods Base, so the main power goes, so the lifts are out. This fog comes in and so the helicopter is out. The security door jams so we can't use the stairs all day, and when we do get the door open the stairs are no good anyway, even though a quake like that shouldn't have done any damage. For that matter, how did a quake so minor start an avalanche so big, a one-in-a-hundred-thousand-year event, Clara called it, from just a *tremor.*

'No, something is going on here, something deliberate. *She* knows,' he added, with another glare to Rita. 'It's all in that book of hers. I read it again last night. It's your fault, Richman; you were the one talking about it. And now I can't help wondering if something really does want us trapped here.'

The others met this long outburst with a moment of strained silence.

Then Richman said coolly, 'So you think one of Rita's *presences* is to blame for all this? You mean, a presence here in the Mount?'

Kushal looked stubborn, then confused. 'The Mount? Well, I don't know. I thought . . . in her book, I mean, there aren't supposed to be presences in places where lots of people have lived. People drive presences out, that's how it works, isn't it? And the Mount has had climbers all over it for years, and huts up here, even before we began construction.'

His look to Rita was too pleading for her to refuse, despite the vast sea of reluctance that flooded up in her. She gave a cautious nod. 'According to what's in that book, you're right; there should be no presence left here in the Mount. Not anymore.'

'According to the book,' Richman echoed, eyes dancing. 'As if you didn't write it yourself. But fine then,' and now he looked back to Kushal, 'if there's no presence in the Mount, then where is it?'

Kushal glanced at Rita, but when she gave no sign of answering, he said, 'In the Wheel, of course. In that bloody great mountain out there.'

The billionaire smiled easily once more. 'But that can't be, can it, Rita? I've read that book too, don't forget. The Wheel is miles away from us, and I'm sure you explained somewhere that none of your presences can act across so much distance. They're strictly local. Or have I got that wrong?'

Rita flushed, and replied stiffly, 'No, that's what I wrote. It shouldn't be possible.'

'There you go then, Kushal. There can't be a presence here in the Mount, and even if there is one in the Wheel, it can't reach us. So you—'

'But I'd never seen the Wheel when I wrote that book,' Rita interrupted. 'It's . . . it's not like any other place on Earth. If I had come here back in those days, then I might have written differently.'

Richman only frowned at her silently, almost sadly, as if in disappointment.

It was Kennedy who spoke next. The security chief had been sprawled back on a couch, staring at the ceiling, as if indifferent to the entire conversation. Now he lifted his head and said, 'Would someone mind telling me what the fuck you all are talking about? What the hell are *presences*?'

His employer glanced at him with cool amusement. 'You *still* haven't read her book? How many times have I asked you to do it?'

Kennedy shrugged. 'I don't read fiction. Especially science fiction.'

Richman laughed, gave a rueful shrug to Rita, then turned back to his security chief. 'Well, I'll explain it to you then. Of course, it all sounds a bit crazy if you just lay her theory out there, so I'll start with the story of how Rita here came to believe what she believes, or what she *used* to believe. I'm taking this straight from the second chapter of her book. I remember it quite well, it made such an impression.' His smile returned to Rita. 'Unless you want to tell it?'

She stared back without trying to hide her discomfort. 'No, thank you.'

'Okay then.' He addressed Kennedy. 'It all started when Rita was only a girl, fifteen or so, from memory. She was a very well-off only child. Her father was already famous by then, and very much in-demand. And it so happened that he came to work on a house that was being built in a unique position.

'Oh, not as unique as *this* position, but still . . . Imagine a tall sandstone sea cliff—somewhere south of Sydney, quite remote, on the edge of one of those huge national parks they have around there. Scooped into this cliff was a big cave with an overhanging ceiling and spectacular views across the sea and down to the surf below. Somehow, the very rich owner of the block of land behind the cliff got planning permission to tunnel down and build himself a house in the cave. And he hired Richard Gausse to design it. Where was it again exactly, Rita? I can't recall the name . . .'

Rita hunched silently in her chair, not looking at Richman anymore. She could remember the name of the place all too well, but only shook her head—fuck him if he thought she'd say it aloud.

'Well, forget the name,' the billionaire went on, 'it doesn't matter. The house was designed on four levels, half dug into the solid rock of the cliff, half extending out into the cavity under the great arch of the cave roof. From above and behind the house was invisible, but from within it opened to views of the sea and to the waves crashing against the rocks. By all accounts it was going to be beautiful, if it had ever been completed. But of course, it never was. At least, not quite to the original design.

'Rita and her mother came to visit one day. There was some mix-up; they were supposed to be meeting Rita's father at the site, but Richard was away on some errand, so Rita and her mother ended up there alone. And, according to the book, Rita began to notice that something didn't feel right.'

Still Rita refused to look at Richman, barely able to believe that he was really going to make her relive this awful moment, and in public. And he didn't even have the details correct. Yes, on that terrible day, her father was away when she and her mother arrived—he had forgotten they were coming to see the house, and had gone to argue with a contractor over defective window frames. But they hadn't been alone at the site, not in the beginning—there were more than a dozen workmen busy about the place.

That's why, at first, nothing felt wrong at all. Not with so many people around.

But it was late in the day, and soon the workmen began to drift off. The foreman was the last to leave, and he assured Rita's mother that Richard could not be long much longer, that he would certainly come back to the site, as he had left his briefcase, which he always took home with him at night. So if they wanted, they were welcome to stay and wait for him. (It was the days before mobile phones, when a simple call could have solved the matter.) The site was quite safe to wander about, all the structural work was complete, only the fitting out remained.

So they waited, Rita and her mother, quietly exploring the four levels. The house was indeed beautiful, all glass walls and light and open terraces, the sea somehow visible from everywhere, even underfoot, and it was a warm, lovely evening. But even so, Rita began to grow uneasy.

It was a feeling that had been stealing upon her as the workmen left one by one, a sense of not wanting them to go, and especially, as it dwindled to only the foreman, of not wanting to be alone there with her mother. But now they *were* alone, and her anxiety was mounting minute by minute. It was like nothing the fifteen-year-old Rita had ever experienced before, as if someone who hated her and meant her harm was hovering at her shoulder, on the cusp of violence. There was no one there, she looked multiple times, but the sensation would not go away.

'Finally,' Richman went on, 'the two of them ended up on a lower balcony overlooking the drop down to the ocean, ninety feet or so, if I remember right; the book is quite detailed. Four stories overhead, meanwhile, was the giant overhang that formed the roof of the cave. Now, that overhang had been checked by structural engineers, and they were quite sure that it was solid, that there was no way it was likely to collapse any time soon, certainly not in the house's expected lifetime.'

Not in a dozen lifetimes, the engineers had said, Rita remembered. True, the very fact that this was a cave set within a sea cliff predicated that the roof would collapse one day, when the ocean finally ate away its foundations. But the estimates spoke of the event being centuries off, if not millennia.

374

Still, before she and her mother stepped onto the balcony, Rita almost said something. Almost. She wanted to demand, or beg, that they get out of there, that they go up to the top floor and escape to the surface. That's how strong it was, the sensation of hostility and resentment, of not being wanted by something that was all around them.

But then they were out on the balcony, and the ocean was a glowing blue in the sunset light that streamed over the cliff top above, and the wind gusted warm and salt-laden, and her mother lifted her arms and said, *Oh, this is lovely.*

Her last coherent words.

'But secure or not,' said Richman, 'a chunk of the roof came down. Though just before it did, Rita somehow knew it was going to happen, and tried to shout a warning to her mother.'

No. Again, it was not quite like that. Rita hadn't known what was going to happen. Rather, the sensation of latent hostility in the air suddenly turned to a malicious glee, and its focus lifted. Rita looked up then, and saw the great boulder already falling. The cry she gave was too late, far too late.

Richman carried on relentlessly. 'Not in time, however. A rock the size of a car detached from the overhang and fell four stories to slam into the balcony, smashing a great hole in it. Rita's mother almost got out of the way, but it glanced her, and she ended up hanging from the edge of the hole.'

Rita was lost to memory. The concussion was all but silent, so easily did the tumbling boulder obliterate the balcony. Only when it hit the sea below did the rock arouse any thunder. And left behind was her mother, hanging at the edge of the huge hole, dangling over the ocean far beneath. She was not holding on deliberately, it was just that her left wrist had become trapped in a jagged crevice of concrete and reinforcement bar that lay exposed by the destruction.

From that single wrist, the flesh laid open to the bone, she hung for several long moments, writhing in disbelief and shock. Her legs kicked wildly beneath her as if for purchase, and her free arm flailed as she tried to rise to take a hold. But even if there had been purchase or a hold it wouldn't have mattered, for the boulder had shattered her legs and arm, and all three limbs were disjointed, jangling ruins.

Even so, she may well have survived, if it had ended there. She would never have walked properly again, but she might have lived.

But the sensation of malice that had surrounded Rita had not abated. Even through her terror and shock, she was aware of it, distracting her from what she should have been doing—which was going to her mother's aid. Instead her attention was drawn, helplessly, back to the cliff top again.

There, another great chunk of stone was readying itself to detach.

No, it was being *readied* to detach.

That was the only way she could describe it. The boulder was not quite as large as the first, but it was big enough, and directly over her mother, and it was being *wrenched* from its position. It was not yet free, but in a series of jolts and shivers, it was bit by bit splitting away, as if unseen hands were tugging at it, over and over and over again.

And the sensation of glee, of vengeance, of retribution, was overpowering.

Rita turned back to her mother, who was still trying frantically to lift herself by her painfully trapped wrist, blood streaming from a cut on her forehead (it was only later that Rita would realise that she herself was cut all over from flying stone splinters) and for a moment their eyes locked.

Then came the final cracking sound above, and the rush of something huge in the air.

'But then a second boulder broke loose,' Richman concluded, 'and carried another piece of the balcony away, and Rita's mother with it. So she died. A terrible, tragic accident, you might think. But that was not how Rita as a girl saw it.'

Rita herself might not have been in the room for all the attention that Richman gave her, he was speaking now only to Kennedy. In any case, she was trapped in the past, helpless all over again as her mother vanished in a blur of grey and a booming clap of thunder. She was alone, standing on a ragged edge of concrete, staring down to the rocks below, and at what was left there, smeared and bloody, already being washed away by the surf.

And finally, for the teenage Rita, just before hysteria took her, before she descended into the screaming catatonia in which she would be found by her father when he arrived only five minutes later, her final memory of the event was of the unmistakable mood that exuded from the cave all around, even as it faded away. It was no longer hostility, or even glee. Now it was of accomplishment.

Of vindication.

'You see,' Richman explained to his security chief, 'Rita came to believe that her mother's death wasn't an accident at all. That it had been something quite deliberate.'

Kennedy spoke at last. 'What, that the overhang was sabotaged? By who?'

The billionaire shook his head. 'You don't understand. Rita didn't blame any human agency. She blamed . . . well, the cave itself, the overhang, for deciding to fall on her mother.'

The security chief frowned a glance to Rita. 'A piece of rock *decided* to fall?'

'Well, more correctly, a *presence* in the rock,' said Richman. 'Something that had existed there ever since the cave was formed, and which had survived for centuries because the cave was so remote that hardly any humans had set foot there.

'That last thing is the key, for if enough humans *had* set foot there, then the presence would have been forced out. Humans weaken presences, you see. Kill them, eventually. Indeed, the one in Rita's cave was already dying because of the construction, because of all the workers on

377

site every day. If those men had hung around that evening, it wouldn't have been able to do anything at all. But Rita and her mother were left alone, so it had just strength enough to do this last thing, before it faded away completely.'

Rita held her gaze stubbornly upon the floor. She was furious, to have her life laid out like this, but she couldn't argue or even deny anything the billionaire was saying. She had written it all exactly this way in her fucking book.

'Jesus,' said Kennedy with a puff of breath. 'I knew it was all meant to be pretty crazy, but you're kidding me. Kushal, seriously, you believe this shit? You think there's a *presence* here?'

The builder was hesitant but determined. 'Look at all the problems we had here during construction. All the mishaps, all the things that went missing, all the people that got injured, the people that *died*. I've worked on a lot of sites, and if I'm honest, this one was different. And the way we have been trapped here, it's *orchestrated*, can't you feel that?'

'Well, *I* don't believe it,' offered Madelaine. But her tone was full of ready sympathy. 'I'm sorry, Rita. It must have been terrible beyond belief, to witness such a thing. And yet even so, what you claim is not something I can credit. But what about you, Walter? It was you who made us all read that book. You invited Rita to come here. Why did you do all that? Unless you believe the things she claims?'

Rita lifted her gaze at last. The billionaire's smile was ironic. 'Believe? I don't know about that. But I've come across similar ideas before. I remember when I was just a young climber cutting my teeth in the Himalayas the local Buddhist folk would tell us tales about the mountains we crazy Westerners were always so keen to climb. They believed that certain of those mountains—not all of them, but most of the prominent ones—were inhabited each by a guarding spirit, a local god, if you will. Which sounds rather similar in principle to Rita's presences.'

'The notion of such deities is not unknown in Hinduism either,' muttered Kushal.

'Indeed,' conceded Richman. 'Anyway, these spirits, according to the legends, did not welcome humans climbing their mountains, and always resisted those who first attempted it, dogging them with avalanches or bad weather. That's why, the local folk said, it was always so difficult to be the *first* to successfully climb any given mountain. Or even to be the second or third to do so.

'But here's the kicker. Once a mountain has been climbed a *few* times—four times, five maybe—then eventually the spirit will despair of protecting the peak, and depart. And after that, according to the Buddhists, the mountain will become easier and easier to beat. And the funny thing is, that's how it really *works* with mountains. Everest, for instance, was a hell of a struggle for Bourdillon and his team to climb that first time in the fifties, and for the next few expeditions too. But these days scores of people more or less walk up it every year.

'So is it all true then? Are there really local gods up in the hills? Of course not! It's mythical nonsense! Mountains get easier to climb purely because of improvements in mountaineering techniques and equipment—and because these days half the climbers in the world are really just tourists going up routes where someone else has already fixed ropes and ladders. You don't need the death of some local god, or of a presence, to make sense of it.'

And with that, the billionaire sipped his drink as if the matter was now beyond dispute.

Kushal, however, shook his head slowly. 'But by your own logic, Walter, if there *was* a presence, or even a local god, in the Wheel, then it would still be there. After all, the Wheel has only been summitted once. Not many times. Just once, and only with great effort, after many deaths. And since then, it has not at all become an easy mountain to climb.'

'You're right about the effort,' said Richman. 'Who knows it better than me?'

'But that's it exactly,' pressed Kushal, more disturbed than ever. 'You! Isn't it another strange coincidence, too much of a coincidence, that you,

ANDREW McGAHAN

the one man in all the world who has defeated the Wheel, are one of the
six of us trapped here now, trapped *because* of the Wheel? That doesn't
sound like just bad luck to me. That sounds like revenge.'

Richman laughed outright. 'What's got into you tonight, Kushal?
Revenge? What revenge? As I keep saying, we're completely fine up
here. *I'm* completely fine. So if some angry minor deity in the mountain was out to get me, then it's failed, even after it's done its worst. So
what's to worry about?'

Madelaine pursed her lips. 'And yet, Walter, you *are* worried. You
have been worried for some time, since construction began. You think
something is not right. And so you brought Rita here, to see if she could
tell you what is wrong—and you brought me and Kushal here so that
we could listen to what she has to say, and then rebuild and redesign
this place in whatever way might fix the problem.'

'I'm sure I don't know what you mean,' said the billionaire, still
smiling easily. 'I invited Rita here purely for her father's memory.'

'Oh by god in heaven,' declared Clara, slamming her drink down.
'Walter, just tell Rita what the fuck it is you want already. What you've
always wanted. Tell her you want a damn lustration.'

There was a beat of shocked silence in the Saloon, everyone staring
at the major-domo. Rita had never heard Clara speak with anger in
the whole time she had known her, let alone directed at her employer.
Richman gave no response, however, only regarded his employee with
a long gaze of chill indifference.

It was Kennedy who broke the impasse. 'What in hell is a lustration, might I ask?'

The billionaire broke his gaze away from his major-domo to smile
thinly at the security chief. 'It's a Latin word, and it means a ceremony
to get rid of bad luck. You can read the damn book yourself, if you
want to know more. But don't worry, there isn't going to be one performed here either way.'

'Why not?' complained Kushal, gesturing to Rita. 'If she's here, as you wanted, and she can really do what she claims in her book, then—'

'I said *no*!' For the first time frustration ruffled the billionaire. 'I don't need any damn magic tricks to make me feel safe in my own home.'

'Then why bring her here at all,' Madelaine insisted, 'if not for that?'

'I was curious, that was all. You were here with her father during the construction. You saw how Richard became convinced that the building was cursed or something, how he started talking about Rita and her book. He went on and on, insisting she had the answer. It was probably some kind of dementia, I think now. Still, the problems we had with this place were real enough. So sure, I got Rita here to check her and her theories out for myself. But now that it comes down to it, no, I don't believe a word of it—and what's more, *she's* so mixed up about it all that she'd be useless anyway. Isn't that true, Rita? You couldn't do a lustration now if your life depended on it, could you.'

All gazes swung to Rita, Kushal's in hope, Clara's and Madelaine's in surmise, Kennedy's in outright contempt. She flushed. So that's what it was all about, that's why she had been brought here: because Walter Richman's Observatory—at least according to her now dead father— needed a lustration.

God. Her father, suddenly a believer in presences—what an irony that was. And as for Richman, how dare he toy with her so long before finally making himself clear. But none of it mattered. There was only one answer she could give. She shook her head. 'No. It's been years. I don't even . . . I wouldn't know where to start anymore.'

'There you go then,' concluded Richman. 'Can we have an end to all this now? Trust me, tomorrow, when this fog blows away and a helicopter comes, you're going to wonder what the hell you were all getting so worked up about.'

And for a second night running, the billionaire called an end to the evening by stalking off towards the Library and his private domain.

And for a second night, Clara, after a pause, followed after him.

▲

But that wasn't quite the end for Rita.

Back in her apartment, she had no interest in sleep. Opening another bottle of wine, she sat in the darkness of the living room, all the lights turned off, and as she drank she stared out into the night beyond her balcony. There was nothing to see out there but the fog swirling, illuminated to a dim orange by an unseen light somewhere above her flat, but she stared on all the same, heedless.

She was thinking about Richman and wondering why he was lying.

For he *was* lying. To her, to the others, probably even to himself. *I don't need magic tricks to make me feel safe inside my own home!* he had said in an uncharacteristic flash of anger.

And in doing so had revealed himself.

For he *was* afraid in his own home, of that much Rita was sure. Why else would he have called her here? Out of mere curiosity, as he claimed? Or, as he also claimed, because her father had been concerned that something that was wrong here—because her father, after a lifetime of dismissing Rita and her book, had in his dying year changed his mind?

No. A man like Richman didn't act on the basis of what other people believed; men like Richman implicitly trusted only their own opinions. So he too must be worried about his Observatory. He must *know* something is wrong here; he must even know, or suspect, why. It was just that, having now come to the necessity of admitting his own fear, of asking for help, his pride was baulking. Even after the avalanche, after the great wave and all its destruction, still he hoped that he could ride all this out without having to admit to his need; worse, to his vulnerability.

But who knew—maybe he was right about the last bit, maybe they *would* ride this out. Maybe a helicopter finally would appear tomorrow morning, and by tomorrow night they would all be safely back in Hobart, and the Wheel would be denied its prize, if Richman truly was the prize.

Yet Rita's sense of foreboding had not abated. What if they were still stuck here tomorrow night? Or even the night after that? And why did she feel so sure that the worst was yet to come? What could be worse than what had happened already?

Then again—she yawned a moment, took another sip of wine—all of this was beside the point. There was only one question she needed to answer, and that was the one Richman himself had asked her. Did she *believe* anymore? And if it really came down to it, could she do anything to help?

Could she perform a lustration?

Was it possible?

At length she went to the closet and pulled out the warm coat and fur hat she had been given two nights before. Donning them, she turned to the balcony airlock door. The weather panel showed the temperature at a bitter minus seventeen degrees Celsius, though there was still little wind, at least.

She passed through both doors and stepped out into the fog-laden night.

And Christ, it was cold. The air nipped at her exposed brow like a headache. Worse, the stone flags, though purposely rough for grip, were slippery underfoot. But she crept her way to the balcony edge, reassured at least by the solid stone wall that rose chest-height there, and by the fact that the darkness and fog hid the awful plunge downwards.

Steadying herself, she stared eastward. She could not see the Wheel, of course. Nothing was visible other than billows of fog rising before her, dim in the glow from the unseen light source above, driven by a movement of air that oozed up the face of the Mount and onwards over the peak.

But she did not need to see. Even without trying she could sense the vast gulf that opened before her, nearly three thousand metres down to the ocean, and ten kilometres across the middle airs to where, immense beyond imagining, the wall of stone and ice thrust up in brute strength.

So much anyone would sense, perhaps—it was a basic human aware-ness. But now Rita closed her eyes, and for the first time since she had arrived at the Observatory, for the first time anywhere in some twelve years, she tried to reach out deliberately with her *other* awareness, probing at the Wheel. Yes, on the Terrace, after the avalanche and the wave, she had been overwhelmed by the hostility that seemed to flow from the mountain, but that had been a passive act on her part, without volition, a reaction perhaps purely of shock after the disaster. Now, she was reaching out by her own will, by free choice.

And she could not help but wonder—am I really doing this? She felt like an alcoholic who, after many years on the wagon, leaps from the carriage on a whim and raises a drink to her lips . . .

Ah, and wasn't alcohol a relevant point? She had drunk too much wine tonight. Even her old self, when she was still practised at this, would never have been able to detect anything in her current state, not with her special senses so deadened by drink.

And the Wheel was too far away. She had never interacted with a presence at such a distance before. Even if the entity in the mountain really was strong enough to influence events here in the Observatory (could that be?) it did not follow that *she* was strong enough to reach it in reverse.

Indeed, she could feel her mind dissipating helplessly in the great gulf of mist and air between her and the Wheel. No, this wasn't going to work, she was too drunk, and it was too far, and there were a million other reasons, not least of which was her doubt that she even had *special senses* anymore. Not without drugs in her system, anyway, or maybe an adrenalin surge of shock and trauma. Which meant it was all delu-sional bullshit in either case.

And fuck, she was over-thinking all this; of course it wasn't going to work. If it was possible at all, then it must be a natural process: it was not and never had been an intellectual exercise.

She strained a moment longer, trying to visualise in the way she once had, then puffed out a sigh—effort wasn't the solution, she knew that—and with a shrug gave up the attempt.

And as she did so, in the instant that passed between having her eyes closed and opening them, there came a fleeting vision, a glimpse of something that was immediately gone, but the weight of which left her staggering back from the rail.

Jesus!

It was the same; it was same entity she had sensed after the earthquake, it was still there, suffused through the great mass of stone that was the Wheel, a presence vast beyond all her reckoning, faceless, nameless, but *there*. And still its enmity was bent unrelenting upon the Observatory and the humans within it. And holy Mary, its *strength*.

She shuddered, backed up to the airlock door and fumbled at the handle before fleeing inside to warmth and safety. And to more wine, a lot more wine, to block out any chance of even inadvertently opening her mind to so much malice again. What actual threat the vision portended, she did not know, the connection had been too brief to get any sense of the intention in the mountain's hatred. Perhaps if she had held the connection longer, some answer might have come. But there was no way in all hell was she going to try to find out.

Commune with that thing out there? Or for that matter, attempt a lustration with it?

They had to be fucking kidding!

5

PRIESTESS

**Extract from *The Spawn of Disparity*
by Rita Gausse, 1995**

My own journey into an understanding of presences began a year after my mum's death.

That year was an awful time for me. Not only because I'd lost my mother, devastating enough for any fifteen year old, but also because at the same time I was questioning my very sanity.

Others questioned it too.

My father, for one. It started straightaway, as soon as he arrived at the cliff house to find his wife dead and his daughter hysterical. I was raving at him about rocks falling on purpose, about how it was no accident, that the cave had *executed* Mum. He didn't believe me, of course. He thought I was overwrought. When he got me to a hospital they gave me some kind of sedative, and before I knew it I was waking up in bed at home, as if it had all been a dream. Except it wasn't a dream. Mum was still dead.

In the weeks following, Dad tried to convince me that it had really been just an accident, terribly bad luck that no one could have predicted. But I wasn't buying it. I knew what I'd seen and felt that day, and nothing Dad said could convince me otherwise. We argued. I accused him of trying to brainwash me into denying the truth, he accused me of using Mum's death for selfish, grandiose attention seeking.

The fights got pretty ugly. I mean, we were already in opposite camps anyway, a workaholic middle-aged father and a hot-tempered teenage daughter, who had never until then spent much time together. Bad enough, but now we could both add grief and blame and guilt to the bonfire.

In the end I was bundled off to board at school, and to endless sessions with a therapist, neither of which did any good at all, beyond making me more and more furious, and more and more hateful to Dad. It was no surprise that I began to rebel in other areas—smoking, drinking, sex, you name it.

Meanwhile, the house in which Mum had died was approaching completion. There had been a delay in construction of some months, while the coroner held an investigation. The finding was of accidental death. Even the structural engineers who had declared the cave stable were spared any blame. It seemed there had been a hidden flaw within the rock, impossible to detect by any standard measure. Afterwards, the owners of the house were allowed to resume building, with various design alterations, and reinforcement of the cliff face above. A year after my mother's death, it was almost ready.

I learned of this one weekend when I was home from school, by overhearing a phone conversation between Dad and one of his colleagues. And immediately, I knew what I had to do. I had to go back to the house. I had to stand in that same spot again. I had to prove to myself that my memories, however bizarre and terrible, were not lies.

It took a series of huge rows with Dad for me to get my way. I was helped by the fact that my otherwise clueless therapist suggested to him that it might give me some closure. Looking back, I can see why Dad didn't want to do it. The house must have had horrible memories for him too. No matter what the coroner said, he must have blamed himself and his design for his wife's death. I blamed him, at least in part, for if he hadn't built his stupid house in the cliff in the first place, then none of it would have happened. Still, he loved Mum, I can't deny that, and no doubt he was as gutted by her loss as I was.

At last it was all organised and permission granted, and Dad and I drove up to the coast to the house. We had it to ourselves, the owners had agreed to steer clear for an hour or two; reluctantly, by report, but I had demanded that the house be empty when we arrived. It had been empty when Mum and I had been there, and somehow I knew that the emptiness was important.

And yet as soon as we walked in, nothing was really the same. An incomplete building, no matter how cluttered with tools and ladders and plaster dust, will always feel vacant, whereas a finished house filled with furniture and family photos will always feel occupied, even when no one is there. We were alone, yes, but I felt no sense of any presence lurking in the background as Dad and I walked about, there was only an air of comfort and wealth and beauty.

Oh yes, the house was unquestionably beautiful, even I had to admit that, no matter what it had cost me. My father had ceased work on the project after Mum's death, handing it over to another architect, but that new architect had made only minor structural changes to the original design, so it was still very much my father's vision, and I could tell that despite everything he was proud of it. Which, of course, only made me hate it all the more entirely.

But that was beside the point. All I really cared about, as we moved from floor to floor, was locating that forbidding presence I had felt on the day Mum was killed. And to my increasing alarm, I couldn't. There was no sense of hostility or brooding threat this time. There was no sense of anything at all.

We made our way to the lower balcony, to the exact spot where Mum had died—or as close to it as was possible now, as the balcony had been redesigned as well as rebuilt. And still I felt nothing out of the ordinary. I stared down at the rocks where her broken body had been smashed to pieces. The memories roused by the sight were horrific, but no *special* unease stirred in me; no hairs rose on the back of my neck; I felt no proximity of an *other*.

A panic began to grow in me. Had I imagined the whole thing? Was Dad right all along? Even worse, was my idiot therapist right too?

Then I looked up, to the great overhanging roof of the cave, to where the boulder had worked itself loose, and there were tears in my eyes now, of frustration and terror and doubt.

And that's when it came.

Not a sense of a presence, but of . . . of an active absence of a presence. It was not that there had never been anything there; instead there was a spiritual cavity where something *had* been, just as there was a physical hole in the cave ceiling, where the boulder—the two boulders, in fact— had fallen.

And I understood then. I was looking at a grave. Not of my mother, or at least not only of my mother, but of the thing that had killed her. It too was dead now. It had been extinguished by the completion of the house, by the occupation of the family that called it home. The entity that had been so angry and vengeful over the intrusion of humanity into this previously untouched place, had, after its last display of fury, bowed to the inevitable, and died.

I felt that loss keenly. The cave was infinitely a lesser place without it, merely an overhang of rock, meaningless. And in that moment everything changed in me. My hatred evaporated, replaced by pity. The best way I can describe it is to imagine that my mother had been killed, say, by some wild animal that was itself endangered and dying. A Bengal tiger, perhaps, or a polar bear, a creature forced by dwindling habitat and hunger into an area it did not belong, where by ill luck it encountered and killed a human, only to be later found dead itself of starvation. I would not hate such a creature, I would only pity its wretched final hours, and lament the fate of its species.

That's what I felt, overwhelmingly, in the instant that I stared up to the rock ceiling. Whatever had lived here had been dying when it attacked my mother, lashing out in its fear and desperation, and now it was dead. And it was my father's house that had killed it.

I looked at the man beside me with a suddenly renewed loathing. He was a killer! On behalf of his super-rich clients, he was a destroyer of something that he had no right to destroy. If it had been just this one cave, that would have been bad enough. But this was what he did *everywhere*. He worked almost exclusively with remote and unspoiled locations; he was famous for his 'submerged' style of design, which in particular dug into and transformed locations of natural wildness and beauty, made them habitable for man.

I did not know then for certain that presences existed in many places, but I already suspected it. And what my father had done to this cave, he was doing all over Australia, all over the globe.

It is no surprise, then, that things only got worse between us, after that.

▲

I went away from the cliff house with a whole new perception of the world around me.

In fact, I soon realised that there are two worlds. One consists of the regions that mankind has inhabited densely for years—cities and towns—and those places, no matter how beautiful (think of Sydney Harbour, say) are desolate and empty of anything *other*. Whatever presences inhabited them before humanity's advent are now long dead.

The other world is to be found away from the towns and cities, but not necessarily *far* away, and it is not necessarily what people call wilderness. I began skipping school, and catching busses and trains out of Sydney, to go roaming in the countryside, searching for places that might possess *presences* (as I started to call them) the same as the cave. And I found them. In scrub gullies, along overgrown creek beds, in quiet forgotten places that humans—although they lived close enough—rarely bothered to venture.

Things were *there*; I could sense them as clearly as if they were beacons.

Later I would travel more widely, to distant native forests and to remote alpine meadows, and would find still more presences—but remember, it was never anything to do with the forests or the meadows themselves.

Presences are products purely of *landscape*, they inhabit formations of stone and earth and water, not trees or plants.

And those formations have to be singular, out of the ordinary, as I've already explained. Not *every* hill or gully or lake possesses an inner awareness, no matter how remote. But a hill that is sharper than those around it, a gully more steep and narrow than most, a lake unusually deep and dark; *these* places have something, a self-knowing, a presence.

It is this consciousness, so alien to our own, that mankind senses when confronted with dramatic scenery in some lonely place. And alone or in small numbers, passing by, our own consciousness is no threat to the presence in the landscape. But when we come in greater numbers, and settle permanently, and build over the landscape, then our mass consciousness is lethal to the presence that preceded us. Poisoned, suffocated by us, it withers and dies.

But not willingly, not in silence, and not without protest—though in truth, the invading humans will rarely be aware of that protest. They may get a bad feeling about a place, they may fall victim to unlucky accidents there, they may experience a fleeting regret that, in the name of progress, a hill must be levelled, or a river tamed, or a lake drained dry. But only a few have the ability to detect the presences directly, or even to communicate with them.

But I'm getting ahead of myself.

At eighteen I was done with school and free to go wherever I wanted. And I went. I spent the next two years drifting all over Australia, seeking out remote and unvisited landmarks to see what, if anything, I might discover there, *feel* there.

It was a gypsy life, involving a lot of camping, and also a lot of hanging around bookshops and libraries, reading up on alternative philosophies and religions. Inevitably, I fell in with certain crowds of fellow nomads. Sometimes it was hippies (I've known my fair share of communes), sometimes it was conservationists, or bushwalkers, or birdwatchers, or four-wheel-drive enthusiasts, sometimes it was gun-toting ferals protecting their scrub marijuana patches, and once it was even a mob of wiccans dancing naked around a desert bonfire . . .

But I was none of those things myself, and though I picked up bits and pieces from each of those groups, none of them could sense what I sensed, or could teach me anything about it.

So I had to teach myself. In time I learned what sort of landmarks might possess consciousness and what types wouldn't. I learned the type of mental state I needed to be in, to best sense the presences. I learned of their individual nature, of their ancientness in some places, and of their fleeting immediacy in others. I became expert in an Australia that no one other than myself seemed to know.

But I spoke very little about my developing ability. As far as my friends were concerned, all this time I was simply partaking in the same generic 'nature is good' vibe that they espoused themselves, be it via meditation, or bushwalking, or the cultivation of pot, or Gaia worship.

The fact that I would go off into the bush for hours or days in search of unusual land formations was just considered to be my particular nature kink. I even developed a modest fame as the girl who had a knack for locating previously unknown 'power sites' in the bush. For once I found a place with presences—a rocky outcrop, a dark gully, a hidden water-hole—then when others came there, even if they were blind compared to me, they could still feel *something*.

And it was because of this modest reputation that, not long after my twenty-first birthday, the second great change in my life arrived.

At the time I was at a crossroads, living in a commune in the scrub outside of Bairnsdale in eastern Victoria. I had accepted the truth of presences, but was beginning to wonder what practical use that was to me. I had no career, no home of my own, and no particular purpose in life. Worst of all, I had no money. I worked the occasional odd job here and there, but for urgent funds, to keep my car going, or to travel, or often just for basic supplies, I resorted to my rich and famous father, who always coughed up.

Not that either of us was happy about it. He, of course, disapproved of my whole wastrel existence, and hated having to enable it. And just as strongly, I disapproved of him: his whole career was based on destroying the very things that I had come to find the most precious, which made it indefensible that I took the money he earned from it. Hell, I even attended protest rallies *against* some of his projects, although I was careful to not reveal my true last name, or my parentage, to my fellow protestors.

So I was searching for a way out of the impasse, when one day I received an unusual request.

It came from a family who had just moved onto a bush property in the hills north of Bairnsdale, not far past the little town of Bruthen, and on the east side of the Tambo River. This was pretty wild country, much of it state forest, and with no road access at all when the Tambo flooded, but the block these people had bought was a beautiful one, seventy acres or so on a hillside overlooking a creek, and with long views down a forested valley.

They had expected to be very happy there, but instead, something was wrong. Something they thought maybe I could help with.

Intrigued, I drove up to see them. And sure enough the place was lovely. Indeed, it was striking, for halfway up the hill a large stone shelf jutted out from the slope, perfectly level. This natural platform was about fifty yards broad and deep, and was fronted by a cliff a good twenty metres high: a very unusual formation for that part of the country. And not surprisingly it was on this ready-made base that the family had started to build their house.

There were five of them in all, the two parents and three children under the age of ten. They had moved in about a month before, having built a track up to the platform, and then dragged a caravan up there to serve as a camp while they built their home proper. But though the spot was as gorgeous as they had hoped, with no other house or sign of civilisation in sight, they had found their time there to be disturbing rather than restful.

Something wasn't right, they told me. They felt *unwelcome*. And it wasn't merely because they were roughing it; they were used to that, they had been living in places like this since they had been married. But unlike any other of their bush camps, here, on the broad, empty stone platform, there was an air, they insisted, of sustained hostility.

In the daytime it was bad enough, but at night it had become downright frightening. Noises came out of the darkness, groans and shrieks that most definitely were not made by any animal, and the children were plagued by nightmares and fits of sleepwalking. The oldest boy had disappeared entirely one night, and was not found until the next morning, wandering bewildered and naked down by the creek.

They had begun to wonder if there was something unusual about the stone platform. Having heard, through mutual friends, that I was good at discerning 'power' in such spots, they hoped I might be able to tell them something more concrete. Could it be, they asked, an Aboriginal thing? There were some markings on the lower cliff that might have been faded paintings and worn carvings. Could the platform be a sacred site of some sort?

Of course, as soon as I saw the place I knew it would host a presence. As for a sacred site—well, to this day, I don't know. The markings on the cliff might have meant something, they might not; they were too faded to say if they were man-made.

But in truth the whole issue of presences and their relation to Aboriginal mythology is something I'm still pondering. I've visited many supposedly sacred sites over the years, and while some are bare of anything *other* (perhaps because they've become tourist attractions, or have been built over) those that remain un-trampled do indeed have an attendant presence, often a very strong one.

Given that, it seems to me that surely there must be a link. Surely, all those millennia ago, there were Aboriginal shaman who shared my ability to sense presences in the landscape, and perceiving those presences to be gods or spirits or demons, then declared the sites sacred, and off limits.

It's an interesting thing, actually: the fact that Indigenous peoples never chose to *live* in an area that they declared sacred. Such zones might be visited at certain times and as part of certain rituals, but human contact was kept very limited. The traditional explanation of this is that they did so out of awe and respect. But I wonder. What if those earlier peoples in fact recognised, as I came to, that presences, for all their apparent power, are able to be killed by human habitation? What if they kept away from their sacred sites to ensure that the presences there endured—to save their own gods, indeed, whereas we Westerners seemed so determined to destroy ours?

It's an intriguing thought.

But in any case, to get back to my story: I agreed to spend a night there on the stone platform, and to report anything I might learn.

The family I dispatched off to Bruthen for the night, as in those early days I assumed that I needed isolation for the experience to work, though I have since realised this is not so. As the sun set behind the western hills and the long evening deepened towards dark, I got a fire going, more for company than for warmth. It wasn't at all cold, but it felt lonely the moment the family was gone.

And it got lonelier as it got darker. The scenery that had seemed so lovely in the afternoon—the hillside, the valley, the creek—now took on a sinister air. The nakedness of the stone platform, the angle of the slope above and the sheerness of the cliff below, the way the trees were positioned in groups, as if it huddled and conspiring, all of it seemed increasingly askew in the fading light. The fire burned brighter, but the darkness grew ever larger all around it, and I began to sense a malign intent in the air, a feeling of being watched by unfriendly eyes, inhuman eyes, not eyes at all, but a watching, waiting alertness.

It was the presence of the platform, no mistake, and it was angry. Indeed, not since the death of my mother had I felt a presence that was so hostile, and so wishing of harm. No wonder the family had been having a terrible time. It was all I could do to sit there myself as the evening inched towards midnight, so potent was the sense of threat.

But at the same time, I understood why this was happening. The presence that had attacked my mother had been in its final extremity, lashing out before it was itself extinguished—and the same was true here. The presence in this platform had existed since the stone itself was moulded into shape, but now humans had arrived, permanently, five of them, their consciousness suffocating the platform's own. And so, amid my dread, I also felt regret.

And somewhere in the depth of the night, the presence became aware of that regret.

Now, for all my experience with presences, it remains difficult for me to describe exactly in what form they sense we humans and our minds. I suspect that usually we appear to them as a grating intrusion, not thinking beings at all, but merely a kind of static that crowds out their own awareness, faint maybe at first, but as more and more of us arrive, building to a din in which the presences drown.

But for the first time, there on the platform, I became aware of a presence gradually becoming aware of *me*. Me uniquely, not merely an annoyance, but a creature with consciousness. And what made the connection, I'm sure, was that the presence could sense my sadness at its incipient extinction: an emotion, perhaps, it had sensed in no human before.

In turn, I could sense something beyond its anger and pain, and that was gratification—gratification precisely that its anger and pain had been recognised. I do not pretend to fully grasp the thoughts of a presence, if indeed they think at all, in a way we would accept. But I could feel that my simple acknowledgement of its existence and of its impending death was dissolving away its anger, even though the fact of its death remained unchanged.

Indeed, it did not fear death. After all, an end comes to all presences sooner or later, as the landscape shifts and changes over the ages. But what presences do fear and resent, I suspect, is death coming unnaturally, caused by beings too brutal to even recognise the thing they are killing. *That's* why presences lash out against intruding humans, their animosity a malaise in our hearts: not merely in self-defence, but in outrage at the insult of not even being acknowledged in the first place.

It was at this point that I took off my clothes. There was nothing sensual in this, I had long learned by then a truth shared by many belief systems, from the hippy communes through to the wiccans, that baring one's body to nature is mirrored by a more fundamental baring of the psyche. And indeed, it had helped me before, being naked, to attune myself to landscapes around me. But now I did it more to express to the presence within the stone platform my goodwill towards it, to expose my own vulnerability as a naked creature of flesh and blood.

Unclothed, I sat by the fire and opened my arms to the night, pouring out my sympathy and empathy to the thing that surrounded me in the darkness, cold and ancient and inhuman as it was. I even tried to share with the presence the memory of my own mother's loss.

And the night heard me. From the shadows and the stone I received in response a clear sense that the presence recognised what I was doing, and that it acknowledged my mother's death. There was no sympathy: it saw her death as the fair price to be paid for the destruction that had been wrought by the humans in the cave. But it accepted that the price had been paid, and that the matter was done.

I understood then that my regret, appreciated though it was by the presence in the stone platform, would not be enough to assuage its anger. There must be a higher price paid if the presence was to accept its approaching end. A price of pain, of suffering. And then it came to me, the real word for what I was considering. Not a price, but a *sacrifice*.

I didn't hesitate. There was pocketknife nearby in my camping gear— I picked it up and, carefully but deliberately, I made a cut across my wrist. Then I turned my arm and dripped my lifeblood onto the ground, onto the native stone of the platform.

And the blood was accepted.

It was like a vast sigh; the night seemed to take a great breath, full of portent, and then to exhale with a rush of grief and resignation. And with that, the hostility in the air began to fade, the menace in the shadows slipping up and away like an invisible bird. Suddenly I was alone on the platform, my arm dripping blood, and the stone was empty and harmless all around me. The presence was gone.

I dressed and bandaged my arm and waited out the rest of the night until dawn came, but the sensation of a watching otherness never returned. The hillside and the platform felt like any other place in the bush now, still beautiful, but no more than that, stripped of its awe and malign strangeness.

When the family returned with the rising sun they looked askance at me, sleepless and half-manic with exhilaration, my bloody arm wrapped in a rag. But I assured them that the place had been 'cleansed' and that they could reside there untroubled, that their home would welcome them now.

And so it did.

▲

That was my first lustration. Not that lustration was a word I used at the time. I had no word for it. That first morning, indeed, I didn't even consider that I would ever do such a thing again.

But I was wrong. The family I had helped were very grateful, and they weren't reticent about telling other people what I had done. Soon word was spreading through the underground bush networks about a woman with a special talent.

Within weeks I was getting requests from people in similar situations, folks who had built houses in remote areas, places where no one had ever built before, and who were experiencing an inexplicable unease upon the site. Some thought they were being haunted by ghosts, or stalked by demons, or cursed by witchcraft; others wondered if they were picking up on electromagnetic movements within the earth, precursors to earthquakes maybe; one lone man was even convinced it was extra-terrestrial aliens that were plaguing him at his little hut up in the hills.

But in common they all felt that something in the landscape around them wasn't right—and so they called on me to do what I had done for that first family, to cleanse their property of whatever was disturbing it, and to bring peace back to their lives.

And time and time again, I did exactly that. The problem was never ghosts, electromagnetism or aliens, of course. It was always because a presence existed somewhere nearby, protesting at the intrusion of the newly arrived humans. But by spending a night alone with each of these threatened presences, acknowledging them, and shedding a symbolic amount of blood in sacrifice, I could placate their hostility, and send them, in dignity, on their way.

Except—as I started to wonder more and more—why *should* they have to be sent away? Why did the presences have to die? Just so a human family could build themselves a new house?

It didn't seem fair.

So I began to try something new. After spending a night in commune with a presence—but not dispatching it—I would explain to the landowners what was happening, and enquire as to whether they could build their house elsewhere on their property, out of the presence's way. Just a hundred metres could be enough to make a difference.

True, often there was nothing to be done, the house was built, or the owners were resolute, and I'd spend the next night doing my usual lustration. But sometimes the clients were amenable; a construction site could be shifted, or the layout of a farm altered, and the presence could be saved. Indeed, this has become my preferred option, and I now see myself as an advisor on how to *preserve* presences as much as a facilitator for aiding their departure.

But in any case, the ceremony, the lustration, remains much the same. Even if I have convinced the owners to preserve a presence, I still let blood for it, as payment for its suffering.

But why *lustration*?

Well, I've been aware from the beginning that I am treading quite a well-worn path in this. After all, priests and priestesses have been making blood sacrifices for the same reason—to placate or dispel local gods or demons—since the dawn of human history. It still goes on daily in many cultures of the world. It's really only in the latter days of Western and Middle Eastern civilisation, swamped by monotheisms or atheisms or various other contemporary *isms*, that the notion has fallen out of favour.

Needless to say, I do not actually consider myself a priestess, for I believe in no god, not even of the local variety. Presences have nothing to do with divinity. Nor do I consider myself a witch, nor a medium, nor anyone who has anything to do with magic or the spirit world or an afterlife. I have just this one ability and talent, and beyond that I claim no beliefs or dogma or authority.

Nevertheless, in searching about for terminology to describe what I was doing, I settled upon a religious term from ancient times: lustration. It derives from the Latin *lustratio*, a ritual to cleanse an area of malign influences, or perhaps of the memory of violence that has occurred on the site. Attendant with the ceremony, there was often a sacrifice to appease the local spirit being driven out.

The parallels with my 'cleansings' are obvious. Indeed, the fact that the notion of sacrifice has been retained throughout the ages fascinates me. After all, the blood I spill, or the cattle and sheep that ancients sacrificed to their deities, is of no earthly use to the presences or spirits that are being placated. So why does the sacrifice have any effect at all?

I have no sure answer. I only know that my payment, however token, is accepted.

But like many a priestess before me, I now charge a fee in turn for my services.

At first, I had no interest in making money from lustrations. What I did was as much for the sake of the presence as it was for my human clients, so money never entered my head. But some of the places I was visiting were interstate, or even overseas, so I did not protest when my clients began to reimburse me for my travel and living expenses. And in time I saw that if I was to make this my life's calling—which it seemed to be—then it was only sensible to charge a rate which enabled me to do it properly.

Hence my professional lustration career was born. In the years since (I am now twenty-five) I have performed perhaps a hundred such ceremonies. And yet still the truth about presences remains unheard-of in the wider world, known only within an underground circle of alternativism and mysticism. With this book, however, I hope to change all that.

It is time I, and the reality of presences with me, emerged from the shadows.

I can't tell you how excited I am.

BOOK

FOUR

1

ONE DOWN

RITA CAME AWAKE WITH A groan. Throwing off the tangled sheets, she found herself bathed in sweat, her limbs trembling as if from heavy labour.

What? Had something happened? Her sleep-fogged memory was full of some undefined struggle, as though in her slumber she had been held down by an oppressive, suffocating force, fighting in vain to wake up but unable to do so.

She sat up, glanced at the curtained windows. A dim grey glow shone at the edges. It was six a.m. The pounding in her chest fell away, and slowly the recollections of the previous day came to her: the failure of rescue to come, the hope of escape down the emergency stairs thwarted, Richman's harassment of her last night, then her foray out onto the balcony to attempt contact with the Wheel, and wine, far too much wine . . .

No wonder she felt like shit.

What was she even doing awake so early? It must have been well past midnight when she had gone to bed, though she didn't remember falling asleep—unconsciousness seemed to have hit like a black slab. But maybe it was just the alcohol that had given her the nightmare sense of oppression.

She shrugged the memory away, climbed from the bed, went to the windows and pulled the curtain aside. A wall of dank grey greeted her.

Damn. More fog. As thick and dark as yesterday. And—she glanced at the weather panel—actually *colder* than yesterday. Minus twenty-two degrees Celsius. Small, sharp spikes of white had formed on the parapet rail where she had stood last night, the ice coalescing out of the misted air.

Ice. Ice . . .

Something about its dull gleam made her uneasy. She couldn't say why. She had no intention of venturing out there, and here in her apartment it was perfectly warm and safe. And yet . . . she could not shake the feeling that somewhere, something vile was waiting. Something to do with ice.

It slipped away again. She looked at the bed, but even though she still felt tired, she did not think she would be able to go back to sleep. Wandering into the kitchen she gazed at the coffee-making equipment a moment, and at the fridge, full of food, if she wanted to cook breakfast. Then she shook her head. It wasn't coffee or food she wanted, it was human voices and light, something to dispel the silence and the creeping anxiety left over from her dreams.

Would anyone else be awake yet? Kennedy had mentioned something about an early start—there were more things he wanted to try in the Control Room. And some of the others could well be up and already breakfasting in the Dining Hall. They might even have a fire going. Decided, Rita went back to the bedroom and dressed.

Out in the hall, the quiet pressed against her like a chill, the dim lighting and the windowless walls giving an air of eternal, timeless night. She glanced down the passage towards Madelaine's and Kushal's apartments, hoping that one of them might appear, company for the walk. But neither did. She moved numbly down the hall to the Well and the Helix Staircase, and began the long climb.

Was it colder out here, or did it just feel that way in so much space? High above she could see the Atrium dome, its windows blue-grey with the approaching dawn, but there was no sound anywhere other than her own tread on the carpeted steps. No friendly voices from above, no music. And when at last she came to the top and looked about she saw no one in the Dining Hall or the Saloon.

Was she the first up after all?

The gloom and silence were preying heavily on her now. Oh, to see some proper sunlight shining in. But overhead the fog against the windows of the dome still only hinted at the coming day. It was a twilight time, night not yet banished.

The great wedge of glass that contained the lower waters of the Terrace Pool had become, by night, a black monolith since the power failure.

But she noticed it was not entirely black now. She stepped closer. In normal times, an observer on this level would be able to watch swimmers in the pool as if they were fish in an aquarium. Of course, no one swam there now, but in some strange undersea effect the grey ghost of dawn above had made the whole mass of water glow subtly.

She peered up, remembering their inspection of the pool the day before—had it frozen over yet? Normally, the surface above was a silvery roof through which the sky was a distorted shimmer. Now she saw only a hazy fixed whiteness. Yes, it looked to be a solid sheet of ice, complete from edge to edge.

Except . . .

She stared, her face against the glass. In the centre of the pool's surface there was a flaw in the ice, a pattern of dark shapes, five of them, seeming to protrude down from above.

What could they be? She stared a moment longer, a terrible suspicion dawning as the shapes resolved into something recognisable.

Then she was screaming.

▲

By luck, at almost the same moment Clara emerged from the private elevator in the Library.

Otherwise, no matter how Rita might have screamed, no one would have heard her, no one would have come running. She would have been left there alone with the thing hanging above her in the pool, screaming until she went mad. But the major-domo was there at her side, staring up to where Rita's rigid finger was pointing.

'Oh god,' Clara said. 'Come on, there might still be time!'

That broke Rita out of her paralysis. There might be still time? Sweet Christ, did that mean . . . ? But no, it was too appalling to consider.

She hurried after the major-domo. They ran up the stairs to the Conservatory, and at the air-lock doors did not even pause to pull on overcoats—though the weather panel was flashing orange for caution, the temperature reading minus twenty-five degrees Celsius—but passed straight on through to the Terrace.

The cold! Rita might have been naked for all the protection her indoor clothes gave. A breeze was blowing over the top of the Mount, no great gale, but it was enough to make the mist stream forbiddingly across the Terrace, and for the chill to be knife-sharp against every inch of her skin. But she followed after Clara, hastening across the icy ground as swiftly as she dared.

The pool emerged from the mist, a curved shoreline of black stone, beyond which was a frozen sweep of white. They paused on the rim. So dense was the fog that the further side of the pool was barely visible, but at the same time everything was glowing within the mist as dawn grew in the unseen sky. They could see well enough.

Too well.

At the centre of the pool, a dark hunched shape rose from the unblemished whiteness.

A human, embedded in the ice.

That is, the *torso* of a human, chest down, hunched over the ice, shoulder blades to buttocks visible, the body naked, frosted white and unidentifiable even as to sex.

Everything else, the person's head, and their arms and their legs, were—

Clara broke the horrified silence. 'It can't be. It couldn't . . . happen like that.' She cast her gaze about desperately a moment then lunged aside to a low stone seat. Its top was hinged, and raising the lid, she drew something forth. It was a lifesaving buoy, an orange ring attached to a line. The major-domo unravelled the stiff rope, then extended one end to Rita. 'Hold this—I'll go out. Pull me in if the ice gives way.'

Rita took the rope dumbly, and watched as the former mountain climber, the ring hooped over one shoulder, ventured cautiously out upon the slick surface. The ice seemed solid, however—there was no cracking, no shifting. There were no tracks across the whiteness, no footprints, no path of something being dragged, no sign at all of how the body out in the middle of the pool had travelled there.

Clara stood over the shape now. Her hands hovered helplessly a moment, as if she was unsure how to touch the thing. At last she tried to grip the torso about its midriff, but Rita could see how her bare hands recoiled from the cold. The corpse—for a corpse it surely was—was as frozen as the ice.

'I can't . . .' Clara called across in confusion. 'There's nothing to grab onto.'

Rita could only nod. She had seen it for herself, from below. The figure's arms and legs, and its head, were buried in the ice, extending through into the water beneath, they were the five shapes that had so puzzled her as she stared up to the surface. Two arms dangling down, hands spread wide in supplication, two legs splayed and limp, and finally a face, locked in the ice, drowned, staring at nothing . . .

'I need an axe,' the major-domo added, an uncharacteristic hysteria fringing her voice. 'We'll have to cut . . . I think . . . Oh Jesus, I think it might be Kushal. It's fucking *Kushal.*'

And sure enough, once everyone else was roused from their sleep to confront the horror, the builder was the only one absent.

But it was some hours, even with the help of several axes, before they could retrieve the body, and confirm its identity for certain.

▲

Later, after they had hacked Kushal free and stowed him, still frozen grotesquely in a crouching position but draped at least in a blanket, in one of the kitchen's walk-in freezers (yes, they could have left him on the Terrace, where it was even colder, but that had been psychologically impossible) they gathered, numbed, by the fire in the Saloon.

It was noon by then, and still the Observatory was wrapped in its grey shroud. The only difference now was that the wind had picked up, so that the fog outside had begun to stream across the Terrace and past the windows, and a subtle thrum underlay the silence within. There had still been no hint of an approaching rescue, no helicopter or plane to be heard, no ship's horn from below in the harbour. It was as if the world beyond the fog had ceased to exist, and there was only the Observatory left.

Looking at her grey-faced companions gathered before the flames, it seemed to Rita that everyone had aged years within a single morning. The annoyance and perplexity of their entrapment had become something infinitely more grim and baffling. A man was dead, his absence as acute as a missing tooth. Yes, they had known already that people must be dead, possibly many of them, down at Base, drowned by the great wave. But this was different. This death had struck not amid the thunder of a natural disaster, but silently in the night, in mockery of the warmth and luxury and security of their high fortress.

Inexplicable.

'How could it have happened?' Richman finally asked softly. They had been asking the same question all morning, but now the billionaire looked up from the fire and at each of them, as if the time had come to settle the matter once and for all.

'I can't see how it could have,' answered Clara wearily. 'I've been going over and over it, but nothing about it adds up. I mean, forget poor Kushal for a minute, and how it was that he got stuck in the ice. The ice *itself* doesn't make any sense.'

'The ice?' asked Madelaine, her usually stylish hair still mussed from being woken rudely by Rita five hours ago, with no time to tend to it since. 'What do you mean, the ice doesn't make sense?'

'I mean, it was nearly six inches thick. But yesterday the pool had barely begun to freeze over. There's no way the ice should have been able to get so thick so quickly, not unless the temperature went down to minus sixty or worse overnight out there. But that kind of cold is unheard-of on the Mount. Higher up on the Wheel, yes, maybe, but . . .'

'Look, the pool froze,' said Richman, impatiently. 'I don't see that it matters how it froze, it's a fact that it did. All I want to know is how Kushal got trapped there. Why on earth was he even up on the Terrace last night? Naked, for Christ's sake. Had he gone mad? Was it . . . was it a suicide?'

The word lingered in a short silence, the flames in the fireplace crackling.

Madelaine shook her head. 'If so, there was no note in his apartment. No. It's impossible. I knew him. He was not unhappy about anything.'

It was Rita and Madelaine together who had searched Kushal's apartment for any clue as to what might have happened. But there was nothing. Kushal had retired at the same time as the rest of them last night, and all indications were that he had gone straight to bed. The clothes he had been wearing during the day were neatly folded over a chair in the bedroom; a book—Rita's own book, she noted to her discomfort—was resting page down on the side table, next to an empty whisky glass; his toothbrush and some medications sat neatly on the sink in the bathroom; the bedside lamp was switched off, and the bed had clearly been slept in.

But at some point he had thrown the covers back. And on the floor, as if discarded hastily, were a man's pyjama pants and shirt. Nearby, slippers lay unused. Suggesting that Kushal had risen, taken off his clothes, and then, naked and barefoot, climbed all the way up to the Conservatory, and finally walked out into the deadly minus-twenty-degree chill of the Terrace.

Why would he do that? Why would anyone, unless forced, maybe, at gunpoint? And indeed, Kennedy's first suspicion had been of foul play, theorising that someone—one of the five of them—must have invaded Kushal's apartment and marched him at gunpoint out onto the Terrace.

Except that it hadn't happened. Immediately after raising the possibility, Kennedy had descended to the Control Room and summoned up the security camera footage of the previous night.

And there, plain to see, appearing in the hallway outside his apartment at 1.55 a.m., was Kushal, quite alone, tall and solid and completely naked, walking with a slow, calm deliberation towards the Helix Staircase. He seemed to be fully awake; his eyes were certainly open—though the resolution of the security camera was not sufficient to read any expression there—but at the same time his gait had the manner of one drugged, or perhaps sleepwalking.

The cameras next caught on him the Helix Staircase themselves, then in the Atrium, and then in the Conservatory. All the while he moved in the same slow, abstracted manner, never glancing to this side or that, never veering from his course. Which led him at last to the airlock doors. He slid the inner door open calmly, and passed through to the second.

But here the all-seeing security was foiled. For although there were indeed more cameras out on the Terrace, and although they were still functioning under the emergency power protocols, the Terrace lighting was not, and between the fog and the night, the cameras were all but blind. A little indirect lighting did leach up from the Atrium below, and perhaps a vague shape was caught at one point, moving near the pool's edge, but otherwise there was nothing but phantoms of mist.

'It cannot have been suicide,' Madelaine repeated. 'I don't care what your cameras saw. He was *fine* when he went to bed last night.'

'That's not exactly true,' said Clara, her expression thoughtful. 'He was upset about the stairs collapsing, remember. He wasn't his usual self at all.'

Richman shook his head. 'He would hardly kill himself over that. But dammit, even if he did intend suicide, how the hell could he have ended up like that, half in and out of the ice? He would have had to walk out into the middle of the pool and cut holes in the ice to put his arms and legs and head through. But what did he use to cut the holes? He had no axe, and there's no sign anyway that the holes were hacked out, the ice was snug around his arms and neck and legs. Okay, maybe, if he'd walked out when the ice was still thin, then he could have forced his arms and legs through it, but of course if the ice was that thin it would never have supported him to walk out there in the first place. But if the ice was thick enough to hold him up, he could never have sunk his hands and feet through it without an axe or something. It's impossible either way. It's like he was simply hanging there, in midair almost, while the ice formed around him.'

Clara was gazing at nothing. 'Maybe he was.'

'What?'

'Oh, I don't know. There's no way to explain it. But Kushal himself would find this another interesting coincidence, don't you think?'

'And what does *that* mean?'

The major-domo glanced at Rita and then to her employer. 'He was the one most concerned about what's happening here, about whether or not there is something deliberate behind it, something that comes from the Wheel. He was the one who thought Rita should perform a lustration. And as I understand it, a lustration would *weaken* whatever force lies in the Wheel, maybe even kill it entirely. So you don't find it strange that of the five of us, *he's* the one who dies in a way that seems overtly impossible?'

Richman laughed sourly. 'So what are you saying—the Wheel did this? The Wheel made him walk up to the Terrace, naked, and then held him there over the water while it froze solid?'

Clara was unperturbed. 'Did he look like he knew what he was doing, in those videos? He's walking like a zombie. I think something had a grip on his mind, something forced him out there.'

'Oh for fuck's sake . . .'

'Rita?' asked the major-domo. 'In the old days, did you ever experience anything like this? Did your presences ever . . . hypnotise people?'

Rita was already shaking her head. No, god no, there had never been anything like this. She had known presences to give people nightmares, and there had been the young boy, at the site of her very first lustration, who had been sleepwalking. But to make a grown man walk heedless to his death, to hold him above the water as it froze? 'No,' she said. 'Even back then, I never saw anything like this.'

Clara said, 'And yet you claimed in your book that these presences of yours are capable of killing people. Your mother, for one.'

Rita swallowed. 'Yes, but that was the only death I witnessed firsthand. The presences I dealt with were usually not as strong as that.'

The major-domo was implacable. 'But you say also that there are bigger and stronger presences in storms and in giant waves and the like, and those things can certainly kill people.'

To that Rita had no answer. It was true, she had written exactly that, believed it; she had experienced for herself the ferocity of the monstrous presence within the jet stream during the LA flight, had been in terror for her life because of it.

Yes, presences could kill. But when they did, it was a swift, unthinking action. The sudden fall of cave roof, a tornado's whirl, a rogue wave rearing and crashing in a few terrible moments. The idea that a presence could coldly reach out across the sea and take hold of a human's mind and body, one human among six, marking him out for reasons of its own, and then guide him to a point of execution . . .

No, at that even her old self would have rebelled. It could not be. And yet, how else to explain what had happened? What *else* could have made Kushal do what he had done?

Richman was staring at his major-domo. 'Are you really buying into all this, Clara? You think a ghost did this to Kushal?'

Clara shook her head. 'No. I don't think so. I just wanted to reason out how Rita—or how her book—might have explained it.'

'Trust me, natural causes are more than explanation enough,' said Richman. 'Whatever the reason—suicide or sleepwalking—Kushal went up to the Terrace and ended up in the pool and drowned. Then, by some fluke, he froze in that weird way. I don't know *what* the fluke was, but I've seen enough bizarre shit on mountains in my day to know that ice can do freakish things at times. Right?'

Clara, his fellow mountain climber, gave a reluctant nod of agreement.

'Then let's leave it that,' the billionaire concluded, 'and forget all the other bullshit. We've got enough problems as it is.'

'Like no rescue coming,' said Madelaine. 'Even though you promised it would.'

Richman gave a puff of frustration. 'If only this damn fog would lift!'

Kennedy, who had been hulking silently in a chair all the while, looked up. 'Fog or not, we should have heard a plane or helicopter at least circling about by now. And we haven't.'

'I know, and I can't think why that is. Someone has screwed up massively somewhere.' Richman straightened, gathered himself. 'But fine. If rescue isn't coming, then we have to rescue ourselves. The first thing is to get down to Base. Agreed?'

His gaze swept the group, and then settled significantly on Clara. Rita stared at the major-domo in sudden alarm, understanding. But Clara herself was gazing at the fire and gave no answer.

Kennedy nodded slowly. 'If it can be done, then yes, getting down to Base seems a good start. But,' and he too now looked at Clara, 'can it be done? Can someone really get down those stairs?'

'Like I said,' said Richman, with a certain impatience, 'I'd be happy to try. But in these situations it's not about who *wants* to go, it's about who *should* go, who has the best chance of getting safely down. And ego aside, I know that's not me.'

Bastard, thought Rita in increasing foreboding. *Tell him to fuck off,* she willed at Clara. *He can't make you go down those damn stairs.*

'It's a matter of what's best for the group,' Richman went on. 'That's how it works in business, that's how it works on a mountain, too.'

Clara looked up at last, directly at Richman, her eyes dark with an emotion too private to be understood by the others. (Was it, Rita wondered, disgust?) 'But *you* want me to go?'

The billionaire faltered for just an instant, then was all easy assurance. 'No one is insisting. It's your call entirely. If you think you can do it.'

'Jesus,' Kennedy swore, but only looked away without any explanation.

Rita too felt herself on the brink of protest . . . but to say what? After all, what right was it of hers to tell Clara what to do, or even to judge the sanity or otherwise of an attempt to descend the stairs? Richman and Clara were the experts here, mountain climbers both—surely they knew better than Rita did what was possible and what wasn't.

But even so, this was all wrong.

'Well?' Richman asked.

Clara nodded. 'Okay, Walter,' she said, and something final and weary about her tone made Rita guess that the major-domo had said exactly that to Richman too many times, and that Clara was sick of it, and that was why she was leaving him.

Richman was oblivious. 'Excellent. What we need to do now then is get you fitted out with some climbing gear. With any luck you won't need it. Still, I know there's some stuff in the Museum that isn't too old: ropes, harnesses, carabiners . . .'

Clara nodded, then, strangely serene, glanced to the others. 'Don't worry. I know none of you like the look of those stairs, but it shouldn't be that hard, even if a few of the flights have fallen. There's still the main scaffold. I've climbed far worse.'

Yes, thought Rita, her glance going to the major-domo's booted feet, *but that was when you had all your toes.* But again, the calm competence in Clara's gaze defied her, prevented her from protesting aloud. If Clara thought she could handle the stairway, then she would know, wouldn't she?

And anyway, what else was there, truly, to be done? Should they just sit here, trying not to think about dead Kushal, crouched obscenely in the freezer, and waiting vainly for the fog to blow away, for a rescue helicopter to come? What if another day went by with no change? Wouldn't they then be back in this exact position tomorrow, only a day more impatient and anxious? And what if, meanwhile, someone else went sleepwalking?

No, something had to be tried.

Poor Kushal, of course, had wanted a lustration performed. But even now, indeed especially now, Rita knew that she would not, could not, do that.

Which left only Clara. And two and half thousand metres of ladders.

2

THE STAIRS

IT WAS THREE P.M., AND Clara stood at the top of the emergency stairs, ready to begin.

Richman, Kennedy and Rita were with her, gathered on the concrete lip at the head of the great shaft—Rita battling every second against her vertigo. Madelaine had remained up above, standing watch in the Conservatory. Her job was to listen for a rescue helicopter or plane in the fog, then sound an alert if she heard anything. The other three would see Clara off, and then move to the Control Room to best monitor her long climb to the bottom.

Clara herself was going through her equipment for the last time. From the Museum she and Richman had scrounged a collection of ropes, slung now in neat loops over her shoulders, and a harness, off which dangled a multitude of clips and loops and other tools, the names and purposes of which Rita—although she had listened to Clara and Richman discussing them all expertly—had already forgotten.

In addition to the climbing gear, Clara also carried, in a backpack or clipped to her harness, two torches, a knife, two rolls of industrial tape, two bottles of water, some energy bars for food—for even at best she expected to be several hours in the descent and would need her strength—and finally, hanging from a belt, one of the walkie-talkies.

There were intercom panels all the way down the shaft, one every twenty-five flights, that would enable her to report directly to the Control Room. But of course there was no guarantee that the intercoms would be working all the way down, or at the bottom, if she reached it.

Patting all this down and mouthing a checklist to herself, Clara finally gave a nod, straightened, and looked at the others. 'Okay then.'

It was time.

Richman said, 'Don't forget, give us an update at least every half hour, by intercom or by radio, whichever works the best.'

'And don't push your luck,' added Kennedy. 'You find things are really unstable down there, just come back up. Rescuers will get to us eventually either way, whatever happens, so there's no need for any crazy risks, just for the sake of it.'

Clara considered him levelly. 'I don't think this *is* just for the sake of it. That's the problem.' Her gaze moved briefly to Richman. There was a message bright in her eyes—or so it seemed to Rita—but she said nothing aloud, and he gave no response. And with that, the major-domo turned to the gap in the railing, and the abyss that waited beyond.

Her first step down was an experimental one, testing the topmost rung of the first flight of stairs. It held without a quiver. She dropped several more steps, clumping with heavy deliberation, and still the ladder appeared firm and fast. (To Rita's unease, the major-domo was facing outwards as she went, as if she was on a normal stairway, and not, as Rita would have done, face inwards, as on a ladder. But indeed, though steep, the stairs were not quite vertical.) A few more rungs, then Clara was on the first landing.

She paused there a moment, seeming to test the feel of the little steel-mesh platform under her feet, then nodded. 'So far, so good,' she said, with a glance up at the others. 'I'll see you all later.' Then she was moving calmly down the next flight.

The three at the rail watched in silence, leaning out to see better, even though, for Rita at least, this brought the full horror of the shaft into view. The scaffold tower and the stairway within, now that it had a human on it for scale, only looked all the more flimsy, a construction of straws, while all around the throat of the shaft gaped black and awful.

Four flights down, Clara paused again and looked back up at them one last time. The major-domo did not speak, but Rita had a sudden flash of what they must look like from below, the three of them watching from the safety of the rail, secure on the platform of concrete. She felt suddenly ashamed.

Then Clara was moving once more, from landing to landing, back and forth down the opposing angles of the ladders. Soon she was ten flights down, and nearing the place where the first of the disjointed stairway was adrift of its moorings, its lowest step hanging nakedly out over the gulf.

Rita's hands tightened on the rail, watching from above. Clara paused at the top of the askew ladder and studied it for a time. The gloom seemed thicker down there from Rita's viewpoint, and indeed Clara pulled out a torch and played its beam probingly about. Finally, still with no glance up, she swung herself lightly—and terrifyingly, to Rita—out onto the crossbeams of the scaffold, her back to the open plummet of the shaft, and in a series of quick movements descended hand over hand to the intact landing two flights directly below.

Jesus, Rita thought, letting out a shaky breath. *Holy fucking Mary cunting Christ.*

But Richman sounded only pleased. 'Good girl,' he said. 'Piece of cake.'

Below, Clara was already moving on. Within a minute she encountered the second unseated ladder, and bypassed it in a similar swift manner, with no need of ropes or other gear. After a few minutes more her small figure was lost between the gloom of the shaft and the criss-cross of the ladders.

Even so, the watchers watched. After an interminable while, a sudden torch beam stabbed out to the walls of the shaft far below, searching some unseen detail, but then it flicked off again. And after that, though they waited still, nothing.

She was gone beyond sight.

'If I yelled,' said Kennedy softly, 'do you think she'd still be able to hear us?'

'Probably,' replied Richman. 'But I wouldn't do it. You might distract her just as she was about to swing out from a platform again.'

They all stared down a moment longer, the air of the shaft rising gently and yet with an unpleasant insistence against their faces.

'Then let's get up the Control Room,' said Kennedy, voice even lower. And off they went.

▲

The facts about the emergency stairs—as laid out by Kennedy from the design schematics available in the Control Room—stood stark in Rita's mind.

It was exactly two thousand three hundred and ninety metres from the top of the stairs to the base of the elevator shaft. The rungs on the ladders were each twenty centimetres apart. That meant five steps to a metre, or nearly twelve thousand steps in all, divided into nearly twelve hundred flights. Intercom panels were placed at every twenty-fifth landing, which added up to forty-seven of them in total.

Clara made her first report from the fourth of those intercom panels, some one hundred flights, and two hundred metres, down the shaft. Already, she had descended the height of most of the taller skyscrapers of the world. In normal conditions, it might have taken her about fifteen minutes. On the earthquake-damaged stairs, it had taken her just under an hour, and she was not even a tenth of the way down.

'Hullo up there,' came her voice, hollow over the speaker that was set into the main control desk. 'Can you hear me? Is this thing working?'

'Roger,' answered Kennedy, manning the desk while Rita and Richman looked over his shoulder from chairs behind. 'We hear you. How goes it?'

'Slow. No insurmountable hurdles yet, but lots of the flights are partially dislodged, so I've had to go carefully, climbing every now and then. And it'll only get harder. Looking down, the lighting fails completely in another twenty flights or so.'

God, thought Rita. Bad enough to descend through that echoing void in the gloom of the emergency lighting. In no light at all, other than that of a torch . . . it made her feel clammy all over.

'Well, good luck,' said Kennedy. 'And from now on, if you can, call us from every intercom panel that you pass, just to confirm you're still okay. Otherwise we'll only get worried up here.'

'Will do.'

And she was gone.

The three of them waited, saying very little, glancing at the clock on the wall as it slowly ticked away the minutes. Restless, Rita's gaze roamed repeatedly to the bank of video screens that showed images from the Observatory's security cameras. There was little to see there for the most part, only empty rooms, or halls down which no one walked, or doorways that never opened.

But one camera showed life. In the Conservatory, Madelaine was sitting in a wicker chair, reading a book. From time to time, when Rita happened to look at the screen, the designer's head would be raised, staring out into the mist on the Terrace, her pose alert, as if maybe she was hearing something. But always, after a few moments, she relaxed, and returned to her book.

After twenty minutes the intercom crackled. 'I'm at the next panel,' came Clara's voice. And Rita reminded herself that this meant she was twenty-five flights further down. 'I was right. Lights are out here, and as far as I can see they're out the rest of the way down. I'm carrying on by flashlight.'

'Very well,' said Kennedy.

And they waited again.

▲

It was another hundred metres down that the major-domo met her first real obstacle.

'Four flights were completely gone,' she reported from the following intercom. 'And most of the scaffolding too, just the main uprights left, and the anchor points to the shaft itself. I had to drop straight down by rope. Which is fine, but it might be a problem if any of the rest of you have to come down this way. Up until now there's been nothing a beginner couldn't handle, but an eight-metre down-climb on a free rope might be a bit of a challenge.'

'More to the point, can you get back up?' asked Kennedy. 'If need be?'

'Oh yes, I've left the line there. I have plenty more yet, if I need to do it again.'

'Fair enough,' said Kennedy. And Richman was nodding his approval.

So it was only Rita, seemingly, who was horror-stricken at the idea of shimmying down a rope amid the blackness of that awful shaft, with nothing but your own sweat-slippery grip between you and a drop that was still over two kilometres deep . . .

▲

Forty minutes later came this.

'You guys up there—these intercom panels, they have numbers on them. Like, this one is ES37. I'm assuming that stands for emergency stairs intercom number thirty-seven, yes?'

Kennedy nodded to the mike. 'Correct. The numbers are there so that someone on the stairs—maintenance workers or whoever—can tell the Control Room exactly where they are in case of emergency. They count upwards from the bottom, so that means you're thirty-seven intercoms up.'

Rita did the calculations in her head: if there were forty-seven panels in all, then Clara was ten intercom panels from the top, with a panel every twenty-five flights, or fifty metres . . . that meant she was five hundred metres down.

'That's what I thought,' came the disembodied voice, doubtful. 'But in that case there's been a screw-up during installation, because the panel above me said ES36, I'm sure of it. And it should have read ES38, right? If the numbers count upwards?'

Kennedy and Richman exchanged a glance. 'Someone put a panel in the wrong place, I guess,' said the security chief into the mike.

'If Kushal was here, I'd give him what for about the sloppy work,' replied Clara. Then, appalled, 'Oh, shit . . . I can't believe I said that.'

To which no one replied.

'I'm going on,' said the major-domo.

▲

In the world outside night had fallen. Rita could see it on the security monitors: various windows around the Observatory were captured by the cameras, and they had all gone dark. Three hours now they had been sitting in the Control Room. She felt—not bored exactly, she was too tense for that, but she was impatient with so much waiting. The worst of it was that Clara was not even a third of the way down—there would be hours more of this yet.

'I'll go up and get us some food,' Rita declared. 'Will sandwiches do for everyone?'

The two men nodded, eyes on the intercom. 'And some coffee too,' said Kennedy.

Rita bridled a moment at the order, given as offhandedly as if to a waitress, but then let it go. What did it matter right now anyway?

She climbed up through the service tunnels, very much aware that for the first time she was alone there and relying on her own sense of direction to navigate. She remembered the poor cleaning woman who had been lost in these same passageways. Yes, Rita had found her quite unharmed, but if Rita herself lost her way now, who was likely to find *her* in this all-but-empty Observatory?

But the fears were groundless; she arrived in the kitchen without incident. Before attending to food or coffee, she passed on through the Dining Hall and on up to the Conservatory, where she found Madelaine dozing lightly in the chair, her book fallen on her lap. Rita touched her shoulder gently.

'Oh,' said the designer, starting awake and blinking up at Rita. 'Hello there; I must have drifted off a moment. Is there any news?'

'Not yet. Clara is fine, but finding it slow going. There's still a long way left. I thought I'd make us all sandwiches.' Rita glanced to the windows. It was dark out there, but light from within leaked out to the Terrace, and against the glass the fog was racing swiftly by in swirls and eddies. A low thrum could be felt underfoot, matched by an occasional moan and whistle from the eaves of the Conservatory—the wind playing. It had strengthened in the last few hours. 'Nothing to report from up here?'

The designer stared at the fog. 'No. I thought I heard a sound out there a few times, but it never came to anything. Just phantoms.'

'Well, are you hungry? Do you want to help me out in the kitchen?'

'No, I'm fine. I'll think I'll just stay here and keep watching and listening.'

'If there wasn't a plane or helicopter all day, there won't be one now, at night.'

Madelaine was unmoved. 'Even so,' she said, her eyes still upon the swirls beyond the glass.

Rita lingered a moment, uncertain. Something seemed a little off with the designer. Then she glanced up to the corner where she knew the security camera had to be—though she could not see it, it must be camouflaged as one of several light fittings in the vicinity. She felt oddly sure that back in the Control Room this very instant the two men were watching her, wondering why she was simply standing there as Madelaine sat unmoving in her chair.

'Okay then,' she said, and turned away. 'I'll be in the kitchen if you change your mind.'

'Fine,' said Madelaine.

▲

Long after the sandwiches had been eaten and the coffee drunk, Clara reported in from intercom panel ES28—still well short of halfway, but nearly a full kilometre down the shaft now.

'I'm taking a break here,' she said. 'Knees are playing up a bit, all this downhill work.'

'Check,' said Kennedy. 'And no surprise, that's nearly five hours you've been on the go now. Let us know when you move again.'

Silence fell for a time.

Richman muttered unhappily. 'At this rate, it'll be dawn before she gets down.'

Kennedy gave him an admonishing look. 'All the better. That means it'll be daylight when she reaches Base, whatever is left of it.'

The billionaire gave a distracted nod, and the silence fell once more.

Rita sat back in her chair, her thoughts on the woman a thousand metres below, in the depths of the Mount, on one of the tiny landings, her legs stretched out to relieve the aching muscles of her thighs. Climbing down so many stairs, it would be bad enough for anyone— but it would be even worse, surely, for someone whose feet were . . .

She said to the men, 'I've never wanted to intrude before, but . . . Clara's feet. How badly were they affected when they were frostbitten?'

Richman and Kennedy looked at each other, but didn't speak for a moment. Then Richman said, 'She doesn't like to talk about it. She considers herself fully functional; that's all that matters.'

But Kennedy gave a snort. 'She lost the forward half of each foot, she needs prosthetics just to walk. This must be goddamn hell for her.'

The billionaire set his lips tightly. A blush had risen in his cheeks, making his normally handsome face seem suddenly blotched and harassed. 'She's still the best climber here, toes or no goddamn toes. I don't see *you* shimmying down any ropes.'

Another silence.

The intercom clicked on. 'Getting a bit warmer down here,' came the hollow voice.

'Makes sense,' answered Kennedy. 'You're a kilometre lower down than us.'

'Right.'

It was banal chitchat. Rita sensed that the major-domo had called in just to hear a human voice in reply. The isolation down there in the dark—she would probably have the torch switched off to save on batteries—must be oppressive.

'Hey, Clara,' said Kennedy abruptly. 'Give that walkie-talkie a try, see if it works from down there. Mine is set on channel four.'

'Good idea. Give me a moment here,' came the reply. And Rita imagined the major-domo turning on the torch to fiddle with the radio.

The security chief had hefted his own walkie-talkie, watching it expectantly. After a long few moments the thing blared into life with a burst of static, followed by a garbled undertone of what was evidently Clara talking, although the only word Rita caught was *over* at the end.

Kennedy pressed the *Send* button. 'Say again, Clara, if you hear this. You're not coming through. Repeat, say again. Over.'

Another burst of static blared, then the air seemed to clear a little, and just audible came the strained words, half shouted, 'Testing, testing, one, two, three. Over.'

'Gotcha,' said Kennedy. 'But it's pretty shitty reception, so I'd stick to the intercoms, if you have the choice. Over and out.'

'Roger, understood,' came the answer, heavy with static again. 'Over and out.'

For five minutes there was nothing further. Rita stared at the clock, and at the video screens, and at Madelaine, who was still in the

Conservatory, either reading, or staring at the windows, even though there was only blackness and fog out there.

Then, from the intercom, 'Okay, that's enough of that. I'm on my way again.'

▲

Midnight approached, and far below, Clara's pace was slowed by more collapsed sections, forcing her to descend by rope. These down-climbs did not seem to present her any great difficulty, to judge by her tone on the intercom, but she clearly found them frustrating. It was just before twelve that she finally called in from panel ES24, which meant that she was at last halfway down, nine hours into her ordeal.

'Congratulations,' said Kennedy.

'Fuck that,' was Clara's tired response, before bidding them adieu and moving on.

More slow time passed. It was good news, but even so, boredom was overcoming the tension within Rita; she was yawning repeatedly. What she really wanted to do was to go to bed in her apartment, but it didn't seem right to abandon the climber below, even though obviously only needed one person to monitor Clara from the Control Room, not three.

Her gaze flicked every now and then to the security screens. At one point she saw to her surprise that, up in the Conservatory, Madelaine had left her seat and was standing at the glass wall that looked out over the Terrace. The designer was staring intently into the blackness, her pose alert, as if just drawn there by some sound or movement.

Rita watched the scene for perhaps three minutes, but the camera could reveal nothing beyond the glass. In all that time Madelaine did not move, nor did her alert air seem to relax.

Then Clara called in from the next intercom panel, and Rita forgot about Madelaine for a few moments. When she looked back, the designer was in her chair again, reading once more.

▲

One a.m.

'All right,' came Clara's voice over the speaker, 'this is getting ridiculous. The last panel I passed higher up was ES21, but now this one says ES22. I passed ES22 half an hour ago. This should be ES20. Whoever installed these things needs a swift kick. Not only have they got the panels out of order, they have repeats of some numbers. It could really lead to confusion, if there was an emergency down here.'

'Noted,' said Kennedy. 'Sounds a stupid mistake. So you're really at ES20. You okay?'

'Oh, I'm fine. No problems.'

But to Rita, the climber's annoyance and weariness was palpable.

And she still had a long way to go.

▲

Ten minutes later.

'Okay, that's it, I give up. This panel says ES21 again, and I know perfectly well I'm at ES19. I'm going to ignore whatever the numbers say from now on. I have eighteen more intercom panels until the bottom, that's all I need to know. You got that?'

The three in the control room exchanged glances.

'Roger that,' said Kennedy.

▲

Just after two a.m., the intercom buzzed alive. 'Lights!' Clara shouted. 'I can see lights moving below me, way down, maybe at the bottom! Flashlights! I think I can even hear shouting down there!'

The three in the Control Room had been sunk in a stupor. Now they came instantly awake. People! People must be alive at Base after all!

'Have they seen you yet?' Kennedy demanded. 'Have you yelled down to them?'

'I've tried. I've shouted all I can. But I don't know. I haven't heard an answer. This shaft is weird with noise. But they should hear me. I'm at—I mean, I *should* be at panel ES16 now, so that only leaves about eight hundred metres to the bottom.'

'What does the number actually say?' asked Kennedy, frowning a little.

'ES24. But that's bullshit.'

'Okay then,' the security chief said. 'Keep heading down, and keep trying to get their attention. But be careful, don't rush, don't forget it's dangerous. Call us the second they answer.'

'Check,' came the voice.

▲

But the report from the next intercom down might have come from a different woman. The excitement was gone, replaced by a tired confusion.

'I don't know what happened. I haven't seen any lights for the last ten minutes now. Haven't heard anything either. I've been shouting, but there's no answer, not a sound. Just pitch-black all the way below me. It's like I imagined the whole thing.'

Kennedy was shaking his head. 'Don't start second-guessing yourself, do you hear me? I'm sure what you saw was real. Maybe . . . maybe there were people inspecting the bottom of the shaft for a few minutes, and now they've gone again. Or there could be other explanations. The point is that there are people alive down there, that's all that matters.'

'I suppose so.' But again, the weariness in her voice belied the words. And Rita thought she could detect something else in Clara's voice now, beyond frustration and disappointment. It might have been loneliness. And why not? After eleven hours on her own in that lightless shaft, creeping further and further away from all companionship, anyone would be craving some human contact.

Kennedy sat up abruptly. 'Wait a minute, Clara, I'm a fool. All I have to do is buzz on the intercom from up here and see if anyone at the bottom answers. I can't believe we didn't do this straightaway. Stand by while I give it a go. Ignore the ring. I'll hang up and call a second time when I want you.'

He clicked off, punched the letters ES into the intercom keyboard, then hit the *Talk* button.

'That call goes to every intercom in the shaft, all forty-seven of them, right?' Richman asked. 'You can't just call the one at the bottom?'

Kennedy nodded as the tone sounded. 'From here, you can only dial all the shaft intercoms at once, not one at a time, and from the shaft you can only talk to the Control Room, nowhere else. It was the simplest way to set things up. Remember, the comm system down there is meant only for maintenance or emergencies, not everyday use—it was pointless to give each intercom its own number.'

Rita was leaning forwards eagerly. The intercom tone, a flat electronic buzz, sounded over and over. *Pick up, pick up, someone,* she willed.

But no one answered.

Dispirited, Kennedy hung up. He paused a moment, then rang the shaft again.

Clara answered. 'Anything?'

'I'm sorry, there's no answer. They must have left the shaft altogether.'

The climber below was a long time replying. Then, very flat, she said, 'I don't think there was ever anyone there. I think I was seeing things.'

'Clara,' said Kennedy sternly, 'I told you, don't second-guess yourself.'

'I'll tell you one thing,' the climber replied in an irritated tone, 'it's getting damn hot down here now. Is it getting hotter up there?'

Kennedy raised a perplexed eyebrow. 'No.'

'Lucky you,' was the muttered answer. 'I'm moving on again.'

▲

Clara's next report was yet another reversal in tone, suddenly fierce and vindicated.

'There *has* been someone here,' she declared. 'There was another section out, almost four whole flights gone, and someone has strung a rope there, just like I've been doing higher up.'

'See, I told you,' said Kennedy. 'You didn't imagine those lights.'

'Yes.' A laugh came, somewhat unsteady, distorted through the speaker. 'Thank god, thought I was going mad for a bit there.'

'But there's no other sign of who they were? Just the rope tied? Nothing else?'

'No other sign. I suppose whoever it was must have given up at that point. No surprise, really—they still had about two kilometres to go to the top of the shaft; they probably thought the stairs were too damaged for them to make it. Strange they didn't try to use the intercoms, though.'

'Maybe they didn't know the shaft intercoms run on Observatory power. They must have thought there was no point trying to call.'

'I guess . . .' But the confidence was gone from the climber's voice once more, as if some disturbing realisation had come to her.

'Everything all right, Clara?'

'Oh, it's nothing.'

'What's the number of the panel there, by the way?'

A pause. 'I'm not looking at the numbers anymore, I told you that. Moving on.'

▲

'Fuck, it's getting hot in here,' was the comment from the next intercom down. And truly, even through the distortions of the speaker, the climber below sounded flushed and out of breath.

'Is it time you took another break?' Kennedy enquired. 'You've got water. Rest and have a drink.'

'Descending shouldn't be this hard,' Clara was complaining, almost talking over the security chief. 'Hard on the knees, yes, but it shouldn't be so goddamn tiring. I'm glad this is nearly done.'

'The heat,' Kennedy said. 'There's no sign of a fire or anything below, is there?'

'No, all dark down there. I wish it was dawn already, I might be able to see some light at the bottom, even just a bit, coming down the entrance tunnel. It's only five hundred metres now.'

Kennedy said, 'I know it doesn't matter, but just for my sake, what's the panel number there?'

'It's wrong, I can tell you that.'

'But even so . . .'

'It says ES26. Like I said, nonsense. I'm really at ES13, if my count is right.'

Kennedy didn't speak for a moment, giving a look to Richman, and Rita was aware of a slow curdling of the mood in the Control Room.

'Okay,' the security chief said carefully. 'Well, we'll stand by for the next check-in.'

'Roger that.'

And she was gone.

Richman was staring at Kennedy. 'Is that mike off now? She can't hear us?'

Kennedy nodded. 'It's off.'

'Then what the hell is going on here? Has she been climbing *up* again without realising it? That rope she found—just like hers, she said. So *is* it hers? Has she doubled back on herself?'

Kennedy gave a worried shrug. 'Hard to believe, but it would explain why the panel numbers haven't made any sense, if she's been going up and down all this time without realising it.'

'But how could that happen, for Chrissake? I mean, I know it's dark and all in there, but climbing up is not the same as going down! She'd have to be out of her head to not know the difference.'

'Maybe she is.'

'What do you mean?'

'I've just been thinking. How is the elevator shaft ventilated, do you know?'

The billionaire fell silent a moment, struck by the notion. Then, 'You think the air is bad down there? That she's hallucinating?'

'I know it can happen in old mine shafts,' said Kennedy, 'if there's no air being pumped in. Carbon monoxide or other gasses that are heavier than air can sink to the lower levels, and anyone who enters there is immediately poisoned or suffocated. Is air pumped into *this* shaft, do you know?'

Richman pondered a moment. 'There were a few issues during construction, I remember. Men fainting and so on. And some vents were dug laterally to help—but no air is actually pumped into either of the elevator shafts. They're not like mine shafts, after all, they're open at both the bottom and the top, so air circulates, it doesn't get trapped.'

The security chief thought. 'But if the quake did damage at the bottom, and sealed the lower end of this shaft, then the air could have gone stale down there. Or worse, exhaust gasses from the generators up here might be sinking down the shaft, making it downright deadly.'

Rita said, 'So the lights she saw, they might really just have been a hallucination?'

'Could be,' said Kennedy.

'You have to get her up, then! It's dangerous down there, she might suffocate!'

'Wait a minute, wait a minute,' Richman interjected. 'We don't know that yet. She sounds fine enough to me. The intercom numbers might genuinely be messed up, like she says, and someone else really might have climbed part of the way up and strung a rope. Let's wait and see. We can't talk to her now until she gets to the next panel anyway.'

'There's the walkie-talkie,' said Rita.

'Which is next to useless. I say we wait until the next panel and see how she is then. Okay?'

He was talking to Kennedy now, not to Rita, and the *okay* wasn't a question, it was an order.

'The next panel,' the security chief nodded.

▲

There was a long wait. The clock on the wall ticked to three a.m. On the security video screen, Madelaine was out of her chair again and at the glass wall, staring out into the night on the Terrace. What could she see out there? Why didn't she go to bed?

The intercom crackled, and then Clara's voice came, angry. 'What's going on up there? Have you sent someone down behind me?'

'What do you mean?' asked Kennedy.

'I can see lights above me—a flashlight—way high up. Who is it? Who's coming?'

Kennedy looked significantly at Richman—what more proof was needed?—and the billionaire raised a hand in surrender.

The security chief addressed the mike. 'Listen to me, Clara, how does the air feel where you are? How's your breathing? Normal?'

'What? My breathing is fine. Who did you send down, I asked? Tell me!'

'We haven't sent anyone down. There's no one above you, so I don't know what lights you're seeing, or if they're even real. Here's the thing, Clara, we're worried that the air might be bad down there and that you might be getting disorientated. What's the number on the panel you're using now?'

'The numbers again? I told you—'

'Please, Clara. It's important.'

'Well, it's ES27. But . . .'

Rita bowed her head: that confirmed it, the panel before had been ES26. The major-domo was climbing upwards now, not down. Worse, she was nowhere near the bottom, she was merely circling about at the halfway mark.

Kennedy said, 'I see. Have you found any more collapsed sections with ropes already fixed? The same sort of rope that you're using?'

'How did you—?'

'It's your *own* rope, Clara. You've been wandering up and down the stairs without realising it for a while. You've become disorientated.'

'Are you crazy? I'm fine.'

'No, you're not. We think you're getting slowly poisoned. You've got to keep coming *up* now, and only up, to get out of the bad air.'

'Not a chance. I'm almost at the bottom, I'm not going all the way up again!'

'You're not at the bottom. You've been going backwards. You're about halfway again.'

'I'm . . . I'm not listening to this. You've got it all wrong. I'm going on down.'

'No, Clara, don't do that.'

'I'll report from the next panel. Goodbye.'

'Clara? Clara?'

But there was no reply.

▲

There followed a long, anxious interval. Kennedy made repeated calls on the intercom and the walkie-talkie, but there was no response from the climber below. They had no choice but to wait.

At last the intercom burbled, and Clara was there, her tone curt. 'I'm at ES09 now. Only four hundred and fifty metres to go.'

'The panel actually says that?' Kennedy enquired carefully.

'Of course not, it says ES26, but I know where I am. I'm making good time, that last section was easy, though it's getting hotter and hotter. I've dumped my pack to save on weight and effort. Just got the rope and the torch; that's all I need now.'

ES26. So Clara was heading down again now. The worst option.

Kennedy was shaking his head. 'You dumped your pack? I don't think you should have done that. You need that water and food. And you're going the wrong way. You have to come *up*.'

'Rubbish.'

For the first time, Richman leaned forwards and spoke into the microphone. 'Clara, it's Walter here. Listen to me. You're not thinking straight. It's like . . . it's like when you're climbing, like you're at eight thousand metres without oxygen and without acclimatising. You know how crazy climbers can get in situations like that, and they don't even realise it, they think they're fine. They'll even climb up when they think they're climbing down. You've seen it yourself, how climbers have to be talked down over the radio by people at base camp. That's what's happening here. We're trying to talk you back up. You have to do as we say.'

The woman below wasn't buying it. 'I've been fucking oxygen-deprived, Walter, for real. Do you think I wouldn't know if I was going through that again? You guys aren't here. You can't see what I see. I'm fine, I tell you. And I'm going on. It's only a few hundred more metres. You'll see soon enough.'

'It's a mistake,' Richman said gravely.

But again, only silence answered.

▲

'No. I won't be doing that,' said Richman.

Kennedy and Rita were staring at him. Half an hour had passed, more than time enough for the major-domo to have reached the next intercom panel, whichever direction she was headed. But Clara had not reported. Nor had she answered the walkie-talkie. It was clear then what had to be done. Someone had to go down the shaft to get her. But that someone would need climbing experience, which neither Kennedy nor Rita possessed, and that only left . . .

'None of us are going down there,' the billionaire added. 'No matter what.'

'She needs help!' Rita insisted.

'She does,' Richman agreed stonily. 'But we can't offer it to her. She's on her own.'

Kennedy was looking sternly unhappy. 'Jesus, Walt. If she's only halfway down—'

'Don't you get it?' the billionaire cut him off. 'It's too dangerous. If the air is bad, then whoever goes down to help will end up just as confused. We don't have any breathing equipment here. There are oxygen masks and cylinders in the Museum, but they aren't charged. Why would they be?'

'But to just leave her . . .'

'It's exactly like I said, when I talked about mountain climbing. She's a climber disorientated at eight or nine thousand metres without oxygen, and we're climbers a few thousand metres down who don't have any oxygen either. We'd like to go and help, but we can't, because if we go to the same altitude, we'll be just as weak and confused as she is. It takes a team of four or five climbers at least, with oxygen or even altitude suits, to bring a stricken climber down from high up. To try it alone is as good as suicide. The same basic reasoning applies here.'

Rita struggled with various protests on her lips, but spoke none of them aloud. The argument was a sound one, even if she did not believe that it was soundness that made Richman refuse to attempt any rescue. At least, not soundness alone.

But was *she* going to volunteer to go down into that terrible pit? She was excused, of course, being no climber. But if she had in fact had climbing experience, would she dare go anyway?

'We wait,' Richman concluded. 'We hope that she contacts us again, and then we do our best to convince her to come up. But that's it.'

And the other two found they had nothing to say. On the security monitor, Rita noted distractedly, Madelaine had not moved apparently for perhaps over an hour, she was still at the windows, staring entranced out to the darkness.

▲

It was four thirty a.m. before Clara reported again. 'I told you fools I was fine,' came the voice, though it hardly sounded like the major-domo anymore, it had gone bitter and hectoring. 'See, the panels have come right again, and this one says ES04. I'm only a hundred flights from the bottom now. Satisfied?'

'Can you actually see the bottom then?' Kennedy asked neutrally.

'Not yet,' came the voice, defensive. 'It's all dark still. But I can hear noises down there.'

'Noises?'

'People. Talking down there.'

'Well then, if you shout down, they'll hear you in turn. Have you tried that?'

'No, no,' said the climber evasively, 'I don't want to alarm anyone. I'll wait.'

Kennedy shook his head sadly. 'Clara, trust me, you're not where you think you are.'

'You're lying! You're trying to stop me getting to the bottom, getting out! Well, it won't work. I'm going on—and I won't call again until I'm down!'

Another click, then dead air.

Kennedy sighed.

'Try calling the shaft again,' Rita said, suffused with horror, 'just to be sure. Even if she's confused, she might really be hearing people from the bottom. They might answer, even if she won't.'

The security chief sighed and shook his head, but punched *ES* into the intercom keypad.

Once more, no one answered.

▲

At five a.m., leaving Kennedy to man the intercom, Rita and Richman descended through the service tunnels to the top of the elevator shaft.

439

'Because you never know,' Rita had argued, aware of how desperate she was starting to sound. 'If she's completely delusional, she might have been climbing up for the last few hours. She might be in earshot of the top, or we might be able to see her. If she could hear us yelling, then maybe . . .'

So they went, and came to the concrete platform overlooking the immense drop into darkness. Peering over the edge as far as she dared, Rita could see nothing but the steel ladders and scaffolding veering away into nothingness. Richman, leaning out far more confidently over the rail then she would ever dare, apparently saw nothing either.

'I'll give a shout,' he warned, and after Rita had stepped back a bit, he cupped his hands and bellowed, 'Ahoy there! Clara! Can you hear me?'

The call ran echoing down the shaft, but to Rita's ear it seemed to be quickly stifled, lost in the steady slow creep of air that rose from the depth of the pit. Richman called again, and again, and each time the noise vanished down into the darkness.

No response came.

'You feel the air moving, right?' Rita asked.

Richman moved his face experimentally. 'Yes. Slowly. Rising up the shaft.'

She nodded. 'But if that's so, then how can the air down there be bad?'

'You're right.' He considered a moment. 'But then I was never sure the air was bad anyway. If it was carbon monoxide down there, Clara would be unconscious or dead already, for one. And any other gas or even a simple lack of oxygen would disable her in time. But she's not disabled. Something has got into her head, but she's still moving fine.'

'Then what is it?'

His eyes were dark. 'I have no idea. But I know what Kushal would say, if he were here. He'd be quoting your book at me again.'

She stared. 'You think the Wheel is behind this? You think the *mountain* has got into her mind?'

'I'm not saying *I* believe that, no. But the rest of you seem to think such things are possible.'

Rita considered him narrowly. 'But wait a minute: if you don't believe the air is bad, then why won't you go down and help her? What's the real reason? Is it just that you're too scared?'

But the billionaire didn't rise. 'The air might be bad, it might not be, breeze or no breeze, but until I *know* either way, I'd be a fool to take the risk. But feel free to go down if *you* want to try.'

And it took only a glance into the abyss, at the half-detached ladders dangling, knowing that worse waited further down, entire collapsed sections traversable now only by rope, for Rita to admit that no, she would not be going down.

'Let's go back up then,' said Richman.

▲

Back in the control room, Kennedy was repeatedly dialling the shaft intercoms, in the hope that Clara might be passing by one as it rang.

'Nothing?' Rita asked.

'Nothing. You guys?'

'No luck either.'

They sat down to wait again.

Rita glanced at the security monitors. Madelaine had vanished from the Conservatory screen. No doubt, thought Rita, she had done the sensible thing at last, and gone off to get some sleep.

▲

It was nearing six a.m., just as the first hints of dawn would be paling the sky outside, that the next call from Clara finally came over the intercom.

The voice was scarcely identifiable anymore as the calm, unflappable woman that Rita had known these last few days. The major-domo sounded beaten and disconsolate, at wit's end.

'I don't understand. I don't understand. I should be at the bottom. I've gone down past five panels since the one I called from. So where is it?'

Kennedy was gentle. 'Can you see anything below you?'

'No. No. God, my feet hurt.'

'What number is on the panel you're at now.'

'I'm not going to tell you.'

'Tell me, Clara.'

A groan. 'It's impossible.'

'What does it say?'

'It says ES negative one.'

'What?'

'Negative one!'

Kennedy's expression was pitying. 'But Clara, you know there isn't a—'

The major-domo wasn't listening. 'I can't have gone past the way out, I can't have missed the exit tunnel. I'd have seen that, wouldn't I? Even if the shaft and the stairs go lower than ground level. Does the shaft go lower, do you know? How much lower? I point my torch down and there's nothing, no bottom! Where's the damn way out?'

'Calm down, Clara. You're not reading the panel right. The shaft does not go lower than ground level. There is no intercom negative one.'

'I'M LOOKING RIGHT AT IT!' It was a shriek over the intercom, the panic vibrating even through the small speaker. Then softer, almost a sob: 'Don't tell me what I can and can't see, all right?'

'Then forget about the way out or the bottom. Forget all that. Come back up.'

Weary. 'It's too far. My feet hurt too much. I cut my heel on some metal. There's a lot of blood.'

'You cut your heel? Through your boots?'

'Of course not.' The tone was chiding. 'I took my boots off a long time ago.'

Kennedy eyes went wide. 'You're . . . you're barefoot down there?'

Rita too was staring in shock. Clara had taken off her *boots*? She had bared her maimed feet, her toeless half feet, to the metal stairs?

'Oh yes,' said the climber, blithely. 'I got rid of all my clothes. It's better this way.'

'Your *clothes*?' Kennedy sounded as if the breath had been knocked from him. 'Clara, what are you thinking? Can't you see? You're delusional. You have to stop going down. You have to go back to where you left your shoes, and then keep on coming up.'

'No, no.' The climber below sounded vague and careless now, as if on the verge of sleep. 'I'll go down. I'll keep going down. This hole has to end somewhere. It can't go on *forever.* Goodbye for now.'

And she was gone again.

Kennedy immediately tried to call back on the intercom, and then the walkie-talkie.

No answer.

The three of them looked at each other. There was no need to vocalise what they were each surely thinking. In Rita's mind at least the image was very clear: the major-domo, confused and naked, far below in the shaft, limping on bloody feet down the staircase in a vacant, sleep-walker's daze.

Just as Kushal had appeared on the security camera footage.

On the way to his death in the pool.

▲

Clara's final call came some forty minutes later, just as the three listeners—exhausted and strained to breaking point after their night-long sleepless vigil—were on the verge of giving up.

A squawk rose from the intercom, and then a whisper, 'Negative nine now. I'm underground, way underground. I still can't see the bottom. There isn't one. But it's all right. I understand now . . .'

Kennedy broke in. 'Clara, please. Tell me exactly where you are. What can you see?'

'You wouldn't believe me. But you'll see for yourself, eventually.' A small laugh came, a giggle, from a mind that was lost. Rita could not imagine it coming from the mouth of the woman she knew. 'Are you there, Walter? I'm talking to you.'

Richman swallowed. 'I'm here.'

'Good, good,' crooned the voice from the abyss. 'Because it's not me that it wants, you know, not really. Or any of the others. It's you, Walter, you bastard. It's *you* it wants, because of what you did up there. That disgusting thing you did.'

'Clara . . .' warned Richman lowly.

'You did it to me too,' muttered the voice. 'And I let you. But no fucking more. I quit, Walter. I quit as of this minute.' There was a pause, then, quite calm and clear, she added, 'Jumping now.'

The link clicked off.

'Clara!' Kennedy yelled into the dead microphone, useless as it was. 'Clara!'

For a beat there was nothing.

Then, bizarrely, there did come the blare of an intercom connection being made, and a strong clear voice was shouting at them excitedly.

But it wasn't Clara.

It was Madelaine, calling from the Conservatory. 'There's a helicopter! I can hear a helicopter outside! Come up! They're here at last!'

3

ON THE TERRACE

THEY WENT, THE THREE FROM the Control Room, abandoning the woman below in the shaft. Richman, Kennedy and Rita were up and running through the service tunnels, madcap, so eager were they, after the long night, to escape the underground darkness and to see the sky and a helicopter promising rescue and salvation.

Morning greeted them as they emerged into the Dining Hall and the Atrium—but here was disappointment, for the light was the same pale grey that they had known for the last two days. Fog still turned every window of the dome overhead into a monochrome slab. The Mount remained swathed in cloud.

Yet at least a helicopter had come. They hurried across the Atrium. Could they hear the aircraft yet? No. Not from inside. There was only an unearthly quiet in the Atrium, without even the thrum of wind. The blustery conditions of last night must have eased. That was good, that would only help.

They dashed up the spiral stairs and so came to the Conservatory. Madelaine was not there. Was she outside in the fog? Rita moved to the airlock doors and searched the mist through the glass. Yes, there, out on the Terrace, a shadow figure was moving back and forth—indeed, now it came to the glass. It was Madelaine, peering inwards.

The designer saw them, beckoned urgently. 'Hurry up!' she called, her voice diminished through the thick glass to a faraway bird call. 'Hurry up, come out here, before it goes away!'

Kennedy was already yanking back the inner door as he grabbed one of the jackets from the stand, Richman following close behind. The weather panel, Rita took an instant to note as she clutched a jacket of her own, was orange, and read minus twenty-nine degrees Celsius.

Then she was following the men through, out into the infinity of grey.

The air clamped vicelike on her brow, set her throat afire. The fog itself seemed to consist of drifting ice crystals. She fumbled to button her overcoat and pull the hood closer about her face, then jammed her hands deep into the pockets. The two men and Madelaine were huddled out at the centre of the Terrace, and she hurried as best she could on the ice-slick ground to join them.

'I don't hear it!' Kennedy was saying when Rita came up, his face—frost already forming on his upper lip—turned to the invisible sky.

'Wait,' the designer replied excitedly, breath puffing as a denser cloud into the fog before disappearing, her cheeks so bright red they seemed to shine in the gloom. 'Just listen!'

They all stood silently a moment. The mist oozed without sound about them. Just visible off to one side was the frozen-over pool, a dark hollow at its centre marking the spot where they had dug Kushal from his horrid resting place. But no sound of rotors came. Rita thought she would have to remove her hood if she was to have any hope of hearing—

But there!

Now it came, fading in like a tuning radio signal, an insectile vibration in the air—the throb, both high and low, of whirling blades.

'Not close,' was Kennedy's verdict, his neck craned to stare into the mist. 'High up still, east I think, maybe above the cloud level.'

'But it's *someone* at long last,' said Richman. To Kennedy, 'Can you tell what type of chopper it is? Big? Small? Civilian? Military, even?'

The security chief listened a moment, the sound rising and falling as the unseen thing seemingly turned to and fro above the cloud. 'It's not small, but then it wouldn't be, not if it flew here from Hobart. Military, maybe, or a big air-sea rescue craft.'

'Can they land up here in this fog?' Rita asked of both the men.

'Probably not,' answered Kennedy. 'Not without an improvement in visibility. But they should be able to land down at Base.'

'Then they can't help us?'

'Not this minute. But Christ, at least they've finally arrived. Three damn days!'

'Oh, they'll land up here,' said Madelaine.

The other three glanced at her in surprise, so confident was her tone. The designer was not looking at them, her eyes were to the heavens, her glowing face almost beatific in the gloom.

'They'll land up here,' she repeated. 'I've known all night they were coming. I could feel it somehow; I could feel it through the fog. Someone was on their way, someone would arrive today.'

Rita remembered suddenly that Madelaine had missed all that had transpired in the Control Room overnight. She said, 'Listen, Madelaine, we don't know what happened to Clara. She got halfway down the shaft, but something went wrong . . .'

The designer did not appear to have heard. 'I couldn't wait; I had to come out here to see. They're getting closer now, don't you think?'

. Rita hesitated uneasily. Did the designer understand? Clara was in trouble; she might be *dead*. Overhead, the helicopter sound swirled once more. Was it louder? Nearer? Rita couldn't tell. The noise seemed to shift about in the mist, coming from different points at different times.

'They can't land in this soup, I tell you,' Kennedy insisted. 'You'd need a special radio location beacon to have been installed up here, and then the right instruments on the chopper.'

Madelaine only smiled. Belatedly, Rita noticed something strange about the way the designer was wearing her coat. The rest of them had the furred hood pulled up and the front buttons all fastened, with their hands plunged deep into the pockets, but Madelaine's hood was down and her coat was hanging open, revealing her light house-dress beneath, while her hands, completely bare, were clasped almost prayer-like over her breast. It was bizarre. She had been out here longer than any of them, and she was, in effect, half naked to the deadly cold air.

Indeed, how *much* longer had she been out here? Rita was unable to recall exactly when was the last time she had observed Madelaine, over the security camera, still in the Conservatory. Four in the morning, five in the morning?

'Madelaine? Aren't you cold? How long have you been standing out here?'

The designer shrugged. 'I came out in the dark. It was so lovely, and I wanted to hear.'

The dark? What did that mean? A half-hour ago? An hour? More? But that was madness, dressed the way she was. Now that Rita looked closely, she could how thick the frost was on Madelaine's lips and in her eyebrows and hair. Worse, the fingers of her bare hands were an ominous greyish-white, and the red of her cheeks was like a wound.

'You need to get inside and . . .' Rita began. But then she trailed off as the sound of the helicopter swelled suddenly, very loud, as if the machine was passing low overhead. They all stared up, ready for a dark shadow to appear through the mist, rotors shimmering in a blurred circle.

No shape appeared. The sound lifted, seeming to bifurcate as it did so, as if two helicopters were sweeping away in opposite directions.

'What the—?' Kennedy demanded.

'It's just the echoes,' Richman assured him. 'It's just the way sound gets twisted around up here.'

Rita shook her head, cursing the mist. If it would only clear for a moment, allow just one glimpse of open sky and of the helicopter. For two days this damn cloud had held them, as much a part of their prison as the solid rock of the Mount itself.

'The fog doesn't bother them,' breathed Madelaine, 'they can see us easily.'

Something was seriously wrong with the designer, but Rita was too distracted to concentrate on that, the air was too full of noise now; it was as if there were not one or even two helicopters circling the Mount, but a whole squadron of them.

Even Richman's assuredness seemed to waver. 'What on earth are they up to? Why are they just circling the fuck around?'

Rita addressed Madelaine finally. 'Look, your hands, they must be freezing. Put them in your pockets at least. I'm asking. Please.'

The designer ignored her still. 'They told me to wait for them out here. Just me, they said. But I thought I should call the rest of you, even so.'

The roar beat at Rita in confusion; she couldn't think. It didn't even sound like helicopters to her anymore; it was too big, too far away.

Kennedy was shaking his head, his voice a yell. 'This isn't right! That's not a chopper!'

'What do you mean?' Richman shouted back. 'Of course it is. What else could it be?'

Abruptly, a new sound wailed out across the Terrace, the whooping of a siren. Rita had heard it once before, it meant something terrible—but when, and what? She couldn't remember.

Then an amplified female voice, calm and clear, was sounding from hidden speakers, loud enough even to cut through the roar in the sky. *Emergency. Strong winds approaching. Seek shelter. Emergency.*

And god, *now* Rita remembered: five days ago, her tour of the Observatory with Clara, the major-domo explaining about the winds that could descend from the Wheel, about the Doppler radar that monitored the mountain constantly, about the . . .

Kennedy's expression was stricken. 'Jet stream! That's the goddamn jet stream coming down!'

Horror filled Rita. Yes. That's what Clara had said. The jet stream. The monster that Rita had met all those years ago in the sky—it was descending to Earth now, to blow *here*, across this very Terrace!

Emergency, the voice repeated. *Strong winds approaching. Seek shelter. Emergency.*

Rita turned aghast to the east, to where the Wheel reared, unseen in the fog. And there was no mistaking it. The roar in the air no longer sounded anything like a helicopter. It was a ripping, whistling, jet-engine sound now, the sound of winds halfway supersonic in speed tearing down the face of the Wheel, the tumult loud enough to be thunderous from even fully ten kilometres distant.

And when those winds hit the sea, Rita remembered, they would be turned and pushed westwards towards Theodolite Isle, the streams of air focussed and piled upon the island by the arced shoreline of the great mountain.

Focussed and *accelerated.*

'Inside!' Kennedy was yelling. 'Inside, quick, we don't know how long we have!'

The four of them were maybe twenty yards from the airlock doors. Kennedy and Richman were already running, and Rita followed.

Yes, Clara had told her that the alarm was no cause for panic, that it was designed to sound within plenty of time to get to safety, that there was no need for wild haste, they had only to make an orderly withdrawal. But it was all very well to be told that on a fine sunny day when everything else was normal—it was another matter entirely in this fog, with the hellish roar filling the sky, and amid the litany of disaster that these last few days had produced. Rita *was* in a panic, and like the men, she ran helter-skelter.

Except, where was—?

Rita stuttered to a stop, turned. Madelaine had not moved; she was still gazing serenely up into the fog, as if no disaster threatened.

There's plenty of time, Rita told herself. She forced her legs to move, stomping back across the Terrace towards the designer. It couldn't be thirty seconds yet since the alarm had sounded, and they surely had at least several whole minutes.

'Madelaine, what are you doing? We have to get inside! Can't you hear the alarm?'

The designer finally seemed to become aware of Rita. 'But I can't go now. I want to see them. *You* know what I mean. You've seen them before; you've heard them. I didn't believe you at first. But last night— last night I began to understand.'

Rita stared, appalled. Presences. The fool of a woman was talking about *presences*; she thought that was what was coming down from the sky.

'Madelaine, no, it's the jet stream; it's terribly dangerous; it's going to hit here any second, more powerful than anything you've ever experienced. You'll die if you get caught in it. Come inside!'

Rita had hold of the designer's arm, tugging at it, her own panic growing all the while. The sound from the east was fiendish, the wind would by now be ravaging across the intervening sea . . .

'Madelaine, *please.*'

The designer was immovable, and there was nothing rational in her eyes. 'But you can wait with me,' she said, and now she was holding on to Rita. 'You can help me when they come.'

Jesus.

'Rita! Madelaine!' came Kennedy's shout, barely to be heard over the approaching cataclysm. 'What the hell are you doing? Come on!'

Rita turned, pulling at Madelaine and trying to pull free of her at the same time. Kennedy and Richman were hesitating at the airlock doors, not yet going in—but not coming to help her either.

'She won't come!' Rita shouted to them. 'We'll have to drag her in! Help me!'

Kennedy hesitated, took several uncertain strides forwards. Richman, however, retreated a step within the doorway, stone-faced.

Then, awful, the air stirred about Rita. Not a hurricane blast, not the jet stream yet, only a precursor gust that set the fog dancing, then died. But the temperature seemed to plummet in an instant, ice lancing at Rita's skin like blades.

Kennedy froze, backpedalled. 'Leave her! Just get the fuck inside! It's almost here!'

'Madelaine!' Rita pleaded.

But the designer was lost, gazing upwards. The wind returned, another gust that rose, then fell, then rose again. Madelaine let go of Rita and raised her arms to the fog. It was swirling in great slow whorls and billows now, opening to tantalising vaults of clear air. Rita was reminded, in a chilling flash, of a video she had once seen, showing the sandy ocean floor stirring gently as only a few feet above great breaking waves crashed and raged and foamed.

And now a new note keened, close and immediate. It was the piping of something immense and fast whistling across the uppermost point of the Mount, across the top of the Cottage raised on its knoll, across the peak of the Lightning Room, maybe only fifty metres above Rita's head.

'Run!' came the scream from behind her.

She ran.

It was only twenty yards, Kennedy waving her in madly, like some crazed airport worker directing an airliner to its gate. Only twenty yards—but five yards out a gust dropped from above, instantly hurricane force, a scream in Rita's ears. Disbelieving, she went reeling sideways and fell. Something peppered her skin and clothes—was it grit, blown loose from the stone floor? Then the scream ebbed, leaving her to scramble to her knees and flounder to the doors, where Kennedy grabbed her and hauled her through.

For an instant longer he hesitated, ready to slide the outer door shut. 'Madelaine!' he called.

The gust that had knocked Rita over had not touched the designer. Still far out upon the Terrace, she remained upright, her arms spread and raised. Even as Rita looked the wind roared anew and Madelaine's coat streamed out behind her like wings, her dress pressed flat against her body. 'I'm here!' she cried to the heavens. 'I'm ready to go now!'

A hammer blow of air, as wide as all the mountaintop, swung out of the sky. It was visible somehow, like a shockwave in the fog. The roar became a freight-train howl, metal screaming on metal, and the world outside turned to madness. Madelaine staggered, then was thrown backwards, light as a toy, even as the outer airlock door was torn from Kennedy's hands and slammed shut. He and Rita, both on their knees, scrambled through the inner door where Richman heaved it closed behind them. There was an instant of silence in the Conservatory as Rita and Kennedy lurched upright. Then, outside, the wind bellowed afresh, louder than ever.

And did not stop.

'Holy shit,' uttered Richman.

Rita stared out. The jet stream had come. It raged in stupefying brutality across the Terrace, blasting from gust to gust. But it was not, Rita could sense even in those first instances, the jet stream in its natural state, not as she had experienced it in those tortured moments of the LA flight. This was no freely flowing river of the upper airs.

This was a jet stream that been captured by the stony heights of the Wheel, a jet stream that had been dragged, furious at the insult, down from its proper home in the high atmosphere, and then herded and enraged and strengthened threefold by the immovable arc of the great mountain. It was a jet stream driven mad by the Wheel, and then inflicted here upon the naked summit of Observatory Mount.

She gazed transfixed. Gust after great gust hit the mountain, shaking the very bedrock, but with no trees to bend beneath it, with no external curtains to flap in it, with no rain to be driven by it, with just a bare arena of stone across which to blow, the only visible indication of the speed of each gust was the fog whipping across the Terrace. But even judged by such an insubstantial medium, that speed was staggering, too fast for the eye to follow, too fast for the head to turn, a mad career, east to west.

She was safe, Rita reminded herself. The Conservatory windows were of thick and specially toughened glass, inset deep into the walls which were themselves part of the stone of the mountaintop. None of it was going to blow away; she was as secure as if in an underground storm cellar. A bomb bunker. But even so, she shrank back from the glass. For the panes were flexing inwards. Not cracking or smashing, true. But the force it would take, to make glass so thick, and so solidly embedded, *flex* like that . . .

She tore her gaze away for an instant to consider the weather panel by the door. The figures glowing there were scarcely believable.

Temp: −43C

Wind Av: 249 kph

Wind Max: 338 kph

Then she was staring back to the windows, remembering the most horrifying fact in all this, and searching for . . . yes, there.

Out upon the Terrace, defenceless beneath the wind, Madelaine lay flat to the ground.

At first, Rita was amazed that the designer was even still there, that the initial gusts had not simply blown her clean off the peak. There was nothing out there to hold onto, no shelter.

Except, no, that wasn't quite true. Here and there about the Terrace large glass panels were set flat into the ground. They were the tops of the window shafts that opened into the Atrium dome below. Around these glass panels low fences had been erected, made of metal posts and stainless-steel wire. Their function was to protect the panels, to make sure no one walked on them and damaged the glass.

Madelaine, in falling, had managed to grab hold of a post of one of these fences, and she held there still, her hands white around the steel as her long coat beat in the shrieking air above her like a whip.

In fact, her position was further protected by the eastern parapet of the Terrace. The low stone wall, though only a little above waist height, was enough to divert the full force of the jet stream slightly upwards and over the spot where Madelaine sprawled. Rita could see the curve of the wind in the way the fog moved, as clearly as in a wind tunnel.

Madelaine was even free to shift her body minimally. As Rita watched, the designer inched one of her hands to the lowest wire of the fence, and began to edge herself sideways, crablike, towards the airlock doors, her nearest hope of salvation.

'No, damn it,' Kennedy moaned. 'Not this way. Go towards the parapet, you fool, get in under the lee there. Don't come this way!'

Rita stared at him blankly.

'She won't be able to get in this way,' Richman explained to her, his face pale with shock. 'We can't open the doors. They lock automatically from both sides at winds of over two hundred kays.'

'So override the lock!' cried Rita, her gaze returning to the creeping figure out in the tempest. 'Get the door open and let her in!'

The billionaire was unmoved. 'You don't understand. There's a reason for the protocol. In winds like this—Christ, look, it's gusting near four hundred now—you don't dare open the outer door. The inner door wouldn't take the strain. And if the inner door goes, then you've got a pressure differential in here that would pop all the windows in the place, and then all of us would be dead. Not just her.'

'Anyway,' said Kennedy more grimly. 'I doubt we could get the outer door open even by force. Look at the way it's buckling in its frame.'

It was true. The sliding door was holding, but it was bowed inwards and contorted. Rita could not imagine the strength it would take, quite apart from the courage, to venture out there and somehow wrest it open to the nightmare beyond.

But then what of Madelaine? The designer had inched another foot closer as they debated. Her head was down as if she did not dare raise it to look, but somehow she knew which direction to take. Except that it was the wrong direction.

And the wind mounted still. There were no longer separate gusts that Rita could discern; there was just an everlasting blast that scaled higher and higher in ferocity. On the weather screen, the average wind speed and the maximum gust read the same.

410 kph.

Out on the Terrace, Madelaine had come to the end of the fence. Still ten metres at least of open stone remained between her and the door.

'Don't try it, for the love of god,' moaned Kennedy. 'Just stay the hell there.'

But Madelaine would not be able to stay there, Rita could see that. The wind was only getting stronger; the shelter of the parapet would never be enough. The designer's fingers, cut and black with blood, were already slipping from the wire. Inevitably she would lose her grip and be blown away, she had no choice but to make the attempt . . .

At last Madelaine lifted her head, just by a fraction, and looked their way. Her face was white, almost unrecognisable to Rita, its expression pure bewilderment and terror, as if she had just woken up to find herself in this horrific predicament, with no memory of how she came to be there.

And perhaps it was true, Rita thought. Perhaps Madelaine had been in a kind of fugue state before the wind came, which would explain why she had behaved so strangely. Perhaps she had only come back to herself when she was thrown to the ground. Had it been the same way with Kushal? After sleepwalking to the pool, had he awoken, too late, to find the ice sealed around his limbs, so that he could only scream uselessly into the water as he drowned? And what about Clara, lost and dazed upon the endless stairs, counting the wrong numbers?

Across the wilderness of wind and whipping fog, and through the glass, Madelaine's gaze met Rita's; one woman trapped and doomed, *knowing* she was doomed, the other, only yards away, safe and yet helpless. It was unspeakable. Finally the jet stream mounted again on itself, shaking the Mount more profoundly than ever, a banshee scream, and Rita let her gaze shift to the weather readout, to see there the impossible figure of five hundred and two kilometres per hour. When she looked back, Madelaine was bowling away across the Terrace, limbs and coat flailing like a broken umbrella.

Rita gave a sobbing cry, expecting to see the lost woman disappear over the western parapet—but in fact the tumbling scarecrow was halted short of the edge, fetching up instead, with sickening force, against a second of the stainless steel fences.

'Oh dear god,' breathed Kennedy.

For now the designer was displayed as if crucified upon the wires, propped up face on into the jet stream, her head held against one of the poles, her arms pinned outflung, her torso bent beneath her and her legs trailing behind, their bones already broken, to judge by their unnatural angle.

But her face . . . The wind tore at it savagely, deforming it into a loose, hideous mask of gaping eyes and bloodied mouth, flapping about her skull. Her clothes, meanwhile, were shredding as if blades were cutting in the air, her overcoat tearing away in strips, followed quickly by her flimsier garments beneath, until she was suspended there quite naked, other than a last few rags that somehow hung on.

521 kph, said the readout.

Rita had a hand to her mouth, feeling vomit rising with her horror. Naked. Naked. Kushal had been naked when he died. And Clara as well, down in the pit, had declared that she had thrown off all her clothes, even her shoes. And the man in the sauna. And the one on the Lightning Room.

All of them, naked.

Was that what the Wheel demanded of them? That its chosen victim must be stripped to bare skin before the mountain inflicted its punishments? Would they all end up naked this way—Rita and Kennedy and Richman too—before they died?

And still Rita could only stare. The designer's body, stripped of its stylish apparel, was stout and pale, but in truth it was scarcely human anymore, so mangled was it by the wind, the skin rippling and stretching in ways beyond bearing.

539 kph, said the readout.

'Jesus, I hope she's dead,' Kennedy was praying. 'Jesus, let her be dead already.'

But Madelaine was not dead. Her battered face—it had turned blue, either from the lethal cold or from some sort of internal haemorrhaging—turned purposefully even now, slowly, laterally across the gale, so that the sockets of the eyes looked once again towards to the airlock doors. But if there were eyes within the sockets still capable of sight, Rita could no longer tell, and did not want to know.

566 kph, said the readout.

And now the fence itself was bending. Unburdened, it might have withstood the jet steam, but with Madelaine's body acting as a sail, the steel uprights were surrendering to the onslaught, leaning further and further. And still the ruined face, flapping red about the mouth, streaming blood into the air, seemed to stare at Rita, safe in the stillness behind the Conservatory glass.

Then the fence gave way completely, and Madelaine tumbled backwards once more. And yet even then she was not set free. Entangled from the waist down now in a long snarl of stainless-steel wires, fixed at their further ends to mooring points set deep in the stone, she flailed about like some misshapen kite, lifted into the air and slammed down upon the ground, again and again and again.

580 kph, said the readout.

Not a shred of clothing remained on her now, she was only a mass of white and blue and red flesh, and she must be dead, she must surely be dead, her skull crushed as her head was driven into the stonework, over and over again.

And yet somehow Rita knew that even now there was a mind alive in that shattered body, blinded and dazed beyond belief by the violence done to it, but thinking still, aware still . . .

Then, even though Rita would have thought there could be no scale of ferocity left to the jet stream, it notched higher yet, like thunder and shattering steel and a thousand women screaming all at once. The windows bent so much under the strain that everything went blurry outside as if through coke-bottle lenses, and Rita was sure, as she cowered, that the wind readout clicked over to six hundred kilometres per hour before flashing an error signal and going blank.

Then one of windows gave an awful crack, a jagged fracture appearing in the glass. At the same moment, Kennedy clutched Rita and dragged her away, leading down the stairs to safer quarters in the Atrium below, following Richman who had already fled.

And so they saw no more.

▲

Hours later, after the jet stream had withdrawn, rising to its usual haunts far above, they crept carefully up to the Conservatory once more, and found that the cracked window had held anyway.

But out on the Terrace, in the fog that once again swirled lazily in air gone calm, all trace of Madelaine, and the fence in which she had been entangled, were gone.

4

THE RITUAL

SO NOW THEY WERE JUST three.

'We'll withdraw to the Cottage,' said Walter Richman, as they stood surveying the deserted, wind-blasted Terrace. His handsome face was as drawn and haggard as if five years had passed since Rita's arrival, not five days. 'And lock the doors.'

Rita and Kennedy glanced at him questioningly. The Cottage? Locked doors?

'Madelaine was alone all night before she died,' explained the billionaire. 'Clara was alone down in the shaft. Before that, Kushal was alone in his apartment. So, the three of us aren't going to let each other out of our sight until rescue finally gets here. And we're not going to set a foot outdoors again.'

Rita stared at him, the questions rising to her lips. Yes, his proposal was sensible, but what did Richman now think was happening here, what did he believe was *doing* this to them?

But the billionaire forestalled her. 'Wait,' he said. 'First, if you or Kennedy want any gear from your rooms, we should collect it now.'

Together, they descended first to Rita's apartment, where she gathered up her luggage, then went to Kennedy's quarters in the other guest wing, which until now Rita had not visited. That done, they returned to the upper levels.

And already, as they climbed the Helix Staircase, then passed through the Saloon and the Library, the Observatory felt abandoned in their wake. As they passed through each great chamber, it seemed to Rita the space was in the act of becoming a ruin, an artefact, never again to be inhabited.

They came to the secret lift in the Library—the only elevator in the whole building that still functioned under the emergency power protocols—and rode it in silence up to the Cottage. And the feeling of desolation only grew in Rita. Below them now all the Observatory, with its great Atrium and its Halls and its Cavern Pool and its Games Arena (which she had never beheld and probably never would) and its guest wings with room enough for dozens of visitors at a time, and with all its luxurious appointments and priceless art, and its miles of service tunnels and other secrets, all of it was left untrodden now by a single soul.

So quick, Rita thought hollowly. Was this how the end always came to houses, to cities, to civilisations? One moment there was life and order, then the next, simply, it was gone?

The lift chimed their arrival.

Stepping out into the foyer and then into the living room, there was comfort at least in the smaller dimensions here, in the simulacra of a normal home. Of course, it was anything but a normal home. But the evidence of that remained hidden by the fog that was grey against every window. Rita chose to concentrate on the familiar, on the warm colours of the walls, the welcoming couches by the fire, and in the kitchen, beckoning, the coffee equipment.

She got the water boiling, then joined the men flopped in exhaustion on the couches. The shock of the morning's events still filled the air between them, like a painful ringing in their ears after an explosion they had somehow survived.

'We need sleep,' said Richman. 'Or at least god knows I do. But before that, we need to work out some strategy. We need to work out . . . well, what's going on here, and what we're going to do about it. There can be no more kidding ourselves.'

This last was offered almost as a rebuke to Rita, as if she had been the one who had been kidding herself, as if she was the one in denial. A weary anger rose in her and immediately vanished. 'So you accept that it's the Wheel behind all this?'

The billionaire gazed at her emotionlessly. 'We're under attack; I know that much, and it's not just the earthquake or the avalanche or the wave. Those could have been natural things, maybe they really were. But now something is getting into our heads, and there's nothing natural about that. Look at Madelaine . . . she *wanted* to stay out there on the Terrace, no matter the alarms, no matter that she was going to die if she did. It was like she was hypnotised. And Clara, you heard her down there, she wasn't herself anymore. And Kushal too. Three times it's happened. That's no coincidence; that's organised.' He paused, then at last gave a slow nod. 'So is it the Wheel behind it all? Yes . . . I think maybe we have to say it is.'

But Kennedy, even after all he had heard and witnessed, balked at this final step. He shook his head stubbornly. 'The Wheel is a just a mountain; it's a pile of rock; it can't get into people's heads.'

'How do you explain it then?' said Richman. 'What's making us *act* these ways?'

The security expert searched about, threw up his hands. 'Maybe it's something in the water, or the air, or something we ate, something toxic. That plus the earthquake and lack of rest. I don't know.'

Richman turned to Rita, 'But *you* know, don't you? You know it's the Wheel.'

Rita simply nodded.

The billionaire stroked his jaw. 'Your father told me it was, months ago. All the things that were going wrong here during construction, the accidents, the deaths. He tried to convince me it was the Wheel, and that we needed you here. But why would I have believed him? I'm a rational man; I need proof, and he didn't have any proof. If he'd come up with something concrete I would have listened . . .'

Rita said nothing. So now it was her father's fault, for not being convincing enough.

The billionaire went on. 'In the end, it was only when he died that I began to wonder.'

'When he died?' queried Rita. 'Why then, exactly? Dad died from a heart attack. It had nothing to do with the Wheel.'

Richman nodded easily. 'Of course. I just meant that after he died I had to be here more to oversee the project, and so I began to realise firsthand that something was wrong with this place.'

Kennedy had been heedless of the exchange, preoccupied. Now he said suddenly, 'Okay, let's say for a second that it *is* the mountain doing all this. Why, for fuck's sake? What does it want?'

Richman considered him mildly. 'To get to me, obviously, that's what. Because I beat it, I climbed it, because it *lost* and I *won*. Now that I've come back, the Wheel wants its revenge.'

'Do you hear yourself? It's a piece of *stone*. It's not alive. It can't hold goddamn grudges.'

The billionaire dismissed his security chief and turned once more to Rita. 'I should have called you in from the start. I should have got you here to do your little magic trick before we turned the first sod over.'

A lustration, Rita realised. By *little magic trick*, he meant a lustration. Even when he was asking for her help—and he *was* asking for her help, wasn't he?—he had to belittle her art. But again the anger faded. After all, she herself, for the last ten years and more, had scorned her own faith.

She said, 'It wouldn't matter if you had called me. I wouldn't have come. Not for that.'

'And now?'

'Now what?'

His patience snapped. 'Are you going to perform a fucking lustration, or aren't you?'

She blinked, and the urge in her was to tell him to fuck off, that this was his problem, not hers. Except it wasn't just his problem. Oh, the Wheel wanted *him* and him alone, she was sure enough of that. But it seemed intent on cutting its way through the rest of them first, each of them that was trapped here.

So it was her problem too.

She sighed. 'Yes. Yes, I suppose I am.'

'Okay. Okay then. Now we're getting somewhere.' The billionaire drew a hand across a sweating brow. 'So, how can we help? What do you need from us to get set up?'

'You want me to do it *now*?'

'Can you think of a better time? Can't you feel it? We've got a moment here while things are quiet, while the Wheel is . . . spent, I guess is the word. You think waiting will make things better?'

He was right. There was a sense of *lull* now, of the malice that surrounded them being, for the moment, exhausted. But it would build again. It would build again fast. So yes, they shouldn't wait.

'All right,' she said, 'all right. Just give me to a moment to think. I haven't done one of these in over twelve years, you know.'

She pondered as the men watched her. God, was she really going to go through with this? She had not forgotten her attempt of two—or was it three nights ago?—to make deliberate contact with the Wheel. It had been awful, and that was before anyone had died, before she had known how lethal this could all be. The idea of reaching out to the mountain now filled her with a dread that was nauseating.

But again, to not try it, to sit here and wait for the rest of the day to pass and night to fall, and for the Wheel to regain its strength and then . . . Who knew what then, or who it would target next?

So, yes, she was really going to do this.

In the kitchen the electric kettle piped to show that it was done, breaking her reverie.

She said to the men, 'I'll need coffee and some food before I do any-thing.' She hesitated. 'But for the lustration itself, well . . . in the old days, it helped if I'd taken certain substances first.'

'Drugs, you mean?' asked Richman.

Rita nodded. But, of course, it was more than a matter of *help*. Towards the end, lustrations had been all but impossible without the extras.

'What kind of drugs?' Richman pressed.

'Small amounts of LSD were very good. Marijuana was also useful. But mostly, the last few years I did this, it was cocaine.'

'Jesus,' swore Kennedy. 'You were high all the time? People *paid* you to do this shit?'

Richman glanced without expression at his security chief. 'Coke we've got, yes, Kennedy? But I don't know about pot or LSD.'

Kennedy, too, was unabashed. If his habit had ever been a secret, it hardly mattered that it was out now. 'Oh sure, coke, yes, I got. LSD, no. But I do know that Eugene liked a joint recreationally, so there might be some pot in his apartment.'

Rita blinked. She had not given the IT specialist a thought in days now. Was he even alive still, down at Base? Was anyone alive down there?

'Okay,' said Richman, 'we'll go down together and look in a few minutes.' He studied Rita again. 'Drugs aside, what else do you need?'

'A vantage point,' she answered. 'Usually in the old days I'd do this on a hilltop, or by a waterfall or deep in a cave or the like. The idea was to get as close to the presence in question as I could.'

Richman considered. 'Obviously, we can't get you closer to the Wheel. But the Lightning Room is the highest point of the Mount, and if not for the fog it would give you the best *view* of the Wheel.'

Rita felt a shiver of dread, of some distant foreknowledge confirmed. The Lightning Room. Yes, yes, of course it would be there . . .

'And if we get you all that, then you can do your thing, your lustra-tion?' Richman demanded. 'You can make all this stop? If there's really a presence in the Wheel, you can force it to go away?'

She shook her head. 'I have no idea what I can do anymore. Even in the old days I never tried anything on this scale. Make it go away? No, I doubt that. At best, maybe, I can placate it. Enough so that it might leave us alone until rescue comes.'

Richman was disappointed. 'That's all?'

'*All?*' Rita retorted hotly. 'It'll be a fucking miracle if I can get us that much!'

'Okay, okay.'

Shaking her head, Rita got up to make the coffee. The fog, she noted, pressed thick to the windows, making her think of a spy dressed in grey trying to eavesdrop on all that was said.

▲

An hour later—one p.m. by the clock, but time had ceased to have meaning—Rita sat cross-legged on Walter Richman's bed in the Lightning Room, and set a lit match to the end of a freshly rolled joint.

She was alone, having banished the men to the floor immediately below, down the winding, narrow access staircase cut into the rock—close enough for them to come quickly if she called out, but far enough away to not be a distraction.

In the old days, especially towards the end, she had not been so shy about being watched during a lustration, even if she was naked. But she wanted no observers today—and she sure as fuck wasn't going to be taking her clothes off. Back then, the nudity was all about getting physically close to the earth, about removing all barriers between her and a presence. But with the Wheel there was no need of that, the mountain was already all too palpable.

She took a deep drag of the joint, coughed for a few moments from the unfamiliarity—it had been a while, god knew—then inhaled again.

She contemplated as the hot smoke permeated her lungs. The nudity and other fripperies could be abandoned, yes, but not this, not the altered state of consciousness that the drugs provided. Yes, there had been those times, from the traumatic first event onwards, when she had made connection with presences spontaneously. But in those instances the connection had usually been too uncontrolled, too wild, to be of any use as a lustration.

She took another puff, already feeling the cotton wool numbness at her extremities.

The danger was, of course, that the pot might simply put her to sleep. She had eaten down in the kitchen, and drunk three strong coffees in a row, but still, it was over a day since she had slept, and the exhaustion in her was very real. But thankfully Kennedy's cocaine was ready to come to the rescue there. Three lines of it lay already set out on a little mirror lying flat at her side.

The cocaine to keep her mind alert, and the marijuana to open it up.

She looked up to the glass walls of the Lightning Room. She was facing east, directly towards the Wheel. There was nothing to be seen through the fog, but Rita could feel the mountain out there, vast and potent, dwarfing her by a factor of billions. Sweet Jesus . . .

She heaved a deep breath, took another toke, and then waited the coughing out.

It was very quiet. Listening hard, she could hear nothing but her heartbeat and the crackle of the joint in her hand. Beyond that, the silence was profound, as solid as the stone floor below, the many feet of it between her and the next floor down. There was not even a whisper from the air-conditioning ducts, though the room was pleasantly warm against the freezing air on the other side of the glass. Her father had done his work too well; the room was perfect.

To sleep here would be wonderful, Rita decided, taking a last drag from the joint, now down to a nub. The bed was firm yet inviting beneath her, and as vast as her entire bedroom back at home. And oh, the temptation to lie down now in the grey warm gloom, and to surrender to sleep, her mind slipping away into oblivion, where there were no problems, nothing to fear. It need only be for a few minutes . . .

Her head bowed drowsily, but an instant later she started upright as the joint was suddenly scorching in her fingertips. She stubbed it out in the ashtray firmly, and picked up the small mirror. Time for the cocaine—and not a moment too soon.

She fumbled with the rolled-up US fifty-dollar bill (donated by Kennedy, Richman had no cash on him) and snorted two of the lines, feeling clumsy and idiotic, so long had it been. When she was done, she wiped at her nose and waited as the numbness took hold in her nostrils, and as the familiar tart aftertaste leaked at the back of her throat.

No particular rush came, and there was no change to the languor of the marijuana, but her underlying exhaustion faded, as if a new reserve of strength had been tapped inside her. Not an adrenalin surge, something smoother and more fluid, something almost lazy in its power. True, it was surely just the cocaine, but it felt entirely natural.

And *good*.

She was ready now.

Sitting up straighter, she addressed the eastern windows and the great wall of fog. It came to her that she had never done a lustration before by daylight. Always, in the past, she had performed these rituals by night, as often as not by a burning fire. But then the gloom of the mist was almost like night anyway, and as for a fire, that had only ever been an extra, for effect's sake, it had never been a necessity.

She was distracting herself with these thoughts, she knew. Playing for time. She was scared, that was the truth of it. Scared that it would not work anymore—and even more scared that it would.

But—she reminded herself, forcibly—the alternative was to sit in this luxurious trap and wait until the next one of them was taken. She no longer hoped that rescue would come in time to save them. Not while this fog held. She could not even fool herself that she might be the one who was left until last. Richman would be the last. It was *him* the Wheel wanted isolated, not her or Kennedy.

So she had to do this.

She glanced to her side. Lying next to the mirror and the last line of cocaine was a box cutter knife. Marijuana to expand the mind, cocaine to energise it . . . and a blade to draw the blood.

If it came to that.

She pushed the fear down, focussed again, looked up towards the hidden Wheel, and gingerly, carefully, sent her mind out questing.

Out, out through the thick glass and into the mist beyond, into the damp grey and the biting cold and the shifting of the middle airs, here three thousand metres above the sea. Her eyes were closed now, but she saw not blackness but the glowing grey of the fog, and she searched through it eastwards, suspended above nothing, only a disembodied thought now, but listening, wide open to receive.

And at last, through the mist, the Wheel advanced like the coming of night. The fog did not dissipate, but within her mind the mountain became visible anyway, dark, shadowed, but with clarity, as if she beheld it on a clear moonlit night, all of it, stretching to either side of her in its immense arc of forty-five kilometres, surrounding her, leaning over her, twenty-five kilometres high.

She quailed a moment, almost withdrew her mind there and then. All she had to do was open her eyes and shake her head and she would be back in herself. The Wheel was just too overwhelming, too heavy a weight of stone and ice. She had forgotten, during these last few days, lost in cloud, just how crushing the mere sight of it could be.

But she held on somehow, until the dizziness and vertigo settled. Then, cautious once more, she let her mental eye begin to climb. Up, up, she gazed, past the frowning lower slopes, past the snowfields, now swept bare and bleak by the great avalanche, past the snouts of glaciers hanging perilously, past the chasms of the great couloirs, past all whiteness of snow or ice and on to the naked faces, sheer and terrible, of the upper half of the mountain. And then onwards still, far into the airless, waterless, warmth-less stratosphere, all the way up to the uttermost crest, cut hard against the black sky of space, where, remote but clear, the summit clenched, the very Hand of God . . .

Out of nowhere, Clara's last words from down in the abyss of the shaft came to Rita. *It's you, Walter, you bastard. It's you it wants, because of what you did up there. That disgusting thing you did.*

Disgusting thing? What disgusting thing was that? What crime had Richman committed upon the summit that the Wheel could not forgive? Or was it just the crime of standing there at all?

Rita shook the thought away. It didn't matter. She searched again, probing beyond the mere visible face of the Wheel now and opening herself to the essence of the mountain entire, to the awareness that existed within the heart of so much immensity of stone. She was ready to find hatred there. She was ready to find rage. She was ready for resentment to bear down upon her, weighted with all those billions upon billions of tonnes of rock and ice.

But instead, sensed at first almost as only the faintest of emanations, a dying echo from the high cliffs, but then strengthening as she focussed upon it, until like a tide that had turned and was now quickly flowing towards its full flood, came another emotion, one she had not expected at all.

Not anger . . . but grief.

Rita let her mind's eye play across the mountain. She had encountered grief before during lustrations, yes, in presences that were dying, that were being slowly extinguished as humans gathered about them with the poisonous consciousness of man. Presences could indeed mourn their own deaths, their passing too soon from knowledge.

But this was different.

The presence within the Wheel was different. Entranced, Rita drank it in, a consciousness that had been forged half a billion years ago by the trauma of the Wheel's birth, by the wrenching of such unimaginable weight, tectonic plate grinding inexorably against tectonic plate, so high into the sky.

It was a circumstance unique in all the world, and it had produced, in its violence, an awareness, a presence, that was likewise unique.

And the Wheel knew it. The great mountain understood that not only was it different from its immediate surrounds, as did any presence, it understood that it was different from any other formation to be found upon the entire *planet*, that it was the only one of its type and kind, that there had been no other like it before, and never would be again, in all the age-long life of the Earth.

In the vast loneliness of that realisation, the presence of the Wheel had looked beyond itself to the wider world—an ability that Rita had never sensed before in any other presence. It had looked, and had discovered the existence of all the lesser presences about the globe, in their thousands and millions. Only little entities of little landscapes, but alive and aware, bright sparks in the darkness, and the only companionship the Wheel could find.

But in the millennia since, no more than an eye-blink by the eon-long standards by which it judged time, the Wheel had been forced to watch as one by one those same presences were killed, a constellation of candle flames being doused long before they were due to fail, as human consciousness ravaged across the planet, erasing all other thought.

Until even the Wheel's own turn had come. People had arrived in their hundreds and scaled its unscaleable heights, and one had even stood atop its inviolate pinnacle, and the mountain had been unable prevent it. Oh, that brief invasion had not been enough to *kill* the presence within the Wheel, or even to injure it beyond indignity and insult. But it was a sign that the mountain well understood.

It too would be killed soon, at humanity's hand. One day, be it a century from now or a century of centuries, people would return to the mountain, not in their hundreds but in their thousands, and they would remain, even at the summit, and then even the mighty presence of the Wheel would be drowned in their noxious thoughts, and so expire, as so many of its lesser cousins had already expired.

It was for all this that the mountain mourned. For itself, and for all of its kind. The acuteness of that grief cut at Rita's mind and heart like an icy edge. Yes, there was anger there too, and the slow smoulder of rage and the desire for vengeance. Why else, after all, would the Wheel have done what it had done in these last days, if not to be revenged? But the anger was almost a minor note, lost in the symphony that was the Wheel's sadness and loss.

And that gave Rita hope. Rage she did not think she would be able to placate. But sadness? That was another matter. Sadness, perhaps, she could assuage.

For after all, she shared the Wheel's grief. Not its response to that grief, not the violence it had enacted and was enacting, but the mourning for all that was being lost, yes, that she shared. And for that, in part, she was prepared to pay.

She summoned the sadness now, and sent it flowing from the well of herself towards the monolith of the Wheel. It was a daunting prospect, so small was she and so limited was her store of empathy, when proffered to the towering mountain. But she persisted nonetheless, giving all that she had.

And she was heard.

For a moment, the great tide that was the Wheel's grief slowed, a thoughtful ebbing as it became aware of another mind, one alien to it, and yet one somehow able to tune itself to the mountain, offering it sympathy, offering it understanding.

The Wheel might have lashed out then, spurning the offering, but it did not. The tide held in abeyance, considering, weighing, not yet rejecting and not yet accepting; acknowledging, but not prepared yet to be placated. If it was to cease to flow—so the silent pause within Rita's mind seemed to say—it needed not only shared grief, but also something actual, shared pain, shared loss.

A sacrifice.

Rita took a deep mental breath. Yes, she recognised this desire, having sensed it in so many other dying presences. There was always a need for recompense in exchange for destruction, for a payment in exchange for withdrawal, for a fee to be offered, no matter how small or symbolic, as long as it was *real*, as long as it was given in life source.

In blood.

Unseeing, her eyes closed, her mind still adrift in the fog, Rita reached for the box cutter at her side, and slid out a quarter inch of the blade.

See, she said wordlessly to the mountain, *see what I am prepared to do for your sake.* And for a further moment the tide waited, withholding, watching in cold silence to be paid the price.

Where to cut? The place of easiest access, Rita decided, given that she was clothed. Her arm. Eyes still closed, she shoved up her sleeve, and then traced the razor edge slowly along the smoothness of her wrist, the pressure just enough to pierce the skin.

Yes, she felt the cut open, and a wet warmth well forth. There was virtually no pain. But then it wasn't about the pain; it was about the life-blood that would be released. Rita turned her wrist as she cut, holding it out over the edge of the bed, and felt the tiny droplets go, spattering to the stone floor. She projected the sensation to the mountain.

Did the Wheel hear and see? Did it accept? It was too early to tell. Rita cut for another slow inch, knowing without sight that it would soon be time to stop, that already she had inflicted a wound maybe three inches long that would bleed copiously for many minutes before clotting. She had cut no major blood vessel, it was not life-threatening, but it was still blood aplenty, and more than enough.

But when she went to raise her hand, the cut complete, she found she could not lift it.

What?

Suddenly the box cutter was a stone weight and her arm was power-less to control it, powerless to lift it away . . . and, she realised with a surge of horror, powerless to stop it cutting. The blade was still tracking slowly along her arm, coming to the fold of her elbow. Smoothly negotiating the bend, it began to slice along her upper arm.

Her eyes snapped open, staring down. It was no illusion. Completely beyond her volition, her hand and the knife within its grasp were continuing the cut. She could neither halt nor even delay it. She could only gape at the blood that was running down her wrist and onto the bedspread, more and more of it . . .

Abruptly she became aware of a new mood in the Lightning Room, immensely strong.

It was glee, and it came from the Wheel. Even with her eyes wide open and her mind shut and the entire lustration forgotten, still the sense of the presence around her was overwhelming. And it was laughing at her. It had *tricked* her.

There was no gentle grief, no mourning sadness in the mountain. Or rather, there had been *once*, but it had long since curdled into rage. And not just any rage, but an all-encompassing, cruel, pitiless fury. The Wheel sought no understanding or atonement or placation from humanity; it sought only destruction. And who better to inflict that destruction upon than the man who had defiled the mountain's undefiled peak, the man who stood as symbol of all humankind's contempt for any awareness other than its own.

Yes, the Wheel would kill Walter Richman. It would glory in doing so, and it would kill anyone else it needed to, in the effort to render him helpless and alone. As for the pretensions of a woman who had the temerity to offer the Wheel sympathy, to try and atone for mankind's misdeed with a trivial flow of her blood—well, the Wheel was going to show her now how much blood would *really* be needed.

All the while Rita could only stare. The blade was almost up to her shoulder now, still remorselessly slicing her skin. But then, an inch short of the shoulder joint, the knife stopped, and after a moment her hand lifted away. It wasn't her doing, however. No part of her body was under her control; she was watching through a TV screen instead of her eyes.

Now the box cutter hovered above her lap. Her thumb moved to the catch that adjusted the blade. It had been set at a quarter inch, but now her thumb pushed, and a full two inches of naked segmented razor extended out wickedly.

Her other hand, moving likewise on its own, now pulled back her skirt to reveal her legs crossed beneath her, and to expose the pale and defenceless expanse of her upper thigh. There, beneath a crisscross of ancient shallow scars from the past, secure within her flesh, pulsed her femoral artery.

Oh dear god.

Panic suffused Rita, but she could move nothing, do nothing; there was not even a surge of heartbeat, so divorced was her consciousness from her body. The Wheel held her fast in its grip, moving her like a fluid puppet, and she understood exactly now how Kushal must have felt as he walked to his death, and Madelaine too, and poor lost Clara.

The knife lowered to her thigh.

And yet even in her terror, her most coherent emotion was not fear of death or pain, rather it was one of embarrassment at her own stupidity—that she had walked so open-eyed into this trap, that she had surrendered herself so willingly to the Wheel's control, that she had bought the knife with her, and even begun the cutting of her own accord!

The blade dipped, made contact with the skin. Even though she was otherwise unconnected with her limbs, the steel sent an exquisite thrill of threat through her mind. Then as she watched, helpless, her hand pressed down, and the point of the blade sank into her flesh, slow, steady, deep.

No, she was screaming in the prison of her skull, but it did no good. The Wheel was going to kill her by her own lustration, and it was going to force her to watch every slow second of it.

Buried deep, the razor began to cut, and already blood was flowing, not yet the bright vermillion of arterial blood, and not yet the spraying heart pump of arterial pressure, but any moment—

Her head rocked violently. Then rocked again. Her eyes rolled, dazed. *What?*

Kennedy stood before her, his hand raised and open from having slapped her, his mouth contorted in anger, yelling something, though she could not hear. And when she did not respond, for she could not, he clutched madly at the wrist of the arm that held the box cutter, and tugged it upwards.

Rita watched, a distant spectator, as the blade withdrew a fraction. But then the arm was fighting him (*the* arm, not her arm) and pressing down again, sawing, sawing at her thigh, and the security chief did not seem to have the strength, for all his brawn and size advantage over her, to stop it. She was stronger than him. The Wheel was stronger.

Baffled, Kennedy gave up the fight and glared at her for an eternal instant, as if searching in her eyes for reason or volition. Apparently finding none, he raised his hand again, now clenched into a fist. Rita stared at it in her daze. The fingers were curled hard and tight as stone, and it was utterly beautiful.

He reared back, and with all his strength—she could discern the practised way he threw his entire bodyweight into the movement—he hit her high on the cheek, and in the explosion of pain she knew joy and relief before oblivion swept her away.

5

MEDICATIONS

CONCUSSION, MARIJUANA HANGOVER, COCAINE COME-DOWN, sliced wrist, hacked thigh . . .

Rita considered the list in a darkness that seemed to heave like a small boat on an unsettled sea. Concussion, yes, she might well have concussion, to have been hit as hard as Kennedy had hit her. And the rest, the drugs, the wounds, were already established facts. When she woke up, when the darkness lifted and the boat stopped rocking, she was going to feel fucking awful, her head would be throbbing, her arm and her thigh on fire, her thoughts scrambled . . .

Except, wasn't she awake already, to be thinking this? But what was she doing in a boat?

Her eyes slipped open and there was the world waiting for her, slightly blurry but quite solid. She was not on a boat at all, though the seasick feeling didn't leave her; she was in the living room of the Cottage, stretched on one of the couches. Far away by the tall windows were her two fellow prisoners, Richman and Kennedy, talking, their backs to her.

She tested her limbs cautiously. Immediately there was pain, the stiff, bound sensation of wounds only freshly sutured and crusted over, the hurt seeming to come more from her arm than her leg, even though she knew that the wound in her thigh was the more serious. Someone had stitched and bandaged her, and she assumed it was Kennedy, because of his military and security training.

She glanced down. Someone had also stripped her to her underwear to do the first aid, and then wrapped her loosely in a blanket. And god her head hurt, though really it was more the whole left side of her face, which felt terrifically swollen. Was there a fracture there? A cheekbone? Her jaw even?

But none of that mattered. The important thing was that her hand lifted when she told it to lift; her toes curled when she ordered them to curl; she could move her dry lips and lick them with her tongue. There was no one, no *thing*, controlling her body anymore. She was her own property again.

Celebrating, she tried to rise against the cushion, and fell back with a groan as her head pulsed, and the stitches in her limbs gave coinciding shrieks. Darkness hovered again.

'You awake?'

Rita gazed up. She had not seen them move, but somehow the two men were now at her side, staring down. It was Kennedy who had spoken.

She did not dare nod. 'More or less.'

The security chief's stern face softened slightly. 'Thank god. I was worried I'd knocked you into a coma. You'll be in pain. I stitched you up, but I haven't given you any medication yet, because I wanted you to wake up again first. Do you understand?'

A tiny nod this time.

The relief withdrew from his expression, his gaze hardening. 'So what the hell happened up there? Why were you trying to kill yourself?'

Talking was painful, but she forced it out, firm. 'It wasn't me. It was the Wheel.'

'Oh, come on! I was there. I saw. *You* were cutting your own leg. No one else.'

But Richman was nodding with a light of understanding in his eyes. 'The lustration went bad, is that what happened?'

Rita gave another minimal nod.

'Tell us everything.'

But Kennedy was shaking his head. 'Wait, dammit, she needs some pain relief first, and some water; she'll be dehydrated. Let me get her comfortable first, then she can tell her tale.'

The security chief disappeared to the kitchen for a time, returning with water, a pot of tea, and a several pills. Before swallowing the latter Rita, as a vet and medical professional, demanded to know what drug they were. Kennedy duly told her, and she forgot immediately. The water was delicious, the tea, very sweet, even more so. Meanwhile, Kennedy checked her dressings to be sure all the bleeding was stopped, and finally wrapped her in a thick dressing gown and propped her up on the couch. Only then did Rita, as best she could, still sipping on the tea, report what had happened in the Lightning Room.

'Jesus,' said Richman, when she was done. 'So there's no way we can deal with this thing?'

Rita shook her head, the pain drifting in her skull as she did so, but only mild now. The pills were working. She felt as if she had just downed four or five glasses of wine very quickly. Not drunk, but definitely out of sync with the rest of the world. She put her tea aside, sank back into the couch.

Kennedy was still wrestling with his scepticism. 'I'll give you this much at least,' he said finally, 'you certainly *acted* like someone who was possessed. There was nothing that recognised me in your eyes at all. But to say it was the Wheel . . .'

Richman wasn't listening. 'Then that's that,' he pronounced. 'If we can't negotiate with it, we have to focus strictly on survival, on staying alive until rescue comes.' His eyes went to the windows. 'At least the fog is lifting at last. That'll help.'

Rita followed his gaze. It was true, she saw to her dim surprise. Beyond the glass, the weather had changed. A breeze had arisen, and the mist that had clung so thickly while she was in the Lightning Room was now rolling past in fragments and billows, first thin, then thick again, then offering a glimpse of a cold, pale sky. But it was so dark. Evening was coming on. She must have been unconscious for several hours.

'Too late to be of any use to us today,' muttered Kennedy. 'We're stuck here one more night at least. That's if *anyone* ever shows up.'

Richman shook his head. 'I don't know why no helicopter has come from Hobart; it makes no sense at all. But even forgetting that, we haven't got much longer to wait. There's the *Aurora Australis*, remember? It's due to dock here some time tomorrow, by our arrangement. Sure, it might be a day or so late, if bad weather delays it. But even the Wheel, no matter how strong it is, can't close down the whole damn Southern Ocean. The *Australis* will be here.'

Kennedy shrugged. 'Even if it does come, how does that really help us if we're still stuck up here? We can't use the emergency stairs.'

'Christ, it'll be a *start* . . .'

Rita could only wonder at the men's blindness. Tomorrow, the day after, it didn't matter: the ship would be too late, no matter *when* it arrived. The Wheel—she was sure of this, having shared her soul with the mountain—knew with exactitude how long it had before any rescue intruded, and it would be careful to finish the three of them off before then. In its malice and cunning, the Wheel was master of all timing here.

Richman and Kennedy's conversation had moved on while she had drifted.

'No one is to be left alone again,' Kennedy was saying. 'We knew it was a risk leaving Rita on her own up in the Lightning Room, and look what happened. So, lesson learned. We three stay in each other's sight. We stay awake too, and we check on each other all the time, to make sure none of us is losing it. The next question is—where do we hole up? Here? Is there anywhere safer we could go?'

Richman seemed to consider a moment, as if debating some point privately, then nodded. 'I can't really think of anywhere else.'

'Maybe we should barricade ourselves in a storeroom or something, down in the main residence,' opined Kennedy. 'Or in the Control Room maybe. Take food and water for the night. With the cameras there, we could watch everywhere else.'

But Richman was decided. 'There's nothing and no one to watch. We're the only ones here now. No, the Cottage is the securest place.'

A stray thought wandered into Rita's world. Something to do with Kennedy's mention of the Control Room. Something unfinished.

She spoke. 'Clara.' The men turned to look at her, and she explained in a pained whisper. 'Do you know what happened to her yet? Have you tried to contact her . . . since this morning?'

Kennedy shook his head. 'Aside from going back to the Control Room, there's no way to communicate with her from here. Other than with that thing.' He nodded to a walkie-talkie that lay on the coffee table. 'I've tried, but no answer. The signal might not even be reaching her, way down in that shaft.'

Rita said, 'Maybe she's not in the shaft anymore. Maybe she made it down and got out.'

Kennedy's gaze allowed no such hope. 'I think we have to face the facts about Clara. You heard the state she was in at the end. And unlike you, she had no one with her to snap her out of it.'

Rita could not deny the truth of this. She had felt what it was like to be in the Wheel's grip, the impossibility of fighting against it.

Richman was gazing moodily at the windows again, where banks of fog were fleeting by against the growing darkness. 'Clara gone, and Madelaine, and Kushal, and all the people down at Base. Christ, I don't understand this. All this death—and *why*? Because I climbed a mountain? Why is that such a crime? How do any of us deserve all *this* in response?'

Rita, dozing again, smiled to herself at his frustration. Richman was doubly blind, if he hadn't worked it out yet. But *she* knew. It was the one useful thing she had taken from her near-death encounter with the mountain. It had possessed her, yes, but she had seen into its heart in return.

'I mean, *someone* was going to climb the Wheel sooner or later,' Richman went on bitterly. 'What does it matter who, exactly? And it's not as if we stayed when we got to the top, or changed anything up there. We left straightaway and took everything with us. We treated that mountain with goddamn *respect*. So why all this, and why now? Is it because of the Observatory? Because I chose to build a house here? Is that supposed to mean I've defiled something? Defiled what? The Mount here was hardly pristine before we came; it was covered in crap a century old, all those huts and bunkers and radar dishes. I cleaned all that up. I made it *better*. And Jesus, this is what mankind *does*, we build things where there were no things before. If we didn't, the whole damn planet would still be a wilderness. Everyone does it everywhere. So why single *us* out? What's the problem *here*?'

Yes, thought Rita calmly. In one way he was right, fool that he was. He had only done what all humans had done throughout history, be they rich or poor. Humans explored and climbed mountains, they built homes where there had been no homes before, they spread and multiplied, and the presences of the landscape withdrew before them. It was the way of things. Yes, maybe on rare occasions the landscape struck back, and people died, as Rita's mother had died. But not often. And there had never been anything like this, never an attack so prolonged or of such magnitude as was happening here.

So why was this different? What entwined Richman and the Wheel in such mortal enmity?

Rita almost giggled in her drowsy state. The irony of the answer was too delicious. Fiendishly so, despite the fact that the consequences spelled her own doom as surely as Richman's.

It was his own pride, of course, his towering ego, that had caused all this. For when Richman had defeated the Wheel all those forty years ago, he had claimed it solely for himself, and himself alone. He had allowed no one else to share the summit with him, to share the glory of the victory. And in that monumental act of conceit, he had sown his own fate.

The terrible truth was this: if he *had* shared the Wheel, if he had let the hundreds of other climbers in his team ascend to the summit in turn, as he had promised them, then none of this would be happening. The presence within the Wheel could never have hoped to avenge itself upon hundreds of individual climbers. Indeed, it may not even have survived their intrusion, especially if Richman had left all his camps in place, so that even more climbers, in the years following, had continued to reach the summit. Faced with a ceaseless parade of humanity, the presence within the Wheel would have dwindled and died like so many lesser presences before it.

Instead, by ruling out the summit for all but himself, Richman had not only ensured that the presence within the Wheel survived, he had also made himself, one lone man, the sole focus for the mountain's rage and hatred.

For forty years the mountain had nursed that hatred, untroubled by climbers save for on its lower slopes, and building its reserves of strength to immense potency, waiting for the day when Richman would come back within striking range. Indeed, *calling* to Richman, willing him to return, luring him with his own vanity to revisit the scene of his triumph, and, in his pride, to build his home there.

And so Richman had come.

And still the mountain had forborne its vengeance, waiting all through the construction of the Observatory, allowing no more than a hint of its malice to radiate upon the Mount. Even that hint had been enough to disturb those on the site, to drive several of them to their deaths. The Wheel could have done worse at any time, had it chosen to. But instead it had waited, ever patient, until the one man it wanted was in residence, relaxed and unguarded. Then, with exquisite timing, it had finally struck.

Not to just kill him. No. It was content to kill hundreds of others, but it did not want Richman himself dead, not immediately. It had a slower form of torture in mind for him. And now he was almost alone. Soon his last two companions would be gone, and once they had been dealt with, then the Wheel would take possession of Richman and—

Rita blinked, coming back to herself with a shock of alarm. She opened her eyes to the room. God, for a second there she had *been* the mountain, she had been sliding out of her body once more, and letting the Wheel slide back in, insidiously.

She shook her head, welcoming the pain it summoned, the way it cut through the haze of medication and exhaustion.

Was it real, what she had been dreaming? The fate the mountain held in store for Richman—she had received only a hint of it, only the dimmest suggestion, but it had been . . . abominable.

The men, meanwhile, had moved again without her seeing it. They were at a different window now, looking westward, and it was almost full night. Sky was visible above the thinning fog, the blue-black of late dusk. But there was a fringe of orange too, low, beyond her sight, the afterglow of sunset.

'We'll have stars tonight,' Richman was saying, 'and a clear sunrise in the morning. The mountain is losing its grip, I tell you. We've outlasted it. All we have to do is get through this night intact.'

But whatever Kennedy's murmured response to this was, Rita did not hear it. Already she was drifting away again on the medication.

The mountain losing its grip? Richman could not be more wrong. All the breaking up of the fog meant was that the fog had served its purpose, and could now be dismissed. And if the Wheel had finished with its cloak of cloud, then that only meant it had some other device at the ready to deploy against its target. Something even worse.

Whatever else she did then, she must not sleep; she must not let down her guard. She must remain alert through this coming night, against what was surely to come.

And so thinking, she succumbed completely, closed her eyes, and began to snore.

6

THE WITCHING HOUR

SHE WAS NOT ALLOWED TO sleep uninterrupted, however. Over the next several hours, she was woken at intervals by Kennedy, usually with a gentle touch to her shoulder. 'It's to check for concussion,' he told her the first time. 'It's okay for you to sleep, but I need to make sure you can be woken easily.'

'Fine,' she would grumble, and then mumble her answers to the questions he asked her: what was her name, when was her birthday, did she know where she was, was she in any pain?

Then she would sleep again, and when woken once more would find that an hour or so had vanished. At some point the men must have cooked dinner, for dirty plates and cups suddenly appeared on the coffee table. Another time she woke without prompting and found that music was playing softly on the stereo, something classical that she did not recognise. The men were at the windows, talking as they gazed out, and beyond the glass the fog was gone. 'Look at the temperature,' Richman was saying, 'it's back up to zero, it's almost warm out there now.' And for some reason, even as she drifted under again, the notion of warmer weather filled Rita with unease.

In between, her sleep was blessedly dreamless, the unconsciousness of the drugged. But pain hovered in the background, her face, her arm, her leg, coming ever closer as the time passed, until finally she swam towards consciousness again, stiff and sore even as she lay unmoving. She knew she would not be able to drift off again. Not without more pills.

She opened her eyes. The living room was silent about her, no music, no voices.

What were the men doing now? She turned her head a little and she found that she was gazing at a small clock that sat on a low table by the couch opposite, an antique of some kind.

It was one o'clock. A nothing time, she thought, a time for insomniacs and invalids. Sunset was far behind, dawn still hours ahead.

She shifted stiffly on the couch, now very sore indeed. She needed those pills, and also, her bladder was complaining. She'd have to get up. Could she do it without the men? Propping herself on one elbow, she rose painfully to a sitting position—and saw that in an armchair at the far end of the couch Richman was sprawled, fast asleep. His hand was draped next to a half-empty wine glass on a side table, and his chest rose and fell slightly with a soft snoring.

Well, that was surprising. Wasn't the idea for the men to both stay awake through the night? Rita shifted her gaze further about the room, searching for Kennedy. *He* must be awake at least, if Richman was dozing. But he was nowhere to be seen.

Stranger still.

A dim rumble came, an undertone to the billionaire's snoring. Rita recognised the sound, faint though it was within the cocoon of the Cottage. It was thunder, from far off out in the night.

Her gaze moved to the windows. Was rain on its way? A storm? At first, she could see nothing through the glass, only darkness, and reflections of the living room interior. Then came a pale blue shimmer from somewhere off to the west, and after a long pause another faint rumble sounded. Yes, a storm was out there, but still some distance away.

For a few moments more she remained propped as she was, staring at the windows, her mind not fully emerged yet from the medicated sleep, thinking nothing, detached still from the waking world. Again the blue shimmer trembled out in the night, and for the third time the low rumble muttered against the glass, almost gentle, a lullaby that might soothe her back to sleep. It faded to silence.

And then, a new sound.

Her detachment vanished. The noise was barely audible, high and thin and far off, but she knew screaming when she heard it, and this was the awful scream of a man in utmost terror.

She sat up, ignoring the pain that ignited everywhere in her body. The screaming went on, demented, bereft of all poise or dignity. It had to be Kennedy, but where was he? The sound was so distant, on the bare threshold of hearing.

She turned to the snoring Richman. 'Wake up! Wake up! Something's wrong!'

Richman stirred, opened his eyes groggily to stare at her un-comprehendingly.

'Why are you asleep?' she hurled at him. Her feet were on the floor now, dizziness and nausea threatening. 'You two were supposed to stay awake and watch each other!'

Richman only blinked at her, dazed, then gazed down at himself in amazement. 'I didn't . . . I mean, I don't know . . . I was just . . .'

'Shut up!' Rita hissed. 'Listen.'

He obeyed.

They listened. The screaming went on, more regular now, though still high with terror, shouted words, but too muffled to grasp. It came, Rita decided, from one of the floors overhead.

'What the fuck?' breathed Richman, lurching to his feet. 'What's happening up there?'

Rita herself had risen by now, clutching the robe about herself, her wounded leg protesting wildly. 'How the hell could you go to sleep?'

'I didn't! Kennedy and I were just sitting here, talking. I don't remember even feeling tired.' His eyes went to the clock. 'Christ, but that was two hours ago! Come on! We have to get up there.'

He was hurrying for the stairs. Rita followed, limping painfully, feeling the fire of individual sutures tugging free in her thigh. Thunder muttered again, and the screaming above renewed in pitch.

'Christ,' Richman moaned as they climbed, 'what the hell is *happening* up there?'

The Wheel, Rita thought. Whatever it was, this was the Wheel at work again, and this time it had chosen Kennedy. But what had it done? What could be so terrible that it could make a man as tough and capable as Kennedy scream that way?

They had climbed one flight to the level of the guest bedrooms, but still the desperate shouts came from far above, so Richman led the way further on, to the level of his private bedroom and office. Here the screams were louder, and words were at last discernible.

Help! Jesus, fuck, help!

But the cries still came from above, and there was only one level left: the Lightning Room.

They dashed up, Rita not caring how many stitches she tore. Round and round the stairs in the tunnel of stone they went, emerging at last to the platform beneath the open sky, roofed only in titanium framed glass, where that very afternoon Rita would have died, had not Kennedy saved her.

Fucking help me!

Richman and Rita gazed about in bewilderment. The room was dark, but shadows could be guessed at, and none of them were Kennedy. And yet, bafflingly, his cries were immediate now, close.

Get me off this!

Overhead, they still came from overhead. Rita stared up in confusion, and then—

Lightning flickered. It was only sheet lightning, hidden within cloud, pale and blue, but it was enough to briefly turn the exterior world to day. There on the mountaintop, surrounded by glass, it was as if Rita hung suspended in midair. Faraway below was the black sheet of the sea and her back was to the Wheel, but now another titan reared to the west, soaring high above her and dropping far away below. It was a great mass of roiling cloud, the storm, much closer than she had thought, and much larger. Great thunderheads were already looming over the Mount, frozen in an instant of their own internal lightning, but potent with motion, updrafts and downdrafts racing in misted chasms, dragging curtains of dark rain.

But revealed also by the lightning—it flickered again as Rita stared, as if to confirm the impossible thing—was a silhouetted figure, a man, spreadeagled across the glass ceiling overhead.

A man *outside* the glass.

Help me! Kennedy screamed, his voice strangely deadened, even though he was only a few feet above them, for he was on the wrong side of glass that was inches thick, glass that was bulletproof. And Rita could still not understand in the darkness what he was doing there, or what help he needed.

Get me fucking loose!

Thunder rumbled again, louder now, a long tumble of boulders clashing in the middle airs. Kennedy screamed above them and Richman was fumbling at the bedside table until finally he found a lamp and switched it on. It was dim, only a reading lamp, but the night withdrew at last, and through the glass Kennedy could be seen in full.

He was naked, contorted strangely upon the crest of the glass and titanium dome—and Rita grasped finally the reason for his terror.

He was trapped there.

Clenched about his left wrist was one manacle of a pair of handcuffs—his own handcuffs, presumably, the ones that Rita had seen him wear on his belt—and the other manacle was locked around the base of the stout bar of iron that speared up to the night and to the storm from the peak of the roof.

The lightning rod.

But that wasn't all. If he had been otherwise free, Kennedy could have risen to his feet and so lifted his hand clear of the rod to escape. But he wasn't free. A second set of handcuffs—the security chief must have carried two pairs—bound one of his ankles to the top rung of the ladder that climbed the outside wall of the Lightning Room to give access to the roof. Stretched out flat on the glass, fully extended between the ladder and the rod, he could scarcely move.

Get the fucking bolt cutters! he was yelling at them, eyes and mouth wide in the gloom. *There's a set up here with me. Do you see them? Get up here and cut me loose! A fucking storm is coming!*

The storm. Thunder grumbled once more from all about. There were still no actual forks of lightning visible, only the blue flashes from within the massing clouds, but inevitably, as the storm crossed over the Mount, a bolt would strike the lightning rod. Why, they had all discussed this very topic only four, no, five days ago. The rod always got hit, Eugene had said. Multiple times for every storm. And when it did . . .

In her final horrified understanding, Rita traced the line of the grounding cable that was meant to run from the base of the rod across the roof, then down the side of the room to the bedrock of the Mount. The line had been cut, she saw. The upper end was now wound around the rod, and the lower end had been tied roughly about the security chief's cuffed ankle. Which left only Kennedy himself as the single link now between the rod and the ground.

Blue light flickered bright overhead, starker than before, and thunder boomed loud, and the man on the roof writhed to stare up at the sky, screaming, and tugging manically at the handcuffs. But the rod was of solid iron, and the access ladder was of titanium alloy, and both had been fixed there with strength enough to withstand all manner of gales and tempests. His struggles were in vain.

The bolt cutters! he howled.

Richman cried, 'I see them!' To Rita's amazement, the billionaire then dashed to the stairs and disappeared downwards. What was he doing? Where was he going? But then she remembered. There was no access from the Lightning Room itself to the narrow balcony that ran, below eye level, around the base of chamber. That balcony—it was for the use of staff, to clean the glass—could only be reached via a small door in the tunnel below.

She stared up, helpless, as Kennedy contorted and struggled and peered wildly at the storm-filled sky. She saw the bolt cutters finally, a large pair of them, lying at the base of the sloping roof, near Kennedy's feet, out of his reach.

The picture formed with hideous clarity in her mind of how it must have been, how Kennedy had ended up in this hellish predicament. After all, she had experienced herself what it was like for the Wheel to take possession of her limbs, and to move them beyond her will, even to her own destruction.

Such it must have been for Kennedy. Having dispatched Richman to slumber, the Wheel must have seized hold of the security chief and guided him as an automaton to do its bidding: namely, to collect his handcuffs and the bolt cutters—the latter from who knew where— and then to ascend, naked, to the balcony of the Lightning Room, and finally up the ladder and across the glass roof.

Had he been aware all along of what was happening to him? The way that Rita had been aware as her own hand had hacked away unstoppably at her thigh? Had he been forced to watch, helpless, as his body, under the Wheel's impetus, cut the grounding cable, then cast away the cutter, then handcuffed itself first to the rung of the ladder, and lastly to the base of the rod, trapping himself there irrevocably?

Had the Wheel been that cruel? Had it released his limbs, and given him back his voice to shout for help, only when it was too late, only when the first flashes of lightning began?

Hurry the fuck up! screamed the trapped man, calling not to Rita, she knew, but to Richman, who still had not appeared outside the glass.

The sky flared blue again, and this time Rita caught a glimpse off to one side of a naked bolt etched against the night, and the thunder when it came had a deadly crack before the rumble.

Oh Jesus god shrieked Kennedy above her. Rita stared about uselessly, as if something might appear, something with which she could smash the glass, but there was nothing in the room but the bed, and some low chairs, and the lamp, and anyway, the glass was smash-proof, that was the point of it.

Again a streak of lightning flared, the sky turning brilliant, and she saw once more the soaring chasms of cloud churning, before the thunder cracked and the man attached to the lightning rod screamed and tugged insanely at his bonds.

What was keeping Richman? Rita had just resolved to descend herself to see when the billionaire appeared once more at the top of the stairs, his expression bewildered and harassed.

'I can't get the fuck out,' he swore. 'The door is locked and the keys are gone.'

What are you doing? screamed Kennedy from above. The security chief was scarcely recognisable as himself, stripped of his suit and of his air of brute resourcefulness, his naked flesh pale and shrivelled in the freezing air. *Help me!*

'I can't!' Richman called back. 'The keys! You must have taken them out there with you!'

Smash the fucking door then!

'He's right, smash it down!' Rita echoed. 'What are you even doing back up here?'

The billionaire shrugged desperately. 'The door is bombproof, like every other external entry. I'm not going to be able to just break it down, not without some heavy tools or machinery.'

'But we have to *do* something!'

'I don't know wha—'

He broke off as above them a great forked network of fire blazed, and thunder cracked splittingly. Illuminated in the shutter flash, a giant black cloud seemed to be reaching down to the Mount, bursts of rain lowering from it like fists.

Oh sweet god help me! Kennedy screamed as he fought, staring up, rapt, to the monster.

Neither Rita nor Richman moved. Rita was frozen, sensing (and perhaps even Richman could too) a terrible coherence gathering in the night beyond the glass, her nerves singing with a tension that rose and rose. All was dark overhead now, the storm invisible, but the blackness grew heavier every instant, more pregnant with electric potential.

Damn you, Richman! Kennedy screamed. *Damn you and your fucking mountain!*

His last words. For in answer the lightning descended from the sky.

Rita remembered enough of her school lessons to know how lightning worked, how a grasping network of feelers came creeping down from a thundercloud until one reached the ground or some other point, and then the main stroke leapt *upwards,* but that it all happened too fast for the human eye to discern anything but a single flash.

Nevertheless, staring up into the impending doom of the storm, she *saw* the fingers come searching down, in two main branches, for all the world like the fingers of two elongated hands, questing in the potent air for the right path by which to make the fatal connection between sky and mountain.

The instant seemed to be drawn out agonisingly. Down, down, the glowing tendrils reached, grasping all about in the middle airs above the Mount. Kennedy's body was arched in a final paroxysm of effort to escape, but it served only to thrust him up towards the groping fingers.

And then one feeler, having jagged far to one side of the lightning rod, jagged back in a single gleeful leap, and touched the iron tip.

The world blazed stark white, a burning river of silver cleaving the night in two, the main bolt searing up into the darkness, a million-fold brighter than the trailers. The light alone threw Rita to the floor even as the thunderclap hit her like a falling wall. The concussion was stunning, shattering everything surely, all the glass of the Lightning Room . . .

Yet when the blaze was gone an instant later, and the thunder was rolling away into the night in thumping echoes, Rita's dazzled gaze revealed that the glass dome remained perfectly intact, and that it was only Kennedy who was broken.

She didn't know what she had expected, perhaps that he would be reduced instantly to smoking cinders. But it was not so. He had not been set on fire, no smoke rose from him, but his spine appeared to have been snapped. At least, Rita could not imagine how a human body could be bent back on itself in such a way if the spine *hadn't* snapped.

Even so, he wasn't dead.

Indeed, as the thunder faded, she could hear that he was still screaming, although incoherently now, a stroke victim's gurgle. And though his arms still flailed in an effort to escape, his lower half was unmoving, and something in the way his head moved suggested that his eyes had been blinded.

Then the sky ignited again. There were no warning feelers on this occasion, just another explosion of light and noise as electricity scalded the iron rod a second time, and squinting into the glare, even as she cowered down, Rita could see Kennedy's broken body arch again in orgasmic spasm as the energy coursed through him.

But lightning doesn't strike twice. Except that she had already been warned that here upon the Mount it often did strike twice, and anyway, natural laws no longer applied, for this was the Wheel's doing. And then she thought of blood being boiled by the electrical surge, and of muscles and tissue cooking even as Kennedy yet lived, and was sure she could hear him scream through the thunder.

Then the lightning hit again.

And again.

And did not stop.

Rita was huddled on the floor now, weeping as the detonations pummelled her over and over. The bolts were harmless to her there within the Faraday cage of the room, but each blast wrenched at her heart and at her sanity, until she was screaming herself at the tumult to *Stop, stop, stop*!

And then finally it did.

The continuous thunder drained away, and she could take her hands from her ears and peer up to see what was left on the roof above.

And yes, *now* there was smoke rising—but oh Christ, Kennedy still wasn't dead. His limbs, especially his cuffed arm and leg, those that had carried the charge, were charcoal-blackened, and the rest of him was reddened strangely, reminding Rita of cooked meat upon a frypan, but he was *moving* still, writhing, his head shaking from side to side.

Die, she willed. *God, please, just die.*

Something white and hard and the size of a brick fell from the blackness above and smashed against the glass like a gunshot. It was followed quickly by another. Rita stared beyond Kennedy's tortured form into the upper night, and in the light from a faraway lightning flicker saw that the entire sky was descending, a mass of falling white shapes. Then she was ducking her head instinctively as she realised what she was seeing—hail.

The stones seemed to strike all at once, the din even worse than thunder, sharper and crueller and more painful to the ear. Rita huddled in terror, arms over her head, for surely the glass must smash. And surely, surely, she couldn't be hearing through the wall of noise the wet smack of ice upon flesh and the ripping of skin and the crunch of bone.

She should flee, she knew—she should be scrambling for the stairs to get out from under the dome that could give way at any moment, but she was incapable of movement, could only remain in a crouch as the murderous din went on and on.

Until it, too, finally stopped.

It was raining by then, but only the normal, heavy rain of any storm, and with the depletion of the hail she sensed too the withdrawal of the influence of the Wheel. Not an exhaustion of its influence, merely a cessation; its hunger for the moment sated, leaving the storm to blow without hostility.

She dared at last to look up. Amazingly—and she had to tip a mental nod to her dead father for his design—the glass of the dome was *still* intact, its strength proof against any onslaught.

Kennedy, however, had been made of less stern stuff. He was reduced to bloody tatters. His chained arm had broken away at the elbow, the upper limb still dangling from the cuff, while the rest of him had slumped down upon the ladder, a sodden mass, blood and brain matter and other bodily fluids streaming away across the dome in the rain. But yes, dead at last, unquestionably. There was not enough of him left in one piece to possibly be alive.

Lightning flickered through the downpour, and thunder rumbled from nearby. Rita noted even through her shock that although the Wheel's malign guidance was gone, lightning could still strike the peak, and now with the grounding cable severed and even the link of Kennedy's body broken, it might no longer be safe here, even on the inside.

She turned to Richman to say that they must leave, that there was nothing to be done for Kennedy now, not until the storm was over.

But Richman wasn't there. She peered about the dim space, but no, he was nowhere within the Lightning Room. When had he gone? She couldn't remember. He had been there when the first bolt of lightning struck, hadn't he? Yes, but after that? She couldn't recall. Had he dashed off in a last attempt to reach Kennedy? Or had he fled simply in horror of the lightning and the hail, as Rita herself should have fled, once the end was inevitable?

It hardly mattered either way. Lightning flashed again and cracked loudly, too close for comfort. Rita moved at last, limping down the tunnel stairs, her wounded leg burning and stiff, now that the adrenalin had left her. She felt weary and sick and despairing. So it was only the two of them now.

But when she regained the living room, Richman wasn't there. And though, increasingly exhausted, she climbed the stairs again and searched his private quarters and the guest bedrooms and everywhere else she could think to look in the Cottage, she could not find him anywhere else.

It wasn't the two of them at all.

It was just her now.

The billionaire had vanished.

7

ALONE

IT WASN'T UNTIL THE END of her third frantic search through the
Cottage, when Rita spied herself in one of the guest bedrooms' full-
length mirrors, that she finally gave up her quest for Richman, and
forced herself to take stock.

Her reflection was appalling. With her swollen cheek and tear-
reddened eyes, she was a stick figure wrapped in an oversized robe that
was falling off one shoulder to reveal a bra strap and her bloody, bandaged arm. The robe itself was wet, she noticed, around the groin. How
had that happened? Had rain leaked through the dome of the Lightning
Room, cracked by hail? Then she realised: at some point in the horror,
her full bladder must have emptied itself. She hadn't even noticed.

Jesus. Suddenly she stank to herself of urine and sweat and blood.
She needed a shower, but there was no question of that until she found
Richman. There was no way she could shut herself in a bathroom and
stand under running water, deaf to what was happening around her,
deaf to anything that might be creeping just outside the door, while she
was still on her own. And oh god, she couldn't really be on her own,
could she? Alone? In this terrible place?

Which set her off on another circuit of the Cottage, even to the point
of trying the little door that led out onto the balcony around the Lightning
Room, even though she knew Richman could not be out there, would

never go out there while the storm still blew. But it was locked fast anyway, as Richman himself had said, and there was no sign of any key.

At last she drifted aimless and distraught to the guest bedroom in which she had left her luggage when they had all moved into the Cottage—there had been no chance to actually sleep there. She stripped, wiped herself down with a damp towel, then put on fresh underwear and clothes. She should have changed her bandages too, blood was oozing from her thigh after all her exertions, but she couldn't face that yet. The mystery of Richman's disappearance was too urgent.

Where was he?

Had the Wheel taken him? Had Kennedy's gruesome execution merely been a distraction, during which Richman, the true target, could be snatched away to some unseen end?

No. Of that much, Rita was sure. Attuned as she was to the moods of the Wheel, she knew she would have felt it if the mountain had already claimed its prize, the vengeful exultation would have been overwhelming. And there had been no such sensation. The Wheel had killed Kennedy, and then withdrawn patiently to prepare its next move.

So Richman could not simply be *gone*. He had to be somewhere. He had to have taken the chance in the Lightning Room to abandon Rita for a reason of his own, and he must be hiding from her still. And yet patently he was not in the Cottage, the place was simply too small and too plainly laid out for him to have secreted himself there.

Which left only the Observatory below.

She shivered at the thought. Lord, she did not want to go down there again, to return to all those cavernous, empty halls. The Cottage, even after Kennedy's death, at least felt partially secure. To go back to the Observatory, to its immensity and silence and shadows . . . it made her heart shrivel.

And yet what choice was there?

No choice. The loneliness was unbearable already, and besides, she was angry now. How dare Richman just desert her like that, without a word? If for no other purpose, she wanted to find the billionaire to berate him for his selfishness, for putting her through *this*, on top of everything else.

Gathering her resolve, she crept down the stairs to the living room. All was quiet there. The couches were empty, the blanket where she had slept remained thrown aside as she had left it, likewise the plates the men had left on the coffee table. Beyond the windows rain still sluiced heavily across the Terrace, and thunder murmured in bass support, but again, it was only weather now, not an enemy.

The enemy was her own fear.

She moved first to the airlock doors that led down to the Terrace, to check, as she had already three times in the last half hour, that they were locked. They were. So if Richman had left the Cottage, he must have gone down by the elevator.

She went to the lift. There was a key by the doors that could be turned to lock the elevator in the up position, securing the Cottage from any entry via the Observatory. Rita had seen Richman turn that very key yesterday, and listened to him explain its function. She had hoped to find it unlocked now, and the elevator car gone, for that at least would prove her theory that Richman had gone below.

But the key was still in the lock position, and when she turned it, and pressed the button, the elevator doors opened immediately, the car waiting at the ready. She stared at it in pained concentration. So . . . so that meant that Richman had *not* gone down? Or was there a way to send the car back up? But why would he bother? And either way, he couldn't have reset the key from down there, could he?

Or could he? What if he was in the Control Room now? Wouldn't that give him access to all sorts of security systems? Maybe the lock could indeed be reset from below, in which case, had he done so just for this purpose, to confuse her search?

But why? Why vanish in the first place, and why hide his tracks? It made no sense.

She rubbed her aching head. No, she couldn't reason it all out; her mind was too fogged with pain and shock. She should do something about the pain at least. The medical kit that Kennedy had used on her must be lying about somewhere, and it must be a proper, hospital-grade kit, because he had dosed her with something powerful, god knew. She should find it, take some more of the pills.

Ah, but then she would probably fall asleep—and for an instant the temptation to do just that was near irresistible. To simply sleep! To block out this nightmare and descend into oblivion! It would be so lovely, and after all, when she woke up it might all be over, rescue might have come, and she would have spared herself hours of suffering.

Or—she reminded herself with tremendous effort—she would never wake up at all. Drugged, she would have no resistance to the Wheel whatsoever. It could walk her half-conscious body off the side of the Terrace, for all she would know about it. So no, she could not, must not, succumb to the lure of painkillers and slumber; she must accept the throb and ache as best she could, and stay awake.

With a bitter sigh, she took a step into the elevator, and pressed the *Down* button.

As soon as the doors closed and the car began to descend, her terror returned. What if *this* was what the Wheel had been waiting for, to trap her alone in a stalled elevator with no help that could possibly reach her? The car was so small, and there was no one to call, no one to notice now if she vanished . . .

But in moments the car slowed, stopped, and at the chime the doors slid soundlessly open to reveal the shadowy expanse of the Library.

Calm down, Rita told herself.

She stepped out. Despite her own admonishment, she could not help a nervous glance to either side, as if Richman might be lying in wait to spring at her. Which was stupid. Whatever he was up to, he wasn't some crazed killer.

But nor—she stared from corner to corner—was he anywhere in sight in the Library.

A whisper came from behind and Rita jumped, looked back. Christ, it was only the elevator door—the fake bookcase—sliding shut. *Stop it*, she told herself again. Then, taking a shaky breath, she made herself walk towards the Saloon.

But god, it was cold down here. Not actually freezing, maybe, but it felt much colder than the Cottage. This was, what, the fourth day now since the main power supply had failed? The emergency generators could obviously keep the intimate rooms of the Cottage warm, but here in the vaster spaces of the Observatory, the native chill of the upper Mount must be finally beginning to seep through.

It was darker down here as well, the few lights falling too dimly in so much space. Also, it was silent. Cocooned in rock, the Library was disturbed by no sound of rain and barely any rumble of thunder. There was only the rich, secret quiet of opulence, of polished oak and soft leather, and of unopened books slowly decaying.

Hand to her mouth, as if to stop herself from screaming, Rita moved on past the tables and shelves and couches, and saw Richman nowhere.

She came to the Saloon and found it similarly empty and dim. But here the sense of abandonment was even more acute. It was in the small details—unwashed plates on a table, a bottle lying on its side on the bar, a couch shoved out of alignment—that stood out because they would never be attended to now, or tidied up. Humans had departed this place. It was if she were walking through Tutankhamen's tomb only moments after it had been sealed, knowing that nothing would change, nothing would move, for the next three thousand years.

But was that true? Was the Observatory genuinely abandoned *forever*? Would no one ever live here again, walk here? Rita could not know that, but she *felt* it, of that there was no denying.

She moved on into the Atrium, its dome lost in shadows and its windows showing only rain-streaked darkness. No one was there. She

503

glanced into the Dining Hall and saw that it was empty. She peered down into the well of the Helix Staircase but no one moved on the twin snakes of the staircases. Of course, the guest wings waited down there, beyond sight, and all the other levels. At some point, she would have to descend into the heart of the Mount, if she really meant to search.

But not yet. She turned from the well and passed through the great arch into the Entrance Hall, pausing in the threshold to gaze down the long line of cathedral pillars to the furthest end. It had taken her breath away when she had first beheld it, now it felt bare and freezing and dead, a mausoleum in which no one had ever been buried and never would be, a pointless construction. And behind every massive pillar, Richman might be hiding.

Her skin crawling, she inched down the long aisle, the quiet weighing heavier and heavier on her, though here there was at least a whisper of rain from the tall windows and from the ceiling panels. The faces in the paintings of Richman's art collection stared down at her silently from their hanging places, and human statues carved by long-dead masters observed her motionless as she passed by. At length, she came to the oval cavity and the stairs that led down to the private Museum in the crypt.

Richman would not be down there, Rita told herself, not wanting to descend the steps. Why would he be? But then, why would he be anywhere? And yet he must be somewhere, so . . .

Step by step, she descended. And there he was, waiting for her at the bottom, arm raised and triumphant at the very summit of the Wheel, the image life-size, printed on stone. But she had remembered that she would see this, and was ready for it. More disturbing was the hulking pressure suit, standing somehow alert and alive on its dais. It was all too easy to imagine eyes staring from behind the mirrored glass of the faceplate, to imagine that any moment the arms would stir and the gloved hands reach for her. Easy, but nonsensical. Richman would not be hiding in his old suit. Still, it took all Rita's self-possession to turn her back on the thing and search the rest of Museum, to be sure he was not secreted somewhere else there amid the relics of his glory days.

Was it getting even colder? The chill seemed very real now. Maybe it was just that the crypt, clutched particularly tight within the frozen rock of the Mount, was always lower in temperature. But Rita could sense too a psychic edge to the chill, as if the room was the focus of a bitter ill will—and she remembered then that the Museum was a testimony to Richman's victory over the Wheel.

No, this was no place to linger, not at a time when the mountain was extracting its revenge. She fled as soon as her circuit was complete.

Back in the Entrance Hall rain still hissed black against the windows. Reluctantly, Rita forced herself onwards between the pillars and the watching statues, and so came at last to the foyer at the Hall's end, with its altar-like stone within. Richman was not there, and Rita spared only a wistful glance at the elevator doors by which she had entered this prison, all unknowing, five, no, six, days ago. She knew the lift was defunct, that there was no escape that way. Her eyes were drawn instead to the great painting that hung on the foyer wall, *The Triumph of Death*.

It seemed bigger than she remembered, as if it had swollen in accord with the desolation of the Observatory around it. Death indeed now triumphed here. Ah . . . but what was it Kennedy had said, when he and Rita had stood in this spot? That's right . . . he'd said that Richman liked this painting because the billionaire could not see his own death in it, that he saw it as proof of his own triumph *over* death.

But as Kennedy had pointed out, all the deaths in the painting were man-made; they were killings by war and poison, by hanging and torture. There were no deaths at nature's hand. Nowhere upon the canvas was there a body frozen in a pool. Nor a body flayed to death by the wind. Nor one fallen and lost in an underground labyrinth. Nor one blasted apart by lightning. Which only proved it. The painting was a fool's deceit, a comforting lie. The truly mortal danger lay somewhere else entirely.

For the billionaire, for everyone.

Far away, a metal thing fell and clattered, echoing from beyond the Entrance Hall.

Rita froze, listening, but the sound did not repeat. She almost called out, but could not bear the thought of her voice echoing in the cathedral space. Instead, she hurried in a silent, painful shuffle down the aisle, and so came again to the arch. From there, she peered into the Atrium and the chambers beyond: the Saloon, the Library, the Dining Hall.

Nothing. No one. Nor could she spy any object that might have spontaneously fallen: a tray carelessly placed on the edge of the bar in the Saloon, perhaps, two or three days previously, and only just now toppling off because of the vibrations she had caused as she had walked by a few minutes ago . . .

Fantasy. There was no tray. Nothing had fallen. Had there even been a noise at all? How could she be sure of anything right now, when there was only herself to confirm it?

So . . . what to do next?

She moved frigidly to the top of the Helix Staircase, gazed down into the heart of the Mount. It was a pit of spiralled shadows that seemed to swirl as if actively revolving. Nauseated, she thought again of all the rooms down there—the guest apartments, the recreation wing, the storage levels, and knew that she could never search them all, not alone in this silence. And even if she did, Richman could elude her effortlessly, so it was pointless.

Defeated, she leaned against the balustrade and took several ragged, tearful breaths. Then a sensation came creeping, raising the hackles on the back of her neck. She lifted her head, stared about.

She was being watched, she was sure of it. Someone was observing her.

Someone was *laughing* at her.

There! Far overhead in the Atrium dome, where the night and rain darkened the windows, she could discern a small black protuberance. It had to be a security camera. She could remember, from her night in the Control Room, that there had been a screen displaying from on high this very place in which she stood, at the top of the stairs.

Someone was watching her now, on one of those screens, watching this very second as she gazed up. It could only be Richman. He must be in the Control Room, must have been watching her all along as she searched fearfully through the halls.

Why was he there? Was what he hoping for? Was he trying again to make contact with Base or with the outside world, by radio or telephone? Or had he merely chosen it as a place in which to barricade himself, with the all-seeing security eyes to show him what was happening in the rest of the building? She couldn't imagine, and it didn't matter. All that mattered was that she now knew where he was.

So, the Control Room. It would mean venturing into the service tunnels, into their maze of twists and turns, all on her own. She had done it once before, yes. But now, god, it would be bad . . .

But it was that or give up on confronting the billionaire. And her anger was greater than her fear. She was walking already, moving towards the Dining Hall. He would see her, of course, on other cameras, he would know she was on her way, but there was nothing to be done about that.

Beyond the Dining Hall she passed through the servery area and into the banquet kitchen. It, too, was empty and evocative of the people who had been there—minor messes littered the counters, a disorder that would remain uncorrected for all eternity now. Rita only hurried through, and turned into the first of the service tunnels, the doorway to the Observatory's underworld.

Signage and arrows on the walls pointed the way to enigmatic destinations—*SC1-4, RD1, GR, SD1-12, SE*—but for Rita they may as well have been hieroglyphics. She ignored them, summoning the memory of her earlier visits to the Control Room. Along this tunnel to a landing, down one flight of stairs to another landing off which four tunnels opened, take the left tunnel, straight ahead through two more junctions, and she would be there.

She set off, arms hugged to herself because here too the cold was deeper than elsewhere. Presumably the service passageways had never been as fully heated as the public zones. Nor as well lit, even before the lighting had switched to emergency power. Now, in the chill gloom, the tunnels felt like the concrete pipes of some under-city stormwater system, empty for the moment, but still dank and forbidding, and never meant to be inhabited.

The tunnel bent left and right, then, sure enough, she came to a landing and a stairwell running up and down. She descended one flight and came to a second landing with four passages extending off. She took the left tunnel and held straight through two junctions . . . but instead of coming to an unmarked door, she found herself descending a steep flight of stairs to a T-intersection, with not a door in view.

Well, *this* wasn't right.

She retreated, consulting her mental map. That left-hand turn at the second landing, was it meant to be left as you faced down the stairs, or left as you faced *up* the stairs? She came back to the landing and this time took the opposite tunnel. But after a single turn, it arrived at a dead-end space off which three doors opened, all of them locked, but none of them, she was sure, the Control Room.

What was going on? She couldn't be that much out in her reckoning, could she? But actually, was it supposed to be just one flight down to reach the correct landing, or two flights? She remembered now that the first time she had been shown the way, she had been able to hear the emergency generators running from somewhere further down the stairwell. She hadn't heard anything this time. That must be it; she had to go one level lower.

She retraced her steps and descended a second flight down. Her leg, after so much walking, was becoming seriously painful, and the bandage was wet about her thigh, but at least, yes, *now* she could hear the dull roar of the generators from below. She was on the right track again. But from this third landing, which tunnel was it, the left or the right?

She went left. But that only led to another intersection, and more dead ends with locked doors. When she was making her way back to the main stairs to try again, she somehow found herself in a new passage that twisted about confoundedly and dropped down several levels of stairs without any chance of an exit, before debouching into a long low chamber lined with more doors and tunnels still, none of them familiar. She spun about, stared.

Fuck.

She was lost.

She pushed her frustration, and her fear, down. She couldn't be *that* lost, the tunnels all led eventually to the public zones that she knew, so she had only to keep trying doors and passages, and eventually she would emerge somewhere to get her bearings.

But the thought was only limited comfort. It was so dark, and so cold, and so silent. God, what if the power should fail? She didn't even have a torch! She hurried back up the twisting tunnel, but now could recognise nothing, none of the intersections or passages, and so she made turns at random. She needed to climb several levels up, she knew, and so took ascending stairs whenever she could, but often there were only downward-leading flights, and overall, it seemed, she was descending deeper and deeper.

Then another horrid thought came. What if she was not merely lost, but instead had been deliberately misled? What if this was the Wheel's doing, playing with her mind? Not possessing her completely, not making her sleepwalk to her death, but confusing her just enough to trap her forever in these passageways, always taking the wrong turns?

Panic rose in her then, and she shuffled madly on for a time, pushing at doors that did not open, lurching this way and that at each crossway, a black claustrophobia roaring in her head, desperate for fresh air and for the sight of something, anything, other than the endlessly blank concrete walls.

And so it was that, having blundered down who knew how many levels, she finally came upon a sight that she *did* know: turning a corner, she beheld a collection of shining metal pipes that emerged from the bedrock to enter a side-room room that was filled with gleaming tanks and machinery.

It was a filtration room. For a pool. For the Cavern Pool. It was where she had found the lost cleaning lady, all those days ago. Yes, she was sure of it. She hurried on. She only had to turn left here, and go through the door at the end, and then . . .

With something like a sob, Rita emerged into an alcove lined with shelves piled with fluffy towels. Two steps beyond that and she was out on the paved terrace that fronted the Cavern Pool. She spun there, glorying in the familiar scene, the great cave, the huge pool, the beach chairs. Oh, how good it was to recognise something, to know exactly where she was. True, she had strayed miles from her original route to the Control Room, but who cared? She was free, she could find her way now, she was—

Her elation drained away abruptly, and she paused, cold once more. She was . . . no better off at all, really. Nothing had changed or improved. She was still alone, still trapped within the Observatory, and Richman was still missing.

And, now that her relief had faded, an unpleasantness in the air began to bear down on her. The Cavern Pool had changed since her last visit. The chill had invaded here too, and all the waterfalls and fountains that had filled the cavern with noise were now silent. But worse, there was a mildewy, stagnant, neglected smell about the place . . . of water that had stood undisturbed for too long.

Of course. Under the emergency power protocols, the heating and filtration down here had been suspended. Rita stared out over the pool. Its surface was dark now that the underwater lighting was switched off, and here and there were flecks of a white, oily scum.

No, she wouldn't want to swim here anymore. It would be black in the tunnels and grottoes now, the water silent and undisturbed, and who knew what bacteria or moss or algae would grow in there as the years mounted and no one came to turn the lights or the filtration back on . . .

But there was another smell too. What was it? Not watery or mouldy at all, but a ranker, sweeter smell. Like . . . like meat boiled and left to . . .

Oh. Oh lord. She turned to the doorway that led to the sauna wing, remembering the tales of the man who had died in there, alone and forgotten in the steam room, his body baked so long that it cooked, the flesh soft and beginning to fall away.

They had gutted the place afterwards, she had been told. They had removed every tile and stone of the old sauna and replaced them with new. But Christ, that smell, oozing out to hang in the cold, still air. They must have missed something, there must be some crack or crevice into which the bodily fluids had leaked and then escaped detection, only to emerge now that the air circulation had failed.

Hand to her mouth again, Rita fled the Cavern, stumbling out through the swing doors to the landing at the base of the Helix Staircase. There she paused, heaving in deep breaths until the panic receded. *Idiot*, she told herself. *Fool*. Most likely she had just imagined the dead-man smell. The stagnant pool air had triggered a memory, and her own loneliness and morbid fantasy had done the rest . . .

But god, what she would give to see another human face right now. Anyone.

There was no one, however, just the great silence of the Observatory, and the vast emptiness of the well, soaring up with the Helix Staircase to the Atrium dome high, high above. The windows were still black way up there, but if the storm still blew outside and thunder boomed, this deep down in the Mount there was no sound to indicate it.

Rita expelled a final tremulous sigh, felt her heart settle back almost to normal—at least, as normal as it could be, with her bruises aching, and her gashed leg singing, and her nerves stretched taut. But what should she do now? Should she try again for the Control Room? Did she have the nerve to delve into the service tunnels once more?

No . . . she didn't think she could face that. But if not, then she was giving up on finding Richman. And what did that leave? Where could she go? Where would be safe? How could she stop the Wheel from seeping into her mind, and finishing her off?

What, in Christ's name, in the depths of all this disaster, was she supposed to *do*?

No answer came.

Her gaze fell upon the only other passage that opened from this level, a wide hallway curving off into gloom. It led, she knew, to the Games Arena: the site of her father's death, and the one place in all the Observatory she had never visited.

Even now, she could not explain why she had always put off going in there. After all, her father's heart attack could have happened anywhere; it did not matter that it had happened *there*. But even so, every time it had been suggested, by Clara or Eugene, or even by Richman, Rita had always told herself that she would go another time, another day, not then, not yet.

She did not want to go there now, either. But Richman *knew* of her aversion to the Arena, and if his intention was to hide from her, then it was possible he might be in there. After all, she could well be wrong about him being in the Control Room, that had only been a hunch, a feeling . . .

She crossed the landing, peered down the passage. It wasn't level, but rather descended away, paved with flagged stone, bending as it went, its end out of sight. And she noted an interesting thing: unlike most of the other large chambers of the Observatory, which were orientated north–south, it seemed that the Arena must lie off at a right angle, to the east, if her sense of direction was true.

She bit her lip, hesitating, then frowned. *Goddamnit, go and look, it's just a gym or a basketball court or something, that's all.*

She walked down the curved hall. It ended in a level space backed by a set of swing doors. She pushed them open a crack and was surprised to find complete darkness waiting beyond. That was unusual. Even on emergency power, most of the Observatory had remained at least partially lit, whether the rooms were in use or not. So why not here?

She opened the doors further, took a step inside. In the light that entered from behind her, she saw a floor extending away into a gloom that appeared limitless, except that on the fringe of the light she could recognise what looked like the edge of a multi-lane running track.

She took another step inwards, hand outstretched behind to stop the doors closing and leaving her in blackness—but she need not have bothered, for with that step she heard a subdued click, and a light glowed to life on the inner side of the door. It must have been set on a motion sensor. And then she was staring in wonder as another light came to life, further away, and then another still further on, and more still after that, receding.

Hundreds of lights.

A gym? she thought inanely, mouth agape. *A basketball court?* How had she got it so wrong? She remembered now that Clara and the others had told her that the Arena was bigger than that. Much bigger. But she'd had no *conception* . . .

What she saw now, illuminated dimly by a ring of lights that seemed to curve off into infinity, was an open space so vast that for a moment she thought that she had stepped outside, that maybe the whole side of the Mount had fallen away here, leaving her exposed to the night sky. Her second thought was that by some magic she had walked onto the playing field of a great sports stadium.

But the Arena was not quite either of those. She stood at the entry to an immense dome, carved from the solid rock of the Mount, perfect in its shape and staggering in its size. Rita had thought that the Entrance Hall was big, or the well of the Helix Staircase, or even the Cavern Pool with its watery sense of space. But this . . .

She was walking forwards now, out across the expanse of the void, marvelling at the spectacle. As she did so she crossed the running track, springy underfoot and marked with ten lanes. Perhaps her impression of a sports stadium had not been so wrong, for she saw now that the track circled the entire rim of the dome's floor, a full four-hundred-metre circuit. Olympic ready. And within its ring lay a huge expanse of artificial turf, a playing field, again full scale, white chalk lines marking it as a soccer pitch—or so it appeared to Rita's unsporting eye; it could just as easily be for rugby, or perhaps US-style football.

Incredible. Oh, the space wasn't a true stadium, there were no grandstands, and the dome of the roof, astounding as it was, was still lower than would be the case if fifty thousand fans were intended to fit inside. But even so—a complete football pitch, a four-hundred-metre running track, and all of it hacked from the inside of a mountain!

The labour of it! The expense! The indulgence of it too, the near obscenity. Of all the excesses Rita had witnessed in the Observatory, this wonder impressed and appalled her the most. To cut out so much rock, at such unthinkable cost, and why? Just for one man's recreational needs! Just to create a chamber that might see a half-hour's use each day. Just to provide Richman with a track to run around, and a field to kick a ball about, when a simple elevator ride down to the Base could give him the same anyway!

There was even more to the place, Rita saw now, glancing behind her. To one side of the door by which she had entered, glass walls opened to a deep recess which contained the more conventional gym she had expected, with exercise machines of all sorts gleaming in the dimness; while on the other side of the door, an arch opened into a second, lesser cavern that was angular and dark, but which seemed to be a court for either basketball or tennis.

Amazing.

And outrageous.

She had walked almost to the centre of the football pitch. The upper reach of the dome was now some fifty metres overhead. Huge banks of lights clung there, dark now, but presumably, when power was available, they could illuminate the playing field to daylight brightness. At other places, cables extended down, and dangling from their lower ends were various box shapes, speakers perhaps, so that music could be played while Richman ran his laps.

She could only imagine the arena all lit up, and with sound booming. No wonder the others had been so eager for her to see it. For all its simplicity and functionality when compared to the more ornate sections of the Observatory, and for all its wastefulness, the sheer overkill of its existence, it was undoubtedly the triumph of the entire residence, the pinnacle of her father's design.

And here, she realised, her thoughts suddenly cold, in his own monstrous work of beauty and arrogance, her father had died.

She lowered her gaze to the artificial turf; she was standing almost on the dot in the centreline. She had a strange sense of certainty that it had been right here, in the middle of the great space, that it had happened. Why did she think that? All she really knew was that he was somewhere in here, inspecting his work.

Richman was the one who had found him and sounded the alarm, at dawn, when the billionaire came down for his regular morning run. So Clara had said. But that meant, surely, that her father had arrived here even earlier, in the middle of the night, or in the pre-dawn.

Did that make sense? Why would he be making an inspection tour at such an hour?

Rita turned slowly, the sensation suddenly very strong once more of being watched. No one was in sight on the playing field or on the running track, but in the shadowy depths of the tennis court or the gym, who could be sure? Alternatively, if Richman was in the Control Room after all, then no doubt there were more security cameras here in the Arena that he could be using right now to watch her.

Or was it something else that made her skin crawl, not Richman at all? Some*one* else.

To Rita's unease, a persistent image was forming in her mind. An image of her father, here in this place of his death, unseen, but present and close somehow, perceiving her, observing her.

But that was nonsense. She was no believer in ghosts, nor even in an afterlife. It was a truth that had often amazed her clients, back in the old days—that someone who communed regularly with unseen inhuman presences refused to credit the possibility of *human* spirits. But to Rita it had always been quite simple: presences existed as fact, she felt them as a tangible experience, whereas she had never experienced anything to suggest that ghosts were real, or that there was a nether-realm after death from which return was possible.

And yet . . . she could not shake it, a sense of familiar proximity, of *him*. More than that, of an urgency in him, a need to communicate.

Occasionally, in the old days, she had been asked to speak to ghosts that her clients were certain haunted their houses, and she had tried it once or twice, opening her mind on a cursory level, and felt nothing. But those purported hauntings had lacked any relevance to her. This was her own father. If it was really possible to send messages from beyond death, and if he indeed had such a message, then shouldn't she at least make an effort to hear it?

Rita closed her eyes and sought to calm her thoughts. She had taken none of the drugs that would usually aid her in this, but then, so otherworldly was her state right now, injured, alone, exhausted beyond measure, terrified, that she was already more or less in an altered reality anyway.

Explicitly, she sought for no inhuman presence, in no way opened herself up to the machinations of the Wheel. Instead, she sought rather for something warmer and more familiar, for a vestige of an emotion that would be human, that was of warm flesh and blood, not of cold stone. She searched for her father as she had known him when she was a small girl, and he was a hero who could do no wrong.

Nothing. Nothing. Or could she . . . On the very edge of sensation, as ambiguous as half-heard notes amid static, was there something there? An echo of trauma, of an experience that was not hers, but another's? Of a mistake made, and of suffering, and of a dying word whispered in the dark?

Of a warning, meant for her?

A voice said, 'Hello, Rita.'

She shrieked, opened her eyes. The echoes of her own cry shimmered back at her from the walls, but there was no one else there.

8

THE VOICE OF GOD

LAUGHTER, SOFT AND YET ALL-ENCOMPASSING, sounded throughout the Arena. Rita spun about, staring. No one was there, and indeed the laughter did not sound as if it came from close to her; it came from above and all around, a voice from the heavens.

Then, 'It's only me, Rita.'

She drew a breath at last into frozen lungs. Not her father, nor any kind of voice from the beyond, but Richman, only Richman, his accent recognisable now, amplified as it was in the sepulchral air.

'Don't bother looking for me,' the voice went on, in a tone of friendly advice. 'I'm nowhere near; I'm just watching you on the cameras.'

Rita could pinpoint the source of the voice now. It came from all about, yes, but in particular it came from the closest of the boxes that hung down from the dome, hovering maybe twenty feet above her head. She had guessed right; they were speakers. But could she communicate in return?

'Can you hear me?' she said to the darkness above, and the box hanging there.

'Indeed,' came the reply. 'The security system is wired for sound as well as images.'

'You're in the Control Room,' she accused. 'I knew it. I was on my way there.'

Another laugh. 'So I assumed, before you got lost. I was watching you all the while. I saw where you made your wrong turn. I can show you the right way, this minute, if you like. But the Control Room won't do you any good. I'm not there. I'm not in the Observatory at all. I'm still in the Cottage.'

'Bullshit. I looked everywhere up there.'

'Not everywhere, you didn't. I'm in the Cottage's safe room. You've heard of such things, I assume? For protection against terrorists and kidnappers and the like? Well, one of the key security features of *this* safe room is that the entrance to it is very cleverly hidden. Even knowing the room exists now, you could come back up to the Cottage and search for days, and you'd still never find it.'

Rita could only stare upwards, the strangeness of the whole situation overcoming her for a moment, as Richman's smooth American tones sounded with perfect fidelity through the dim gulfs all about her. It was surreal. And *safe room*? Yes, she'd heard of such things in the homes of rich people, but wasn't there usually another name used?

Then anger came. 'You left me. You left me in the Lightning Room with . . . with what was happening to Kennedy . . . and you ran away.'

There was no apology in the amplified reply. 'I took the wiser course of action, whatever you choose to call it. A business decision, really. At this point, everything aside from self-preservation is an illusion. Especially any notion of altruism. My intention is to wait this thing out in the one safe place left.'

'And the rest of us can go to hell?' Rita queried in disgust, realising even as she said it that there was no *rest of us* anymore. It was just her.

'You think I should have invited you in?' mused Richman lightly. 'But why should I trust you? I've already seen that the Wheel can control you. For all I know, it would make you attack me.'

She frowned up at the dome. 'You don't think the Wheel can control *you*?'

'It hasn't yet, so as far as I know it can't. And even if it can, it doesn't matter now.'

'Why? What makes you think you're so safe in your little prison cell?'

'Oh, it's no cell. It's a whole suite, very well appointed thank you; kitchen, bedroom, bathroom, living area, plus a second fully equipped Control Room in which I'm sitting right now. There's also food and water and other stores, enough to keep me comfortable for at least a month. And all of it is secure as hell, with just the one bombproof entry now locked behind me, and no exterior windows or doors.'

She grinned, hoping there was a camera above her that would show the grin in all its contempt. 'And none of that will mean a thing the next time you fall asleep, when the Wheel takes over your body and makes you open that bombproof door from the inside, and walk right out into the open.'

Now came another laugh, satisfied, as if Richman had been waiting for this very point to be made. 'Even then, I'm safe. It's a final security feature of this place. Imagine if I was in here but terrorists outside were holding my staff or loved ones hostage, threatening to kill them if I didn't come out. In that situation some misguided nobility might indeed get the better of me. But there's a switch here that, once thrown, makes it impossible for anyone, even from the inside, to open the door for a pre-set time. I've thrown that switch, set for seventy-two hours. So Wheel or not, I'm not going anywhere for three days. And by then . . .' for the first time the confidence in the amplified voice faltered a modicum before recovering, '. . . by then, this thing will be over, and someone will have come.'

Panic room, Rita was thinking, yes, that was proper word, not *safe* room. And god yes, Richman had panicked indeed, if he was prepared to lock himself away for three days with no possibility of escape, even if rescue came this very minute.

Only, was he right? In his cunning and cowardice, had he truly preserved himself against the Wheel? And if so, then Rita herself was now the only target remaining out in plain sight.

An astonishing bitterness possessed her. Yes, yes, it would be just typical somehow, wouldn't it? He might survive this indeed. The one man to blame for the entire disaster might be the only one to walk free of it, as people like him always did.

As the *rich* always did.

There it was. She had refrained as best she could, up until this point, from disliking Richman based purely on his wealth and privilege, from being biased against him simply because of her own relative poverty and powerlessness, but for once she could not resist the sheer hatred. Fuck him. Her life was in peril. Kennedy and Kushal and Madelaine and Clara were already dead, along with hundreds more down at Base, all of them innocent in this affair when compared to Richman, but *he* would walk away with no price paid other than the loss of money.

Fuck him.

With the air of moving on, the voice asked, 'So, can you sense anything of him there?'

She looked up, distracted. 'Who?'

'Well, your father, of course. You're standing right where he died. I took it for granted that you were trying to make some connection with him.'

Rita blinked. Yes, she had been doing exactly that, and the result had been . . . had been what? Only an enigmatic hint of . . . something.

She said, 'What was he doing here, when he died? The truth this time, not the story.'

There came a hesitation from above, but then Richman seemed to breathe a sigh, as if none of this mattered anymore. 'It's the truth that his heart killed him. But you're quite correct that he was not down there for any mundane reason. He was naked, for one thing, when I found him. His clothes were in a pile next to him. I think—I can't be sure of this, mind—I think he was there trying something that *you* inspired him to do. I think he was trying to perform one of your lustrations. And had his heart attack in the attempt.'

'What?'

'I'm guessing. But he'd been talking about you, and your book, and the concept of lustrations, in the days before he died. We'd been having so much trouble here, more than you know even now. And he'd come to believe, and had come close to convincing me as well, that there was truth in your beliefs after all, and that we needed to do something. He didn't tell me that he was going to try it himself, but when I found him that morning, it was pretty clear.'

Rita was lost for a response for an instant, grappling with disbelief and with a thousand implications. 'But . . . even if he . . . why here, in the middle of this awful place?'

'I can't say. He was still alive when I found him, just, but he was no longer coherent, so I didn't get an explanation as to his reasons.'

There was evasion in the response, Rita sensed. Richman at least had his own guess as to why her father had come *here* to attempt a lustration. She could guess too: this huge chamber, of all the Observatory's reshaping of the Mount, was the greatest insult to the native stone, the most unnecessary, the most likely to infuriate the Wheel. So where better to begin placating the Wheel than here in the Arena?

But if that had indeed been her father's reasoning, it was fatally flawed. The Wheel was in no mood for placating, and how easy would it have been to strike down a man with an already weak heart. She had a sudden vision of him clutching at his chest and falling to the cold grass, lying there alone, dying, and knowing it. And for the first time, grief—actual, immediate grief—keened in her.

'Did he say *anything* at all,' she asked of Richman, 'at the end?'

'Not that I understood, I'm afraid.'

But here Rita felt rejection rise in her, a protest that seemed to come from some other source, almost as if someone else was listening to this exchange, and could stay silent no longer. Richman was lying. Her father had indeed spoken final words, and Richman had indeed heard and understood them perfectly well. And those words were . . . were . . .

Damn it, she had been on the edge of it just moments ago, before Richman interrupted. She searched again, and yes, it was still there, a sub-aural ringing within the emptiness of the Arena, a whisper of a dying breath, a warning . . . no, not a warning, but a request, a plea . . . *It's too strong . . . don't . . . I beg you . . . don't call her . . . don't bring Rita here.*

Oh god. It came in a rush of knowledge now, as if she had been right here, watching.

Her father had tried to stop all this. He had failed in his attempt at a lustration, but in doing so he had experienced the savage strength of the Wheel, felt how deranged with hate it was, and knowing that he had planted the idea of summoning Rita in Richman's mind, he had requested, with his dying breaths, that Richman not do it. He had *begged*.

And the billionaire—fucking Walter Richman—hearing this, had flatly ignored him.

Jesus. Rita felt sick. She couldn't stand there a moment longer, not on the very place where it had happened, not while Richman was watching from above, gloating over the video screens in his private room. It was too claustrophobic suddenly, too airless. She went stumbling away across the artificial turf towards the exit and escape.

Richman's godlike voice pursued her effortlessly, coming from speakers ahead and behind her. 'Why did he try it at all? I can only assume he hoped that your ability with presences was in some way hereditary, that as your father he might have a similar talent. I wish he had left well enough alone, however. He might be alive still. He was planning to invite you here, to tell you that he was sorry for all those years of not believing you. I only did what he was going to do, when I asked you here. Don't forget that.'

Liar, Rita thought, fucking *liar*. She had come to the edge of the field and was crossing the running track, the exit beckoning ahead.

'Where are you going now?' Richman's amplified query came.

Where indeed? She didn't care, as long as it was away from here, away from his smooth rich voice. She shuffled through the doorway into the passage that led back up to the well, but she had hardly gone ten paces along it before god spoke again.

'You can't escape me, if that's what you're trying to do. I can follow you everywhere.'

She paused. The voice was not as all-surrounding as it had been in the Arena; it had a thinner quality here, tinny, but yes, there, set within the ceiling was a small black hemisphere from which Richman's voice emanated.

'There are cameras and listening devices and speakers covering pretty much every inch of this place; you should know that by now. Well, actually no, not every inch. There aren't any cameras or microphones in the bedrooms or bathrooms. It's purely a security thing, it's not about voyeurism.'

Rita was limping on again. She came to the well, gazed up at the dizzying whorls of the Helix Staircase. And yes, there were more of the black hemispheres here too, dotted around the walls.

'Just so you know,' Richman's voice informed her from the nearest of these, 'in case you have it in mind, you can't come back up to the Cottage. I've locked the lift by remote control.'

Fuck.

But the last thing she wanted to do was give him the satisfaction of knowing he had guessed rightly. 'Why are you following me then?' she snarled to the atmosphere. 'You're safe in your Cottage and your room, so why do you care what I do?'

'Oh, it's nothing personal,' he replied. 'But I need to be watching, in case the Wheel takes control of you again. If it does, I need to see what happens. It might be helpful to me later.'

Still there was no apology in his tone, no shame, just unshakeable self-justification. And in that brute drive for his own survival, Rita heard the overture of her own death. If the Wheel came for her, he would do nothing but watch coldly, and learn from it what he could for his own advantage.

But would the Wheel come for her? She was not its prime target, of that she understood. Surely its time, its energy now would be focussed on Richman, and him alone. But if Richman was truly unreachable there in his refuge, then might not the mountain, denied, strike out in its anger at whomever it could reach?

The anger was back. Fuck him. She said, 'I wouldn't be so sure that *you're* safe, even in your little spider hole. The Wheel doesn't need you out in the open; it can still make you harm yourself, just like it did to me. You must have knives in there with you, and other sharp things, if not a gun.'

Was his laughter a little more forced this time? 'I'm not as dumb as you, Rita. I'm not going to open my soul to the damn mountain and invite it in. And I'm not going to let it hypnotise me like it did the others. I've got enough of Kennedy's cocaine in here to keep me wide awake for as long it takes, plus I've got a mental discipline that someone like you can't even dream of. It's a mountaineering thing. If you can't keep control of your own thoughts on a high peak, if you let your mind wander, then you die. Not all climbers have it, true. Clara didn't, not really. But I do.'

And damn him, he was probably right. That was the genius of sociopaths, after all. It was their very inhumanity that gave them endurance.

Rita had set foot on the stairs, climbing without knowing where she was going, her injured leg so stiff and swollen she could scarcely bend her knee anymore, the material of her pants stretched tight about the thigh. But up she climbed in spite of the pain, three times, four times around the spiral, until she came to the guest level, the two wings extending off north and south from the landing.

She paused, considering. Should she return to her old apartment? Would she be any safer there? She did not really think so. There was no 'safer' to be had in this situation. But after hesitating, she left the landing and headed down the southern hallway anyway, for sheer lack of an alternative.

Then the lights went out.

There was no flicker, no warning: blackness swallowed her with a silent snap, and she reared back instinctively, almost as if a wall had appeared from nowhere right in front of her.

She stood, frozen, her hands partly outstretched, eyes bugged wide. But there was nothing to see, not a hint of light anywhere.

'Sorry about that,' came the godlike voice out of the darkness. 'Seems there's a bit of a problem in the generator room. Those gens really aren't meant to run so long unattended; there's supposed to be an engineer on duty to look after them, to change oil and filters and so on. I'm getting "engine overheating" warnings up here, so I'm afraid I've been forced to cut power back to the barest necessities. But never fear, some lights are still on up on the main levels.'

It was more bullshit, Rita knew. Oh, it might be true that the generators were not meant to run so long without maintenance, but that they had developed a fault at this very second? No, that was pure crap. Richman had turned off the lights deliberately. For some reason, he did not want her lingering down here, hiding out in her old apartment. He wanted her up in the public sections of the Observatory.

And there was nothing she could do, no light she could create. If she'd had her phone, she could have used its torch, but she couldn't even remember where her phone was. It had been useless ever since the disaster had taken out the coverage.

Shit. She did not want to go up—not if it was what Richman wanted—but she couldn't fumble around down here in the blackness forever either. It was just too awful, too close. Even when dawn came (god, how many hours away was sunrise?) no light would reach down to these sections.

Reluctantly, she turned around (or hoped she had) and inched back the way she had come, eyes casting about for any glow or glimmer at all. Finally, she sensed that she was moving into an open space once more, and looking up, she could see high above the faintest of glows from the top of the Helix Staircase. She let out a long shaking sigh, and after a moment more, began to slowly climb.

The time, what was the time? It felt like it had been a week since Kennedy's death, but she went back over all she had done since then— searching the Cottage, getting lost in the tunnels—and in truth it might have been only two hours, certainly no more than three. Which made it maybe four a.m. The winter sunrise was still hours away yet.

She laboured on, gasping with pain from time to time as her leg stabbed sharply. But in spite of her physical exertion, the air felt colder as she rose. Was she just imagining that in the dark? No, the chill was palpable, as if a freezing draft was curling its way down the stairs. What was going on?

She reached the top. Disappointingly, the Atrium level, with all its grand rooms, was almost fully dark. The faint light she had seen from below came from higher up still, from the Conservatory, a glow spilling down the small spiral stairs.

She was too hungry for that light to care now what Richman was up to; she just wanted to see electricity burning. She limped over to the stairs, began the final ascent. Ah, but the cold draft was even worse here, a stream of freezing air in her face.

She came to the Conservatory. Its wide floor was in shadow, but behind the bar, two lamps glowed to illuminate the shelves and the bottles there. That was all. Richman had left her no other relief from the darkness. And all around, night pressed at the glass walls and windows. The storm had long since blown out, it seemed, for all was silence now.

But the cold!

Rita saw the reason then. The airlock doors leading out to the Terrace—both the inner and outer doors—were standing open.

That was supposed to be impossible, she knew. There was supposed to be a failsafe mechanism that forbade both the inner and outer door being open at the same time. Nevertheless, there they stood, ajar, a passage clear to the open air.

Fascinated, she drifted closer. The doors could be opened both manually and automatically, she knew—so had Richman done this by remote? Were *all* the external doors throughout the Observatory like this now, wide open? And at that thought Rita felt a frisson of new fear, for if that was the case, then how quickly would the whole building be reduced to freezing? How long before she could not survive here at all?

The lights behind the bar flicked off, and darkness slammed down again.

Rita whirled. *Fuck fuck fuck.* He had done it again, the bastard. But why? Why lure her up with light, and then deny it to her?

What did he *want*?

She stood motionless, trying to calm herself, listening in the silence. Nothing moved, nothing threatened, there was just the cold.

Eventually, as her eyes adjusted, she found that in fact she could see, just a little. A pale illumination was coming from *outside*, through the windows. Not electric light, but the faint wash of starlight, and yes, moonlight. There, overhead: the waning Moon, riding high in the pre-dawn sky, was peeping in and out between slow-moving shreds of cloud, the last remnants of the storm, maybe.

It wasn't much, barely dispelling the darkness within the Conservatory, where Rita could detect only shadowy shapes and the outline of the windows. But through the airlock doors, out on the Terrace, everything was awash in a blue glow . . .

She stared. Why, the entire area was sheathed in ice. It was not snow, not hail, but a clear frozen coat of water that somehow caught the moonlit and magnified it. Every edge and corner on the Terrace was delineated clearly, like a ghost landscape under the dark heavens. It was beautiful.

But so, so cold. The air oozing in from outside nipped at Rita like teeth, although the weather screen by the doors was dead along with the lights, so there was no way to know the exact temperature. She took a coat from the rack, wrapped it about herself as defence, and edged closer.

Her every nerve was singing in alarm (she must *not* step through those doors) but she was also fascinated beyond measure by the silver-blue light, and the stillness of the night out there.

She stopped at the threshold, gazing through the opening. The ice, the silence, was entrancing. It came to her that in the entire Observatory, *this*, the Terrace, was the only truly engaging place. Everything else was underground, hollowed out caves and tunnels, no matter how well camouflaged. But the Terrace remained close to what the peak of the Mount had always been: a summit beneath the sky.

And something called to her from out there. Something in her cried to stand under an open heaven, free at last of rock walls and rock ceilings and the eternal night of underground.

But it was madness, surely, to step through that inviting outer door. Two deaths already had been inflicted out there, and no matter how calm the air might seem now, how gorgeously the ice might glitter, how native and natural the peak might seem, it could all turn in an instant; she knew that. In her right mind, she would never consider it.

So was she in her right mind? Or was she being hypnotised again, as she had been in the Lightning Room? Was this the feeling that lured Kushal out onto the Terrace to his doom, and then Madelaine, after her long night of staring through the glass?

Rita experimented mentally. Do I *have* to go out there? No, was the answer. Could she step back from the brink. Yes. She took two steps backwards, and felt no tension rise in her, no contrary voice demanding that she go forwards instead. Her will seemed entirely her own.

But she wanted to go out.

She glanced around, feeling Richman's eye upon her once more. He was silent, but he must be watching on his screens, for after all, he had driven her to this very spot, presumably for a purpose.

Did *he* want her to go through the doors? She felt it suddenly as a truth—he *did*. These doors weren't open by accident. He had overridden the failsafe system, then forced her up here using darkness as a spur, all in the hope that she would accept the invitation and step out and find . . .

Find what?

Her death?

Was that what he was doing? Was he making it as easy as he could for the Wheel to reach her? Nowhere was more exposed than the Terrace, nowhere would she be more vulnerable. To lure her out there would be to place her utterly at the Wheel's mercy, and the Wheel had so far shown no mercy at all, so that was as good as . . . as good as . . .

Sacrificing her to the mountain?

In his place?

Yes. That was exactly what he was doing, exactly what his billionaire instincts were no doubt telling him he must do, if he was to survive. Such brutal logic would even appear to him as a virtue, as a hard but unavoidable choice that a weakling would ignore, but which the strong-willed must take.

The piece of shit.

She stared at where she knew the camera was, letting disgust fill her gaze, even though her expression would be unreadable to him in the dark.

Fuck you, arsehole.

And yet still she wanted to go outside.

Her gaze returned to the Terrace, where the ice glimmered in soft lines. To the left, a monstrous shadow loomed in the night, the Wheel, hulking over the little Mount. There would no defence against it out there, nowhere to hide. And even so, knowing it was a trap set by her host, knowing how deadly it would be, *still* she longed to stand out there.

Why?

She extended her inner senses minimally, cautiously, and felt nothing, no threat, no awareness in the atmosphere, either benign or hostile. There was only a sense of . . . what? Abeyance? Yes, something like that. Vast perils still hung on the horizon but in this instant, all the elements, the ice, the Wheel, the night, the Terrace, were waiting, all powers held in cessation for a moment that had not yet arrived.

And that moment was not quite imminent. If she stepped out into the air, the Wheel would not suddenly seize her. She would, although vulnerable and as crushable as a mite, be safe.

She blinked. Madness. Madness. Her very thoughts were being manipulated, surely. Why else would she ever go out there?

And yet she went anyway.

Treading as if to make a single noise would break the spell, she moved one deliberate step at a time through the inner door and then paused at the outer. Nothing happened. The inner door did not slide shut behind her, no wind stirred ahead on the Terrace. In the sky, the Moon shone pale.

She moved again, taking two steps, three, clearing the outer door and then several paces further, out into the open air, silent all the while, treading with the most extreme care upon the ice floor.

Still nothing, and behind her the doors did not slam shut and trap her outside. Perhaps having opened them both simultaneously, against all the protocols, Richman could not now shut them. Perhaps he didn't want to. No matter. She was out there now, right or wrong.

The night held its breath, as did Rita for a moment, feeling her brow and cheeks and the flesh of her nostrils burn with the cold. But oh, the air felt so fresh, so alive with possibilities, she had to inhale it, no matter how painful. And the sky!

Away to the north, a black bulk of cloud was dwindling, still with shimmers of lightning within, the storm dying in the final hours of the night. But overhead and to the south and west stars blazed, glittering dust against black. And rearing vast against them was the Wheel, its West Face, like the icy Terrace, shining faint silver in the moonlight.

It was beautiful beyond bearing. Rita seemed to be able to behold the mountain entire; its every rising bastion and precipice; its every fang of rock or wasteland of snow or perched glacier of ice; its shadowed couloirs, great and small; its bare upper faces of stone; its summit ridge, so high, so far above, and yet still, in the crystal air, etched brilliantly against the Milky Way. The mountain's majesty, its might, its imponderable, unbearable, crushing weight of age and stone; it was *there* above her.

She could not help it. She fell to her knees under the weight and wonder of the mountain, enraptured and horrified at once, too trans-fixed to feel even the knife-cold of the ice beneath her.

She did not open her mind to the Wheel, she made no invitation, the force of it simply flooded in, and she was defenceless against the flood, a beetle impaled upon a pin. The mountain, unlike the Moon, was not waning, not even after all its efforts of the last five days. No, it was waxing to the peak of its power. And that power was all-encompassing.

Tears bit coldly in her eyes. She seemed to feel herself spinning with vertigo, and all she could think of was the breaking wheel, the torture device from *The Triumph of Death*, the wheel of torment and mortality. She was fixed upon it now, and would die thus, as it spun faster and faster. She was a mote on the crest of a wave about to violently break and she was helpless in every way to stop it. The Wheel would spin on and on until her limbs were flung away . . .

But then, unaccountably, the breaking wave released her and passed on; the terrible sensation of whirling stopped abruptly, and with a jagged lurch the night righted itself. She was still alive. On her knees and gasping and freezing, but alive.

The mountain had let her go.

She stared, baffled beyond relief. The Wheel had held her, effortless in its supreme strength, examining her in the fullness of its loathing, and then, instead of destroying her, it had tossed her aside.

She gazed up at the great mass, the silvered precipices of its West Face brooding with a vast single expression of age-long, inexhaustible anger. And she read there an astonishing thing.

The mountain did not want her. The focus of its titanic malevolence lay elsewhere. It wanted Richman, and only Richman now. Rita was a microscopic thing not worth even contempt anymore.

But no . . . that wasn't quite right either. The Wheel had killed the others all too willingly, just to isolate Richman, so why not her?

The West Face above was immovable, not deigning to answer. Ah, but she could read it now. And again, the irony. The mountain was letting her go for one reason only: because Richman wanted her dead. It had recognised his intent in luring her out here into the open, and it was the Wheel's freezing pleasure to foil that intent.

Beyond that, her fate was of no interest to the mountain. But even so, staring up, she caught a last fleeting consideration of her before it forgot her entirely, an acknowledgement that she at least had the ability to discern its true nature. For the sake of that ability came one stern and final warning, delivered without voice and without mercy.

Flee this place if you wish to live.

Flee now.

Then she was dismissed, might never even have existed, as far as the mountain cared.

And still she could only kneel and weep and stare up in stupefaction. Flee? Flee? Flee how, flee where? There was nowhere in the Observatory, nowhere upon the whole Mount, where she could escape the Wheel's wrath when it came. For that wrath—she could feel it growing like a cataclysm ready to fall upon Richman—would be all-consuming.

In which case, she must flee the Mount entirely. But that could only mean . . . ?

Oh no. Not that.

Yes, that. The emergency stairs. They were the only way down and out of here.

But Clara, look what had happened to Clara, and she had been an experienced climber, she had been able to face those teetering ladders without fear. Rita had never climbed, was terrified of heights; she would panic at the first challenge, and fall, screaming as she plummeted into the shaft. And if she was to die on the emergency stairs anyway, what did it matter if she died here in the Observatory instead? Why put herself through the dread and agony of descending into that awful shaft, for the same result?

Except . . . she might not die on the stairs, that was the appalling truth of it, she *might* not. Whereas if she stayed here in the Observatory, even if she hid herself away in the lowest, smallest room in the under levels, as far as she could get from Richman and from the vengeance that would fall on him . . .

She stared again to the summit of the Wheel, an argent dagger against the stars, and at last she could behold what was gathering there.

Not with her eyes exactly, and not with her mind, but with some terror-inspired combination of both, she could see. The unchanging, unmoving air of the high stratosphere was moving and changing now, perhaps for the first time in millennia. Currents were circling slowly around the summit, winds blowing where by rights no wind could ever blow. And though they looked slow from far away, Rita knew that up there, twenty-two thousand metres above her, the revolutions were in truth howling gales, gaining in strength as they spun and spun, a giant whirlpool, round and round about the peak.

Whatever was coming, whatever punishment was to descend upon the Mount and upon Walter Richman, it was beginning up there. And when it was ready, when it fell, it would be unimaginable.

Rita groaned, rose convulsively from her knees, and went stumbling and slipping across the ice towards the Conservatory doors.

Her choice was made. Between the horror of the stairs and the horror of what would descend from the mountain, there was no comparison. Better to tumble to her death in the shaft than to face what was being summoned by the Wheel high above.

Rita skittered through the airlock doors to the firmer footing of the interior, then made for the spiral stairs. As she went, she glanced up to the watching security camera. She felt no responsibility or loyalty to Richman, he deserved none. Even so, she summoned her breath and called a warning to him. 'You're gonna die up there, if you stay here. Can you see the Wheel from your little hidey-hole? Because if not, it's a shame you can't go outside now and take a look.'

Then she forgot him and went lurching down the stairs. Her wounded leg protested immediately. Jesus, how was she going to manage the thousands upon thousands of steps in the shaft? It didn't matter. She would find a way.

She gained the Atrium and hesitated a moment, staring about. It was still very dark down here, the moonlight no more than a hint through the dome overhead. She could just make out a path to the Dining Hall, but it would be pitch-black in the kitchen, and even worse in the service tunnels.

How on earth would she find her way down to the emergency stairs? Then she remembered, yes, back when this had all started, when she and the others had first been marooned, they had gathered together an assortment of torches to have handy, just in case the emergency generators failed. They had left a couple of those flashlights waiting on the sideboard in the Dining Hall, she was sure.

She limped forwards again. Which was when the godlike voice sounded once more, booming softly through the gloom of the Atrium.

'Nice try,' said Richman, sounding amused. 'What am I supposed to see on the Wheel?'

She glanced ceiling-wards. 'You really don't have a window? You can't see the mountain?'

'Windows would be a weakness in a safe room. And I don't need one anyway. I've got one of the external cameras turned to the Wheel, set on night vision. There's nothing there.'

Rita shrugged as she passed into the Dining Hall. Well, she had warned him; it was more than he was owed after what he'd done, but the fool was determined to be blind. No camera in the world—night vision or not—could capture those ominous movements around the summit. It was a strangeness that had to be felt as much as seen.

'Your funeral,' she muttered, and paused in the dark, groping about first to locate the sideboard, then feeling across its surface. Yes, she had them, two LED flashlights, small but powerful. She slipped one into the pocket of her coat, flicked on the other one, and passed into the kitchen, chasing its beam.

She grabbed two small bottles of water from a shelf and added them to her pockets. She should probably hunt out some food as well, she knew—when had she even eaten last?—but the urge to be gone was too strong, there was no time.

She plunged into the service tunnel. Awful. In the hard white light of the torch, the concrete walls looked even starker than her visit of only hours earlier. But on she went, her footsteps echoing in the darkness. She must concentrate, she must not get lost in here again.

Don't think about the route, she told herself, just *walk* it, you've done this before. Down one level, left at the bottom—and Christ, now she remembered, not straight ahead through two junctions, but *left* at the second junction, then hold on around a rightward bend—and ha, thank god, there it was, the Control Room, right where it was supposed to be.

To her surprise, the door was hanging open. She paused to look in, veering the torch beam about. Everything was dead, the computer and video screens blank, the server towers no longer blinking their green and orange lights. Well, it was only to be expected, Richman was in command from his second Control Room now. All that mattered was that Rita knew the way to the emergency stairs from here.

She set off again. Another level down she passed by the generator room. Its door was shut, and, at her try, locked fast, but she could hear the muted roar of the beasts within. Oh yes, Richman could turn the lights back on any time he wanted, the bastard. But there was nothing Rita could do about it.

She pushed on, and the roar faded to silence again behind the thick walls. Another two levels down and she was there, at the threshold of the service elevator and the emergency stairs.

She had feared, on her way down, that Richman might have closed the bombproof security door, barring her escape route. But no. Or perhaps he did not even know she was here, did not guess what she intended. Perhaps he could not track her on his cameras in the darkness of the tunnels.

She crept across the threshold and onto the concrete lip. She was careful at first to keep the torch focussed solely at her feet, to not let the beam stray to the yawning abyss of the shaft. But the sense of unseen space opening all about her in the darkness was simply unendurable. At the rail, she tremulously aimed the torch down, and forced herself to look.

And oh god . . .

Deprived even of the dim emergency lights, the shaft was a circular well of freezing dark. The beam reached no further down than a few dozen metres, etching out starkly the gantry of the useless elevator on one side, and on the other the first few flights of stairs, so thin, so insubstantially attached to the scaffolding, or worse, hanging askew . . . and beyond that just a plunging blackness, infinite.

She couldn't really be going down there, could she? Clara had gone down, a mountain climber with gear, afraid of nothing, and been driven mad by what she found. Was Rita really going to follow?

A voice crackled into life behind her, and she started so violently she almost dropped the torch, almost sent it tumbling two and a half thousand metres into the blackness, turning and turning and turning, its spiralling beam marking its fall . . .

'You're seriously fool enough to try this?' came Richman's inquiry, scratchy now; the only speaker available to him at this point was the intercom by the elevator doors. There was, Rita remembered, a camera somewhere here too, but it was the last camera he would be able to track her on; there were none down in the shaft, only the blind intercom system. 'You're going to *climb* all that way? In the dark? You're going to shimmy down the ropes that Clara left behind? Very daring, for a non-mountaineer.'

'What does it tell you that I'm prepared to try this, rather than stay up here, after what I saw happening on the Wheel?' she said.

'Goddamnit, there's nothing happening on the Wheel!' And the sangfroid was gone.

'Have you been outside and looked?'

Silence.

She laughed. 'Oh, I forgot. You can't go outside, can you, not for three days. Well, it's by your own hand that you're stuck here. So fuck you.'

And with that last word of bravado, and before the panic could overwhelm her again, she set foot on the first flight of steps and climbed briskly down, out of his sight, and into the ordeal of the shaft.

9

THE UPPER STAIRS

TWO DAYS EARLIER, WHEN SHE had watched Clara venture down these same stairs, nearly as steep as a ladder, Rita had sworn to herself that if *she* ever had to do likewise then she would not climb face-outwards, as Clara had, but rather face *to* the steps, as if it was an actual ladder she was descending.

But she had not known then that she would be descending in darkness, that she would need to be holding a torch continually. To climb down a ladder with only one free hand, trying awkwardly all the while to illuminate the rungs below her feet as she went—no, that would be horrible. She went face outwards, the torch lighting her way, her other hand clutched fervently to the rail.

But it was horrible anyway. It would be so easy to overbalance, so easy to tumble forwards into the eager air. Her initial rush lasted all of four flights down, switching to and fro, before the reality began to sink in, the shaft expanding around her as vast as the throat of a volcano, and the stairs shrinking to wisps of slippery metal beneath her feet.

She slowed, each step becoming harder, and on the fourth landing she froze, legs shaking, her grip on the rail locked. Another five or six switchbacks below, the torch clearly picked out the first of the ladders that had come askew, breaking away at its lower end from the landing, leading now into the open abyss. *No, no, no . . .*

She couldn't do it. Clara had avoided the broken ladder by simply climbing down the scaffolding itself, but *Rita* could never do that. She could never scramble like a spider between the crossbeams while the awful drop sang its siren song beneath . . .

But fuck, she had known she would have to, otherwise why come here at all?

Paralysis held her for some minutes, her breath coming hard, nausea swirling a red mist at the edge of her vision. She wanted to go back. More than anything in her life she yearned to go back, to climb the ladders to the solid stone of the passages above, to be safe, to be held secure . . .

But even in her terror she could remember the slow swirl of the air about the peak of the Wheel, and could feel from afar the threat implied by that movement. Maybe that slow swirling, which was not slow at all, was already moving down the sheer face of the mountain, ice crystals glittering as they were torn from the rock by some unspeakable potency. And of the two terrors, the stairs or the mountain, still the second was greatest.

So even as she hung there, impaled by one fear, she knew she *must* keep going.

With an act of supreme will, she unclenched her hand and forced her numb legs to move, her blocks-of-ice feet to seek for the next step down, and the next. Two flights, four, her heart beating hard, then she was at the top of the loose ladder.

Could she descend the ladder and maybe leap (god, *leap*?) across the gap to the lower landing? Rita set a foot on the first rung, then withdrew it instantly as if stung, for the flight immediately quivered at her touch, and a thin metal shriek rang out, a bolt snapping, maybe, or a weld breaking free.

Fuck fuck fuck.

No choice. She placed her torch in her coat pocket, beam pointed upwards. It was the best she could do for light, as she would need both hands here, no matter the cost. Then she reached to the side and took hold of the scaffold—there was a crossbeam at chest height—and stepped sideways, one foot at a time, onto a beam level with the landing. And there she clung, frozen again, for a minute more.

Move, you useless bitch.

She moved. Her hands slick with cold sweat, her mouth set in a rictus, she let one leg—her bad leg—sink below the beam, lower and lower, until her arms were outstretched above, and still her foot only dangled in midair, while her even good leg was bent nearly double and about to give out.

Then—bang—her swinging foot found metal, and locked there. *Oh fuck god thank you.* She let her whole body sink, her bad leg holding out, just, her arms dropping to the next rung. Before doubts could assail her, she down-climbed two rungs more, a jerky windmill of awkwardness. Then she was nearly a whole flight down, and giddy with success.

But she was only halfway. Because of the switchback pattern of the ladders, the next landing down was on the far side of the scaffold, beyond her reach. She had to descend *two* flights, to the landing directly below the one she had left.

She sucked in air. *You can do this.* She swung her bad leg free once more and climbed another rung down. A pause, and then again she sent her foot searching, found metal, let her weight settle—and with a metallic click the crossbeam under her shoe gave way completely to go clattering away into oblivion, leaving Rita hanging by her arms.

She let out a formless wail, scrabbled to climb back up, but her bad leg couldn't rise that high, and her slick hands were losing grip, and—

She fell.

A metre, no more, onto the lower landing. It rebounded with her weight, shuddered a moment, then held. She lay in a heap on the grating, legs bent painfully beneath her, arms wrapped around a railing support, her eyes closed as she wept helplessly. *Oh god oh fuck oh Jesus Christ . . .*

But in time she got up again, wiped at her red eyes, and continued on down.

▲

If Rita had thought about it at all before, she might have supposed that terror could not be an endless state of mind. No matter the peril, no matter how prolonged the danger, surely exhaustion or boredom would set in eventually, numbing the worst of the fear.

But it wasn't like that. For the next hour—although time was the merest guess—as she forced herself downwards step by step, not once did the acuteness of her terror ease.

Nor did she become in any way accustomed to the hideous ladders. Each new flight was a different experience in instability, some of the ladders trembling silently under her feet as if about to break free, others groaning and complaining with metal-stressed voices, even as the rungs held firm.

Twice more in that period she was forced to climb down by the scaffold to avoid damaged flights, and each time was worse than the last. The accumulated experience only made it harder, not easier, her fears of a misstep, or of another beam giving way, building with every attempt.

And even when she did not slip or fall, she took no reassurance from it, only leapt ahead in her mind to the next gap that would come, and the even worse collapses that she knew awaited her, from Clara's account, still further below.

Also because of Clara's account, Rita did not try to measure her progress. She did not, for instance, count each ladder as she climbed. With twelve hundred flights to descend, it would be too cruel to watch how slowly the tally mounted. More importantly, she ignored the numbers on the intercom panels when, every now and then, she passed one by. For that was how poor Clara had been led astray. Either the panels themselves were misarranged, or—as Rita thought more likely—the Wheel had got into Clara's mind and made her see numbers that weren't there. Either way, Rita would not tempt the same fate.

542

She even stopped searching downwards with her flashlight, to see what lay ahead. The shaft was always a limitless gullet beneath her, awful at every glance, crushing her spirit. So why look? Better to simply face what she must face when it arrived. So she focussed her beam only on her shoes and on the rungs underfoot, and crept on down.

It was a shock, thus, when she turned at a landing to move to the next flight and found nothing to step onto, no stairs at all, and hardly any scaffolding remaining, only a vast vacancy and darkness dropping away.

For a moment she stared down, mesmerised, her foot wavering in midair as if it wanted to carry on regardless and walk out into the void—then she was clutching convulsively to the rail, pulling back and sinking to her knees in terror.

God, she had almost walked into *space*. The ladders, half the gantry supporting them, it had all tumbled away in the earthquake . . .

But then, as her heart laboured, she saw it—a rope. It was tied fast to the last solid crossbeam of the scaffold, and dangled into the darkness. Clara's rope. With dread fascination, Rita played her torch down its length. Four flights below, the scaffolding appeared to reassemble itself, as if out of nothing, and the rope was tied firmly to the landing there.

No no fuck no.

Shimmy down that, like a kid on some obscene piece of playground equipment?

Was she fucking *kidding*?

And yet, if she could not go down, then she could only go back up. And strangely, it was the thought of recrossing the three gaps she had already crossed, of climbing back *up* the rickety scaffold, that daunted her most. Down it was.

Only, how? She hunched there, staring at the rope and the awful distance to the lower landing. Four flights equalled eight metres. Only eight metres. But it might as well have been a thousand miles, the way the gulf of the shaft mocked and tempted.

Never had Rita felt so trapped by indecision, so bereft of company, so far from human advice. No one could assist her here, and yet if she didn't get moving she would simply linger on this perch until the time stretched into days, until she weakened from hunger, and in exhaustion simply toppled off.

Except, she didn't have that long. She had only a matter of hours. Whatever it was that was coming down from the Wheel, it would hit before the day was out, and in her gut the warning was inarguable: she could not be anywhere near the top of the Mount when that happened. Not even the lower shaft would be protection. She had to get to the bottom, and then escape through the exit tunnel, and fast.

With a sigh, she once again put the torch, beam up, in her coat pocket, to free both of her hands. Then she addressed the rope. She took hold of it, testing it for give, and found only a little slack, so well had Clara secured the lower end. Clara herself must have climbed down a freely swinging rope, but then tied it off to make it easier for anyone following.

Easier? Fucking easier?

Rita gritted her teeth. She had to do this, must do this. Hands gripped tight, she hefted herself slightly and wrapped her legs around the rope. There would be a proper way to do this, no doubt, a mountaineer technique of shimmying down a line, but she did not know it. All she could do was loosen the grip of her legs a little, and then relax her hands—

Oh fucking lord.

She slipped maybe a foot, the rope burning like a hot wire against her wounded thigh. But she came to a stop when she tightened her grip again. And so, after a pause, she repeated the exercise.

Down she went in a series of lurches, each one making her injured thigh shriek more stridently. Worse, the blood from the bandage was making the rope damp, it felt greasy and slick to her hands. But, damn it, she couldn't do this with only one leg to scissor around the line, she needed to use both.

Down she dropped, and down again, and all the while the rope, tied though it was, danced and swayed under her ill-disposed weight, so that sometimes it felt she was swinging far out from the landing below and hanging ludicrously over the void.

Halfway, more than halfway. And she was sliding faster now, the rope slipping smoothly between her blood-wet legs and hands, but that was okay, she was in control still, she was in—

How it happened she did not know. The rope somehow caught around her ankle and then jammed hard around her knee: the shock of the sudden stop tore her hands from the rope and with a sickening flip she was dangling *upside down,* her arms flailing wildly as only her legs still held to the line.

A sudden blackness had possessed the shaft; she could see nothing; she was going to fall and die. But then her scrabbling fingers brushed against metal below, the grating of the landing. She let go with her legs and slumped with a wet thwack onto the platform.

Thank you thank you thank you she prayed, curled up in a foetal position and eyes squeezed shut, praying—not to any god certainly, she was an atheist as much as ever, but sometimes there was no other form of expression. She had made it. And then, as she shuddered and cried through her closed eyes, it came to her that really she should be thanking Clara, for if the major-domo had not strung the rope, then Rita could not even have got this far.

And what had happened to Clara, for her troubles? It was something that Rita had avoided thinking about, but now, as she lay there recovering, the major-domo, having trod the same path, seemed a very immediate presence to her.

Was Clara really dead? They had all assumed she was, but there had been no confirmation of it. Her last communication could have meant almost anything—and after that there had been only silence. Still, what could that silence mean other than that she had met her end somewhere down here—that the Wheel, having toyed with her so long, had ended it finally?

And yet again, maybe, just maybe, she was *not* dead, but alive somewhere below, insensible and deranged perhaps, but not dead. Maybe Rita would even meet her if she climbed down far enough, and then they could help each other, Rita to bring Clara back to sanity, and Clara to assist Rita with the technicalities of the remaining climb.

It could be, couldn't it?

Rita opened her eyes, found only blackness. Her flashlight must have switched off in the last tumble. She fumbled for it in the jacket pocket, felt horror suffuse her. It wasn't there. It had fallen out. She scrabbled about on the platform, searching for a mad instant, before she remembered her second torch. *It* was still there, thank god, in the other pocket, and gasping in relief she switched it on.

Light, beloved light. But search as she might on the landing, the first torch was nowhere to be seen. It must have gone, plunging away down the shaft. Curious in a dreadful way, Rita switched off her second torch, then peered into the void. Was the first torch still alight down there? Would she be able to see it, from two thousand metres above?

But in the blackness she could discern nothing other than the phantoms that shifted and expanded within her own blind eyes.

And if she called down into that blackness, would Clara answer?

Rita shuddered, clicked the torch back on. No, she would not be shouting into the abyss, the very idea was terrible. And she would have to be careful now, painfully so, with her sole remaining flashlight. If she dropped it, she was done for. And even if she didn't drop it, how long would the battery last? These newer LED flashlights were vastly more long-lived than the older incandescent models, she knew that much, but even they couldn't go on forever.

Another reason not to linger. She had to move. The refuge of this landing, reached with such hardship, was illusory. There was no refuge anywhere in the shaft, it lay only at the bottom, through the tunnel and so finally to the outside world.

Groaning, Rita rose to standing, and then set her foot gingerly to the descent once more.

▲

Back and forth she went on the switchback ladders, down and down, the sameness monotonous, but also endlessly terrifying, as each flight tilted differently under her feet, or gave a different groan or screech. Now and then would come a gap, and another debate within herself, wearier each time, before she gathered the nerve to climb on the scaffold.

And still it got no easier; still her fear did not relent. Still she felt, every second, the acute exposure of her position, the frailty of the thin metal that held the stairs to the scaffold and the scaffold to the walls of the shaft. And even if the whole thing did not collapse beneath her, then at any instant she might simply misstep and plunge over the rail.

How long could a mind bear this kind of strain, she found herself marvelling, before the screaming started, and the mad rush to oblivion?

And yet, even though she was listening acutely all the while for the fatal sound of metal parting, it was some time before she realised that a whispering had arisen around her in the shaft.

It came from above and below equally, almost a radio static mutter, and when she finally paused to listen to it more attentively, still she could not make any sense of it. She descended another four flights, ears cocked and eyes wide. Now the whisper was coming more strongly from below, and she could, straining her hearing, resolve it into words.

'Rita. Rita . . . Are you there? Talk to me, Rita. Just press the *Talk* button.'

It was Richman on the intercom system. He did not know exactly where she was, she reminded herself, the shaft intercom didn't work that way. He was merely broadcasting on all panels at once, and she was drawing near to one now.

Ignore him, she told herself.

Ignore him. Don't talk to him. Let him rot unanswered in his precious safe room.

Ah, but it was a voice, a human voice, here in this soulless stone purgatory, where she had no company but echoes and the cold air running up from the unseen depths. And besides, he would only go on whispering at her if she didn't reply.

So when the intercom panel appeared three landings further down, she paused there, her finger hovering over the *Talk* button.

'Rita, Riiita,' he was crooning, like a man trying to lure his pet cat out of hiding. 'I know you can hear me somewhere down there . . .'

Her finger pressed home. 'What the fuck do you want?' she demanded, her own voice surprising her, it was so ragged and high and strange.

'Rita!' came the response in a delighted tone. 'How far down are you?'

She had already noted the panel number, even without wanting to. It read ES41, which made it the sixth panel down from the top, which meant that she had come down one hundred and fifty flights. God, was that all? That meant she still had over a thousand flights to go. So many, so *many* . . .

But she wasn't going to tell Richman any of that. 'None of your fucking business,' she rasped. 'So, again, what do you want?'

'Oh, only to report that everything is fine up here. I don't know why you're risking your life down in that hole when the worst is over. The sun is out, and there's no wind, so when the rescue helicopter comes it'll be able to land with no trouble at all.'

She stared bitterly at the little speaker. Oh, the cunning bastard. It was a lie—or a wilful denial on his part—but oh, how she wanted to believe it. For if everything was calm and sunny up there, and if a helicopter did come, then she could stop this, she could stop the torment. She need not even attempt to climb back up, she could simply remain here on this landing, which felt perfectly solid, and wait for professional rescuers to reach her. Maybe they would have to abseil down, maybe they would get the service elevator restarted and bring it to her level. But either way, she could *stop,* the fear could *stop.*

She couldn't hide the hateful weakness in her voice, the hope against hope, when she spoke again. 'You can see all that on your TV screens? You know for sure that everything is okay?'

His response was cheery and swift. 'Better than that, I've been outside. I was lying about that whole "time lock on the door" thing. I've been out and I've been on the Terrace and looked up at the Wheel, and I tell you, it's a beautiful day out there.'

The perverse flicker of hope in her died. Definitely he was lying, the sunniness in him was as brittle as chalk; even through the distortions of the intercom she could hear that.

It was just more bullshit. He had not been outside, and everything was not okay, even from what he could see on his security screens. And now he was trying to convince her to come back up, to . . . well, why exactly? What did he want from her?

Maybe just company. Maybe he had begun to sense what Rita had already sensed, the disaster brewing above him, and he could not bear his isolation. Maybe it was as simple a need as that. He did not want to be alone. He wanted her back.

But maybe, a wiser part of her whispered, it had occurred to Richman, locked in his self-imposed cell with his cameras, that she might in fact reach the bottom of the shaft and escape.

He would not like that. Even if he survived the nightmare that was coming, he would not want *her* to be a fellow survivor. For the story she would tell of their ordeal would not be the same as his, would not be at all flattering to Walter Richman. And she understood by now how much that would matter to him. Enough, certainly, for him to be willing to discard her life in the meanwhile.

In which case, all he was trying to do here was to confuse her, to either goad her into making the mistake of going back up the shaft, or to at least delay and bewilder her, so that she might, like Clara before her, become lost and despairing.

She clicked the button a last time. 'I'm gonna survive this, Richman. Just watch.'

And then she was moving on, limping down the next flight of stairs as fast as she dared.

'Good luck!' his voice spat behind her. 'You'll need it, if even Clara couldn't make it down. You'll fall sooner or later, and down you'll go, tumbling over and over, screaming, hitting the walls, the rock tearing an arm off here, a leg off there; I've seen what it's like, what a fall can do to a human body . . .'

It went on, but she was two flights down now; the voice had shrunk to a mutter once more and she could ignore it—even though he was right. She still had impossibly far to go, and for all she knew the greatest horrors still lay ahead of her, and she was already at the borderline of her willpower.

She could not win here.

But she crept on doggedly, and when, an eternity later, she passed the next intercom panel—ES40 it said, which was the right number, for what that was worth—the speaker was silent.

▲

A long, ragged interval followed.

Rita had given up trying not to look at the intercom numbers whenever she passed them, her resolve worn away. Indeed, she was counting them down now, her target intercom ES24, which would mean that she was halfway to the bottom. She celebrated every milestone. ES35. Then, much later, ES30. Just six intercoms to go.

And another thing: all the numbers were in their proper order, so she had guessed right, the panels had not been incorrectly installed, and poor Clara *had* been misled by the Wheel into seeing things that weren't there. But the mountain had no interest in Rita. She was being left mercifully alone.

So she might make it.

She might really make it.

But as she passed by intercom ES29, there came a sudden sharp vibration through the stairs. It swiftly grew into a jolting tremor, kicking at her legs as she clung to the railing, teetering dangerously. A low rumble sounded up and down the shaft, and the stone of the walls seemed to flex, setting all the spider's web of the scaffold and the stairs swaying and creaking, and raising a storm of dust from every surface, particles dancing in the beam of Rita's torch.

Terror flew back at her in a sickening wave. What was happening? Was it the end?

Then the movement calmed, and she was alive still, the stairs holding firm. But her alertness only grew the more taut, for, from far above, there came an even stranger sound: a faint, high-pitched whistling, a hooting as of wind. Then silence.

Oh sweet holy motherfucker.

It was starting up there. Whatever the Wheel had summoned, it was getting close.

What was the time? If it had been, say, five a.m. when she had begun, then surely it must be at least eleven a.m. by now, as impossible as it was to believe in this shaft that there was daylight anywhere in the world. And she still had more than halfway to go. At this pace it would be after dark by the time she reached the bottom, and that was too late. She had to move faster, for she knew in her heart that if she wasn't down by sunset, if she wasn't out from under the Mount before nightfall, then she would not make it down at all.

A hopeless sob escaped her, but she forced herself to stagger down the next flight, trying to go with greater speed, willing her injured leg, stiffened taut now, to bend and bend again. And so on, down the flight after that, and the flight after that . . .

551

In time, she fell almost into a doze as she went, terror notwith-standing. Only to be awakened when a voice was suddenly laughing raucously up and down the shaft.

'Rita! Ha! Can you hear me down there? You should have listened to me! I told you!' It was Richman again, hailing on the intercoms.

She stared down blearily, saw that there was a panel only two flights below her. As the billionaire's mutterings and laughter echoed in the darkness, she limped down to it. It read ES24, the halfway mark, but that did not seem to matter now. She pressed the *Talk* button. 'What are you talking about?'

'There you are! How far down are you now? However far it is, it doesn't matter, because you're going to have to come back up!'

'For fuck's sake, *what*?'

The billionaire's distorted voice was gleeful. 'Clara! I've talked to Clara!'

Rita stared at the hateful little speaker in shock. 'What do you mean—Clara?'

'She's alive after all. She made it out. But *you'll* never do it. You'll have to come back up.'

'Clara is out? Since when?'

'Since yesterday. But she lost her walkie-talkie, and it took her until just now to find another one that works, so she could call and let me know.'

Since yesterday? Clara wasn't dead at all, but had escaped and been free for a whole day? But . . . but her last message. *I'm jumping now.* What had that meant? 'What happened to her?' Rita demanded. 'What happened to her in the shaft?'

Laughter. 'She didn't jump; she just lost her mind there for a while; she had a blackout; she doesn't know for how long, a few hours prob-ably. When she came out of it she had climbed almost to the bottom. But that's where it gets really difficult, climbing wise. The stairs, the gantry, everything is gone completely down there, and she was out of rope to rappel with. So she had to free climb—tough, technical climbing—down the wall of the shaft itself. She barely made it. You never will, Rita. Never.'

'But she got out?'

'Yes, yes, she got to the tunnel and got out. She says it's a hell of a mess outside; half of Base is washed away. But not all of it. The security office is still standing. That's where she found the radio.'

Conflicting emotions raged through Rita. Hope, fear, doubt. 'Is there help down there, did she say? Are people alive? Has a ship come yet?'

'People are alive, I don't know how many, but yes, help is coming. Clara found the satellite phones, too. She's been talking to Hobart. They've had all sorts of troubles getting choppers in here because of the weather, but there're two on the way right now to take us all out, due in an hour or so. You have to come back up, or you might get left behind.'

Rita sagged against the panel. Thank every god imaginable, rescue at last. And yet, and yet . . . here was Richman again, insisting that she go *up*. Could it be another trick? Was it true, what he was saying about Clara? And what about the Wheel?

'Richman,' she said, 'did you feel a tremor a while ago? And hear . . . I don't know . . . but is there any wind blowing up there?'

He sounded puzzled. 'There're no tremors, no wind. Why are you still worrying about that?'

She frowned. The tremor had been very real; he must have felt it. Was he lying?

She pressed the button again. 'Can I speak to Clara myself? Can she call me on this?'

A pause. 'No, no, she can't, not from where she is. The intercom system in the shaft only talks to the control rooms up here. Remember?'

Damn. She did remember; it was true. But what about the rest of it? The tale of Clara's survival? Despite her doubts, it sounded tantalisingly plausible. It explained Clara's long silence, if she'd been in a fugue state for hours, and lost her radio in the shaft, and then had to search for another amid the wreckage of Base . . .

If only it didn't mean that Rita had to go *up* again. For even if rescue was really coming, even if a chopper would be landing on the Terrace an hour from now, there was still the Wheel to consider. It was not done with them, not done with Richman—something awful was coming, and Rita knew she had to be at the bottom of the Mount, not the top.

She said, 'Is Clara *sure* I can't follow her down and get out the way she did?'

'Not a chance,' Richman came back confidently. 'Coming up is your only hope.'

But there was a peculiar edge to his voice. An eagerness, it seemed to Rita. An enthusiasm that didn't fit. After all, hadn't Richman already shown that he didn't care if she lived or died; indeed, that he probably preferred the latter? Why then was he suddenly so keen for her to be rescued alongside him?

In any case, was it really out of the question for her to keep going down? Consider: a helicopter would be landing at Base as well as up at the Observatory, to pick up Clara, right? If Rita could just get close to the bottom of the shaft, even if she couldn't quite reach ground level, then surely the rescuers would be able to find a way to climb up to her?

Yes, yes . . . anything would be better than going upwards. Upwards felt *wrong*.

But something warned her not to tell Richman about this, not yet. She chose her words carefully, pressed the button. 'Okay. Okay, I'll get going. I'll call you when I've made some progress.'

'Excellent.' The relief in him was, once more, too eager, too quick. 'You're doing the right thing, Rita. I know things got pretty hairy these last days, but the worst is over now. You'll see.'

'Fine,' she said. 'Over and out for now.' And took her finger from the button. No. No, she did not trust him, or that eagerness, at all.

She turned to the stairs once more, playing her torch beam over the flights below. Yes, she would continue on down and at least see for herself, at least be sure that the way was really blocked, before she even considered going up again.

Was there a faint tremor beneath her feet—and again, was there, just within hearing, a distant piping sound from high, high above?

She shook her head. Maybe it was phantoms. Maybe everything was okay up there.

But she headed down anyway.

10

THE LOWER STAIRS

IT WAS PERHAPS ABOUT AN hour later—outside, in the normal world, it must now be past noon—that Rita saw the thing, hanging below her.

She had been in another of her walking dozes, hurrying as fast as her fear would allow, still in constant terror at every groan and shiver of the stairs, but her thoughts, from sheer monotony, drifting away. Within the small pool of her torch beam the ladder she climbed was eternally the same ladder, rung by rung leading down to the same steel grate, and then, when she reversed direction, it would be the same ladder again. The uniformity was hypnotising. And all around, the walls of the shaft were unchanging.

Or was that, in fact, true? A doubt came dimly, and Rita paused upon the next landing, played the flashlight across the shaft walls. Was the colour different? She was sure that, when she began the climb, the stone had been a grey-blue. But now the walls were almost an ochre tan. Could that mean that the quality of the rock itself was changing, as she sank deeper into the heart of the Mount? And god, she really was in the belly of the great spire now, wasn't she, with all those vast tonnes of stone above her, pressing down. If she thought about it too much the shaft itself seemed to squeeze and shrink . . . and oh, it would be so easy to lose one's wits in this awful place.

Like Clara had.

Stop it. Clara made it out, remember? Clara is fine. And so will you be.

It helped. Rita took a water bottle from her pocket and drank. It was almost all gone, the water. She should have brought more, not to mention some food, the very notion of which made her feel faint. But why was she so thirsty? It wasn't hot in the shaft; it was cold, with a steady flow of chill air rising from below. Blood loss, maybe. Her injured leg was soaked, that was a lot of fluid to replace . . .

Her thoughts wandered again, dangerously vague. Funny how Clara had said that it was actually hot in the shaft, so hot that she had taken her clothes off. She must have been very confused.

But she made it out.

Rita put the bottle away, wearily turned her torch to the next flights below.

And saw it.

Far down, at the limit of the torch's reach, something was hanging in the shaft.

A white bundled shape. Rita stared in puzzlement, not understanding how the thing could be suspended there. It seemed to be floating in midair, in the wide vacancy between the stairs and the curved wall of the shaft. But then she realised that whatever the thing was, it was connected to a long rope that hung from one of the lateral support struts—the narrow iron beams that, here and there, stretched from the tower of the elevator scaffold across to the shaft walls, steadying the entire structure.

Was it a bag?

Clara had mentioned throwing her backpack away, hadn't she? So was that it?

But it didn't look like a bag. In the torch beam shadows it looked more like—

Oh god. Oh no. Not that.

It couldn't be, Rita told herself. She stared a moment longer, unable to tell, then went clambering down the stairs, heedless of any danger. She had to get close; she had to see for certain.

Maybe a dozen flights down she stopped and aimed the torch again. The thing was there, no more than ten metres below her now, dangling motionless over the abyss, white and hideous in the light. And there could be no doubt anymore.

It was all a lie.

Clara hadn't got out.

Clara hadn't made it to the bottom. She was hanging dead in the torch beam.

In mute horror, Rita let her gaze rise up the rope from which the body dangled. The line was tied in a knot around the horizontal strut, which speared out just below where Rita stood.

Tied. So, after sending her last message—*jumping now*—the major-domo, lost in the Wheel's spell, must have shimmied out along the strut, fixed the line, then dropped into the empty air.

Had she done it to hang herself, like some criminal executed on a gallows?

If so, she had failed cruelly, for the rope must have tangled about her as she fell. Clara now dangled not upright from her neck, but almost sideways, with her feet uppermost, the rope looped about each of her legs, spreading them wide apart. Her arms were lashed helplessly to her sides by another loop, and the final noose about her neck had yanked her head back grotesquely, forcing her tongue out and making her dead eyes bulge as they stared up.

Oh no no no . . .

The major-domo was naked, other than the adornment of the rope. And finally Rita was answered as to the mystery of Clara's frostbite. For yes, each of her feet was missing not only its toes, but the whole lower half, leaving only blunt stubs of heels. And the heels were bloody. She had hobbled to this final end on feet cut and crippled by the metal stairs.

Rita moved again, descending the last few flights to come level with the corpse, her torch beam held on the atrocity all the while. Tears blurred her vision, but she was mute, too torn with pity and grief to weep, or to even give vent to profanity.

She was level with Clara finally—but there was nothing she could do. The body hung a good three metres out in space. Rita could not reach to cut it down, could not even ease the obscene indignity of its pose. Clara must simply hang there, as she had through the last two days, choked and dead like this, while high above the others had worried, and then forgotten about her in their own troubles.

But—oh fuck, had she died straightaway? Or had she woken up from her Wheel trance to find herself like this? Please god let it be that she died without waking up, let it be that she hadn't lingered like this, agonisingly aware, but her arms trapped, unable to help herself in any way . . .

Then suddenly rage was sweeping Rita's grief aside. Fucking Richman. Clara had been dead all along; she had never reached the bottom. *Never.* He had lied again; he had fabricated *all* of it, the whole fantasy about the major-domo escaping. It was deception, designed yet again for one purpose: to get to her.

It was unspeakable. In her fury, she turned brutally from the dangling corpse—there was nothing she could do for it, nothing—and stomped heedlessly down the ladders again, flight after flight, until she came to the next intercom panel.

There, she stabbed the call button and hissed into the mike. 'You bastard; you fucking bastard. Clara is dead. I just found her. She never got out.'

There was a pause, then a clatter of static. 'What? What did you say?'

'Clara is dead! I just found her body! She's hanging from the end of a rope!'

'What?' Richman sounded bewildered. 'What are you going on about? I was talking to her just five minutes ago. She's fine.'

'Stop it, just stop the fucking bullshit, all right? I've seen her damn body; I know what you're trying to do, and it's not working!'

Another pause, then Richman again, sounding deadly cold. 'Rita, I don't know what game you're playing, but Clara is alive. I've talked with her. You're the one who's lying. Or maybe . . . Christ, how long have you been in that damn shaft now? You know how confused Clara became, maybe the same is happening to you? Think. How come you didn't notice her body on the way down, but only discovered it now that you're heading up again? Makes no sense.'

'I'm not going upwards, you fool, I'm still going down. And I'm not losing my mind. But Clara did, and it got her killed. I've *seen* her.'

'No, goddamnit, you haven't!' Richman was angry now. 'You *can't* have!'

A chill curled in Rita. The billionaire's anger sounded genuine. It was not the embarrassed annoyance of a liar caught out in his lie, or even the defiance of a shameless conman doubling down—it was the alarmed irritation of a man hearing news that conflicted with his own reality.

And it came to her starkly: Richman really believed that Clara was alive.

For a second she doubted herself instead. Could *she* be the one imagining things? Had she hallucinated the corpse? Reluctantly, she played her torch beam upwards—and shuddered. Clara was still there, dangling above now like some awful broken sack, half lost again in shadows, but real.

Rita lowered the flashlight, her vision blurred with new tears, and pressed the *Talk* button. 'Richman, when you spoke to Clara on the walkie-talkie, did you really recognise it as her voice? It couldn't be someone else that you're confusing for Clara?'

'Of course fucking not! I've known Clara for years. Do you think I don't know her voice when I hear it? And why would someone else say they were Clara if they weren't? You're not thinking straight, woman.'

One of us isn't thinking straight, Rita noted, but it wasn't her. Richman was being deliberately misled—his thoughts, his very hearing, were being played with. And it could only be the Wheel doing it. The mountain was toying with him.

She tried again. 'Richman, listen to me. What's happening with the weather up there? Are you still watching the Wheel on your screens?'

'That again? Look, the mountain is fine, the weather is fine. Let it go, already.'

He sounded sure—but if the Wheel could convince Richman that he was talking to his dead major-domo on the radio, then surely it could also make him see whatever it wanted him to see through the cameras, and hide what was really happening.

Even as Rita pondered, another tremor rumbled and shook the shaft, rattling the stairs. And once more a sound sighed down from above, a distant whistle of wind that rose and fell, as if a gale had blown briefly in the passageways at the top of the shaft.

But apparently the billionaire could hear none of it, feel none of it, see none of it.

She gave a final effort. 'Walter, look, I don't know if you can really leave your room or not, but if you can, for the love of god leave now and head down. It might not be too late.' She didn't believe that; it *was* too late, but surely it was better that he try, rather than sit there meekly to await his end.

But the reply was only scathing. 'Fuck you, I know what you're doing with all this crap about Clara. You'd do anything, say anything, to try and put me in danger, now that rescue is here.'

'Rescue? You really think that's coming? You said the helicopters were less than an hour away. Shouldn't one have landed by now?'

'They're coming! Clara is in constant contact with them via satellite phone. They've struck stronger headwinds than expected, that's all. But it'll only delay them another hour at most.'

Rita shook her head. For the first time there was a hint of mania in his certainty. And maybe none of this mattered anyway, maybe he truly was trapped in his safe room by the time lock, come what may.

Enough then. She could no more help Richman than she could help poor Clara, hanging above.

Time to move. 'I'm sorry,' she said into the intercom, as her farewell. 'I don't know how to convince you. Good luck.'

She turned away, ignoring the tide of invective that spewed from the speaker in her wake, and returned to the ordeal of the descent.

▲

Now she was on unexplored ground.

It was doubtful that poor Clara had made it much further than this, before the Wheel took her mind away and sent her climbing randomly up and down over the same section of stairs. So there would be no more fixed ropes to help Rita in the difficult spots. She was on her own.

On the other hand, she could at least dismiss Richman's tale about the stairs having collapsed entirely near the bottom of the shaft. That was a report he had supposedly received from Clara. It was possible thus that the stairs remained intact all the way down.

So she had to hope anyway. But in fact her progress, in the hour or so following her final conversation with Richman, was more torturous than ever. The stairs only deteriorated the deeper she went, with more and more ladders wrenched askew, forcing her to climb again and again on the scaffolding, dropping painfully from beam to beam, knuckles white on the metal. Terror assailed her afresh every single time, and there was still so far to go.

And Richman would not shut up. She had sworn to herself that she would not speak with him again, but there was nothing she could do to stop him hailing the intercoms. His voice, sometimes a faraway mutter when she was between intercoms, sometimes a hectoring shriek if she was passing by a panel, was her constant companion in the darkness.

'Clara called again,' he was saying at one point as she passed by a speaker. 'She doesn't sound very dead to me, you know. And she's worried about you, Rita. She says you're crazy for not going back up.

She says you're going to die down there.' And his voice sounded almost dreamily detached now, as if envisioning something pleasant.

By the time she approached the next panel down, he had moved on, by some process of free association, to the subject of her father. 'Of course, Richard always said you were unstable. Yes, he was happy that you two were talking again, but it was his belief that the death of your mother permanently unhinged something in you. He thought that maybe if you hadn't been so set against men and against marriage, that maybe if you'd had children of your own, it might have fixed you . . .'

Good god. She shut it out and shuffled down more ladders until his voice was reduced again to indistinct mutterings. But when she came to the next intercom, he was still on the same theme.

'Displacement, he thought it might have been. Delusions of grandeur. All this nonsense about *presences* that only *you* in all the world can detect. It's one way to feel special, I suppose, when you aren't special at all. Was that how it was? The daughter of a man like him, born without any of his talent, and denying her own womanhood, cooking up *something* that would make her important?'

Rita raised an eyebrow. So Richman was not even a believer in presences anymore? It was all *nonsense*, something *cooked up*? After everything that had happened, and was happening still, he was suddenly a master of reason, a sceptic?

Blind fool.

For all the while, the signs were clear that the final cataclysm was brewing up above. Tremors were shivering through the stairs every few minutes now, and strange moans and whistles and thuds sounded again and again from the top of the shaft. And down where Rita was, the slow ooze of air from the bottom had strengthened to a gusty upward breeze, drawn by some vacuum-like hunger above.

Oh yes, it was a warning, she must hurry, she must hurry. It must be mid-afternoon by now. But shortly after passing an intercom panel marked ES14—which meant she still had three hundred and fifty flights to go, or seven hundred metres, nearly a third of the journey yet—she came upon exactly what she had been fearing most, ever since finding Clara.

It was another collapsed section. Two ladders and most of the scaffolding had fallen away, leaving a complete gap of four metres, a naked drop without a single crossbeam that might be climbed down. Yes, Rita had previously descended gaps just as wide—but this time there was no rope, ready strung, to help her do it. Clara had not made it this far.

Rita crouched on the upper landing, shining the torch about in growing panic. And that was another thing, the torch itself—was the beam getting dimmer now? How long had it been since she switched it on? Four hours, five? It wouldn't last forever. But forget that for now, it was a distraction. *Concentrate. Think.* How the fuck was she going to get down to the platform below? There was nothing but air.

Well, no, that wasn't quite true. The load-bearing upright struts of the scaffold still remained in place. One of them ran from her landing to the landing directly below. Couldn't she use that to climb down, just as she had used Clara's ropes?

Except that it wasn't a rope; it was a steel girder, smooth and sharp-edged. She could not hold onto *that*. She would slip and plunge away in the darkness, the walls of the shaft rushing by, tearing off her skin, the wind wailing in her ears—

Stop it. Stop thinking. Just do it. Force yourself to move. You have no choice anyway.

And maybe even fear itself does approach prostration eventually, for without any of the moans of her early forays over the abyss, Rita only swung in grim silence down onto the strut, the torch stuffed once more in her pocket. Her arms and legs wrapped around the steel, the corners digging into her flesh, she began her sliding descent, for all the world like a slow-motion fireman on a pole.

Bizarrely, as she slid she was suddenly aware of Richman's voice, wafting up on the cold breeze, lecturing. 'It's what a superior mind, all superior minds, realise at the ultimate point of decision, and it's this: there is no right and wrong, there is only the decision, and the act, and the results of the act, victory or loss, survival or death, nothing else . . .'

Jesus. *That* tired old shit now?

Fuck. Stop. Ignore him. She was a metre down, three metres to go to safety.

Then abruptly the shaft throbbed and rumbled around her, and the girder seemed to warp like a bowstring under her grip. Another tremor! She clung there an absurd moment, a hapless rider at a vertical rodeo, then the metal kicked her free.

For the second time, she fell.

And for the second time, she crashed into the landing below, and was saved.

But the impact was harder this time, much harder. She slammed face first into the grate, her nose blossoming with pain as if broken, her shoulder hitting too, and a bone—a collar bone, maybe—snapping audibly. But worst of all, by the far the worst, she felt the torch being jolted free from her pocket, watched as it bobbled a moment on the platform. She reached for it and missed, then shrieked as it went over the edge, tumbling, dropping irretrievably away into the abyss, the beam drawing endless circles, mapping the shaft as it went, an eternity of falling, until the light snapped out all of a sudden, either hitting the ground or some other obstruction, and then—

Darkness. Utter lightlessness. And silence, thick, as the tremor passed, leaving only the whisper of Richman's voice rippling along the shaft walls, like an echo of the disaster, '. . . someone like you would never understand, for, as the saying goes, to a creature born in a cage, freedom itself is the crime.'

▲

Rita made herself move on quickly.

Yes, she could have given up there and then. She could have curled into a ball of catatonic despair, or retreated into hysteria, shrieking into the void until the darkness could be borne no longer, and she threw herself off her ledge to end it.

But she allowed herself none of these luxuries. Instead, before terror could paralyse her, and before even taking stock of her injuries, she reached out in the blackness, found the first step of the next descending ladder, and on her hands and knees began to crawl her way down, lizard-like, pressed flat to the rungs, feeling ahead with the touch of her bruised fingers. One flight down, then a landing, then turn, hands groping blindly, to find the next flight, and so on.

It could be done; it could be done.

That mantra, and the fact of motion, was enough to make the terror withdraw a fraction.

Now she could take stock, even as she crept on. Her nose was bleeding, or at least it was warm and wet whenever she put a hand to it; and there were other cuts on her face; and her left shoulder cracked with every moment, the pain fresh and sharp compared to the throb of her wounded thigh. She was, in all, a wreck: exhausted, delirious, losing too much blood altogether—but so what? She was still capable of movement, that was all that mattered.

Fine. Except that she was blind now; she might easily, even at a crawl, plunge off a landing by mistake. And what if she came to another gap, a collapsed section, a missing ladder? What if, searching for a rung that wasn't there, she simply overbalanced and went tumbling down? Even if she didn't actually fall, another such gap would be the doom of her anyway, as it could never be crossed in the blackness.

But that didn't matter either, not until it occurred. In the meantime she must move, and move, and not let herself scream.

In the intensity of such focus, it was some time before she realised that Richman had stopped talking. The only sounds in the shaft now, other than her own, were the faint rumbles and groans caused by the tremors. They had become almost continuous, an eternal, half-heard thunder. That, and the whisper in her ears of the air rising around her, the breeze tugging more and more insistently, a nagging alert that the fatal moment above was coming closer.

Ignore, ignore, just move.

Down Rita clambered. Already she had lost count of the flights she had descended since dropping the torch, nor was there hope any longer of getting her bearings from the numbers on the intercom panels. She must merely forge on in her blindness until some end was reached— the bottom, or some impassable gap and the inevitable fall to her death, or simply until insanity took her completely.

Then Richman suddenly spoke again, loud, almost in her ear, making her jump even in her crouch, as if he had touched her in the dark. But of course it only meant that she must be alongside an intercom speaker. Yet it wasn't just his voice that shocked her out of her stupor, it was what he said.

'I took a piss in the Hand of God. Did you know that, Rita? I pissed on it.'

Her eyes went wide in the blackness. His voice had lost its hectoring tone. Now it was reflective, and perfectly sane-sounding, for all that he must be speaking from pure madness.

'No, seriously,' he said, as if in answer to her thought. 'Nobody knows it, because I've never told anyone before, even though I was asked all the time about what I did on the summit, what I saw in the cave there. Of course, I'm only telling you now because you'll be dead soon. Do you hear? When the helicopter comes for me, I'm not going to tell them you're down there. I'll tell them you vanished, that I don't know where you went. We'll all fly away without you, and no one will find your body for months.'

She nodded to herself. Unquestionably, he was mad. For one thing, he had forgotten that, by his story, Clara was alive and knew Rita was in the shaft. Even his own crazed logic was collapsing.

Richman chatted serenely on. 'Now, I know what you're thinking—you're thinking that I was in an altitude suit when I reached the top of the Wheel, sealed and pressurised, so how could I take a piss? Well, fair enough, obviously I didn't simply hang my prick out at minus seventy degrees and in almost zero atmosphere. It's not even possible, in a suit. There's no zip, no fly. But the urine is accessible—it's captured via tubing and stored in a compartment in the thigh, and that compartment can be opened and emptied without removing the suit. Are you following all these details?'

Rita almost nodded again, as if he could see her. She was hesitating on the landing, knowing that she should keep moving, but bizarrely fascinated by his tale. Was it true, had he really done it?

'So there I am, in the Hand of God, and I step into the cave, and I know that no one can see me there. I look around and there's nothing of interest, it's just an overhang of rock, nothing there at all, for all the stupid myths that people believe. And I think to myself, should I leave some mark that I was here? Carve my name in the stone?

'Then it comes to me, something even better. I pop the urine compartment and pull out the container. The piss in there is not fully heated; it's a half-frozen mush, not quite solid, not quite liquid. And quick as I can, I smear it all around the cave. Most of it is boiling away as I go, but enough of it clings there to make it worthwhile, frozen to the walls forever.

'And that's the point—forever is exactly how long it will be there. As long as the Wheel itself stands, my piss will be on its summit. Is there a better way to say how much I fucking *own* that mountain? I owned it on that day; I've owned it ever since; I own it still, and there's nothing the Wheel can do about it. Even after all the shit of these last few days, I'm still here, my house is still here. So I've beaten it again.

'You can feel that, right? With your precious special senses? The Wheel has spent its *all* in this attack; it's got nothing left. And what's more, it won't get another chance. It took it forty bloody years to save up the strength to try and get me this time, so if it wants another shot it'll take forty years more—and by then who cares, I'll be long gone.

'So I win.

'Do you get that?

'I *win*.'

Rita started moving again, not needing to hear more. And lord, the question wasn't whether or not he was mad now, the question was had he been mad all along, even when he was young and famously leading his huge team in their efforts against the Wheel? To scoop out his frozen piss to slather about the summit . . . was that a sane act? But then what did madness or sanity even mean to people like him, when money and power were their only standards?

It was all irrelevant. Movement was all that mattered. Because whatever else Richman was right or wrong about, he was dead wrong in thinking that the Wheel was exhausted. Rita's every sense shrilled that it was instead coming to the full flood of its power, and to the long-awaited fulfilment of its vengeance upon the billionaire. And he was oblivious.

On, on she pressed, crawling in the blackness, the breeze gusting in her face, almost a wind now. Sometimes she reached too far with her groping hands and overbalanced and fell chin first to the step below, banging her broken nose, or wrenching her fractured shoulder, reigniting the agony. But she let none of it stop her; there was less time than ever, the urgency in the air a greater prod than all the pain in the world. She had to get out, had to.

She didn't know how many intercoms she must have passed in the darkness without hearing a word from Richman, but suddenly he was calling out once more from a speaker close at hand, piercing and exultant. 'Do you hear that, Rita? Do you hear that sound? There's a helicopter out there, at last. It's landing on the Terrace. Listen to it!'

He left the channel open, apparently so that she could hear the noise of the helicopter in the background. And the thing was, she *could* hear something: a droning over the speaker, tinny and distant, yet powerful, rising and falling.

But it didn't sound like a helicopter to Rita. It didn't sound like anything human at all. It reminded her of the hum a swarm of bees would make, or worse, a swarm of wasps, rising furiously to attack an intruder. But it wasn't bees or wasps either.

She knew what it was.

It was the voice of the Wheel, ululating in full cry now around the Observatory.

11

THE BOTTOM

THE INTERCOM CLICKED OFF AT last. Rita lingered a few moments by the panel anyway, wondering. What was Richman doing now up there? Was he looking eagerly from screen to screen in his safe room, trying to spot an imaginary helicopter landing on the Terrace, on an imaginary calm, sunny day? Was he so far gone, maybe, that he could actually *see* that?

But lord, even down here, something like two kilometres below Richman, the imminence of disaster was becoming ghastly. The stairs trembled constantly under Rita's hands, jolting fiercely now and then, and the wind was starting to race up the shaft, moaning through the scaffolding as it went.

She must keep going. Yet she hesitated still, wondering if she should call Richman back on the intercom, to try one last time to save him, to tell him what was really happening. Even in the dark, she might be able to find the button. But no . . . it was too late, she knew, much too late. *Move.*

She crawled on again, down flight after flight. She gave no quarter to the pain any longer, or fretted about what would happen if she came to a gap in the stairs. There was only the urgency, and the wind streaming upwards, beating against her. Soon she could hear little else but the rush of it in her ears.

Faster, faster she pushed, heedless of anything but escape now—and yet, what was that scratching sound that barely cut through the din?

Then she had it: she was passing by another intercom panel, and Richman was yelling through it, she could just discern his words.

'I told you! I told you! The chopper has landed and Clara is right outside my door now. She's banging on it. I can hear her yelling. I can't open it, but she says they've found a way to get in anyway. It'll only take a little while, then I'll be gone!'

And Rita had time to shape only a single thought, horrified: that whatever it was that was banging on Richman's door, it was not his major-domo, it was nothing remotely human at all . . .

Then she was plunging on into the wind, and really it had grown into a gale now, a vast inhalation drawn by the impending catastrophe above, roaring up the shaft, stinging her already battered flesh and making the stairs clank and sway on their loosened moorings. Awful, awful, nothing she had known had ever been as bad as this, the darkness, the shout of the wind around her, the fear that she had only minutes left to live, that once more she was a tiny mote caught upon a giant wave that was about to break.

Then she fell again.

Her hand groped out, found only the wind, and she tumbled into nothingness, screaming soundlessly. For an immeasurable instant she plummeted into the gale. Then she hit metal again, hard, the breath slammed from her so completely it did not seem, as she writhed and rolled and came to a stop, that she could ever get air back into her lungs.

But at last breath came, gasping and convulsive, and amazingly nothing seemed broken, or at least broken any worse than before. She must have toppled only a flight or two, and maybe even the wind had helped, uplifting and slowing her fall, even as its awful voice bawled endlessly at her.

There was no time to stop, no time to wonder. She righted herself somehow in the nightmare dark, crawled on again. Down and down, thinking nothing, hoping nothing, deafened, but feeling great thuds and contortions from the stone tube around her, the whole Mount hunkering under the assault.

Then she came up against a barrier of some kind, a great tangle of metal. She clutched about in the dark, felt steel all bent and twisted, piled heaps of it. It must be wreckage fallen from above, ladders and scaffolding, all tangled together. The blockage seemed huge, as if it filled the shaft from side to side.

But she must not stop. She ducked belly flat and squirmed beneath the mess. There was just space enough down along the ladder. Jagged points tore at her skin, ripped her clothes to rags. *Naked*, she thought crazily, t*hey were all naked when they died*. But at last she was through, and the stairs seemed clear once again. Down another flight, and another. And then—

The ladder she was descending ended, and she felt something utterly shocking under her hand. It was stone. Flat, smooth stone. Not metal, not the grill of one of the landings. It was bedrock.

She scrabbled about in wonder. Stone, stone—it was the bottom of the shaft!

She had made it, despite everything she had made it!

She was weeping again, her bruised cheek to the ground. Her hands now came upon a wall. She groped along it sideways for a metre or so, and yes, it curved as it went, it was the shaft's circular wall. There was no mistake. She was down!

But—

Her scrabbling became more urgent. Where was the way out? There should be a door of some sort here, opening into what would be a long tunnel that led away through the base of the Mount to the final exit. But as she continued to crawl along the curving wall, occasionally climbing over wreckage fallen from above, she found nothing. Where was it?

The wall went on. Goddamn, it couldn't be that long of a circuit, could it? Had she already completed a full turn? How could she know in the dark? She pushed on, and it was only when she was clambering over a third piece of wreckage that she finally realised: it was actually the same piece of wreckage that she was climbing over for the third time. She stopped, blinking blindly.

There was no door.

She huddled there a moment, eyes wide and unseeing and terrified. There was no door. But that was madness. Terror raging through her, she completed another circuit, again found only smooth bedrock, refusing her. She had been tricked! It was all a lie, there was no tunnel, no exit. She had come all this hideous way only to be trapped.

She collapsed then, sobbing. Beneath her, the cruel stone was throbbing with earthquakes, and the wind was an ecstasy of noise, the Mount groaning in mortal pain. It was almost time; it was almost the end, and she was blind. There was nowhere she could go now, nothing she could do; she was defeated; the shaft had won; she was going to die here.

No, said a voice.

But not a voice. Rita did not stir in the blackness, she remained huddled and weeping on the floor, but her mind seemed to withdraw from herself now, lifting away and then looking down on her own body, even though there was no light to do so. And in that withdrawn space, she was not alone.

You don't need to die, said the voice calmly. *You only need to think, and you can live.*

She regarded this statement with bemusement, strangely unworried. Who was speaking to her? No one else was in the shaft. It wasn't a presence, not as she had ever known one. And it certainly wasn't the Wheel; the voice had none of the lofty austerity with which she associated the mountain. And yet she wasn't alone.

So who was there?

Who spoke?

The voice ignored her. *There is indeed an exit, and you have all the clues you need to find it.*

Clues?

Can you feel the wind anymore?

The wind? Rita could *hear* it, god knew, but now that the voice drew her attention to it, she could no longer *feel* it. It wasn't shrieking around her anymore; the air where she lay was almost still. And yet from over her head the howling went on. So from where was the air being drawn into the shaft?

And think, the voice continued, serenely, *would the exit tunnel connect with the absolute bottom of the shaft? Does that make sense? Wouldn't there need to be a certain amount of space left spare at the bottom to fit things like the elevator workings and the foundations of the gantry, a level below the level where the tunnel enters? So, if you've reached the very bottom, then that must mean . . . Can't you see the answer?*

And then she could. In an instant she was plunged back into her ruined body, with all its pain and defeat, and the reassuring company of the voice was gone as if it had never been there.

She reared up off the floor.

Of course, of course. The exit must lie one or two flights *up* from the absolute bottom. In her maddened blind descent she must have passed it by. All she had to do was go back up.

She clambered across the juddering floor, found the ladder unerringly, and crawled upwards. At the first landing she groped about but could feel only vacancy on either side—it wasn't here.

She climbed again, up another flight. At its top she found herself ascending into the full force of the wind once more—but the gale was blasting at her from side on. She stared into it sightlessly.

Yes, this had to be it; she had to be facing the tunnel now. She crept forwards into the wind, and her clutching fingers passed from the steel of the grating to suddenly encounter rough concrete.

God yes! This must be a platform, like the one at the top of the shaft that extended out from the curve of the walls to meet the stairs.

She crawled on. The concrete bucked beneath her suddenly as another quake hit, a big one, tossing her to the ground. Where was the damn door? She was still so blind—was she even facing the right way anymore? She groped in panic.

And then she heard it, a thin screaming that cut through the roar of the wind. It was a voice coming from an intercom panel, the last of them. She must be right by the entrance to the tunnel.   .

Hurry. She lurched upright, tottered towards the sound, and found a wall, and yes, a corner, a doorway, an opening from which the wind yelled in its ultimate frenzy. And from the intercom, a matching yell. 'The Hand of God!' Richman was crying. 'The Hand of God!'

Now, was Rita's only thought, *it's happening now. The end. Get out or die.*

She fell forwards through the doorway, and even as she did so, there came a mighty thud and clatter behind her, and she knew that more of the scaffolding had come tumbling down from high above, and that she had been an instant from death. Again.

But now she was in the tunnel. There was still no light, but she crawled forwards into the scream of the wind, across a carpeted floor that leapt and shook like a living thing, quake after quake. *I am not reborn yet,* she found herself thinking over and over. *I'm not reborn yet, but I'm in the birth canal . . .*

How long was this tunnel? A hundred metres? Two hundred? Either way, it must be traversed on her hands and knees, for the wind was too strong for her to stay on her feet. From time to time she raised her battered head to stare briefly ahead into the blackness, eyes stinging, hoping to see a glint of daylight ahead—if it *was* still day—but every time the midnight-dark in the tunnel remained unrelenting.

Around her, the Mount wrenched and heaved, and she was beginning to discern a terrible pattern to it now, a repetition to the quakes.

Then at last, through slitted eyelids, she saw it, a pinprick star ahead of her in the black. A light, far away. She put her head down and forced herself into the gale for another age, then looked up again, and yes, it was now unmistakably a rectangle of light, a doorway, glowing a dark orange, as if a fire burned beyond—or the last glow of sunset.

Could it be, could it really still be day outside? The *same* day? Had no more than ten hours elapsed during her ordeal in the shaft?

She was weeping again, exhausted, elated, barely able to force headway into the gale: it was howling with ever more frenzy through the tunnel. Quakes pounded the ground beneath her again and again—and finally she realised, appalled, what it was about the pattern that she recognised.

She had witnessed this before, long ago, at the moment of her mother's death. After the first great rock had shattered the balcony on which they had been standing, leaving her mother hanging on its edge, Rita had looked up and seen the second great boulder being readied to fall. Some force had tugged and tugged at it, until finally it broke away.

The quakes that came now, shaking the whole Mount over and over, were exactly the same. They were a determined wrenching, a heaving, to break something loose—as if some great hand had taken hold of the Mount and was trying to haul the peak up by its very roots.

Out, out, she had to get out! She laboured forwards, and now dust and tiny flecks of stone were raining down from the tunnel roof with every great heave. Despite the roar of the wind she could hear or sense the clatter of more steel collapsing back in the shaft, the great staircase, the tallest ever built, collapsing like so many chopsticks.

Ahead, daylight taunted her. She could now see that the tunnel opened into a foyer of some kind, a couch was visible, and beyond that a wall of glass in which all the panels were shattered. The sliver of sky beyond was now a bushfire red . . .

Stones were raining on her, hurting, and the wrenches had become massive, slamming and slamming and slamming. But the threshold was before her at last; she was crawling through the dust and debris into the foyer, the light dazzling even though it was no more than the last afterglow.

Just a few metres more.

But now she was thrown to the floor, even as she reached for freedom, the earth kicking catastrophically, titanically, *slam, slam, slam*, and behind her the tunnel was collapsing and flying stone splinters were lacerating her back.

The wrenches came again, a crescendo.

Slam, SLAM, SLAM.

Then—

SLAM.

With a single, shuddering reverberation, it all stopped, as if the gears of some mighty engine had abruptly seized. The wind caught, then snuffed out like a flame. The ground fell uneasily still, seeming to pant in exhaustion under Rita's hands. There came a patter of stones and other debris raining in the ruined tunnel behind her, followed by silence.

Then a new sound arose, from outside, a low crumbling noise that built quickly to a roar, a thunder. It was the sound of something immense falling, tumbling slowly down the side of the Mount. It *was* the Mount, or some large part of it, collapsing down itself. It rose to an unbearable din, and the earth shook a final time as vast weights crashed to the ground outside, tremendous, godlike thumps. Then it faded away once more to silence and stillness.

Rita lay unmoving, waiting. But the quiet only stretched out, ringing in her ears. Whatever had happened out there, it was done.

She rose unsteadily, dust- and blood-streaked, half-naked in torn clothes, her face blackened, one eye swollen all but shut, covered in muck, her injured leg useless—and yet she limped determinedly towards the outer doors. She must see it herself; she must *know*.

Upright, she walked out from under the Mount at last, seven days and five hours since she had first entered Walter Richman's house.

Outside, dust was everywhere. Through the haze Rita could only guess at the vast heaps of rubble that now lay in ramps against the Mount, both to her left and right. God only knew how much of Base had been buried. But her amazement was reserved for the sky. Above the dust, the heavens were clear. She had been certain through these last hours that some kind of storm was raging over the top of the Mount. But the red sunset sky was cloudless.

She walked further out from the mountainside, the dust thick on her skin, choking in her throat, but her gaze still turned upwards. Gradually the higher slopes of the Mount came into view, and then finally the summit region. But it was all changed, the familiar shoulder shape of the peak had been scored with mighty rifts and scoops, great chunks had been cleaved away and thrown down, reshaping the summit entirely.

But that wasn't the most shocking thing. Above the summit, something shimmered in the twilight air. At first Rita thought it was the funnel of some colossal tornado writhing over the Mount. But then she realised that it was not really a visible thing at all, it was a vortex made of force as much as of air, a whirlwind that only eyes such as hers might see.

She followed its length, winding sinuously though the upper airs, an invisible tube of tightly spinning potency, lifting away and withdrawing towards its source, and that source was the Wheel.

The Wheel! She faced it fully now. Its western face was bathed in the red of the sunset, accentuating its own crimson hues, so that it soared up as an infinitely massive wall of ruby, glorious, shining all the brighter the higher it climbed, until its upper third was almost too dazzling to contemplate, the red turning to gold and then, at the crystal point of the faraway summit, to searing white fire.

The Hand of God. It was from there that the unseen funnel had descended, and to that freezing height the funnel was now retracting. But even as it went, the whirling tube was still spun tightly about its core, and held there, within the grip of the wind, was the prize for which all this had been fought.

That prize was already several kilometres above Rita where she stood, already too small for human eyes to discern. But by some other sense Rita beheld it even so, and recognised what it was. High above, and being carried higher by the wind-formed hand, was a miniscule human figure.

Alive, she was sure of that. Tiny limbs flailed, seemed to clutch at the void in search of a hold, as if falling, even as the figure rose.

Alive, even as it ascended beyond the regions breathable to man, even as it was drawn higher into the sterile stratosphere. For the shape was cradled and treasured, it seemed to Rita's special senses, within a pocket of air that the Wheel's long arm had created for that very purpose, to carry the prize unharmed and aware to the uttermost heights.

How high exactly, Rita would never know. For at last the distance was too great even for her enhanced sight, and the dot that was Walter Richman vanished against the golden glow of the upper mountain, twenty-five kilometres above her head. Even the funnel itself receded from her view.

But a last sensation came down to her from the high summit. A voiceless clarion of satisfaction and exultation. The Wheel, victorious.

Then a cloud seemed to pass over the sinking sun. The golden mountain dimmed to an enormous shadow, and night came on, cold, and Rita was coughing from the dust in her throat.

She staggered in her pain and weariness, took directionless steps. What now? All around through the dust she could see only the great ramps of rubble, and beyond them the wreckage of Base—earthquake and tsunami and landslide had all wrought their havoc here, and she recognised nothing.

But no, there, one structure still stood intact, a multi-storey resort-like building, set on a rise and made of solid concrete: the staff block. Its lower floors looked ravaged yes, but the upper levels less so. And on the balconies—god, the relief!—figures were emerging tentatively now, to stare up in wonder, pointing to the Observatory.

Rita glanced up herself to the summit of the Mount, saw again the great rifts and scoops that had been torn from the peak. She could not see the Cottage from this angle, but she knew all the same that it would bear similar scars. And that one such rift had laid open Richman's special safe room, tearing away its walls, so that the whirlwind could pluck the billionaire out into the open air, and into the gleeful grip of his nemesis.

And when, exactly, she wondered, had his sanity returned? When had he realised that he was caught within the wind's grip, defenceless in midair, stripped of all aid of money or power, and being whirled aloft, higher and higher, to his death?

And how long exactly, she wondered, with a last look up to the fading summit of the Wheel, would it be before the mountain, savouring its slow revenge, would let that death occur?

Shuddering, she dropped her gaze once more. The people on the staff-building balconies had noticed her now, and were signalling, calling.

Night deepened. Painfully, she began the long limp down the slope towards them.

EPILOGUE 1

Selected articles, July through December, 2017

Billionaire out of Contact. *Emergency services in Tasmania have confirmed that all communication with Theodolite Isle, controversial home to billionaire climber Walter Richman, has been lost for over twenty-four hours since an earthquake struck the region on Saturday afternoon local time.*

A spokesman said that although the quake was only moderate in strength, 5.1 on the Richter Scale, communications at remote locales can often be easily interrupted. A rescue helicopter is being dispatched early Monday morning, and nearby ships have been put on alert.

Concerns Grow for Missing Billionaire. *Climbing billionaire Walter Richman and his staff remain uncontactable into a fifth day. Repeated rescue flights to the remote location have been forced back by weather that officials have described as being 'as poor as have ever been experienced'. Ships in the area have been diverted to the island, but the nearest, Australian Antarctic research vessel* Aurora Australis, *remains some two day's sailing away yet. Walter Richman has only lived on the island some three months, after the completion of his controversial residence there early in . . .*

Rescuers Reach Stricken Isle, Cannot Land. *Rescue helicopters yesterday reached Theodolite Isle in the face of hostile weather, but were unable to make landing there in high winds and limited visibility, before being forced to turn* *back. Pilots reported that the little they could discern of conditions on the island suggested that the port facilities there had suffered severe damage. It is now being speculated that though the earthquake of six days ago was not strong, it may have caused a large-scale avalanche or landslide upon the nearby Wheel, resulting in a catastrophic tsunami . . .*

BREAKING NEWS—*Second Quake Strikes Missing Billionaire's Isle.* *Australian earthquake monitors are reporting that at around 5 p.m. local time a major quake registering 7.9 struck in the region of Theodolite Isle, some seven days since an earlier quake cut off communications there. Officials meanwhile hope to have rescuers on site within twenty-four hours, with weather in the region improving at last, and with the Australian Antarctic research vessel the* Aurora Australis *now less than a day's sail away . . .*

BREAKING NEWS—*Disaster on Billionaire's Isle.* *Reports of massive devastation are coming from Australian Antarctic research ship the* Aurora Australis, *which at dawn this morning finally docked at Theodolite Isle, eight days since communications there were lost, and following a series of earthquakes. It is not known yet if there are casualties, or if . . .*

BREAKING NEWS—*Billionaire Feared Dead. Many Others Missing.* *It is now feared that Walter Richman, billionaire and renowned mountain climber, may have perished in the series of quakes and a massive tsunami that have struck Theodolite Isle over the last eight days. Fears are also held for many of the over one hundred staff members who work on the island. Numbers of survivors have not yet been confirmed, but it is thought to be low . . .*

Survivors Talk to Investigators. *The forty-seven known survivors of the disaster on Theodolite Isle, now in emergency care in Hobart, have been giving detailed accounts of their ordeal to the authorities. The official death toll currently stands at seventy-three, with another twenty still missing, including billionaire Walter Richman . . .*

Daughter of Architect Among Survivors. Ms Rita Gausse, the daughter of the renowned Australian architect Richard Gausse, is the sole survivor from those who were stranded in the residence atop Observatory Mount (a house designed by her father) during last month's disaster there. It has been reported that she and five others, including billionaire Walter Richman, influential construction magnate Kushal Mangalam Ambini, and famed interior designer Madelaine Reynard, were marooned atop the mount by the tsunami that devastated the island below.

Ms Gausse is reported to have escaped down an emergency stairway. The fate of the other five remains unknown, nor has any sign of their remains so far been located.

Inquiry Announced into Billionaire's Death. A Coronial Inquiry has been launched by the Tasmanian Department of Justice into last month's disaster on Theodolite Isle, which resulted in the death of at least ninety people, with many still missing, presumed dead, including billionaire Walter Richman. The terms of the inquiry will include . . .

Irony of Billionaire Climber's Death. Friends and family of billionaire Walter Richman have reflected upon his life and death at a memorial ceremony held in New York yesterday to mark his passing.

The main speaker, business associate and former climbing partner from the 1975 conquest of the Wheel, Daniel Simmonds, said, 'He loved that mountain. He was more at peace there than I ever saw him anywhere else. He did not fear the Wheel and its formidable reputation as so many of us did. Oh, he respected it, but he knew it lay within his own capabilities to conquer it, and he was right. It did not surprise me in the least that he finally built his house as near to the Wheel as possible. It was only fitting. That he died there might be seen by some as an irony: the man who conquered the Wheel conquered by it in turn. But I'm sure he would not have seen it like that. He would have seen it as truly coming home . . .'

Assessors Report on State of Billionaire's Home. Engineers have finished their assessment of Walter Richman's stricken residence atop Observatory Mount, and of all the other facilities upon Theodolite Isle, in the wake of the disaster there in June.

A preliminary report suggests that the Observatory residence, Walter Richman's grandiose mansion excavated into the top of the Mount, has suffered too much damage to be salvageable, with many sections of the multi-storied complex remaining inaccessible due to collapse or landslide. In fact, a submission will be made to the Coronial Inquest into the disaster that the extensive excavations into the Mount's summit may well have contributed to the summit's collapse during the second quake.

At the foot of the Mount, damage to the port and town of Base is equally severe, but it is thought that at least the port facilities and the weather station can be returned to working order . . .

Billionaire Officially Declared Dead. Some five months after the disaster that destroyed his home, billionaire mountain climber Walter Richman has been declared officially dead by Tasmanian courts. Though Richman's body has not been recovered from the ruins of the Observatory residence, it has been ruled that as his last known position was within the section of the residence most heavily damaged by the second earthquake, now inaccessible, it was legally reasonable to assume that his remains lie there. His estate and business empire, estimated to be worth in excess of seventy billion US dollars, will now pass to his family . . .

What Now for the Wheel? In the wake of the disaster upon Theodolite Isle in which billionaire climber Walter Richman and ninety-two others lost their lives, the focus has rightly been upon the recovery of the deceased and the treatment of the survivors. But with investigations into the disaster now winding up (the Coronial Inquest has finished with submissions and is due to report its findings next year) the climbing community has begun to discuss what all of this means for future expeditions to the Wheel.

The Wheel itself suffered little damage from the quakes that so devastated Theodolite Isle. And while a moratorium on all climbing was immediately called after news of the disaster broke, by the summer of next year climbers will fairly expect that the mountain will be open to them again. Much of the West Face's snow cover was lost in the avalanche that caused the terrible tsunami, but all the major routes up the mountain—as far as can be told—remain open. However, without the support facilities that were available on Theodolite Isle, mounting a major expedition upon the Wheel will be troublesome for some years to come.

'It's a real pity,' said one climber from the assessment team sent to study the Wheel. 'I've never seen the mountain look friendlier, strange as that might sound. With the snow cover gone, it's like the Wheel has shrugged off a whole lot of ugly weight and mean attitude. It's a hard thing to explain to non-climbers, but all peaks have moods, and to me, even after all that's happened, the Wheel is looking like a happy mountain.'

EPILOGUE 2

Selected articles, 2037 to 2120

October, 2037. Consolidated Press

The Mysterious Death of Walter Richman . . . Of all Richman's intimate business companions and staff with him on Theodolite Isle during the disaster only his personal IT specialist, Eugene Morris, survived. But as Morris's own published account of the event describes, he departed the upper residence some minutes before the initial earthquake struck. His tale is a gripping one to be sure, telling of the tsunami that struck the lower parts of the island, and of the subsequent adventures of the forty-seven people who survived it, marooned for a week in the ruins before rescue finally arrived. But he can shed no light on what was transpiring above in the Observatory during that time, nor reveal how Richman and the others perished.

Only one witness could possibly do that: Rita Gausse, daughter of the Observatory's designer, and a guest to Richman that fateful day. But in the twenty years since, she has refused to do so.

There is, of course, her testimony at two inquiries, one into the disaster in general, and one into the death of Richman in particular. And on the face of it her tale is simple enough. The six people trapped in the Observatory, Richman included, decided at first to merely wait for rescue. Then, as rescue did not come, personal assistant to Richman and former mountain climber, Clara Lang, made an attempt to descend the complex's emergency stairway, even though it had been badly damaged by the quake. The others waited another two days, but as it appeared that Lang had not succeeded in reaching the bottom (her body has never been found) Gausse herself then made an attempt. And succeeded, just before the final quake struck, destroying the Observatory and claiming all the others.

Which is all fair enough, as far as it goes. But in the twenty years since then, the silence of Ms Gausse, a veterinarian based in rural Victoria, is curious. The world, after all, has been eager ever since the disaster to know how a man like Richman behaved in the crisis. Accordingly, Ms Gausse has been offered a cavalcade of international book deals, film deals and television deals, all giving her the chance to elaborate on the dry details of her testimony, and all of them offering considerable financial recompense. But she has refused involvement in all of them.

Why?

Is it merely because, as Ms Gausse claims, she has no desire to relive what was undeniably a stressful experience? She received significant injuries in her escape, requiring surgery and long recovery, and in the years since has lived on a remote bushland property where, she declared to this reporter, she is 'quite happy thanks and just wants to be left alone'.

Or is it because, as has been increasingly rumoured, the Richman family has pressured her to remain silent. The great Richman dynasty endures, after all, even following the loss of Richman himself. The billionaire's second wife and his two sons inherited the bulk of his many enterprises, and it seems, if sources are to be believed, that they do not want details of Walter Richman's last hours known.

It is idle to speculate, maybe. Did the dauntless conqueror of the Wheel perhaps not respond to the crisis with calm and courage? Was there panic and disorder in the Observatory before the final end? Did something even stranger take place upon that lonely mount?

Only one woman can say.

And, calmly, she chooses not to.

March, 2120. Paranormal News

A Multiplatform Experience for Seekers of the Truth in the 22nd Century. *Mystery in the Hand of God*

Of all the many Hand of God myths that have circulated in the climbing world through the centuries since the Wheel's discovery, perhaps the most intriguing is also one of the most recent, for it emerged in the days after the second successful ascent of the Wheel, which took place in 2075, one hundred years exactly after the first ascent.

This second ascent, known as the Anniversary Expedition, was mounted specifically to honour the 1975 achievement. It was a far simpler affair, however, than that earlier vast and unwieldy expedition. Walter Richman's team consisted of hundreds of climbers and support staff, and their efforts involved the laying of kilometres of electrical cables and water pipes up the mountain. In comparison, the Anniversary Expedition consisted of only six climbers, and not a single metre of cable or piping was required, leaving the Wheel pristine.

Of course, there had been a century's advance in technology between the two teams. There was no need for the Anniversary Expedition to lay cables or pipes, for instance, because everything was airlifted directly to the climbers by heavy-duty drones; standard prop-drive models below ten thousand metres, and c-pulse drones above ten thousand. The expedition's water and food, their climbing equipment, the batteries for their suits and huts, the huts themselves, all of it was toted up the West Face to wherever the climbers happened to be. Likewise, all waste was carted away by air, leaving no trace behind.

In fact, as the drones were capable of carrying loads of up to two hundred kilograms each, the climbers themselves could easily have been airlifted directly to the summit, though that would hardly have been sporting. But it did prove crucial on two occasions—once, at eleven thousand metres, when a climber fell and shattered a femur; and again at sixteen thousand metres, when another of the climbers developed appendicitis. In both cases, the stricken individuals were safely airlifted from the mountain, leaving the remaining climbers free to continue their ascent.

The act of climbing itself was also a much simpler affair. This was no 'siege' assault on the Wheel, as was Richman's, with its torturous placing of camp above camp, requiring endless trips up and down the mountain. The Anniversary team was climbing 'Alpine' style, which meant one ascent and one descent, and they did it at a speed that would have astonished Richman's team. The 1975 ascent took nearly two years: the Anniversary climb was done in a mere fifty-nine days.

This was largely due to the drone system, of course, but advances in pressure-suit technology can also claim some of the credit. Richman's suits were bulky, stiff and tiring to work in. The Anniversary suits, by comparison, made of environment-reactive 'smart fabrics', were scarcely more burdensome to wear than a thick jumpsuit.

Which is not to claim that the Anniversary ascent was without travail. Two injuries have already been mentioned, and the climbers faced all the usual dangers to be found upon the Wheel: ice and snow and avalanche, airless altitude, deadly cold and freakish winds. The Wheel threw it all at the Anniversary team, just as it had thrown it all at Richman's climbers. And like Richman's effort, the Anniversary Expedition was staggeringly expensive, the drones and smart suits being state-of-the-art, prototype equipment. Climbing the Wheel may have become easier, but it remains to this day a sport reserved for the very, very rich.

In any event, against all difficulties and in record time, the remaining four climbers of the Anniversary team made a last camp on the Wheel's summit ridge on 11 August 2074, and the next morning set out on the last leg of their ascent, just as a hundred years earlier Richman and his three companions had set out for their own summit push. However, *this* time there was no debate as to how many of the climbers would actually be allowed to stand upon the Hand of God; the Anniversary team had sworn that they would all do so together, or none of them would.

And so it transpired. Late in the day, with the sun trending westwards in a fine blue sky, the two men and two women scaled the last few metres of the ridge and stepped onto the flat palm of the summit.

Before them rose the curved fingers of the Hand of God, the famous summit cave waiting darkly beneath. No one had stood there or looked into that cave since Walter Richman himself a century earlier, only to forever keep secret what he had seen.

Eagerly, the four climbers crowded about the cave and looked in.

And then . . . ?

Well, this is where it starts to get weird.

▲

In truth, there should have been no space for rumour or conspiracy theory to thrive, because the whole world was supposed to share the climbers' view that day, via footage beamed live from the climbers' helmet cameras. But an untimely glitch in the broadcast facility on the support ship made live transmission impossible, so it was decided that recorded footage of the summit moment would have to suffice.

And indeed *some* footage, showing the climbers reaching the Hand of God, was later screened to a fascinated audience.

But there was no footage showing the inside of the cave. Pressed as to why this was, expedition officials had excuses ready. It had been decided 'in advance', they claimed, to not film the cave in any detail, out of respect for the mountain, which should be allowed to keep its last mystery. After all, hadn't the great Walter Richman done the same?

Which was fine, said critics, except that there had been no mention of this decision about the cave in any of the planning stages of the Anniversary Expedition. In fact, the intention had seemed just the opposite, to *show* the cave. So what had changed? To which the climbers and the officials said only this: *No comment.*

Soon enough, however, a different account of the summit day began to circulate through the climbing world. According to these rumours, what happened was this: what the climbers saw in the cave was so shocking that they decided there and then it could never be revealed.

Because it was impossible. There could not be a corpse at the top of the world, where only one other human had ever stood.

And such a corpse! Even if—an unlikely scenario—some secretly mounted expedition had reached the peak of the Wheel without anyone else knowing, and even if one of its members had died at the summit, the body would not look like this body, *could* not look this body.

The man was—supposedly—all but naked. There was no sign of an altitude suit, no trace of any climbing gear at all, just a few shreds of clothing that proved (in later testing by forensic scientists, so the rumours ran) to be no more than a pair of Levi's jeans, a white cotton shirt, light underwear and socks, and a pair of casual sneakers.

Baffling enough. But what was worse were the signs suggesting that the man, unsuited, in an environment without air and at minus seventy degrees Celsius, had survived for some time in the cave. How else to explain what had happened to his skin? Bits of it were torn off, especially about his hands, feet and buttocks, leaving livid bloody holes in him, perfectly preserved in the frozen conditions, and proving that he had been bleeding and therefore alive at the time of the injuries.

Corresponding patches of torn skin, the story goes, remained stuck at various points on the icy walls of the cave. It was as if the man had blundered from place to place under the overhang, grazing up against the brutal cold of the stone, his skin freezing on contact, so that he had to tear it away to be free. As one of the four witnesses was supposed to have said, 'It was like that damn cave had eaten him alive.'

Then there was the matter of the position of the corpse, and the expression on his face. As all climbers know, freezing conditions can be cruel to dead bodies, posing them in all sorts of undignified or strange poses. But even so, none of the four witnesses had ever seen anything like this, for the wretched corpse was apparently kneeling on all fours, the head turned up torturously, the flesh gone to alabaster, the eyes to unseeing veined marble, and the mouth drawn back to teeth of ice, as if pleading, or begging, or imploring . . . but for what?

For rescue? For mercy?

And even that, as the tale went, wasn't the most shocking thing. The most shocking thing was that the climbers recognised the man's face.

Who better to recognise it, after all? The Anniversary team had spent much of their preparation studying Walter Richman and his great achievement of a century earlier. They had read his books, they had seen dozens of photos of him and watched hours of videos. His face was as familiar to them as each other's. So yes, they knew him when they saw him, kneeling frozen in the Hand of God.

▲

A fantasy? A ghost story?

Of course it is, most would say.

Still, there are questions that linger. The whole macabre tale could be dispelled in an instant, for example, if just a few seconds of actual footage from the cave, or even a single still from the recording, had ever been released. But no such proof has ever been forthcoming.

Why not?

And after all, the whereabouts of Walter Richman's body remains unknown. His death in 2017—in the series of earthquakes that destroyed his grand home on the summit of Observatory Mount—is an established fact. But his corpse was never found. It could only be assumed at the time that he lay buried within. As it is assumed to this day.

But assumption is not proof.

What is more, even before the Anniversary Expedition took place, there had long been strange rumours about Richman's death and the events leading up to it. The source of these reports is supposedly a manuscript that many have heard of but few have seen. Known as the Gausse Manuscript, it was, apparently, found in the estate of a woman named Rita Gausse, who was the daughter of the famous architect Richard Gausse, the designer of Richman's Observatory residence.

Now, it's a fact of history that Rita Gausse was staying with Richman as a guest at his grand house when the disaster began. It's a fact too that she was the sole survivor of the six individuals who were in the residence when the first of the quakes struck. But other than her testimony to the official inquest, in which she pleaded ignorance in regards to the manner of Richman's ultimate end, she never in her lifetime made further comment upon what she had witnessed.

According to legend, however, after her death in 2049, a printed manuscript was found with her belongings, which, among other autobiographical matters, detailed Richman's demise.

Of course, this manuscript, even if it really exists, has never been seen publicly, and even by repute it was full of many ludicrously far-fetched claims and events, which perhaps explains why Ms Gausse never released it during her lifetime: no one would have believed her. But what is interesting is that Walter Richman's descendants, owners still of vast commercial enterprises, went to some lengths and expense to purchase Ms Gausse's estate, including all writings and documents.

At the time, a spokesman for the family said merely that Ms Gausse's papers included historically valuable documents pertaining to her father's life and to the building of the Observatory, which Richman family archivists were eager to obtain. No mention was made of any *book*. But of course, if the book indeed existed, then the Richman family could now ensure it never saw the light of day.

For the tale the manuscript told—according to the rumours—was very different to the official finding of Richman's death by natural disaster. More damningly, it was deeply unflattering of Richman himself, painting him as grossly narcissistic and even accusing him of contributing to the deaths of the others trapped in the Observatory.

Still, would that matter? Isn't this all ancient history? Maybe, but on the other hand, Walter Richman remains today much as he was in his lifetime, a titanic figure in the history of climbing, a hero, an inspiration who died too soon in tragic circumstances. His family and their companies still trade heavily on the aura that he left behind. They would not want that image tarnished. Which would explain why, if the manuscript exists, they purchased it, and kept it hidden.

But does it also explain why, seventy years after the Gausse book was found and suppressed, four climbers who had no apparent connection to the Richman dynasty, decided to keep secret something so monumental as the discovery of Walter Richman's corpse atop the Wheel? Maybe it does, for though it was not known at the time, the Anniversary Expedition was funded by—you guessed it—the Richman family. It was done through various subsidiary companies, but researchers have since followed the paper trail, and there is no doubt that the entirety of the money was provided by the Richmans.

The four climbers, in other words, were in the pay of those who on no account would want it known that Walter Richman died, gruesomely, atop the very mountain he conquered.

Still believe that the whole tale is nonsense?

Well, only the Richman family knows for sure. And as has been the case for a hundred years and more they remain aloof in their world of wealth and privilege, and feel no compunction to tell the rest of us. As for the Wheel, no one has successfully climbed it since the Anniversary team. So for now, the Hand of God keeps hold of its secrets.